The Apples of Vermont

A Novel

R.L. Carroll

RED LEAD PRESS
PITTSBURGH, PENNSYLVANIA 15222

ISBN: 978-0-8059-8522-1
Library of Congress Control Number: 2007927914
Printed in the United States of America

First Printing

For more information or to order additional books, please contact:
Red Lead Press
701 Smithfield Street
Third Floor
Pittsburgh, Pennsylvania 15222
U.S.A.
1-800-834-1803
www.redleadbooks.com

For J.C.

For Bob Hall, passionate English Literature Professor par excellence, who angrily said to me in 1978, "You don't know a sodding thing about literature!"

I know now that he was absolutely correct.

For Ronald McCall, my 8th Grade English Teacher, who sent me to the dean's office twice in one week for too much talking in his class. This culminated in my receiving a week's worth of detention. The next week, Mr. McCall instructed our class to write a three to five page short story. I wrote about a Math Teacher, Donald McPhall, who, when not teaching at his junior high school, lived in a tree in a large downtown park, ate from garbage cans, and generally terrorized the old people, as they sat on the green benches talking, reading newspapers, and feeding the pigeons. Mr. McCall gave me an 'A' on my very first short story, and he wrote, "This is really excellent literature Mr. Carroll! Someday you're going to make a whole bunch of money writing cheap drug store novels."

I hope now that he was absolutely correct.

The Moon

❖ ❖ ❖

Chapter One

The wonderful thing about a *Polaroid* camera—when sufficiently provoked of course—is that one can duck around a corner, find another room, an alcove, a foyer, a cul-de-sac, a closet, perform a dropping-of-the-trousers-snapshot-of-the-derrière ceremony, place the still undeveloped photo into the hand of the unsuspecting target, and be several miles away, cruising down a two lane blacktop, top down, listening to Sinatra croon, "Fly Me to the Moon," as the target slowly understands the message:

That is exactly what Salome Apple did to her confused, arrogant, obnoxious, macho, gauche, violent, cock-of-the-walk, yet somewhat perceptive father, on the day of her fourteenth birthday, after he announced that she would be making a trip to the doctor's for a gynecological report regarding the exact status of her hymen. The problem was, of course, she had neither car to burn tires for dramatic effect, nor car stereo for comfort of soul. And, of course, had she the latter, in 1974 it would have been *Fleetwood Mac's* "Heroes Are Hard to Find," not Ole Blue Eyes belting out an American Standard. (Once she had used, unbeknownst to him, two of her father's Sinatra albums to balance the antique armoire in her bedroom, however.)

Salome Apple needed no automobile; she was hauntingly beautiful, and with her waist-length red hair, piercing bank lamp green eyes, five-foot six-inch petite frame, and well developed upper region, a ride from some guy heading south on Highway 7 past Rutland Vermont was ineludible. And, if at first he missed her, the poster board sign with the large painted hitchhiking thumb and words **BIG APPLE** could not be missed. It was a proven commodity for Salome, a formula of basic hetero masculine mathematics—eyes to sign=eyes to Salome=ride. So Salome was not worried, when she placed the undeveloped photo in Bubba Apple's hand and ran from the farmhouse. Her duffle bag was packed and waiting with the finished poster board, under her favorite elm, next to the stream, which ran through the middle of her father's 1000-acre orchard on Highway 7.

Salome Apple was old soul wise. As is usually seen, when one knows that a parent, mate, or society is repressing the external life, one's internal wisdom and creative life grow proportionately—until, of course, separation finally occurs from said source of repression. On the inside, Salome was a voluminous creative ant farm. A good radiologist with a metaphysical fluoroscope might have seen a maze of tunnels, some of which were burrowed through to the surface, others ending prematurely in no particular direction. But whichever way those tunnels ran, curiosity was the permeating essence of the trip.

When precocious Salome was only nine years old, she wondered what it must feel like to be losing a mate. So she told Selma Greenwood, the thirty-seven year-old soon-to-be-widowed Head Librarian of the main library in Rutland, "I heard that your husband is quite sick with cancer. I'm so very, very sorry that you have to go through this. If you need somebody to talk to, I'm here for you." Selma Greenwood was so moved, she would always remember young Salome's kindness, and she would always try to watch out for her. That was it; once you knew Salome, you automatically became one of her protectors.

As he eased up on the accelerator when he saw the sign and fully braked when he saw her, 170 pound, six-foot three-inch, brown-haired, hazel-eyed Anthony Kulpa, hadn't even the most miniscule notion that he was about to be categorized with the above mentioned group. The oddness of the sign had first attracted him, but when he saw Salome, he remembered just how frustrated he was with being nineteen, having been away at his first year of college at the University of Vermont in Burlington, and having not gotten laid. "You'll do better if you quit telegraphing your need," his twenty-seven year-old brother had recently told him on the phone. "Stop going to the typical places where guys usually go to look for women. Instead, try shopping malls, grocery stores, laundromats, and especially museums. And remember, women want sex just as much as men!"

'Since you seem to know so much about women and sex, what about hitchhikers?' Anthony Kulpa thought, as he leaned across the seat to roll down the window of his '68 *Dodge Draft*. "You're heading to New York City?"

"Yeah," Salome responded.

"I'm going to Long Island. I can drop you at a train near The City."

"Thank you," Salome said, while checking Anthony out through the car window. 'Eighteen or nineteen,' she thought. 'Scruffy attempt at a beard…beginning to grow his hair out…new college boy probably...cute.'

"I'd really appreciate that." Salome sat down in the *Dodge*, put her duffle bag on the floor, put the poster board sign in the back seat, and then closed the car door. She asked, "Do you live on Long Island?"

"Nah," Anthony said. "I have a photographer friend who lives out there with his parents, and I'm staying at their place for a week." Then Anthony added, "Would you mind…rolling the window up…got the air on. Oh…and you can put your bag in the back also…give you more room." 'Damn…she's hot!' he thought.

'Hmm…he has a friend who is a photographer!' Salome thought. And then she said, "This way, I can use the bag as a footrest," and she demonstrated. 'I can also bail quickly if needed,' she also thought.

"You live in Rutland?"

"I've been…living in Rutland…kind of…yes," Salome said and then added, "What about you…since you don't live on Long Island, where do you live?"

"I'm just finishing summer school after my first year at UVM, but my home is Florida," Anthony said, while adjusting his position to conceal a growing problem.

Salome, aware of, and flattered by, what she saw Anthony doing, said, "Summer school? You got stuck in summer school? Today is August 6th… I guess your whole summer has been ruined…hasn't it!"

"Yeah…I just barely passed this year. I had to retake two classes this summer to not flunk out. At least I don't have to be back until the middle of September," Anthony said, now finally content with his lower *ajustement.*

"Well…at least you got in. Why did you want to go to college in Vermont anyway? Didn't you say you were from Florida?"

"I've always loved the Burlington area…I have relatives who live there and across the lake in Plattsburgh. I've been spending summers there since I was a baby."

"Do you live with one of your relatives up there?" Salome asked, and then realized that question was probably getting too personal.

Anthony, who was neither alarmed nor cognizant of what Salome perceived as possibly being too personal, said, "No…I share an apartment with two other guys…about four blocks from campus."

"What do you want to do after college?" And then curious Salome thought, 'What's up with all of this personal shit? Am I suddenly Mike Wallace?'

"You mean…what do I want to be when I grow up?" And Anthony smiled and thought, 'I want to be your love slave!' But he said, "I'm in Pre-Law. I want to be a corporate attorney. What about you?"

"Well actually…I was thinking about modeling, that's why I'm heading to New York. I need a portfolio though…is your friend real expensive?"

"He probably is," Anthony said. "Darius is only twenty-four, but he is already well known, and he demands top dollar…His photos are regularly featured in major magazines…But I'll tell you what, I need to stop, get gas, and use a restroom." And then Anthony turned off of the highway into the lot of a large convenience store/gas station. "I'll call him from a payphone and ask what he'd charge you."

"That sounds great! Thanks!" Salome said.

"By the way…I'm Anthony…Anthony Kulpa," Anthony said, as he was exiting the car. Fifteen minutes later, he came back to the car and said, "Darius wasn't home, but their housekeeper suggested that I bring you along to talk with him. She also said they have a huge house, and she's sure that Darius wouldn't mind if you stayed a few days."

"What about his parents?"

"They're in Alaska at their other home."

"I don't know…" Salome said. "This kind of sounds like, 'Would you like to come up and see my etchings?'" And then Salome realized that this was something probably nobody ever said, but—the cheesy cliché it is—was probably etched into every post World War II young girl's mind.

"No….no…it's not like that at all," Anthony said. 'Of course it's like that!' he thought. "Look…," Anthony gulped hard, "…I won't deny that you are unbelievably beautiful…and if given the chance, I'd love to ask you out…But this is strictly an offer of help…You said you needed a portfolio, and it looks as if I've hooked you up. All I can say…if Darius Malcovitch is willing to shoot you without charging an absurd amount…you will be one lucky supermodel-to-be!"

"How did you meet this guy?" Salome asked.

"He stayed at our family's motel last summer, and I met him through my brother."

"So you're staying there a week?"

"Yeah…I figured I'd relax…go to The City…see a show…and then head to Mad Beach next week…for the rest of the summer."

"Mad Beach?"

"Short for Madeira Beach, Florida. It's on the Gulf of Mexico off of the coast of St. Petersburg."

"Is that near Miami?" Salome asked, while trying to remove a speck of dirt from her eye, a birthday present, from her time standing on Highway 7.

"No…Miami is on the other side of the state. St. Petersburg is on the western side of the state...the Tampa Bay Area."

"By the way," Salome said, having finally dislodged the unwelcome gift, "My name is Salome Apple." Salome immediately felt her *faux pas*. She had been totally engaged in thought over the pros and cons of heading to Long Island with Anthony, and what she had forgotten, was that she was planning on using her older sister's identity.

"Salome…that's a beautiful name…that sounds like something else." (Years later, people would say her name sounded like *Sallie Mae*, the place one mailed student loan payments.) Anthony, who then thought, that one probably needed to be eighteen to be photographed and promoted to most of the modeling agencies in New York, and suddenly feeling that perhaps Salome wasn't eighteen, said, "I'm nineteen...by the way."

The fourteen year-old Salome, aware for some time that her age would be problematic if she ever had to leave home, fortunately, had recently found her older sister's old driver license, from when petite, five-foot six-inch, blonde-haired green-eyed Jennifer, at eighteen, had decided to dye her hair as red as Salome's. Salome had discovered the driver license in the bottom of a drawer, after she had begged Jennifer to borrow a green top. Jennifer, at twenty-one, having just completed a nursing program at Mt. Sinai in New York City, was home for the summer trying to "figure things out." She begrudgingly had agreed to loan her youngest sister the green top with a "Don't stink it up!" thrown in. Luckily, other than hair color, Jennifer and Salome looked very similar. And because Jennifer looked a young twenty-one—and an even younger eighteen on the picture of her old license—and Salome an old fourteen, it was possible for Salome to pass for Jennifer. "I'm twenty-one," Salome said to Anthony.

A fairly intuitive Anthony immediately doubted that Salome was twenty-one. He responded quickly, "So you were born in..."

Salome, who knew that some wouldn't accept twenty-one as her age, and that her sister's birth date on the license would be a constant source of quizzing, said, "I was born on the last day of September in 1952."

"Unbelievable!" Anthony said. "You're almost twenty-two...and I just turned nineteen...You're almost three years older... You look so young!"

"I get that a lot," Salome said. "All of the women in the Apple family look young. Even my grandmother at seventy-six looks great."

Anthony could not take his eyes off of Salome. She had to motion with her hand twice to get him to pay attention to the road and not her. Once they almost hit a guard rail. Salome was simply the most beautiful woman, to whom he had ever spoken. And she was not only beautiful, she was approachable. 'Well,' Anthony thought, 'she's approachable only because she's currently a captive in my car.' He then thought about his brother's advice, and how hard it was for him to emulate Felix, with all of the sexual conquests that Felix had had by the time he was nineteen. Anthony just hadn't found his own way yet, when it came to getting lucky with the ladies. Beginning conversations with women, chit chatting, with an agenda of asking them out, usually petrified Anthony. Although today, he felt totally at ease with Salome. And then Anthony thought about his brother again, how angry Felix could make him, and he accidentally verbalized that which he had meant to keep private, "What the hell does he know anyway?"

"Who are you talking about?" Salome asked.

"My brother...Felix," Anthony answered, now embarrassed by blurting out private information to a stranger.

"Why are you mad at your brother?"

"He thinks he knows everything about everything!" And then a still totally bedazzled-by-Salome, Anthony, spilled some more, "He hasn't thought clearly about anything...since the incident at the motel twelve years ago!"

"What incident did you have at a motel twelve years ago?" Salome asked curiously.

Anthony realized at that moment that he really wouldn't make a very good CIA operative, and then he thought about his promise to Felix. But then he decided, since he had already mentioned it, 'Fuck it...why not talk about...*some* of it?' So he said, "Like I told you... my family owns a small motel on a beach in Florida...My step-mother slipped and fell down several stairs at the motel on an outside staircase...she ended up a paraplegic...It was a nasty scene...My brother feels responsible for the mishap...It's screwed him up since he was fifteen."

"Why does your brother feel responsible?" Salome asked.

"That...I don't want to discuss!" Anthony stressed firmly.

@@@@@@@@

Stocky, six-foot one-inch, short red-haired, green-eyed, fifty-four year-old Bubba Apple was still screaming at his wife about Salome. When he was very angry—which was quite often—he would point his crooked middle finger in the face of whomever he was addressing, and his voice would take on a kind of honking geese sound with an elongated nervous vibrato on certain words and expressions. "WHYYY...JEEESUS CHRIIIST...sons of bitches running WIIILD around here!"

"Calm down Bubba, and stick that finger someplace else," his wife of nearly twenty-four years, Pauline, said. "It's your own fault. Telling your daughter on her fourteenth birthday that you want proof of her virginity...for God's sake Bubba!"

"She's running WIIILD...and you know that Pauline!"

"I know that Salome has good common sense," Forty-six year-old, medium built, five-foot six-inch, blonde-haired, blue-eyed Pauline said. "Besides...what do you suggest? We're living in the middle of the 1970's. Chastity belts haven't been in style for a long time."

"WHYYY...I'll LOCKKK her up in her bedroom until SHEEE's 21!"

Hearing this as she entered the room, Jennifer Apple, number one daughter of Bubba and Pauline said, "You talking about locking up Salome? You do that Bubba...and you'll screw up yet another of your kids for life!" In the

Apple household, since any of the six children could remember, mom had always been "Mom," and dad had always been "Bubba."

Bubba turned toward Jennifer, crooked middle finger trembling, "WHYYY...I SHOULD LOCK ***YOUUU*** UP TOO…running with that married New York City doctor!"

"I'm twenty-one, he's getting a divorce, and we're not running together," Jennifer said smiling. "Neither of us," Jennifer said, extending her middle finger in her best Bubbaesque manner and pointing it at him, and then preparing her throat with his nervous catch, "IS MUCH INTO JOGGING!" And then she continued, "We are into SLEEEPING together, however!" And then Jennifer sat down at the dining room table to brush her long blonde hair.

"Don't brush your hair at the dining room table, Jennifer!" Pauline said with some annoyance.

"Aw…Mom…there's no food on the table," Jennifer said.

"I don't care," Pauline said. "You know how I feel about…"

"Okay Mom…enough…I've stopped…I'm sorry," Jennifer said.

"Like I said, Pauline….running WIIILD around here."

"OH MY GOD," Pauline said, much in the same way that Sandy Denis had said it in *The Out-of-Towners.* "You can't control your childrens' lives forever! Mind your own business, Bubba! The best thing to do when Salome comes back for dinner is to not even mention the photo."

"What photo?" asked Jennifer, fighting her urge to start brushing again.

Pauline picked up the photo of Salome's naked tush from the table, handed it to Jennifer, and told her the story. Jennifer began what seemed like just a miniscule chuckle, but it quickly segued into a very hearty belly laugh. That laugh provoked Pauline into doing that which she had been desperately fighting, laughing herself, while Bubba was still in the house. And, in the time it would have taken Sinatra to sing a chorus from "Moonlight in Vermont," both Jennifer and Pauline were hysterical with impunity.

Bubba slammed the front screen door and screeched something about, "CHORES…JEEESUS CHRIIIST!!…IN THE BARN…"

When she finally could spit out the words, Jennifer said, "I don't know how you've put up with Bubba all of these years, Mom." (In later years, Jennifer would tell her then husband, Dr. Colin Morgan, the married gynecologist she had not been jogging with, that on that day, after seeing Salome's picture, she had literally wet her pants from too much laughter.)

"I'm a tough little Indian!" Pauline said. (And, of course, years later, Salome would point out to Pauline that that expression was politically incorrect. Upon trying "tough little Native American" for a few years and finding it syllabically displeasing, Pauline would eventually revert to "Indian," and explain that she was referring to those who came from Calcutta, Delhi, and Mumbai etc.)

@@@@@@@@

Anthony and Salome were smoking, quietly listening to an eight track tape of "The Dark Side of the Moon," and enjoying the ride down Highway 7 when the car overheated. They were in western Massachusetts, the Berkshires, and Anthony pulled the car off of the road onto a small flat surface of brown grass that was just large enough to accommodate two vehicles. He opened the hood, took a look, and sat back down in the car. "It's my top radiator hose. No big deal…I've got *AAA*, and they'll tow it to a gas station for free. And it won't cost that much to fix…it's just the time involved. We'll probably be sitting around here for a couple of hours at least. Do you want to hang with me or not? I'm sure you could just stand here and get another ride."

"I'd probably have to walk up the road a little, so any guy who wants to stop won't think that you're involved in the deal!" Salome said laughingly, and then she used her elbow to give Anthony a light little jab in the side.

"You're probably right about that," Anthony replied with somewhat more of a serious tone.

"You're a nice guy and I've enjoyed your company," Salome said. "I'm also beginning to trust you a little…so I think I'll keep riding with you."

Anthony couldn't suppress his smile. "It looks as if there's human activity down the highway…do you see all of those cars in what looks like a parking lot?" Salome saw what Anthony was referring to, about 1/4 of a mile down the curving Highway 7. After Anthony convinced Salome that he felt it was safer for them to leave the car and go exploring for a phone together, they headed toward what they both thought looked like a business.

The sign in front read: **Arrowhead: The Home of Herman Melville.** Anthony and Salome headed for the author of *Moby Dick*'s souvenir store to find a phone, and they saw a little sign over the store's door that said: **"Come on in. You'll find a whale of interesting items for sale."** (Years later, when Salome would tell Felix about the sign, he would say, "You should have told them you were visiting psychiatrists from the Freud Institute in Vienna, and you were looking for the Captain Ahab Center for Better Mental Health." And even years later than that, when Salome would think of what Felix had said, she would wish that she had been able to respond at that time, "I should have told them we had car trouble, and we were looking for *Ishmael's 'Thar She Blows!' Radiator Shop*!")

After *AAA* had been called and Anthony had been informed that it would take at least an hour for them to get there, he suggested to Salome that they get something to eat in the Arrowhead Coffee Shop. They both ordered coffee, and then they decided to split the Mobius Fish Strip dinner.

While they sat waiting for the food, Salome said, "Have you ever played 'Truth or Dare?'"

"When I was in the eighth grade," Anthony responded, while working on one of those silly restaurant table puzzles. In this case, it was connect the dots to make a whale.

"Okay...well then put your mind back into the eighth grade mode... truth or dare?"

"Do we really have to?" Anthony whined.

"Well...if you're scared..." Salome said sarcastically.

"Okay...okay...I guess we're playing this game."

"Truth or dare?"

"Uhhh.... dare...I guess."

Salome was a little disappointed, yet she didn't show it. "I dare you to get up and give a speech to this coffee shop."

"What the...?" Anthony stammered out. "A speech on what?"

"Anything you choose."

"This is crazy!" Anthony said.

"Ah ha!...I kinda like crazy," Salome said.

And, of course, since Anthony was willing to be whatever she wanted because he wanted her, he got up and said, "LADIES AND GENTLEMEN...IF I CAN HAVE YOUR ATTENTION." The fourteen or fifteen people in the coffee shop looked up. "I would like to call your attention to someone wondrous and rare...a woman of true beauty and class. Ladies and Gentlemen...I give you the next great American Supermodel...Miss..."

Salome tugged at Anthony's sleeve, and then she motioned for him to put his ear to her mouth before he continued, "You better make that *Jennifer* Apple," she whispered.

"*Jennifer*?"

"It's my older sister's I.D. that says I'm 21...it also says my name is *Jennifer*."

"...Miss...Jennifer Apple!" And Anthony started to applaud, which, of course, started the entire room applauding.

Salome was not so disappointed now with Anthony's choice of "dare." He had shown himself to have major brass ones—an attribute that Salome had always admired and tried to emulate—and he had just covered her back.

"Kinda interesting...considering how you've been bullshitting me since I picked you up...that you wanted to play 'Truth or Dare,'" Anthony said.

"Kinda necessary when I don't know what kind of pedophilic creep might be picking me up!" Salome shot back.

"Kinda risky being obviously underage and heading to The City to be a model," Anthony said with true concern.

"Kinda necessary when one's father is an asshole!"

"That's kinda interesting," Anthony said.

"What you told me about your step-mother and your brother's guilt is kinda interesting too," Salome said. "And I loved your speech by the way," she added.

"Thank you...you are beautiful and classy ...but I don't want to talk about my family!" Anthony said forcefully. "I don't want to lie about anything, and I don't know you well enough yet to tell you the whole story. Listen...If I don't feel I can be totally honest about a subject...I'd rather just avoid it...And I can't believe that I brought this up in the first place!... Look...I'll promise not to lie to you...if you'll promise me the same."

"I won't say that yet," Salome said, "But when I tell you that I'll never lie to you...I'll never lie to you."

"I can live with that," Anthony said softly and added, "Truth or dare?"

"Truth always," Salome said with total seriousness.

"I see," Anthony said. "Okay then...here's your question: How old are you really, and how many men have you slept with?"

And in that moment in-between the initial shock of hearing something so entirely Bubbaesque, with the realization that sometimes brass ones can bang too hard and leave one black and blue, and in that instant in which the personas of two individuals were quasi-slammed and burned indelibly into her mind, as the potential for being one and the same, and in that nanosecond in which she needed to reject what she feared she already knew, Salome lightly bit her lip and slowly said, "I have never slept with anyone! Jesus Christ...I'm just fourteen...and I've been living in Rutland all of my life!"

@@@@@@@@

Jack and Jimson Apple were fixing the fence that ran behind the barn at a 45-degree angle and separated Bubba Apple's 1000 acres from the smaller orchard owned by their hostile Greek neighbor, Gus Strattus. The barn had been built in 1952—just before the birth of Jennifer, two years after Bubba and Pauline had bought the orchard—right next to the Strattus property line as a kind of spy station, and it featured a dark little bathroom with a sixty-watt bulb directly over the john. There was just enough light for Bubba to look at one of the many catalogues or men's magazines that were piled up against a wall for his perusal, whenever he would sit daily and ponder his kingdom.

"Are you getting serious about Penny Walters?" Eighteen year-old, blonde-haired, green-eyed Jack Apple, number two son of Bubba and Pauline, asked his brother, seventeen year-old, red-haired, blue-eyed number three son, Jimson Apple.

"Why...because I took her to the prom?"

"Well you did spend a bunch of money for that night, the limo, the tux, the..."

"The motel room in Burlington!" Jimson finished, with a big Cheshire Cat-like grin, as he shifted his six-foot, 160-pound body to dig a new fence post hole.

"So it was just about getting laid?" Jack asked, but he already knew the answer. It was really just an older brother messing with his younger sibling. And although their hair and eye colors were different, and Jimson was ten pounds heavier and two inches taller, it was impossible not to see or hear that Jack and Jimson were brothers. When it came to dispositions however, that was a whole different situation. Jack was easy going, in the past he had never gotten too angry about anything. But Jimson was a serious person, with a much more volatile temper.

"Well…that was part of it. You know the deal...Lizzie ditched me for Harold Williams. Going out with Penny was rebound stuff," Jimson said.

"I can see you paid attention to Moses this year…huh!" Jack said.

"Moses" was the name given to Mr. Wheeler, the teacher most kids wanted for twelfth grade English in 1974 at Rutland Central High School. He was called Moses, because, with his long flowing white hair and beard, he looked that old. And, with his clever way of teaching, by turning a simple English class into a Psychology/Philosophy/Sociology/Anthropology class, he was easily the most popular teacher at Rutland Central High School. "Until recently…just about everyone at your school would have said, 'Lizzie Mitner? Sure…she's marrying Jimson Apple after high school.' Nobody knows why you guys broke up," Jack added.

"And it's nobody's business!" Jimson said, in an irritated way. "Stop asking!"

Jack, who had been hoping that he could be the one to win favor with Bubba by telling him the real story about the breakup of Jimson and Lizzie, began to sarcastically thank Jimson for the brotherly trust when they both heard Bubba shout from the barn, "WHYYY...JEEESUS CHRIIIST!!!…MY ASS IS GLUUUED TO THE SEEEAT!!!" Jack and Jimson ran into the barn's bathroom, and they found—what Jack would later describe as the apple red-faced Bubba—glued to the toilet seat with his pants hiked up in the best way possible. (Years later, when Jack would describe to Felix the look on Bubba's face, Felix would say, "I guess if somebody had found Kerouac glued to a crapper, his face would have been beet red!")

"WHYYY...THAT LITTLE BITCH SALOME PUT GLUUUE ON THE SEEEAT!!!" Bubba yelled.

It was nearly impossible for Jack and Jimson to keep straight faced, but, realizing the wrath that awaited them, somewhere down the road, if Bubba felt that they endorsed what was currently happening to him, they both fought their natural inclinations and dealt with the situation in a kind of simpatico stoical way.

"How do you know Salome did this?" Jack asked delicately, allowing himself to remember, just a month ago, when he and Bubba had had a nasty argument, that Bubba had brought his knee up into Jack's crotch and doubled him over.

"WHYYY...SHEEE'S RUNNING WIIILD!!!" Bubba screamed.

"Yeah, but…there's no proof she did this," Jack said, trying to lessen some of what appeared to be imminent danger heading his younger sister's way. Jack did fear getting on Bubba's bad side, but Jack's desire to garner the same respect that Bubba gave to his older brother, nineteen year-old number one son, Bruiser, was ebullient enough to take the chance.

"WHYYY...SHEEE GAVE MEEE A PICTURE OF HER NAKED ASS...BEEEFORE RUNNING OUT...THAT MISERABLE LITTLE BITCH!!!"

Jack pondered why Bubba hadn't just reached out in his typical Bubbaesque way and grabbed Salome, if she had indeed handed him a picture of her naked butt. He wondered if Bubba were slowing down. But he also knew that question might win him some physical abuse, so Jack left it unasked.

"What should we do Bubba?" Jimson asked.

"WHYYY...YOUUU DUMB ASS!!! GET...A COUPLE OF WRENCHES FROM THE TOOLBOX!!!"

Jimson figured out that Bubba wanted them to unscrew the bolts from the seat to the base of the toilet. He looked behind Bubba and saw that the bolts were 1/2 inch, but when he returned from the toolbox he had also brought a couple of monkey wrenches, just in case he had misdiagnosed the hardware situation.

Jack and Jimson knelt on each side of Bubba in the narrow space allowed on both sides of the john, and worked in earnest at getting the rusted seat bolts to budge. Jack even went and got the squirt oil, but to no avail.

While both sons were independently thinking about how to tell Bubba that God Himself would have difficulty in loosening those bolts, Bubba was fixated on an expression *his* father, Rev. Ignatius Apple, used on occasion about so-and-so being, "crazier than a shithouse rat!"

Bubba Apple, aka Blanchard Apple Sr., was born in April of 1920 in Wedowee, Alabama, to the Baptist Reverend Ignatius and his wife Salome Apple. Salome Apple, nee Gorge, named her only child after her father, the then (and presumably still) deceased one-time mayor of Wedowee, Blanchard Gorge. Ignatius had agreed to that first name for his son, but Salome had to accept Merewether, the name of the then (and presumably still) deceased one-time undertaker of Wedowee, and father of Ignatius, Merewether Apple. Bubba would never tell anybody ever, not even Pauline, his middle name. Only years later, when he passed away, would his family ever learn that information. And if his son, Blanchard Jr., hadn't needed to bring in his birth certificate when he began junior high, and hadn't noticed what his real name was, and hadn't gotten so pissed off that an explanation had been needed (everybody had always called him "Bruiser" since he was small, a name he would live up to years later, by winning the 175 Lb. Division of the Vermont State High School Wrestling Tournament two years in a row as both a junior and senior) Bubba would never have told anybody that Blanchard was *his* own real first name either. Bruiser, aka Blanchard Jr., had handled well, hearing how he had been named, once he knew he was named for his father. Bruiser already looked exactly like Bubba, so having his name made him feel proud. Bubba, on the other hand, would always hate his real name.

"Bubba…these bolts are going nowhere," Jack finally said nervously.

Bubba, suddenly awakened from his reverie, was surprisingly calm.

"I figured as much," was all he said. "Go and get the small electric power saw and orange extension cord. There's an outlet above me in the light socket." When Jack returned with the equipment Bubba added, "Be real careful cutting through the back of this seat, Jack. Don't cut me…and don't let the blade touch the porcelain bowl either."

The orange extension cord with its three prongs would not fit into the outlet in the light socket with its two inputs. Bubba said, "There should be an adapter in the toolbox."

After Jack, most carefully, cut the back of the toilet seat away from the bolts, Bubba stood up, clutching his pants in the front, and attempted to pull those pants over the seat glued to his rear. This did not work very well however, as Bubba was wearing size 38 pants and his ass was currently a 56.

Jack had to become a potty Picasso, a rear end Rodin, and sculpt with the power saw, very carefully, the circumference of the toilet seat. "Go to the house and get the keys for one of the trucks," Bubba told Jimson very calmly.

At that moment, twenty year-old, medium built, five-foot eight-inch blonde-haired, blue-eyed Cindy Chumwell, number two daughter of Bubba and Pauline Apple, was telling her mother on the phone, "It's all set. Dick's orders came through. We leave on the twenty-fourth of August at 1730 from Tokyo International, and it's not soon enough for me. I've had enough of Japan. I guess it was worth the extra six months here for Dick to finish out at Plattsburgh Air Force Base though. Anyway, we arrive the next day in Miami. We're spending a week with Dick's parents, and then we'll see you at Burlington Airport on the second of September at 2030 hours."

"I can't wait!" Pauline said. "I get to have you home for a whole month, and then you'll be living only two hours away."

"I know…it'll be great. It's been so strange for nearly three years. I get married right after high school, and boom! I'm living in Japan."

"Do you think Dick will get transferred from Plattsburgh in a few years?" Pauline asked.

"Well…we won't have to move anywhere else…unless we want to. Dick's deal…for next year…to re-up…with a cash bonus…was six years at the Plattsburgh base. After that, we'll see. He'll probably retire and look for something civilian…Wow!...I was just kicked by either Tonya or Dick, Jr.!"

"Do you know how happy I am that my first grandchild is going to be born in Vermont and not Japan?" Pauline asked rhetorically. "I hope the long plane ride is okay for the baby," she added.

"My doctor gave me a big thumbs up on that. And by the way…I hope you won't be too disappointed if I have the baby in Plattsburgh instead of Rutland. It's just too..."

"I know…two hours away when a baby is coming is too far," Pauline finished for Cindy.

Jimson pushed through the screen door and interrupted his mother, "I'm grabbing the truck keys, Mom, we have to take Bubba to the emergency room."

"What's wrong with Bubba?" Pauline asked with concern.

"Well…it seems as if Salome left some *Krazy Glue* on the toilet seat in the barn, and Bubba got stuck to it," Jimson said with laughing eyes.

"OH MY GOD!" Pauline said. "Is he still stuck out there?"

"No…Jack cut the seat off of the toilet and shaped it with the power saw. Now we need a doctor to do something about the glued part."

"What's wrong?" Cindy asked on the phone. When told the story of the photo Salome had given Bubba and what appeared to be more of her current hi-jinks with the glue on the toilet seat, Cindy laughed out, "That's Salome! She's the youngest, but sometimes I think she has the biggest…"

Before Cindy could get the word out, Pauline said, "I have to follow Bubba to the emergency room. I'll call you later."

"Okay Mom, I'll talk to you later. Love you. Give my love to Bubba also." And Cindy hung up.

@@@@@@@@

A little while later, at Rutland General Hospital, Bubba was sprawled belly down across a small operating table in the emergency room.

"Hey Bubba…I'm gonna numb up your backside a little with this," said Dr. William Wicks, doctor on call at the ER of Rutland General Hospital, fellow VFW member, and long time acquaintance of Bubba's.

"Not like the WAAAY you've been numbing up the backside of Augusta Smith's WIIIFE I hope, Bill!"

"Now Bubba…don't you go spreading that bullshit! I'm not fooling around with Maggie Smith!" Dr. Wicks said, and then he gave Bubba just a wee bit more of needle jab than necessary.

"Right Bill…Ouch! WHYYY…JEEESUS CHRIIIST…you SON OF A BITCH! That hurt!…Then how come your van was parked out in front of the Smith place all last WEEEKEND…while Augusta was AWAAAY in Boston?" Bubba expressed in his usual Buabbaesque way.

"I didn't know he wasn't home," Bill Wicks said, "I went over to talk to him about a plumbing job…and my car wouldn't start. That's all there is to it."

"YOUUU were probably checking out his WIIIFE'S plumbing!" Bubba said with a smirk.

"Bubba…when are you going to learn to just shut your mouth? You start a rumor like that and it's just going to create trouble for no reason. If one of your kids just glued you to a crapper, it was probably because of your big mouth and you deserved it. Now listen for the last time…I am not fooling around with Maggie Smith! My basement keeps holding water, and I remembered I needed to speak to Augusta about it as I was driving by his place."

Bubba, who didn't totally believe Bill Wicks, because Maggie was flirtatious with all men and Bill hadn't gone out with anyone in the two years since his wife had died, was getting ready to keep the discussion going when Bill added, "Bubba…with all of the skin I'm cutting off of your butt here, you are going to be very sore for a couple of weeks. You'll have to sleep on your stomach. I'll give you something for pain that will knock you out at night and help you to sleep. I'd also like to keep you in the hospital for a couple of days, to keep an eye out for any possible infection."

"That's RIIIGHT Bill," an annoyed Bubba said, "KEEEP MEEE in this hell hole for a couple of days to jack up MYYY bill. Does the hospital give YOUUU a commission?"

"You know Bubba I should just throw you out of here. I should let you get an ass full of pus, so I can drain it and cause you more pain!" Bill Wicks said, and then he told a nurse to go out to the waiting room and get Pauline.

"WHYYY...JEEESUS CHRIIIST…Bill, you just have to get Pauline involved in this don't YOUUU!"

Pauline, who had followed in her car with Jennifer, pushed through one side of the double doors of the ER operating room and said, "Are you giving Bill trouble, Bubba?"

"WHYYY…the bastard wants to KEEEP MEEE in here for a couple of days," Bubba said. "Has Salome come home? I'm gonna KILLL her!"

"Look Bubba!" Pauline said with some anger. "If Bill says to stay in the hospital…you're going to stay in the hospital. End of discussion! And when you see Salome…you're not going to do anything to her except to apologize. What you said to her was just miserable!"

"SHEEE'S a MISERABLE bitch. She's running WIIILD," Bubba said. "She has no business SLEEEPING around at her AAAGE!" And he pointed his crooked index finger at Pauline.

"OH MY GOD," Pauline said. "She's not sleeping around Bubba, and point that finger of yours elsewhere! She comes to me all of the time and tells me just how wrong you are about her. ON HER BIRTHDAY Bubba! HER BIRTHDAY! She's told me before, that the other girls her age don't like her because she's so beautiful…that other than Selma Greenwood and Geneva

Liberty, the only friends she has are boys. She realizes that most of these boys would like to date her, but at the moment they're all just friends!"

"Yeah...right," said Bubba.

"She's not jumping in and out of bed with boys!" Pauline emphasized.

"Not JUMMMPING," said Bubba. "More like HUMMMPING!" he added, sounding like Big Daddy in *Cat on a Hot Tin Roof.*

"Bill...can you give him something that will knock him out?" Pauline asked.

"I've got something hanging here below my right shoulder that will do the trick!" Dr. Wicks said, making a fist and shooting a stare at Bubba.

"I'll bet Maggie Smith would SAAAY that knockout punch of yours isn't TOOO far below your right shoulder!" Bubba shot back with a stare.

"Fuck you Bubba!" Dr. Wicks said as he stormed out of the room. He then added, "Your boys should have left you glued to the crapper!"

As Dr. Wicks was pushing through one side of the double doors, nineteen year-old Bruiser, number one son of Bubba and Pauline Apple, was pushing his way through the other. "Salome glued you to the crapper?" Bruiser asked his father with a laughing smirk. "She's a miserable bitch!" he said, echoing Bubba's earlier sentiments.

"When she gets home, I'm gonna lock her in her room!" Bubba said.

"That's what she needs," Bruiser added.

"Now look how you've messed up your son," Pauline said. "He'll never find a woman who will stay with him, and if he ever has a daughter, he'll treat her with disrespect."

"Aw Mom," Bruiser said. "I would never let my daughter become a slut like Salome."

Pauline walked quickly over to Bruiser and slapped him across the face. "Don't you ever talk about your sister...my daughter like that again! Bubba's the A-hole here, and you better stop idolizing him, or you're going to end up a very lonely man." And then Pauline turned to Bubba and said, "I'm going to find Bill Wicks, and I'm going to tell him to check you in here for observation. You're going to stay in the hospital as long as Bill says, and you're going to shut up and do what he says. You got that Bubba?"

"But Pauline..."

"Shut up Bubba!" And then Pauline left the room. She found Bill Wicks, and he agreed to admit Bubba into the hospital. She started to leave when Jennifer, who had been talking to her married doctor friend on the pay phone in the waiting room, and wasn't too pleased with the tenor of the conversation, said, "Wait Mom... I need a ride."

"That Bubba!" Pauline said. "I just want to get home."

"Yeah...," said Jennifer, "a few vodka and tonics sound pretty good to me too."

Chapter Two

Take a picture of this: a red clay-splattered, pale white moon-painted, green kudzu-strangled, termite infested, thirty year-old Baptist church, on a pretty oak-canopied street in Wedowee, Alabama at 10:07am, on Sunday, April 11, 1927, the day of Bubba's seventh birthday. Inside, along with Bubba and his mother, Salome Gorge Apple, the forty plus parishioners are sitting in their highly polished pews, and have been pronouncing prayers, singing psalms, and humming hymns for over an hour. They sit attentively, as Reverend Ignatius Apple begins one of his hyperbolic fiery philippics about a damned afterlife. "America is becoming the new Sodom and Gomorrah. Gangsters have the blessing of Satan as they fill our cities with liquor, drugs, prostitution, and NEGRO MUSIC! THE JEW has infiltrated all areas of business, entertainment, and GOVERNMENT! And although they've attempted to cover up his lineage and teach him how to look like a Christian, so they can run him for governor of NEW YORK, how can FRANKLIN DELANO ROOSEVELT not be one of them? ROOSEVELT is a MARRANO! He pretends he's a Christian in public, but behind closed doors he secretly practices his HEATHEN RELIGION! Oh…THE JEW has become particularly polished at vocalizing his denial of OUR SAVIOR—with so many of them becoming LAWYERS! And when I pray to JESUS every morning and every night, I thank HIM for letting me live in a town like ours. A place unlike our larger northern cities, where our northern Christian Brothers and Sisters have had their lives WRECKED by money loving gangsters, THE JEW, and uppity NEGROES who greedily grasp after that which is not theirs. But Satan also works his evil in our smaller towns, WHEN WEAK-WILLED

MEN produce that devil drink in their own BACKYARDS!" As he emphasized "backyards," Reverend Apple shot a stern glance over at Tom Powers, cotton grower and master of moonshine. Everybody in Wedowee knew he made the stuff somewhere on his 600-acre farm—somewhere where the cotton wasn't being grown—and most of the town's men, including Sheriff John Owen, were his customers. "And SATAN also appreciates those who IGNORE sin," Reverend Apple continued, as he shifted his glaring gaze to Sheriff Owen. "If all you think about is MONEY, then you are thinking like THE JEW! Remember that JESUS threw THE JEW out of the temple for thinking only about MONEY," and Reverend Apple looked back at Tom Powers, "so perhaps I should do the SAME THING!" Reverend Apple continued, "But I am a Christian, and to be a Christian one must be merciful. So I will be merciful and pray and pray and pray for the souls of any TRANSGRESSORS who might be sitting before me NOW and are currently thinking like THE JEW. Because I know IF THEY'LL ONLY LISTEN to how they will SUFFER when this life is over, if they'll only IMAGINE how those HOT FLAMES must feel burning their flesh for ETERNITY, if they'll only..." At that moment Reverend Ignatius Apple began gesticulating, jerking his head and left arm in an uncontrollable motion. At the same time, spittle was drooling off of his chin. His eyes became glazed over, as he fixed them upon the large crucifix on the back wall of the church. A couple of men from the front pews rushed up on the pulpit, thinking that Reverend Apple was having a heart attack. Bubba tried to go up and help his father, but his mother held him back. Reverend Apple violently pushed the helpers away and shouted, "SINNERS! SHIT! DISSIMULATE NO MORE! FUCK! YOUR SOULS ARE MINE! BASTARDS!" And then just as quickly as the herky-jerky stuff had started, it stopped. Reverend Apple used the arm of his suit jacket to wipe the spittle from his chin, his eyes went back to normal, and he continued, "LISTEN TO WHAT A CHRISTIAN MUST DO TO FIGHT SATAN! If they'll only ask FORGIVENESS...and feel how Christ COMPELS THEM to FIGHT SATAN! I pray to JESUS for them, and ask HIM to help them to SEE THE LIGHT." And with that having been said, Reverend Apple quickly ended the service with the Twenty-third Psalm.

In 1927, in Wedowee, Alabama, and everywhere else for that matter, nobody had yet heard about the hideous disease called Tourette's Syndrome. When Ignatius Apple's gesticulating and swearing became more pronounced in public, people postulated that he was fighting Satan—not just for himself, but for everyone. So Ignatius' shaking, drooling, and swearing rants were always welcomed at *The Wedowee Coffee Shop*, Jim Taylor's Barber Shop, or Jack Jackson's Hardware Store. The townsfolk always felt particularly blessed when in the presence of Reverend Apple during one of those moments, and the common response was, "Thank you Lord, for sending us a true Christian warrior to help us battle Satan." By then, Tom Powers had seen the light and had stopped selling illegal moonshine. But, of course, that didn't stop people from drinking. Now everyone who liked to drink, including Sheriff John Owen, had to drive an extra two miles to see Marcus Tucker, a non-parishioner who had always been Tom Powers' main competitor. Yes, Reverend Apple was welcome everywhere, except when children were present. The common response when children were present was to cover their ears. When a child would ask, "Why can't I hear what Reverend Apple is saying?" The parent would respond, "You are not ready to understand Reverend Apple's way of battling for us yet. When you're older…" (And, of course, young devoted Jewish children would be told the same thing by their parents, if they attempted to study *Kabballa* before the age of forty.)

Meanwhile, the governing board of the Wedowee Baptist Church decided by June of 1927 that the children should not hear Reverend Apple in church either. And although Bubba regularly heard his father at home during his Satan-battling moments, and he had accepted his parents' explanation as to the importance of what was happening, he too was denied admission into church on Sunday mornings. The pride he had always felt, from watching his father preach from that pulpit, was suddenly taken from him. No longer would the children attend an hour of Sunday school and then join the adults for the second half of the service, which included Reverend Ignatius Apple's sermon. Instead, they would stay the full two hours with their teacher, the ancient Mrs. Moss, and she would do a children's version of the service complete with a children's sermon in class.

On this August afternoon in 1974, after Dr. Bill Wick's sedative had kicked in, and Bruiser had left his father in the semi-private room with the man in bed 505A mumbling something incoherent about Watergate, Bubba was dreaming about his father's swearing on that pulpit in Wedowee in 1927. He was also remembering what he overheard Jerry Tucker, Marcus Tucker's seven year-old son say to two other boys at school, "My father says that Reverend Apple is crazier than a shithouse rat!" And all that was getting slammed in Bubba's dreamy, delusional mind at the moment, along with an article about Tourette's, from an unsolicited mailed science journal, that he had recently read while pondering his kingdom in the barn. Bubba awoke in a terrible mood thinking, 'crazier than a shithouse rat, Tourette's, and the apple doesn't fall far from the tree!'

A nurse's aide, who walked into the room just a few moments later said, "Mr. Apple. We need your dinner selection for tonight."

"WHYYY…What difference does it MAAAKE?" Bubba said in a nasty way. "All of the food is SHITTT here anyway!"

"I'm so very sorry you're unhappy with the food, Mr. Apple," she said in her most diplomatic way. And, of course, Bubba was just assuming that the food was no good since it was hospital food, and he had no idea that his daughter Jennifer's friend, the soon-to-be-divorced doctor that she had not been jogging with but had recently been arguing with, had a brother who was CEO of *HOSPCHOW*, the largest provider of food and hospital kitchen personnel in the world, and at her request in the last year to Dr. Colin Morgan after a particularly wonderful afternoon of sex, and at his request to his brother after his brother had trounced him 6-2/6-1 in a particularly vigorous best 2-out-of-3-sets Sunday morning tennis match, that Mick Morgan was more than happy to make sure that Rutland General Hospital was placed in the upper tier of customers. They always received the best of everything. "You have no dietary restrictions listed on your chart, so you are welcome to use your phone and call outside of the hospital for delivery of anything you'd like," the nurse's aide said. And, of course, 'As sore as your ass is gonna be when that anesthetic wears off, why don't you phone out for a huge bucket of prunes, Mr. Big Mouth!' was what she was thinking.

"And WAAASTE my money on a delivery fee? WHYYY...JEEESUS CHRIIIST...YOUUU people must think I'm made of MONEEEY!"

And the nurse's aide left with, "If you need anything Mr. Apple, just ring the bell."

Bubba decided he wanted Pauline's food, so he called her to ask for a plate later. The phone kept ringing. "WHYYY...JEEESUS CHRIIIST... Where the HELLL is SHEEE?" Bubba said loudly and then slammed the phone down.

The man in bed 505A, still dreaming about Watergate said, "She accidentally erased the tapes."

"What the HELLL are you talking about?" Bubba yelled at his roommate.

"Rosemary Woods. She's probably left Washington by now," he said, and then he fell back asleep.

@@@@@@@@

"Look...Salome...once again...I shouldn't have asked that question. I'm sorry," Anthony said, just as Van Morrison's "Moondance" was ending on the radio. The radiator hose had been fixed, and although there had been moments of chit-chat during the past hour or so on the road that had almost broached the tenor of conversation prior to Anthony's question, that ill-at-ease feeling had and still permeated the *Dodge*. Anthony had apologized back at the coffee shop, and Salome had responded, "Just forget it," but Anthony realized it wasn't forgotten.

"I don't know why I was so tactless, Salome. We just met...a question like, 'how many men have you slept with?' is none of my business anyway."

"You were tactless," Salome said in slow deliberate syllabic pronunciation, "because you have the same battle with misogyny that my father has!"

"Mis...? What was that word you used?" Anthony asked.

"Misogyny...hating women. You see all women as potential whores. We're all just sperm receptacles to you. You think women are good for just one thing," Salome said, and then watched as they sped by some guy hitch-hiking on Highway 7.

"That's not true!" Anthony protested. "I've had a lot of female friends in my life."

"Yeah?" Salome asked. "You have any female friends now? You know, someone you can call and ask to crash at her place for a day or two? Someone you can borrow money from by saying, 'I have a date tonight with this incredible woman. Could you loan me a few bucks?'"

"Well...not really," Anthony said, as he swerved into the left lane to avoid a manure truck, whose idiot driver had pulled directly in front of him. Anthony quickly rolled down the window and gave him the finger.

"That's because you don't have any female friends. You have female acquaintances...women you'd like to fuck who haven't let you yet...and they're just in a 'holding pattern' until you either do 'em or forget about them," Salome said, stressing the word "fuck" for all of its shock value.

"Are you saying it is impossible for me to have female friends that I don't want to fuck?" Anthony asked, feeling some excitement.

"No...I don't believe it's impossible for men and women to be Platonic," Salome said. "Sometime, in the future, you may be able to develop a strong non-sexual relationship with a woman. But you're not in that place now. You probably have some issues with your mother."

"What's my mother got to do with this?" Anthony asked.

"You're in college and you've never taken a psychology class?"

"No I haven't," Anthony responded, somewhat pissed off that his intelligence was being examined. "I have to take one this year at UVM, it's part of the sophomore requirement."

"Well...you're gonna have to read some Freud. You'll learn about the Oedipal Complex, and how young boys have a secret desire to kill their fathers and marry their mothers, and then get pissed off at their mothers for choosing their fathers instead."

"That's such bullshit!" Anthony said, annoyed with this conversation.

"It's true!" And Salome reiterated, "Young boys, at a very young age, have a desire to replace their fathers with themselves."

"Where did you hear such horseshit?" Anthony demanded.

"I read a general psychology textbook last year, while I was grounded in my room for a month...thanks to my asshole father," Salome said, remembering back to that particular rage. "It was in a big box of books that my Aunt Clara sent over after my Uncle Wilbur died. The son/mother thing is fairly common," Salome continued. "There's also a daughter/father thing, although I forgot what it's called. Anyway, in most cases, this is why people have issues with their parent of the opposite gender. The reason you hold women in such low regard is because you probably hate your mother."

And that caused the old hurt to surface in Anthony's countenance. With certain celerity, Salome could see the change in Anthony's expression, from annoyance to hurt. And she said, "What's up with your mother?"

And Anthony, having battled with the onerous hurt for years, said, "I hate my mother for abandoning me just before my second birthday, and having made no effort to contact me in the past seventeen years. I don't know if she's alive or dead. When she was alive, I hated my step-mother for trying to replace my mother, and I hated all of the extra work I had to do because she ended up in a wheelchair. She's dead, but I still hate her. But how does this fit into all of your psychological theories? I hate my father also, but I've hated him always...for driving my mother away...because of the affair he had...with the woman who would later become my step-mother...And I hate him now...for blowing his brains out last year!"

@@@@@@@@

Pauline and Jennifer Apple, having consumed four vodka and tonics, were sitting on the living room floor giggling. "A Blastoff?" Pauline half-laughed/half-spoke. "And *who* thought of this drink?"

"I told you Mom," Jennifer said. And then doing her Bubba impression, complete with pointing figure she continued, "WHYYY you're not PAAAYING attention WOMAAAN!" Pauline was laughing tears as Jennifer continued in her own voice, "Colin named the drink. We were sitting in his Manhattan apartment and he said, 'Hey...if *Gatorade* enters a body so much quicker...what do you think'll happen if we mix it with vodka?'"

"Blastoff!" And Pauline laughed some more and said, "Why don't you go get us some *Gatorade*? I want to try that drink."

"Because I'm too drunk to drive," Jennifer said.

Fortuitously, Bruiser walked in and Pauline asked him to go.

"Jesus Christ Mom...Don't you guys think you've had enough?"

"We're just fine!" Pauline exclaimed, "Just go to the store and get me some *Gatorade*, Bruiser."

"Okay...okay...I'll have to do this quickly. I need the car to go check out another dog near Middlebury," Bruiser said, while snatching a piece of candy from the candy dish on the coffee table.

"Middlebury! You're going to drive up there now?" Pauline asked.

"This is a great deal. This puppy comes from an award winning line of Walkers, and he's only $700. He'll be ready to tree bear for next year's season in September," Bruiser said.

"But you already have four dogs. All they do is yelp all of the time," Jennifer said, somewhat annoyed at the number of times her sleep had been disturbed since she had returned from Manhattan.

"You should have gotten used to sleeping through a lot of noise, having spent the last couple of years in New York City!" Bruiser shot back. "Hey... shut the fuck up! I took the $5,000 that Uncle Wilbur left me, built the kennel out there by the barn all by myself, went to Georgia and bought two award winning Red Ticks, went to Burlington and bought two award winning Walkers, and doubled my money last year taking idiot hunters to tree and shoot bear."

"Yeah...well one of those Red Ticks, Gertrude you call her, just trees kitties!" Jennifer laughed out.

"Shut up you miserable bitch! Gertrude is great at treeing coons. With all the damage that coons do, Gertrude made me close to $1000 last year. All *you* can tree are married doctors!" Bruiser said nastily.

"Hey fuck you nature boy!" Jennifer shot back.

"Both of you stop the swearing," Pauline said. "Bubba's not here tonight, so I'd like to enjoy one evening without all of the foul language."

"Okay Mom. I'm too busy to stand here arguing with my pinhead sister anyway, so I'll go get your *Gatorade* and then head up to Middlebury."

"Take one of the trucks," Pauline said, "I don't want puppy pee in my car."

"Okay Mom, I'll be back in a few," Bruiser said as he grabbed the truck keys from the hook in the kitchen and headed out the screen door.

"Hey Jennifer, be nice to your brother," Pauline said after Bruiser had left. "He's not really college material...he always struggled in school...and there aren't too many decent jobs in this part of the state. I give Bruiser lots of credit. He could have just worked for Bubba forever, and perhaps that is what he'll eventually do, but to pass that state test...to become a fully licensed Vermont State Wilderness Guide...I have to give him credit, that was quite a feat."

"Yeah, well he's gonna lose his license," Jennifer said, "if he doesn't stop shooting bear out of season."

"OH MY GOD YES," Pauline said. "I told him that. He's been real lucky so far."

Changing the subject Jennifer asked, "So what do you want to do for dinner, Mom? I'm getting hungry."

"Well...after the drinks...I'm not in the mood to cook. Jimson is having dinner at a friend's house, and Jack is working at the gas station until 11:00 pm. Don't know when Salome will get home, and Bruiser will be gone a few hours. Let's just get a couple of pizzas delivered," Pauline said, "In case anybody shows up hungry later, we'll have plenty."

"What about Bubba? You know he's gonna want you to bring him food. That was probably him calling before."

"I'm sure that was Bubba. To hell with Bubba tonight, let him fend for himself!" Pauline stressed.

Bruiser, quickly back from his two-block-down-Highway-7-store-sojourn, plunked the *Gatorade* on the table, and said, "See ya!"

"I hope Salome gets home soon...I worry about her," Pauline said.

That got Jennifer thinking. With cautious effort, she made her way up the stairs to Salome's room. She looked through Salome's armoire, bureau, and closet, and she saw that a good portion of Salome's clothes were gone. 'She's still got my green top!' Jennifer thought, as she looked for Salome's large duffle bag, and discovered that it was gone also.

Jennifer, head spinning from the drinks, walked slowly down the stairs. Pauline had already called for pizza, and there were two "Blastoffs" mixed and waiting. "Most of her clothes are gone," Jennifer said, "I think Salome has run away."

"OH MY GOD NO!" Pauline said.

@@@@@@@@

Bruiser Apple turned off of Highway 7 at the old Four Corners dirt road. He was about eight miles south of Middlebury, as he headed east a few miles toward Ripton, along the Middlebury River, on this other unnamed dirt road. Since Pauline had made him take the truck, there was work that could be handled today instead of tomorrow. He found the spot where he usually hid the vehicle, and he took his six plastic one gallon milk containers, made the five trips to the river, and watered the thirty female marijuana plants he had scattered and safely growing in the woods along the base of The Bread Loaf Mountains. No, perhaps Bruiser wasn't "college material," but he had certainly understood the two horticultural books he had purchased in a head shop in Burlington that had taught him how to grow pot. He had used the seeds from some great *Maui Wowie* that a friend, Jr. Liberty, had brought back from Hawaii. And, after the fourteen male plants had been extracted, Bruiser was originally left with thirty-four healthy budding females that were due to be harvested right around Labor Day. And, of course, since not many people were growing marijuana in the northern states in 1974, and since most people didn't even know what a marijuanna plant looked like in 1974, Bruiser had very little to worry about in the way of either pirates or law enforcement officials. But Bruiser wasn't complacent. He had learned how to grow his plants horizontally, so although each plant was between seven and nine feet long, none was more than four feet high. His biggest problem had been the deer and bunnies, who apparently hadn't noticed the plants in their infancy, but had waited and feasted on four nearly mature plants in the past month. (Years later, when Bruiser would tell Felix that, Felix would remark, "I never knew that deer and rabbits were so smart. I guess good things do come to those who wait!" He would also add, thinking of the Steinbeck novel, "It's too bad that you didn't have Lennie Small around to help you with your rabbit problem!")

A third horticultural book would finally solve Bruiser's dilemma. He learned that he needed human hair. So, covertly, Bruiser had made several trips to Burlington and had visited several different beauty salons. He had waited until late in the business day at each salon, and then requested the cut hair on the floor for a science project he was allegedly doing at school on "How Mold Can Affect Hair." All of the ladies in the salons, although surprised, were happy to accommodate and have somebody else sweep their floors for free. Bruiser had collected five huge plastic garbage bags of human hair, hid them for a week in the basement of the barn, cut up and mixed in plenty of garlic cloves, and urinated several times in each bag. He had then placed this cornucopia of odious smells around the scattered pot plants. This procedure had been completely successful, as the deer and bunnies, expecting a free lunch, had to finally throw up their paws in disgust and say, "Fuck this shit! This stinkhole is somebody else's turf!" (And, of course, this same kind of turf procedure would always work—with graffiti—in the neighborhoods of New York City.)

@@@@@@@@

A few hours later, after Bruiser had returned with the pup he bought in Middlebury and was sleeping soundly, after Jack and Jimson had come home and were in Sandman Land, after Jennifer had consumed two Blastoffs with Pauline and was lights out with sheep counting her, after Bubba had been given another sedative, and was now dreaming that he was fourteen and at some kind of an amusement park called Wacky Wedowee World, listening to his father deliver yet another mercurial monologue—this time about the loaves and FUCKING fishes—Pauline was sitting up totally sober, keeping vigil for a phone call from her youngest, her anguish having totally overtaken the effects of six drinks.

The phone rang. "Hello...Salome?" Pauline nervously asked.

"It's me, Mom," number two daughter Cindy Chumwell said all the way from Sendai, Japan. "I know it's nearly 2400 your time, but I just got back from the doctor. I was kind of scared."

"What's the matter sweetheart, is everything okay with the baby?" Pauline asked, shifting her concern from Salome's plight for the moment.

"Everything's fine," Cindy said. "After I spoke to you earlier, at about 1330, I noticed that I was bleeding...I got scared that's all. I walked over to the base doctor's office and got checked out. I just got back. Everything is normal."

"Thank God!" Pauline said. "I couldn't stand anymore bad news right now."

"Why...what's going on?" Cindy asked. "You answered the phone thinking it was Salome. Is she still gone? Is Bubba up ranting and raving waiting to give her hell when she gets home?"

"Bubba isn't even here. Bill Wicks made him stay in the hospital, at least for tonight. He wanted to keep a watch on Bubba's butt, after cutting it, to make sure that there wasn't any infection," Pauline said. "He doesn't know yet that Salome has run away. And since he's the one who drove her away, the hell with him, I'll tell him tomorrow."

"How do you know that she's run away?" Cindy asked.

"Jennifer found...that half of Salome's clothes...plus that big green duffle bag that she loves...were all gone."

"What do you think Bubba will do?" Cindy asked after gulping.

"I imagine he'll go see Gene Fowler over at the state police, or Rutland Sheriff Glenn, or both," Pauline said and then added, "He'll probably want to file a Missing Persons Report."

"Well how about you, Mom? Don't you want to file a report?"

"Not yet. I trust Salome. She may be only fourteen, but she's very wise. I know she hasn't spent a penny of the $5,000 Uncle Wilbur left her, and that she had nearly $1200 saved up anyway from babysitting and birthday presents from the past few years. She probably figured something out with the money. I just hope she isn't out there hitchhiking with more than $6,000 in her pocket! She had to have figured something out...Wait a minute. Listen Cindy, let me call you tomorrow. I have an idea that I need to follow up on."

"Okay Mom," Cindy said. "Call me anytime tomorrow and let me know what's happening. Please don't forget, Mom!"

"I'll call you sweetheart...I promise. Give my love to Dick," and then Pauline hung up.

Pauline immediately opened the drawer of the nightstand table and took out her address book. She found Selma Greenwood's phone number.

The phone rang five times before a sleepy Selma Greenwood answered, "Hello?"

"Hi Selma...It's Pauline Apple. Sorry to call so late...but you know our agreement."

"I know Pauline. I did hear from her an hour ago, and I was going to call you in the morning. It seemed kind of late tonight," Selma said, hoping that Pauline wasn't annoyed with her. Attractive forty-two year-old Selma Greenwood, sat up in the bed and pulled the auburn hair out of her eyes.

Pauline appreciated that her daughter could always find safe haven with Selma. Although Salome and Pauline had a wonderful relationship, there were times when Salome felt more comfortable talking to an adult woman who wasn't her mom. In the past five years, Salome had found that she could trust Selma with anything, and that Selma's accurate acumens were a source of great comfort.

"Where is she, Selma?" Pauline asked with a voice full of stress.

"You know our deal, Pauline. I won't ever betray Salome, but I'll keep you abreast of how she's doing," Selma said.

"That's not going to work this time!" Pauline emphasized. "She's only fourteen, and she's a runaway. I'm sorry Selma, but Bubba's in the hospital, and I'd love to work things out with Salome before he comes home."

"What's wrong with Bubba?" Selma asked, as she used just about all twenty-five feet of the extra long cord to carry the phone into the bathroom with her.

"Your buddy Salome left some extra strong *Krazy Glue* on the toilet seat for Bubba...The boys had to use a power saw to cut the seat from the toilet...and then Bill had to cut the seat off of Bubba's butt...Bill wants him to stay in the hospital at least tonight...keep a watch for possible infection."

Selma couldn't suppress her laughter, and while she was tinkling she said, "At least it isn't something life threatening!"

"Well it's life threatening to Salome, if Bubba gets a hold of her," Pauline said kind of half-seriously.

"What would Bubba do?" Selma asked, while flushing the toilet. "Would he beat her? Lock her up for the rest of the summer?"

"He might beat her," Pauline said. "At least he'll slap her across the face and ground her in her room for the rest of the summer. But that's certainly better than something happening to her hitchhiking! Look Selma, I have to talk to her. Where is she?"

"When she called an hour ago, she was on the outskirts of New York City." And then realizing that a slight variation in the truth would be better for Pauline and Pauline's family's sake, Selma added, "She was picked up on Highway 7 by a couple of nice college sisters from UVM. She said that they had offered her a place to stay on Long Island for the week, and they were sure it would be okay with their parents," Selma said, now back in bed.

"What is she going to do then? Does she have her savings with her?"

"She said that she was going to find a room in New York, sign up for a one-year GED prep course, and then get her high school diploma by the time she's fifteen. And since she knows that she can attend a community college with a GED, it's her intention to be enrolled in college at fifteen also," Selma said, which was what Salome did intend. As for the nearly $6200 that everyone in the family assumed Salome had in the bank, in reality $5500 had been given in the last year to Selma to keep in case Salome had an emergency, and the nearly $700 Salome had stashed with her stash in a small metal box in her bedroom floor under a loose plank between the scantlings, she had taken with her. Not wanting the Apples to make life even more difficult for either Salome or herself, Selma decided not to say that she was to send the $5500 to Salome when Salome was settled. Instead Selma said, "Salome has all of her money with her. She said she had most of it in hundred dollar bills, and that it was hidden within the lining of her boots. She said that in the next day or two she plans on depositing most of what's left in a bank in New York

City, after she pays a couple months of rent in advance on a room someplace."

"That money will run out quickly in New York. How does she plan on supporting herself while she's studying to get her GED?"

And, of course, since Selma wanted to propitiate a profession for Salome that Pauline could possibly live with, and knowing how the Apples would see that modeling at fourteen with a bogus ID saying "Jennifer" was parlous, Selma said, "Salome said she knows she can find a waitress job anywhere, that there are a million places to eat in Manhattan. She plans on living simply for the next year, with just work and study occupying her time. Salome is a real smart girl," Selma added. "I believe she will be successful and make it all the way through college."

"No doubt," Pauline said. "I know she's smart enough to do anything. But she's too young to be doing this now. She should just come home and graduate normally with her class in three years from Rutland Central High School. She should be with her family now. Later, she can go off to college."

"Well," Selma said, "You know that Bubba is the problem. Salome has cried to me too often about him. She finally decided that she cannot be around him any longer."

"That crazy son of a bitch!" Pauline stressed. "If I didn't love him I'd divorce him."

"Yeah...love is strange," Selma said, thinking back to her three-year topsy-turvy marriage. Her husband, Robert Greenwood, had died from cancer five years ago.

"Regardless of what Salome wants to do, and no matter how much I trust her to do well, Bubba is never going to allow his fourteen year-old daughter to live alone in New York," Pauline said. "And you know he'll get the FBI involved if he has to."

Selma suddenly gulped hard, imagining a future interrogation with the FBI. What would she do? She wanted to protect Salome, and secretly she admired Salome's quixotic modeling vision, but there was something in her past that nobody in Rutland knew anything about, and she certainly wanted no part in discussing anything with the *federales*.

"Do you really think that the FBI will be real interested in a fourteen year-old runaway girl, especially if she calls them regularly to say she's okay? It seems to me that they're just too busy for all of that!" Selma hoped.

"That depends on how much of a stink Bubba raises," Pauline said. "And I just can't imagine Bubba not doing everything to bring her back."

"If and when she calls again," Selma said, thinking that it would behoove her for this thing to end before the FBI got involved, "I'll tell her to call you."

"OH MY GOD PLEASE, Selma!" Pauline half-cried out, "Tell her I love her and we can work this out."

@@@@@@@@

"My second generation Italian Catholic father, Frank Kulpa, met my second generation Russian Jewish mother, Beverly Jenkowitz, in New York City in 1943, while he was on a thirty-day leave from the Navy," Anthony told Salome. Just stating the hatred of his mother, step-mother, and father, had been the necessary confession that opened the door to a comfortable cathartic conversation with Salome. "He met her on day one of his leave, proposed on day 6, was turned down until day 13, they married on day 27, honeymooned until day 30, and then he was in Europe for 2 years. While he was gone, a grandparent I never knew, Sophie Jenkowitz, the six-year widow of Chaim Jenkowitz, another grandparent I never knew, apparently softened her hard-line attitude toward her only child marrying outside of the Jewish religion, and didn't change her will as she had originally threatened, died, and left my mother a duplex on Ocean Parkway in Brooklyn and nearly $100,000 in cash, stocks, and bonds. When dear old dad's hitch with the Navy was up in 1945, he convinced my mother to sell the duplex, move to Madeira Beach, Florida, and buy a small three-floor twelve-unit plus owner's duplex motel right on the Gulf of Mexico."

"So you grew up right on the water?" Salome asked, fascinated with every punctilio in Anthony's pontification. But as Salome would say on the days in which she believed in astrology, "It's my Leo nature to be curious."

"Yeah...it was kind of neat watching the Sun go down over the Gulf of Mexico every evening," Anthony semi-sarcastically said.

"Tell me more about your family."

"My parents bought this small motel, *The Breakers*, on Madeira Beach in the summer of 1945. It features 300 feet of beachfront on the gulf. It is three floors and shaped like a big U. In the middle of the U is a swimming pool and shuffleboard court. On the first floor is a game room complete with two pool tables and four bridge tables, a small laundry room, lots of storage space, two two-car garages, and the office. There are twelve rooms for rent on the second floor. Nine of those rooms are efficiencies for overnight or short-stay rentals, and three are one-bedroom apartments that we rent by the year. On the third floor, on each side of the U, is an apartment that is more like a small house. Each of the two apartments on the third floor has three bedrooms and two baths. Our family lived in the southern apartment. The northern apartment was saved for the Malcovitch family, the wealthy parents of Darius, the photographer whose home in Amagansett we'll be staying at in about twenty minutes," Anthony said as they crossed Hampton Bay. "Darius' grandparents had rented that same apartment for more than twenty-five years, from when the original owners had built the place in 1925. It was part of the deal my parents cut with the former owners, to always allow the Malcovitchs to have that apartment. Darius' parents took it over in the early 1950's, and kept it until they had a major falling out with my father in 1963. And if you knew the incredible amount they'd pay to stay there from January 3rd until early April each year, demanding that the place remain unoccupied for the other nine months, you could understand how financially hurt we were after that dispute. There wasn't a mortgage on the place, my mother's money had purchased the motel for cash in 1945, but the Malcovitch money paid the entire overhead and put all of the food on our table for the whole year. That allowed my parents until 1957, and then just my father until 1963, to use the monies from all of the other rents for savings."

"Why was there a falling out in 1963 between them and your father?" Salome asked.

"One thing good I can say about my father is that he was no racist. He rented one of the one-bedroom apartments by the year to a black man. In 1963, two years before Civil Rights Legislation would make it illegal to discriminate, there were no motels or hotels renting to black people on the beaches along the gulf in the St. Petersburg area. No motel other than *The Breakers* that is, and Darius' father wasn't happy about it. My father was ostracized by all of the other hotel/motel owners, as well as all of the other beach businesses. His picture was in the paper so many times with police articles about threats to the family and vandalism to the property, it got to the point that when we'd want to eat out or go to a movie, we'd have to drive across Tampa Bay to Tampa." Anthony said, and then lit a smoke.

"Sounds like your dad was quite a man," Salome said, and then lit one herself.

"Yeah...well that doesn't excuse all of the other shit he pulled!" Anthony said, getting angry thinking about it.

Salome, realizing that discussing more dad/mom issues might have to wait, said, "So how did you meet this photographer, Darius, last year, if his family stopped staying at your place in 1963?"

"It was after the season was over in June. Darius parked his *MGB* in the lot, walked into the office, and asked my brother if the big apartment on the third floor was vacant. My brother said, 'Yes,' and asked him how he knew about it. Darius told Felix who he was, and about his wonderful childhood memories of that apartment. Remembering Darius from a decade earlier, Felix said, that he didn't believe 'that the sins of the fathers were passed on to the sons,' and he rented Darius the place for a month."

Salome suddenly felt uncomfortable and said, "Yeah, but if Darius' parents are assholes, and they had a falling out with your dad, how come we're staying at their place?"

"Well," and Anthony smiled as he threw his cigarette butt out on the highway, "Darius' father is the A-hole, his mom is wonderful. Anyway, they're both in Alaska with Darius' younger sister and brother for the summer. He told them that my name was Anthony Greene, that I was a nice Jewish boy attending the University of Vermont in Pre-Law, and that he had met me while doing a major photo shoot in Burlington."

The irony didn't escape Salome, and she said, "So you and I are both using aliases?"

"Kinda necessary," said Anthony, "when staying for free at a racist's mansion on Long Island, a racist who hates my family."

"Kinda funny and kinda sad," Salome said. "Kinda wonderful also," she continued, thinking about herself, her siblings, Anthony and his brother, and apparently Darius too, "how the children have grown up with better values than past generations." And then reflecting on Bubba she added, "My dad may be an asshole, but I don't recall him ever being a racist."

"Do your parents have any black friends…not just acquaintances but real friends…and for that matter do you?" Anthony asked, seeing an opportunity to pay Salome back a little for the embarrassment over her 'you don't have any females friends really' discussion from earlier.

"Well other than the older woman I called earlier, Selma, Geneva Liberty is my best friend, and she's black." Salome continued, "And Geneva's brother, Jr., is my brother Bruiser's best friend. But no, my parents don't hang out with any black couples in Rutland…but then they don't really hang out with anybody as a couple anymore…We do have a number of black employees at the orchard...What's your point?"

"I guess I don't have one," Anthony said, pleased nonetheless that he had a chance to put Salome on the defensive. Then he tossed in, "Truth or dare? And I promise my question won't be as personal as before."

Salome didn't feel like playing, but Anthony reminded her that he hadn't felt like playing in the coffee shop at Arrowhead either. "Truth," Salome begrudgingly said.

"Would you marry a black man?" Anthony asked with a twinkle in his eye.

"If I loved him," Salome shot back with lightning-like speed. And then she added, "And you?"

"I don't think I'd want to marry a black man!" Anthony said.

"Come on wise ass, you know what I mean," Salome said, and then gave him the same kind of elbow poke in the sides that she had given him in the Berkshires earlier.

"I'd marry a black woman if I loved her," Anthony said and then added, "My father used to say that intermarriage was the way to solve the world's racial problems. I grew up believing that."

"Wow!" Salome said. "It sounds as if your father was a Hippie before there were Hippies."

"He was part of the Beat Generation in the 1950's, before the Beatniks, before the Hippies. As a matter of fact, for many years the Beat Writer Jack Kerouac stayed at our motel."

"I never heard of him," Salome said. "What did he write?"

"Several novels," Anthony said and then added, "Probably *On the Road* was his most famous or *The Dharma Bums*. He died in St. Pete. in 1969. My father attended his funeral....Also, when Felix was in graduate school in Literature at NYU a few years back, he had a professor who bad-mouthed Mr. Kerouac...called him a 'delusional drug using deadbeat writer.' My brother always liked Mr. Kerouac...so his response was to write a big paper for that Modern American Literature class...I don't thoroughly understand it...but Felix said that his paper showed...how the passivity of drug use by Kerouac...while sitting in the back of a car typing his stories across America...was more noble...and did a lot less damage...than the machismo notions of Hemingway—having to battle a big fish or to kill a bull."

"So your brother is real smart," Salome said. She wanted to ask why Anthony's brother felt responsible for their now deceased step-mother becoming a paraplegic, but she decided that could wait, along with questions about Anthony's real mother's abandonment and Anthony's father's suicide. Instead Salome asked, "What ever happened in 1963 with the black guy at your motel?"

"Mr. Younger is still staying with us. Walter Lee Younger is our best friend, and kind of our surrogate father, because he's nineteen years older than Felix and twenty-eight years older than me. Just like your best friend, Selma, is twenty-eight years older than you."

"What does Mr. Younger do for a living?" Salome asked.

"He's done a lot of different things in the past eleven years. Last year, my brother convinced him to try college at the University of Tampa Bay. He easily aced his first year there. Now he's all excited...wants to go to graduate school...become an anthropologist."

Salome, thinking of her own impending college fate down the road, said, "So he's able to work his way through college without a problem?"

"Well," Anthony said, as they pulled the car through the brick gate and started up the drive toward the Malcovitch mansion, "Walter Lee mostly lives off of the lawsuit money he won against both a homeowners association on the Southside of Chicago and the city of Chicago itself."

"Why...what happened?" Salome asked.

"In 1962 his family's home was fire bombed in a white subdivision of Chicago...Clybourne Park I think it was called...The bombers were seen wearing KKK white hoods... but it was later proven that was just a masquerade...it wasn't the KKK who had done the bombing...it was actually the Clybourne Park Home Owners Association...And the head of that organization...I think his name was Lindner or something similar...also worked for the Housing Commission in the mayor's office. Walter's mother, sister, son, wife, and the child she was carrying all perished in the bombing."

"OH MY GOD!" Salome said, sounding a lot like her own mother.

Chapter Three

Bathed in full moonlight, the opulent Malcovitch mansion resembled a Mediterranean patrician's palace. Anthony hopped out of the dead tired *Dodge* with Salome's *Polaroid* and popped off a few pictures for posterity.

"What a house!" said Salome, as she posed for a photo in front.

"I've gotta pee!" said Anthony, as he gave the camera to Salome and she took his picture in the same place.

"Hey Anthony...remember...my name is Jennifer...okay?" Salome mentioned for the second time in five minutes.

"Me remembering your name isn't going to be your problem," Anthony said with a concerned smirk. An attractive African-American woman in her late thirties answered the doorbell. "You must be Anthony," she said. "And this is the friend you mentioned on the phone earlier. I'm Annie Harrison, and I'm the live in housekeeper and cook. Young Mr. Malcovitch hasn't returned from his photo shoot in Pt. Jefferson, although he should be home within the hour. In the meantime, let me show you to your rooms."

"Thanks so much Miss...or is it Mrs. Harrison? My friend here is Jennifer," Anthony said, as he walked into the foyer caring both his and Salome's duffle bags.

And Salome said, "It's *Ms.* Harrison, Anthony!" And Salome turned to her and said, "It's a pleasure to meet you."

"It's Annie. Young Mr. Malcovitch prefers if I call him Dari when his father isn't around."

"I heard the father is an A-hole!" tired Salome blurted out and then embarrassingly flipped with, "I'm so sorry! That was a stupid thing for me to say."

"But girl...it was right on the money!" And Annie burst out laughing and slapped Salome lovingly on the back. "I like you already Jennifer," she added.

"I'm sorry, but I need a bathroom desperately!" Anthony grimaced. Annie led Anthony and Salome upstairs and showed them their bedrooms. Their bedrooms were right next to each other, both huge with separate sitting areas and private bathrooms. Anthony rushed to check out his private bathroom. Annie mentioned that although it was after midnight, she had been keeping spaghetti and meatballs warm for everybody. Also, she said that she had made "the best damn garlic bread on Long Island!" Anthony and Salome were starved, so after washing up and changing, they both quickly headed downstairs to the kitchen table.

"I hope you like my cooking," Annie said. Annie was a wonderful cook, with a creative flair in the mixing of flavors. Although tonight's spaghetti and meatballs was just great comfort food, her garlic bread, indeed, was a taste sensation. Her particular secret with the garlic bread and with most of the dinners she cooked was that she used a blend of several different types of peppers, which—particularly for the seafood—left a wonderful not-too-hot-not-too-sweet taste in the mouth. She even made her own breadsticks with peppers, and they were as magnificent as her garlic bread. She was ahead of her time, in that this type of nouveau Southwestern cooking would be made very popular fifteen years later in Manhattan by another Long Island chef. Two of the tragedies in Annie's life thus far, had been not being able to find the right guy to love her, and not being able to find the right person to financially back her in a restaurant. Bringing an accountant and an attorney with her to prove just how much money could be made with a restaurant in the right location, the subject had been broached with the wealthy Mr. Malcovitch. And although he loved Annie's cuisine, his distrust in the abilities of an African-American woman to succeed as an entrepreneur had caused him to reject the idea. His official rejection for public posturing had been, "I run a satellite guidance corporation complete with an assembly plant here on Long Island, and a large salmon seining business in Alaska. I know nothing about the restaurant business, and I'm just too busy to diversify any more."

"But don't you see," Annie had said. "With your salmon business, the only real cost would be the shipping of that fish back to New York. I would feature my special peppered version of the salmon at our restaurant, and in no time we'd be booking reservations six weeks in advance. Think of all the money we could make at a chichi Manhattan place at $19.95 a pop!"

"I'm sorry Annie, but no," had been Gregor Malcovitch's final reply. His wife, Elizabeth Malcovitch, had thought Annie's idea was sound, but she knew better than to question her husband's business decisions. Darius thought the idea was terrific, and he had been saving a bundle of money from the ridiculously high amounts he was now able to command as a well known photographer. He figured within the next year or two with the cash he would have, plus his credit line, he would be able to go into business with Annie. Recently he had thought, 'I wonder...will dad sell the salmon to me cheaply?'

And when Darius had told Annie Harrison his intent, she replied, "You're a wonderful young man, Dari. If you can pull off your end of the deal, we'll make a fortune. Oh...and FYI, I've had a notion to try rolling that peppered salmon in a macadamia nut and onion breading. If it's good, I thought that would be a second variation of my peppered salmon on the menu." A week later she tried her new idea, and she received all kinds of accolades from the Malcovitch family. In fact, Gregor Malcovitch had slipped and said, "This should be on the menu of a restaurant somewhere!"

"Your spaghetti and meatballs are wonderful," Salome said. "But this garlic bread is to die for."

"I agree," said Anthony. "If I'm ever awaiting execution in The Big House, this garlic bread is definitely going to be a part of my last meal!"

"Thank you both so much," Annie said with a big smiling face. "Since you'll be staying here the better part of this week, I'll make you my special salmon one night. You've never tasted anything like it. Tomorrow night we're eating out in Manhattan, because after I told Dari that you had called earlier, he said that he could get great Broadway tickets for the four of us."

The idea of a Broadway play really excited Salome. A year earlier she had seen her first Broadway show. She had taken a long day trip by bus to Manhattan with her junior high class to see a Wednesday matinee of *Man of La Mancha*. She had been in love with Broadway ever since.

"What play are we seeing?" Salome asked excitedly.

"Oh this should be great, it's gotten rave reviews!" said Annie. "We're seeing *Johnson and Boswell: The Musical.*"

"I read something about that play in *The Burlington Gazette*," Anthony said. "Apparently it's about the greatest literary critic in the history of the English language, Dr. Samuel Johnson, and his biographer, James Boswell." (A week later when told what play they had seen, Felix would remark, "Dr. Johnson is the second most quoted man in our language just after Shakespeare, and he put together the first modern English dictionary. And Boswell's biography is the greatest biography ever written, because it includes so much of Dr. Johnson's literary criticism within it. But the notion of a musical about them seems absurd!" Anthony would reply, "I don't know anything about literary criticism, but I thought the musical just sucked!")

Twenty-four year-old Darius Malcovitch entered the house, saying, for Annie's benefit, "Lucy, I'm home! You've got some splainin' to do Lucy!"

And Annie replied in a whining Lucy Ricardo voice, "Whyyy can't I be in your show...Ricky?"

Darius came into the kitchen, not seeing his guests at first, and said, "Wasn't it silly naming that character Ricky Ricardo? I mean that makes his name in English Ricky Ricky!" And then upon seeing Anthony he said, "Anthony...I'm so glad you're here. Welcome to our not so humble abode."

Anthony got up and gave Darius the old Hippie handshake, interlocking thumbs instead of palms, and said, "Thanks for having us."

Darius said, "It's my pleasure." Then he switched to a standard handshake and said, "Save that other handshake for all of the other schmucks!"

Anthony was delighted, because although it had seemed that the one-month friendship developed last year back at the motel between Darius and Felix would last a lifetime, now it felt as if Darius were including him too in his inner cabal. "This is my friend Jennifer."

Darius reached for her hand, kissed it and said, "*Enchanté Jennifer.*"

Salome, who had taken French for a year in junior high school, and had grown up in a house in which her mother—from French-Canadian lineage—occasionally spoke French on the phone with Salome's aunt, Clara, was able to respond very formally and in a perfect French-Canadian accent, "*Enchanté de faire votre conaissance, Monsieur Malcovitch*!"

And, in that instant in which their eyes met, it was all over. Whether it would last or just be mere amorous caprice was uncertain; nonetheless, the Earth moved, the Moon winked, the kitties cried, and the hearts sang Ca Thump Ca Thump. 'My God,' thought Salome. 'Anthony is nice with his long skinny self, and I want to get to know him better, but Darius is a hunk! This guy obviously works out. Those arms look like they could hold me up forever.' It was true, Darius had Popeye-like arms, and his legs were also well developed. He did workout continually, and every year he spent outside athletic time, rock climbing in either Utah or Alaska, and skiing in either Colorado or Austria. 'And that face of his! Perfect features. Beautiful blue eyes. Sexy blonde hair with an expensive haircut.' Salome had never been so smitten.

'What a stone cold fox!' Darius was thinking. 'I'd like to bend her over this kitchen table and do her right now!'

Anthony, sensing the immediate chemistry between Darius and Salome was pained to ask, "So how much would you charge Jennifer to do a portfolio? She wants to be a model, and she wants to see if any of the agencies can give her work."

And Darius gave the answer that Anthony feared he would, "Nothing. For a friend, it would be my pleasure to offer my services at no charge. How about tomorrow, Jennifer? I'll do the standard photo portfolio for you, and then make several copies for you to leave at different agencies in Manhattan. I also know how to type up a good resume for a model."

Anthony kind of glared at Darius, and Salome was sensing the testosterone thing happening with Anthony. "That would be incredibly kind of you," she said.

"I assume you're going to be here until at least the first of the week,"

Darius said hopefully. "You'll need at least next Monday and Tuesday to drop off your portfolio at all of the different agencies. Although there is one agency in Manhattan where I can probably get you in this Saturday if you'd like." Darius then added, "I have to leave on Wednesday, and I won't be back until after Labor Day, but you're both welcome to stay here until just before my family returns on the twenty-fifth of August."

"Where are you heading on Wednesday?" curious Salome asked, and then thought, 'Shit…I'm still being Mike Wallace!'

"Out to Utah on my *Road King*, for both business and pleasure. I'm doing a shoot for *National Geographic* at Zion Park, and then I'm going to do some rock climbing."

"Wow!" Salome exclaimed. "You have a *Harley-Davidson Road King*?"

"Yeah…and two other bikes besides. I'll show you guys my bikes in the morning, okay?"

"That would be really neat," Salome said. Anthony, who could care less about motorcycles, and realizing that he had an apparent major problem now in his attempt to woo Salome, said nothing.

Darius then said, "By the way, I assume you've brought an assortment of clothes to model in."

"I have a few outfits," Salome responded. "Do you have an iron and board I can use tomorrow morning?"

"No problem. I'm sure Annie wouldn't mind taking care of that for you though."

"Nah…I can do my own ironing."

"Did you bring a bikini?" Darius asked.

"Yes," Salome said, noticing the grimace on Anthony's face. 'What the hell,' she thought. 'I *just* got a ride from him. And yes, I kinda like him, he's fun to be with, and I do want to spend more time with him and get to know him better, but Darius…'

"What size are you?" Darius asked, guessing a 6.

"I'm a size 6."

"I have a whole assortment of size 6 in my studio, on the other side of the house. I have formal wear, business suits, casual outfits, and bikinis—especially in size 6. So if what you have tomorrow doesn't really work for you, we'll find something that does."

"Thank you," Salome said, exchanging a quick knowing look with Darius.

The next morning when Darius awoke, he found Salome and Anthony in the backyard on the beach. They were sitting under the big umbrella, around the big circular wooden table in wooden beach chairs, smoking cigarettes, drinking coffee, and watching the Atlantic Ocean. Anthony had a portable radio on, and David Bowie's "Moonage Daydream" was blasting from a station in The City.

When the song ended, Anthony turned off the radio and said, "Good morning."

Darius asked, "You guys been up a while?"

"About an hour and a half," Anthony said and added, "About three cups of coffee worth."

"Did Annie make you breakfast?"

"She wanted to," Salome said, checking Darius out in the strong morning light. "But we said we'd wait for you."

After they had eaten breakfast and were getting ready for a look at Darius' bikes, Darius asked Annie, "Where should we go to eat before the show tonight?"

"Well perhaps we should let your guests decide," Annie said.

"I like everything," Salome said.

"I like everything except liver and onions," Anthony said.

"Have you ever had Polish food?" Annie asked.

Both Anthony and Salome shook their heads, "No."

"Want to try it? It's really just good hearty peasant food," Annie said.

"Annie turned me on to Polish…Ah…bigos, borscht, and babka. Great!" Darius said. Anthony and Salome both wanted to try it. "We can park the car in the East Village near the restaurant—take a cab to the show."

"I can't wait to see *Johnson and Boswell: The Musical*," Salome said.

"It's a hot ticket," said Darius. "Fortunately, a friend of mine…"

"Yeah I know," Anthony interrupted with a trace of bitterness, "You're obviously well-hooked."

Darius led them into the six-car garage that housed his three motorcycles in one of the garage spaces. "That 1955 *Indian* over there doesn't run, but I'm hoping to have someone work on it in the near future. I just got it a few months ago for hardly anything." Anthony wondered what "hardly anything" meant in Malcovitchian lingo, but he didn't ask. "Over there, on the left, is my 1970 *Sportster 883*. That's a smaller *Harley*. And here is my 1971 *Road King*. I rode this big boy up the Al-Can Highway in the summer of 1972 to Alaska." And Anthony thought, 'I always think of motorcycle riders as potential organ donors.'

"Do you ride?" Darius asked Anthony.

"I'm not really interested in motorcycles," Anthony said. "They're dangerous, and the noise gives me a headache. But…hey…everyone's got a thing."

"How about you?" Darius asked Salome.

"I love *Harleys*!" Salome exclaimed. "My brother, Jack, bought a used 1969 *Harley Ironhead* last year. He taught me how to ride it, and I'm allowed to use it everywhere on our property. He won't let me take it on the street yet."

"Well maybe on Sunday morning we can take a short ride out to Montauk Point and see the lighthouse. That *Sportster* would be perfect for you, and Anthony can ride on the back of the *Road King*," Darius said, knowing that Anthony would obviously decline.

"I'm so happy!" said Salome.

"You guys go. I'll pass," said Anthony. And then he thought, 'It's hard to dislike Darius, but in this case the dude is a real cock-blocker. Now I wish I had never brought Salome here.' And then he thought, 'I wonder if muscle boy here would still be interested in her if he knew she were only fourteen?' Anthony already knew, as beautiful as Salome was, as much as he thought he might be falling for her in just one day, she wasn't worth going to jail for. Yet, until Darius was in the picture, he had fantasized on the trip about the possibility of just waiting for her to be legal. (And in the next week when he discussed this with Felix, Felix would tell him: "Wait for nobody! That's the way it goes in relationships, in that we may end up as conduits for whomever we're with at the moment, to wherever they may be heading.")

"So Jennifer, are you ready to make history by shooting the first pictures that will most assuredly catapult you into supermodel stardom?" Darius finally asked, when it was apparent that they were finished looking at the motorcycles.

"I sure am," flattered Salome said. "Let me get that iron and board, and I'll be ready in thirty minutes."

"This will take a few hours, to take enough shots and find the right ones that will make your portfolio perfect. And then I'll need you to sit down and give me information, so I can construct an intelligent resume for you. With Friday afternoon traffic heading into The City, we should leave here around 3:30 to have time to eat before the show."

"3:30 it is then!" said Anthony. "I'll just hang out on the beach, swim, sunbathe, smoke a couple of joints, and listen to music while you two conduct business." And he thought, 'Man...I've got no claims on Salome so I can't gripe...but this still sucks anyway.'

"While you're ironing, I'll call my friend at the agency who might be able to see you on Saturday," Darius said, and then he left the room.

"Are you gonna be okay...all by your lonesome this afternoon?" Salome asked Anthony.

"I'll be fine," he replied, but he didn't have much of a poker face.

And so after the phone call to Mitch Leopold Model Agent Extraordinaire had been successful, and after Salome had been squared-away for an early Saturday afternoon appointment in The City, and after having worn what Darius had in his chic women's wardrobe, including two very tiny bikinis that had looked incredible on her, and after Darius had been able to knock out enough great shots and do her resume in just under two hours, they all piled into the Malcovitch *Range Rover* at just after 3:30.

The drive to Manhattan had been easy, the Polish food a sagacious pedestrian's epicurean delight. Salome was still thinking about Darius' question during the shoot, "Would you like to do a few nudes to put yourself in a situation to make a lot more money from the men's magazines? I have a good friend at *Boner Magazine*, the number one men's magazine in the world." Salome was still wondering if she had done the right thing by declining, as they walked out of the theatre after having seen *Johnson and Boswell: The Musical*. It was raining and difficult to flag a cab.

"Damn! It's raining!" Annie said, covering her hair with her opened *Playblurb*, the ink running from the opened page listing the magazine's staff.

"A little rain won't kill you!" Darius joked.

"Don't you know that water is kryptonite to a black woman's hair?" Annie retorted quickly.

After they had walked two blocks briskly, they were finally able to flag a cab. While heading toward the East Village, Annie was the first to give a critique of the show. "Well that was certainly unusual," she said. "The guy who played Dr. Johnson continually sounded like Paul Robeson singing 'Ol' Man River' with different lyrics."

"And the lyrics were kind of obscure," Darius said. "One would have to be totally acquainted with Johnson's life to understand some of the references." One of the songs, "Poor Scotland," based on something that Johnson had said in 1768 went:

If one man in Scotland gets possession
of two thousand pounds, what remains
for the rest of the nation?
Patriotism is the last refuge of a scoundrel,
the true patriot will never feel such
indignation.

Another number was: "Should You Give or Take the Wall?"

Should you give or take the wall when you're
walking down the street, should you stay inside
during summer, to escape the summer's heat?

"That seems profound!" Anthony said, tongue planted firmly in cheek. Other numbers were: "I'm a Lexicographer, I'm Just a Harmless Drudge," when Johnson puts together the first modern English dictionary; "Oh My Tetty!" a torch song for his wife just after she dies; "The Gesticulation Rag," a kind of strange dance number, with the dancers continually in resupinated positions; and, what Anthony would describe as a "very Gay little ditty," a number called "Walking Through the Hebrides," that featured Johnson and Boswell at times walking and skipping hand in hand.

"What did you think Jennifer?" Darius asked.

"It was different, but I really enjoyed it. Thanks so much for the ticket," Salome said diplomatically. In reality she hadn't really enjoyed the play too much—she had not been able to understand the references—but she also knew that she was partially to blame, because her mind had been fixated on the pros and cons of modeling nude.

"I thought it was just stupid!" Anthony said. I wish Felix were here."

"Yes…your brother Felix, a true Man of Letters…he would have had an interesting take on this production," Darius said.

On Saturday, Anthony drove Salome to Mitch Leopold's modeling agency on West 23rd Street and 10th Avenue in Manhattan. On the way he tried to make his case to Salome, that she should drive down to Florida with him that following Wednesday, stay awhile on the beach, and if she had to get back to The City before he would be passing through around September 18th , he would purchase a plane ticket for her.

"Yeah, but I wouldn't be able to stay at the Malcovitch mansion then, and I would come back to New York City with no job and no place to stay," Salome said.

"Well how about we find you a room today, after your appointment, and I'll pay the first month's rent. That way you'll have some place to return to," Anthony said kind of pleading.

"Well today is August 8th, if you're not coming back through New York until September 18th, I'd actually have to pay two months rent," Salome said and then added, "Look...unless this Leopold guy offers me something today, or the other agencies I plan on visiting Monday and Tuesday offer me work right away…and if I have a room squared away…I'd consider going to Florida with you. I've never been there, and it's my desire to go everywhere in this life. And, of course, Salome also thought at the same time, 'Darius is going to be gone until September anyway, I might as well check out Florida.'

"Deal!" said Anthony with a smile. "I'll even pay the rent on a room for the first two months."

As for the address on her resume, Darius had used his own address on Long Island. For the phone number, Darius had used his private line and put a generic message on his answering machine. He told Salome, "You can just call here and speak to Annie once a day on my parents' line before my dad gets home around 6:00. She knows how to retrieve the messages from my phone, and she'll pass them on to you." Salome figured that on the road she could do the same thing, and that she could also give Annie the phone number of *The Breakers* on the beach.

"And you'll spring for a plane ticket, either on the road or from Florida, if an incredible job offer comes up?"

"100% we are in agreement," Anthony said happily.

"Okay. Let's see what happens today, Monday, and Tuesday," Salome said. "And let's see if I can find a room to rent today. Also, I need to call Selma quickly before my appointment, so please find a pay phone."

@@@@@@@@

"Hey Selma…it's me," Salome said when Selma answered the phone at the library. Selma Greenwood, Head Librarian of the main Rutland Library for six years, still worked on Saturdays. She told the staff that she liked working Saturdays, but in reality it was the only time she could communicate by phone with her sister.

"I'm so glad you called. Listen Salome, I've got a real problem," Selma said with loads of agitation in her voice. "Your running away may get me into major trouble with the law!"

"What are you talking about?" Salome asked totally stupefied.

"I'll tell you the story from the beginning Salome, but you'll have to promise me that you'll never…and I mean NEVER," Selma screeched at a volume of about 30 decibels higher, "tell ANYBODY what I'm about to tell YOU!...OKAY?"

"SHHH!" said several people in the library.

"Selma…I love you like a sister. I'll protect your secret my whole life," Salome said. And indeed, Salome would keep that secret her whole life.

"Well…I have to tell you this…because you need to know the truth…you need to know why I just can't have Bubba getting the FBI involved…after you've been missing for a while…why I can't be questioned, and more importantly…why I can't be fingerprinted BY THE FBI!"

"SHHH! said several people in the library again.

"OH MY GOD!" said Salome, again sounding like Pauline.

"But I think I have a solution to both of our problems. I mean…unless you've decided to just come home anyway."

"If it means jail time for you Selma, of course I'll come home," Salome said and meant.

"I love you for saying that Salome, but if you'll do exactly what I say you probably can stay away…without me having any problems. I don't know if this will work…I mean…I'm pretty sure…I know I can sell your mom on it…it's Bubba who'll be the tough nut."

"What are you thinking Selma?"

"Well…first of all my name is really Ida Laplotski," Selma said.

"Laplotski?" Salome asked.

"And my people were Polish Jews."

"But I've seen you in our church for years!" Salome exclaimed.

"I was never that religious as a Jew anyway, so it was easy for me to pretend to be a Christian. My real birth certificate says Ida Laplotski. My *obtained* birth certificate says Selma Underwood. My marriage license says Selma Greenwood. Anyway, forget my real name. Always call me Selma."

"It will always be Selma 100%...I promise...But tell me the story!"

"I will," Selma said, "But let me tell you how we can handle this first."

"Okay," said Salome.

"I have a sister, Ivy Laplotski, who lives in New York City, in Queens, and I spoke with her this morning as I always do on Saturdays. She's in Manhattan on Saturday mornings at her research job, working at the Museum of Natural History, and she always stops early at a different pay phone to call me. She has a phone in her apartment, but she only uses it for local calls. She especially never calls *me* on that phone line, for fear that she's wiretapped...and that the FBI might be listening."

"OH MY GOD SELMA...What did you do?"

"I'll tell you that in a moment...don't worry...I'm not a murderer!" Selma kind of laughed. "Anyway, my sister lives alone in a nice two-bedroom apartment in Flushing, Queens, off of Parsons and 71st ...we'll tell your parents her name is Ivy Underwood...and she's willing to let you rent a room from her for awhile...You can stay...until Bubba takes the heat off. The deal is, there can't be any phone calls coming in from your family in Rutland. Because even if Bubba accepts this and allows you to stay in New York at my sister's, any reference to me by one of your family members over the phone, might get the FBI listeners putting two and two together."

"I understand," Salome said, completely flabbergasted by all of this.

"But there's a way around that too," Selma said. "You can get a phone service in New York...a phone number with the Queens area code for people to call you...that answers for you in the voice you record. Then you just call your service a few times a day from a pay phone to get your messages. Nobody will ever be able to catch you live answering the phone, but you'll just say that you're in the city working two jobs or at the library studying for your GED test all of the time."

"That could work," Salome said. "And by the way, unless I get an immediate offer either today, Monday, or Tuesday from the modeling agencies where I'm visiting and dropping off my portfolio..."

"You've put together a portfolio already?" Selma interrupted.

And Salome told Selma about Darius. "If nothing's happening by Wednesday, then I think I'm going to head down to Anthony's motel in Florida for five weeks. So I better see your sister today, and I better square-away that phone service deal on Monday or Tuesday."

"Ivy will be home after 7:00 tonight. I told her that you would probably come over. But she doesn't want to meet your new friend Anthony or anybody else. She said that if she does this, nobody can ever come over and visit you. Nobody can ever actually know the physical dwelling where you're staying. That means that you're going to have to discourage family members from visiting."

"I'll worry about that down the road," Salome said. "My immediate problem is how to ditch Anthony tonight."

"You'll have to figure that one yourself, my friend."

"Where do I get my mail then?"

"You're going to have to rent a post office box in Flushing."

"Okay…I guess that will work. But even if you can sell Bubba on the idea of me staying with your sister, he'll still want to talk with her. And if he can't dial into her apartment…"

"I've got the solution to that also. Ivy is going to call Bubba today at a little after 5:00 from a pay phone. I spoke to your mom earlier, told her *only* about my sister's offer and your progress, and she was okay with it. She's getting Bubba at the hospital this afternoon…"

"Why's Bubba in the hospital?" Salome asked.

And when told the repercussions of her glue job, Salome just laughed. "Your mom will make sure that Bubba is home for Ivy's call," Selma continued. "Ivy will tell Bubba that she's having trouble with her phone, and that it won't be working until Tuesday afternoon when the repairman is supposed to come, and that's why she's calling from a payphone. Then on Tuesday, you'll call Bubba, make nice nice, and give him your phone number. If he asks for Ivy's number also, you'll just have to tell him that you don't remember it…You're just gonna have to avoid giving up her number!"

"Phew! This is a lot of work, but it could actually work!" Salome said. "Give me directions on how to get to your sister's in Queens." And after Selma had told Salome where to get off of the E Train, and what bus to take up Parsons to 71st Street, Salome said, "I need to get to my appointment. But first…what's up with you and the law?"

And then Selma told Salome exactly why the FBI was interested in finding her.

@@@@@@@@

"WHYYY…JEEESUS CHRIIIST…Pauline! I don't give a rat's ass that I was SLEEEPING! You should have WOOOKE me up to tell me that she had RUN AWAAAY yesterday!" Bubba bellowed, on his belly, from the backseat of "Bluebird," Pauline's 1973 *Oldsmobile*.

"Well I'm sorry Bubba," Pauline said. "You know that Bluebird and I had to take my sister Clara…to Burlington Airport early yesterday morning… to catch a connecting flight at JFK to Paris. The flight out of Burlington was delayed, so I just kept Clara company for a couple of hours. By the time I got back to Rutland, did the Friday supermarket shopping for the week, kept my usual hair appointment, and made you your dinner…it was 8:00. When I brought you that plate of chicken stew, you were sleeping soundly. I thought it would be better to just let you sleep through the night. So I left the stew next to the bed with an 'I love you' note and came home."

But last night's slumber had not been too pleasant for Bubba. He had had the third in his trilogy of door-opening-childhood-memory dreams, since having been admitted to the hospital. Most of these memories had been suppressed since 1942, when he was in the infantry in the North African Campaign, and a mortar shell had gone off just above the foxhole where Bubba and another army soldier were taking cover. Bubba never remembered exactly what had happened, just that he woke up days later in a hospital in Tripoli. He had forgotten a good portion of his childhood memories since that blast, and it was only because of Bill Wicks' current cocktail combination of a liquid Valium drip plus synthetic morphine tablets, *Percodan*, that had reawakened some of those memories.

The year was 1937, Bubba had just turned seventeen, and on this Sunday he was coming into manhood in what was now a tradition at seventeen for boys and eighteen for girls in the Wedoweeian First Baptist Church sense; he was being allowed to hear his own father preach in church. Most of the parishioners of the church still considered Reverend Ignatius Apple the apposite augur apostle of post-worldly pronouncements, but some of the parishioners were mumbling quietly amongst themselves about the need for a change. Reverend Apple turned to his flock and said: "Our JEW PRESIDENT ROOSEVELT, is doing everything he can to get our CHRISTIAN brothers involved with this JEW WAR in Europe! We are still pretending we are NEUTRAL, but we are sending MILLIONS OF DOLLARS to the JEW interests in Europe. Why should good CHRISTIAN blood be spilled for the JEW? Let the JEW fight his own battles, and he can see if the NEGROES want to help! Send the JEW and the NEGRO to go fight in Europe!" And then Reverend Apple started drooling, and his left arm and leg were doing what would be called years later "The Funky Chicken." Then in a very deep voice he shouted, "SON OF A BITCH," he straightened up, wiped his chin, and was back to normal. In Bubba's dream, his father's words were getting all mixed up with the picture of an African-American soldier's face. Bubba was just beneath the surface of remembering that it had been the African-American Sergeant Terence Boler, who had carried his unconscious body two miles to the Med-Evac Unit and saved his life in 1942. Bubba had never had the chance to thank him, because Sergeant Boler was killed the next day. Bubba had never had the chance to tell his father, "It was a black man who saved my life," because his father had died in

1941 just before Bubba went off to boot camp in Georgia.

"You should have WOOOKE me, Pauline. I'm gonna have the cops drag her ass back HOOOME!" Bubba said, pointing his crooked finger backwards at the car door by his feet.

"No you're not!...Look Bubba, it won't do any good to force Salome to come back here...She'll just keep running away, because you don't know how to keep your big mouth shut! So here's what we're going to do...We're going to let Salome stay at Selma's sister's place in Queens...what's her name...Ivy Underwood...for say six weeks...We'll give Salome a chance to prove herself. We'll go down and visit her after she's had a chance to find work, enroll in the GED course, settle in a bit, and gotten over her rage with you...And if everything is working out with Selma's sister and everything else looks good...we'll let Salome stay longer. But who knows, Bubba... I'm betting that Salome will be lonely and she'll want to come home in five to six weeks anyway...and especially if you let her know that you love her...and all is forgotten on your end." Then Pauline realized that she had made a pun and she said, "On your END Bubba!"

"That's SOOO funny Pauline."

"That's the smart way to handle it Bubba, because we can't search the whole planet for her...and she could easily leave again and never speak to us. And I swear Bubba...if that ever happens because of YOU...I'LL NEVER SPEAK TO YOU AGAIN!"

Bubba knew better than to argue with Pauline on or at this point, so he said nothing. Pauline said, "So you're gonna be real nice to Selma's sister when she calls later...you got that Bubba?"

"I got that Pauline," was all he said.

As Pauline slowly approached the turn for their farm, she saw Jack at the mailbox. "Hi Sweetie," Pauline said. "How was work last night?"

"It was real busy Mom. I've still got a headache from all of the people in the station, and also having to listen to Old Man Strattus yell this morning."

"You take something for it?"

"Yeah...it hasn't worked yet."

"What did Gus Strattus have to say?" Bubba said from the backseat.

Jack moved closer to the car, now realizing that Bubba was in the back, and he said, "He had to bring one of Bruiser's dogs back again. This time, the dog ate one of his chickens. He was real pissed off. He told me, to tell you, that if another dog of ours comes onto his property, he's gonna shoot it, and then dump the dead carcass in front of our mailbox."

"WHYYY that big dumb GREEEK son of a bitch!" Bubba yelled, "I wish the dog had KILLLED his God Damn rooster!" All of the Apples were fed up, having to hear that rooster at dawn, for nearly five years now, since Gus Strattus had decided to diversify, and to include eggs as part of his farmer's repertoire. And, of course, the Stattus household was also fed up, with having to hear Bruiser's yelping dogs five or six times daily.

"Well maybe if you had let him keep that waterline way back when... Bubba," Pauline said. She was referring to something that had happened in 1950 when they had first purchased their orchard. Gus Strattus, who had bought his place in 1945, had constructed an aqueduct running from the stream on their property over to his property, approximately twenty-two feet away. Since the main well on the Strattus property was beginning to dry up, and subsequent well drilling efforts had yielded little result by 1948, for the two years prior to the arrival of the Apples, Gus Stattus had just been tapping that stream to water his whole 300-acre orchard. It annoyed Bubba when they bought the place, so Bubba had made Gus Strattus disassemble the aqueduct. Pauline had thought that it was no big deal to let the neighbor tap into their water source, but Bubba was having none of that. He did jokingly say to Dr. Bill Wicks at the time, "WHYYY...we could just let him KEEEP that aqueduct...and we could dig our septic tank just UPSTREEEAM from it...and then his apples would get FERTILIIIZED by the shit of the Apples!"

"Where the HELLL is Bruiser?" Bubba asked Jack.

"He took one of the trucks to run errands...about an hour before Old Man Strattus showed up."

"I want that God Damn KENNELLL fixed TODAAAY! If you see him, Jack, send him to MEEE!"

And as Pauline pulled the car up to the front door she said again, "Remember Bubba...You're gonna be real nice to Selma's sister later."

"Isn't SHEEE married?" Bubba asked. "What does her husband think about a FOURTEEEN year-old moving in with them?"

"Selma said that her sister never married. She taught junior high science in New York City for ten years, and then she took a job doing scientific research for a museum."

"Do YOUUU think that this spinster can KEEEP an eye on Salome?" Bubba asked with more agitation in his voice.

"Well she did handle boys and girls Salome's age as a teacher for ten years," Pauline reiterated.

And later that day, at a few minutes after 5:00, Bubba kept his word. On the phone, Ivy Laplotski was just obsequious enough to gain Bubba's trust, and she managed to totally control the conversation, so that Bubba never got the chance to ask for her phone number. He had accepted Pauline's plan of a six-week trial for Salome in New York City, and he told Ivy, "JEEESUS CHRIIIST...tell Salome that I love her...and I'm SORRRY."

@@@@@@@@

Salome told Anthony after the meeting with Mitch Leopold, "He had nothing for me now, but he said that he might call in the next few weeks." In reality, that's exactly what Mitch Leopold had indeed said, along with, "If you'll do some nudes, I can get you $2500 for two days work." Then Salome told Anthony about "a friend of Selma's in Brooklyn, who had a room to rent, but had been so brutalized by her ex-husband, that she had moved in secrecy, and she wasn't able to handle meeting new men yet, and that Salome had to go see her alone at 7:00 that evening, and that even though it all sounded kind of freaky, it was a good thing for her."

And Anthony replied, "Freaky? It sounds like absolute bullshit!" But he really didn't have any claims on Salome, so he reluctantly agreed to just meet her at 10:00 at this coffee shop in the West Village right next to where the E train stopped. And, of course, the first thing that ran through his mind was, 'I wonder if she's meeting Darius somewhere tonight?' And, of course, the second thing that ran through his mind, when he looked at a subway map, was that the E train didn't even go to Brooklyn.

After Salome had been buzzed into the security building where Ivy Laplotski lived in Flushing, and she had taken the elevator to the third floor, she pushed the ringer on the door of 3-D. When the door opened, she said with much surprise, "SELMA! How the hell did you get here so fast today?"

Ivy said, "I'm Ivy. I'm Selma's twin sister."

"OH MY GOD!" Salome said, now sounding more and more like Pauline. "Selma never told me she had a twin…Selma…you devil!" And as she walked into the apartment she added, "What's it like to be a twin?"

And Ivy answered all of the standard twin questions, and then she told Salome about some of the practical jokes that she and Selma had played as kids on their parents. Then Ivy mentioned that their dad had died when they both were twelve, and that he had never been able to tell his daughters apart.

"Is your mother still alive?" Salome asked.

"Yeah," Ivy said. "She's in a nursing home a few subway stops from here."

"Does she ask about Selma…Ida?" Salome asked.

"She doesn't have to," Ivy said. "She suffers from what is now being called Alzheimer's Disease. She hardly remembers anything, and it's been more than two years since she remembered anything about the FBI and Ida. I just alternate between being Ida and myself when I visit her, so she thinks that both of her daughters are living happily together in Queens."

Chapter Four

The apartment was a monolith to apathy. To the left of the front door, the main dining area was now seating a party of seven—big black plastic garbage bags in seven of the eight available chairs around the table—and having booked reservations for today's brunch, and having slipped a little something into the maitre d's hand, yet still waiting patiently at the bar against the wall discussing current movie pictures and listening to a hackneyed lounge lizard version of "Moon River," were six more big bags of trash. The lucky seated garbage bag diners at *Chez Felix's Café de Crap* had selected and been served the Early Bird Special *du jour*, which featured a few cases of empty disseminated *Budweiser* cans and several nights worth of *A & S Pizza* boxes with two or three moldy slices left in each. The visiting Miami Palmetto Bug Family—the flying southern cousins to the New York City Cockroach Family—were finishing their breakfast at the buffet in the kitchen. This morning's meal on the counter section of the restaurant had consisted of two half-eaten moon pies; an opened butcher's wrapped paper sheet of moldy three week-old cappicola; a two week-old opened carton of 1/2 and 1/2; six slices of *Kraft American Cheese* on a cutting board; a black 1/2 eaten banana; an opened container of sour sour cream; a tilted nine-tenths empty bottle of *Cuervo Gold*; several sliced empty lime rinds; and loose kosher salt scattered everywhere. And, of course, dessert in the kitchen sink had been wonderful also. The Miami Palmetto Bug Family had feasted on pieces of four week-old congealed fried chicken, still in the frying pan; two two week-old dishes of cereal, with pieces of *Post Raisin Bran* and sugar stuck to the insides; a dinner dish with flecks of pork fried rice; a sauce pan with pieces of stuck cheese grits; and a mostly empty *Swanson's T.V. Dinner* sectional tin, with Salisbury Steak, mashed potatoes, green beans, and apple cobbler. And, after having eaten their fill, the Bug Family had leisurely strolled through the ground level labyrinth of the Museum of Scratched Rock Albums, carefully avoiding *The Rolling Stones*' "Sticky Fingers," and retiring to their rooms for the day in the little wall crevice partially covered by *The Beatles*' "Let it Be." And all the while, the orange and white two year-old tabby cat, Petomane, was oblivious to both the Miami Bug Family and his own stinking litter box.

After the huge garbage truck on Gulf Boulevard in front of *The Breakers* had finished compacting its Sunday morning load, and he could finally hear the ring on the outside staircase, and he decided that he was closer to the apartment's phone than to the office's, Felix Kulpa—avoiding the thirty-third step—bolted up the remaining stairs to his unlocked apartment. He stubbed his right big toe on the claw-foot leg of a small Victorian end table, in his attempt to answer the phone before the broken answering machine did nothing. "Fuck...that hurt!" Felix said and then he thought, 'And it was probably Hollywood calling!'—although it had only been just twelve weeks since he had begun submitting his manuscript—'calling to let me know that they've cast Richard Dreyfus to play my protagonist and Jessica Lange his love interest in the movie version of my novel.' Felix could see the title, *All the Seats Were Occupied*, along with the names of Richard Dreyfus and Jessica Lange looking particularly good on a movie theatre's marquee. 'Yeah... well...it probably would have been a made-for-T.V. movie deal anyway,' Felix continued thinking, 'with Bill Bixby and Meredith Baxter-Birney.'

Walter Lee Younger came in from the strong sunlight, and barely avoided crushing a spilled box of *Post Raisin Bran* on the floor. He said, "Hey 'Licks...let me hold a square."

Felix gave Walter Lee a cigarette and said, "*No problemo*, Home Lee."

Walter Lee laughed and said, "So now it's 'Home Lee' huh...last time it was 'Ug Lee!'"

"Yeah...well if you don't start buying your own cigarettes again, it's gonna be 'Niggard Lee' next!"

Walter Lee then did his usual Fred Sanford shtick when Felix came up with a particularly good zinger; his right arm would stick out rigid with his hand looking as if it were pushing against something, his left hand would go up to his heart, he would roll his eyes back and move his head around and act all woozy, and then he would sit down and laugh a true guffaw. When his funny bone was particularly touched, forty-six year-old extremely fit, although hair starting to gray, Walter Lee Younger, could laugh and cry for hours. And sometimes for several days, whenever he'd see Felix, he'd start laughing and crying all over again.

With tears in his eyes, Walter Lee said, "You best be not calling me

'Niggard Lee'...in front of no Brothers...Mistuah Charlie!"

"Hell no," Felix said. "I'll just call you 'Boy!'"

Walter Lee, still laughing, said, "You be in fine form dis morning'... Mistuah 'Licks!" And then Walter Lee got a good whiff of the apartment and said, "I know I ain't been by your crib in awhile...but wat you white people done been cooking all up in here? It be smelling like bar-b-que *Port o' let*!"

Felix laughed and said, "Yeah...well...my Jewish neurotic clean freak self has been taking a vacation."

"I can see and smell that!" Walter Lee laughed. "What's going on with you 'Licks? You used to keep this place spotless. Now it looks as if you're getting ready to do a photo spread for *Better Shitholes and Gardens*."

"I know man, I'll clean it up before Anthony gets here in a few days. I keep all of the rooms in this motel immaculate daily...you know I do Walter Lee...it's just that I haven't felt like cleaning up in here for a while."

"Well...hey," Walter Lee said, "I heard the women really go for the cluttered el stinko look these days, 'Licks. This place been helping you score big time?"

Petomane came over and rubbed himself against Felix's leg, did his meowing routine, and thought—in an Edward G. Robison/Johnny Rocco kind of voice—'Hey asshole human...Round Boy Felix...I'm hungry...Feed me now!'

Felix said, "In a few minutes Peto," And then he said, "Well that's kind of it Walter Lee. I've just gotten real tired of playing pick up games with women, so I don't care if this place is a mess at the moment. I mean...I know I've been real lucky with the females in the past few years...I'm just bored with the game right now. After Tatiana left me, I guess it was important for me to attract other women. Okay, I've proved to myself that I've still 'got it.' Ho hum. Hell...I didn't even feel particularly guilty...when I picked up that pretty forty-something frustrated housewife across the street at the supermarket...just after learning that my father had killed himself...Hell No! First I thought, 'Fuck him for doing that,' and then I fucked her!"

"It's been a necessary phase in your life, that's all," said Walter Lee.

"I can't understand it anyway. What do women see in me? My brother Anthony has the good looks...170 pounds, six-foot three-inches, a real handsome face, no hair all over his back! Yet, he feels insecure about himself. I think...he may still be a virgin...at nineteen!"

"No way!" said Walter Lee.

"I think so," Felix continued. Now look at me...230 lbs, six-feet tall, stocky, and I have as much hair on my body as a Siberian bear. But I don't seem to have a problem attracting women. I'm just sick of talking to them. "

"That's because you have the poetic rap my friend. And when the ladies hear your deep baritone voice, it gets them all gushy inside."

"I didn't think you cared, Sweetie!" Felix said, adding a little hand swish with it.

"Oh I think you're ugly as shit," Walter Lee said. "But I'm hip enough to know what the other gender sees in you. Now come on 'Licks...women are a good thing," Walter Lee said, while swiping another cigarette from Felix.

"Yeah...they're a good thing in bed. In relationships, they're duplicitous divas. Look Walter Lee...I've always been straight up with every woman I have ever dated. I've never been the quintessential cock hound with a little black book and women dangling on strings. And with Tatiana, I wore my soul on my sleeve. And every female I've ever known...has stuck it in my ass...without the *Vaseline*."

"Well...you were married to Tatiana for five years...that's a whole different thing," Walter Lee said, snatching Felix's lighter from the table.

"It's just the same type of shit, but at a more grandiose level. I mean...way before Tatiana, when I was going out with Ellen Jameson in high school, she was also seeing some schmuck from a high school in Tampa at the same time, and she kept us both jerked around. And then there was the so-called civilized breakup with Amy What's-Her-Name during my first year at NYU in 1965. She calls me on a Saturday morning, a couple of months after we've stopped dating, and asks if I'm free that evening. I ask her why. She says she misses me, and would like to hang with me Platonically. I'm not busy, so I figure what the hell. We meet at some Spanish restaurant in the West Village, talk about going to have a beer and listening to some music after dinner, and then as I'm leaving the men's room after we've eaten, I overhear part of her conversation on a payphone on the other side of this partition. Apparently the guy she would rather be with has suddenly had his evening freed up, so she agrees to meet him back at her place at 10:00. When she gets back to the table, she feigns a headache, says she would prefer skipping the beer and music, and would like to just go home...Bullshit!"

"Seriously my brother...it's all just a part of the weeding out process," Walter said.

"It looks as if you've been doing okay with that woman you've been weeding out!" Felix said. "I haven't seen you around too much lately."

"Yeah...Sylvia and me are cool...for now. But what's really on your mind 'Licks? I know the last couple of years haven't been easy for you, but I assumed you were getting adjusted. I mean...with all of the women I've seen you bring up to this place...that seemed like a good thing for you...in the aftermath of all of the tragedy."

It had indeed been a couple of tough years for Felix, with Tatiana divorcing him two years ago and his father's suicide last year in April of 1973. He had begun writing his recently completed novel in November of 1971 to deal with the pain of Tatiana's moving out with another man, and the therapy from writing had been the metaphorical catharsis of crunching cartilage that had carried him all the way through the divorce and beyond in 1972. But since he was still writing the book in April of 1973 when Frank Kulpa had killed himself, the novel had then taken a completely different direction from the original outline of romantic betrayal—and now included suicide as a form of betrayal also. Still, both the book and his ability to attract pretty women had seemed like ongoing therapy. Now that he was finished—that time that is usually wonderful for a writer, because just *living* allows new things to be gathered up for the next story—Felix's novel still hadn't slayed all of his internal dragons yet, and his desire to keep hooking up with women was on the wane too. Both events always seemed correlated to Felix, who would describe a sexual encounter with a new woman as, "working on a new story." He told Walter Lee what was going on, and Walter Lee said, "Well...perhaps you're still rewriting the old story...even though you think you've just finished it."

Walter Lee's observation seemed particularly astute, and Felix told him so. Then, goofing on an Orson Welles wine commercial that was being run incessantly on television, he added, "I will write no line...before it's time!"

Walter Lee laughed and then said, "Hey man...you're going to Europe next week...that oughta square away your shit...You'll be seeing all kinds of new things...and it will probably clean out your head a little...get you ready for a new story...In fact...I can see you sitting outside in a little café on the Left Bank...drinking espresso...discussing existentialism...with some beautiful Bohemian French babe...before you get her to the boudoir and boink her booty!"

"Maybe so," said Felix. "It just all seems so futile at times. I really loved Tatiana."

"I know you did man, but you can't let yourself be so obsessed with the past. We both know that it was your father's obsession with your step-mother, Terry, that probably led to his demise when she died."

"Yeah, I know," Felix said. "I just wish I knew my father better. I wish I knew why my mother left a few months before my eleventh birthday and Anthony's second, and Dad never explained anything to me."

"Your father was very private about his personal life. I knew the man since 1963, and never once did he mention why your mom, Beverly, had left in 1957. He did say to me once, after he had been drinking more than I had ever seen him drink, 'Walter Lee, Terry is the love of my life.' And he said that in the late 1960's, several years after her accident in 1961."

"I know he really loved her," Felix said with some sadness, "But I wish it had been...."

"You wish it had been your mother that he had loved like that instead," Walter Lee finished.

"Yeah...you got it," Felix muttered. "I just wish he would have answered some questions about Mom. I asked him many times to talk about her, but he always refused. Now I'll never know the whole story."

In April of 1973, before driving out to a little lake in an undeveloped future subdivision off of Ulmerton Road in St. Petersburg, and ending his life with a .045 service revolver's bullet to the right temple, Frank Kulpa decided to share some personal things about his life with his sons Felix and Anthony. Unfortunately, since he had composed the letter on the typewriter in the motel's office, and had placed the letter and envelope in the back pocket of his pants, and had forgotten to leave it behind in the apartment, and had to stop at a *Quick Rip Convenience Store* to use their stamp machine, address the letter back to the motel, and find a corner letter box before ending his life, and since that letter would be taken from the box by Ernie Gatler on his route that evening, and brought to the letter sorting table in the Madeira Beach Post Office, where mail sorter Gabe Neuman, would attempt a strike over the proper bin's plate, but not notice, that instead he had thrown a ball way outside and missed the zone completely, and since that would send the letter down into a crevice between the wall and the letter sorting table, and since even years later, when the Madeira Beach Post Office would have bar code sorting machines and even machines that attached bar codes to letters that had none, but that letter sorting table with bins was still being used for "undeliverable mail," and since that letter sorting table with bins would never be moved until twenty-two years later when a new post office had been built, the following letter would not reach Felix until late September of 1995:

> *April, 1973*
> *To My Dear Sons Felix and Anthony,*
>
> *I know, upon hearing what I've done, you'll both be very hurt, perhaps even angry with me. I'm so sorry to hurt you, I love you both very much, and I wish that there were some other way. My dear boys, I have less than six months left to live anyway, as I have been diagnosed with an inoperable lung tumor—lung cancer. I'd rather not let you see me go out like that, so I've decided to go look for Terry on my own terms.*
>
> *Before I say goodbye, I know an explanation about some things in my life is necessary, in particular about your mother. I truly loved your mom when we first married in 1943. But something happened to her after you were born in 1946, Felix. Honestly, your mom acted as if her privacy had been invaded by having a baby. For a long time, she wouldn't even hold you. One psychiatrist I spoke with said it was the longest case of Postpartum Depression, nine years worth, he had ever seen. Please understand boys, I did love your mom. But after seven years of absolutely no intimacy, I*

couldn't stand it any longer. I started seeing Terry downstairs. After having lived for five years with a husband who had suffered a stroke and was in bed all of the time—three of those years here at the motel—with no intimacy either, she had her needs too. So, in 1953, we became lovers, vowing to keep our families intact. In early 1954 her husband died, and later in the year, your mom caught me with Terry. We had a major fight, which ended, when I took your mom to bed. The result of that one night was the birth of my beautiful second son, Anthony. Your mom said, even though I had allegedly raped her, and she couldn't stand it that her body was to be invaded a second time, she would go ahead and carry the child to fruition, so that Felix could have a sibling. And that's what she did. She demanded that I not see Terry if she stayed and had the child, so I quit seeing Terry until early 1957 when your mom finally left. Our divorce was handled quickly, and a 15-year mortgage was placed on the motel so I could buy out your mom's half. In return, she signed away her rights to you boys. I have no idea where she is, I haven't seen her since that day in divorce court in the summer of 1957. Terry and I married a month later, and she gave me a whole new life to love. And even after her accident in 1961, when she could no longer use the lower portion of her body, I loved Terry as I had never loved any other woman in my life. My life is over, so I want to be with her. I finished paying off the mortgage on the motel last year, so now my two sons will own the place free and clear. And, there is almost two hundred thousand dollars in my checking and savings accounts for you to split. Love each other as brothers, and always stay close. I wish I had stayed closer to my brothers and sisters inBurlington and Plattsburgh, but I'm very glad that my sisters and brothers love my sons—although they speak very little to me. And Anthony, I know you'll find someone wonderful to spend your life with. And Felix, I know that you'll find an even better love down the road that will make you forget about Tatiana. I'm just sorry that I'll never know my grandchildren. I love you both very much, and I'm very proud that the two of you are my sons.

Dad

"Well maybe you're not supposed to know the whole story 'Licks," Walter Lee said and then added, "Maybe that is meant to be the fire in your belly that'll help you write for the rest of your life. Maybe that's just what's needed for you. Hey…the prom queen doesn't usually crank out a literary masterpiece. Most great writers had dysfunctional childhoods."

@@@@@@@@

Leaving Wednesday at four o'clock in the morning had been a smart move for Anthony and Salome, as there was hardly any Long Island rush hour traffic yet on the highway heading toward Manhattan. The only traffic they encountered was more than an hour later, when they were in Brooklyn on the Belt Parkway approaching the Verrazano Narrows Bridge. Once on the bridge heading towards Staten Island however, all of the traffic was going in the opposite direction, heading north toward the long work day in The City.

Anthony turned off of I-278 before the Goethals Bridge—the middle bridge of three bridges to the west that connect Staten Island to the rest of the continental United States—and took 440 South, down the western side of Staten Island, through the Canyon of Odors, by the largest landfill dump in the United States. He was heading towards the Outterbridge Bridge, the southern most way to escape from Staten Island. (When told about this part of Anthony and Salome's sojourn a few days later, Felix would say: "I wonder if one can define 'escaping' as ending up in New Jersey!")

The trek was smooth down the Garden State Parkway to the beautiful southern tip of the Jersey Shore, Cape May, and the car ferry ride across Delaware Bay to Lewes Point, Delaware was wonderfully relaxing. After disembarking the *Dodge*, and driving diligently an hour's duration through Delaware, Anthony and Salome headed south along the Eastern Shores of Maryland and Virginia towards the Chesapeake Bay Tunnel Bridge. By the time they crossed that bridge and were in Virginia Beach, Virginia, it was one o'clock in the afternoon, and Anthony and Salome were both ravenous. Anthony, remembering an expression that Felix occasionally used, said, "I'm so hungry, I could chew the ass out of a rag doll!" So the starved travelers stopped at *Captain Bligh's All You Can Eat Seafood Restaurant*, destroyed a few pounds of crab legs and Chesapeake Bay scallops each, and when they walked out of the place toward the parking lot at 3:00, Salome said, "I'm so stuffed, about the last thing I feel like doing is driving anymore…Maybe we should stay here tonight."

And Anthony responded, "That's fine, I'm pretty bloated too. It would be neat to relax by the Atlantic Ocean out on the beach in the sunshine."

And Salome said, "I'm not going anywhere near that ocean."

"How come?" asked Anthony.

"Sharks!" Salome emphasized.

"We were by the Atlantic out in Darius' backyard and you seemed okay with it."

"We were hundreds of feet away from the water. And if you noticed, I never went any further than the table and chairs under the umbrella."

"Well…first of all, sharks hardly come this far north," Anthony said.

"I don't care, I'm not taking any chances!"

"And secondly, the odds were much greater that you'd be hurt on that little motorcycle spin you took on Sunday with Darius than attacked by a shark on Virginia Beach."

"I don't care about your logic," Salome stressed. "I trust myself on a machine. I don't trust a dumb creature. I'm not going anywhere near that water!"

"Fine," Anthony said. "But you're gonna have a real lousy time at my place in Florida, since being on the beach next to the Gulf of Mexico is what makes it so special. You're not gonna go swimming for five weeks?"

"I'll swim in the pool, and I'll sit on the beach a few hundred feet away from the water."

Salome stopped Anthony before he went to check in at *The Crustacean Beach Inn* and said, "What do you want to do about our sleeping situation?"

And Anthony responded, "If you really want me to get two rooms I will. But it would be a hell of a lot cheaper to just get one room with a queen-sized bed. I promise I'll keep on my side of the bed."

"I know you're a gentleman Anthony," Salome said. "One room with a queen-sized bed is fine with me."

Later, after they had checked in at the hotel and went to their room with the queen-sized bed and spectacular ocean view, Anthony said, "Felix is going for a month to Europe on Monday, and I promised him I'd run the motel until September 16th. Walter Lee will run it from the September 16th through the 19th when Felix gets back. Walter Lee and I both have to start college at our different schools on Thursday, September 20th. For now however, we can stay out on the road and check out a few different cities for a few days before Florida…if you'd like. I want to be at the motel for Felix's twenty-eighth birthday this Sunday, August 16th that's all, and then he leaves the next day."

And Salome thought that was a wonderful idea, she was curious about a number of places in the South. So they changed into their bathing suits and took the elevator down by the pool at the rear of the hotel. The beach came right up to the pool, and a patron could sit on a beach chair on the sand about 200 feet from the water. There was a strong chop on the ocean this particular day, so the waves made it up about twenty-five feet onto the beach. After staring at the water for a few minutes, brave Salome dropped her towel on a chaise lounge, and ran down barefoot to just touch the water with her toes. She quickly ran back.

"Wowdy-dow!" said Anthony, and then he held his left hand up to his mouth like a microphone and said, "Shark Two this is Shark Leader One, we've almost got her lured into a false sense of security. Be ready to pounce the next time she gets to where the water touches the beach." And then he held up the other hand as a microphone and said, "That's a big Roger Shark Leader One. I have her spied with my little shark eye. We'll have Salome bits for dinner tonight!"

"Hey knock it off," Salome said with some slight annoyance, "Do you know how much courage it took for me to do that?"

Anthony smiled and said, "I'm proud of you!"

"Okay wise ass," Salome said, "At least I did a little something to tackle my fear...let's see you take a ride on the back of Darius' *Road King* to tackle yours!"

"That's okay, you're right," Anthony said, because he wasn't in the mood to discuss Darius or motorcycles.

The next morning at about 7:30, Anthony and Salome headed west on Highway 58 across Virginia. Two hours later, when they came to I-95, they turned south into North Carolina. Two hours later than that, as they were approaching Fayetteville, North Carolina, they saw a billboard advertising massages at the next exit for ten dollars. "My back is killing me," Salome said. "I'd love a back massage."

Anthony, totally aware of what these type of massage parlors really were, smirked and said, "Well perhaps you can get a real deal back massage there." And so Anthony pulled off at the next exit and found the place. The three barely-clad girls, barely legal, all giggled when Anthony told them what Salome wanted.

"We'll give your baby the massage of her life," one of them whispered in Anthony's ear.

"Look...here's twenty dollars," Anthony whispered back. "Just give her a really good legitimate back massage."

"What if she asks for something else?" The young girl whispered back.

"Well I guess that will be between you ladies," Anthony said.

"And how about you big boy...you want the works?"

Anthony looked up at the Bill of Fare, and saw that "The Works" included a "Hand Release," and was a mere twenty-five dollars.

"Nah...I'll pass," Anthony said. "I'll just sit here in your waiting room."

After they were back on the highway, Salome said that the massage had been great, and that her back felt wonderful. Anthony asked her where she would like to stay for the night.

"I've always wanted to see Charleston," Salome said. A little while later on the way to Charleston they were both thirsty, so they pulled off of I-95 at an exit and found a little fruit stand that featured orange juice. Salome spotted something interesting at the stand, plastic bags of Benne Wafers, and she asked the African-American woman behind the counter about them.

"They've been in the South since slave days," she said. "And their origins are African." And so Anthony and Salome munched on Benne Wafers and drank orange juice, and a few hours later they checked in at *The Prince of Tides Beach Resort* on Charleston Beach.

The beach in back of the hotel was beautiful, and once more Salome ran down barefoot and just touched where the waves stopped on the beach.

"Shark Leader One this is Shark Two," Anthony joked with the phony mike in his hand again, "We've picked up her trail again further south. Preparing for pounce mode."

"That isn't funny!" Salome said, and for the third time in a week she elbowed Anthony in the side.

The next morning they took a tour of Savannah, Georgia, and later that Friday they headed toward Florida to spend the night on Jacksonville Beach. As they were getting ready to cross the Florida state line, Salome said, "Are there really alligators everywhere in Florida?"

And Anthony laughed and said, "We usually have them roaming around wild in downtown St. Petersburg."

"Stop it Anthony! Gators scare me as much as sharks."

And Anthony did his mike shtick again with, "Gator Two this is Gator Squad Leader One, we're taking over for the sharks in this sector. She's getting ready to cross the state line, over." And then Anthony continued, "That's a big 10-4 Gator Squad Leader One, we'll get her in Jacksonville."
"You keep making fun of me, but don't forget that paybacks are a bitch!" Salome said. And then she added, "Have you ever eaten gator tail?"

"Yeah," Anthony said. "And really, it does taste just like chicken."

"Can we get gator tail sometime in the next five weeks in Florida?"

"That's no problem at all," Anthony said. "I know just the place on St. Petersburg Beach to take you."

Saturday morning when Anthony awoke, he immediately started pestering the sleepy Salome. He said, "I must have *Big Tim's Bar-B-Que* in St. Petersburg today! It's as if I'm a salmon returning to my spawning ground when I cross the Florida line. No other food will do! I'll stop and get you anything that you want, but nothing is going past these lips today until *Big Tim's* ribs and sauce have been there first." Salome said she could wait too, after Anthony reiterated what a gastronomical treat it would be. So they drove the four hours to St. Petersburg, went crazy at *Big Tim's*, and Anthony bought a slab to bring to Felix.

"What about Mr. Younger?" Salome asked.

"He's strictly a vegetarian," Anthony replied.

They pulled the *Dodge* into the parking lot of *The Breakers* at just after

2:00 Saturday afternoon. "Are you sure it's cool to tell your brother and his friend the truth about my name and age?" Salome asked for the third time in the past hour.

"He's my brother, he loves me, and I've certainly kept some big secrets for him," Anthony said.

Felix was in the office doing some paperwork, and he immediately came around the counter and gave Anthony a big hug and kiss when he saw him. Anthony returned the affection and said, "I brought you some *Big Tim's*."

"I can smell it, and my mouth is watering!" Felix said.

"But first...Brother Felix...I'd like you to meet Salome Apple."

Felix shook Salome's hand and said, "Salome. What a beautiful Biblical name. 'The Dance of the Seven Veils,' for King Herod...and asking for the head of John the Baptist for her mother...The famous painting...The Oscar Wilde play...The Richard Strauss operetta." And Felix thought, 'Damn...she's incredibly beautiful!'

"I don't know about any of that stuff," Salome said. "All I know is that I was named after my grandmother." And then she thought, 'Felix is certainly bigger than his brother, but not as tall. But he's got real sexy eyes and a sexy voice!'

Walter Lee Younger walked into the office and said, "'Knee! It's great seeing you," and Walter Lee gave Anthony a big hug. "Even though I can smell that you've brought some cooked rotting flesh all up in here!"

"Well go eat a big bowl of broccoli, Walter Lee!" Felix said. "Besides, the meat won't kill you before the tobacco does."

"I know that 'Licks, that's why I quit buying cigarettes."

"So I've noticed," Felix said.

"Walter Lee, I'd like you to meet Salome Apple," Anthony said.

"Nice to meet you," Walter Lee said, and 'Hot damn...she's a fox!' is what he thought.

"It's nice to meet you too...Mr. Younger," Salome said, and then she thought, 'What a distinguished looking middle-aged man.'

"Please...call me Walter Lee," he said.

"Let me take you guys up to the apartment to settle in. Besides, I want to do some damage to those ribs," and Felix ushered everybody out of the office and hung the 'If nobody's here please ring the bell' sign on the front door.

@@@@@@@@

A couple of hours later, Salome was taking a bath in Felix's apartment. Felix had told her to use the big bathroom with the tub while she was visiting, and that he and Anthony would use the smaller bathroom that just had a shower. Felix popped open a can of beer for Anthony, took one for himself, and said, "How old is she Anthony?"

"How old does she look Felix?"

"Fourteen," Felix said.

"Well you've hit the number right on the head, but she has a driver license that says her name is Jennifer Apple and that she's twenty-one."

"Are you fucking nuts...driving a fourteen year-old across state lines? Have you been *schtupping* her?"

"Nah," Anthony said. "Not that I wouldn't like to, but I don't want to go to jail."

"Hey it doesn't matter whether you're doing the horizontal bop with her or not," Felix stressed. "You're nineteen. She's fourteen. You took her across state lines. They'll bust you for Statutory Rape regardless."

"Are you serious?" asked Anthony.

"Serious as a heart attack," Felix said. "If you don't believe me, ask Walter Lee. Or better yet, I have a friend who is a criminal defense lawyer, maybe you remember him...a friend of Dad's...Al Levinson. Let's give him a call. I'll tell him that you're writing some kind of bullshit paper over the summer and you need to know the law. You can listen in on the extension in my bedroom." And Felix made the call to lawyer Levinson at home, and lawyer Levinson confirmed, much to the chagrin of Anthony, everything that Felix had been saying.

"Well what can I do? She's here now with me, and I promised her that she could stay until I was heading back up north." And then Anthony told Felix about Salome's modeling plans, the stay at Darius' house, how Darius thought she was twenty-one, the competition from Darius, the freaky woman, who hated men, who Salome was renting a room from, allegedly in Brooklyn, where the E train doesn't go, Annie Harrison's garlic bread and peppered salmon, *Johnson and Boswell: The Musical*, and how he thought he might have fallen in love with the fourteen year-old Salome in just over a week.

"You oughta just put her ass on a plane tomorrow," Felix said. "Yeah she's beautiful alright...but I've already got her sized up."

"What do you mean?" asked Anthony.

"She's the type of girl who uses her smile much like a gun. She's happy to do whatever is happening at the moment...and she'll act so pleased that you've turned her on to something new. But ultimately...she's just passing through...and she'll use your money along the way."

"Aw come on Felix," Anthony said.

"Has she paid for anything since you've met her?"

"Well no...but I've invited her...so I should pay."

"Like I said...she uses her beauty as a weapon. Of course you've invited her...your tongue is hanging out and you drool every time you see her. She's got you by the balls my dear brother...because you're just so horny, and she is fucking beautiful. But look at the facts…she's fourteen, so you can't have her. But you've already said that you thought you might be in love with her, although you also said that Darius, although he doesn't know her true age yet, has probably stolen your chances…even if she were old enough to give you chances. It's a losing situation Anthony…and I don't want you to get hurt."

"I know," is all that Anthony said.

@@@@@@@@

Two evenings later, after Felix had taken off for his month long trip to London, Amsterdam, Paris, Madrid, Lake Geneva, Monte Carlo, and Venice, Anthony and Salome found a bottle of tequila in Felix's apartment along with limes in the refrigerator. After several shots of tequila, lime, and salt, their inhibitions started to break down. Anthony was so drunk, he told Salome a story that he had thought he would never tell anybody. "Look…I always knew that my brother loved me…and I always looked up to him...But from the time I was six or so…he always seemed so distant...He would always talk to me and answer anything I asked...He always took the time to be a good brother…but I could always tell that there was something troubling him just behind his eyes…Last year…a couple of evenings after our father's funeral… he admitted that when he was fifteen…he took the back of a hammer…and pulled out all of the six nails on the thirty-third step of the outside staircase to our apartment...When our step-mother Terry…came up the stairs carrying a full basket of clothes from the laundry room…that step slipped from beneath her…and she fell backwards down all of the steps to the ground…She landed wrong…permanently injured her spine…and ended up a paraplegic for life…My father built a three-floor ramp for her up to the apartment at a gradual angle…it wasn't too steep…for her motorized wheelchair…he also built handrails…for her safety…Because she died of pneumonia…six years ago…due to the respiratory problems that came with her spinal cord injury…and because our father was never the same after her death…and he decided to end his own life…Felix now blames himself for both deaths."

Salome was really drunk too, and she felt very close to Anthony once he had shared Felix's story. She didn't know how she felt about a fifteen year-old who had attempted murder and had put another human in a wheelchair, but she knew she liked Anthony a lot. She thought about Darius for a moment, but that was on down the road. She leaned over and said, "I've wanted to kiss you for a long time," and she did just that. Salome and Anthony started to make out passionately, and Anthony totally forgot how old she was. He lightly tweaked one of her nipples with his fingers. She moaned and said, "Why don't we go into your bedroom?" And in Anthony's bedroom, they pulled off each other's clothes, and Salome said, "I want to fool around with you Anthony, but I'm not going all of the way…that just ain't happening." And so they explored each other's bodies within the parameters of not going all of the way, and they fell asleep in each other's arms. But as Anthony was drifting off, he saw himself standing in front of a judge and saying, "She said her name was Jennifer, and she showed me her driver license that said twenty-one! We didn't go all of the way your Honor!"

@@@@@@@@

"Red Leader One, this is Seagull Six. We're approaching the drop zone."

"That's a Roger Seagull Six. Prepare to open the ass bay doors on my mark!"

It had been two weeks since Salome and Anthony had arrived in Florida. They had been two wonderful weeks, as Salome and Anthony were now sharing the same bed and—within the parameters of not going all of the way—exploring each other's bodies every night. By day they would hang out at the pool and watch the front desk. A few times Walter Lee had taken over in the office, allowing Salome and Anthony a trip to *Sunken Gardens*, in downtown St. Petersburg; a trip to *Busch Gardens*, in Tampa; a lunch at *Ted Peters' Famous Smoked Fish*; and a dinner at *Silas Dent's*, in which Salome finally got to try gator tail.

It was four o'clock in the afternoon on this particular Saturday, and Salome sat on the little landing between the thirty-second and thirty-third steps on the outside staircase leading up to Felix's apartment. One would head up thirty-two steps to the little landing and then have a choice. If you went left to step thirty-three, you were going to the Kulpa apartment. If you went right to step thirty-three, you were going to what used to be the Malcovitch apartment. At first, Salome wondered why Felix had chosen step thirty-three to loosen. Then she realized doing that protected anyone heading to the other apartment. Salome tried to imagine what it would be like turning to the left, losing her step, and falling backward down thirty-three stairs. She put herself in that position and tried to act out the part. What she found was that the angle didn't make sense. She could see if she had indeed slipped on the thirty-third step, she would fall backward on the landing and hit her head on the other thirty-third step heading towards the old Malcovitch apartment. It was almost impossible to make herself fall at the necessary angle to turn off of the landing and head straight down the thirty-two steps. She sat back down on the thirty-second step, her back against the landing.

"Seagull Six this is Red Leader One. Open your ass bay doors."

"That's a Roger, Red Leader One. The ass bay doors are open."

"Drop load on my mark Seagull Six, five, four, three, two, one…release!"

And, of course, legend has it, that Sir Isaac Newton first began thinking about the Laws of Gravity, when an apple fell from a tree and conked him on the head. Salome Apple first began thinking about those Newtonian Laws, when spiraling down with the accuracy that a World War II bombardier would have envied, the seagull shit hit her precisely in the middle of her head. "WHY JESUS CHRIST...SON OF A BITCH!" she yelled.

The next afternoon, Salome heard the Madeira Beach Bank's clock chime four times at four o'clock. That reminded her of the seagull shit incident from yesterday, so she looked up into the sky. She saw a flock of seagulls passing over the motel, and at precisely the same time as yesterday, she saw them drop their tawdry cargo on the motel. Salome bolted up the steps, and saw that the fresh seagull shit had landed on and all around the thirty-second step.

The next day at precisely four o'clock it was raining, so the seagulls decided to stay home, but at least the thirty-second step got washed. But the following day, and the day after that, Salome noticed that at approximately 4:00 every afternoon, *The Breakers* became ground zero in Seagull Potty World. A theory then began to maturate in Salome's never-think-inside-of-the-box mind. She noticed that there was an overhang from the roof of the motel that protected about half of the width of steps thirty-three and higher on each side of the landing, but steps thirty-two and lower had no such covering. Curious Salome then used the stairs that accessed the roof from Felix's apartment, and she went up to see what the top of the motel looked like. And although there was all kinds of debris on the roof, Salome noticed that there wasn't any seagull dookie. She wondered why the gulls didn't just bombard the roof. Not having taken Seagull Psychology 101 or having read *Jonathan Livingston Seagull*, she had no answer. But she did deduce, that whatever it was about step thirty-two that attracted the seagulls—that's where they were attracted nonetheless. Step thirty-two was the first exposed step from top to bottom, and it was the one that kept receiving the goods. Still working on her hypothesis a few days later she asked Anthony, "When your step-mother fell, what happened to the loose thirty-third step?"

And Anthony said, "You really want to play Sherlock Holmes don't you! Okay...the thirty-third step went flying and landed on the ground."

So like any true student of the scientific method, Salome kept observing the data over the next few weeks. It was becoming fairly conclusive to her that the seagulls had a thing for step thirty-two. A few afternoons before she and Anthony were scheduled to leave, she had Anthony watch the 4:00 seagull sorties. Then she brought him up to step thirty-two and said, "It wasn't the loose thirty-third step that caused your step-mother to fall and become a paraplegic. Yes, Felix did intend on hurting her...but he failed! He may be guilty for the attempt, but he's innocent of the result. Your step-mother slipped on seagull shit on the thirty-second step, she fell straight backwards, and her full laundry basket flew out of her arms, and part of that basket touched the loose thirty-third step and knocked it to the ground. We need to tell Felix that he's innocent!"

"Wow…I can't believe…with all of the times I've cleaned seagull crap from these steps…that it never occurred to me…that most of it was on the same step…Wow! But *we* aren't going to tell Felix squat about this theory. If he knows that I've told you about this, he'll never speak to me again!"

"But you need to tell him," Salome stressed. "He's your brother, you love him, so perhaps you can relieve some of the burden he's been carrying for thirteen years. Just tell him that you came up with this idea, that's all!"

"Maybe so," Anthony said. "But it's going to take the perfect moment for me to tell him about this, because I know how hard he's been working at forgetting it."

Unfortunately, it would be years before that perfect moment.

And, of course, Salome's newly discovered Holmesian-like sense of property/injury deduction, in The Case of the Slippery Seagull Shit, years later, would be the sine qua non to her successful fifteen-year career as a top notch insurance claims adjustor.

Chapter Five

The orange-purple September sky at sunset over the Gulf of Mexico was a Madeira Beach Chamber of Commerce picture postcard, on this sad last evening in Florida for Salome and Anthony. Anthony walked along the beach softly singing to himself, "*The Moon may be high, but I can't see a thing in the sky…I only have eyes for youuu.*"

Walter Lee got within less-than-shouting-needed-range and said, "I'm sorry to see you go 'Knee."

"I'm sorry to have to go Walter Lee," Anthony said, as he and Walter Lee continued walking together along the shoreline. And, of course, Anthony would miss Walter Lee. But what he really meant was, "When I drop off Salome in New York City, I'm heading back to Burlington alone."

"I know you're going to miss Salome when you leave her in New York City," Walter Lee said, "But maybe that's for the best 'Knee. She *is* only fourteen. Don't get me wrong…I know that in other cultures around the world…girls are married at fourteen. When my sister was alive, she introduced me to a friend from Nigeria whose sister had married at thirteen. In that culture, in parts of India, in a number of other places it would be okay. But hey…in 1974, if you do a Jerry Lee Lewis in these good ole United States, you're going to jail. Look…'Knee…you're a grown man, and you're gonna do what you're gonna do. But I've known you since you were seven years old…I've watched you grow up. And unfortunately, since you don't have a parent around to give you parental advice…I just thought I'd stick my big nose in."

"Thank you," Anthony said. "I love you too, Walter Lee." And then

Anthony patted Walter Lee affectionately on the back as they continued walking. "It's too late though…I'm already totally zonked with Salome. I don't care if she's fourteen, and if we have to live in Calcutta."

First, Walter Lee thought of conjuring up the cliché, "If you really love something let it go…," and his second vagary might be, "Well perhaps you guys should indeed move someplace where it's legal." Instead, Walter Lee decided to delve into more dangerous territory, and he asked, "Is she in love with you too?"

And Anthony had to be honest, "I don't think so Walter Lee…I don't think so."

While Anthony and Walter Lee were walking on the beach, Salome was up in the apartment on the phone with Bubba. Since that first Tuesday away, when Salome had called home, and given her parents her phone number and her post office box address in Queens—telling Bubba that she didn't want to inconvenience Selma's sister Ivy Underwood, by using either her phone number or apartment's mailbox, and with all of the college catalogues she was ordering, that were too big and would be kept for her to pick up at the post office anyway, how getting a box at the post office was a good idea—Bubba had been fairly amiable during their phone conversations.

"SOOO…you're working at another POOOLOCK place?" Bubba asked.

"Yeah," Salome lied, "The two sisters on Long Island…uh…Annie and Harriet…turned me onto Polish food at this place in the East Village called *The Polish Palace* before they took me to that Broadway show I told you I saw."

"Johnson and SOMETHING," Bubba said.

"*Johnson and Boswell: The Musical*," Salome said, and then she continued her mini saga. "Anyway, I discovered that I love Polish food….and the place was real busy. I asked if they needed a waitress. They weren't hiring at the moment, but they took my name and number. I needed to land some kind of a job immediately, so when I noticed a "Help Wanted" sign for a waitress in the window of another Polish restaurant a couple of blocks away, I went in, got hired, and began the next day. When a job opened up at *The Polish Palace* I grabbed it, since their food is much better, they're busier, and I'll make better tips."

Felix's cat, Petomane, came over and started prancing back and forth against Salome's leg, meowing loudly and thinking, 'Ummm…nice…it's too bad I only have an inch and a half dick.'

And Salome whispered, "I'll feed you in a few minutes Peto!"

And Petomane thought, 'Food would be nice you chesty wench, and then I'll either go spend some quality time in the box, or go out and look for some cootie cat that I can handle!'

"WELLL," Bubba said, "YOUUU better not eat too much of what you're serving, or you're gonna get real fat!"

"I thought you'd be happy with that," Salome joked. "If I got real fat, that would certainly keep the boys away!"

"I want you to be able to land Mr. RIIIGHT when you're older," Bubba said with seriousness.

"Thanks Bubba," Salome said and then added, "So I'm working at this new job at the restaurant four days a week from noon to eight o'clock, and then five nights a week from nine o'clock to two in the morning I do janitorial work on the fifty-second, fifty-third, and fifty-fourth floors of a big skyscraper in midtown."

"What about school?" Bubba asked.

"My GED Prep Class is Monday through Friday in the mornings from eight until eleven in Flushing, and then I hop on the Subway across the street and head to Manhattan."

"When do you SLEEEP?"

"I work at the restaurant Thursday through Sunday, and I do the janitorial job Monday through Friday, so there are only two days in which both jobs overlap. I can sleep in Saturday and Sunday mornings, and I can take a nap Monday, Tuesday, or Wednesday afternoons, but I usually spend that time at the library."

"I'm very impressed with how hard YOUUU are working," Bubba said. "I love and MISSS you," he added.

"I love and miss you too Bubba," Salome said, hardly believing that those words had just come from her. "Can I say hi to Mom?" she added.

"Uhhh…SHEEE'S not here at the moment," Bubba lied and looked over at Pauline. Pauline was sitting on the sofa listening to the conversation and shaking her head 'No!' "SHEEE won't be back until LAAATER."

"Eight o'clock at night and she's out?" Salome asked with suspicion. Since Pauline had night blindness, it was rare for her to go out in the evenings anymore.

"Well…Cindy DROOOVE, and they picked up your Aunt Clara. It was some KIIIND of important errand!"

"Okay Bubba," Salome said, feeling that something might not be right. "How is it having Cindy back from Japan?"

"It's good… I MISSSED her," Bubba said.

"Is Dick okay as a houseguest?" Salome asked.

"Dick is Dick!" Bubba said with a touch of sarcasm.

Salome laughed and said, "Well give my love to everybody. Tell Cindy I won't forget to mail her that 'I Love New York' t-shirt that she asked me for. And tell Jennifer that I'll also mail back her green top…washed! And tell Mom I love and miss her."

"Okay Salome," Bubba said and hung up.

Earlier that day, after having been summoned into her doctor's office with Bubba for a consultation, two days after having had a colonoscopy in which the pathology had come back positive for colon cancer, Pauline had decided that she didn't want Salome to know. She knew that Salome would immediately come home, and Pauline didn't want to disturb what seemed to be working for her daughter at the moment in New York City. But Pauline didn't feel up to lying to Salome when she had just called, ergo she feigned being absent. Fortunately, the colon cancer had been detected early. Dr. Paul Emerson had told Pauline and Bubba, "It doesn't appear as if the cancer has gone beyond this one localized place in your lower colon. I will cut out this small piece of lower colon, and it will be fairly easy to stretch and sew the rest together. Then, with one eight-week radiation protocol of twice per week, you should be as clean as the proverbial whistle." The surgery would be in three days, with the radiation beginning two weeks later. To avoid a temporary colostomy, Pauline's diet for three months would be liquids only.

And, of course, even with the encouraging news from her doctor, Pauline's thoughts still ran to her own mortality and how little time we actually get to be alive. She was only forty-six, and the last thing she would have ever thought to worry about was colon cancer.

Salome fed Petomane and Petomane thought, 'Yumm!...screw Round Boy Felix...take me home with you!'

Salome then made a pitcher of frozen Margaritas. She brought it along with three glasses, and a small bowl of salt, down to the beach table they always used. The timing was perfect, as Anthony and Walter Lee were walking back to the motel anyway.

They sat around the table drinking Margaritas, watching the day turn into night, and after several minutes of silence Salome finally said, "Thanks for being so great to me...to us...while we've been here Mr. Younger."

"If you don't start calling me Walter Lee..."

"I'm sorry...Walter Lee...you've been wonderful."

"You're a very nice young lady, Salome. And since I lost my own family 12 years ago, and part of my adopted family just a little more than a year ago, 'Knee-'Licks is the only family I've got." (Walter Lee would always call the two Kulpa brothers "'Knee-'Licks," a name that, years later, would be used for a popular character on the television series *Star Trek Voyager*.) "I hate to see 'Knee go."

"I'll miss you too, Walter Lee," Anthony said again.

"Anthony told me about your family tragedy," Salome said, "But I just haven't known if I should mention it."

"I appreciate that your apprehension comes from a place of sensitivity," Walter Lee said. "But I can talk about it...twelve years has made it easier. One thing I've learned is just how precious this life is, and what a burden it is for us as human beings to have to think about death." Petomane meandered out by the beach table and Walter Lee noticing him said, "For the kitty cat, he just lives and doesn't worry about the future. Oh sure, if he's under attack he'll instinctually fight for survival. But Petomane doesn't sit around and wax philosophic with other kitty cats about what happens when this life is finished."

And Petomane thought, in his Edward G. Robinson/Johnny Rocco voice, 'Says who? This is only my third life and I still have six more to go, so it isn't a pressing issue yet! Besides, I *know* after the ninth life, me and my peeps will all go to our spiritual other world, Katmandu, and that eventually, the mother ship will land and take all of us, no matter which life we're in at the moment, back there too.'

"But we humans were given the opposable thumb, which gave us the ability to grasp objects in our hands. A definite advantage over other animals, in that we could pick up a stick, clobber those animals, and then eat them. Later, we learned how to use our hands to grow crops so we didn't have to eat animals. And our human hands built everything on this planet including a way to leave the planet also. So physically we were given this ability, and mentally we were given the brain to figure out all of this mechanical stuff. We were also given a major burden that came with the brain, the ability to see our own impending deaths and to have to wonder what the purpose of it all is. We were also given hearts that break, when we have to experience the deaths of those we love."

Anthony, thinking about his father's suicide just over a year ago, said, "Or hearts that get tougher when we're angry about someone choosing to end his own life."

Salome looked at Anthony and said nothing. Walter Lee said, "Hearts getting tougher might just be a way to mask the pain, but that might be necessary to do…for a while."

"Well…one can't live in Hurtville forever," Anthony said.

"No, but one has to do some time in Hurtville, before hitching up the *U-Haul* and moving on to Toughville," Walter Lee said and then added, "And usually our stay in Toughville is just temporary, until we remember our previous lives in Hurtville and continue on down the road to our final destination of Wellville."

"It sounds as if you've been in all of these towns before," Salome said. "Tell me…is Wellville the same as Goodville?"

"I think so," said Walter Lee. "Wellville feels like Goodville to me. After my family was killed in that racist firebombing in 1962 in Chicago, I fell apart. I wasn't killed, because I was out chauffeuring my boss to O'Hare Airport that night. I come home to find that I had lost my mother, my sister, my son, my wife, and the unborn child my wife was carrying. And what hurt equally to losing them, was that I had lost the opportunity to make something of myself for them while they were still alive."

"I'm sure your family loved and respected you Walter Lee," Anthony said.

"Well...I am happy that by agreeing to move to the house in the white subdivision that my mom had purchased...that I pleased my family. They all said that I had finally come into my manhood...but it was touch and go there for awhile. I almost accepted the Clybourne Park Home Owners Association offer to buy the house from us at a substantial profit, and for years after the bombing I wished that I had. It took a lot of years of talking to your father, 'Knee, for Frank to convince me to see a professional. Then it took a lot of therapy sessions with that psychologist, Chuck Coaker, to no longer blame myself for having not hung tough in the first place...by insisting on taking the money from the people who clearly didn't want us around."

"So you no longer blame yourself?" Anthony asked with some trepidation.

"No I don't," Walter Lee said. "Owning a home after so many years had been a dream deferred for my family. This house was what everybody wanted, so we took the chance. Of course, I also carried guilt for a long time over wasting $6500 of the ten thousand dollar life insurance policy that my father had left us a year earlier, by getting conned by one of my so-called friends into a so-called business deal. For a long time I thought that if we had the ten thousand to put down, we could have gotten a mansion in a black neighborhood and then I would have had a nice house and an alive family."

"And you've given up that notion also?" Anthony asked.

"Yeah...I owe your father, Frank, for helping me with that one. He pointed out that my mother had already spent $3500 down for a house in a lily white neighborhood before I had blown the other $6500, and if she had wanted to put all ten thousand down on a mansion in a black neighborhood, then that's what she would have done. And he was right. I finally figured out that I'm here now, and that we don't get a lot of life to live before we have to leave. And you were right Salome, I have spent lots of time in Hurtville. I was there for a long time after the tragedy. I drank up pretty much all of the money I had in the world at the *Green Hat*, my favorite jazz bar. I'd listen to the music and stay drunk. Then one day a life insurance check arrives at my rooming house. I owe my landlady two months back rent on my room, and she recognizes the envelope as an insurance check. She comes down to the *Green Hat* and gets me. My mother had left a ten thousand dollar life insurance policy just like my dad had. I straightened up real quick when I saw that check. I figured I had been given a second chance to prove myself to my family, and perhaps they would be watching to see what I would do. I bought a used car, and decided that I had had enough of Chicago for one lifetime. I decided to head to Toughville. By now, news was coming out in the papers that the bombers of my house were not really the KKK...they were members of the Clybourne Park Home Owners Association...headed by that asshole Lindner...the guy who tried to buy us out in the first place. Then when the story broke that Lindner also worked for Mayor Dailey's Housing

Commission...I went and saw a lawyer. He said that we would make a lot of money from the lawsuits, but that it might take six or seven years. I hired him for nothing out-of-pocket, just one-third if we won the suits. I had to make several trips back to Chicago for court appearances, once while there were riots in Lincoln Park during the Democratic Convention in 1968, and eventually, in 1970, we won the suits...and I became fairly wealthy. These days...although I still miss my family...I think I'm living in Wellville."

"Didn't Felix and Tatiana meet you in Chicago in August of 1968, and you actually planned that trip to see your lawyer around your participation in that demonstration? Didn't the three of you get arrested?"

"I see 'Knee!" Walter Lee said. "So you know the whole story... Well, that's true...I actually owe the beginning of my political awareness to your father and step-mother, 'Knee."

"How's that?" Anthony asked.

"Well first of all, if you never heard the story...In February of 1963, I was driving along the beaches on the west coast of Florida, fantasizing that I could find some Brother or Sister who owned cottages in the ghetto section of the beach...a place for black folks. I'm on the beaches immediately to the west of St. Petersburg, and I drive north over the John's Pass Causeway from Treasure Island to Madeira Beach. A few blocks later I see this place called *The Breakers*, conspicuous only because it was the only place that didn't have a 'No Coloreds' sign hanging near the office. I thought, 'What the hell...let's see what the deal is here.' I parked my *Chevrolet* in the lot, and your father was walking out of the office as I was walking in. I asked, 'Is your sign broken?' And he said, 'What sign are you talking about?' And I said, 'The one that says "No Coloreds."' And your dad said, 'We've got lots of coloreds here, unfortunately they're all colored white!' And I knew that I liked the man right away. I told him that I might be interested in a long term rental. He gave me a good deal on my one-bedroom place on the second floor. It turns out that his writer-friend, Jack Kerouac, had just moved out of that apartment and into his mother's house in St. Petersburg. The apartment had been vacant for less than a week when I rented it."

"Did you get to meet the writer-friend of Anthony's dad?" Salome asked.

"Yeah I did. Frank brought me into his house for an impromptu visit when we were in his neighborhood, and later I got a few dinner invitations with Frank. His mom, 'Murmur' he called her, was an exceptional cook."

"Anthony told me that Mr. Kerouac passed away in 1969, but is his mother still alive?" Salome asked.

"Yeah she is," Walter Lee said. "And I feel guilty, because I haven't seen her in years. And by the way 'Knee, did anyone ever tell you the story about when your dad and I were at Jack's and the Beat Poet, Allen Ginsberg showed up?"

"No, I never heard that story," Anthony said.

It was 1968, and Frank and I were over there on a Sunday afternoon for dinner. We were watching this quiz show on television, *G.E. College Bowl*, when there's a knock on the door. Frank answers the door since he's the closest. This balding guy with a long beard and long hair on the back of his head comes in. Jack makes introductions, and then Allen Ginsberg sits down and says nothing. Finally, about twenty minutes later, Ginsberg gets up, walks to the center of the room, turns toward Jack, points his finger and says, 'You, my friend, have gone from great writer to great alcoholic. You sit and drink whilst babies burn!'"

"He really said, 'whilst'?" Anthony asked.

"Really said, 'whilst,'" Walter Lee said. "Then Jack, who was drinking but could hold his load real well, stood up in the center of the room nose to nose with Allen and said, 'And you, my friend, have gone from angry Beat to happy Hippie, with nary a twitch of the Id!'"

"Wow!" said Salome. "That's quite a story. What has Allen Ginsberg written?" she asked.

"Probably his most famous poem, which is pretty long by the way, was called *Howl*. It was published in the 1950's," Walter Lee said.

"So go on with how my father helped mold your political views," Anthony said.

"Well it wasn't just Frank, it was Terry too," Walter Lee said. "Your father told me that he started to think deeply about life, philosophy, and politics in the late 1940's. His marriage to your mom, Beverly, was apparently a rough marriage. He didn't speak much about that period in his life, but he did say once that when Beverly began to ignore him after Felix's birth, he turned to books about philosophy, psychology, politics, and religion. I know he was very well-read, because between 1963 and 1970 I read his entire library. And Terry already owned and had read most of your father's books when they got together, and she had another fifty books that Frank and I read. The three of us saw the stupidity in the House of Un-American Activities Hearings in the early 1950's, felt the Rosenbergs had been setup, knew the Vietnam War was just designed for the military-industrial complex to rack in tons of dollars. By 1963, Terry was in a wheelchair, and except for Felix's wedding in 1966, she didn't travel far. Frank didn't want to leave her alone anyway, so I went myself in late 1964 to protest the War in Vietnam in Washington D.C., after the so-called Gulf of Tonkin Incident had increased our troops from 26,000 to 160,000. I also joined with my Freedom Riding white Brothers and Sisters in the South in 1964 and 1965...and was back in D.C. in the summer of 1965 at a massive Civil Rights Demonstration with Martin Luther King, Jr."

"And what about 1968 in Chicago?" Salome asked.

"By then Felix and his wife Tatiana had come into the same political fold, so the three of us met in Chicago and went to the demonstrations in Lincoln

Park. We were arrested and held in the Cook Country Jail for three days. Felix got the crap beat out of him by the cops. They broke his nose."

"Oh my God!" Salome said. And then she asked, "What were those demonstrations about?"

"First, in April of 1968, Dr. Marin Luther King Jr. was assassinated in Memphis, Tennessee. Then in June of 1968, Bobby Kennedy was assassinated in Los Angeles, California. Senator Kennedy had just won the Democratic Primary in California that night, and he was definitely headed toward being the Democratic nominee in the presidential race that year. As a matter of fact, the Republican Party probably wouldn't have even run Richard Nixon—the man who would become President of the United States in 1968 and had to just resign a few weeks ago—against Bobby Kennedy, since his brother John Kennedy had already beaten Nixon in 1960. Anyway, Bobby Kennedy's platform was simple: 'Elect me in November of 1968, I'll take over in January of 1969, and within ninety days of becoming your President of the United States, every single one of our soldiers will be back from Vietnam.' After Bobby Kennedy was killed, the Democratic Party ran Hubert Humphrey for President. Vice President Humphrey was much more conservative in his approach to ending Vietnam, and Nixon beat him anyway. Now, in 1974, they're finally talking about meeting in Paris next year to end this bullshit war. We've lost almost 58,000 troops since our involvement in this Vietnamese Civil War, double of what we would have lost if Bobby Kennedy had indeed ended the war by April of 1969 as he had promised. Felix, Tatiana, and I were in Chicago adding our voices to the dissent, over anyone gaining the Democratic nomination whose intent wasn't to immediately end the war in the same way that Senator Kennedy had said that he would."

"Wow!" said Salome again.

"And you guys went to Woodstock in the summer of 1969 also," Anthony said.

"It was Frank and Terry who got me thinking about politics in the first place, but it was Felix and Tatiana who got me involved with psychotropic drugs and Rock Music in 1968."

"What are psychotropic drugs?" Salome asked.

"L.S.D. primarily," Walter Lee said. They turned me onto the stuff in the summer of 1968. Got me high, sat my ass down, and made me listen to "Turn On, Tune In, and Drop Out," a record by Dr. Travis Leary. Then, they made me listen to "Sergeant Pepper's Lonely Hearts Club Band," by *The Beatles*, "In Search of the Lost Chord," by *The Moody Blues*, and "Are You Experienced?" by *The Jimi Hendrix Experience*. The next summer we played the hell out of "Tommy," by *The Who*, before the three of us drove up to Woodstock. I learned a lot about myself during that period by listening closely to the lyrics...everything became so amplified on the L. S. D....I learned that *compassion* was most important...hate needed to go...and how important it is to be in the here and now. One can always intellectually theorize about the here and now...but on acid...it's no longer theory. So yes, I just had to go to Woodstock. But I'd like to think that I furthered Felix and Tatiana's musical knowledge also, with my collection of *Motown* Soul, R & B, and Jazz."

"I was born too late. I would have only been..." and then Anthony shot a look over at Salome, "fourteen in the summer of 1969! What I missed out on by being born too late!"

"Well look at all you're gonna get to see down the road, that I'll miss out on because I was born too early!" Walter Lee said. "Anyway, I'm not interested in acid or any other drugs now. But it was my acid experiences that led me into reading about psychology first, and then Eastern religions. That's kind of where I'm at today. I particularly like studying different cultures and the affects of religion on those cultures. Did Felix tell you that I've decided to go after graduate degrees in anthropology?"

"He sure did," Anthony said. "I can't wait to call you Dr. Walter Lee Younger, and to get you to autograph whatever book you write."

"My sister, Beneatha, was always going to be the first doctor in our family, and I used to give her hell for being so selfish and tying up our money with her college tuition. Also, I used to kid Beneatha about her desire to discover her African roots. I hope, wherever she is now, she knows how sorry I am for all of that. And I hope she'll see, that my graduate work in anthropology, that comes from doing research in Nigeria...is my way of paying tribute to her."

"I'm sure she does, and I'm sure she will," said Anthony.

@@@@@@@@

It had to have been a fluke...an accident...although Freud would say there are no accidents. "Of all the airports, in all of the cities of the world, why did she have to pick mine?" Bogie might have said. I was sitting at JFK Airport, in the Freddie Laker Sky Train Terminal, waiting for my flight to London, and although starting a much longed for vacation, in a lugubrious mood...when she walked in my direction. I had to bring my newspaper up with great lubricity to not be seen. There she was, the love of my life, my ex-wife, Tatiana Orlonsky Kulpa, strutting like some soubrette across the stage, suitcase in tow, dressed to the nines, obliviously walking in front of me, and then alighting in a seat, not ten feet away, that faced me. I kept The New York Times in front of my face without peeking for five minutes, and then I decided to make my getaway, exit stage left, to a group of seats further away from the gate. I went to stand up, and I almost drove the top of my head into her chin, as she was standing just three inches in front of me. "How did you know it was me?" I had asked. And, "I smelled you!" had been her response. And I laughed. And she laughed. And she sat down next to me and we talked. She was on the same flight, but continuing on to Paris where she now lived. It had been a year since she had ditched her gynecologist-lover, Dr. Peter Wunderlich, in New York—the asshole who had examined her little nook-nook in his office, and then stole her from me in August of 1971, when she had moved out of our efficiency apartment in what was then called the Lower East Side, and is now called the East Village, but has always been called Alphabet City on 10th and C in Manhattan—and had since moved to Paris. She was still painting, and, with her perfect Parisian French, was working part time in a chic boutique along the Seine. We had convinced a nice older lady to swap seats so we could sit together to London, and then somewhere, over the Atlantic Ocean, she had rediscovered that same old Ca Thump Ca Thump for me that she had once had, and that I had never lost. She convinced me to spend my entire vacation with her in Paris, and I convinced her to get off in London and we'd travel to Paris together. And after we had eaten fish and chips in London like true tubby trenchermen, we took the ferry to the Continent, and then the train to Paris, and then a taxi to her flat on Avenue de la Grande Armée. And that evening, and for the next three days before she had to return to work, we made love as if it were new love. And all the food we desired was delivered to us, so we could stay in bed. And now, dear journal, it's been nearly five incredible weeks, and I have to leave tomorrow. I'm awaiting her arrival from work, and wondering how this conversation—the one we've been avoiding—will go tonight. I want Tatiana to marry me again.

And so, dear journal, there is hope. Not for now, not this instant, but for somewhere in the future. L'homme propose, la femme dispose...the man proposes, the woman disposes...or decides. Tatiana has not ruled out marrying me again. She asked me if I'd move to Paris and live with her. I explained how I wanted to give Anthony his crack at college and law school, and if I moved to Paris, Anthony would either have to leave college in Vermont and move back to run the motel, or else agree to me selling the place...which might not be in our best interest. I explained how the agreement I had with Anthony was that I would deal with the motel now for nine months a year...with him running it during the summer...for up to ten years...until he finished college, law school, and some traveling and general fucking around. I told Anthony I wanted to turn it over to him by the time I was forty. And Anthony agreed that he would take over, and use one of the storage rooms on the first floor to build a small law office. After ten years went by...somewhere before my 50th birthday...we would decide what to do next...whether to just sell the place. I could not move to Paris right now, Anthony needed to do his thing, and it would not be fair to him. And Tatiana said she understood, and that she had loved the summers we had spent at the motel, helping out first Frank and Terry and then just Frank, and how she loved hanging with Walter Lee, and how she remembered how silly I could be, like the time I kept talking as if I were Lennie Small from Steinbeck's novel, "Of Mice and Men," in front of strangers on the beach and in the coffee shop, regularly going into, "Ah please George, tell me again about the place we're going to have, and how we're going to live off of the fat of the land, and how I get to tend the rabbits!" And how I had kept doing that, until she had finally figured out that I really wanted her to play George, and when she had finally responded, "We're going to get a little place with some land. We'll have a little stove in a sitting room, and when it rains, we'll just keep warm while listening to the rain drops on the roof. And if a friend comes over, we'll invite him to stay, and by golly he would. And when there's a carnival in town, we'll just take off from working and go to it. And you get to tend the rabbits," how I had dropped out of character, because she finally had gone into character, and how I then snatched her into my arms and had kissed her all over her face and said, "I will always love you, Tatiana," and how that scene had regularly played in her mind during the last three years that we had been separated, and also during the past almost five weeks that we had been together. So we walked through the wooded area along the Champs Elysses, noticing the mid-September yellowing-orange Plane Trees, and then we continued our trek, around L'Arc de Triomphe in L'Place de l' Etoile to Montmartre. We walked halfway up Montmartre and sat and relaxed in this little blues club, Chez Moustache, listening to the music, holding hands, and looking into each other's faces. Then we took a taxi back to her apartment and made love one final time. We decided we would talk on the phone regularly, and during Christmas she would come to Florida for ten days. And, if I could get either Anthony or Walter Lee to watch the place for ten days in April, I would return to Paris, and she would come back to Florida for a month in June, and we would see how things were going. And if things were going well between us a year from now, she would consider marrying me again. I know things will be going well.

@@@@@@@@

Jimson Apple ran into the dining room with Bubba running close behind, "WHYYY…don't think you can get AWAAAY from me, YOUUU dumb son of a bitch!" Bubba yelled.

"Aw shit Bubba," Jimson said, running around the dining room table avoiding Bubba, while Bubba tried desperately to catch him. "I didn't mean to run the tractor into the ditch and fuck up the axle. I'll pay you back I promise."

"WHYYY…you'll MAAAKE a down PAAAYMENT now!" Bubba said, as Jimson faked as if he were moving around the left side of the table, and Bubba sold Jimson that he had accepted that direction. But they had both come around the table in the other direction, and Bubba's right fist had met Jimson's left cheek and knocked Jimson to the floor.

"You fat bastard!" Jimson shouted. "I'm gonna kill you some day!"

"WHYYY…how about TODAAAY?" Bubba said, and then he kicked Jimson in the butt, while he was still on the floor. "How can you BEEE so

STUPIDDD?" And then Bubba walked over to the refrigerator and snagged a beer.

Dick Chumwell, twenty-two year-old son-in-law of Bubba and Pauline, walked in and set the bucket of *Kentucky Fried Chicken* and paper bag full of biscuits and quart containers of side dishes on the dining room table. As he walked by Jimson on the floor he said—not to imitate Bubba, but just to say something—"How can you be so stupid?"

"Hey fuck you! You're a real dick, Dick!" the aching Jimson said, and then he got up, ran up the stairs, locked his bedroom door, and called Lizzie. Dick went and got his own beer.

Pauline's doctor had called immediately after Bubba's conversation with Salome earlier, and he had asked Pauline to come and check into the hospital that night. He wanted to start her on a special controlled liquid diet that would clean out her colon before Monday morning's scheduled surgery. Cindy and Jennifer had taken Pauline to the hospital. Jack was working at the gas station until 11:00 pm. Bubba and Dick had just returned from a late VFW meeting, and Jimson had been doing necessary chores all day in the orchard. Bruiser had left early in the morning for Buffalo, New York. He had to pick up cooler components for the business, and shipping it would take too long.

"He's a total asshole, and I can't live here anymore," Jimson said to Lizzie on the phone.

"Well...we have been talking about moving in together anyway," Lizzie Mitner said. It had been nearly a month since Jimson and Lizzie had gotten back together, and they both had just started their freshman year at Rutland Community College. They were discussing renting this unfurnished house in downtown Rutland, next to the library, where Lizzie worked part time as an assistant to Selma Greenwood and the other librarians. And, of course, the problem would be Lizzie's parents, how they would react. Her mom, Barbara Mitner, might handle the idea of her seventeen year-old college daughter living with a seventeen year-old college boy. Maybe. But no way would her father, Vermont Highway Patrolman Jonathan Mitner, handle it.

"Let's do it this week," said Jimson. "We've got plenty of money. You said after tuition and books, after your grants, you'd have about $2,000 left this year. I have the $5,000 that Uncle Wilbur left me, plus after tuition and books this year another $2200 I've saved up. We can get nice furniture and a nice used car or truck."

"Oh...I'm sure we could handle it financially," Lizzie said. "But my dad won't let it happen. I already checked on this, I have to wait until I'm eighteen in January to legally move out. So why don't we get the place, fix it up, you move in, and we'll have a place to hang out and fool around together. I'll just have to go home to my parents' house at nights until January."

"It's a done deal," said Jimson.

"Just don't tell anybody that we've rented this place together now," Lizzie stressed. "You should sign the lease alone, and tell your parents that a couple of other guys are moving in."

"That's a done deal too," said Jimson.

@@@@@@@@

The trip back to New York was painful for Anthony, but he did his best to put having to say goodbye to Salome in a couple of days out of his mind. He was trying to just enjoy what time he had left with her. He had suggested, and Salome had agreed, to taking a different way home—up I-75 to Atlanta, I-85 from Atlanta to Petersburg, Virginia, and then I-95 to New York. Salome was excited that she would get to see Atlanta, the self-proclaimed "New York City of the South." They had stopped at a *Waffle House* outside of Ocala, Florida for breakfast five hours ago, where Salome, along with eating eggs, bacon, and raisin toast, had devoured a big bowl of a recently discovered new love—cheese grits. Now that they were on the outskirts of Atlanta, they both were hungry again. Anthony suggested finding a nice restaurant in Underground Atlanta, but Salome said she wanted to try this famous hamburger joint she had seen on television—*The Varsity*.

After having chowed-down on wonderfully greasy burgers, dogs, and fries at *The Varsity*, Anthony suggested that they get a room and stay in Atlanta for the night. They checked in at *The Lester Maddox Inn* on Piedmont Street, showered, changed, and then headed to Underground Atlanta to walk around for the evening. After having seen all there was to see in Underground Atlanta, and after having had a decadent dessert and cappuccino in a commercialized decadent dessert and cappuccino place, Anthony and Salome decided, at the suggestion of a young couple that they had sat next to in said decadent dessert and cappuccino place, to leave the Underground, and head to *Alex Cooley's Electric Ballroom* a few miles away to see some live rock bands. They missed the first group's set and most of the second group's set, but they really enjoyed the headliners, a three-piece group called *Triangulated Crossfire*, who were playing material from their just released first album, "The Grassy Knoll."

The next day was Saturday, and along I-85 near Gainesville, Georgia, Salome asked Anthony to find a payphone. It was still early morning, and Salome wanted to call Selma at the library just after it opened, and just before Ivy made her regular Saturday morning phone call to Selma. Salome wanted Ivy to know that she would be at Ivy's apartment in Queens the next evening. Salome also needed Selma to wire her $500. Although Salome still had $550 of the $700 she had taken with her, she wanted to give Anthony $500 towards his expenses before they parted. The money would be waiting at any *Western Union* later that day under the name of Jennifer Apple, but Salome figured she would have Anthony drop her and then wait a few minutes, and that they would say their goodbyes at the main *Western Union* in Manhattan on Sunday. Salome also asked Selma to wire the other $5,000 on Tuesday to Jennifer Apple, as that would give Salome a chance to settle in at Ivy's, give Ivy a few months rent in advance, and find the closest bank where she could open a savings account. Salome had spent $35 on a Vermont State Identification Card for non-drivers, which looked like a Vermont State Driver License, and she would use that for ID to open up a second savings account, in her real name, in a second bank.

Anthony and Salome spent Saturday night in Petersburg, Virginia, and the next day it was just a seven hour ride to Manhattan. Anthony parked the *Dodge*, with the engine still running, in front of a fire hydrant on Seventh Avenue and Forty-third Street at the *Western Union*, and he waited for Salome to come back. It took her about ten minutes.

She handed Anthony the $500 and said, "You've been absolutely wonderful, but it isn't fair that you've been paying for just about everything in the past five weeks. I want you to have this money."

"I don't want your money," Anthony said. "I invited you, so everything was my responsibility."

Two cops in a patrol car pulled up along side of the *Dodge*, and the cop on the passenger side told Anthony, "Hey buddy...you can't park here."

And Anthony said, "I'm not parking here officer. I'm just saying goodbye and dropping someone off here."

"Well actually," the cop continued, "The sign says 'No Standing,' but I'll give you a few minutes. Don't be here when I drive back by in five minutes!"

"Thank you officer," Anthony said.

"I insist that you take this money," Salome said. "I had a great time, and this shouldn't all be on you."

"I have plenty of money," Anthony said. "You'll insult me by making me take this. I'd much prefer it if you'd keep your money and let me keep seeing you."

And Salome took a deep breath and said, "I've had a great time with you Anthony, and you've rocked my world in ways I can't even tell you. You know, I never told you this before, and you were a real gentleman, after we got through your initial improper first question, for not asking, but what you and I have been doing physically is all new to me. Yes, I have kissed and made out with a few different boys in my life so far in Rutland. But I never let anybody see me naked, I've never been with a boy who was naked, and I have never done the things that you and I have done with anybody else."

"Well good," Anthony said. "That must mean that I'm special and that we have a special thing."

"You are special, and we do have a special thing, and I'll always love you deeply Anthony. But I know that we're not long term, and I know that I have to date other people," Salome said.

"How do you know that we're not long term?" Anthony asked, the words having a hard time escaping around the lump in his throat.

"I just know it," Salome said. "I don't feel Ca Thump Ca Thump."

"Not like Dari Malcovitch, huh," Anthony said with some bitterness.

Salome turned her head away for a moment so she could mumble, "I'm not interested in Harry Malcovitch. He's disgusting!"

But when she turned her face back towards him, Anthony could see that although her words were saying, "no no no," her eyes were saying, "yes yes yes." He also thought it was kind of cute that she would give his wrong first name...kind of like a half-lie. But Anthony knew it had only been five weeks that he had been with Salome, and there had been no promises made.

"Well...can't we just date other people, but also date each other?" he asked.

"I can't do that," Salome said. "If you and I are still dating, it will take away my drive to meet somebody else."

And Anthony understood how problematic that would be anyhow. "I can't believe, with what we've had, that you want to end it so soon," he finally said. "We seem to get along so well," he added.

The cop who had spoken to Anthony before was back, and Anthony said, "She's getting out of the car right now officer." And the cop nodded sympathetically, and he and his partner drove off again.

"We do get along real well," Salome said. "And I would be devastated if I couldn't have your friendship in my life. I can see us being the closest of friends."

"Great!" Anthony said.

"Yellow goes with black, yellow goes with blue, and it goes with red too," Salome said. "Just because we do get along so well at so many levels, it still doesn't mean that we're right for each other as long term mates."

"I understand," Anthony said but didn't mean. "You better go now before that cop gives me a ticket," he added.

Salome grabbed her green duffle bag from the backseat and pulled it over the front seat. She said, "Let me have some sugar," and Anthony turned his face to her and they quickly kissed. She opened the door, got out, closed the door, and said through the open passenger window, "Are you gonna be alright? I just couldn't live with myself if I knew that you weren't gonna be alright."

And Anthony thought, 'I'm sure you could live with yourself regardless.' And he reached across the seat, started rolling the window up, and said, "I'll be fine. I think I'll put the air on." Then he drove away without looking at her in his rearview mirror. He thought about whether he should give Darius a heads up as to her actual age, but he thought, 'Fuck him. It's his problem now. I promised her that I wouldn't tell him, so fuck them both.' And then Anthony realized that he had been thinking too much like Felix lately, but he also now understood why Felix felt the way he felt about women, sex, love, and relationships. 'Felix has it right,' Anthony thought. Then he wondered if Felix would tell Darius how old Salome was, but he decided not to try and persuade Felix one way or the other. That was his call. That was her problem. And he heard himself say in a Rhett Butler kind of way, "Frankly Salome, I don't give a damn!"

It would be hard for Anthony to forget about Salome. And even though two months later he would begin a torrid two-year relationship with his math professor at UVM, a thirty-one year old Russian woman twelve years his senior, Anthony would always think about Salome. It would be three years before he would see her again, however.

@@@@@@@@

It was mid-October 1974, and Central Park was a color masterpiece of artistic stroke. Joggers wore sweats to fend off the autumn chill, and Salome sat drinking coffee on a bench near the carousel—kept warm by the leather jacket, fur-lined leather gloves, and wool cap she had recently purchased at an incredible discount on Orchard Street. The purchases had been Salome's way of celebrating her first full paycheck for eight days of waitress work during a two-week pay period. Incredibly, although she had fabricated the entire story to her parents in Rutland while she was enjoying the Florida sun about being a waitress in the East Village at *The Polish Palace*, when Salome found no modeling work and went looking for waitress work two weeks after returning from Florida, *The Polish Palace* was the first place she had tried. And, of course, just like the way minor characters suddenly appear from nowhere in the middle of great Victorian novels to make needed plot changes, *The Polish Palace* just happened to have had a waitress position that had just opened, and they liked and hired Salome on the spot.

Salome was thinking about Anthony, how she missed him and the great times they had had. She was remembering a certain moment in Florida, the last night, that instant when she had approached the beach table carrying the drinks and Walter Lee and Anthony had approached the table from the other direction. There was a freeze frame etched deeply in her mind of Anthony's face then, a moment in which she might indeed have been in love with him. And although she still believed that the way things had played out was for the best, whenever she thought of Anthony she thought of his face in that moment.

Salome picked up the math book and looked at the next lesson. She had begun a GED preparatory class the first week in October, a month later than she had told her parents, and this class was in Manhattan, about two blocks from the restaurant, and not in Flushing. She had already told her parents that she switched schools to Manhattan, that it was more convenient, and they had seemed satisfied with her explanation. This school offered an eight month class, four days a week Monday thru Thursday, from 8:30 in the morning until 3:30 in the afternoon. And they had a money-back guarantee: "If you take our class, and you show up and do all of the work, if you don't pass the GED Test, 100% of your money will be refunded!" They had a monthly installment plan for tuition, but it was cheaper to pay the entire fee at once. Salome had given them $800 for tuition and $87.50 for books.

Salome worked at *The Polish Palace* the same schedule she had originally fabricated to her parents, i.e., Thursday through Sunday, but the hours were a little longer than she had originally created—from 4:00 pm until 11:00 pm. Thursday was the only day in which she had both school and work. On this late Monday afternoon, Salome decided, after she had done the necessary 25 math problems for tomorrow while sitting on the bench, that she would get a gyro from the street vendor on 59th Street, check her messages from a pay-phone, and head back to Flushing.

"Hi Jennifer this is Darius," Darius' message began.

And Salome thought just how intelligent she had been to not say her name on her recorded phone message. When one called one heard her voice say, "Hi…you've reached 555-7852...and I'm not available now. Please leave a message, and I'll get back to you." And Salome thought she had also been intelligent, having two bank accounts, one in each name, because that was how she had been able to cash her first "Jennifer" paycheck.

"I've been meaning to call you for the past five weeks since I've been back," Darius' message said. "But calling you today is a necessity, because I know of some modeling work I can get you. Actually, it's at the Coliseum, and it's standing up for several hours in a sexy dress, and waving your arms and smiling in front of a bunch of *Oldsmobiles* at the Automobile Show. Anyway, flexible hours, days, for the next four weeks, $20 per hour. If you're interested call me. And hell, even if you're not interested call me. Let's get together." The phone message had been left less than an hour ago.

Salome called Darius, "Hi stranger," she said. "How was Utah?"

"I had a great time, so I stayed two weeks longer," Darius said. "And I took some spectacular pictures of Zion Park. How was Florida?"

"I had a great time," Salome said and added, "And I really liked staying at *The Breakers*. Did you get to meet Walter Lee?"

"We met, but we only spent a few minutes talking. He had a friend from Nigeria visiting the same month that I was there, so he was occupied."

"He's a great guy!" Salome said and meant.

"I would have liked to have gotten to know him better," Darius said. "Most of that month I spent getting to know Felix, and Anthony would sit with us and party occasionally. How are Anthony and Felix?"

"I only got to rap with Felix a little, but he seemed like a nice guy. He was only there for two days before he took off for Europe. And Anthony and I said our goodbyes in September…I guess he's back at UVM in Burlington."

"I didn't know that Felix was going abroad this year," Darius said. Then, avoiding any discussion about Anthony, he changed the subject and asked, "So…what do you think about that job?"

"It sounds great," Salome said. "If I can get flexible hours."

And then Darius gave her the information she needed, where to go and who to see, for the modeling job at the Coliseum. Then he asked her where she was working, and he seemed pleased it was *The Polish Palace*. "Now I can enjoy my favorite food served by my favorite waitress!" he said.

And Salome was thankful that she had used the name Jennifer to get her job at *The Polish Palace*. And although they hadn't asked to see her ID, Salome had figured that they might since they served liquor. Darius then asked if he could come by and have dinner late Friday night, and if Salome would like to go out and listen to music and have a few drinks after her shift. Salome agreed.

That Friday night after Salome's shift, Darius took her to *The Blue Note* to hear Miles Younger' last set of the evening. Salome was carded when drinks were ordered, but her ID was accepted and they both drank a few rounds of Margaritas. They were getting touchy feely with each other in the booth, and when they walked out to Darius' *MGB* after the set was over, Darius grabbed Salome and planted a passionate kiss on her mouth. Salome didn't refuse, and they stood there by the car making out.

"Get a room!" a couple of teenage girls said as they walked by.

"Why don't you come back to my place on Long Island tonight?…My parents are in Boca Raton with my brother and sister for the weekend."

"I have to be at work at 4:00 tomorrow," Salome said.

"I'll drive you there," Darius said.

And so they headed to Long Island. Salome was tired and hammered, and she fell asleep in the car. Darius had to wake her up when they reached his house, and then once inside he led her to his bedroom, next to his studio, on the far side of the mansion. Salome plopped on the bed, and Darius said, "I'll be right back." He went to the kitchen and quietly—since it was already three o'clock in the morning and he didn't want to wake up Annie—made another pitcher of Margaritas. He carried the libation, two glasses, and the salt shaker back to his room. He turned on his stereo low to a jazz station, and then he woke Salome up to have a few more drinks. Salome sat up, and after a good stiff Margarita she was awake again. Then Darius took the glass from her hand, began kissing her deeply with his tongue, and while she was really getting into the kiss, he ran his hand up under her top and bra. Salome moaned loudly. Darius helped her off of the bed and started to remove her clothes. And Salome said, "I really like you Darius…and I'd like to fool around with you…but I'm not going all of the way…that just ain't happening." And then they explored each other's bodies within the parameters of not going all of the way.

A while later, when the first of nearly a year's worth of such physical explorations together were over, Darius said, "Come pose…in the studio."

And Salome, who had been pondering the option of modeling nude since Darius had first broached the idea two months ago said, "I still don't know if I want to do this."

"The pictures will stay right here unless you tell me to do otherwise," Darius said. "You're just so fucking beautiful, I want to take some photographs just for me that's all."

"Do you promise these pictures won't get sent anywhere?" Salome asked.

"They'll be just two sets made…one for you and one for me. Like I said, they won't leave my house unless you tell me to try and get you work."

And so for the next few hours, Salome posed nude in some very provocative positions. Darius used his artistic eye, and his camera captured her in a way that would have given a chubby to a dead man. They were both exhausted when they finally crashed at six in the morning.

The next day they woke up just after 1:00, and Annie was happy to see Salome. "Welcome home Jennifer," she said. And then instead of breakfast, with Darius and Salome's strong approval, Annie warmed up some of her special peppered salmon from the night before. Salome needed clean clothes for today's restaurant shift, so she wore one of Darius' robes while her clothes were being washed and dried in the machines. Darius and Salome had salmon and bagels for brunch sitting at the big umbrella table in the back yard. When her clothes were ready, Salome got dressed and thanked Annie for the wonderful meal and hospitality. Darius then drove her to her job in The City. She was forty minutes late, but it was her first time, so the boss didn't give her hell.

For Thanksgiving and Christmas in 1974 and for Easter in 1975, Salome took the four hour bus trip by herself from Port Authority in Manhattan to Rutland. Other than those times, or when she worked, or when she went to school, or when he worked, Salome and Darius were inseparable. Salome realized by December of 1974, that staying at Ivy Laplotski's wasn't going to work anymore, not with a steady boyfriend who lived on Long Island, and who didn't always want to drive two hours each way or to spend money on a hotel room for intimacy. And Darius was starting to get a little suspicious about where Salome lived, where he wasn't allowed to go, with the lady who couldn't handle meeting men. So although her parents still thought she lived at Selma's sister's, in December, Salome moved into a small one-bedroom apartment in Chinatown, with another young waitress from work, eighteen year-old Jaxie McKenzie. They each had a new twin bed in the bedroom, but the sofa in the living area also folded out into a bed. Whoever had the company, used the bedroom exclusively that night, and the other person would crash on the sofa. And this is how Salome lived through the rest of 1974 and the first half of 1975. At work, with Darius, Annie, Jaxie, and at one bank she was Jennifer. At school, with her family, her siblings on the phone, Selma/Ida, Ivy, and the other bank she was Salome. She finished her GED class in early May of 1975, she took the test, passed, and received her GED in late May. Meanwhile, she and Darius continued exploring each other's bodies—within the parameters of not going all of the way—and Salome submitted the paperwork, and was accepted to the Borough of Manhattan Community College for September of 1975.

Salome made a trip back to Rutland in late May to show her parents her diploma, and she convinced them to let her stay in The City for the summer so she could work six days a week to save money for college.

Meanwhile, Salome had convinced *The Polish Palace*, to let her have thirty days off, from late July until late August. Salome was incredibly excited; she and Darius were riding *Harleys* up the Al-Can to Alaska.

Darius had felt guilty since January of 1975, when his friend the model agent, Mitch Leopold, had dropped by and Darius had shown him Salome's nude shots. Leopold had immediately offered Darius $7500 for the photos and negatives, claiming that—after Darius had said that he was sure that his client did not want these shots coming out in the United States—he could get one of the European versions of *Boner Magazine* to pay him $10,000 for the pictures. And although Darius didn't really need the $2500 cut he would take, and his better judgment told him that Jennifer would be really pissed if he did this behind her back, he decided to take the money from Mitch Leopold anyway. He figured that he'd keep the $5000 for Jennifer, and when she needed money, he would surprise her. He also figured, since the photos would only be published in Europe, that she wouldn't be too angry. As for why he didn't just call her to ask when Mitch Leopold had first made the offer, he had figured that she'd say, "No!" and that she'd be pissed that he had shown her naked self in those positions to anyone in the first place. On this late July morning, as he tied the bindles to the back of the *Harley* seats, he tried to put it out of his mind.

On the back of his *Road King* seat, tied in a tight bindle, were his clothes, inside of his sleeping bag, inside of the two-man pup tent. On the back of Salome's *Sportster's* seat, her bindle consisted of her clothes inside of her sleeping bag. The adjustable aluminum bars that made up the tent frame, the sterno cooking kit, the first aid kit, toiletries, and other miscellaneous items were in the *Road King's* saddle bags. Darius and Salome wore helmets and leathers.

They headed west on I-80 once they were out of New York City. Darius had gone riding with Salome several times in the past year, and a month ago she had passed his "handling the bike in Manhattan" test. So although the heavy honking traffic still worried Salome a little and she sighed a sigh of relief once they had made it over the George Washington Bridge, she had handled her *Harley* in Manhattan like a pro.

After having ridden about eight hours since leaving Long Island, Darius and Salome stopped for the night at a motel along I-80 just on the border of Pennsylvania and Ohio. Salome asked, "Why don't we just camp out?"

And Darius responded, "Believe me...you'll be sick of camping out by the time we reach Alaska. We should enjoy a motel bed while we can."

The next morning they left early and drove across Ohio, Indiana, and half of Illinois on I-80 before stopping for the night. Upon seeing the sign that said I-65 North to Chicago, and that Chicago was only 50 miles away, Salome thought about Walter Lee. She asked Darius, "Do you want to spend a day in Chicago?" And Darius replied, "When we come back from Alaska we'll take I-90 along the top of the United States, and swing down the eastern side of Wisconsin to Chicago."

The following day they finished off Illinois, pressed onward through Iowa, and stopped for the night in Nebraska, after having eaten an incredible and huge porterhouse steak at *Meat and Potatoes*—the self-proclaimed "greatest steakhouse in the world" in Omaha.

Somewhere in western Nebraska on I-80 the next day, Darius got a flat tire. They found a station that fixed it, but Darius said to Salome, "I don't want to take any chances on the Al-Can...it's mostly a 2200 mile highway of hard packed dirt and pebbles. In the next big city lets find a *Harley* dealership. I want to buy a new tire."

They found that dealership twenty-four hours later, off of I-15 North in Helena, Montana. Darius had the new tire put on, and he and Salome crossed into Canada two hours later through the Sweet Grass, Montana border stop. That night they found a nice Victorian bed and breakfast in Calgary, Alberta.

The next day they drove north to Edmonton, and stopped and explored the biggest shopping mall in the world. A few hours later they headed north by northwest, at a forty-five degree angle, towards Dawson Creek, British Columbia—the official beginning of the Al-Can Highway. They spent, what would be their last night for a long while in a motel. They feasted on wonderful brook trout at a small dive in the middle of Dawson Creek that Friday evening. It was an interesting building, because it had been built with half of the building dangling over the creek.

On Saturday they camped outside of Whitehorse, Yukon. Darius remarked, "Aren't the Canadians wonderful with what they provide for free at all of their government run campgrounds?" It was true, in that all of these campgrounds had no fee. They also provided free hot showers, free chopped firewood for cooking or just keeping warm, and free water and dumping facilities for recreational vehicles.

Darius and Salome had to stay an extra day outside of Whitehorse, since one of the 300+ Bailey Bridges (named for the Englishman in World War II, who invented this prefabricated bridge, which could be constructed anywhere within twenty-four hours) along the Al-Can had begun to collapse just outside of Whitehorse. Darius and Salome went looking for some pieces of rubber around Whitehorse. The headlight of both bikes had been covered with a metal mesh covering, and Darius had mounted a small angled plastic shield on the front fender—all in an effort to deflect the pebbles from the road. The final ingredient in this "how to avoid pebble damage" mixture was the cut sheets of rubber surrounding the fuel tanks. Salome's piece of rubber needed to be replaced. Unfortunately, there was no place to find the needed rubber in Whitehorse.

By late afternoon of the following day, Darius and Salome reached Upper Laird River National Park at the top of the Yukon. This national park, in the middle of the snow capped Canadian Rockies, featured an 89 degree hot springs. Darius and Salome met some long-haired freaks floating in the hot springs. These three guys, along with the two children with them, were driving an old army green painted school bus towing a dune buggy made from an old *Volkswagen Beetle*. With all of the mechanical trouble they had had, they were now in the fourth week of their sojourn since having left Bradenton, Florida. Salome and Darius drank wine and smoked pot with the guys while hanging out in the hot springs for a few hours. Afterwards, they all ate together around a fire as night fell. Later that evening the five Floridians crashed in their school bus, while Salome and Darius fell asleep in their sleeping bags next to the fire.

On Tuesday, Darius and Salome entered Alaska through the border crossing at Tok, Alaska. They took South Highway 4 towards Anchorage, because that was the direction of the Malcovitch Alaskan mansion. The Malcovitchs owned 100 acres on the Kenai Peninsula along the Gulf of Alaska, about 80 miles southwest of Anchorage. In addition to the beautiful wood, glass, and stone six-bedroom five-bathroom house, the property included a salmon seining operation, which had docks for their 12 boats and a canning plant. Darius' parents, brother, and sister had just left, electing this year to spend August in France at a rented villa in Nice. Darius and Salome would have the house to themselves for several weeks. The seining operation was run by Eric "the Red" Palance, and he didn't need any help from a Malcovitch during this salmon season. Darius would just go by the next day and slip him a hundred dollar bill and say, "I wasn't here with a girl this summer was I?" And Eric would say, "Who the fuck are you?"

And so, after camping out a couple of hundred miles northeast of Anchorage, the next day Darius and Salome finally reached the Malcovitch property. Along the way, Salome had Darius stop at a big supermarket in Anchorage. Although she didn't tell him, today, August 6th, was Salome's fifteenth birthday, and she wanted to make Darius and herself a special meal.

After dinner was over and too much wine had been consumed, Darius started getting frisky with Salome on the sofa in the den. Salome said, "Give me fifteen minutes, and then come up to our bedroom."

When Darius went to the bedroom, the lights were all off and there were seven candles burning instead. Salome came out of the bathroom in a sexy silk negligee that she had purchased in New York City purposely for this night. She said, "I love you Darius, and I want you to be the first and only." And she and Darius proceeded to remove all of the parameters that had been previously associated with their body exploration expeditions—several times. As they snuggled in each other's arms a couple of hours later, Salome said, "I will love you forever…Darius."

"I will love you forever, too…Jennifer," Darius said.

"I hope you'll love me enough to be able to handle what I'm about to tell you," Salome said nervously.

"What…that I'm not really the first?" Darius asked with a twinkle in his eye.

"No…that's not it. You are the first!" Salome said.

"Then what?" Darius asked.

"Jennifer is the name of my twenty-two year-old sister. My name is really Salome, and today is my fifteenth birthday."

"Ha ha…you're kidding right?" Darius said with a smile.

"I'm not kidding," Salome said, and then she went to her purse and got both Jennifer's old license and her official ID card to show him.

"WHAT? YOU'RE ONLY 15?" Darius yelled. And then thinking about the photographs he had sold Mitch Leopold that had already been published in Europe he said, "I'm RUINED! My professional career is now in the CRAPPER! No magazine WILL EVER TRUST ME AGAIN!"

And Salome said, "What are you talking about?"

And Darius admitted to Salome about having sold the nudes to Mitch Leopold for European publication.

Salome said angrily, "You did WHAT? I can't believe you did that without ASKING ME FIRST!"

And Darius responded, "I can't believe you let me take those shots without telling ME THAT YOU WERE ONLY FOURTEEN!"

And for an hour, Salome and Darius screamed at each other. Then Darius left the house with his checkbook and rode down to the cannery where Eric Palance had a room upstairs. He woke Eric up, wrote him a check for $2,000, and said, "I want you to get rid of that girl NOW! I want you to take her to the Anchorage Airport RIGHT NOW! I want you to get her a ticket for later today, no matter what the flight connections are and no matter what the cost...back to New York! I want you to stay with her at the airport until she's on the plane! The ticket should be right around $1,000, but I've made this check out to you for $2,000 for your trouble and your silence! If you have to wait with her in front of your bank in Anchorage first to cash this, so be it! Just make this work Eric! Get dressed now and go up to the house and tell her! I'll stay here!" And then Darius made two checks out for $5,000, one to Jennifer Apple and one to Salome Apple and said to Eric, "Tell her to pick the one she can cash, and then bring me back the other one! Tell her that this is her share of the amount paid for the European photographs! Tell her also, I never want to see her again!"

At 5:00 pm Alaskan time, a very sad Salome took off on a fourteen-hour plane ride, with stops in Seattle and Chicago, that would land at 11:00 New York time the next morning. And although she had a window seat on the first leg of her flight to Seattle, she really didn't see anything at all...outside of the window.

Chapter Six

Bubba Apple's adversarial neighbor for the past twenty-five years, Gus Strattus, stood photographing the magical Moon over the Sea of Crete, as he and his wife, Helen, were returning to Athens from the island of Ios in the Cyclades Chain, on this warm late evening in August of 1975. They had spent two days and one night on Ios visiting Helen Strattus' great aunt, cousins, nephews, and nieces, and this four hour plus boat ride was just the serene silence that Gus had craved. 'Vacations are nice,' Gus thought. 'Especially lifelong dreams of returning to the land of one's ancestors. But with all of the walking, sightseeing, and talking to the relatives we never knew, I've got a marathon-sized headache!'

Gus and Helen Strattus had already spent two weeks prior to the trip to Ios traveling around Greece, and Gus was looking forward to getting back home. They had seen the obligatory sights in Athens, the Parthenon, the Acropolis, the Erechtheion, and the Nike Temple to name a few. They had traveled to Mykonos; seen the windmills of Rhodes; sat in the Atticus Theatre in Herod; bought a souvenir, in the gift shop of the Temple of Hephaistos; fiddled with their worry beads, while experiencing the awe of "The Doorway to the Sea" in Thera; stood drinking Retsina from a flask, at the Isthmus of Corinth in Peleponnesos; and, after having eaten a very spicy squid dinner at a nephew of Gus' home in Mégara, spent some quality time in the Temple of Halitosis also.

When the taxi driver dropped Gus and Helen off in front of *The Metropolis Inn* in downtown Athens, Helen went to their room and Gus went looking for some aspirin. They were leaving the next afternoon, and with the long trip to JFK, and then the long wait for the plane to Burlington, Gus didn't want to feel lousy while traveling. He found a pharmacy a few blocks away, made his purchase, and then stopped at a little magazine and drink kiosk on the street for something to wash the four aspirin down. While he was in the kiosk, he noticed the large display of men's magazines. He had hoped that this trip to Greece, a kind of second honeymoon, would reawaken some of the lust that Helen once had. At sixty, Gus Strattus still desired sex with his wife. He saw her as he did when he first married her thirty-five years ago—still the most beautiful woman in the world. And although Helen still loved her husband very much, at fifty-seven, she just was no longer interested in sex. With that thought in mind, Gus Strattus decided—in order to get a good night's sleep tonight—he'd have to take matters into his own hands. He thumbed through several different magazines, until he decided to settle for the latest Greek edition of *Boner Magazine*.

Later that night, after dinner, after Helen was sleeping soundly, after he had taken four more aspirin, Gus sat on the throne in the hotel's bathroom with the magazine. He examined closely, page by page, all of the naked women in their provocative poses. When he got to page thirty-three he did a double take. There, to his surprise, in some of the sexiest poses he had ever seen, was his neighbor's youngest daughter Salome Apple. 'She can't be more than fourteen or fifteen,' he thought. He saw that she was using her older sister's name, Jennifer, in the included mini-biography that came with each woman's spread. A wickedly devilish idea came into his mind—a way to give his asshole neighbor a headache, just like the one Gus was currently experiencing. He decided to go back to that kiosk and to buy up all of the copies of the magazine, but first he'd sit here a while with the magazine in his right hand. The art and science of growing apples, as Gus Strattus did for a living, is called Pomology. And, of course, the art and science of what Gus Strattus was doing at the moment is called Palmology.

@@@@@@@@

It was late afternoon in mid-September 1975, and Bubba sat in his favorite chair in front of *The Apple House* drinking a beer. *The Apple House* was the warehouse and store on Bubba's property that was just five hundred feet from Highway 7. When heading south out of downtown Rutland on Highway 7 and crossing Route 103, one would immediately see the huge sign on the right: **Apple Apples: Red Delicious, Fameuse, Northerns, and McIntosh. Gift Boxes, Cider, and Pie. Shipping Available**. And two hundred feet after the sign was the dirt road that led to *The Apple House*. About another 1000 feet further south on Highway 7, where the mailbox was, was the bigger dirt road, which ran back about 1500 feet to the Apple's house. And still another five hundred feet further south on Highway 7 from the dirt road that ran to the Apple's house, was the twelve foot wide stream that ran westward under an unnoticeable little bridge on Highway 7 and through the middle of the Apple's 1000-acre orchard—save for the sharp southwestern turn it took by the barn at the rear of the property. This was the place where the stream was just twenty-two feet from the Strattus' orchard. There was also a dirt road on the property that ran from *The Apple House*, to the Apple's house, to the barn.

Tomorrow was Bubba and Pauline's twenty-fifth wedding anniversary, and Bubba was thinking just how lucky he was to have her for his wife. The shock of hearing a year ago that Pauline had colon cancer had really jolted him, and some of his nasty and violent behavior in the last year, even more so than usual, was a direct result of Bubba becoming more aware of his own vulnerability. A scared animal who doesn't reason things through, usually reacts with violence when under pressure. Fortunately, Pauline was now alright. The surgery and radiation had worked, and just a week ago her blood work had still come back negative. But there was also the fear—although Bubba kept it buried in the back of his brain—that had been awakened during his hospital stay last year, that his father had, and that he might be predestined to get, Tourette's Syndrome. Bubba opened up the jewelry case and looked at the beautiful present he had bought Pauline for tomorrow's anniversary. The white gold heart-shaped pendant featured a nice one carat brilliant cut stone in the middle, surrounded by twenty-five four point diamonds—one for each year of marriage—to equal a total weight of two carats. Bubba was sure that Pauline would love it.

Bubba thought back to how he and Pauline had met. He had been recovering in a hospital in Tripoli after the mortar shell blast near his head had literally cleaned his clock in 1942. Although three months later he would be shipped off to Walter Reed Hospital in Washington, D.C., where he would spend another three months with noteworthy psychiatrists trying to help him to recover from his partial amnesia, before discharging him from the Army in early 1943. The first three months in Tripoli, the attention to him was minimal. In Tripoli, Bubba hadn't remembered that he was an excellent musician. At Walter Reed, after they found him a tenor saxophone like he had requested, the doctors were surprised by Bubba's ability to remember—note for note—more than 200 songs. And they weren't just simple songs, they were complex arrangements of difficult pieces. Bubba could play from memory the Benny Goodman jazz arrangement of "Sing Sing Sing," as well as something classical like Wagner.

The United States Army had no psychiatrists in their makeshift hospital in Tripoli, but the doctors attending to Bubba knew that he shouldn't return to combat, so, when no discharge papers had come back after their request for such, they just let Bubba stay in the hospital. Apparently Bubba had done something fairly heroic—although he couldn't remember exactly what—just prior to the mortar shell going off above the foxhole, because a week after waking up in the hospital he was promoted from corporal to sergeant. (Years later, Bubba would sing to his children, to the displeasure of Pauline: "*Oh Sergeant Apple's Troopers were bastards in the night. The dirty sons of bitches would rather fuck than fight*!")

A month later, while the twenty-two year-old Sergeant Bubba Apple was still in the army hospital in Tripoli, he received a letter from an unknown girl whose school in Burlington Vermont was sponsoring a pen pal program for soldiers overseas. The fourteen year-old girl, Pauline Bouvier, had drawn Bubba's name and Military Unit from a box, just by chance. She wrote:

> *Dear Sergeant Apple,*
>
> *I'm a ninth grade student at Burlington Central Jr. High School in Burlington, Vermont.*
>
> *I picked your name to write to. I think you are very brave fighting for our country. My dad wanted to go fight too, but they said he was too old! (He is 38!) We live in an apple orchard! (My dad raises apples.) Our farm house is in the middle of the orchard. We also run the county ASPCA animal shelter. Whenever I answer the telephone I have to say, "Bouvier Animal Shelter, may I help you?" I have to go do homework now, but I'll write back. I have enclosed a recent picture of myself and my address. I'll write again soon.*
>
> *Very truly yours,*
> *Pauline Bouvier*

Bubba had thought that the fourteen year-old Pauline Bouvier was very beautiful, and he told her so when he wrote back and thanked her for the nice letter. Oh, he wasn't coming on to her overtly, he was just telling a young lady during that unsure time between being a girl and a woman, that she had the goods—at least physically. (What would be called an "Ego stroke" in the 1970's, and what a good loving father might tell his insecure daughter in any era.) Pauline would send Bubba two more letters during his stay in Tripoli, and another two letters while he was in Washington, D.C.

When Bubba was released from Walter Reed Hospital and discharged from the Army in March of 1943, he bought a bus ticket and went home to Wedowee, Alabama. His father had been dead for two years, but his mother seemed to be in good health. Bubba moved back into his old room, and he spent hours in the tool shed—about five acres away from the house—practicing on the saxophone. The Apples had forty wooded acres, but his father, having been a Man of the Cloth, never grew anything on the property. The house sat right on the road, and all of the property was behind and to the sides of the house. There was a barn about an acre behind the house, but the further away tool shed was where Bubba had always practiced "Satan's music" as his dad had called it. Reverend Apple didn't want Bubba to play the saxophone. When his wife's brother had died and left the instrument to Bubba, there had been one bodacious fight between Reverend Apple and his wife. Salome Gorge Apple had won that argument, but her concession had been that the only music that Bubba was allowed to learn was Gospel Music. So Bubba learned Gospel Music with Andrew Taylor, his music teacher at school, and then Bubba taught himself first classical and then jazz in the privacy of the tool shed. Fortunately, there was a sliding window in the front of the shed, so Bubba could look out and change from a Dixieland Jazz version of "When the Saints Go Marching In" to a Gospel version when he saw his father approaching.

Five weeks after Bubba had returned home, on April 11, 1943, the day of his twenty-third birthday, his mother passed away in her sleep. The cause of death was a massive heart attack. Bubba spent the next few months practicing saxophone all day long in the house, trying to figure out if he should leave Alabama, and if so—go where? A realty company from Wedowee offered him $12,500 for the property, a fair offer for 1943, and Bubba contemplated taking the offer. A week later, Edward Blakely, a representative from *Winchester Rifle*, showed up at the front door. At that time, Bubba learned, rifle companies were paying up to $2,000 each for fully mature Black Walnut Trees. Since Black Walnut was the hardest wood one could make a rifle stock from, and since Black Walnut was not all that easy to find anymore, the price paid for each tree was high. Having done an aerial survey from a low flying crop duster over the entire central portion of Alabama, their binoculars had spied approximately fifty large Black Walnut Trees on Bubba's property. Edward Blakely and Bubba went for a walk on the property. Blakely made notes in a little book. When they returned to the house, he asked Bubba if he could use the phone for a long distance call, that he would reverse the charges. Edward Blakely called his boss at the home office, gave him the data that he had just gathered, and his boss gave him the top amount of $90,000 that he could offer. "My boss said I should horse trade with you. But I'm not in the mood for all of that, so I'll just tell you that the most he said I could offer you for your place is $70,000." Blakely would win major points with his boss for saving him 20K.

"WHYYY...I thought you just wanted the TREEES," Bubba said. "I didn't know you wanted ALLL of the property and the house TOOO," he added.

"Yeah...we want your property. There has to be a reason why you have more Black Walnuts in your backyard than any other forty-acre tract in the

South. We're going to turn this place into a research center."

"It's a done DEEEAL!" Bubba had said, and within twenty-four hours there was a certified check for $70,000 in Bubba's hands. (Unlike New York City many years later, when a young couple would buy a house so that their grandchildren would eventually get to close on it, closing on property in Alabama in 1943 was just a twenty-four to forty-eight hour process.) Bubba was allowed to stay in his place for thirty days, but he managed to sell off everything he didn't throw out within ten. So then Bubba packed a suitcase, his sax case, and took it along with his certified check to the bus station in downtown Wedowee. He bought a ticket to New York City.

In New York, Bubba opened up a savings account with his certified check, took an inexpensive room, and began circulating around the jazz clubs on 52nd Street. Eventually, in September of 1944, he landed an audition and subsequent job playing tenor sax with *The Tommy Dorsey Orchestra*. (Salome didn't know it, but those two Sinatra albums that were still balancing the antique armoire in her bedroom had been autographed by Frankie. Although Frank Sinatra had already gone solo by September of 1944, he'd regularly hang out with his old band, *The Tommy Dorsey Orchestra*, and he and Bubba had known and respected each other.)

In June of 1947, Bubba was on his way to a Manhattan recording session at 43rd Street and 9th Avenue in a taxi, when a large delivery truck ran a red light and broad sided the cab with such force, the cab flipped several times and ended up roof down on a sidewalk. Bubba suffered a very bad concussion from the accident, and his brains were rescrambled á la 1942 African Style. Something happened to Bubba after that car accident that would affect his personality the rest of his life. And although, many years later with the help of a psychiatrist, Bubba would finally remember and work through even deeper childhood traumatic experiences than he would begin to remember in the hospital in 1974, that car accident in June of 1947 was a pivotal point in the evolution of Bubba's negative side. Bubba would know the rest of his life there was something wrong with him, and he would look for symptoms of diseases like a true hypochondriac—but he would never tell anybody about it until he told his psychiatrist years later. In 1974, at fifty-four years of age, he would begin to think that his father had had Tourette's Syndrome, and he would become positive that he was on the road to the same fate. A decade later, when Bubba was sixty-four, his psychiatrist would finally convince him, that Tourette's wasn't something that he could suddenly just "get" at this stage of his life.

After that car accident in June of 1947, Bubba lost his interest in music, and he would put down the saxophone and not pick it up again for nearly forty years. His children would never hear him play until the mid-1980's, and whenever Pauline would mention how good he had been, they would usually say something like, "Yeah...sure Mom." Bubba's official reason for quitting

The Tommy Dorsey Orchestra was that he was tired of rehearsing and sitting for endless retakes in recording studios. Everyone was sad to see him go, as most people that he came in contact with, until after the car accident, genuinely liked Bubba Apple. As for supporting himself, between the stock market, the live gigs, the recording sessions, the $20,000 he had settled for with the company whose truck had creamed into his cab, Bubba had managed to nearly triple the $70,000 he had arrived with in New York three years earlier. Meanwhile, his letters with Pauline Bouvier had increased to about one per week in the past year. She was the one thing in Bubba's life after June of 1947 that never upset him. She always made him feel good about himself. So when, in the past several letters, she had mentioned how worried she was that her father, due to major unforeseen financial problems, might lose the orchard, Bubba knew that he had to help.

Bubba had met and liked her parents, Jacques and Ethel Bouvier, the same time he had met Pauline for the first time. That was in May of 1946, when *The Tommy Dorsey Orchestra* had played at the University of Vermont. Bubba had sent Pauline the tickets, and after the show they had all met backstage. The Bouviers had allowed Bubba to escort their daughter for an hour to the diner across the street for pie and coffee, and they had just waited for her in their truck parked in the UVM Theatre parking lot. Now that Jacques Bouvier was in trouble and Bubba had quit the band anyway, Bubba decided to buy a used car, and to head up to Burlington, Vermont.

Bubba arrived in Burlington, was given a room in the Bouvier house, and he immediately bailed Jacques Bouvier out of his financial problems. A month later, after he had gotten both her mother's and father's permission, the twenty-seven year-old Bubba asked the nineteen year-old Pauline to be his wife. She said "Yes," but for the next three years they just stayed engaged. Bubba slept in his own room in the Bouvier house, but it was a common occurrence for Bubba and Pauline to tip-toe to each other's bedrooms late at night. Bubba spent those three years thoroughly learning the apple business, and when the 1000-acre orchard with farmhouse in Rutland became available in 1950 for $160,000, on the advice of Jacques Bouvier—he had actually worked at that farm twenty-five years earlier, and he had helped Old Man Grady, the previous owner, to locate and plant the finest Red Delicious and Fameuse rootstock in all of New England—Bubba and Pauline bought it as a wedding present to themselves. Bubba and Pauline just had $160,000 cash left to buy the place mortgage-free, but they decided to put $110,000 down and put a twenty-year mortgage on the other $50,000.

Now, in mid-September 1975, Bubba thought while sitting in front of *The Apple House*, 'Where the hell have twenty-five years gone?' He was amazed, as it seemed like only yesterday that he and Pauline had moved to this place. To be sure, there had been hard emotional moments in their family just like every other family, like when Jacque Bouvier had passed away in

1965 and the Bouvier Orchard was sold, and Ethel Bouvier, much to her displeasure, had to move to a small house in downtown Burlington. But the years had been good to Bubba and Pauline financially. Most apple growers in Vermont had one hundred-acre orchards. Gus Strattus' orchard was three times the size of a normal orchard and considered large. But Bubba and Pauline's orchard was one of the largest orchards in the state of Vermont. They had been selling more than 30,000 bushels of apples per year in the last five years. And when Pauline had accidentally discovered in 1958, that by mixing all four apples that they grew together made an incredible pie, and she had come up with the idea of buying a large coffee urn and some tables and chairs, and turning part of the store into a dining area that featured apple pie, coffee, and milk, along with the traditional cold apple cider, profits had only increased. The Apple Orchard quickly obtained the reputation of having the best apple pie in the state. Sometimes residents as far away as Burlington, nearly two hours away, would eat their mid-day Sunday dinner at an expensive place, and then take a leisurely Sunday drive and mosey on down to the Apple Orchard in Rutland for dessert. And, of course, they would always buy a couple of pies to take back with them. One doctor from Burlington last year, calling a few weeks ahead before Christmas, came down a day before Christmas and bought fifty pies to give away as presents.

In the beginning, Pauline and Bubba had run the store six days a week themselves—Monday being the only day they were closed. As the children grew up, each child was given a few shifts per week in the store. Nowadays, Jack and Jimson alternated in the mornings—with Jack accommodating Jimson's current college schedule of classes. Jack also worked at the *Rutland Food and Gas* convenience store on Highway 7, Monday through Friday 3:00 pm until 11:00 pm. Bruiser hardly ever worked in the store, as his gruff manner tended to alienate customers. Except during bear season in September and October, since Bruiser now had his own thriving private enterprise with would-be Hemmingwayesque bear hunters, or when he was called to rid some hapless farmer or business owner of his or her raccoon problem, or he was hired as a tour guide, Bruiser did most of the deliveries for Bubba. He also helped Jack, Jimson, and Bubba with other chores on the property. Jennifer had nothing to do with the family apple business, as she worked five day shifts per week, Monday through Friday, as an RN at Rutland General Hospital. Jennifer was well known at the hospital, having spent the previous three summers working there as a nurse's aide, and having been the person responsible for making the hospital's food fabulous. And, of course, the latter was the reason she had day shift with no seniority. Bubba was now working in the store late afternoons, the time slot that Salome had originally filled. And they had recently hired a local older lady, Sally Brown, to cover the store from noon until four o'clock Tuesday through Friday. Pauline hardly ever worked in the store, as during the days she had her hands full working in the kitchen they had built in the back of *The Apple House* in 1962, when the number of pies they needed daily went beyond what their two ovens in the farm house could accommodate. Bubba had purchased eight used pizza ovens in 1962, and they were set up in a second room off of the kitchen. The pizza ovens had sped up the baking process three-fold. The part of the kitchen where the coolers were kept, that housed not only the cider to be served but most of the ingredients that Pauline used in her pies, was kept separate from the oven section by a large fire door, so Pauline didn't have to suffer all morning from the intense heat. Although, during the cold winters, the large fire door was kept open to help warm the place. And, of course, during the September through October harvest, with the exception of Pauline, who, besides pie baking, had to make breakfast and lunch for their thirty workers, *everybody* in the family, including nurse Jennifer, except when she was nursing, and Bruiser, except when he had been privately hired, picked apples. Bubba was currently paying seven dollars per hour cash to his workers. Seven dollars per hour cash to pick apples in 1975 was a high wage, and that was another reason Gus Strattus was annoyed with Bubba.

The next night Bubba and Pauline showed up thirty minutes late to their own anniversary party at *The Butcher Block* restaurant. Bubba had given Pauline her pendant at the house, and Pauline had become so swept up with emotion over Bubba finally buying a gift that showed good taste, her mascara had run from her eyes, to her cheeks, to the top of her dress, which needed to be changed. Bubba didn't tell Pauline that he had dragged Bill Wicks along to help with the purchase, that it had actually been Bill Wick's good taste—along with his sharp eye, when he figured the number of small stones equaled the number of married years—that had made this beautiful pendant hers.

Jennifer said, "Well it's nice of you guys to," and then clearing her throat so she could do Bubba's voice, and pointing her finger also continued, "FI-INALLY SHOOOW UP at your own PARTEEEY!"

Bubba laughed, pointed his finger at Jennifer and said, "WHYYY… JEEESUS CHRIIIST, let your mom EXPLAAAIN WHYYY we are lAAATE!"

Pauline did a show and tell with her new diamond pendant, and everybody "oohed and ahed." At the dinner party was Jennifer's squeeze, Dr. Colin Morgan. He had recently gotten his divorce, and was in the process of getting his Vermont medical credentials. Also, he was looking at beautiful homes in the Rutland area, with an eye toward moving to Rutland with his two children—of whom he had just won joint custody with his ex-wife—getting on staff at Rutland General Hospital, opening his own gynecological office, and marrying Jennifer Apple. Bruiser was there with his grandmother. He had driven to Burlington to pick her up, and she was going to spend a week with the Apples before being driven back to Burlington. Jimson and Lizzie were there; they had been living together since January, and surprisingly, Lizzie's father, Vermont Highway Patrolman Jonathan Mitner, had handled Lizzie's moving in with Jimson the day after her eighteenth birthday with no dissent. He had just told Lizzie, "You're my daughter, I love you, and if things don't work out, you can always move back." Jack was at the dinner, but he was supposed to work. He had to beg George Macy to cover his shift. Pauline's sister, Clara, was also at the dinner, and she had volunteered to drive her mother back to Burlington a week later. Cindy and Dick had driven down from Plattsburgh, New York, with their nine month-old daughter, Tonya. Tonya had had her bottle, and she was sleeping in her stroller in the restaurant. Unfortunately, Salome had to work in New York.

"We made great time getting here, Bubba," Cindy said. We left P-burg at 1730, and even with a diaper-change stop along I-87, we still pulled into the parking lot here at just after 1900! Dick and I came in, sat in the bar, fed Tonya, and had a couple of drinks!"

"I hope you're going to stay at home tonight, and not drive back," Pauline said.

"We were hoping you would say that, Mom," Cindy said. "Dick said he'd like to have a few more drinks tonight...and not worry about the drive back...we didn't know, since you have Grandma staying, if you had room."

"It's no problem sweetheart," Pauline said. "Mom is staying in Salome's room, and you and Dick can stay in Jack's room. I'm sure that Jack won't mind sleeping tonight on the fold-out sofa bed in the den."

"When do we eat?" Dick said. "I'm starved...let's get a waitress over here."

So after the cocktail waitress took their drink requests, the food waitress was called over and everybody ordered. Then the food waitress, a classmate in Lizzie's Freshman English Composition Class, said, "Now help yourselves to our award-winning salad bar." Dick was the first person in line.

Earlier, just as Dick, Cindy, and baby Tonya were coming into *The Butcher Block*, Gus Strattus saw them and avoided letting them see him. He and Helen had finished their meal and paid their bill, and he was walking around the restaurant waiting for Helen to return from the restroom. Gus happened to have noticed the big table in the small private dining room with the sign that read "Apple Family: 8:00." He had then asked the cashier, "A big party for the Bubba Apple family tonight?" And the cashier had responded, "Yes. It's their twenty-fifth wedding anniversary." So Gus hadn't been surprised, when he saw Bubba's daughter Cindy with her husband and baby—who he knew lived in Plattsburgh—coming into *The Butcher Block*. And then he knew, the opportunity he had been waiting for had arrived. Five of the six copies of the Greek version of *Boner Magazine* had already been placed in large brown envelopes, stamped, and addressed. Included was a note half-sticking out from page thirty-three that read: *Thought you'd like to see what the underage daughter of one of our town's leading citizens is doing these days*. So Gus dropped the five envelopes in the mailbox in front of the downtown post office. The envelopes were addressed to Sheriff Glenn, c/o The Rutland Police Department; Mayor Herbert Green, c/o City Hall; Wilson Smith, c/o The Rutland District Attorney's Office; Editor Thomas Handlin, c/o *The Rutland Free Press*; and to Selma Greenwood, c/o The Rutland Main Library. Gus then took the sixth copy of the magazine, with the same note, that he had gift-wrapped in "Happy Anniversary!" gift-wrapping paper with ribbons, a bow, and a "Happy Anniversary Bubba and Pauline Apple" label, and brought it to the *Rutland Taxi* office in downtown Rutland. He told the dispatcher that this had to be delivered immediately to *The Butcher Block*. Business was slow that night, so the only driver on call was sitting in the office. Gus gave the driver twenty dollars and told him to keep the change.

When the "present" was hand delivered to the Apple table at *The Butcher Block* by *Rutland Taxi* Driver Jebediah Witherspoon, he stood there with his hand out, looking for a tip from Bubba.

"WHYYY... JEEESUS CHRIIIST...a gift we have to pay for!" Bubba exclaimed.

"A gift we have to pay for," an on-the-threshold-of-getting-hammered Dick repeated.

"I've got it," Jack said, and he gave the cabbie five dollars,

"I wonder who sent this?" Pauline asked, taking the package from Bubba.

"Let's SEEE!" Bubba said, taking it back from Pauline.

And, of course, after opening it, reading the note, and seeing exactly what it was, Bubba jumped up and shouted, "WHYYY...JEEESUS CHRIIIST! Sons of bitches ARRRE still running WIIILD around here! I'm gonna KILLL her! I'm going to New York RIIIGHT now, and I'm going to drag her ASSS back here until SHEEE'S twenty-one! And don't you try to stop me Pauline!" Bubba said with a stern look at his wife, as Pauline was examining the photos.

"I'll go with you," Bruiser said.

Jennifer, after looking at the pictures and failing to keep the magazine away from her boyfriend, said, "I can't believe she'd do this!"

Cindy, who was holding a scared crying Tonya, thanks to Bubba, didn't have that problem with Dick, as he was already fairly oblivious. He did say however, "I can't believe she'd do this!"

Clara, sitting two seats away from Pauline, leaned around her mother and said, "OH MY GOD, PAULINE!"

Grandma Ethel Bouvier, in-between her two daughters said, "I'm so disappointed in Salome."

Jimson and Lizzie said nothing.

Jack said, "Salome isn't the first girl to pose nude for a men's magazine, and she certainly won't be the last. Why shouldn't she use her good looks to make a ton of money while she's young? This certainly isn't the same thing as being a prostitute."

Pauline was very proud of her son, Jack, at that moment. And although she knew that what her fifteen year-old daughter had done was wrong, and Salome needed to come home now, Pauline was proud of Jack's loving protection of his younger sister. Pauline said, "You're right, Bubba. This is too much. We trusted her, and she obviously lied to us about what she's been doing in New York City. She needs to come home." And then with more force she said to Bubba, "But I don't want you going to New York City to get her! Let's go talk to Sheriff Glenn…I'm sure that Roger and Winnie Glenn won't mind if we drop by their house…even though we're discussing police business. Let's see what he suggests that we do."

"WHYYY BULLSHITTT Pauline! I don't need Roger Glenn to tell MEEE what to do!" Bubba yelled.

Bubba had gotten so loud, and baby Tonya's crying was so continuous, and so many other diners were getting annoyed, *The Butcher Block's* manager, Angus Hoofman, had to come over and ask the Apple family if they could lower the noise. Cindy put Tonya in the stroller, and took her outside for a little walk.

Pauline said with some anger, "You're not going after her in New York City, Bubba! I know what the end result will be if you do that…we'll lose Salome forever. This needs to be handled as a police matter. As a matter of fact…" And she addressed everybody at the table, "It would just be better if Salome were to believe that the police took action because she broke the law. She's underage, she modeled nude, and she broke the law. We should let her think that this…somehow…came to the attention of the police first, and that we only found out about it from them later."

"WHYYY…you want your daughter to have a POOOLICE record?" Bubba asked. "If Bruiser and I go get her, at least SHEEE won't have a CRIMINALLL record! We'll just grab her at her JOBBB tomorrow NIIIGHT!"

"She's only fifteen, Bubba," Pauline said. "What's the worst the police can do to her? The photographer is the one with the more serious legal problems. I'd rather that Salome get scared by a police arrest, and have a minor record, than have you going down to The City and alienating her from us forever! Don't forget, Bubba, there's no way we can keep her from eventually running away again. And the next time she runs, Bubba, we won't hear from her for years."

"The PHOOOTOGRAPHER!" Bubba yelled loud enough to bring Manager Angus Hoofman back into the room. Bubba looked at the photo spread again, and saw that the photographer was listed as, **Darius Malcovitch**: **Amagansett, New York**. "I'll BREAAAK him in two!" Bubba added.

"We'll let the police handle him too, Bubba!" Pauline said.

"Mom's right," said Jack.

"Why don't you shut the fuck up!" Bruiser said to Jack.

"Why don't you eat me…I'm a weenie!" Jack shot back at Bruiser.

Bruiser jumped up and headed for Jack, and Pauline stood up between them and said, "Bruiser sit down! This is my twenty-fifth anniversary, and I'm not going to have my children fighting!"

Manager Angus Hoofman came over and said, "We're getting too many customer complaints. I'm afraid, if you don't lower it, I'm going to have to ask you all to leave."

And Pauline said, "We're real sorry Angus. We just received some very disturbing family news."

And Dick said, "Very disturbing family news."

"I'm not hungry now anyway," Pauline said and then added, "Bubba, let's go see Roger Glenn!"

And so Bubba and Pauline left and drove over to the Glenn house. Roger and Winnie Glenn were surprised yet gracious when they answered the door. After Bubba had shown Sheriff Roger Glenn and his wife, Winnie, the magazine and thrown in a few more "WHYYY JEEESUS CHRIIISTS," Roger Glenn came up with the solution. "You remember my brother, Bill, don't you?" Bubba and Pauline both nodded "Yes." "He's a detective in Manhattan. I'm sure I can get him to do me a favor, unofficially, so she doesn't have a juvenile record." And then Sheriff Glenn called his brother at home and explained the situation. Detective William Glenn was happy to help his brother out. "He wants to know where she lives," Roger said to Bubba and Pauline.

"We know it's somewhere in Flushing, Queens," Pauline said. "We have a post office box for her, that's all."

"We have a PHOOONE number for her," Bubba added.

"We don't want to call and give her a heads up," Roger Glenn said.

"She works as a waitress at *The Polish Palace* in the East Village," Pauline said. "Her shift is Thursday through Sunday, from 4:00 until 11:00. She should be working right now," Pauline added.

"Wait a second," Roger Glenn said. And then after continuing his conversation on the phone with his brother, Roger hung up the phone and said, "My brother is going to pick her up at work right now. He's going to drive her back to Rutland tonight, and spend the night with Winnie and me."

"Thank God!" Pauline said. And she added, "We can't thank you enough Roger," And then she gave Roger Glenn a little kiss on the cheek.

"Hey watch it!" Winnie Glenn said jokingly.

"I can't thank YOUUU EEENOUGH Roger! I OOOWE YOUUU a big FAAAVOR!" Bubba said, and shook Roger's hand.

"Well," Roger Glenn said, "A couple of those wonderful pies and a jug of your cider for my brother to take back to The City would suffice!"

"We'll go home and get pies and cider and bring them back to you right now!" Pauline said, and added, "Once again, thanks so much Roger."

@@@@@@@@

Detective William Glenn was totally discreet in the way in which he arrested Salome. He flashed his badge and asked at the cash register if someone could have her come over and talk to him.

"What can I do for you officer?" Salome asked him.

"Ms. Apple, I'm afraid you're under arrest," he said, and then he explained the situation to her. He then said, "Why don't you tell your employers that there has been some family trouble at home, and that you'll call tomorrow and let them know how things are."

And Salome, although fuming inside at Darius and the situation in general, thanked Detective Glenn. And she asked, "Can we go by my place in Chinatown so I can get my clothes?" Detective Glenn agreed, and after that task had been accomplished, they began the four-hour trip to Rutland, Vermont.

Detective Glenn was a nice man, but he wasn't much of a conversationalist. The little he did say was regarding the photographer who had taken the shots. He asked her, "Would you be willing to testify in court against the photographer who took the pictures of you naked?"

And Salome said, "It was totally my fault. He thought I was my twenty-one year-old sister, Jennifer. The name and age on the driver license I showed him said Jennifer Apple, age twenty-one. And the picture of Jennifer, when she had red hair a few years ago, looked just like I look now. Darius called me Jennifer for a year, and it was only the last time I saw him in which I told him my name was really Salome, and that I was only fifteen."

"What did he do when you said that?" Detective Glenn asked.

"He had one of his workers put me on a plane immediately, and he said that he never wanted to see me again…that I had ruined his good name...And he was correct…it's all my fault…So no, I couldn't testify against Darius."

"Are you in love with Darius?"

"Yeah…I guess I still am. But I blew it…so I'll just have to learn from my mistake. I think I have enough life left to undo the wrongness of this situation by doing good things only."

"I think you're on the right path with that, and I wish you luck," had been the last thing that Detective Glenn said.

They rode in silence pretty much the remainder of the trip, and when they arrived at the Apple house, just after midnight, Pauline was the only one who wasn't sleeping. When she saw the headlights she went to the front door, to keep the doorbell from waking up Bubba.

"I'm glad you're home sweetheart," Pauline said.

"I'm so sorry, Mom," Salome said, and she began to cry.

Pauline came over and held her daughter and said, "We all make mistakes Salome. It's whether we can learn from them." Pauline thanked Detective Glenn, and she offered him pie and coffee. He declined, said he was exhausted, that he just wanted to get to his brother's house and go to sleep.

The next day at 1:00 in the afternoon, after Pauline had left for her hair appointment, Salome awoke to Bubba's bellow next to her bed. "WHYYY... JEEESUS CHRIIIST...I guess you ARRRE a WHOOORE after all."

"I screwed up, Bubba," Salome said.

"OOOH it's worse than YOUUU just screwing up...YOUUU'VE ruined my life and your MOTHERRR'S life in this town. Yeah...I just found out those PHOOOTOS have made their way all over town...you SLUTTT!"

Salome jumped out of bed and started to run past Bubba. Bubba stuck his foot out and tripped her, and although she stayed on her feet, she stumbled into the wall. "Hey FUCK YOU FAT ASS!" she screamed at her father.

Bubba came over, right fist clenched, and punched Salome in the side of her face. Salome immediately began to cry, and through her blurred vision, the pain on the side of her face, the warm liquid of blood running down from inside of her cheek into her mouth, she screamed, "I'M GOING TO KILL YOU...YOU FAT FUCK!"

And then Bubba struck the other side of her face just a little lower. Salome heard a loud snap, the pain was excruciating, and she knew then that her jaw had been broken. "HELP...HELP...," she screamed, in spite of the intense pain when she moved her mouth.

Jack, who had come upstairs to get a change of clothes from his bedroom, which was still occupied by Cindy, Dick, and Tonya, and would remain so for another twenty-four hours, heard Salome's screams. Quickly he ran to her room, where he found Bubba pummeling his sister with his fists. Jack headed to his own room and grabbed his *Louisville Slugger*. He ran back to Salome's bedroom, and yelled at Bubba, "BATTER UP YOU BASTARD!" Then he took his best Aaronian swing at Bubba. He hit Bubba in the side, and the strength of the blow was enough to double-up Bubba and send him to the floor gasping for air.

"Pack your duffle bag," Jack told Salome. "But leave enough room in your bag for a few pairs of my pants, shirts, socks, and underwear." Salome did as Jack said. Then Jack went to his room and took some clothes and toiletries, put them in his sister's duffle bag, and he and Salome ran from the house to the barn. Jack tied the duffle bag to the back of his *Harley's* seat, gave Salome a helmet, put a helmet on himself, and they both got on the bike and took off down Highway 7 towards Salome's apartment in New York City.

@@@@@@@@

It's been almost ten months since I received the terminal treatise of temerity from Tatiana, dear journal. I still wish that someone would sneak in here one night and make me an example of a defenestration crash test dummy. My sobriquet should be "Asshole." My tombstone should read: "Well...Fuck Me!" I still can't believe that I allowed myself to be a sucker again...that I allowed myself to hope...that after the month we had together in Paris in August of 1974, by November of 1974, Tatiana was finished with me again. Her refusal to take my phone calls, and then the Dear John letter. So she found somebody else who was enough like me to keep her interested, and enough not like me to keep her sane. And then to tell me, after all of the times that I thought our love making was the way she liked it, that she was tired of the animalistic hair pulling approach, and how, instead of three orgasms in thirty minutes, how she always had wanted to just stay in bed all day with me talking, with on and off again foreplay, and at times how it would be wonderful to lie side by side, with just enough stimuli to keep me hard and inside of her, but no motion moving toward immediate gratification, and how maybe twelve hours later, when she could stand it no longer, to have just one over-the-top orgasm, and how, her new beau understood what I had not, and how she was so sorry, and that she knew I'd find someone who was right for me eventually...and how...

The telephone rang. "*Ball Breakers*," Felix said.

"What?" asked Salome.

"*The Breakers*," Felix said.

"Is this Felix?" Salome asked.

"Yeah it is...and your voice sounds kind of familiar."

"This is Salome Apple. My jaw was broken earlier today. I got it reset and wired at an emergency room in Pittsfield, Massachusetts a few hours ago. I'm all screwed up on pain pills at the moment, and I need to talk very low and easy to keep from being in extreme pain. So I might be hard to understand."

'Speaking of ball breakers,' Felix thought, knowing how badly she had hurt his brother. "What can I do for you Salome?" Felix asked.

"I've been trying to get Walter Lee on his phone for the past hour. I thought he might be working in the office."

"No," Felix said. "Walter Lee is over at his girlfriend's."

"I've got a real big problem," she told Felix. "I'm going to ask your advice, and I know you must hate my guts because I hurt your brother. How is Anthony anyway?"

"He's doing well," is all Felix volunteered about Anthony. Anthony was living with the math professor, the older Russian woman he had started seeing last year. His grades had been much better his sophomore year, and in his mandatory psychology class, he had indeed been made to read Freud. "What do you need advice about? And how did your jaw get broken?" Felix then asked.

And Salome explained some of the tawdry tale, with some of the Darius details, and details about her and her brother, currently on the lam, and currently hanging out in the West Village. And then she said, "I was going to ask Walter Lee two things. First, I was going to see if my brother, Jack, could get a room at *The Breakers*. He wants to begin this incredible refrigeration course offered in Clearwater, and I told him all about your place."

"I don't know," said Felix. "I'd have to see if Anthony would be comfortable with that."

"Well here's the deal," Salome said. "I have a place to stay in Queens, but I can't take my brother there...she doesn't like men." And then thinking about what had just happened to her earlier today she added, "She thinks all men are abusive. Anyway, Jack would like to leave me today, and head down to Florida on his *Harley*."

"Well let me call Anthony," Felix said. "Call me back collect in thirty minutes."

When Felix told Anthony about Salome's phone call, and what she wanted, Anthony responded that he had no problem with her brother being a tenant. And when Salome called back thirty minutes later, Felix told her that. And then he added, "You said that you were going to ask Walter Lee two things, the first one, your brother staying here, has just be handled. What was the second thing that you wanted to ask?"

"Just advice," Salome said. "I know that my parents have a legal right to keep me home until I'm eighteen. But my asshole father just broke my jaw. Surely, there has to be a way that I can just stay in New York, work, and go to school. I received my GED last year living and working on my own, and last week, I just started my first semester at a community college in Manhattan. All I want is to stay in New York City and work my way through college."

"Which college?" Felix asked.

"The Borough of Manhattan Community College," Salome responded. "Sure...on Chambers Street and the Westside Highway," Felix said. And then Felix thought about how her problem might be solved. It would take some effort on his part. Surely more effort than somebody who had broken his brother's heart deserved. But, regardless of what he had told his brother last year about women like Salome, Felix knew that Anthony was an exceptional judge of character. If Salome's being had touched Anthony deeply enough for him to have fallen in love with her, she must be an extraordinary person. Besides, Felix had a thing for damsels in distress. "Give me your parents' phone number," Felix said. "And call me back in three or four hours. We have to allow a logical amount of time to pass, for you to have contacted an attorney on a Saturday. I assume your brother will be on his way here. You said you had a place to stay, right?"

"Yeah," said Salome. "I'll say goodbye to Jack, and call you later."

After she had hung up the phone, said goodbye to her brother, and enviously watched him drive off on his *Harley* toward Florida, Salome decided she'd hang out in Washington Square Park for a few hours. Besides waiting to call Felix back, Salome knew that Ivy Laplotski never got home on Saturday much before 7:30.

Felix waited a few hours, and then dialed her parents' phone number. Dick answered, "Uh, Chumwell."

"Is Mr. Bubba Apple there?" Felix asked.

"He's spending the night in the hospital."

"What happened?"

And it didn't matter to Dick who he was talking to, he just gave out the information. "He had a couple of ribs broken earlier with a baseball bat."

"Sorry to hear that," Felix said. "Which hospital did you say he was staying in?"

Dick couldn't remember if he had mentioned the hospital's name or not, but he said, "Rutland General Hospital."

"Thanks," Felix said, and then he called Information in Rutland, Vermont for the hospital's phone number. Felix then called the hospital and got connected to Bubba's room.

Pauline, who thought that Bubba had broken his ribs falling from the tractor, and was totally unaware of how badly Bubba had beaten Salome earlier, answered the phone, and Felix said, "Mrs. Apple? This is S. Franklin Smilowitz, and I'm the attorney representing your daughter, Ms. Salome Apple."

"Bubba," Pauline said. "For some reason...Salome has hired a lawyer...he's named S. Franklin Smilowitz...and he's on the phone."

"WHYYY...JEEESUS CHRIIIST....Let me talk to him."

And Pauline gave the phone to Bubba.

"This is Bubba Apple...what do YOUUU want?"

"Well just sit back, relax, and listen," Felix said. "Okay...Your daughter knows that you can legally bring her home again. But if you attempt to do that, she has medical records from the emergency room for treatment of a broken jaw and pictures of the job you did to her face earlier today. We will petition the court to have her placed in foster care until she's eighteen, we will take out a restraining order against both you and your wife, and we will pursue police action against you. Also, my client will pursue civil action."

"WHYYY...I," Bubba started to say.

"I suggest you just shut up and listen Mr. Beat-Up-Little-Girls-Man. I've suggested to my client that we legally cut your balls off, but she would prefer just moving on with her life," Felix said belligerently. "My client has a deal to offer you. This is a one time offer, and you get just one minute to decide, before I hang up the phone. Here's the deal: My client will forget about what you've done, if you'll promise to leave her alone in New York City, so she can work, attend college, and live her life any way she chooses. Any attempt you make to get in touch with her, will be viewed as a violation of the agreement. Also, my client takes full responsibility for the pictures that were published of her. She wants you to leave the photographer, Darius Malcovitch, alone. Any police action against him will also be viewed as a violation of the agreement. You have sixty seconds to decide."

"Can myyy wife at least beee in contact with our daughter?" Bubba whispered. And then, for Pauline's benefit he said, "WHYYY JEEESUS CHRI-IIST…Pauline…This is all about us SIIIGNING a permission slip for Salome…that it's OKAAAY with us…that's she STAAAY'S in New York!"

"Ms. Apple is going to call her mother later and explain the whole story. She has told me to express to you, that she hopes you enjoy the repercussions of that phone call."

"No waaay I can talk her out of that calll?" Bubba whispered.

"It's non-negotiable," Felix said. And Bubba reluctantly agreed.

When Salome called Felix later that night, and he told her what he had done, she said, "Unbelievable!…Felix Kulpa…you're my hero!"

And Felix, looking to plant a seed for his brother said, "It runs in the Kulpa genes."

And Salome, remembering the shark and gator shtick Anthony had improvised on their trip said, "Yeah…I know…both of the Kulpa brothers are exceptional human beings." Salome thanked Felix a few more times before hanging up the phone and heading over to Ivy Laplotski's in Queens. When she rang the buzzer and told Ivy who it was, Ivy was surprised, but she buzzed Salome in. Once in the apartment, Salome, slowly and painfully, told her the whole story. Ivy told Salome she could stay an indefinite amount of time. Salome knew she needed a couple of months for her jaw to heal before she could return to work. She didn't know if her job at *The Polish Palace* would still be available that long, but she would call, tell them that she had fallen off of her father's tractor and broken her jaw while in Rutland, and see if they could save her job. If not, there were other restaurants. She would also call her advisor at school, and ask to get her assignments forwarded. Finally, she would call her roommate, Jaxie, and tell her that she was mailing the rent, and she would move back in a few months. Meanwhile, Ivy Laplotski's apartment would be an ideal place for her to heal.

@@@@@@@@

A few months later on a Sunday, after Salome's face was perfect again, and all of the wires had been removed from her jaw, so she no longer had to eat through a straw, Ivy asked her if she'd like to go along to the nursing home to visit Ivy and Ida's mother, and then get dinner out. Other than a few trips to the doctor, Salome had been cooped up in the apartment, and the cabin fever had become intense. Salome said, "Yes…I'd love to get out."

Ivy Laplotski said, "Don't forget, today I'm Ida with my mother."

When they arrived in Mrs. Laplotski's room, Mrs. Laplotski was looking out of the window at imaginary birds. She paid no attention to either Ivy or Salome, even after Ivy had said, "Hi mom. It's Ida. I'd like you to meet Salome."

And Mrs. Laplotski just kept staring out of the window. Ivy had to use the bathroom. The minute she left the room, Mrs. Laplotski turned to Salome and said, "I know that's Ivy, and I know that you're Ida's friend. How is my other daughter doing? Is the FBI still looking for her?"

Chapter Seven

"*When the Moon hits your eye, like a big pizza pie, that's amore*," the Dean Martin record sang through the sophisticated public address system, as newly married Dr. Colin Morgan and RN Jennifer Apple Morgan, tripped the light fantastic toe, for the first time as husband and wife—the flash bulbs popping, and the guests applauding, hooting, and hollering. There was a nice breeze coming in off of Lake Champlain on this July evening in 1976, and the grounds behind *The Burlington Manor*, directly on the lake, looked particularly spectacular with the enhancement of the wedding flowers, plants, and lights. *The Burlington Manor* was the rococo showplace of western Vermont, and the prices ownership charged for weddings, birthdays, anniversaries, and the occasional bar or bat mitzvah reflected that elegance.

Pauline, watching her daughter and new son-in-law dance on the outside parquetry dance floor, stopped her passing son, Jack, and said, "So you're doing well in that refrigeration course in Florida?"

"Yeah…I got top grades my first semester, and I immediately found a job as a helper with the largest refrigeration company in the Tampa Bay area last January. The job is great. I'm making a lot more money than I was before. Besides, I was getting real sick and tired of having to be up seven days a week at 3:30 in the morning to deliver *The St. Petersburg Times*," Jack said, while looking around for somebody.

"How were you able to deliver newspapers on your motorcycle anyway?" Pauline asked.

"Because I occasionally cover the front desk of the motel, the owner would let me use his pick up truck every morning. I have a set of keys for the truck and the garage. He also lets me keep my *Harley* in his garage."

"How did you find this motel in the first place...what's it called?" Pauline asked.

"*The Breakers*," Jack said. "It was absolute dumb luck," Jack lied. "I figured, since I was going to be attending Tampa Bay Technical Institute in Clearwater, it would be cool to live right on the Gulf of Mexico. I just went cruising on the beaches down Gulf Boulevard, until I saw the 'Vacancy' sign at *The Breakers*. I walked into the office, and the guy behind the counter, the owner, Felix Kulpa, gave me a great deal on the one apartment he had left for rent by the year. He threw in letting me house my *Harley* in his garage. And then he let me use his pick up truck, after I found the newspaper carrier route job. Felix is a great guy." And, of course, Jack didn't mention to his mom, that it had been Felix, ten months ago, who had pretended to be Salome's lawyer on the phone, and who had helped her to win her freedom.

"How much longer is your refrigeration course?" Pauline asked.

"It's a two-year course, and I've just finished the first half. The second half is this coming October through May," Jack said. "And then I'll be certified to do everything in refrigeration, from a huge rooftop central air conditioning unit for a grocery store like *Publix*, to walk-in coolers for *7-11*, to a small AC window unit, to your refrigerators and freezers at home, Mom."

"I'm so happy that you've found your niche," Pauline said. And then she added, "Are you going to move back to Vermont or stay in Florida when you've completed the course?"

"I'll probably stay in Florida," Jack said, while scanning the perimeter again, looking...for her. "It's such a hot state, and coolers and air conditioners break down on a regular basis in Florida." And then Jack added, "I still have the $5000 that Uncle Wilbur left me saved, even though, between buying my *Harley* two years ago and my tuition and books for last year and this coming year, I've wiped out the rest of my savings. My plan is to work for somebody else a few years, save a bunch of money, and then open up my own business...probably in Florida."

"Maybe you'll find a nice young lady along the way to help you," Pauline said with a smile.

Jack, who had just turned twenty years-old, and who secretly had been in love with Salome's sixteen year-old friend, Geneva Liberty, since he had been sixteen himself and she had been twelve, said, "Yeah...maybe." And Jack thought about just how much he missed, not being able to occasionally run into Geneva in Rutland. He had been looking for her at the wedding, when he had been waylaid by Pauline.

"I really wish you'd call me more often sweetheart, I miss you!" Pauline said while touching Jack's face, and then, with a pinch of guilt thrown in added, "OH MY GOD!...Your sister calls me from New York City every

Sunday evening at 7:00...You can't call me once a week?"

"Aw Mom...I could call you once a week...I just don't want to speak to Bubba."

"Neither does Salome...that's why Bubba knows not to answer the phone at 7:00 on Sundays. If you'll figure out a time to do the same thing..."

"Okay Mom," Jack said. "How about Sundays after Salome's call...say 7:30?"

"That would be wonderful, Jack," Pauline said. "And if the phone is busy, just try back a few minutes later."

"Okay Mom," Jack said, and then he added, "How is Salome doing anyway? We haven't had much time to talk in the past two days since we've both been home."

"She's doing wonderfully. She just finished her first year of college in New York, and her grade point average was 3.25...that's better than a B. And she did that spending most of the first semester at Selma Greenwood's sister's place, and by studying herself without going to classes."

"Didn't she have to take tests at school?"

"Her professors were very kind to her. She had a lot of papers to write for most of the classes, and Selma's sister went to the library and got the books Salome needed. Her face and jaw were pretty well healed by the last few weeks of the semester, so she was able to return to school and take her final exams."

"You went down to New York to see her right after you heard what Bubba had done, didn't you?"

"I tried to go see her, but she refused to let me. She said she didn't want me to bother her right then. I decided I had to see her anyway. But I only had a post office box for an address, and I couldn't find Selma's sister, Ivy Underwood, listed in New York City Information. I asked Selma for her sister's address and phone number, but she refused to tell me. I'm still kind of annoyed with Selma for that," Pauline said, her facial expression reflecting the memory of Selma's refusal.

"Well...at least Salome kept in contact by phone," Jack said, and then he added, "Is she still working at that Polish restaurant?"

"No she isn't. They couldn't hold her position. She found another waitress job at an Afghani restaurant, and she's been working there since last December," Pauline said.

"So...you're still not talking to Bubba?" Jack asked.

"Hell no...after what he did to Salome...After putting you in a horrible position...To have to do what you did. He's lucky I haven't divorced him yet and taken half of the business, although I still might!" Pauline angrily said. "My only communication with Bubba in the past ten months has been by notes left on the dining room table," she continued. "If he needs to tell me something, he leaves a note on the table too. If I answer the phone and it's for him, and he's in the house, I have a duck caller I blow to let him know it's his call. If he's in the barn or store, I ring the outside bells. I leave his dinner in the oven every night, and he fends for himself for lunch and breakfast. But I guess, during the harvest, like last year during the harvest, I'll be serving him breakfast and lunch everyday, along with all of the other workers."

"How does he let you know if the phone is for you?" Jack asked, with laughing eyes.

"He keeps his saxophone mouthpiece in his pocket, and that's what I hear," Pauline said.

"How come you just haven't moved out?" Jack asked straight faced, remembering his own anger towards Bubba, refusing to allow the image of his parents blowing on devices, to alert each other to each other's phone calls, to make him laugh at the moment. But in that instant, in which his stoic straight face was struggling, Jack saw some funny scenes in his head: *"Hi Pauline it's Bill Wicks. Is your big mouthed husband around?" "Sure Bill," Pauline would respond. And then Bill would hear the loud,* ***"QUACKKK!"*** *Or, "Let me talk to Pauline, Bubba!" a pissed-off-at-him sister-in-law, Clara, might say.* ***"BLAHHH!"*** *would be what she'd hear. Or, Pauline answering the phone and hearing, "This is Vice President Rockefeller. May I speak with Mr. Blanchard Apple Senior?" And Rocky would hear the loud,* ***"QUACKKK!"*** *Or, Bubba answering the phone and hearing, "This is Pope Paul VI. May I speak with Mrs. Pauline Apple?" And the Pontiff would hear the loud,* ***"BLAHHH!"***

"To where? I don't want to live with your grandmother, your Aunt Clara, or any of my children. That house, orchard and business are half mine anyway. I just moved into Salome's room. I put a television in there and a nice reclining chair, and I eat my dinner on a T.V. tray while watching the news."

"Why don't you come stay with me on Mad Beach for a while?" Jack asked. "The summer is slow for the orchard, I'm sure they could get along without you. So what…if people don't get pie for a couple of weeks. Come stay, I have a big one-bedroom apartment, with an amazing view of the Gulf of Mexico. You can use my bedroom, and I'll sleep on the sofa-couch in the living room. I'm off for the next two weeks, so how about it?" And Jack thought, 'Fortunately, Felix is leaving this week, and he will be gone for nearly a year in Europe. I wouldn't want Mom to recognize his voice.'

And Pauline thought, 'Going to Florida might be fun for a couple of weeks. I'm sure Bubba could handle things by himself, and I could get Jennifer and Colin to keep an eye on him.' But then she remembered that Jennifer and Colin were going to be on a Mediterranean honeymoon cruise for three weeks. 'I wonder if I can pay Sally Brown to make Bubba dinner a few nights each week? The other nights, he can just call out for pizza or make a sandwich.' "That's a wonderful idea, Jack," Pauline said. "I'll call the airlines and see if I can get a ticket out of here in the next few days. That'll give me time to make some arrangements that need to be made before I go."

"Great, Mom," Jack said. "My flight is on Monday morning, but I'm sure I can move it back a couple of days, so I can travel with you. I'm sure Jimson and Lizzie won't mind if I stay with them a couple of extra days." And Jack, who was starting to move away from the table, said, "I'll talk with you later, Mom. I'm looking for somebody."

Pauline answered, "I'll talk with you later, Jack." She then thought about just how hard it was going to be, now that Jennifer had moved out also, to have only Bruiser at the house. She missed not having all of her children at home. And then she thought about how angry she was with Bubba, and how her children, when they came home, refused to stay at the house. Jack was at Jimson and Lizzie's, and Salome was staying at Selma Greenwood's.

Salome, having just finished a conversation with her new brother-in-law's children, twelve year-old James Morgan and nine year-old Erika Morgan, signaled to Jimson and Lizzie, and the two of them followed her into one of the many ladies restrooms at *The Burlington Manor*. Salome removed a small suede zippered bag from her purse, unzipped it, pulled out a small mirror, placed the mirror on the sink's counter, took out a small plastic zip-lock bag containing a brand new eight ball—three and a half grams—of cocaine from the suede bag, opened the plastic bag, and shook a small rock of the cocaine out onto the mirror. She then took a protected one-sided razor blade from her small bag, removed the protection, and then began chopping up the rock into six equal lines. When she finished, she put the protective covering back around the razor blade, returned it to the suede bag, and removed a straw from the bag. She handed the straw to Jimson and said, "At last. I wanted to hit this all morning, but Selma isn't cool about getting high."

Jimson snorted his two lines quickly, gave the straw to Lizzie who did the same thing, and then Lizzie handed the straw back to Salome. Salome snorted her lines, and then wiped the mirror with some toilet tissue, before putting the whole kit away in her purse. The three of them then left the bathroom, walked through the lobby, and stopped when they were outside with the rest of the wedding party. "Wow!" Jimson said quietly, "That's some good stuff. My whole face is getting numb."

"Yeah," Salome responded. "I got it from this guy in The City." What Salome didn't say, was that she had been snorting cocaine almost everyday, since last March. That's when she had met Gustav, a Wall Street computer geek and coke dealer. He was a customer at her restaurant, and he had asked Salome out before she had even served the first course of his meal. Gustav, like everybody else at the restaurant, thought her name was Jennifer, and that she was twenty-three years old. Salome's twenty year-old roommate, Jaxie, also thought Salome's name was Jennifer, and that she was twenty-three years old. Salome knew that she had made a big mistake by withholding her real name and age from Darius Malcovitch, and she was in earnest about wanting to always be truthful, but she knew also, that the only real money to be made as a waitress was where alcohol was served. In order to make a living wage, Salome had to lie about her name and age. And she didn't trust Jaxie's judgment enough to tell her the truth either. Jaxie was a sweet person and great roommate, but she was the type of person who told everything she knew, and some of what she didn't. Salome managed to keep her work life separate from her school life, however. At the Borough of Manhattan Community College, she was fifteen year-old Salome Apple.

Salome was still good at allocating enough weekly time to study, to keep her grades strong, but when she wasn't studying, sleeping, or working—usually high on cocaine—serving food at *Khyber Pass*, an Afghani restaurant on 8th Street in the East Village, she was constantly partying. Gustav Muller got the cocaine from his brother, Hans Muller. The cocaine had been so good, and had made Salome feel so frisky, that the first night she got high with Gustav, she took him into the bedroom, and with no discussion of "parameters," they knocked boots. In the morning, after Jaxie had stumbled into the apartment, post an "unsatisfying-encounter-with-a-loser-who-had-picked-me-up-at-the-bar," and while Salome was taking a shower, Gustav, who had listened empathetically to Jaxie's complaint, proceeded to get her high on cocaine. When Salome finished her shower, she heard the two of them getting their freak on in the bedroom. Salome just made a cup of tea, sat at the dinette table drinking that tea, smoked a cigarette, and read the new *Village Voice* that Jaxie had left on the coffee table. Salome waited until they were finished, and then she knocked on the door. "I need some clean clothes," she said. Jaxie gave her the green light, and Salome walked into the bedroom and grabbed her clothes. While in there, naked Gustav chopped up a few more lines of coke for Salome to snort.

A few nights later, when Gustav brought his brother, Hans, with him over to Salome and Jaxie's apartment, after many lines of cocaine, the four of them had an orgy—swapping partners in the same room, sometimes with Salome taking a break and watching the other three, sometimes with Jaxie taking a break and watching the other three—with the evening's headline attraction being Salome and Jaxie together, while Gustav and Hans watched. Since then, Salome had been seeing Gustav several times a week. He was willing to just give her the cocaine, as long as her sexual favors were keeping him interested.

"This is only the second time that Jimson and I have tried cocaine," Lizzie said. "It makes me feel so good!"

"Yeah...it makes me feel real good too!" Jimson said, while holding Lizzie from behind, his now stiffening package rubbing up against her rear. And Jimson thought, 'Well...this is just the second time that you and I have tried it...But there was that prom night with Penny...the eight ball...the motel room...a couple of summers ago!'

"Hey cut it out...we're in public!" Lizzie protested, with just enough emphasis, to let anyone who was watching know, that this position wasn't her idea, but with just enough lack of emphasis, to also allow anyone who was watching to know, that she, Lizzie Mitner, still had the goods to keep her boyfriend turned on.

One hundred feet away, a fairly intoxicated Dick Chumwell, sat down next to his newly married sister-in-law, Jennifer, and said, "You…look… beautiful."

"Thank you Dick," Jennifer said. "I don't usually hear you give too many compliments."

"I'm…not…bad guy," Dick said. And when he wasn't drinking too much, he wasn't.

"I know you're a decent, respectable man," Jennifer said. "Even though you were a pest in high school!" Jennifer added with a laugh. "And I know you were a hero in Vietnam, that the men you helped think the world of you."

"Just…doing…my job," Dick said, and then he added a burp.

"What exactly did you do over there, Dick, that won you the medal and the promotion? Cindy tried to explain it to me, but I didn't get the whole story."

"I…stationed…Sendai, Japan. Cindy and me…lived off base…small traditional…Japanese house. You know…in…Air Force…I'm… jet mechanic…right? Well…one time…in 1972...was flown…from Sendai…to dirt highway…in Vietnam. A circuit board…for A-10 Warthog…a pilot for Warthog…were waiting…in the C-130 Transport Jet. I took…circuit board…pilot and me…parachuted…into Vietnam. Walked…ran…about three clicks…to broken A-10...mortar fire everywhere…I fixed…A-10... Jumped…into back seat…weapon specialist's seat…pilot was waiting…his seat…took off…from…dirt road…flew back…to Japan. There weren't… many A-10's…in Vietnam…that one…crucial to mission…three days later." This had been an unusual plan, in that the Air Force very rarely fixed aircraft 'on the road.' "Air Force said…I acted…heroically. Pilot and me…promotions…medals," Dick said, while drinking his tenth glass of champagne.

"Well," Jennifer said. "That was heroic. I'm proud that you're my brother-in-law."

"You…never…gave two shits…about me…high school!" Dick said, with some belligerence.

"What do you mean?" Jennifer asked. "I used to kid you in high school, but I never hated you."

"What do you mean?" Dick parroted.

"Stop it Dick!" Jennifer said. "Really…what do you mean?"

"Really…what do you mean?" Drunk Dick duplicated.

"Just leave!" a thoroughly annoyed Jennifer said.

"Always…had…crush on you…Wanted…to date you. You…always

acted...too cool for me!" Dick said, remembering that wound from years earlier.

"I never knew that you were interested in me," Jennifer said. "I always thought you liked my sister, Cindy."

"Guess...settled for...Cindy," a totally blitzed Dick blurted out, and then he got up and walked away.

Dr. Colin Morgan, who had heard the tail-end of Dick's pronouncement as he was approaching the table, said, "What's your brother-in-law babbling about?" And after Jennifer told her new husband what Dick had said, Colin Morgan said, "The nerve of that prick. Hitting on my wife, on her wedding day. Perhaps I should go kick his stupid ass for him! Perhaps we should go tell your sister, Cindy, what her husband has just said."

And Jennifer said, "I wouldn't want to hurt Cindy. Dick was just drunk, and he didn't mean all of that stuff. He loves Cindy. He probably won't remember what he said in the morning."

At that moment, a beautiful and beautifully dressed Geneva Liberty, having just made her way through the lobby of *The Burlington Manor*, and having taken the time to say "Hello! I've missed you," and "Let's talk later," and given a kiss to her old friend, Salome, approached Jennifer and Colin's table with a gift. "This is for you guys," she said. "I'm sorry I had to miss the actual ceremony," she added. "But I had to wait for Nancy Andersen to relieve me at the job, and she couldn't get in any earlier today." Geneva Liberty, an eleventh grader at Rutland Central High School, worked afternoons and weekends at *Claire and Carl's Michigan Dogs* in downtown Rutland. *Claire and Carl's* specialized in hotdogs covered with a meat sauce. (People in Vermont and upstate New York refer to this meat sauce as "Michigan Sauce." And, of course, people in Michigan, have no idea that a meat sauce has been named for their state.)

"That's okay," Jennifer said, while standing to give Geneva a kiss for her gift and thoughtfulness, "At least you made it for the party."

Jack, who hadn't taken his eyes off of Geneva since the moment he had seen her walking through the back door of the lobby, approached her at Jennifer and Colin's table. Their eyes met and they both smiled. "Mister Moonlight," by *The Beatles*, was the song that had just begun, and Jack said, "Hello Geneva. Would you like to dance?" And she nodded, "Yes," and Jack took her hand and led her to the dance floor. They danced closely, and continued dancing closely when "Unchained Melody" immediately followed.

Salome, who was watching, whispered to Lizzie, "Geneva has been crazy about Jack for years!"

"It certainly looks like it," Lizzie whispered back.

Cindy approached Salome and Lizzy and said, "Hey Lizzie...would you mind if I steal Salome for a minute?"

"No problem," Lizzie said, and then she walked off.

"What's up?" Salome asked.

"I was in the lobby before, and I saw Jimson and Lizzie follow you into the ladies room. And for the past twenty minutes, Jimson has been bending my ear, talking fast about a bunch of unrelated subjects. I was wondering if the three of you were high on cocaine?"

"What?" Salome protested, with just a wee bit too much vigor.

Cindy, who picked up on how Salome had responded, said, "Well…you can try to convince me that I'm wrong. But if I'm right, and I've hit the nail on the head, please know that I care about your health and safety."

"I see," Salome said. "You've just finished your first year of Nursing classes at Plattsburgh State University, and now everything is a health issue."

"Well…we did have a long seminar on illegal drug abuse," Cindy said. "And Jimson, who usually doesn't have too much to say, is displaying classic cocaine abuse tendencies. And I did see the three of you walking into that restroom…which is kind of odd anyway."

"I had spilled some champagne on my dress in an awkward place. They were just helping wet down the spot…that's all," Salome stressed, with a little less vigor.

"That still doesn't explain Jimson's motor mouth," Cindy said.

"That's not on me!" Salome stressed with some annoyance. Salome and Cindy had always had this kind of a relationship anyway, with Cindy usually asking Salome questions that were none of her business.

Within every family there is always a dynamic between siblings, and how those siblings interact with their parents. Growing up in the Apple household, Cindy and Bruiser had usually sided with Bubba during family squabbles. Even violent acts by Bubba, although none as violent in the past as the beating of Salome's face and the breaking of her jaw, were rationalized by Cindy and Bruiser. Cindy had yelled at Salome a couple of years ago, "Do you have decent clothes to wear everyday? Do you have a nice roof over your head and good food in your belly? Do you have some spending money in your pocket? Well, thank Bubba for that. He has gotten up early every morning of his life, and he has busted his butt for this family! And if occasionally he goes a little crazy, well that's just the price we have to pay for everything else that he does for us." At the time, Bruiser had enthusiastically agreed with Cindy's assessment. It was interesting how both Cindy and Bruiser not only stuck up for Bubba most of the time, but they were the two Apple children who most resembled him. Cindy and Bruiser had different hair and eye colors, but they both had the definitive Apple look. Jennifer and Jimson, who usually sided with Pauline, carried the Bouvier look in their faces—although their hair and eye colors were different. Salome agreed with her mom always, and, except for the hair color, she looked exactly like Jennifer. Jack always agreed with Pauline's point of view, and he had mostly the Apple look, but he was the only one of the six whose face was truly a hybrid of both parents.

When it came to sibling interactions in the Apple household however, Salome and Jack had always been the closest.

"Well," Cindy said. "You're going to do what you're going to do… since that's how you live anyway. I was just concerned about you, that's all."

"Thanks for the concern," Salome said.

"It would be nice if you'd have a little more concern for this family," Cindy said. "While you've been off gallivanting in New York City and modeling naked, some of us have been here and worrying about Mom. And all Mom can ever seem to worry about is you."

"What the hell is that supposed to mean?" Salome asked angrily.

"While you were embarrassing the family a year and a half ago, we were here in Rutland concerned about Mom and her cancer!"

"Cancer? What cancer?" Salome asked.

"Mom didn't want you to know, because she wanted you to have your chance in New York City. She didn't want you to come home. In September of 1974, she was diagnosed with colon cancer. She had major surgery on her colon, and she had eight weeks of radiation. So while you were modeling nude in New York, that's what we were going through here. And then you get some high powered attorney to scare Bubba into letting you stay in New York…," Cindy said angrily.

"What should I have done?" Salome shot back with anger. "The asshole broke my jaw!"

"And Bubba hasn't had a decent night's sleep since then. He's so sorry. He feels terrible. He's even seeing a shrink weekly. And all you can do is to hate him!" Cindy said with even more anger.

"I don't need this guilt shit!" Salome said, and then added, "Is Mom okay now? Did they get all of the cancer?"

"She seems to be one hundred percent cured," Cindy said.

"Well thanks for letting me know," Salome said, and then added, "I have a phone call to make," Then she started to walk towards the lobby.

"Going to get more high? So you can handle this new knowledge about Mom?" Cindy asked loudly, and then added, "I love your outfit, by the way. What an original idea…a sheer, see-through, lavender mini dress with green flowers. A dress that everyone can see your breasts through! And to top it all off with equestrian lace-up riding boots! This was supposed to be Jennifer's day…but hey everybody…look at Salome!"

And Salome just walked away, giving Cindy her back and her high-above-the-head middle finger. As Salome approached the rose bushes that lined both sides of the brick sidewalk for about ten feet before the back door of *The Burlington Manor*, she accidentally caught the left heal of her new *Doc Martens* on an uneven piece of brick, sending her into a rose bush on the right side of the sidewalk. Salome had just paid $125 for these boots, for the wedding specifically, at *Peter's Punk Clothing and Shoes* on Avenue A and East

Sixth Street in The City—where she had also purchased her rayon lavender with green flowers mini dress for $70—and she was still getting used to walking in the boots. They were very stiff. Salome got up off of the rose bush and surveyed herself. The thorns of the bush had pricked her right thigh through the sheer fabric, and she was bleeding. Fortunately, there was a pocket of air separating her now bleeding thigh from the dress itself, so if she walked, pinching the dress away from her body on the right side, she might avoid a blood stain. Unfortunately, the palm of her right hand was bleeding also, having rubbed up against some thorns in a second rose bush when she fell, so Salome had to grab the right side of her dress with her left hand and keep it pulled away from her body, as she tried to make her way to the restroom without looking too ridiculous. Selma Greenwood was walking out of the restroom at the same time Salome needed to get in, so she held the door for Salome.

"What the hell happened to you?" Selma asked.

"I tripped on a piece of brick, and I fell into the roses. I'm trying to keep the blood on my thigh from touching the dress."

"Well here, let me help you in the restroom."

"That's okay Selma, I'll do it myself," Salome said, and then she asked, "Did you know that my mom had colon cancer in September of 1974?"

"Yeah…I found out in November of 1974. Pauline hadn't told me, but I happen to run into her in the same waiting room at the hospital. She was waiting to get radiation, and I was waiting on a friend, who I had driven to the hospital for the same reason. She told me about it then."

"And you didn't tell me about it?" Salome asked with some anger.

"Your mom asked me not to."

"And you still wouldn't tell me?"

"Salome…look…you know I love you. I see you as the daughter I've never had. But just because I can keep all of your secrets, and you mine, it doesn't mean that we can't also have secrets we share with other people," Selma said compassionately.

And an agitated Salome responded, "You still should have told me, Selma. That's my mother! She could have died! I needed to have been the one to have made the decision…if I wanted to stay in New York, or if I wanted to move back to Rutland, to be by Mom's side."

"I had already decided," Selma said, "That if your mom's condition had become real serious, I was going to tell you anyway. I decided to honor your mother's request, because things were going well for you, and I wanted your mom to continue trusting me."

"I don't care, Selma, I feel betrayed," Salome said angrily. "I'll talk to you later," she added, as she entered the restroom, closing the door on Selma. Inside the restroom, at the mirror, Salome examined her dress closely. The rayon fabric was so sheer, Salome saw that the little rose thorn holes were unnoticeable. She washed her bloody right hand in the sink with cold water, and then she wrapped it in several paper towels. She then dampened a few more paper towels, and took them and several dry towels into one of the toilet stalls. She carefully removed her dress and hung it on the hook provided on the stall's door. The right leg of her pantyhose was ripped to shreds, so Salome removed them and dropped them on the floor. She then noticed that the right side of her panties were covered in blood spots. She removed her panties, grabbed her pantyhose from the floor to discard in the trashcan, and walked out to the sink with nothing on but her boots. She made the water soapy in the sink, and she twisted her panties all around in the soapy water, imitating a washing machine's motion, trying to wash out the blood spots. Then she put clean water in the sink and rinsed her panties thoroughly. Next to the paper towel dispenser, this restroom had also provided a hand dryer. Salome used it for three cycles on her underwear. She then took her semi-dry panties, and drapped them across the toilet paper dispenser. She locked her stall, and sat down on the toilet in nothing but her boots. She took the cocaine kit from her purse, and she placed the mirror on her lap. She spent nearly an hour in the stall snorting lines, thinking about what a bitch Cindy was, what a dipshit Bruiser was, what an asshole Bubba was, and how angry she was at her mom, Selma, and the rest of the family, for having kept her in the dark about her mom's colon cancer.

Lizzie came into the bathroom and said, "Hey Salome, are you in here?"

"What's up, Lizzie?" Salome asked from the toilet stall.

"They're starting to cut the cake. What are you doing anyway? Are you sick?"

"Lock the door, and I'll show you. I'm not sick," a very high Salome said. And then she slipped on her dress, grabbed her purse, walked out of the stall, but totally forgot her almost dried panties on the toilet paper dispenser. Salome took out her kit, and chopped up four gigantic lines on the mirror. Lizzie snorted her two humongous rails, and then Salome snorted what would be her eleventh and twelfth lines in the past hour. She told Lizzie when they were finished, "I'll see you outside in a few minutes, I have to check my phone service in New York first for any messages." Lizzie left, totally wasted on cocaine, and Salome headed to one of the payphones in the lobby. The only message was from Annie Harrison, the housekeeper and cook for Darius' parents. She had left the message for Salome, so she now knew Salome's real name. The news was devastating.

Meanwhile, Bubba, sitting at a table as far away as possible from the outside dance floor, was talking with Bruiser.

"So Mom is still not talking to you?" Bruiser asked.

"WHYYY...I'm lucky she didn't LEEEAVE me!" Bubba said. "And you and Cindy are the OOONLY children of mine who will talk to me. I just gave Jennifer AWAAAY, and she wouldn't even talk to MEEE. I tried to give her a kiss and to wish her luck. I tried to apologize for BEEEING a bad father. SHEEE just turned AWAAAY. I'm sure she would have preferred if somebody else had given her AWAAAY."

"I'll always talk to you Bubba. I think you're a great father, and I probably would have done the same thing to my daughter, if she had modeled naked in a men's magazine at fourteen. I'd probably have kicked the crap out of her if she had done that at twenty-four also!" Bruiser said.

"Well YOUUU would be totally wrong! I started SEEEING a shrink off and on…a couple of years AGOOO…I KNOOOW there has been something wrong with MEEE for a long time, and I need to figure out WHYYY I'm so violent! Your mother was RIIIGHT, when SHEEE told you that I'm not a very good ROOOLE model."

@@@@@@@

"Anthony, again, I can't tell you how much I appreciate you taking a year off from college to do this favor for me, " Felix said to his brother, while both of them were sitting at the dining room table drinking a beer in Felix's apartment.

"Well you know I'm not happy about taking this year off, but you're my brother, I love you, and I know you need this," Anthony said. "And honestly," Anthony continued, "It was coming to the end of the road with Lillie anyway. So I guess not being in the same city with her this year works for me." Anthony was referring to Lillie Belis, the twelve year-older Russian math professor, with whom he had been cohabitating for nearly two years.

"Regardless of Lillie, what you're doing for me is incredibly generous. I set out to tour Europe two years ago, but I decided to let myself get distracted by Tatiana instead. And the only result of that choice, was getting my heart broken, yet again. Then she married the joker that she had ditched me for, a Dr. Ralph Hugo, professor of Animal Husbandry at the Sorbonne, and now, nearly two years later, I'm just beginning to think about other women again," Felix said. "Also, since no publishing house in North America wants *All the Seats Were Occupied*, I'm going to see if I can sell it in Europe…while I begin a new novel over there," he continued. "For you to give me this opportunity, Anthony, to just go…to let the wind blow me wherever…This is the mental douche that I need. I can't tell you again…"

"Then don't tell me again!" Anthony said. "Just get back by the end of March next year, so I can go spend four or five months in Europe myself, before I begin my senior year at UVM the following September."

"I'll definitely be back by the end of March next year…I promise," Felix said.

Felix's meowing cat, Petomane, was rubbing himself up against Felix's leg and thinking, 'Why don't you go to Siam…Round Boy…and bring me back some exotic pussy?...See?...some exotic pussy!'

"I'll feed your kitty ass in a minute, Peto!" Felix said.

"So you and Walter Lee have big plans for your stay in New York City next week?" Walter Lee was going to fly to New York with Felix, hang out with him for a week, and then return to Florida, when Felix headed off to England.

"I imagine we'll see a couple of shows, see some live music, and we'll overeat too," Felix said.

"Sounds great, I'm kind of jealous," Anthony said.

"You'll get your turn next year," Felix said, and then added, "I've got to go do some paper work in the office."

About thirty minutes later, in the office of *The Breakers*, while the Apples were celebrating Jennifer's wedding in Rutland, Felix received a very disturbing phone call from Annie Harrison on Long Island. It was a terrible conversation. She had called to tell him, that two days earlier, while hiking up Le Pic Du Midi in the French Alps with a friend, that Darius Malcovitch had fallen to his death. The body was being returned to the United States tomorrow, and the wake was in three days on Long Island, with the funeral the day after the wake.

Apparently, Darius and his climbing companion, were taking a lunch break on a twelve foot ledge. After Darius had finished eating, he decided to climb fifteen or twenty feet by himself, to try out some different shoes. Darius had been using ordinary rock shoes, but he then thought that it might be easier using the shoes with the crampons, for the higher, icier, and slicker elevation. So he hooked up the rope through his carabiners to the piton, grabbed his pickax, and started a little mini-climb to test the shoes. His French climbing partner, Pierre Manette, would say, "It was inexplicable! The bolt rawl didn't break," he would add. "It was as if the mountain just vomited the bolt twenty feet away from itself, sending Darius over the side, and beyond the width of the ledge where I was sitting, still eating my lunch!" (Later, when a reporter from the magazine, *L' Alpiniste Américain Nigaud*, would interview The Mountain, and ask it, "Why did you spew the climber, Darius Malcovitch, away from yourself?" The Mountain would reply, "*Parcequ'il etáit là*!" or "Because he was there!")

@@@@@@@@

A very drunk, distraught, and totally blitzed Salome, stopped at her mother's table and said, "I can't believe...you didn't tell me...about your cancer!"

"How did you find out about that?" Pauline asked.

"What difference...I know. Why...didn't...tell me?"

"Oh Salome, I love you so much. Of all my children, you're the one I've always seen as having the most potential. I just didn't want to take away your chance for greatness in New York, by telling you some news that would have probably made you move back to Rutland."

"But...that should...have...my choice!" Salome said with some belligerence. "Why...is everyone...making choices...for me?"

"Nobody is making choices for you, Salome," Pauline said. "You make your own choices, and I, for one, just try to support those choices of yours," Pauline said, and then added, "At least...when they're good choices!"

And Salome, whose heart was breaking after having just heard an hour ago of Darius' death, with total anger said, "I see...Mom. You still WANT... ME...TO EAT SHIT...for modeling nude...it ending up...THAT FUCKING MAGAZINE!"

"I'm not trying to make you feel guilty, Salome," Pauline said in a loving way.

"WELL...I...DO!" Salome shouted, and then she sat down at the table, put her head down and cried. She whimpered, "I do feel guilty."

"Sweetheart...that's such ancient history. Can't you forget it? I have," Pauline said, as she leaned over her crying daughter, and stroked her daughter's hair.

Salome stood up quickly, accidentally almost knocking Pauline to the ground, and said, "Well...he's paid...HE'S DEAD!"

"Who are you talking about?" Pauline asked, regaining her balance.

"DARIUS...Darius Malcovitch...photographer...took nude shots. I LOVED him...now HE'S DEAD!" Salome cried, forcing the wail, from deep within her stomach, and around the now totally space consuming lump, currently lodged with *Krazy Glue* in her throat; and then, with her heart pumping double time, she ran away from her mother. She was unaware of her direction, and, at that moment, she didn't care. She tripped over a small shrub, about ten feet from where Bubba, Bruiser, Cindy, and Dick were sitting, and she immediately staggered to her feet, wiping the pieces of dirt, grass, and leaves from her high-clinging dress.

"I can...see...her muff!" The totally hammered Dick said.

"Totally classy...no underwear!" The fashion critic sister, Cindy, said.

"What a slut!" The angry and socially inept brother, Bruiser, said.

"Are you OKAAAY?" The concerned father, Bubba, said.

"I see...London...I see...France...I see...Salome...with no underpants!" The stupid Dick spewed forth.

"I wish I hadn't run out of film for my camera!" Cindy said with a smirk.

The wonderful thing about being a human being is—when sufficiently provoked of course—one can forget about having no underpants on until reminded, then lift one's skirt or drop trou, and declare to a nosey sister, a dipshit brother, an asshole brother-in-law, and a violent father: "Sorry about your film...Guess... you...ASSHOLES...will...just...have to...ALWAYS

REMEMBER…this…here…big…oval…APPLE VERMONT MOON!”

The Earth

❖ ❖ ❖

Chapter Eight

"DEAR BROTHERS and SISTERS...Please LISTEN UP...it BREAKS MY HEART...to have to stand here before you today...to have to CALL ATTENTION to your TRANSGRESSION...to have to BEG YOU to SEE THE LIGHT...BEFORE IT'S TOO LATE. I BEG YOU...to REALIZE...THAT COCAINE IS THE DEVIL'S DRUG!" Felix would pontificate loudly, four years later, in 1980, to the two perp parishioners, charged with purloining his product, who were parked on the tan fabric sectional sofa, in the living room, of the Church of Felix Kulpa, at *The Breakers* on Mad Beach. They had found, in a bedroom drawer, hidden beneath some artifacts that remained as a testimony to yet another failed relationship with a female, in this case, a Hoochie Momma blouse and a knitted bag of potpourri, and subsequently snorted up, Felix's five gram stash of cocaine. Felix would add, still sounding like a man he had never met, Reverend Ignatius Apple, "COCAINE IS THE NEW SODOM AND GOMORRAH! ...It's just ANOTHER way of going to HELL!...and BELIEVE ME...THAT'S NO HAPPY FALL!" And then Felix would continue addressing his flock on the sofa, "What a mood altering... PIECE OF SHIT DRUG! Look at the recent research with laboratory rats! They were STARVED...given no FOOD...given COCAINE instead for DAYS. Then, when given a CHOICE between FOOD and COCAINE, they CHOSE COCAINE EVERY TIME! FUCKING ALGERNON, the genius rat from *Flowers for Algernon*, WOULD CHOOSE COCAINE EVERY TIME TOO!

Hey...drugs aren't the answer anyway. But AT LEAST, in the 1960's, most of us who tried LSD, tried it with an eye towards SELF-DISCOVERY!

Some psychiatrists used it in the 1950's with their patients. CARY GRANT used LSD with his shrink in the 1950's. LSD was the difference between THEORY and EMPIRICAL KNOWLEDGE....and it COVERED UP NOTHING! Oh...one could intellectually discuss the importance of BEING IN THE HERE AND NOW, but with LSD it was no longer talk. One felt, in one's gut, the repercussions of LEAVING THE HERE AND NOW. WHEREVER you were at in your head at the moment...was where you WERE AT! AND LO AND BEHOLD...DEAR BROTHERS and SISTERS, IF you felt good about yourself, then you'd SEE THE LIGHT in the HERE AND NOW! If you TRANSGRESSED INTO FEELING BAD ABOUT YOURSELF...BY LEAVING THE NOW...AND VISITING either THE PAST OR THE FUTURE...you would have a BUMMER! And so...FIGURING ALL OF THIS COSMIC STUFF OUT...BECAME THE COSMIC JOURNEY of the WOODSTOCK NATION!...AND THUS THIS GREAT LESSON FROM ON HIGH...BEGAT FEELING GOOD ABOUT AND RESPECTING THE RIGHTS AND PROPERTY OF OTHER HUMAN BEINGS! AND THE GREAT VERSES...from the BOOK OF ROCK...aided in THIS SOJOURN!" (In the late 1960's/early 1970's, Tedd Webb, a local Rock D.J. in the Tampa Bay Area, would always end his show with, "And remember...if you're not a Head...you're definitely behind!") "The point is...The acid exposed the user TO SELF!...BUT COCAINE HIDES THE SELF, AND COUCHES IT IN LAYERS OF ABSOLUTE PRETENTIOUSNESS! AH...CHIC COCAINE...THE DARLING OF THE JET SET. GLAM LABORATORY RATS...SHOVING WHITE POWDER UP THEIR NOSES IN HOUSES, CARS, CLUBS, THEATRES, TOILETS, RESTAURANTS, AND MANORS ACROSS AMERICA. YAHOO! Jack Kerouac might have written: 'Whither goest thou America with thy bright shiny powder shoved up thy nose in the night...I mean WHITHER GOEST THOU MAN?'" Felix emphasized. And he would continue, "JUST LOOK AT THE BEHAVIOR OF YOU TWO. RIPPING ME OFF WITH A TOTAL LACK OF CONSCIENCE! APPALLINGLY MUTE SUPEREGOS!" And then Felix would get considerably more gentle in his speech, "I really hate cocaine. All it does for me these days, is to shrivel up Winky and make me think I want more cocaine. But most of the women I date like the stuff, and for them, it does act as an aphrodisiac. It used to do that for me, but no longer. Anyway, since my *raison d'etre* is to get schtupped, to that avail, I keep it around. What you guys found and just put up your noses cost me $300, and was good for several nights worth of amorous caprice. Thanks...pay me back! Guess I'll have to invest in a safe!"

On this July day in 1976, as Salome rode on the Long Island Railroad out to Darius' funeral in Amagansett, she sat looking out of the window at nothing in particular. She reflected on Jennifer and Colin's wedding four days earlier, and just how pissed off she was with everyone. After her derrière display to Dick, Cindy, Bruiser, and Bubba, Salome had stormed off to yell at Jennifer, for not having told her about their mom's cancer in 1974.

Salome then had decided to leave Burlington immediately and to head back to New York. She had the key to Selma's house, so she would hire a taxi at the taxi stand in front of *The Burlington Manor* for the four hour round trip to Rutland and back. She would have the driver wait at Selma's while she changed and got her stuff, and then the driver would take her back to the Burlington Train Station. (Salome would forget that her panties—now completely dry—were still draped over the toilet paper dispenser in the restroom of *The Burlington Manor*, until she changed at Selma's.) This would be the driver's lucky day, in that the fare for all of this would be $150 plus waiting time, and by the way that Salome would position herself in the backseat, the view from the rearview mirror would be exceptional. Salome was on her way through the lobby, heading to the taxi stand, when she ran into Jack. Jack became the final victim of Salome's acid tongue. "I…can't believe…you…of all people… acting like…the other Apple assholes… wouldn't tell me about Mom's cancer in 1974," she had said.

"You don't know how much I hated that," Jack had said. "I really wanted to tell you…I got into one hell of an argument with Mom about it. But she is my mother, and she was the one whose wishes I had to respect," Jack had continued. "I'm so sorry."

"Fuck you!" Salome had said.

And now, four days later, on the train towards the funeral of the man she loved, Salome felt like a pariah, an outcast from her family and Rutland. 'Fuck them all!' Salome thought, as she covertly snorted a couple more lines of cocaine, in her seat, her body turned almost completely toward the window, about ten minutes before the train was at her stop. And not to be told about her mom's condition by her best friend, Selma, was particularly painful. Salome thought, 'Last December I went to a payphone and called Selma immediately, after her mom in the nursing home with Alzheimer's, clearly asked about Selma and indicated that she knew that Ivy wasn't Selma.' Selma, once told, hadn't felt her mother's question was any big deal, and she had told Salome last December, "That's the second time that Mom has come out of her obscurity this year, on a temporary basis, and asked questions about the FBI and me." And on the morning of Jennifer and Colin's wedding, Selma told Salome, "Mom asked for me again last week." Nonetheless, Salome had been loyal enough to Selma to phone her immediately—she hadn't even said a word to Ivy—the minute their mother had displayed knowledge of knowing that Selma had a problem with the FBI., and that Ivy really wasn't Ida. Salome felt that Selma should have given her an immediate heads up, the instant she had learned of Pauline's colon cancer in 1974.

"*Such is the problematic nature of lies, and especially lies of omission,*" Felix would write in his journal, many years later, in the late 1990's, after a visit from a hurt friend. He would add: *As human beings, particularly when it comes to the relationships we have with those we care about, we have all faced, or will face, or are facing, the dilemma of what to say and what not to say. Somebody we care about asks us not to mention something to somebody else we care about. Are we betraying the second person by keeping quiet? A couple, who have had a long relationship with another couple, see one from that couple with whom they are friendly, out romantically with someone else. Do you tell the mate that his or her partner is a philander? Perhaps the one doing the philandering has decided to end things, that very night, with his or her paramour. Perhaps a lesson has already been learned, and now that couple will have marital bliss for the next forty years, and the one who was unfaithful will never be unfaithful again. Are we betraying the innocent party by not mentioning our observations of unfaithfulness?* Felix would continue: *Some say, "What they don't know can't hurt them." But maybe it's, "What they don't know always hurts them." I don't know.*

Many years later, still in the late 1990's, after Felix would let him read the previous journal entry, Dr. Walter Lee Younger, Professor of Anthropology, would respond, "That whole 'what they don't know won't hurt them versus what they do know' argument is all sophistry."

Back in 1976, at the Amagansett station, Salome hired a cab and gave him the address of the synagogue. She was about a half hour late and the service was well under way, when she slipped into the back and found a seat next to an older couple. Salome looked down at her dress once she was seated, and she noticed that she had to straighten out her now wrinkled hemline. She was dressed in a nice conservative black dress, and she was wearing granny-style black shoes with a matching handbag.

Salome sat listening and not understanding the Hebrew, wanting to cry, but the cocaine made her feel too good to cry. At the end of the service, as the family members at the front of the *schule* were sadly walking down the aisle to exit the building and to drive to the cemetery, Darius' father, Gregor Malcovitch, stopped when he saw Salome. "What's SHE doing here?" he bellowed. "SHE'S the harlot who lied to my son and caused him so much grief! SHE'S the underage model who hurt my son's reputation! GET HER OUT OF HERE!" Gregor Malcovitch yelled. And Salome quickly looked around the synagogue and noticed, that the angry faces of most of the people reminded her of the scene in *The Graduate*, after Dustin Hoffman's character starts banging on the glass of the church and interrupting the wedding. Salome quickly exited, still unable to cry, but feeling like the harlot who

Darius' father had just described.

Once outside, Salome walked down the brick street, looking for a payphone to call the cab driver who had brought her, his business card clutched in her hand. Felix quickly caught up with her and said, "That was pretty cruel... what Darius' father said."

"Felix! My hero!" Salome said, with a grimacing face and a forced smile, "It's great seeing you!" She hugged him and kissed him on the cheek.

Felix, who quickly figured out by Salome's countenance that Anthony had been correct in his assessment, that she indeed must have been in love with Darius, returned the kiss to Salome's cheek, and said, "I know this must be painful for you."

"I liked Darius a lot," Salome said, as she looked down at the ground.

"I did too," Felix said. "But I can tell that it was more than that for you," he added.

"Look Felix...I care about Anthony. I don't want him to know that I was in love with Darius," Salome said, with pleading eyes.

"He already had that figured out," Felix said. "Walter Lee said he would stay and watch the motel, if Anthony wanted to come to the funeral. Anthony said he didn't want to go, that he was sure he'd see you, and that 'He'd be doubly unhappy, both being at Darius' funeral, and being able to read the level of your love for the man.'"

"I'm sorry Felix. Who can ever figure out how the heart works? As much as I care about Anthony, as close as we became, it was just a different sensation when I met Darius."

"I understand," Felix said. "Sometimes it's that instantaneous thing with someone else, sometimes it takes a while to discover. And when it isn't instantaneous, and when a couple goes through the dating process 'to see,' it's always problematic when half of the couple falls in love and the other half doesn't."

"That's right," Salome said.

"Although I've stayed loyal to my brother, and part of that loyalty had to be accepting and even assimilating some of his anger toward you, I understand what the human heart goes through when it comes to how relationships work. My only problem now is how honest I want to be with Anthony, when he asks me specific questions about seeing you here, and what we discussed."

Having changed her mind that quickly, Salome said, "Be honest with him. Perhaps Anthony and I will learn how to be Platonic friends...in the future." And then Salome added, "By the way...again...I'll never be able to repay you for playing a lawyer on the phone with my parents last year and winning me my freedom! Felix Kulpa...you'll always be my hero!" And then Salome gave Felix a better hug, with her breasts pushed into his chest, and then she planted a wet kiss on his lips.

Felix thought, 'Oh my!' and he felt something that sounded like a Ca Thump! travel through his being. And then, as he was going through a series of distractions, pointing out different buildings to Salome with his right hand, so she wouldn't notice the pants adjustment that his left hand now had to make, Walter Lee came walking up. "Salome! It's good to see you," he said, and then he hugged her and gave her a kiss on the cheek.

"Walter Lee!" Salome said, with a return kiss to his cheek, "I get to see another of my favorite people, even though these circumstances are pretty terrible."

"I know," Walter Lee said. "I didn't know Darius that well, just shot the bull with him a couple of times for about a half hour back at the motel, but he seemed like a nice guy."

"Walter Lee and I already had plans to spend this week in New York City, before we learned of Darius' death. I would have come to Darius' funeral anyway, but you probably wouldn't have, would you, Walter Lee?"

"Well…unless 'Knee had wanted to come, and you needed me to watch the motel, I wouldn't have missed it," Walter Lee said. And then he continued, "To let Gregor Malcovitch see, that the darkie who just happened to have the apartment beneath his in 1963...the nigger who caused him so much angst, by being all up in his motel back then…has enough wherewithal to spend his own money on a plane ticket…and to come all the way up here to New York, to pay respects to his son…I wouldn't miss the expression on his reactionary, racist, honkus face."

"Has he seen you yet?" Felix asked.

"Nah…I'm gonna make sure that I shake his hand at the cemetery though," Walter Lee said. "We need to get to the car, so we can follow the crowd there," he added.

"Do you need a ride to the cemetery?" Felix asked Salome.

"No. They don't want me there. I'm gonna get a cab back to the train station."

"Why don't you follow the crowd to the cemetery in the rental car, Walter Lee. I'll go with Salome in a cab to the train station, drop her off, and then have the cab take me to the cemetery. I'm sure there's only one *Forest Lawn Cemetery* in town, and the cabbie knows where it is."

And so Walter Lee followed the crowd in the new *Chevy Impala*, and Felix waited with Salome for the cab. While they were waiting, Salome asked Felix, "Would you like a couple of lines?"

"Of coke?" Felix asked.

Salome nodded her head, "Yes," and then said, "Stand by this little alleyway behind this doctor's office and keep watch. When I have your lines chopped up, I'll call you."

And Felix kept watch, while Salome chopped up and snorted a couple of medium-sized lines for herself. Then she put together a couple of gargantuan-sized rails for Felix and called to him. Felix walked down the alleyway, saw the amount on the mirror and said, "You really want to fuck me up, don't you!" And then he snorted it all.

The cab came a few minutes later, and on the way to the station Felix asked Salome what exactly Gregor Malcovitch's outburst had meant at the funeral. And, of course, as so often is the case when one is snorting cocaine, one's lips can become totally uncoiled and flap away free and easy. As high as she was, Salome felt totally at ease in now revealing everything. She told Felix in considerably more detail than he had heard before, about some of the specific positions she had posed in at fourteen, and how her father suspected their Greek neighbor in Rutland, Gus Strattus, of circulating the pictures around, when she was fifteen. Felix said, "I see," but at that moment, he had just a wee bit more empathy with how most fathers might react in a similar situation with a fifteen year-old daughter, although he still felt it was horrible that Bubba had broken Salome's jaw. And then Salome told Felix about her *Harley* trip to Alaska, her confession to Darius, how Darius had reacted, on the night of her fifteen birthday, after they had done it for the first time, and how sorry and guilty she still felt. And Felix thought, 'Anthony probably doesn't need to hear all of these details.' And finally, she told Felix about her waitress job in the East Village—invited him and Walter Lee to come in for dinner that week, which Felix accepted—how well she had done at the Borough of Manhattan Community College her freshman year, and how she planned on transferring to NYU, Felix's old alma mater, after her sophomore year at BMCC. She also mentioned, Gustav, her new Wall Street boyfriend.

And then Felix told Salome about what had happened after his chance encounter at JFK with Tatiana two years ago, and how they had spent five weeks together in Paris, and how they were supposed to get back together in Florida during Christmas of 1974, but how Tatiana had then kicked him to the curb for somebody else in November of 1974, and how she was now married to that guy, and how screwed up Felix had been over that for more than a year, and how now he was finally going to see all of Europe for eight months.

At the train station, Felix jumped out of the cab, walked around to the other backseat door, and opened it for Salome. Salome got out of the cab, fixed her scrunched-up dress hemline again and said, "I'm at the restaurant every night this week except Monday and Tuesday from four until midnight. Please come by."

"Walter Lee and I, will definitely be by!" Felix said. "I'm kinda stoked to try 'Gani food anyway." And then Salome gave Felix another intense breast hug, planted another wet one on his lips, and walked into the station. "Oh my!" Felix verbalized this time, as he made another pants *ajustement*. 'Yeah,' Felix thought, 'There's a whole bunch of stuff I probably shouldn't tell Anthony.'

@@@@@@@@

After the burial at the cemetery, Felix and Walter Lee headed toward Port Jefferson. Tatiana's parents lived there, and Felix wanted to say hello as long as he was out on Eastern Long Island. Felix had a great relationship with the Orlonskys, and even these days, now that Tatiana was married to someone else, Felix would still talk with the Orlonskys on the phone every few months or so. The Orlonskys both liked Walter Lee very much also. Tatiana's father, Dr. Igor Orlonsky, who had his proctology office in the lower left corner of their Victorian house, loved jazz and talking jazz. Whenever he would see Walter Lee, that would be the main topic of conversation. The last time the Orlonskys had been on Mad Beach, about five years ago, Walter Lee had taken Igor to a great jazz club, *Downstroke*, in Tampa. Tatiana's mother, Katarina Orlonsky, was a high school art teacher in Port Jefferson. She was also a fairly well known artist, although she would say, "I don't have half of the artistic ability of my daughter, Tatiana." And that was probably true. Katarina had the name and the sales, but Tatiana had the gift. Katarina had always seen something extraordinary in Felix, loved him as a son, and had actively campaigned to convince her daughter that she was crazy to not be with him. Felix was happy to be heading to their house.

"I met the most incredible woman at the funeral," Walter Lee said, after he had turned the traffic report on the car's radio off.

"Well I guess a funeral would be one of those alternative sites that I always told Anthony about…a place to find women, where most men aren't looking," Felix said.

"Yeah…well that did put a certain tone in how I handled this," said Walter Lee. "Especially, since the woman, Annie Harrison is her name, works for the Malcovitchs as their chief cook and bottle washer, and she's pretty broken up about Darius. She had raised him since he was twelve."

"Oh yeah…Annie. I've never met her. I've just spoken to her on the phone a few times," Felix said. "But Anthony said she was aces. He also said, she made the most incredible peppered salmon, peppered breadsticks, and garlic bread."

"Yeah…well…I guess she's putting her grief on hold, because I'm gonna get to try that peppered salmon on Tuesday."

"I thought you were a vegetarian," Felix said.

"I'll eat fish and dairy. Anyway, she invited you also, but I told her that you were busy."

"What?" asked Felix.

"Come on 'Licks…do me this solid. Ole Man Malcovitch is taking his family, just to get away from here, down to their condo in Boca for a week on Monday. I asked Annie out for dinner, but she suggested we come over there for dinner on Tuesday instead. I think I really dig this lady, and I'd love to spend some quality time with her alone...if you wouldn't mind 'Licks."

"*No problemo*, Cunning Lee," Felix said, and then laughingly added, "You want to go munch on Annie's peppered fish...alone!"

Walter Lee burst out laughing, and then he said, "I've got your peppered breadstick right here!"

Felix laughed and then said, "But Walter Lee...what's up with Sylvia?"

"Sylvia and me are still cool," Walter Lee said. "But we've had an agreement since jump, that we were just gonna be maintenance lovers."

"Maintenance lovers?"

"Yeah...we both knew early that we weren't right for each other...long term. But we both kinda liked each other's company...both in and out of the bed. So the deal was always...it'd be cool...when either of us left the relationship for somebody else," Walter Lee said, while flipping a cigarette butt out on the highway. "The term 'maintenance' just means that we're keeping my big boy and her cootie cat in shape...don't want any atrophying body parts...while waiting for Mr. and Ms. Keeper!"

"Well that sounds like an interesting relationship. I'm kinda surprised that you're just telling me about this now, Quiet Lee!"

"I've been too busy listening to you and your honky heartbreak stories!" Walter Lee said laughingly.

"Well how's this then...let me entertain you still," Felix said. "I just got turned on big time, both physically and mentally, to the girl my brother has been desperately in love with!"

"Whoa...Salome?" Walter Lee asked, with an eyebrow raised.

"Yeah," Felix said. "Not only did she give me, that old army officer, Major Wood, two times, when she shoved her tits deep into my chest while hugging me and giving me one of the nicest non-tongue wet kisses that I've ever had, but after communicating from the soul with her, I've decided that she's really an exceptional girl."

"It can't be good if you want her," Walter Lee said.

"Oh...I want her alright...I'd just never do anything about it...not with my brother involved."

"What's up with the Kulpa boys...wanting this here young nookie?"

And Felix went into some shtick from a *Cheetch and Chong* album:

> *"Mr. Johnson...you've been charged with molesting this twelve year-old girl. How do you plead?"*
> *"I plead 'Insanity!' your honor!"*
> *"Insanity?"*
> *"Yeah...Insanity your honor. I'm just crazy about that young stuff!"*

"Bailiff...whack his pee-pee!"

"It wouldn't matter, even if Salome weren't jailbait, I still wouldn't make a move on somebody that my brother either loves or had loved at one time. That wouldn't be within my set of ethics," Felix said.

"I don't know," said Walter Lee, playing Devil's advocate, "There have been some great writers who have believed that moving the Earth itself isn't too much of a task...when it comes to going after someone that they truly, deeply, and thoroughly love. What's a brother...when one might have to move the Earth for that kind of love?"

"And there have been plenty of lessons learned in great literature about unethical love too," Felix said. "Whether it's planned perversity like *Dangerous Liaisons*, or a *faux pas* of fate like *Oedipus Rex*, unethical love usually gets punished. There are plenty of stories, in which brothers, or even a father and son, fight tragically over the love of the same woman. And, if one may define 'infidelity' as being 'unethical' also, it's no coincidence that Tolstoy has things not work out too well for his protagonist, Anna, in *Anna Karenina*. And even something in Contemporary Literature, like this great new novel by John Irving, *The World According to Garp*, punishes infidelity. In this story, the protagonist, Garp, has a fling with the babysitter, and the protagonist's wife, Helen, has a fling with one of her graduate students. The result? In a car accident, which is linked by the writer both metaphorically and literally to the two affairs, they lose one child, and another child has an eye put out. True, Garp and Helen manage to come together and heal later in the novel, but the author needed to take us through infidelity and its tragic multifaceted repercussions first."

"I get it," Walter Lee said. "But aren't you a hypocrite? I know you've boinked a few married women, all up there in your 'Licks lair!"

"You're right...I have....like I told you before...I had some of the best sex of my life with a married woman, on the night I found out that my father had blown his brains out!" Felix said. "I was a real piece of shit...but I've changed. I decided over a year ago, Walter Lee, to never ever involve myself with a married woman again. It's a load of bad karma!"

"I see!" said Walter Lee. "The new 'Licks. You never told me. And you called me 'Quiet Lee.' But let me ask you something, 'Licks..."

"What's that?"

"You still got that thing for Grace Slick?"

"Yeah...I've always thought that she was hot," Felix said.

"Well she's in a Common Law Marriage, and even has a kid, with one of the other group members, Paul Kantner, in *Jefferson Airplane*..."

"It's *Jefferson Starship* these days," Felix said.

"*Jefferson Starship*," Walter Lee said. "Would you still do her...if given the chance?"

"I guess...if I it were okay with Paul Kantner!" Felix said.

"Well...what if it were okay with the husband of the woman you schtupped a few years ago...the night you found out about Frank's suicide?" Walter Lee asked.

"That doesn't matter anymore. It kinda feels to me these days...if people have taken official vows...I want nothing to do with being in the middle of that...regardless of... if they encourage me to do so," Felix said.

"Well...I'll bet Paul and Grace have taken some kind of vow....even if it wasn't in a church or on the steps of city hall," Walter Lee said, enjoying his role of Devil's advocate, just a wee too much.

"You're probably right," said Felix. "I misspoke myself. I'm taking Grace off of my list...even as we speak."

"It doesn't matter," Walter Lee joked. "You're too ugly anyway. Grace Slick would never let you anywhere near her white rabbit!"

And Felix laughed as he was pulling up into the Orlonksys' driveway and said, "Whoa...dude...look into the mirror...Unphotogenic Lee!"

@@@@@@@@

The next day was Sunday, and Felix and Walter Lee both woke up in the morning around ten. Igor and Katarina Orlonsky had insisted that they stay in Port Jefferson for dinner, and it had been quite late before Felix had felt sober enough, after countless Margaritas, to drive back to The City. Felix and Walter Lee both showered quickly and headed out of *The Hilton* on 52nd Street and 6th Avenue, to walk around the Broadway District and to look for possible tickets for a show that evening or afternoon. Felix reasoned that the Sunday matinee show for that day might have more cancellation tickets available.

As they were looking along, Felix fired up a joint. "Here," he said to Walter Lee. "This will help with the hangover."

Walter Lee took a good toke and handed the joint back to Felix and said, "I wonder how things are at home."

"I called Anthony while you were in the shower," Felix said. "The first thing he asked me was if I had seen Salome at the funeral. I told him that I had, and that you had, and that the three of us had spoken for just a few minutes."

"Did he ask if it seemed as if Salome had been in love with Darius?" Walter Lee asked.

"Of course," Felix answered. "I didn't want him to have any false hope, so I told him that I thought so. But I didn't feel like getting into everything that had been said, so I didn't say whether or not Salome had confirmed my initial assessment."

"I see," said Walter Lee, who added, "Don't Bogart that joint!"

Felix took another toke and passed it to Walter Lee and said, "Anthony also said that Jack and Salome's mother, Pauline, is a wonderful person. She had Jack go to the *Publix* and get a bunch of food, and she's had Anthony up to the apartment for dinner twice."

"'Knee and Jack keeping quiet about Salome having stayed at the place in 1974?" Walter Lee asked.

"Yeah their lips are sealed. Also, apparently we had this Brazilian bombshell check in for a week with her seven year-old daughter. Anthony took a fancy to her right away, asked her out, and Pauline babysat the girl, while Jack watched the desk," Felix said.

"A Brazilian bombshell?" Walter Lee asked. "Well good for 'Knee. It's been awhile since his Bolshevik babe. I hope he got his pipes cleaned!"

Just as they turned a corner, and Walter Lee had handed the joint back to Felix, they saw a straggly-haired guy of about Felix's age, whizzing against the stoop of a brownstone in broad daylight, oblivious to the passersby. Felix took a big toke on the joint, handed it back to Walter Lee, and said, "From Woodstock Nation…to URINATION!"

That line put Walter Lee into the guffaw galaxy, and the tears of laughter began pouring from his eyes.

"Don't get the spliff all wet…Sill Lee!" Felix said, snatching the large roach from Walter Lee, and attaching a small alligator clip to it.

They continued down the block, stopping at the now-opening various Broadway box offices. When they turned south on Ninth Avenue, they spotted a young African-American child of about eight. He was dressed in his Sunday best, and he had a big blue ribbon pinned on his suit jacket. "Well LOOKEE here," Walter Lee said, "We got us an AWARD winning NIGGER!" That line nailed Felix. He was laughing so hard, he just flicked the roach out onto Ninth Avenue, put the clip in his pocket, and sat down in a plastic chair, which had been provided for the smoking customers of the laundromat in which it sat in front of.

"You can't sit there!" some Chinese guy, apparently the owner of the laundry, came out and said to Felix.

"I'm an inspector with the company that makes this chair," Felix said. "I just wanted to see if it was up to standards," and then he and Walter Lee moved along.

"Well…sheeet…Mr. Licks…at least he spoke to you. If I had sat on his fucking plastic chair, he would have called The Man!" Walter Lee said.

"Why's that?" Felix asked.

"Oh…I see…you been too busy chasing skirts to keep up with the politics, all up in these here northern cities. Well let me explain it to you. The Asians hate the blacks. They're more racist than you crackers!"

"Who you callin 'a cracker?' I live in the South, but I'm just a transplanted northern Jew-wop!" Felix said, and then he added, "Although I'm enjoying this banter…before I forget, Walter Lee, Salome wants us to go eat dinner at the Afghani restaurant where she works. She's there every night except Monday and Tuesday," Felix said.

"Let's get some breakfast," Walter Lee suggested, as they passed a little coffee shop. "All this jive talkin done got me hungry!" And then Walter Lee added, after they were seated, "How about Wednesday night?"

"That sounds cool," said Felix. "I'm leaving from JFK at 10:00 am on Friday. When's your flight back to Tampa?"

"2:00 Saturday afternoon," Walter Lee said. "I'd love for us to see a couple of shows this week," he added.

"Well…since most Broadway shows don't run on Monday, it looks as if today, Wednesday, or Thursday is about it for us," Felix said. "If we get seats for Wednesday, we'll just go to the Afghani place on Thursday night."

After they had wolfed down breakfast, they continued their quest for seats to at least one Broadway show. They finally got lucky at the *John Fiedler Theatre*. They were able to get great orchestra seats for the Thursday night performance of the Tony winning *Neville Chamberlain: The Musical*. After they scooped the tickets, Walter Lee said that he still had a headache and that he wanted to go take some aspirin and a nap. He left and headed back to the hotel, and Felix, lit another joint, and continued his trek around midtown. As Felix walked, he thought about Salome, and about youth in general. Those thoughts segued into early 1966, when he had first seen Tatiana Orlonsky.

Felix had begun his Freshman year at NYU in September of 1965. Within a month he was dating Amy, a girl he met in one of his classes. He could never remember Amy's last name, so Felix always thought of her as Amy What's-Her-Name. By March of 1966 he and Amy were finished, and Felix attended his first anti-Vietnam War Rally in Washington Square Park. It had been a definitive moment in Felix's existence, because even though theoretically Felix had agreed with his father's, step-mother's, and Walter Lee's anti-Vietnam War sentiment, at nineteen this was the instant, the epiphany, the political and personal impasse passed, in which he knew exactly where he stood. And, at the same instant, in which both Felix and Tatiana Orlonsky had been individually consumed by the dynamic speaker's presentation, their eyes had met from ten feet away, and they had also been consumed by each other. They kind of wandered together, meeting in the middle of the ten feet that had separated them, and stood and listened to the speaker. The speaker, a beautiful woman of about 5' 6" with extremely long auburn hair down between her knees and ankles, Ida Laplotski, was a student in the graduate program of Library Science at Columbia University, and she was also a staunch active member of the *Weathermen*, a radical anti-Vietnam War student organization. She was quoting from the speech of a Republican candidate for Senate in 1932, a two time Congressional Medal of Honor winner from World War I, retired Marine Corps Major General Smedley

Darlington Butler, whose speech, "War is a Racket!" which warned early about the Military-Industrial Complex in this country, had created much controversy after being delivered, in-between the end of World War I and the beginning of World War II. The speech was remarkably emotional and full of facts, and it began:

> *"War is a racket. It always has been. It is possibly the oldest, easily the most profitable, surely the most vicious racket. It is the only one in which the profits are reckoned in dollars and the losses in lives.*
>
> *A racket is best described, I believe, as something that is not what it seems to the majority of the people. Only a small 'inside' group knows what it is about. It is conducted for the benefit of the very few, at the expense of the very many. Out of war a few people make huge fortunes.*
>
> *In this last World War a mere handful garnered the profits of the conflict. At least 21,000 new millionaires and billionaires were made in the United States. That many admitted their huge blood gains in their income tax returns. How many other war millionaires falsified their tax returns no one knows.*
>
> *How many of these millionaires shouldered a rifle? How many of them dug a trench? How many of them knew what it meant to go hungry in a rat-infested dug- out? How many of them spent sleepless, frightened nights, ducking shells and shrapnel and machine gun bullets? How many of them parried a bayonet thrust of an enemy? How many of them were wounded or killed in battle?"*

After a very emotional Ida Laplotski had read all thirteen pages of Major General Butler's speech, she ended her own speech with: "Don't ever forget: Vietnam is a war, in which the white man, who stole the land from the red man, sends the black man, to go kill the yellow man!"

Ida Laplotski had literally taken Felix's breath away, but when he looked up into Tatiana's eyes he said, "Hi. I'm Felix Kulpa."

"And I'm Tatiana Orlonsky," she had replied. Thus began their relationship. They were married in a large synagogue wedding in Port Jefferson five months later, in late August of 1966, Felix was twenty, Tatiana was nineteen. Frank, Terry, Anthony, and Walter Lee had all flown up from Florida for the wedding. One of Frank Kulpa's sisters, Maria Thomas, had driven down with her husband from Plattsburgh. Maria, who had never been very close to her brother Frank, was indeed very close to her two nephews Anthony and Felix. After they were married, Felix and Tatiana honeymooned for a week in Paris. Felix had allowed Tatiana to become so entwined in his soul back then, that now, a decade later and divorced, she was still very much a suppressed living part of him. And it had been that magical speech by Ida Laplotski, that had forever grafted together, Felix's view of the world with the love of his life Tatiana Orlonsky. Felix would always remember and love Ida Laplotski for that speech, for that moment, although he had never met her. In April of 1966 Felix began writing for an East Village underground newspaper, *The Community Liberator*, under the name of "Che," and Tatiana did all of the illustrations for that paper under the name of "Frieda." In May of 1966, after they had moved in together, the FBI first called Felix and Tatiana looking for Ida Laplotski. Felix had no idea what had happened to her. He and Tatiana both told the FBI that they had never met her, and had never seen her again after her speech in Washington Square Park. In New York, at least six times, Felix would repeat that answer for the FBI. Later, in Florida, he would say the same thing a few more times. Now, in 1976, Felix still had no idea what had happened to Ida Laplotski, and he didn't know if the FBI had ever caught up with her. He had heard recently what Ida had allegedly done, why she was wanted, but the FBI hadn't told him that. They had always refused to answer that question. They would also refuse to answer how they knew exactly how to find where Felix and Tatiana lived. When they had moved into together, into their first and only place, in the East Village, they had sublet from one of Felix's friends, Michael Keigh, and he had kept the apartment in his name. Since all of the utilities except the phone were provided, no accounts had ever been opened in either Felix or Tatiana's name, and they had even used—with Michael's permission, since he had moved back with his parents in Brooklyn for awhile—his phone and phone number. Felix would always pay the phone bill monthly, by money order, in Michael's name. Yet, the FBI had known exactly where to find Felix and Tatiana. It was always a phone call at home, never a visit, and the questions were at times annoyingly personal.

Once, in late August of 1969, an Agent Shamus Scrotham asked Felix, "So who did you like better at Woodstock, *The Jimi Hendrix Experience* or *The Who*?" And Felix had said, while toking on a joint so noisily, making such loud "SWOOOSH" sounds that even an FBI tenderfoot would have to know that there must be some hootch being inhaled on the other side of the line, "*The Who* really rocked, but Jimi is my man! But hey…since you know I was at Woodstock…that must mean…that you were there also! Did you like the way that Jimi played 'The Star Spangled Banner?' Did you like *Country Joe and the Fish*'s 'Fish Song?' Did it annoy you that the brown acid was bad?"

And Agent Scrotham didn't answer. Instead he asked, "Who did Walter Lee like?"

And Felix decided to goof even more on this dickwad…to make up a bogus band…so he said, "He really loved *The Ho Chi Minh Memorial Bhang Band*, and especially their mega-hit 'The Running Dogs of Imperialism.'"

And that conversation had ended with Agent Scrotham saying, "Well…peace on you!" and then abruptly hanging up the phone.

Another time an Agent Phil Ashow asked Felix, "So when are you and Tatiana gonna have a kid?"

"Fuck you!" Felix had said, before abruptly hanging up the phone.

@@@@@@@@

And so dear journal, it's been an interesting ten days since I last saw Walter Lee. We scooped Broadway tickets on a Sunday, and the next day we saw Al Hirt at The Blue Note. Tuesday, Walter Lee went over to see Annie Harrison and he never returned to The City. I meandered around the West Village most of the day, ate a steak at dinnertime, and went to The_Bottom Line on 4th Street that evening to hear Frank Zappa. I loved the way he did "Cosmic Debris," "Saint Alphonso's Pancake Breakfast," and the twenty minute version of "Call Any Vegetable." There is no doubt, that Frank Zappa, from an earlier album, is responsible for one my favorite quotes of all time: "T.V. dinner by the pool, I'm so glad I finished school!"

On Wednesday morning I called Walter Lee about going to eat at Salome's place that night, but he said that he and Annie weren't going anywhere. I had a great 'Gani meal, Salome served me, and afterwards we went out, had a few beers, and listened to some folk music in Washington Square Park.

I called Walter Lee on Thursday morning to remind him about the play that night, and he said that he and Annie weren't going anywhere. I asked him if he wanted my ticket, to take Annie to the play. He said again that he and Annie weren't going anywhere. I called Salome to see if she could possibly take off and see the play with me. She had me call her back, and when I did, she told me that she had fixed it, that she had changed up with another waitress for the following Tuesday. I got last minute reservations for dinner at Tavern on the Green up in Central Park, so Salome and I had a nice meal with a scenic view of the park, before the show. Afterwards, we both agreed, that the show was ridiculous. If I were still in graduate school, I would have had fun writing a paper about this turkey! I mean…come on! A musical about Neville Chamberlain, the naive English Prime Minister who cut a deal with Hitler? Not only were the songs stupid, but the sets were totally underwhelming. There's a scene in which Neville is singing, "Germany is our Friend," and behind him, stage right, there's a wall with a big hole in it with "THIS WAY TO ENGLAND" painted over the hole. And as Chamberlain sings, apparently unbeknownst to him, Nazi soldiers keep goose-stepping from stage left to stage right and going through the hole…apparently heading to England. And they must have been horribly under-budgeted in this grandiose production, because the same Nazis keep making their way, behind the curtain, back to stage left to goosestep yet again to stage right. Walter Lee and I both had had misgivings about this play right from jump, but we were Johnnie-Come-Latelys, so we took what we could get. Anyway, after the show, Salome and I headed down to Little Italy for a deca-

dent dessert. Even with the stupid play, what a great evening. Phew! Salome is something else! It's too bad...

I was NYC history at 10:00 am on Friday from JFK, so I called Walter Lee from the terminal at 9:00, to take my leave of him. (Hey...what do you want...I'm heading to England...I need to practice up on my English!) A groggy Walter Lee answered the phone and said that he and Annie weren't going anywhere. I said good-bye, and told him I was on the way to Limey Land, and that he shouldn't forget his flight to Tampa the next day. Again he told me that he and Annie weren't going anywhere. Note to self: check on Walter Lee later today or tomorrow!

Nothing interesting to report about the JFK terminal experience this time, and the old man I sat next to on the plane, slept for most of the six hour trip. I sat next to the window, taking all six hours to reread the 454 pages of my unpublished novel, "All the Seats Were Occupied." I read the novel pretending I was reading it as Tatiana. I think all writers do that. You write for someone in particular, and then imagine the face and thoughts of that person while that person is perusing through what you've written.

I had a nice room reserved at The Ambassador, at Quayside, with a great view of the Thames, but it was after midnight early Saturday morning before I finally got to the room, so I ended up crashing until two o'clock the next afternoon. On Saturday I went to Westminster Abbey to see Poet's Corner, but that section was closed on weekends. So I just walked around London. On Sunday, I was in Hyde Park sitting on a bench at the place where people deliver diatribes, "Speaker's Corner," when I heard her. This nice looking, well-endowed blonde in her mid-thirties, ranting on about the United States' new concept, called "Limited Nuclear War." She was explaining, just what that meant, that it might be feasible for the United States and the Soviet Union to fight a nuclear war in Europe, thereby lessoning the chances of the bombs making their way back to the United States and the Soviet Union. "Fuck the United States!" she said. "If they think they can escape from the fate that they may cause in Europe."

After her speech I just had to talk to her, so I went up and introduced myself. She told me that her name was Miep Van Kreneek, she was Dutch, currently living in Paris, and on vacation for the week in London. I invited her out for a meal, she agreed, and we ate and discussed everything from rock music to politics. We didn't even notice that almost three hours had passed while we were in the restaurant. Not only did Miep speak English perfectly, with very little of a Dutch accent, but it turned out that she taught Dutch and English at the University of Paris. She said that she was aware of an available position there, for someone who could teach Victorian Literature and who had a rudimentary knowledge of French. Although I didn't come to Europe looking for a job, I did come with the idea that I was going to allow the wind to just blow me, in whichever direction it happened to be blowing. She told me that a friend of hers had loaned her a car, and asked if I'd like to take a drive with her the next day, to Norwich, a coastal town about two hours northeast of London. I said, "Why not?"

So the next day we headed to Norwich. The minute we were outside of the city of London, I reached inside of my trousers and pulled out a couple of joints from the twenty or so I had rolled in NYC and stashed in a baggie, wrapped in three more baggies, with a layer of Bounce separating the second baggie from the third—just in case some pot-smelling dog had gotten too close to my ass at Heathrow! Since we weren't crossing any borders, I stashed the rolled up bag(s) of joints in my pants pocket. We got pretty baked on the way to Norwich. Which reminds me of a joke: "Why did the Siamese twins move to England?" And the answer, "So the other one could drive for a change!" I found the sensation, of being the passenger on the American driver's side of the car, pretty weird. I was glad that Miep knew exactly what she was doing.

At Norwich, we stayed at a friend of Miep's, Anneke de Stataan, a Dutch woman from Amsterdam, who had grown up with Miep. They had graduated the same year from the same high school, and they were both thirty-three. Anneke had some cocaine, it seemed liked the same ether-based stuff that Salome had back in New York, and I got rocked during the next few hours. Anneke left the living room, and a few minutes later she called to Miep from the bedroom. Miep went into the bedroom, and I lit a cigarette and flipped on the Tellie. I was watching a BBC special called, "The Importance of Storage Jars," when I heard the sounds of female moaning coming from the bedroom. Suddenly Winky said, "Aw shit! It looks as if we're not wanted here!" A little while later Miep called out from the bedroom, "If you're hungry, would you like a sandwich?" And thinking that about the last thing I wanted at that moment was food, I said, "No thanks." And Miep said, "Oh, that's too bad. Anneke and I thought that you might like to come in here and make a sandwich!" And Winky woke right up and said, "What are you waiting for Round Boy?" What an incredible afternoon/evening/night/middle of the night/next morning/next afternoon. I had jumped into bed with two women before, but I had never tried Double Dutch. I finally got around to calling Walter Lee the next afternoon, and all he said was, "Me and Annie aren't going anywhere."

Later that afternoon, Miep said that I had to leave for a couple of hours, that there was somebody coming over that I couldn't meet. That sounded a little dubious. I hoped it wasn't a husband, and that Miep had been straight with me when she had said that she wasn't married. She also had said that Anneke was divorced, and that her ex-husband lived in San Francisco. So I walked around Norwich for a few hours, and when I got back to Anneke's place, Miep had already packed our bags and she said, "We must return to London tonight!" Hey…I was Mr. No Agenda…just passing through…so I said, "Okay." We said our goodbyes to Anneke, and we headed back to London.

When we had driven a few blocks from Anneke's, Meip said, "So are you gonna come to Paris, take the job, share my place, pay half the bills, and be my lover for the year?"

And I said, "Well that sounds great, but I have to return to Florida by the end of next March…it's a promise…so I can't take a job for the whole year."

And Miep said, "The end of March is when the Spring vacation begins. So you won't tell them that you have to leave then, but when that time approaches, you'll feign some kind of a family emergency. They'll be able to find an incompetent substitute for the last two months of school."

"That really wouldn't be fair to my students," I said.

"Well…Just make sure to teach them everything that you think is important, but just cram it all in between September and March…"

"Yeah…well…that could be done," I said. "But I know Paris fairly well, I was hoping to see a lot more of Europe during these eight months."

"So be a typical European," Miep said. "Coming from the United States, you probably don't realize just how small Europe is. You can come live and work with me in Paris, and every weekend we can go to a different country."

And that idea seemed appealing to me. Then I said, "I didn't come with much pot, because I figured that I would just cop a few weeks worth—legally—in Amsterdam. Then I figured, wherever I went in Europe, I would just return every few weeks to Amsterdam to cop again. I'll need to go there pretty soon."

"I have a little pot at my place in Paris," Miep said. "And we can go to Amsterdam this weekend if you like. But I need to head back to Paris, after we return the car to London."

"Wouldn't it be easier to just head to Amsterdam before going to Paris?" I asked her.

"Are you going to come to Paris with me, and be my lover, partner, and friend for the year?" Miep asked again. "Because I need to know that, before I'm gonna say anymore. If you're not interested, I'll be happy to drop you off at the next town, at either the train or bus station."

And I said to myself, 'Self…Miep's pretty easy on the eyes, and she's incredible in bed, and she obviously likes women, which means that I probably won't be limited sexually to just her, and the job sounds nice, and the weekend trips around Europe sound great, and I do love Paris.' "Okay," I said. And then I added, "You keep saying, 'for the year.' What if it turns out that we have such a good thing going, we want it to continue longer?"

And Miep said, "I know it will only last a year. I feel that inside."

"Okay than," I said. "For a year! For eight months!"

"For eight months then!" Miep said. Then she pulled the car over to the side of the road, popped open the trunk, unzipped her suitcase, and showed me the kilo of cocaine that was well packed inside.

"Wholly shit!" I said. "How much coke is that?"

"A kilo," she said.

"You realize in England that's probably a Life Sentence?" I asked.

"It's pretty bad getting caught with this amount," Miep admitted. "But the profits…I've got a real sweet deal going here. About every three months, my friend in London, the one who loaned me this car, gives me the cash for a kilo of cocaine. Anneke in Norwich has the buying connection. That's why you had to leave for a cou-

ple of hours. He came over and we did business, but he never wants to meet anybody besides Anneke and myself. And it took four of these deals before he was willing to meet me."

"I see," I said, as we got back into the car and took off.

"It's too sweet of a deal to pass up," Miep said. "The coke is so pure, I'm able to charge 1500 quid more per kilo than it costs me. Anneke and I split that. Also, first we take out two ounces of pure, then we're able to walk on the rest of the kilo…with two ounces of Mannitol…they never even know…it's such high quality stuff. So, every three months or so, Anneke and I each make 750 quid plus an ounce of pure cocaine. And I don't have to go across any country's border to do it! Like I said, it's a sweet deal!"

And I thought to myself, 'Coke, cash, cootie cat, and companionship on The Continent. Not a bad deal.'

"I want to drop this kilo off in London with the car, and then get my ounce to Paris. I don't want to go anywhere near Holland with an ounce of coke, because as little as they care about pot or hash, their jail sentences for coke are triple the harshness of any other European country."

"I understand," I said. And then Miep pulled a little device called a "bullet" out from her pocket. It had a few grams of cocaine in it, and it could be adjusted to administer the same amount of product with each snort. We hit that bullet all the way back to London. We dropped the car off, took a cab to the ferry, took the ferry to the train, and took another cab from the train station to the beautiful Paris condo that Miep was renting from a family friend, in the Montparnasse Quarter on Rue Ledion, between the Porte de Versailles and the Porte d'Orleans.

We just finished another love fest on her bed, the sheets got all funky and need to be changed, and Miep is showering—she has this thing about showering alone—as I sit here, pen in hand. And so dear journal, depending on how my interview goes, it looks as if I'm back in Tatiana Land for a spell…yet again.

And you know dear journal, what's really kind of ironic, is that Tatiana always criticized me for hating parties. She always liked meeting new people that way, but I always hated being in a place surrounded by strangers, and being forced to mix and mingle. And yet, without that kind of staged, phony, "Alright everybody…it's 9:00…it's time for the party to officially begin" pressure, I absolutely adore, being on a vacation, and meeting new people, like the way I just met two interesting people, Miep and Anneke. Somehow, meeting new people, just inadvertently, out in real life, in different situations, and "relying on the kindness of strangers," is just so much more my style.

@@@@@@@@

In December of 1976, sixteen year-old Salome returned to Rutland for Jimson and Lizzie's wedding. And although she was still pissed at everyone in the family, Salome no longer showed anything but cool when in their company. She wasn't really that angry with her mother anymore, she hadn't stopped calling her on Sunday evenings at 7:00, and Salome had come to understand, that since the sickness had been her mother's, her mother kind of had the right to call the shots. Salome, still annoyed with Bubba, understood his motivation, as her mother's husband, to do what his wife had requested. Salome also had forgiven Selma, realizing that Selma had tried to handle everything to everyone's, including her own, best interest. Selma had cried, when Salome, calling from The City, had asked if it was still alright if she stayed at Selma's house. "How can you ask me that?" Selma asked. Most of Salome's anger was aimed at her siblings, Dick, and Bubba. She felt that her brothers and sisters, perhaps with the exception of Jack, had always treated her as an inferior. Her brother-in-law Dick was just an asshole, and she still didn't forgive Bubba for having broken her jaw.

"I KNOOOW you don't want to talk to MEEE," Bubba said, as he walked by Salome in the backyard of *The Burlington Manor*. I just want to SAAAY, although you HAAATE me, I'm very proud of YOUUU!"

"Thanks Bubba," Salome spit out quickly, and then she walked away.

Cindy walked over to Bubba and said, "She still won't forgive you, huh Bubba?"

"NOOO," Bubba kind of half said and half cried. "SHEEE probably won't EEEVEN after I DIIIE!"

"Well Bubba, she'll grow up and get over it. Look, with some of the shit that she's pulled, that we've all had to forgive...Eventually, she'll learn that forgiveness is a two-way street." And Bubba just nodded and walked away.

Salome stood talking with Jimson and Lizzie. "Oh...that's alright," Salome said to Jimson. "I understand now. Mom made you not tell me."

"That's right!" Jimson said.

'Yeah...well...I wonder just how big that gun was that Mom stuck to your head? You know...the one that made you do something that you really didn't want to do?' Salome felt like saying but didn't. Instead she just smiled and walked away. Salome had snorted a few lines of cocaine, and she had drunk a couple of glasses of wine, but she refused to let herself become as blitzed as she was at Jennifer and Colin's wedding. She was sick of being this dysfunctional family's fodder, and to that avail, Salome had decided before the wedding to keep things at a minimum partying-wise. 'And I don't care if it is their wedding,' Salome thought, since she hadn't offered Jimson and Lizzie any cocaine this time, 'they can pay for it like everybody else.'

And, of course, Salome never paid for her cocaine, at least not with money. Gustav had given it to her free, while he had found her interesting in bed. About a month ago his interest had waned however, when he had gone ga ga over some German girl he met while getting a gin and tonic at *The Gramercy Park Hotel*'s bar. Fortunately for Salome, as Gustav's interest waned, his brother Han's interest waxed. So, along with a 3.4 for her third semester in college, Salome now had a new boyfriend.

"Hope...you forgot...your underwear again," a drunk Dick came by and just had to say to Salome.

And Salome thought for a moment about just saying 'Fuck You!' and walking away, but then she decided against that. That would be too easy. This asshole needed to hear a few things. And today, since she had controlled herself with the mood altering substances, Salome decided to use her brains instead of her guts in the response. "I really hope you enjoyed last July's presentation of my naked ass and vagina," she said, while touching herself. "And although my sister, Cindy can be very attractive when she chooses, I know that you're a closet pedophile Dick, and that you've always wanted me. You love my long red hair...you can just imagine me wrapping it around your cock, can't you? Ummm...that's good...isn't it? And you love my nice firm tits, with their silver dollar nipples...don't you? You'd love to put them in your mouth...wouldn't you? And you can see yourself doing things with my mouth and with my other orifices...can't you Dick? Ah...that's so good. So just remember Dick, when you take your wife to bed for the thousandth time, and it's good but you're kinda bored...just remember, that you'll never, ever be able to touch this luscious body, and that if given the choice between you and the rest of the animal world...I would rather fuck a pig!"

@@@@@@@@

And so dear journal, today has been very strange. I'm a lucky boy...kind of. Today is January 17, 1977, and my novel has been out in Paris, Lyon, and Nice for six whole weeks! I'm lucky, because it finally got published...in French! Over here it's called, "Tous Les Sieges Etaient Occupés," and they gave me the equivalent of about $750 American dollars as an advance. The problem is, my publishing company has no sister affiliates anywhere in the English-speaking world, so the chances of Anthony, Walter Lee, or any other non-French speaking person I know reading this are nil. However, it was a different matter with the totally- fluent-in-French Tatiana, and with my old French-speaking buddy—the one from whom, years ago, Tatiana and I had sublet our East Village place— Michael Keigh. I sent Michael a copy of the novel a month ago, and I expected to hear from him soon. He was a busy financial wizard these days.

When I saw Tatiana at a little café on Rue de Poe, she flew out of her chair, hugged and kissed me, and said, "Congratulations Felix! You did it! I figured you must be in Paris doing book signings and lectures. I've been looking through the paper daily, hoping I'd find somewhere in public where I could see you."

"Well, nobody considers the novel significant enough yet, to have me do that stuff," I said.

"Well I'm sure that will change as more people read it, " Tatiana said, and then she added, "I thought it was incredible!"

I had gotten her recent address from the Orlonskys on Long Island, and I had sent her a copy a month ago, but I still gulped and felt the need to ask, "You read it?"

"Of course! And thank you for dedicating it to me," she said.

I guess there's no feeling for a writer quite like knowing, that the person for whom he has written, has read and enjoyed the story. Some unpublished novelists will send their chapters out piecemeal to friends and family, because novel writing is a long, lonely, and arduous process, and an artist needs a little gratification every once in awhile. A painter can whip out a marvelous painting, in most cases in a very short time, and say, "See what I've been working on!" And his friends, family, and critics will either like it, hate it, or pretend that they like it. Even a short story or a poem is usually available for perusal within a few days, a few weeks, or a few months. But a novel…that usually takes a few years. And since most people think that one is being pretentious when one says, "I'm writing a novel," and since most people usually smile and think, "Sure you are buddy!" it takes a man or woman of true steel to work in obscurity for a few years with only the inner voice to guide. Fortunately, I was one of those people. When I think of how hard it was, how often I wanted to show what I was writing to my brother, my surrogate father and best friend, and especially to Tatiana, and how I fought those impulses…I'm kinda amazed at myself! I never let anybody read any part of the story as it was being written, but I did show Walter Lee and Anthony a few of my more clever journal entries—which did eventually make their way into the book. And, of course, this is no longer an issue once a novelist has had a novel published. Then nobody except the editor gets to read anything new until it's published.

"I can't tell you how pleased I am that you liked my story," I said to Tatiana.

"Your protagonist, Joyce Bloom, is a very strong and well defined character," Tatiana said. "I love the dream she has…what is it, in Chapter Three?…in which she can't see herself in the mirror…because her fear gets in the way…and then Joyce becomes a mirror…and the personified fear tells Joyce that it can't see itself in her either!"

"Thank you," I said.

"Although, with some of Joyce's indecision, in regards to her man and whether she should stay or not, it kinda felt like you were taking a shot at me! Were you taking a shot at me, Felix?"

"Maybe at some levels…I mean, you hurt me, and I'm a writer, so what did you expect? But what I didn't do is to create the Joyce character to be you, so that I could run her through just some thinly veiled fiction and make her look stupid. I've taken material from my life, my family's life, and my life with you, and I've spread it all over the place. I mean…what are any of us, but the sum product of our physical and emotional experiences? The hurt, angst, and humor from my life, gets all mixed up into a gigantic stew. And then when I write, as I develop characters, this stew mixture just spews itself out in various forms. There are times when the males in my story are saying things that I've heard females say. Conversely, do you remember

that whole part of Chapter Seven, when Joyce releases her religious angst on her father? Well that came from a piece of dialogue that Walter Lee had told me that he had had with his mother when she was alive. So no…I didn't take any specific shots at you. I didn't start that novel with the intent of ripping you a new one. Yet my being was so overloaded with hurt, from my mother leaving when I was eleven and never having gotten back in contact with me, from you leaving what we had three different times, from my father's suicide, and for something else, that I've never told you about, happening when I was fifteen. That hurt had to manifest itself somehow and somewhere through my characters. But don't ever forget…Joyce isn't really you. She's me. Every character in that novel is me. I didn't do anything in this novel that every other writer hasn't done before. I took my life experiences, and I wrote a story. The difference is, you don't know the personal lives of other writers, but you do know mine, so it seems more like autobiography to you."

"I understand," Tatiana said.

And changing the subject, I asked, "How are things going with you and Professor Hugo?"

And that caused Tatiana's countenance to change immediately, "We're not getting along at the moment. As a matter of fact, he moved in with his brother."

"Do you want to talk about it?" I asked.

"You know…you're probably the exact person with whom I should talk," Tatiana said. "Because a big chunk of the problem I'm having with Ralph, is that he wants a child."

"And you can't have children," I said, and that caused Tatiana to put her head down on the table and to cry. I immediately walked behind her, and kind of semi-held her in her chair, as I rubbed her shoulders.

"You were always so understanding about that!" she sobbed.

"Well, you knew that I always wanted a child, but for me, you were the love of my life. So the primary relationship with you was more important than having a baby. I had always thought that we'd probably adopt a child or two one day."

"And you knew that I was open to that idea," Tatiana said.

"Yeah."

"Ralph doesn't want to adopt. And it isn't as if I tricked him, that I let him fall in love with and marry me without telling him that I couldn't have children."

"I know."

"You know, Felix, I think about you a lot. I can't believe that I always had this wanderlust, that I just couldn't stay put with you. I don't know why I wasn't happy, because I do know, that I've never loved anyone like I love you. I wish I knew why I've had to hurt you," Tatiana said.

"I wish I knew too."

"Let's go make love, Felix," Tatiana said. "It'll be like old times."

And, of course, as hard as it had been, for me not to show friends and family, chapters of my novel as I was writing it, it was even harder for me to say, to the five foot four inch, well-endowed, continental-nosed, shoulder-length black haired, blue-

eyed, angelic-looking, love of my life, Tatiana Orlonsky Kulpa Hugo, on January 17, 1977, "I'm flattered that you still want me, and you know that I love you as I have never loved nor will ever love another woman. But I don't fool around with married women. Not even married women who were once married to me."

Chapter Nine

Thursday, May 19, 1977 was a day that had begun ordinarily enough. In New York City, Salome was sleeping in. She had worked at the restaurant last night, and a late party had detained her until a few minutes after one o'clock. A day earlier, Salome had finished her fourth and last semester at BMCC. This had been her best academic semester yet, a 3.8 GPA she figured, after having grilled her professors about her grades before they were posted; that would put Salome's cumulative GPA for her first two years of college work at 3.6. She had applied to NYU in February for admittance in September into the College of Arts and Science, and in early April she had been notified of her acceptance. As a backup plan, Salome had also applied to and been accepted by CUNY, the agency who decides which university in New York City one will attend. They had assigned Salome to Hunter College on 68th Street and Lexington Avenue in Manhattan, but they had also given her the option of Queens College in Flushing. Finally, Salome also had been accepted by the University of Vermont in Burlington. Salome's plan was to work fulltime at *Khyber Pass* for the summer until late August, and then Hans had promised her a two week vacation with him to Germany. Salome had no interest in attending her own graduation, and she had opted to check the "will not attend" box, when the questionnaire had arrived with a return stamped envelope in her Flushing post office box.

Cindy had phoned Pauline earlier this morning from Plattsburgh to tell her that her classes in Nursing at Plattsburgh State were going well, and that Dick was thinking about joining the Plattsburgh chapter of AA, because he had promised that he would no longer be drinking by the birth of their second child. Pauline, who was getting ready for a few hours of apple pie baking, and had the phone cradled between her shoulder and ear as she bent over from the dining room chair to tie her shoe, stopped in the middle of making the knot and asked, "What? Did I hear you correctly?" And Cindy had told her mom that indeed, there was another Chumwell on the way. Little Tonya Chumwell could now expect a special Christmas present, and the name of that present would be either Karla or Dick Jr. Cindy had asked Pauline if she could give Bubba the news herself, and Pauline had alerted him of his need to pick up the phone with the loud **QUACKKK!** of the duck caller, just before he walked out to open up *The Apple House* for the day.

Jimson and Lizzie Apple, sitting at a wooden picnic table on the porch of the small house they had recently purchased, were having coffee and discussing the possibility of having a baby sooner rather than later. This was the same house on Main Street next to the public library that they had been renting, and the previous owners had cut Jimson and Lizzie a sweet deal. Both Jimson and Lizzie, like Salome, just had finished their final semesters of community college for an Associates Degree, but unlike Salome, they were both excited about the pomp-and-circumstance-in-cap-and-gown show, soon approaching on the following Saturday at Rutland Community College. Lizzie was working fulltime for the summer at the library next door, and she had been accepted as a junior in the School of Education at UVM in Burlington for September. Lizzie wanted to be a high school Social Studies Teacher. Jimson was working fulltime for the summer at the orchard. Also, he was studying for the Vermont State Correctional Officer/Prison Guard Examination coming up on a Saturday morning in June in the auditorium of the Chittenden County Correctional Center. Jimson, having struggled academically for two years, and having barely squeaked by—mostly due to Lizzie's paper writing skills and her ability to push him and to help him study for tests—had decided against any further academic frustration, electing instead either to luck out with a state job or just to work for Bubba indefinitely.

Jack was just finishing his last week at Tampa Bay Technical Institute in Clearwater, Florida, and he had already been hired fulltime by *Tampa Bay Refrigeration*, the company with whom he had been working part-time, to begin immediately at 42K yearly. In 1977, in St. Petersburg, Florida, forty-two thousand dollars a year was a very good starting salary for most professions. Jack had accepted the offer, with the proviso that there be a thirty day delay before he had to begin. Jack wanted to cruise on his *Harley* out West for a little R and R first. Fred Wadkins, the owner of *Tampa Bay Refrigeration*, had raised his eyebrow when he heard that, because this was the start of his busy season, but then remembering what a good employee Jack Apple was, he quickly acquiesced to Jack's demand. When Jack would return at the end of June, he would be given his own company van equipped with a two-way radio. And, like the other refrigeration techs in the company, Jack would be allowed to drive the van home at the end of the work day. But the most important thing in Jack's world at the moment, was that the frequency of communication with Geneva Liberty had increased to several letters and several phone calls monthly. Geneva would be staying with her aunt and uncle in Los Angeles for the entire month of June, and unbeknownst to her, Jack would be riding his *Harley* all the way out West I-10 to surprise her there.

Jennifer and Doc Colin were very much in love and they were preparing for the summer arrival of his children. The joint custody deal that Dr. Morgan had struck with his ex involved the two children staying in New York City for the next two years, in which his son would graduate junior high, and his daughter would graduate elementary school. The children would then spend the following three years with their father and step-mother in Rutland, graduate high school and junior high school respectively, and then the son would head off to college and the daughter would return for three years in Manhattan to finish high school while living with her mother. Summers were to be alternated, with the parent who didn't have the children for the lion's share, still getting two weeks in the summer with them anyway. And all holidays were alternated. A few months after their marriage, when all of the new construction gremlins had finally been exorcised, Jennifer and Colin had moved into their beautiful wood, stone, and glass five-bedroom four-bathroom home. The house had been built on seven acres of land, and it was situated twelve miles west of Rutland directly on Lake Bomoseen. And recently, Jennifer and Colin had purchased an old Victorian house on West Street in downtown Rutland that they had converted into *The Woman's Center*. Dr. Morgan's office was moved there, and Jennifer, who had just completed her Nurse Practitioner Program on weekends at UVT in Burlington, now ran the center. She could handle most of the medical problems, and, by law, she could write prescriptions for females. The more difficult problems were given appointments with her husband. On this morning, Jennifer was at *The Woman's Center* and Colin was making grand rounds at Rutland General Hospital.

Bruiser, using one of the Apple family's trucks, picked up his partner Jr. Liberty in front of his place, just south of Rutland on Deep Hollow Road. He jumped out of the driver's seat and Jr. jumped in.

"Did you chow down?" Jr. asked Bruiser.

"Nah…I had some toast. Jesus Christ…the smell of the bacon was making me sick this morning!"

"I had some *Post Raisin Bran*," Jr. said. "It's strictly cereal, milk, and sugar in the a.m. for this Brother," Jr. added.

Bruiser had made slightly less than eight thousand dollars and a year's worth of stash in both 1974 and 1975 from growing marijuana alone. And although, as a sideline, this might satisfy some pot aficionados, Bruiser had discovered, as many small pot growers do, that greedy desire for more. It was so simple; if he increased his planting he would increase his profits. His pot, which kept coming from clones of the original *Maui Wowie* he had grown in 1974, just kept getting better and better with each new generation. He had named his boo "Western Vermont Wacky Weed," and it had already garnered quite a reputation. It had become the darling of the fraternity houses at both UVT in Vermont and at Plattsburgh State University in New York. And although Bruiser had commanded one hundred dollars per ounce from the few distributors he knew well and trusted, an amount that was nearly three times of what an ordinary thirty-five dollar commercial ounce of marijuana had been going for, nobody complained. In fact, Jr. Liberty, who had been one of those distributors in previous years, and who always called Bruiser's pot "That Thing"—"Hey man…you got any more of That Thing?"—had told Bruiser that one hundred dollars an ounce wholesale to him was no problem, because he had no problem selling the stuff at two hundred dollars an ounce retail. Whereas two people would split a spliff of commercial weed and get a mild buzz and still be able to function, Bruiser's pot was so good, just two tokes put the user in la la land and looking for a place to take a nap. (A year later in 1978, upon hearing about his pot growing adventures first alone and then with Jr. Liberty, Felix would suggest to Bruiser that he and Jr. should have named their marijuana "Kettle." Bruiser would ask, "'Kettle?' Why 'Kettle?'" Bruiser would add, "Jesus Christ…that's a stupid name!" And, of course, Felix would say, "Because then every time that Jr. mentioned the name of your marijuana…it would be the black calling the pot Kettle!")

Last year, Bruiser had decided to ask Jr. to be his partner. Bruiser had figured it out mathematically, that with a partner, even after the partner took his half, there would still be considerably more money than by working alone. Bruiser had also decided that he liked the idea of someone watching his back. When he went bear hunting, he never just took his dogs and went alone. What if he hurt himself at the orchard and was in no physical shape to water the desperately thirsty and hidden plants? He needed someone who knew where everything was. It had just seemed wiser to Bruiser to have a partner, so he had approached Jr. and Jr. had readily accepted.

Jr. and Geneva Liberty lived with their retired grandparents on their grandparents' nonworking farm. Both grandparents were too old and frail to make it down the rickety wooden steps into the basement of the barn anymore, so that had become Bruiser and Jr.'s grow room. Just in case Gramps did open the door to the basement and peer in however, Bruiser and Jr. had cleverly constructed a lightproof wall that separated the first twelve feet of the basement from the rest. Behind that wall, through a secret removable piece of wall paneling, sat row upon row of little baby plants, all growing in little dirt cups, under the eight foot long florescent tube lights.

Bruiser and Jr. had set the tubes just a few inches above the plants, and by using cable around the ends of the tubes and by hammering nails higher and higher in the 2X4's that held the tubes, they were able to raise the lighting as the plants grew taller. Bruiser and Jr. had also installed a quiet dehumidifier. This climate controlled grow room had given the pot growing season a head start last year. The plants had been nearly eight inches high by the third week in May, when Bruiser and Jr. had transplanted them outdoors. In the northern state of Vermont, known for its harsh winters and regularly extended cold springs, one had to wait until around the third week in May before one could be reasonably comfortable that there would be no more new plant killing frosts for a while.

Last year, Bruiser and Jr. had ended up with slightly more than two hundred fully budded seedless female plants, in various sizes, when they had harvested Labor Day weekend. After losing water weight when the plants had dried, and leaf weight after they had manicured all of the chlorophyll-tasting shade leaves—what growers call "sucker" leaves, because they add weight but subtract aesthetics—off of each dried plant, Bruiser and Jr. still had made slightly more than twenty thousand dollars and a year's worth of stash each. This year they were going for it, they were going to become even bigger entrepreneurs. This year they wanted five hundred plants in the ground. For cloning purposes, they had taken nearly seven hundred cuttings. All of these cuttings had come from their best female plants, which genetically assured only great females for the next season. They had dipped a portion of each cutting in *Root X*, a product that promoted grow root growth. If a plant were to come from a cutting, a grow root would be needed first. Nearly six hundred of those cuttings had produced a grow root and had been placed individually in a small paper cup with topsoil. And from those original six hundred cups, nearly five hundred and thirty had survived.

A month ago, Bruiser and Jr. had already scoped out, in a thirty mile circumference, deep in the Bread Loaf Mountains, the new locations where this year's product was going to be grown. They had five areas, all near a water source, four or five miles apart, divided each into two sections, about one mile apart, divided into two patches, about a quarter of a mile apart. Each area would have approximately one hundred plants, each section fifty of those plants, and each patch twenty-five. Two weeks ago, they had spent several days digging the holes and preparing them with time released plant food. Last week they had transplanted into four of the five areas. Today they were finishing up in Area 5, which was where Bruiser had grown his original 1974 and 1975 crop alone. They hadn't used Area 5 last year.

Many years later, in the late 1990's, Felix would write in his journal: *According to what Bruiser Apple told me in 1978, it is fairly easy to see the difference between a male and female marijuana plant. Male plants are not any good for smoking, however, male plants are quite excellent for making rope, clothes, and paper products. As a matter of fact, male marijuana plants could be used as an intelligent substitute for trees in the making of all paper products, which would eliminate most of the damage that lumber companies do by greedily over clear cutting the land—regardless of the clever ads those lumber companies produce to try to convince us otherwise. And economically-speaking, production of paper products using male marijuana would cost about one-tenth of what logging trees cost. And clothes? Although the sight of a Dixie cotton field might still conjure up a romantic picture for some, male marijuana could totally replace cotton. The United States government has been experimenting with both male and female marijuana plants in Oxford, Mississippi for years, and surely their horticulturalists must know, that in the same way a good female plant can be cloned for a better high, a good male plant can be cloned for a better paper and cloth product.*

Bruiser had already been at Jr.'s place this morning at four o'clock to pick up the plants, the same procedure they had used last week, as it was safer to load the truck when Jr.'s grandparents were asleep. Bruiser had put the topper on the pick up last week, and like last week, he had taped black garbage bags on the inside to cover the two windows in the topper. They had then loaded the baby plants in the truck bed in plastic milk crates, and tied the milk crates with rope to the heavy diesel generator that Bubba insisted stay in the bed of this truck at all times. When the topper wasn't on the truck, the truck remained in the barn.

Bruiser had then returned home to eat some toast, and to remind Bubba that he was using the truck in Burlington all day, still running errands for his guide business, as he had been allegedly doing all last week.

"Well...then TAAAKE the CRAAATE of parts...for the sorter...from the barn...and mail them back to TENNESSEEE from the Burlington Post Office. It will TAAAKE two days less if they're mailed from there, and TAAAKE two days less until...WHYYY JEEESUS CHRIIIST...they figure out how to send the RIIIGHT parts back here this TIIIME!" Bubba had said with his usual annoyance at breakfast.

This had presented a problem for Bruiser. Oh sure, there was still enough room in the bed of the truck for the crate, but the closest he had really planned on getting to Burlington today was about an hour south. 'Jesus Christ,' he thought. 'I'm gonna have to make that miserable trip when Jr. and I are done. And I'll be damned if I'm heading south first to drop him off and then doubling back, so Jr. is gonna have to make that B.S. trip too!' "No problem Bubba," is all that Bruiser had said.

When they got to the Four Corners Road, about eight miles south of Middlebury, Jr. made the right turn. Immediately a stone flew up from the dirt and rock road mixture and put a chip in the windshield of the truck. "Well I'll be a son of a bitch!" Bruiser said. "Now I'm gonna have to hear Bubba yell about the windshield."

"Sorry," Jr. said. He was driving the Apple truck, since it was his turn to drop off Bruiser at Section 1 in Area 5 first, and to use the better hiding place for the truck before he tended to his own section. He would pick Bruiser up at the original disembarkation point exactly three hours later.

"It's not your fault," Bruiser said. "It's just Murphy's Law!"

When they arrived at Section 1, Bruiser's took from the bed of the truck his three milk crate's worth of plants, fifty-three to be exact, and six empty plastic one gallon milk containers for gathering water. The arduous task now was to trek about a half mile in through the forest to the first patch, all while carrying three milk crate's worth of plants in dirt filled paper cups, plus six empty gallon milk containers. It couldn't be done. So Bruiser at this section, as well as Jr. at his, would have to double back for everything and make the half mile trip twice. Bruiser would plant half of those plants at the first patch, and then 1/4 mile away, he would plant the second patch. The water source was in the middle of his patches, 1/8 mile from each.

Bruiser, after completing his Herculean tasks, made it back to the pick up point about ten minutes early. While he was sitting waiting for Jr., he suddenly saw a bear cub playing in the brush about five feet away to his right. Knowing bears as he did, knowing that mama bear couldn't be too far away, Bruiser immediately popped the button on the holster of his .041 *Blackhawk Magnum*. He was licensed to carry this weapon, and whenever he went into the woods the gun went with him. He used a rifle to actually hunt bear as a business, but he always wore the handgun for personal protection. Bruiser was a southpaw, so he holstered his gun on the left side. He was in the process of removing his gun from its holster, when mama bear, with a grandiose growl, came storming out from the trees to the left of Bruiser. She was so fast Bruiser had no chance to finish withdrawing his gun. Bruiser knew better than to try and run, so he quickly curled himself up into a ball and tried to look more like an old log than a potential adversary to mama bear. Mama bear was no fool; this creature was a threat to her baby. She attacked him from the left side. Bruiser was pushed over to the right, the huge brown bear ripping him apart. The feeling of knives being jabbed into his flesh from his neck down to his leg was so excruciating, Bruiser's pain sensors went on instantaneous overload. Then momma bear, with a nonchalant strut, left him for her baby in the brush. Bruiser managed to spring back up to a sitting position, and when he did, he noticed that his left arm, from just above the elbow was missing. And although shock was already setting in, Bruiser reached around for the gun with his right hand, withdrew it and fired off a round. He managed to graze mama bear just across her back, and he saw blood on her coat before she ran off with her baby. Bruiser quickly pulled the belt out from the top of his jeans, and he managed to make a tight tourniquet around his left stump just before he passed out.

When Jr. Liberty pulled up a few minutes later, what he saw was a grisly sight. He found Bruiser, and upon seeing his mangled left side with the belt tied around the stump, he immediately vomited. It was obvious to Jr. that Bruiser had been attacked by a bear. Jr. saw that Bruiser was still breathing, and then he noticed that Bruiser's left arm was about ten feet away in the underbrush. He also saw that broken milk crates and squashed milk containers were scattered everywhere. And although he was struggling with his own emotions, Jr. managed to walk over to the underbrush covering the arm, remove the underbrush, take off his own shirt, wrap Bruiser's arm in it, and then put the wrapped arm in the right jumbo-sized pocket of his overalls. Then Jr., at 140 pounds, struggled to get the 185-pound Bruiser onto the passenger side seat of the truck. After Bruiser had been securely seat belted into place, Jr. cranked up the truck and flew down the dirt and pebble road. At Highway 7, Jr. turned left toward the closer Rutland General Hospital. Nearly forty-five minutes had elapsed since Bruiser had been attacked, by the time Jr. screeched to a stop in the circular driveway of the ER entrance of Rutland General Hospital. Jr. ran into the emergency room and yelled for help. Several ER nurses, two EMT workers with a gurney, and one doctor with a stethoscope ran out to the truck. The doctor quickly listened to Bruiser's heart, barked out several orders to the surrounding nurses, and the two EMT workers lifted Bruiser onto the gurney and then brought him into the ER operating room. Meanwhile, Jr. presented the shirt-wrapped left arm of Bruiser to the attending doctor. The doctor thanked Jr., and then as Jr. left to move the truck, he heard the doctor say to a nurse, "This won't do him any good now, but let's keep it on ice anyway." The nurse took the shirt-wrapped arm into the ER laboratory and set it down on the counter. She put on a pair of gloves, removed Jr.'s shirt from the arm, and then dropped the bloody shirt into a medical waste disposal can. She then placed the arm on a metal tray, and filled out a toe tag with Bruiser's name and tied it around the arm. She then placed the metal tray into the medical refrigerator.

Jr. had been thinking of scenarios, ways to disguise where the actual attack had happened, as he had been speeding to the hospital in the Apple's truck. He didn't want the cops anywhere near where they were attempting to grow pot. He assumed that the authorities would want to see where the attack had occurred, to gather evidence, and also as a jump off place to look for this man-attacking bear—so as he went to move the truck from the circular driveway of the ER, an idea came to him. He would have to move the evidence of the attack elsewhere. He would have to send the police in the complete opposite direction from where any of their pot growing areas were located. Jr. headed back to his grandparents' farm in the Apple's truck. In the grow room of the barn, he left his three empty milk crates, his six empty milk containers, and various pieces of rope. He then grabbed a whole box of 30-gallon plastic garbage bags, an axe, a shovel, two fishing poles, a bait bucket, and his tackle box. He drove the legal speed limit back up North Highway 7 to the Four Corners Road, and then he hid the truck back close to where

Bruiser had been attacked. He took the box of garbage bags, the shovel, and the axe, and then he cut up the underbrush into manageable pieces. He gathered up all of the mangled milk crates, shredded empty milk containers, and blood-covered underbrush, and then painstakingly separated the debris into three 30-gallon plastic garbage bags of evidence that he wanted found, like the bloody underbrush, and two 30-gallon plastic garbage bags of evidence he didn't want found, like everything else. He would stash the stuff that he didn't want found temporarily in the grow room, and then, when possible, he would figure out some way to dispose of it. Jr. then used his shovel to flip the blood-stained dirt and to smooth it over. When he was finished, the area looked as if something unnatural possibly had occurred there, but pronouncing it a bear attack would be iffy.

Jr. drove south to Rutland on Highway 7. Once in downtown Rutland, Jr. hung a right onto Highway 4 heading west. He was going to find a fictional area for this very real bear attack, an area that was as far away from his pot growing areas as could possibly be. He had decided that he was going to say, "Well you see officer…me and Bruiser were fishing up there on the western shore of Lake Bomoseen…yeah, yeah, officer, I realize that it's federal land…and that there are 'No Trespassing!' signs posted everywhere… I'm real sorry…I know Bruiser is real sorry too…but the best bass fishing is there…and Bruiser just had to take a leak…so he walked just a few feet into the woods…that's where he was attacked…and yeah, yeah, Mr. Apple…I'm sorry. I know you wanted Bruiser to mail that crate in Burlington…I'm sure Bruiser is real sorry too…It's my fault…I kinda talked Bruiser into playing hooky…but I swear Mr. Apple…me and Bruiser were gonna try real hard to get to the Burlington Post Office before five o'clock." Just as Jr. drove out of downtown Rutland heading west on Highway 4, still in the twenty-five mile per hour speed zone, Bubba passed in the other family pick up truck heading in the opposite direction back to Highway 7. He was on his way home after a visit to *Rutland Hardware*. Bubba looked over at his other truck and saw Jr. Liberty driving it. "WHYYY JEEESUS CHRIIIST!" Bubba voiced to nobody, "That truck was supposed to BEEE in Burlington. Where the hell is that son of a bitch ANYWAAAY?"

A very exhausted Jr. had to walk slightly more than a half mile from where he could leave the truck, schlepping the three stuffed 30-gallon plastic garbage bags of bloody underbrush, a shovel, and an axe. This is where he could sneak through the fence onto the federal land on the western side of Lake Bomoseen. The most opulent houses in the county were on the northern and eastern sides of the lake, Jennifer and Colin had built on the eastern side of the lake, but the western and southern sides were strictly verboten. That was a federal bird sanctuary. Jr. made it to a place that looked good as the alleged spot were the real bear attack had been, and immediately he began doing a little exterior decorating with his shovel. First, he did a preliminary dirt flip, just to get his chaotic juices flowing. There was almost a Primal Therapy thing happening for Jr., in that he would jab into the earth with his shovel and then release a stifled yell. He then chopped down a few of the very thin saplings, and used his axe again on where the tree cut was—chipping pieces of wood from the cut point, so it looked more like breakage due to a bear—and then he scattered the contents of the three 30-pound plastic garbage bags everywhere. He used his shovel to mix up the dirt from that location with the bloody underbrush that had just been scattered. He took one last look around, making sure that he had covered all of the bases, and then he walked back to the truck. After Jr. had dropped off the shovel, axe, box of garbage bags, and the other two filled 30-gallon plastic garbage bags back at his place, he headed to Rutland General Hospital. It had been nearly three hours since Jr. had left the ER, and when he returned and made inquires, the woman behind the desk made a phone call. A few minutes later Sheriff Roger Glenn came down from the ICU waiting room.

"Mr. Liberty," Sheriff Glenn said, "Can you tell me where you have been for nearly three hours since you left Bruiser Apple here?"

"I was in total shock. I just went for a drive to clear my head."

"In the Apple's truck?"

"I'm sorry about that. I hope Mr. and Mrs. Apple aren't too mad at me for using their truck for a few hours."

"Right now…that's about the last thing anybody is worried about," Sheriff Glenn said. Then he added, "Can you tell me what happened?"

And Jr. told Sheriff Glenn the whole fish story. Then Jr. asked with a trembling voice, "Is Bruiser still alive?"

"Yes son, he is," Sheriff Glenn said with compassion. And then he added, "Barely, however. From what I understand, that bear did some major, major damage. I heard that they couldn't reattach his arm, and that there is serious damage to his voice box also, from where the bear ripped his throat." Jr. hadn't even noticed that wound, as the horror of seeing the missing arm had been sufficiently preoccupying. "He is alive, but from what I've heard…and son…I'm just telling you this because you were there, and I know you're his best friend…this is all confidential…so you didn't hear this from me…there's some serious doubt as to him making it. I'm sorry son… Jr.…I just wanted you to be prepared for the worst."

"Can I go see him?" A still-in-a-state-of-disbelief Jr. asked.

"No…I'm afraid not. He's in Intensive Care, and only family members are allowed up there. I need you to come with me now anyway…to show me where the bear attack happened," Sheriff Glenn said. And then he continued, "We'll go pick up Deputy Warren with the crime scene kit at my office, along with Dr. Roberts. Dr. Roberts is a zoologist from Burlington who works for the Vermont Wildlife Commission. He's been waiting at my office for about an hour to see the location of the bear attack."

Reluctantly Jr. said, "Okay."

After picking up Deputy Warren and Dr. Roberts at the sheriff's office, they drove out to Lake Bomoseen. Jr. showed everybody the location of the attack, and Deputy Warren used the crime kit to at least begin examining the evidence on a limited scientific basis. One of the things that Deputy Warren did was to take several small chips of wood with blood from the underbrush. Those pieces of wood would eventually receive DNA testing, to make sure that the blood came from either Bruiser, the bear, or possibly Jr. Liberty. Deputy Warren also dusted the bloody underbrush for fingerprints, just to make sure that this scene of tragedy wasn't an elaborate attempt at covering up an attempted homicide. While all this examining of the location was going on, a still dazed and confused Jr. just sat on an old log watching. After nearly an hour, Deputy Warren called to Dr. Roberts and Sheriff Glenn, and the three men mini-conferenced beneath an old elm tree.

Deputy Warren then walked over to Jr. and asked him for a blood sample and fingerprints.

"Why?" Jr. asked.

"Sheriff Glenn brought me a sample of Bruiser Apple's blood from the hospital, and a set of his fingerprints also. Bruiser Apple's doctor allowed Sheriff Glenn to take the fingerprints from Bruiser earlier in the recovery room. We just want to account for all of the fingerprints and blood."

"Recovery room? Bruiser has had surgery already?" Jr. asked.

"Just to stop the internal bleeding. From what I've heard," Deputy Warren said, "If he survives, he will need several more surgeries."

"My God!" Jr. said.

"I was able to use my small microscope to identify Bruiser Apple's blood on a some branches over there," Deputy Warren said, while pointing to the alleged location of the attack. "Dr. Roberts was also able to identify, under the microscope, a little sample of bear blood taken from a stick. There's a third blood sample over there, and I need to see if it matches yours."

Jr., after looking at the dry cuts and scrapes on this hands, acquiesced to the blood sample and fingerprints. Deputy Warren went to go check things out. About fifteen minutes later, a solemn faced Sheriff Glenn came over to Jr. and asked, "Would you like to change your bullshit story now?"

"What do you mean?" a very nervous Jr. responded.

"We have some problems with what you've told us. First of all, Dr. Roberts, who is an expert in bear attacks, says that this looks more like the manufactured location of a bear attack than a real location. He'll be happy to explain to you how he came up with his theory. Secondly, Deputy Warren, from examining fingerprints, says that there is a very unusual high amount of your prints everywhere. He said that it looked as if you were handling the underbrush way too much. And finally, let me ask you, if this is where you were fishing, and you had to act as a crutch for Bruiser Apple for more than a half mile back to the truck, how come we didn't find the fishing equipment here? You obviously couldn't carry the fishing equipment and get Bruiser Apple back to the truck at the same time. And with the severity of Bruiser Apple's injuries, I doubt you would have left him unconscious in the truck while you retrieved the fishing equipment."

And thinking quickly Jr. said, "My fingerprints are all over the underbrush, because the underbrush was totally covering Bruiser when I got there. I had to move a lot of stuff to get to him and to recover his arm. As for the fishing equipment, after I left Bruiser in the ER and I took a drive to try and calm myself down, I ended up back at Lake Bomoseen. I walked back to where we had been and I recovered all of the fishing equipment then. The fishing equipment is in the back of the Apple's truck…it's in the hospital parking lot…go take a look."

"So let me get this straight," Sheriff Glenn said. "You went back to the location of a bear attack to recover a hundred dollars worth of fishing equipment. And you had absolutely no fear of running into that same bear again?"

"I wasn't thinking about that," Jr. said.

"I see," said Sheriff Glenn. "So it didn't occur to you that you might be in danger returning to that same spot. Okay. But as a sheriff, as somebody who has had to reconstruct crime scenes for years, I've learned a few things. Some people will always return to a crime scene if they feel guilty. Perhaps the person was responsible for a murder at that location, and there seems to be some psychological need to return. But an innocent victim, somebody who has witnessed cruelty to somebody else or experienced cruelty himself or herself at a particular location, very rarely wants to return to the scene of all that. It's usually considered a big psychological break through when the victim can finally muster up enough courage to return and face that location. I would have guessed, after how you had seen Bruiser all bloody and mangled in the woods, missing an arm, that coming back here would have been the last thing that you would have wanted to do. I would have thought that coming back here now would have been just too traumatic for you. In fact, I was kind of surprised that you didn't put up much resistance when I asked you to come back here now."

"I just wanted to help!" Jr. said. And then he belligerently added, "I didn't do anything wrong. I don't know about any of your psychological theories. I am getting a little bored sitting here now, I'm starved, I stink, and I'm exhausted. So either arrest me or bring me back to the hospital, because I have nothing else to say at the moment."

Sheriff Glenn said, "Look son…if that bear attacked at a different location…and you're pulling my chain right now…do you want to feel responsible if that bear attacks somebody else?"

And Jr. remembered that Bruiser had told him that bears who attack humans don't suddenly get a taste for humans. Bruiser would say that the bear who attacked him would probably never attack another human, as long as another human didn't pose the same kind of threat that he had posed. And although Jr. didn't know what kind of threat Bruiser had been to that bear, he didn't feel that telling the sheriff where the real attack had occurred would necessarily prevent that bear from attacking again. So he said, "I don't feel responsible for anything...anything except convincing Bruiser to come fishing here."

Sheriff Glenn decided not to push the issue with Jr. It was obvious to him that Jr. couldn't be pressured into saying anything else right now, and that Jr. was so traumatized, if he did press the issue, Jr. would probably just shut down. Sheriff Glenn decided to wait a day or two and then question Jr. again. Sheriff Glenn then said loudly for Deputy Warren and Dr. Roberts to hear, "Let's go. I want Mr. Liberty to relax at home." And so mercifully, they quickly left and drove back to Rutland General Hospital.

"You can't get me up to see Bruiser?" Jr. asked Sheriff Glenn again, when they had parked at the hospital.

"I'm sorry Jr., but that's the hospital's policy. You can wait in the hospital's main waiting room, and I'll tell the Apples to come by and find you when they have some news. But I would suggest that you go home son...Jr...and take a shower, eat some food, and get some sleep. You look like hell physically, and I know that you're probably not feeling so hot emotionally either. Go home Jr. Bruiser won't heal any faster, if God will let him heal, with you being here. Take care of yourself. You're no good if you get sick. Would you like a ride home?"

"I think I'll just wait in the downstairs waiting room for now," a tired and despondent Jr. said.

"I'll let the Apples know that you're here," Sheriff Glenn said and then walked away. Jr. sat down in a comfortable chair in the hospital's waiting room and immediately fell asleep.

Up in Intensive Care on the second floor, in private Room 207, a grief stricken Bubba sat in a chair next to Bruiser's bed. Pauline was in a chair on the other side of the bed, leaning over and crying with her head on the bed, her hand clutching her son's right hand. Jennifer sat in disbelief quietly against the wall in another chair. Colin was in the middle of a difficult delivery on the sixth floor of the hospital, and Jimson and Lizzie had just left the room to get coffee in the hospital's cafeteria. Cindy, Dick, and Tonya were on the way down from Plattsburgh, and they were expected any minute. Salome would arrive by bus later that night, and Jack's plane was due at Burlington Airport just before noon tomorrow.

"WHYYY...I...wish this had happened to MEEE...not Bruiser... MYYY beautiful son," Bubba sobbed out from the depths of his insides. "I wish I had SHOOOWN Bruiser more love."

Pauline, who had been called at home about Bruiser's accident while

Bubba was out running errands, had left Bubba a note in the usual dining room place, and then had driven herself to the hospital in Bluebird. Bubba, forty minutes later, upon reading the note, had come immediately to the hospital. Pauline, who had not uttered one single word to Bubba in twenty months, lifted her head off of the bed and looked at him now. As angry as she had been over the breaking of Salome's jaw, she could see now that this Bubba was a shattered man. Pauline had never seen Bubba like he currently was, a man who looked and sobbed as if he had been trampled by a herd of cattle and apparently didn't care if he lived or died. Pauline still loved Bubba very much; he had been her husband and a good provider for nearly twenty-seven years, and he was the father of the son who was currently fighting for his life. She said, "Bruiser knows how much you love him."

Bubba, who was surprised to hear Pauline addressing him directly after nearly two years, looked at her across the hospital bed and said, "Our beautiful son…I'm SOOO sorry Pauline. I love him very much. I love YOUUU very much. And I love Salome and the rest of our children very much ALSOOO. I'm SOOO sorry that I broke Salome's jaw. I've been in therapy for nearly a year and a half now. PLEEEASE forgive MEEE Pauline!"

And Pauline got up and walked around the bed to Bubba, sat on his lap, kissed him several times all over his face, then put her head on his shoulder while they cried together. Seeing this forgiveness scene between her parents in front of her dieing brother was emotionally just too much for Jennifer, and she burst into tears also.

Later, at about three o'clock in the morning, after Bubba had insisted that Jimson, Lizzie, Jennifer, Colin, Cindy, and Salome go home and get some sleep—Dick had taken little Tonya back to the house at just after midnight—Jr. snuck up to Intensive Care. He saw Pauline in the waiting room stretched out and asleep on a couch. He covertly found Bruiser's room and he saw Bubba sleeping in a chair against the wall. Bubba was snoring loudly. Jr. tip-toed up to Bruiser's right side and then tapped Bruiser on his head a few times. Bruiser mumbled something. Jr. tapped a few more times on Bruiser's head, and then Bruiser opened his eyes. Jr. leaned down and whispered into Bruiser's right ear, "I went back to where you were attacked by the bear, and I moved all of the evidence. I moved it up there in the woods…to that federal land on the western side of Lake Bomoseen. I told Sheriff Glenn that we had been illegally bass fishing on the lake, you went into the woods to take a leak, and that's where you were attacked. Okay Bruiser? Do you understand me?"

And Bruiser looked at Jr. and slightly nodded.

"You just get better, buddy," Jr. whispered. "I'll take care of our crop this year. Don't you worry about a thing," he said. And then Jr. left just as covertly as he had come.

@@@@@@@@

And so dear journal, it's July 4th, 1977, Anthony's 22nd birthday. I hope he enjoys celebrating in Paris. I tried calling him before, but there was no answer. It's been nearly two months since we've spoken. I'm still pissed off at him anyway. The nerve of my brother! I'm sorry that my answer to him, when he asked if I could introduce him to Miep in Paris, wasn't the answer that he wanted to hear. Too bad! Our parents are dead, and other than Walter Lee, I'm the kin who has to watch out for my brother. I told Anthony and Walter Lee about my adventures with Miep for eight months. I mentioned the cocaine runs from Norwich to London, the great weekend adventures all around Europe, the incredible sex with Miep, the incredible sex with some of Miep's friends, either alone or with Miep participating, and in general, what a sweet eight months it had been. One thing I didn't do was to mention Miep's last name. And so then Anthony had asked, "Could you put me in touch with her? You know, call her, tell her your Bro is gonna be in Paris, ask her if she would mind showing me around. If the chemistry is there, and you wouldn't mind Felix, maybe I could have the same thing you had until September. If the chemistry isn't there, well at least I'll get a tour, and maybe Miep will be the conduit to some other babe." I had refused, and naturally that had pissed him off.

I told him, "Look dude…I love you…and as your older brother…I feel responsible for guiding you in the best direction. Hooking you up with Miep isn't the best direction. And it has nothing to do with jealousy over the possibility of my younger brother schtupping the woman I'd been schtupping. It's that I don't want you anywhere near a kilo of cocaine! Yeah…I was crazy…And yeah…I'm being a hypocrite. But me taking a chance with the law…and we're talking some serious time here Anthony…at least twenty years behind bars if caught with that amount…that was me and my stupidity. I'm not going to let you be in that position. So no…I will not introduce you to Miep."

And he had said, "Well I know she teaches Dutch and English at the University of Paris. It shouldn't be too hard to find out her last name and to look her up."

And I had begged him not to do that, telling him, "If you do that, ignore me, piss on my leg like that, I just don't know if I'm gonna want to talk to you too much later." And then the son of a bitch went and found her in Paris anyway! I had called her and begged her not to get involved with my brother, and she had agreed to honor my request. But I guess, in person at her university office, Anthony's looks and charm had melted her resolve, because they're living together now. I just hope he makes it through the next two months without getting busted, and that he returns in September to finish his senior year at UVM. Now I feel guilty for asking him to take the year off in the first place. I should have just kept my own mental shit in check last year and not interfered with Anthony's college. But then I guess I wouldn't have gotten my novel published in France.

I have finally gotten over Tatiana. I think it was that moment in Paris last

January that I could have slept with her but didn't. If I had slept with her, I probably would have pushed her into divorcing her husband and remarrying me. She called last April, just after Anthony had left for Europe, to tell me that things were working out with Dr. Ralph. She told me that he had finally acquiesced to the idea of adopting a baby and that he did really love her. I wished her well, and when I had hung up the phone, I suddenly felt free. It felt like the first time that I wasn't just fooling myself, that I was indeed over Tatiana.

Last month I ran into Walter Lee's old lover, Sylvia Morton, in the produce section of the grocery store. She asked about Walter Lee, said it had been last September when Walter Lee had told her about his new thing with Annie since she had last heard from him. I said that he was doing fine, and that he was just ripping through his college classes at the University of Tampa Bay on his way to becoming a professor. I didn't tell her that Walter Lee and Annie Harrison had been flying back and forth from Tampa to New York to see each other a couple of weekends per month since last September. And then something interesting happened. Sylvia said, "You know you're pretty sexy Felix. Why don't you come over and let me make you dinner sometime?" I thanked her for the compliment, and then I told her that she just oozed sex appeal herself. She smiled and said, "Yeah…well I definitely need," and then pointing to her rear end, "more junk in the trunk! A black woman needs a bigger trunk."

"Rolls Royce could not have designed a finer trunk!" I said. And then she kissed my cheek, and headed up to pay for her groceries. Later, I asked Walter Lee how he'd feel if I ended up hitting it with Sylvia. He told me that he was okay with that, so I called her and went for dinner at her place. Dessert was particularly exceptional! She's ten years older than I am, but that doesn't seem to matter. We've been seeing each other exclusively for more than a month now, and it feels as if some kind of new phase has begun in my life...or at least a new story.

@@@@@@@@

It was September 11, 1977, Walter Lee Younger's 50th birthday, and Salome had just finished registering at UVM in Burlington for her first semester in the College of Arts and Science, when she remembered that she had forgotten to send Walter Lee a card. She had included Walter Lee, Felix, and Anthony on her birthday card list for the past two years, but for some reason she had been remiss this year with Walter Lee.

Salome had decided after Bruiser's accident to move back home. She'd given Jaxie her share of two months rent for the inconvenience of the sudden bail out, and Jimson had driven her back to New York City in one of Bubba's trucks one Sunday in June to retrieve all of her stuff. Salome still felt guilty for not having been there during her mom's bout with cancer in 1974, so moving home to help her mom out with Bruiser had seemed the thing for her to do in 1977.

Bruiser was doing surprisingly well. He had had several surgeries on his arm and throat, and although he would never be able to talk in the same way again—for the rest of his life he would always take a deep breath before shooting out small phrases, sounding like a Bubbaesque Darth Vader with Emphysema—he was alive and out of danger in regards to his overall health. He would be going with Pauline to Columbia Presbyterian Hospital in Manhattan this November, for a fitting and subsequent therapy with his new prosthetic arm. After the final surgery on his stump in late July at Burlington Mercy Hospital, after the swelling from that surgery had completely subsided, he and Pauline had recently gone to the same hospital in Manhattan for the first time just a few weeks ago. At that time they had measured and designed Bruiser's prosthetic arm.

Salome had called NYU in late May and explained why she couldn't attend there in September, and then she had called UVM and explained why she just had to attend there in September. At first, UVM didn't want to let her register until the following January. They pointed out that she was way over the deadline for admission in September, that she had not shown that her intention was to attend their school. Salome then explained about the bear attacking her brother. And since just about everyone in Vermont and upstate New York had heard about Bruiser's encounter with the bear, suddenly the Registrar was very sympathetic to Salome's plight.

Seventeen year-old Salome had gotten her driver license in August, and then she had immediately purchased a used standard three speed shift-on-the- floor orange 1970 *Chevrolet Nova*. Salome also had found a job in Burlington as a waitress at a small French restaurant called *Le Cave*. She only worked three days a week, Tuesday, Wednesday, and Thursday from four o'clock until midnight, but since Salome was now living for free at home, and the only real expenses she had were car related—a monthly automobile insurance payment, gas, and maintenance—three days a week was all she needed. Salome still didn't know what her major was going to be at UVM, but she had chosen the College of Arts and Science, because she had assumed that she would get a degree in some field of Liberal Arts. (Her tuition and books were totally covered by governmental loans.) This semester she was top heavy with American Literature classes, because those classes happened to be on Tuesdays, Wednesdays, and Thursdays. It was two hours from Rutland to Burlington, so working and taking classes on the same day had seemed like a good idea to Salome.

Salome was walking through the UVM Quadrangle when she came face to face with Anthony. Salome, at a loss for words, said nothing.

"Hi Salome," Anthony said. "What's it been…three years now?"

"Hi Anthony," she said.

"I see that you're carrying UVM registration papers. Are you going here now?"

"Yeah," was all that she said.

"Felix told me…in 1976…that you had completed your first year of college at BMCC in Manhattan then…So are you starting your third year here now?"

"Yeah," Salome said.

"Well hot damn…you're just a big motor mouth aren't you. Do you…like hate my guts or something?"

"Of course I don't hate you," Salome said. "It's just…with how we parted…it just feels uncomfortable talking to you."

"Well how do you think I feel?" Anthony said. "I was the one with the 'being in love' problem…remember?"

"Yeah…well your problem affected me…tremendously," Salome said.

"Okay…so we both affected each other…but that's history. I know that you loved Darius and that I didn't stand a chance. I've moved on…haven't you? Can't we communicate now as if we were two old friends? I mean…regardless of any hurt I felt about you…I still see you as one of my closest friends. I miss you," Anthony said.

"I miss you too," Salome echoed.

"Are you doing anything right now?" Anthony asked.

"No," Salome said. "I just finished registering and I was gonna head back to Rutland."

"I'm not doing anything now, and my roommates are gone until tomorrow. Why don't we walk over to my place and just catch up? I've got some killer *Jamaican Blue Mountain Coffee*, and I'll make a big pot."

"Okay," Salome said. It was four blocks to Anthony's apartment.

Once inside the apartment, which was really half of a Victorian house, Salome said, "This place is beautiful! Is this the place where you were living when I met you in 1974?"

"The same place," Anthony said. "It's three bedrooms, one and a half bathrooms, and half of the basement. Before I went away last year, I stashed my stuff in the basement and found a guy to sublet my room for the year." And then Anthony went into the kitchen and made a pot of coffee. Salome then asked and received directions to the bathroom. While she was in the bathroom, Anthony went into his bedroom and returned with his cocaine kit. He had no idea if Salome liked coke, Felix had never mentioned that she had gotten him high, but Anthony figured if she did like it, communication would probably be easier. At this point, even though Anthony knew all about cocaine's aphrodisiac effect, he really didn't have any expectation of getting lucky with Salome. Those days had come and gone. When she returned to the dining room table, Anthony had just finished chopping up a few lines for each of them on a mirror. Salome, who hadn't snorted any cocaine since last May, just before Hans had shown absolutely no sympathy about what had happened to her brother and had given her nothing but trouble about moving back to Rutland and then had ditched her, hadn't gone a day without wanting the stuff. All of the problems at home with Bruiser and his condition had put the thought of cocaine on Salome's back burner, but the desire to do cocaine had never left.

"I didn't know that you were into cocaine," Salome said.

"Well…it wasn't until I went to Europe last year that I had even tried cocaine. I liked it immediately, and I hooked up with a great connection in France. Before I left Paris, I shipped myself in Florida four ounces of this incredible stuff. I had it crammed up inside of a beautiful porcelain hollow figurine of Marie-Antoinette. I broke the matching figurine of Louis XVI, and took a piece of that porcelain and glued it into Marie-Antoinette's bottom hole. Anyway, the coke arrived safely in Florida, and Voila!…here's some of it on this tray."

Salome and Anthony spent the next several hours snorting cocaine. When they had finished the pot of coffee, Anthony had made a strong pitcher of Margaritas. As the pitcher of Margaritas began to disappear, when Salome was particularly close to Anthony on the sofa, he just took her face in his hands and kissed her deeply. Salome did not resist, and she began to aggressively take Anthony's shirt off. Anthony picked her up in his arms and carried her into his bedroom. And with absolutely none of 1974's parameters, Anthony and Salome made love, snorted cocaine, and talked through most of the night. Anthony was one of the few people in Vermont who had not heard about the bear attack on Salome's brother. Salome told him the whole gruesome story. And in the middle of the story, when the emotion had just become too overwhelming, Salome finally broke down and cried. And even as the crying was happening, in her mind Salome asked herself 'What's up?' When she was snorting a lot of cocaine in the past, Salome had noticed that she couldn't cry. She had never even gotten around to crying about Darius. In the case of Bruiser, she had figured that even though she was no longer using, that it had been the residual effects of all of the previous cocaine usage that had stopped her from crying. But at this instant in Anthony's bedroom the cocaine had made her cry. Anthony held her for hours listening to every word. When Salome left at seven o'clock in the morning to drive home, she knew she was going to hear about staying out all night from Bubba. She didn't care. The crying, the getting it all out, had made her feel so much better. And making love to Anthony, and remembering what a beautiful and exceptional man he was, put a big smile on her face as she was driving home. She wondered if Anthony might still be in love with her. She had a date with him for this upcoming Friday night, and she couldn't believe just how excited she was about that date.

@@@@@@@@

In July of 1978, *The Breakers* on Mad Beach was loaded with Apples.

Salome Apple and Anthony, who had been an item since the previous September, were using one of the bedrooms in Felix's apartment. One of the rooms on the second floor was being used by Bruiser Apple, and the first real major love of his life, Eileen Hopkins. Bruiser had met Eileen at Columbia Presbyterian Hospital in Manhattan. She was an amputee also, and they had met while doing prosthetic device physical therapy. Bruiser had finally given up on his prosthesis, electing instead to just sew up the sleeves on the left arm of his shirts. Eileen needed her prosthetic lower right leg to walk without crutches. Eileen had lost her right leg in a motorcycle accident while she was riding on the back of her previous boyfriend's *Harley*, and that accident had occurred in North New Jersey just about a month after Bruiser's bear attack last year. Bruiser had been so depressed during the therapy sessions that he wouldn't speak. Eileen Hopkins was an exceptional woman with an incredible disposition. She had helped Bruiser to believe in himself again. (The $41,300 that Jr. had recently given Bruiser as his half of this year's crop sales and that Bruiser had stashed in his safety deposit box had helped too. Jr. had also given Bruiser a year's worth of stash, although Bruiser was slightly annoyed that he had not gotten his choice in selecting his own buds.) Eileen Hopkins had touched Bruiser's heart so deeply, he had taken a big breath and wheezed out, "I could fall…in love with you."

And the two year-older than Bruiser, five foot seven inch medium-sized, brown-eyed brown-haired beautiful Eileen had said, "Good! I've already fallen for you."

Eileen, who lived with her parents in New Jersey, and Bruiser, who lived with his parents in Vermont, had spoken on the phone every single day since they had left the hospital in Manhattan last December. And even though Bruiser would abandon the use of his prosthetic arm, he had stuck around at the hospital and kept up his therapy, until Eileen had completed her therapy and gone home. Bruiser would use one of Bubba's trucks, and he would make the three hour trip to Eileen's house. He had made that trip several times since last December. He was always welcome at the Hopkins home, and they had an extra guest bedroom that he would use. Likewise, Eileen had made the trip to Rutland a few times, and Bubba and Pauline had extended the same hospitality.

When Salome and Anthony had suggested in June of 1978 that they all go for the summer down to Anthony's motel on Mad Beach, Bruiser and Eileen had given a big thumbs up to that notion. And then Bruiser had pulled Salome alone into the other room and wheezed, "Listen…I just want you to know," and Bruiser would take a breath and wheeze out about three or four words, and then take another breath for the next three or four words, "How grateful I am…for the way…you've taken care…of me. I also…want you to know…that I love you…and that I'm sorry…for having been…such an asshole…to you…over the years."

"You're my big brother…and I love you too!" Salome said, and then she gave Bruiser a big kiss. "All that other stuff is ancient history."

Jimson and Lizzie couldn't go to Florida, as Lizzie was back working fulltime at the library for the summer, and Jimson, who had passed his state test, was still in training for the rest of the summer to become a Vermont prison guard. Jimson would also help Bubba and Pauline out at the orchard for the summer, but it was more on a as needed basis. Jennifer and Colin were busy with *The Woman's Center*, and they didn't have any vacation time scheduled until late August when they had Colin's children for two weeks. A sober Dick, who had stopped drinking last November, was working full-time at Plattsburgh Air Force Base for the summer. Cindy, having completed her RN program, was at home for the summer watching Tonya and little seven month old Karla. Cindy was hoping to begin work in the next six months or so.

So in late June of 1978, Anthony, Salome, Bruiser, Eileen, and Geneva all headed down to *The Breakers*. Eighteen year-old Geneva Liberty had asked her grandparents, "Would you mind if I went to Florida and helped Salome with her brother Bruiser?"

And even though Geneva had her own phone and phone line and paid her own bill so that her grandparents wouldn't be involved in her personal business, nonetheless Geneva's shrewd grandmother said, "Have a great time. And give my love to Jack Apple also!"

Meanwhile, Anne Harrison had quit her job with the Malcovitchs on Long Island, and she was now living with Walter Lee in the other three bedroom two bath duplex on the third floor of *The Breakers*. Felix had gladly given Walter Lee that apartment, but he had asked, "You sure you want to give up the vibe of Jack Kerouac in your apartment?" Walter Lee had just smiled at that.

Walter Lee and Annie were looking into what it would take to open up a restaurant on Mad Beach that featured Anne's peppered fish. They felt that they could lease a building, equip it properly, get the inventory they needed, buy a ton of television advertising, and have enough money in reserve to just break even for the first two years, if they had two hundred thousand dollars to start. And although Walter Lee had this amount and could just proceed with Anne, after she had made an incredible dinner in Felix's apartment that consisted of both peppered and nut and onion encrusted salmon and grouper, Bruiser, having thought for several months that he needed a place to invest his money legitimately had wheezed, "I love…this fish. I'd love to invest…in your restaurant." Bruiser thought, 'Maybe Jr. would like to go fifty-fifty in a share.'

Felix said, "Well…if you let Bruiser invest, the Kulpa brothers would like to invest also." Felix, who was still a bit pissed about the Miep Van Kreneek incident last year, shot a glance over at Anthony. Anthony, after consulting with Salome, had nodded in agreement. Anthony had just graduated from UVM in May, and he was beginning Stetson Law College in Gulfport, a suburb of St. Petersburg, in September.

Jack said, "I'd love to invest in a restaurant of yours that made this incredible fish also, Annie. Unfortunately, saving up for my own refrigeration business is a top priority."

Anne and Walter Lee walked off and discussed what just had been proposed. They returned a few minutes later, and Walter Lee said, "If we could find just one more investor, it would be perfect. Because we need two hundred thousand for this first place, if it were four partners putting in fifty thousand each, that would leave Annie and me enough money to quickly open up a second place in just a few months. We've scouted a great location for a second place in downtown Tampa on West Shore Boulevard."

"Would we be involved in that place also?" Felix asked.

"No. Our idea is to make the first place on Mad Beach the flagship restaurant, and to get started we'd like some investors and we'd like to incorporate. And you guys know, that as the years roll on, you'll all make a bunch of money from this place alone. But the other restaurants would be a separate deal...a separate corporation," Walter Lee said.

"Hey Anthony...how about we kick in fifty thousand each and both of us get a separate share?"

Anthony, again asking Salome's advice, said, "That sounds like a good idea." And thus began the *Annpefishco Corporation*. Their restaurant, across Gulf Boulevard and one block north of *The Breakers* would be called *The Careless Navigator*, and it would open in about six months.

Two days later Felix took Bruiser and Eileen to Tampa Airport, both of them had important medical appointments in late July that couldn't be missed. Later that night, when Anthony and Salome were sitting at one of the tables on the beach behind *The Breakers* and watching the Moon, Anthony said, "I love you Salome...I've loved you for four years...since I first picked you up hitchhiking on Highway 7 in Rutland. Would you marry me Salome?"

And Salome, who thought that this might be coming, because of the way in which Anthony had consulted her about investing in Anne and Walter Lee's place a few days earlier, said, "I love you too Anthony...And yes I'll marry you. We'll just have to wait until I'm eighteen in August."

"August 6th to be precise," Anthony said. "Let's get married on your birthday." And then Anthony placed the beautiful 2-carat brilliant cut solitaire diamond and gold band on Salome's finger, and they smooched for a while.

"Where do you want to get married?" Salome finally asked.

"Any place that you want is fine with me. You want to have a big wedding in Vermont? You want a big wedding on the beach here? You name it," Anthony said, still not believing that Salome had agreed to marry him.

"I think I'd like to elope to Reno, Nevada," Salome said.

"Reno, Nevada? Why there?" Anthony asked.

"I don't know. I've always had this gut connection with Reno. I've never been there, I've just seen pictures of the place, but for some reason I feel we should get married there!" Salome said, showing some excitement.

"Reno it is then," Anthony said. "And a honeymoon? I don't care where we go, I just have to be back here in September to start law school."

"Yeah...I'm too late to transfer for my senior year to the University of Tampa Bay for this September...I'll probably have to wait until January. Let's fly to Reno, get married, rent a car, and honeymoon in San Francisco."

"That sounds great," Anthony said. "Where do you want to live when we get back to Florida? We could stay in Felix's apartment for awhile... while we figure it all out. We're investing in a restaurant and I'm going to law school. I'm not going to have much income for a few years, other than profits from the motel, and if we get lucky, profits from the restaurant. We probably should wait on buying a house until I start practicing law."

"Staying in the apartment is fine with me...if it's okay with Felix. And I'll do waitress work while you're in law school. I'll also get my college degree within two years, and I'm sure I'll be able to find a good job and make a better income after that."

"You still want kids...right?" Anthony asked.

"I want kids...but a little later down the road. When we can afford to buy a house, then we can afford to have kids," And then she added, "I don't want to tell anybody in Vermont about getting married until after it's happened. But I do want to tell somebody else now...I'm pretty excited about all this. Let's go tell Jack, Geneva, Felix, and Walter Lee!"

They were walking arm-in-arm towards the office of *The Breakers* to tell Felix, when Jack and Geneva waylaid them just before the door. "You'll never guess what just happened!" said a dreamy-eyed Geneva Liberty. And then she showed Salome and Anthony the 2-carat beautiful marquise cut diamond ring on the white gold band which was now perched upon her finger and said, "Jack just asked me to marry him!"

Anthony smiled at Jack, since they had purchased their rings at the same time and had agreed to pop the question on the same evening.

"How about a double wedding?" Salome suggested.

Love was in the air.

@@@@@@@@

And so dear journal, this Monday is the second wedding anniversary for Anthony, Salome, Jack, and Geneva. It's hard to believe that this is August of 1980, and it's already been two years since I flew out to Reno to be best man for both

Anthony and Jack. I remember how pleased Walter Lee was to be stuck watching the motel. It's hard to believe that Jack and Salome's parents didn't kill them for getting married covertly. Geneva's parents had both died in a car accident when she was four, and her grandparents were both too frail to have flown to Reno if they had been asked. They were annoyed that they hadn't been asked. Geneva was able to smooth things over a bit on the phone, and when her grandfather passed away last month and Geneva flew up for the funeral, she was able to spend a lot of time bonding with her grandmother again. Geneva's grandfather left Geneva some money, but more importantly to her, he left Geneva a beautiful letter of love. Geneva has one more semester to go at the University of Tampa Bay for her degree in Business, and she works four shifts per week as a waitress at The Careless Navigator. Jack is doing well at his job, and he just received his third raise in two years. Jack and Geneva both cover the front office of the motel a few times per week, they don't mind, and they're happy with the low rent I charge them for doing that. They seem to be very much in love, and they are both easy going people who are very easy to be around. Anthony and Salome love each other also, but with all of their cocaine usage, sometimes they can get fairly nasty with each other. Salome has never had an unkind word to say to me, but Anthony can be churlish at times.

The Careless Navigator is booked six weeks in advance, and I can't believe how much money we are all making off of Anne's incredible fish! They opened their second restaurant in Tampa, and then a third place in Orlando. Now they're talking about Miami, Atlanta, and eventually Manhattan. At the same time, Walter Lee is in the middle of writing his doctoral dissertation. Oh yeah…Anne is preggers, and she and Walter Lee are getting married this coming Labor day weekend. Also, Salome told me that Bruiser and Eileen were getting married in November in New Jersey. It seems as if everybody in the world is married or getting married except me!

I eat at The Careless Navigator four or five nights a week. Salome is the maitre d' there, and she is also in charge of all waiters and waitresses. She just received her BA from the University of Tampa Bay in American Literature, and she plans on finding a different vocation soon. Anthony is doing well in law school, just finished his second year, and if it weren't for all of the cocaine usage, I would say that Anthony and Salome have an idyllic lifestyle at the moment.

Well…maybe they're sick of living with me, because I regularly give them hell about using too much coke. I don't use the stuff anymore. At first, because Sylvia and I were an item, and she wouldn't stand for it, I stopped. But after we broke up, I tried cocaine again with the next woman I dated and Winky just took a long nap.

Sylvia Morton and I had a good thing for nearly two years. Sylvia wanted a commitment, but I was having a hard time. And although the idea of marrying her and having a child was appealing, I just couldn't seem to get beyond that 'she's ten years older than me' prejudice. In the beginning that hadn't bothered me, but as time passed I became more fixated with the age difference. I mean Sylvia is beautiful, and I do love her, and she's wonderful in bed, but I'm going to be 34 in fourteen days and she's a month away from 44. That might work for a decade or so, but something tells me, down the road, it will no longer work.

I better finish getting ready. Jack is watching the motel right now, and I'm heading over to this voluptuous Puerto Rican mama's house. I met her while walking on the beach the other day. We walked and talked for nearly two hours, and then I got a dinner invite for tonight. She told me she loves cocaine, so I'm bringing her dessert. I better snag a few grams of my stash from the bedroom drawer before I go.

CHAPTER TEN

"All happy families resemble one another, but each unhappy family is unhappy in its own way," was how Leo Tolstoy began his great novel, Anna Karenina, in the 1870's, Felix would write in his journal in the late 1990's. Felix would then postulate: *On the qualifiers of "happy" or "unhappy," in regards to how one remembers one's childhood, might not those evaluations be directly related to basic mathematical principles? In mathematics, when we add a positive number with a negative number, whether the answer is positive or negative, depends on which number was greater at the start. Hence +50 plus -36=+14, but -50 plus +36=-14. However, when we multiply numbers it doesn't work that way. A positive times a negative is always a negative. Thus +50 times -36 is always going to be -1800. And since multiplication is really the expansion of addition, one might put forth the following metaphorical notion: As long as the family experiences stay for the most part positive for us in our youth, and we just have to add in a negative here and there, there's a good chance that positive is how we will remember our childhood family experience years later. Of course, in adding childhood experiences, we assign the number values to each experience. Was the slap across the face -5 or -50? And in juxtaposition, was the trip to Disneyworld +5 or +50? But when the negative childhood experiences get expanded or multiplied, we will always remember our childhood negatively.*

And in our adult family lives, with our mates, it works the same way. In some families, the 2-carat diamond and emerald ring for the wife on the fifth wedding anniversary, might create a large enough positive numerical value in the wife's mind, to overtake the negative numerical value created by the husband's affair just after the fourth wedding anniversary. In other families, no so-called positive mate-

rial object by the husband will ever replace the negative trauma in the wife's mind. Yet in other families, only by the wife having her own affair, will the marital equation ever balance itself at zero. And Felix would end the journal entry: *Regardless of whether we are children living with our parents and siblings, or adults living with our mates and children, we are the ones, in our own minds, who assign the numerical values of the positives and negatives, and that determines how we see and remember our various family experiences in toto* (total).

@@@@@@@@

"Look Felix…I'm sorry about taking your stash," Anthony said. "I'm getting an ounce tomorrow, so I was just going to replace it then. I figured that you'd never even know."

"Ah…I see…'what they don't know won't hurt them,'" Felix said. "It's more about you violating my privacy…by rooting around in my dresser drawers."

"Don't give me that hypocritical B.S.," Anthony fired back. "How many times, when we were growing up, did you go into my dresser drawer and borrow socks? And then just a couple of weeks ago you told me that you had done the same thing. I never gave you any crap about 'violating my privacy!' So be honest Felix. It's more about *what* I borrowed from your drawer than it is about going into your drawer!"

"Well…I did need it tonight," Felix said. "I was on my way over to Maria Rodriguiz's place…when I noticed that all of the nose candy had been 'liberated' from my bedroom. If you think loaning me a pair of your socks will foster the same effect with Maria tonight…"

During this conversation between Anthony and Felix, Salome just sat quietly on the tan sectional sofa, too embarrassed by having been involved in the theft of Felix's cocaine from the bedroom drawer to say a word.

"Look Felix…if you need cocaine to get laid…perhaps you should reevaluate why you think you can't lure women into bed without it." And although Felix recognized major truth in what his brother had just said, he was unaware that Anthony was now thinking, 'What the hell am I talking about? I was scared silly when it came to finding a smooth technique of getting women from the vertical to the horizontal…until I started snorting coke with them. And if not for the coke…would I have finally been able to win Salome?' Anthony continued, "Regardless of your cute anti-cocaine sermonette a few minutes ago, I know from what Miep said, that you snorted a sandbox full while you were in Europe."

And Salome thought, 'Who's Miep?'

Anthony continued, "And gee…I'm just so sorry that my drug of choice at the moment is not as 'enlightening' as LSD. Says who? Your boy Sigmund Freud used a lot of cocaine, and he seemed fairly well enlightened.

As a matter of fact, his whole…" and then Anthony, remembering a conversation he had with her in 1974, looked over at Salome before continuing, "…Elektra Complex notion…of how young girls have a secret fantasy of replacing their mothers with themselves in regards to their fathers…" Salome smiled and Anthony turned back to Felix and continued, "…was born from his observations of the dreams of Austrian female patients…all of whom Freud had given cocaine." Anthony turned back to Salome and said, "By the way…I enjoyed the Freud part of my undergraduate psychology class at UVM so much…I read a biography of his life."

"Touché!" Felix said. "I guess cocaine, used by a patient with his or her therapist, can be an effective tool. And I guess the same could be said of LSD. The difference is that with LSD, and especially in conjunction with the lyrics of the rock music albums of the time, one had more of a potential to become one's own therapist. With cocaine.…what's really going on feeling-wise inside of the user…usually just gets covered up. The potential for any kind of psychological growth seems stymied. I've been watching you guys for two years now, and both of you regularly display erratic behavior… depending on when you've snorted your last lines. In the mornings, Salome, when you're not using, you look and act depressed and ragged. If I say something you don't want to hear, although you say nothing, you seem irritated and distant. But then in the afternoons, when you've started snorting lines before heading off to work at *The Careless Navigator*, we always get along famously. And you're just the opposite Anthony. You're Mr. Happy Boy in the mornings, because you sit here and do rails before going off to law school. But in the evenings, when you're through studying in the law library and you want to be able to eventually fall asleep so you don't use coke…well, you're psychologically crashing all of the time. You give me attitude over the stupidest shit."

"Or maybe you just say stupid things in the evening, Felix," Anthony shot back sarcastically.

"Oh I don't know," Felix said and then came back with, "Maybe it's just that your evening head is really only concerned with the cocaine gratification that you must deny yourself to sleep, so that which is observant by a non-user, can only sound stupid to you."

"Right!" said Anthony. "How could any of the observations of the great kinda published author Felix Kulpa be anything but brilliant? Guess I'll have to learn French in order to be able to bask in your knowledge."

"Good idea," Felix said, getting really annoyed with Anthony's attack. And then he added, "While you're out getting that French primer, I suggest you stop by the nursery and load up on a new supply of Aloe plants. For two years now, my apartment has looked like a fucking hurricane came through an Aloe greenhouse…with all of the broken branches on the plants…caused by you guys having to shove that lotion up your noses to ease the pain from too much coke."

And Petomane came over and rubbed himself against Salome's leg and thought, 'Yeah…go get some more of those plants with the tasty liquid in them…pretty lady. I love chewing on that shit.'

"Somebody will feed you in a minute, Peto!" Salome said to Felix's persistent cat.

"Yeah…well who says it's *your* apartment anyway? Dad left this motel to *us*, so I guess this apartment is half mine!" Anthony said.

"Well you can have this whole fucking place if you want it!" Felix said. "I was quite happy in New York City. I had finished all of my classes and tests in graduate school at NYU, and I had already received approval on my dissertation topic. I was doing more research, getting ready to begin the first draft, when dad asked me to return to Mad Beach in 1972. He was so depressed about Terry, he didn't feel like doing much more than just staying in bed. He told me that he could neither take care of you nor run the motel properly anymore, and that it wasn't fair how much he was relying on Walter Lee. So, as much as I didn't want to, I came back here to run this place, and to try and keep your seventeen year-old high school ass out of trouble. Other than the one five week break you gave me in 1974, and the eight months you gave me in 1976, I'm the one who has been stuck here for more than eight years. And now it seems that you've forgotten our original agreement. Remember Anthony? It was the agreement that said you'd open up your law office right here at *The Breakers* after you graduated, and that you'd take over the running of the motel for the next ten years. I've heard you and Salome talking lately, about how you'd like to open up an office on West Shore Boulevard in Tampa and buy a house in that ritzy West Shore Village area there. What about the motel? It sounds like you're discarding our agreement. So if you want the apartment and the motel now…fine. The place is yours, and I'm outta here!"

"Don't bother. You can stay here and stare at the Gulf of Mexico, schtupp your cocaine-using babes, write your clever journal entries, and who knows, perhaps your next great epic novel will be published in Upper Volta in the Mossi Language. We'll be moving out this weekend!" Anthony said, and then he stormed out of the apartment. (An historical note: Upper Volta, whose name would be changed to Burkina Faso in 1983 following a *coup d'etat*, does have the Mossi Language as one of its main dialects. However, since French has always been the official language, by August of 1980, a few of that country's inhabitants had already read *Tous Les Sieges Etaient Occupés*. And one young lady, in the capital city of Ouagadougou, would send Felix a fan letter in November of 1980.)

"Anthony was totally wrong," Salome said. "I know how much you love your brother, and I feel your love for me as your sister-in-law also. Let me talk to Anthony…I'm sure he'll calm down. You're right…we do need to stop using the coke. Let us stay here with you until Anthony graduates next

May...we won't ever go through your stuff looking for cocaine again. And I'll try to be more gregarious in the mornings!" Salome added and smiled. Then she walked into the kitchen and asked, "Would you like some coffee?"

"Coffee would be great," Felix said, and then added, "And you're correct...I do love you guys...and I do want you safe and happy. It would be better if you stay until you're really ready to leave. Tell Anthony that I don't want him to leave...I'll just keep my mouth shut about the behavior I see," Felix said.

"Anthony loves you very much," Salome said.

"Well...it's more of a love-hate thing I think," Felix said. "He loves me as his brother, and he knows that his well being is very important to me, but I also know that he resents the relationship that I was able to have with our mom, since I was already eleven when she left. I also know that he's bothered by the special bonding I had with our dad, because of all the political anti-Vietnam War/Civil Rights Movement stuff in the 1960's that Dad and I shared. By the time Anthony was six, our step-mother was already in a wheelchair, and Dad's focus had shifted more towards her. There's also some other stuff in regards to me and our step-mother, that I'm sure Anthony hates me for."

And Salome, who had made a promise to Anthony on a particularly wonderful hot August afternoon in 1974 to never reveal her theory to Felix about The Case of the Slippery Seagull Shit, knew exactly what he was alluding to now. She said nothing.

"So...are you guys going to live and work in Tampa?" Felix finally asked after an uncomfortable silence, after he had gone to the kitchen and was slicing a bagel in the kitchen and added, "Would you like a bagel?"

"No thanks Felix...Look...I swear to you...I had no idea that you and Anthony had any kind of an agreement about him running the motel," Salome said. "I had never heard anything about that until just now."

"I see," said Felix, while wondering why Anthony had never mentioned the agreement to his wife. "Well nothing is written in stone. I mean...we could always just sell this place and make a ton of money. But I had figured, since you and Anthony had put fifty thousand dollars into a twenty-five percent interest in *The Careless Navigator* just across the street, that you guys would want to live in close proximity to your investment. I figured that Anthony would build his law office on the first floor here like he had said, he'd take care of the books and make the major business decisions for the motel for the next ten years, and that we'd just hire someone to live here and run the office fulltime. I didn't think that you and Anthony were going to raise a family at the motel, but I had figured that you'd buy a house either on the beach or in St. Petersburg and stay fairly close to *The Breakers*. The idea was that *I'd* get to break free from the motel and Mad Beach for ten years. And if a business decision required discussion, Anthony would be able to call me anywhere in the world. And now that I have a piece of *The Careless*

Navigator, I was going to handle that business with Anthony by phone also, and just give him my signed proxy for corporate votes."

"Like I said," Salome said, "I had no idea that Anthony had agreed to build his office here and to run the motel for ten years. I wouldn't object to that anyway. We'd always have a parking spot for *The Careless Navigator* and the beach!"

"Okay...good!" Felix said. "I certainly wouldn't want Anthony's agreement with me to cause some kinda rift between the two of you." Felix then took his bagel out of the toaster oven and covered it with cream cheese.

"Nah...I like the idea," Salome said. She then added, "Can I ask you something real personal Felix?"

"Ask me anything," Felix said.

"It's certainly understandable to me, when two people snort a lot of cocaine, how they can end up in bed. And perhaps you were right, coke users are all just laboratory rats shoving crap up their noses without thinking. What I don't understand, since you don't like the drug, is how you can get all of these women high and not get high yourself. Isn't that problematic for you?"

"I remember the different stages of getting high when snorting cocaine, so it's fairly easy for me to just act high with the women I'm with who are using," Felix explained.

"Yeah, but since you don't like the drug...I mean I've heard you deliver a whole bunch of anti-cocaine speeches in the last couple of years...and I hope you don't get pissed at me for saying this...If you hate the drug so much, how can you hang out with, and even provide the drug for, women who do like it? Was Anthony correct, do you think that you can't attract women without it?" Salome asked.

"Attracting women, while I have my clothes on, has never been the problem," Felix said. "I don't think my face is ugly. And although I'm big, I don't think I'm too fat."

"Nah...you're not fat. You're actually very handsome, and you have beautiful eyes," Salome said.

"Thank you," Felix said. He then continued, "I do seem to have the rap when it comes to getting the women into the bedroom. It's just..."

"What?"

"It's just that I'm a hairy beast without my clothes on, and the cocaine seems to help women to overlook that," Felix said somewhat embarrassed.

"I see you without your shirt on all of the time," Salome said, "And it's never looked like anything but natural for you. I've never been skeeved out by the hair on your chest and back, why would other women be?"

"You're unusual," Felix said. "I was reading *Cosmopolitan* in my dentist's waiting room a few months ago, and 2500 American women between the ages of 18 and 40 were polled."

"That sounds painful!" Salome joked.

Felix laughed, saluted Salome, and said, "That was top drawer humor Salome! Upper echelon type stuff!"

"Thank you!" Salome said, proud of herself for apparently having just joined, if only in this instant, the exclusive Felix/Anthony/Walter Lee comedy club. "Continue with your poll!"

Felix smiled and said, "These 2500 women were asked questions about what they like in men physically…what attracts them. When they got to the category of facial hair, it was about fifty-fifty…women who like men with beards and or mustaches. When they got to the category of body hair, although slightly more than sixty-five percent of the women said they liked some chest hair on men, zero percent said they liked back hair. So when I get the ladies high on cocaine, they seem to forget about my bear-like back."

"You were married to Tatiana for five years. How did she feel about your back hair?" Salome asked.

"I don't think she was wild about it, but she never said anything. The times were different then. We were so-called Hippies, and to even mention anything about one's mate's body hair would have been gauche. Tatiana was a real 'Earth Mother' back then also, as she shaved neither her legs or armpits, nor did she give a rat's ass about ever wearing a bikini. So there was a quid pro quo with her in the body hair department," Felix said.

"Well how about now?" Salome asked. "Surely she doesn't let herself go totally au natural in 1980!"

"I couldn't comment on two of the three areas I mentioned before," Felix said. "However, when I last saw her in January of 1977, she was wearing a sexy dress, and her legs were not only shaved, they looked waxed."

"Times and attitudes about hair change," Salome said. "Perhaps you should look into getting the hair waxed off of your back. I mean, I don't think the back hair detracts from you as a man at all…even without a few grams of cocaine in your pocket. The question is: Do you think it detracts from you as a man? And since you apparently think it does, go do something about it!"

"But only women's places do that. I wouldn't feel very manly going to one of those places," Felix said, with a mouthful of bagel and cream cheese.

"You'd be surprised at how many men get waxed." And then Salome added, "Wait a minute. You were going out with Sylvia for two years, and she didn't use cocaine. Was your back hair an issue with her?"

"Nah…she never mentioned it."

"Well there you go," Salome said. "Perhaps rejecting Sylvia because she was ten years older than you wasn't a good choice. She didn't seem to be wrapped up in the superficial. Perhaps you screwed up by not staying with Sylvia."

"Maybe I did," Felix said. "But it's too late now anyway, she's already found somebody else." Felix then guzzled the rest of his coffee.

"How do you know that?"

"I saw her walking hand-in-hand with some guy on the beach last week."

"That's too bad," Salome said. She continued, "Do you mind if I ask you something else, Felix?"

"Anything."

"Why is it so important for you to be with women all of the time anyway? You found Tatiana...and even though the times were different, she seems to have loved you for just being you...at least physically. Sylvia seems to have loved you for just being you physically. Why keep a factory assembly line of women going through your bedroom? Perhaps you need to just cool it for awhile with all of the coke snorting hussy dating, and just wait until somebody like another Tatiana or Sylvia, somebody who is more on your wavelength comes along."

"When I was in high school with a head full of mush," Felix said, "Like all of the other guys, getting women into bed...adding another notch to the belt...seemed to be a young man's 'rite of passage.' After Tatiana devastated me with her infidelity...and by the way...I never fooled around with another woman while we were married...getting women into bed seemed like the psychological reinforcement that I needed. I thought, 'So I'm not good enough for Tatiana huh...let's see if the rest of the gender feels that way.' So each bedroom experience with a woman became another notch in the 'Tatiana was wrong!' belt. My head was stuck in that spot until January of 1977 in Paris. It was interesting, that the moment she decided she wanted me, I no longer wanted her."

"That's not exactly true," Salome said. "You've said that you did want her, but because she was married you turned her down."

"Yeah...that's right," said Felix. "That's more accurate. And I guess I still want her today. It's just that the compulsion began ending in January of 1977 when I could've taken her to bed but didn't, and it thoroughly ended when she called a couple of months later to tell me that she was back with her current husband. I do still want her, but I feel I can live without her these days. I never felt that way until 1977."

"You're a strange guy, Felix," Salome said.

"That's true," Felix said, smiled, and then asked, "In which way specifically are you alluding?"

"It seems to me...if you really love somebody as deeply as you claim to have loved Tatiana...you say 'To hell with all of the moral rules!' and you go after her. I appreciate your sense of morality, Felix. Not sleeping with married women does sound like better karma. But if you knew in the deepest regions of your heart and soul that Tatiana and you were supposed to be together...that it was Kismet...you should have taken her to bed in Paris... and you should have stolen her back from her current husband! Your desire to have her in your life again should have been so compelling...that moving the Earth itself would have seemed like child's play in comparison!"

Felix, who was impressed with how much Salome's vocabulary had grown in the six years since he had first met her, said, "You know...Walter Lee told me pretty much the same thing a few years ago." And Felix thought, but didn't say, 'Yeah...but he said that in regards to how I had felt suddenly smitten by you in 1976!' And Felix continued, "There has to come a point of diminishing returns. The first time Tatiana was unfaithful to me was in 1970, with the dipshit drummer of some band she heard in the Village. She went off with this schmuck for three weeks, but I was happy to take her back. Then she left me for her gynecologist in 1971, and she didn't come back. It was only because of a fluke meeting at JFK Airport in August of 1974, that we hooked up again. But it had become alive for me once more. Then she left me for the third time, three months later, via the phone and letter. Whatever it is about me, that makes it so Tatiana can't stay with me too long, is there in her mind nonetheless. Turning her down in January of 1977 was not only morally correct for me, it was the beginning of the healing process." Felix got up off of the sofa, and carried his empty dishes into the kitchen.

"I understand," Salome said. "So if you've been healing since 1977, and I assume using all of these women to help you heal, how much longer do you think it will be until you're totally healed?"

Walking back into the living room, Felix said, "How about right now?" And then in front of Salome, Felix called Maria Rodriguiz and said, "I'm sorry to call you so late, Maria. And I'm sorry that you've prepared dinner for me. But an emergency just came up at *The Breakers*, and I can't possibly get away now. I'm sorry again, Maria. I'll call you in a couple of days. I shouldn't bother? Okay," and then Felix hung up the phone.

Many years later, in the late 1990's, Felix would note in his journal:
Jean Paul Sartre once wrote, "The definition of 'insanity' is seeing through a game, yet choosing to play it anyway."

"I can't believe you just did that," Salome said.

"What...you've never had your words taken seriously before?" Felix asked. And before she could respond, Felix said, "Now I have a real personal question for you."

"Ask me anything," Salome said.

"When you and I spoke after Darius' funeral, you told me that you had been in love with Darius. You also told me that you weren't in love with my brother, so how did all that change...just 14 months later?"

Salome looked down at the floor first, and then she looked into Felix's eyes and said, "Darius was the first man I was in love with. I was fourteen and he was twenty-four. And although I really enjoyed my time here on the beach with Anthony in 1974, Darius had touched me at such a primal 'I must have him' level, I rejected Anthony and went after Darius. After having had my jaw broken by Bubba, after Darius' death, I just didn't care anymore. And then I hooked up with two brothers, first Gustav and then Hans, and they introduced me to cocaine. I went through a wild period with them in New York. Then I had to deal with Bruiser's tragedy. By the time I saw Anthony at UVM in September of 1977, my world was in shambles, and he was there to help me sort everything out. I had forgotten what a funny, understanding, beautiful, and sensitive guy he is. I wasn't suddenly smitten with Anthony, but during the course of the year, from September of 1977 until we came here during the summer of 1978, I found myself falling in love with him. I knew I loved him as a friend in 1974, but I knew I loved him as my husband-to-be by 1978."

"So all of the coke he had sent himself from Paris before he returned to UVM in September of 1977 had nothing to do with it?"

"I hope you're not calling me a 'coke whore,' Felix," Salome said.

"Absolutely not," Felix said, being aware that he had indeed inferred just that.

"Look Felix…it's true that I was jonesing from no coke when I ran into Anthony in 1977, and that he had cocaine. And yes, it's true that his coke acted as a conduit in terms of our relationship. But I did fall in love with him, and that had nothing to do with cocaine," Salome said with a little annoyance.

"I know," Felix said. "I believe that. I know that you're too perceptive as a human being, to not know if you're in love with someone."

"Thank you," Salome said. "Anthony was wonderful…he helped to fix me. And even before I found myself falling in love with him I had said to myself, 'Anthony really loves me deeply. I could certainly do worse. And I love Anthony's family, both Felix and Walter Lee, so why not let myself fall in love? I could waste years looking for someone who even approached being like Anthony, and since there are so many more things I want to do in this life besides getting married and having kids, why not Anthony?' It just seemed to me Felix, that Anthony and I had such a good thing going…"

"I understand," said Felix. "Hey…I'm happy you're my brother's wife. It's just that I find it interesting that your search for a mate ended at only 18! I mean…that's pretty young to make that decision. For some, it would be double your age, at 36, before a decision on a mate for life could be made."

"So…weren't you just 20 when you married Tatiana?"

"Touché!"

"Like I said…there are other things I want to do with my life. Now that I've chosen Anthony to be my husband and the father of my children, I can concentrate on other important things," Salome said from the kitchen, as she was washing her coffee cup and Felix's cup and plate also.

"Yeah…it seems as if marriage and family is all I've been concentrating on for years," Felix said, walking back into the kitchen to talk.

"Well you did write a novel," Salome said. And then she added as a light-hearted joke, "I wish I could read French better…I know a little!"

"You know," said Felix. "I kid about that all of the time myself. But the truth is, that I'm very honored that my novel was published in French. Some of the greatest prose and poetry has been French."

"I had to read *The Hunchback of Notre Dame* in a World Literature course," Salome said. "Of course I read it in English…I thought it was great." Then they walked back into the living room and sat down.

"It was," Felix said, "But *Les Misérables* was even better. And the French philosophers have always been at the forefront of new ideas. From Jean Paul Sartre's writings on Existentialism, to this new guy I'm reading, Jacques Derrida, and his philosophy of Deconstruction."

"A professor of mine at UTB got into discussing Deconstruction a little, just before the last semester ended," Salome said. "Did you learn about Deconstruction when you were in graduate school at NYU?"

"When I was at NYU," Felix said, "The only Deconstruction going on was to the surrounding blocks around Washington Square Park. This stuff is fairly new, and I'm trying to figure it out now. From what I understand so far, an author writes something, either poetry or prose. This is the 'primary' piece of literature. But then a literary critic comes along and writes a piece on what the author meant in his poetry or prose. This is now a 'secondary' piece of literature, and it 'saturates the text' with what the writer thinks the writer of the primary text really meant. Then somebody else comes along and writes a piece on not only what he thinks the primary writer meant, but also how wrong the writer of the secondary text was. And this goes on and on, until the library has 360 books all trying to figure out what the primary author meant, and all trying to prove that everybody else has it wrong. This is what Derrida would call 'Textual Saturation.' Derrida would say, 'The words must speak for themselves. And even the author has no business telling us what his words mean after the piece has been published.' Anyway, I'm trying to figure all of this stuff out."

"Are you writing anything new?" Salome asked, changing the subject.

"No I'm not," Felix said. "I think I've picked up my journal maybe ten times since 1977. I don't seem to have much to say. I think I said it all in the novel."

"That's your problem Felix…you're not doing anything but running the motel and chasing skirts. You need some reason to wake up in the morning that trips your trigger. You're not writing, and I know it isn't this motel that moves you."

"Well...you're right again," Felix admitted. "How am I going to spend the rest of my life? That 'getting hooked up with a woman and having babies' thing has been a preoccupation of mine, because my life seems so empty being alone. I need to be part of a bigger group…part of a family unit with a woman and child. I guess, besides using women to get over Tatiana, I've also just been searching for a way to not be alone the rest of my life. I guess all of the skirt chasing has both motivations attached."

"I think you'll eventually find that," Salome said and then added, "And it won't take the cocaine."

"I think you're right," Felix said and then added, "So today is a day of change. I'm no longer going to buy cocaine as a tool for getting schtupped."

"Good!" Salome said.

"But let me ask you another question," Felix said. "How much coke do you guys use monthly?"

Salome looked down at the floor and mumbled, "About an ounce per month."

"An ounce per month? Damn! You still scoring from Jesus Narizes in Tampa?"

And Salome just nodded.

"That's $800 you guys are spending monthly on blow! That's a freakin' mortgage payment on a house!" Felix stressed.

"I know," Salome said.

"That's about half of the profits you guys make monthly off of this motel. You've got to stop! Salome, I'm hoping that I'm gonna have some nieces and nephews from you and Anthony. You need to take care of your body. You need to take care of your bank account!"

"I know," Salome said.

"Okay then...let's make this a complete day of change. I'm no longer buying cocaine for any reason. Now I know that you can't make any guarantees when it comes to my brother. But if you stopped snorting that shit, at least what's going on inside of your body would get back to normal, and your bank account would only be depleted monthly by half of what you guys are wasting now. Are you ready to make a pledge, Salome? No more coke for any reason for either of us?"

And Salome looked into Felix's eyes and said, "Yes! It's time to stop!" And then Felix offered his hand, and they shook to the agreement.

Salome then said, "So what are you gonna do? Since you don't feel like writing now, you're taking a hiatus with the women, and you're sick of being stuck at the motel all day...perhaps you should do some volunteer work, Felix. That would occupy your time, and who knows...perhaps that might lead you into a situation where you could find 'a heart of gold.' You need a plan. I have a plan. Anthony has a plan. As a matter of fact, it's just starting to make sense to me now. Anthony has said that he has no interest in being the quintessential store front defense lawyer. He wasn't old enough to have been affected by the Anti-Vietnam War/Civil Rights Movements in the 1960's, so he isn't particularly impressed by a Civil Rights attorney like William Kunstler. I love the music and attitude of the 1960's, but my husband wants to make a boatload of money for us. I remember now that the reason he wants to open up an office on West Shore Boulevard in Tampa, is that he wants to attract a number of good corporate accounts. He doesn't think he can do that with an office here in the motel. He wants to be more visible out there in Big Corporation Land."

"Well that makes sense," said Felix. I guess *I* wanted to live out my Civil Rights defense attorney fantasy vicariously through Anthony."

"If you were a lawyer, Felix, I'm sure that it would be perfect if your office were in *The Breakers*. But that's not Anthony."

"I see that now. I'm sure we can work out something," Felix said and then added, "I wonder what type of volunteer work I could do?"

"Are you crazy?" Salome asked. "You're a Man of Letters. Think of how many kids you could help to read and write!"

"You're right, Salome. I'll go volunteer to help kids read and write." And then Salome said, "Let me change the subject back to something we were talking about before...before I forget! Felix...if you're really too embarrassed to go get your back hair removed professionally, and that's something that you really want to do, if you'll buy an electric clipper, I'll clip the long hair first, and then shave your back for you. It won't be quite as good as waxing, but it will be free and free from embarrassment."

"You mean like once a month?" Felix asked.

"Why not?" Salome said.

"Well...that's an incredibly generous offer, Salome. But I'd feel better if Anthony gave his approval. I don't know how he'd feel having his wife shave another man's back...even his brother's!" Felix said.

Just then Anthony came back into the apartment and said, "Hey look Felix...I'm really sorry. You've been nothing but great to us. I'll try to lessen my cocaine usage, and I'll try not to be an A-hole in the evenings when I'm crashing. Also, I would rather open up an office where I'm more visible to the corporate world. I think that Tampa would be a better decision. However, I haven't forgotten about our original agreement. And although our profits from the motel will be cut, because we'll have to hire someone fulltime to live here and work in the office, I'll still oversee the place...even if I'm living and working in Tampa. Is that okay?"

"Bet!" said Felix. And then he added, "As an act of contrition, would you mind if Salome shaved my back once a month?"

And Anthony looked at Felix with an askew-like glance and said, "I guess that would be okay."

@@@@@@@@

During the Saturday of Labor Day weekend in 1980, just before Walter Lee and Annie Harrison had tied the knot under a big canopy on the beach behind *The Breakers*, Jack and Geneva Apple announced that Geneva was two months gone, and that the baby was due in April. Annie was a month ahead of Geneva, and the two women laughed about how great it was going to be to raise their children together.

Annie said to Geneva, "I know you and Jack are cool in regards to the racial differences, and I know that you two are very much in love, but is Jack living in *Fantasyland* in regards to how the baby is going to look?"

"You mean, because I'm light skinned, is Jack assuming that the baby is going to look Caucasian?" Geneva asked.

"Yeah," Annie said.

"We talked about all that before we got married. Jack really doesn't care if our baby is black, white, boy, or girl. We both just want healthy!"

"How about his peeps?" Annie asked.

"The Apples are wonderful people, especially Jack's mom Pauline. I've thought the world of her for a long time. Jack's father, Bubba, can be an A-hole at times, but he has a good heart. The only thing the Apples were mad about was that we all eloped in Reno and didn't invite them. My brother and grandparents were pretty pissed about that also."

Actually, although Jack and Geneva never knew, Bubba had expressed concern to Pauline in regards to his son and new daughter-in-law's racial differences. "WHYYY JEEESUS CHRIST," Bubba had said. "GENEEEVA is a fine young LAAADY, and I don't care that SHEEE'S black, but there are people out there who will care. I don't want EIIITHER of them to get hurt!"

And Pauline had said, "They'll just have to learn how to be careful...how to sense if they're in the wrong place at the wrong time."

"And how about their BAAABIES?" Bubba had said. "GROOOWING up, those kids are GOOOING to have a difficult TIIIME! In the South EEESPECIALLY!" The one time Alabamian, Bubba, had said.

"Well maybe eventually Jack and Geneva will encounter problems in Florida. I hope not. But if they do, there are cities, like New York, where mixed racial families can probably live safely. I'm sure Jack, Geneva, and their future children will be just fine," Pauline had said.

Just then music blared from the back of *The Trail's End* motel next door. It was the same song that had been played *ad nauseam* for the past year on Mad Beach. A local group, *The Mad Beach Band*, was responsible for "Put Willie Nelson in the White House," which featured the lyric: "*Don't you think it would be smarter, instead of Jimmy Carter, to put Willie in the White House next year.*"

"Sounds like you have a nice family thing happening," Annie said. "I'm envious. I have no siblings. My grandparents all died a long time ago. I never knew my father, and my mom died in 1973. I wish someone from my family could have been here today." And then Anne's eyes became wet and she struggled to get out, "The closest thing I ever had to a brother, the son of the man for whom I had worked for fourteen years, Darius was the son's name, died in a mountain climbing accident in 1976. I wish he were here today to give me away." Annie was crying hard now, and she turned away from Geneva and buried her face into the plastic slats of the beach chair. And, of course, it always hurts deeply when there is a big event in one's life, and someone who had been very important, is no longer alive to witness and participate in the milestone moment.

Walter Lee was sitting unnoticeably on the terrace of his apartment, staring out at the Gulf of Mexico, and crying himself. In Walter Lee's case however, he was not thinking of those who were not here to witness this joyous event. He was thinking that this event wouldn't even be taking place, if those he loved were still alive. "You know I'll never forget you Ruth," Walter Lee said. "We certainly had our hard times when you were alive. We fought, struggled, and yelled. It seemed as if we were fighting all of the time. And I'm so sorry that I was never able to provide you with the nice things...the things that make life easier. But I always loved you Ruth...you were the love of my life. And I hope, wherever you are, that you're okay with me marrying and having a child with Annie. She's a good woman, Ruth. I love her very much. I was just so tired of being alone. I need a companion for the rest of my life, and I'm so sorry that it can no longer be you, Ruth."

And then Felix from the back of the motel shouted, "Okay you poor unfortunate souls. Enjoy your last few minutes of freedom. Brother Bob is ready to perform the ceremony. Best man, maid of honor, bride and groom...it's fifteen minutes until show time!"

Walter Lee had asked Felix to be his best man, but Felix had thought it would be good for Anthony if Walter Lee asked him instead. Walter Lee had agreed. Geneva had asked Salome to be her maid of honor.

Walter Lee and Annie were going to honeymoon in Paris for ten days. When Anthony heard that he had said, "Maybe we can get Miep to give them a nice wedding present when they get to Paris."

And Felix had said, "You know Walter Lee has never liked that stuff, and I don't think Annie has even tried it. Get your mind off of cocaine, Anthony!"

And Anthony said, "I was just kidding, Felix!" But he really wasn't. In fact, until he thought it through, Anthony was planning on asking Walter Lee if he would mind meeting Miep there, and bringing something back from her to him. Fortunately, before he embarrassed himself, Anthony suppressed that particular urge.

@@@@@@@@

In early 1981, senior FBI Agent Fester Daily sat reading *The New York Post* at his desk in Manhattan while having his morning coffee and doughnuts. On the cover was a story of the big ruckus at the Museum of Natural History yesterday, in which representatives of the Algonquin Native American Tribe had staged a protest over the Algonquin exhibition that had just opened. The loud chanting of tribal curses linked together as a song had alerted the museum's security guards that there was 'trouble in River City,' but before they could call the cops and remove the protesters, several of those protesters had spray painted exhibits in red with a big POW. "We are all just prisoners of war in the white man's country!" a quote from one of the protesters declared in the story. "The way this exhibit is being shown is racist, demeaning, and just plain stupid! Members of our tribe should have been involved in the proper setting up of this exhibition!" said another quote. Meanwhile, although not mentioned in the newspaper story, on the eastside of Manhattan, members of the Algonquin Literary Circle were discussing the merits of the novel *Naked Came the Stranger*, by Penelope Ashe.

Fester Daily was reading the rest of the story on page three, when he came to something interesting. An employee of the museum, a researcher named Ivy Laplotski, was interviewed. In the interview Ms. Laplotski said, *"And although I do not condone their methods, the Algonquin Tribe certainly has a good point. This exhibition was set up wrong."* This quote, of course, would get Ivy into trouble with her boss, Thomas Short, the person who had been responsible for how the exhibition had been set up. Fester Daily would say aloud to nobody, "I see…I guess Ivy Laplotski is a Commie bitch just like her twin sister Ida!"

Fester Daily had been the original FBI agent on the Ida Laplotski case back in 1966. He had been a junior agent then, and working with his now retired senior partner, P. Mark Wall, they had followed all of the leads in the case to absolutely nowhere. Reading Ivy Laplotski's comments in the paper, noticing her obviously leftist vocabulary, an idea began to maturate in Fester's mind. In fact he became so excited, he accidentally squeezed his half-dunked *Dunkin' Donut*, and the scarlet jelly ended up squirting all over his shirt and stationary. This was 1981, and with the newly advanced FBI computers, there might be a way to see what else Ivy Laplotski had been involved in, where else she had been, and maybe even nail Ida Laplotski.

In April of 1966, *Weathermen* member Ida Laplotski, as a protest against the War in Vietnam and as a protest for Civil Rights, had been responsible for the compete destruction of a federal building in Birmingham, Alabama. She had parked her car on the street in the back of the building, and then she had snuck onto the grounds. The Bennett Building, located at #1 Government Street, housed both the Draft Board and the local office of the FBI. This was a Sunday night, and the place was completely empty. There were no lights on anywhere. To be sure, Ida had phoned the building from a payphone thirty minutes earlier and had let the phone ring without an answer at least fifty times, and all of the research that previously had been done by the *Weathermen* had indicated that there would be no security guards or janitorial staff there on a Sunday. This building was one of three that the *Weathermen* planned to blow up at the same time—the other two buildings were in Chicago and Kansas City—and they wanted absolutely no loss of life due to the explosions.

The *Weathermen* had a military explosives hook up with a young sympathetic soldier at the Huntsville Alabama Arsenal. Huntsville housed the largest stockpile of weaponry in the South, and Robert Polar, a young army demolitions trainee who had been stationed there and who desperately didn't want to go to Vietnam next, was approached for help by Hugh Stack, a childhood friend from Ann Arbor, Michigan, who was now an active bigwig in the *Weathermen*. Hugh Stack wanted C-4. Robert Polar had then provided him with twelve pre-packed shaped charge satchel bombs, and the training manual that showed how to achieve optimum effect with proper placement.

On this Sunday night, Herbert Whithers was apprehended in Chicago by a passing off duty cop, who spotted him trying to place the last bomb on the southwestern corner of his building. Richard Crevice, the bomber-to-be who had been assigned to the Kansas City operation, was pulled over for a broken tag light on his way to the assignment. The car had smelled like marijuana, and a subsequent search had found his four bombs. He was being held in the Kansas City jail for FBI interrogation.

Ida Laplotski set the timers and placed her four bombs, one against each of the four corners of the building. The bombs were set to go off in twenty minutes, but the third bomb had a shoddy timer mechanism. Ida had just placed the fourth bomb and was leaving the property, when the third bomb went off and blew debris everywhere. The force of the explosion knocked Ida down, and momentarily she lost consciousness. When she managed to gain her wits and get to her feet ten minutes had already passed. She started to walk away from the building, but she had temporary amnesia, so she knew neither of what she had been doing nor who she was. The loud explosion had produced phone calls at the Birmingham Police Station, but fortunately their reaction time was slow enough that they were still safely a few minutes away from the Bennett Building when the other bombs went off. The four story building was reduced to rubble instantaneously, looking as if it belonged in Dresden during World War II. Meanwhile, a confused and disheveled Ida Laplotski, totally forgetting that she had driven a car, had walked through the adjoining neighborhood and was now standing and staring at the I-20 East Expressway entrance ramp. Robert Greenwood, an ACLU attorney from New York City, was driving back home after his vacation and he had gotten off I-20 for gas at this exit. As he approached the entrance ramp to head east to Atlanta for the night, he saw Ida and asked her if she needed help. Ida didn't know at the moment what she needed, so she just casually got into Robert Greenwood's car. As they were pulling onto the expressway he asked her if she had heard the explosions. She just nodded and said that she had no idea where those explosions had come from. They continued driving along, and then suddenly Robert Greenwood recognized Ida.

And although he hadn't been at Ida's emotionally stirring speech in Washington Square Park just a month ago, he had read the context of that speech and had seen her picture in *The Village Voice* a week later. "I know who you are!"

"Well that makes one of us!" Ida had said.

Then Robert Greenwood told Ida about herself. By the time they reached Atlanta, they had listened to accounts of the bombing on four different radio stations and Ida had remembered everything. Robert had figured out that Ida must have been involved, but he didn't care. He found that he was quite smitten with Ida. "At least there have been no reports of human casualties," he had said.

Ida needed Robert Greenwood's help, so she decided to trust him. She said, "I'm totally screwed! I left a car at the location of the bombing with my fingerprints all over it."

"We'll figure something out," Robert had said. And the next morning in Atlanta, after going through the main library's microfiche of all copies of *The Atlanta Constitution* looking for a baby who had died in approximately the same year that Ida had been born, they got lucky. A Caucasian baby girl, in Douglasville, Georgia, had been born very premature and died about a month before Ida had been born in Brooklyn, New York. The Underwood family had named their daughter Selma. When they got back to New York, it was fairly easy for Robert to help Ida open up a post office box under the name of Selma Underwood. A few weeks after sending off the five dollars with a letter of request, a certified copy of Selma Underwood's birth certificate had arrived in the post office box. Robert took care of everything. He got Ida a new social security card, and he took her to take her tests and get her driver license with a new name. A month after having met, Ida agreed to marry Robert Greenwood. At the same time, Robert had gotten sick of living the hustle bustle lifestyle in Manhattan. He found in the *Eastern Law Journal* an opportunity to work for a small law firm in Middlebury, Vermont that seemed to be exactly what he wanted. He married Ida in July of 1966, they bought a small house in Rutland about an hour south of the office, and then Robert took and passed his Vermont State Bar Examination in August. Three years later, in December of 1969, the forty year-old husband of Selma Greenwood died from stomach cancer.

"Since Ivy Laplotski seems to be cut from the same fabric as her sister," Fester Daily said to nobody, "Let's run a fingerprint check on her and see what the cat drags in." Since the FBI's computer system was about fifty percent digitized by 1981, and since Ida Laplotski's file indicated that her twin sister had once taught school in New York City and all New York City school teachers had to be fingerprinted, it was fairly easy to bring up a copy of Ivy Laplotski's prints. In the past, Agent Daily had always tried to run Ida's prints and had always come up with zilch. And since all state employees in

Vermont had to be fingerprinted by the mid 1960's, when Ida had gotten her state librarian license under the name of Selma Greenwood using a doctored Masters Degree in Library Science from Columbia University, she had convinced Ivy to go to Burlington to be fingerprinted for her. When Fester Daily ran Ivy Laplotski's prints through the computer he came up with something interesting. He knew that she currently worked at the Museum of Natural History in Manhattan, but apparently she was also working as a librarian in Rutland, Vermont. "Bingo!" he said to nobody.

Ida Laplotski had made a critical error in April of 1966. The *Weathermen* had gotten some of their research incorrect. If Ida had looked inside of the Bennett Building, she would have noticed that the place was *really* empty. Sure, she had blown up the Bennett Building at #1 Government Street in Birmingham, Alabama, per her radical group's directive. But what none of them knew, was that that was the old Bennett Building. Everything had been moved a week earlier across the four lane highway to the new Bennett Building, which kept the #1 Government Street address, and the old building was scheduled for complete demolition by the federal government a month later. With all of the engineering reports and safety protocols that the federal government would have to pay for prior to a federal building's demolition, what Ida Laplotski essentially did was to save the United States close to $100,000. And, of course, if one told Fester Daily that one would hear, "I don't care. She broke the law, and she's eventually going to be found and sent to jail."

Chapter Eleven

Whether it was luck, fate, or some kind of temporal displacement caused by James T. Kirk and Mr. Spock from the *FSS Enterprise* a few centuries later remains unknown, but on that icy cold Saturday morning in February of 1981, when FBI Agent Fester Daily flashed his badge and asked Lizzie Apple at the front desk of the Rutland Library for Selma Greenwood—the name that had been attached to Ivy Laplotski's fingerprints as a librarian in Vermont—she had to reply, "I'm sorry sir, but Selma is on vacation."

"Is this Selma?" And then he had shown Lizzie the cut out picture of Ivy from *The New York Post*.

"Yes," she had said.

"Do you have any idea where she went on vacation?" Fester Daily had to ask.

And although Lizzie had no idea about Selma's radical past or that her sister was a twin, she had been intuitive enough to realize that an FBI visit on a Saturday in regards to Selma, complete with a cut out newspaper picture of her, by some non-smiling megacephalic-looking flatfoot in a heavy navy blue reefer covering a *Sears* silver seersucker suit, probably wasn't good news for Selma. "I have no idea," Lizzie had to answer.

"Do you know when she'll be back?" Agent Daily had then asked.

"She left last night, and she'll be back a week from Monday," Lizzie had then responded.

Fester Daily hadn't believed Lizzie so he had asked, "I find it unusual that a woman you work with goes on vacation for ten days, and apparently she isn't excited enough about the vacation to brag about where she's going?"

And Lizzie, who could smell trouble standing before her had said, "Selma is probably the most private person I've ever met."

"Thanks," Fester had said before leaving. And then he had thought, 'It's colder out here than Ida Laplotski's tit…I'll bet she went to Florida! I'll check the airline manifests at Burlington Airport,' just before he had slipped on the ice and fallen on his face in the Rutland Library parking lot.

Fifteen minutes later Lizzie had taken her lunch break and walked the two blocks to *Zeus' Heroes* for a sandwich. After placing her order, she had gone next door to the laundromat, used their coin changer for five dollars worth of change, and then she had used their payphone to call Selma at the *Hotel Frontenac* in Quebec City. And although FBI Agent Daily hadn't felt it necessary to ask for a wiretap on the library's phone yet, Lizzie Apple hadn't wanted to take any chances. "*Bonjour…Hotel Frontenac…à votre service*!"

"The room of Selma Greenwood please." The phone had rung seven or eight times before the man at the front desk had come back on and asked in English if Lizzie would like to leave a message. Lizzie had left a message, and a few hours later Selma had called the library.

"From having watched a number of cop shows on television, I think they need ninety seconds to trace a call!" Lizzie had said, "So I'll make this quick." And then Lizzie had told Selma all about the FBI visit, and she had also tried to get some information from Selma about what the problem could possibly be. Selma had said nothing but, "Thank you!" before hanging up the phone. 'Fucking Fester Daily!' Selma had thought.

And now Selma was on the road. She had checked out from the hotel immediately after the phone call with Lizzie. She was hoping that the FBI had just recently somehow made a connection to her in Rutland—having not spoken to her sister this week she was unaware of the story and her sister's quote in *The New York Post*—and that at this juncture the FBI didn't consider her a high enough priority to be watching the borders yet. Selma was hoping there was still enough time for her to slip back into the United States on this freezing Saturday night. She decided to use the smaller crossing at Rouses Point, New York, instead of the larger border crossing back into Vermont on Highway 7. Yesterday she had entered Canada from Vermont on Highway 7. But Rouses Point was closer geographically and it was a quicker border crossing, since it was primarily used either by families heading to Cornwall, Quebec, for the all-you-can eat Chinese buffet, or by sexually frustrated men heading just outside of Cornwall to *Chez Diane* to watch the beautiful naked women dance, and then to head off to a back room with one's choice of a beautiful naked woman for some paid for randy activity. (Regardless of annual inflationary adjustments for said randy activity, according to *The Farmers Almanac*, the price for a *blumpkin* has remained consistently $250 Canadian. And, of course, according to The Bible, the price for too many visits to Sodom and Gomorrah has remained consistently a trip to Hell.)

Selma Greenwood had already put together a contingency plan for an occurrence such as this. She had $20,050 in a special checking account, and Ivy Laplotski had a check made out to her for $20,000 from Selma Greenwood sitting in a desk drawer in her apartment in Flushing.
About once a year Selma would write a new check and send it to Ivy in care of the museum and Ivy would then destroy the old check. Selma would always drive to New York City to mail her letters with a bogus typed return address to Ivy in care of the museum, assuming that if Ivy's mail were being monitored, certainly anything mailed within New York City itself would raise no eyebrows. Selma's small house had no mortgage, and every year when she would send Ivy a fresh check she would also send a fresh power of attorney. Ivy also had a power of attorney from years ago for Ida Laplotski. Once contacted, Ivy would cash the check, sell the house, and forward all of the proceeds.

The house had been appraised at $75,000 a year ago, so Selma was looking at close to a $100,000 nest egg once everything was squared away, because she also had $5,000 in emergency cash—plus everything for yet another identity—hidden in a special lockbox she had installed under the dash of her 1980 *Toyota Corolla* a week after purchasing the car.

When Selma had visited Buffalo a few years ago, she had gone to the main library and looked at the microfiche of past issues of *The Buffalo Post*. And just like years earlier in Atlanta, when her research had yielded the name of Selma Underwood, this time she had found the obituary of a female Caucasian baby in nearby Rochester, who had died a crib death about a year after Ida had been born. Selma, using that child's name, had rented a room in a rooming house in Rochester and had ordered a birth certificate sent to that address. Once she had the birth certificate, she used it to open up a post office box in downtown Buffalo. And once she had the box, she immediately gave up her room in Rochester. Ivy knew that if Selma ever called her at work, quickly said, "It's time!" and hung up, that Selma was on the run, and that Ivy was to deposit the check for $20,000 in her account, wait for it to clear, withdraw the money, and then travel to several different check cashing places in nearby states outside of New York, Pennsylvania, Delaware, Connecticut, etc., and purchase money orders all under $3,000—since anything over $3,000 was reported to Uncle Sam—and to send those money orders to: Amy Rosenberg, P.O. Box 2334, Buffalo, NY, 14212. While doing all of that, Ivy also would drive to Rutland, put Selma's house up for sale, and when sold, forward that money to Amy Rosenberg in Buffalo also. Selma would drive to Manhattan and mail a Saturday morning phone number to Ivy at the museum, and that number would be in the city where Selma would alight for awhile, waiting for the money from the sale of her house in Rutland. When Ivy called that number on Saturdays from a payphone in Manhattan—in order to limit specific information even on a payphone—and

Selma asked, "Is it time?" if Ivy were to say, "Yes!" then Selma knew that somebody had closed on her house, a bank would be writing a check to Selma Greenwood, and that check, with the help of Selma Greenwood's power of attorney, would get deposited in Ivy's account, and that money would be withdrawn over a period of time. Eventually, there would be a plethora of money orders arriving, with different made up return addresses, mailed from different places—as Ivy could work in the travel time.

The post office box in Buffalo had a combination rather than a key, and Ivy also knew that combination. If during a Saturday call Selma ever said, "Make time!" that meant that Ivy had to schlepp six hours northwest to Buffalo in her 1980 *Toyota Corolla* (purchased the same week that Selma had bought hers, unbeknownst what Selma had purchased) and check for an important letter in the box within the next few weeks. The letter meant for Ivy would be addressed to Amy Rosenberg, but Ivy would be able to discern that letter, because it's return address would be the fictional Rick Kimble.

Selma had gotten a New York driver license under the name of Amy Rosenberg in Albany a year ago, when she had convinced Ivy to drive to Albany, meet her, and take her for her written and driving tests. (In 1966 she had exchanged the original Selma Underwood New York driver license that her husband helped her to get, for a Selma Greenwood Vermont license when they had married and moved to Rutland.) Selma had also obtained both a social security card and a passport under the name of Amy Rosenberg, and she had retrieved both of these items from her post office box during another trip to Buffalo six months ago; they were currently sleeping in the lock box under the dash and using the five grand as a pillow.

Until the house was sold, Selma would have to live in close proximity to Buffalo. After receiving all of her funds however, Selma would be "free" to move anywhere in the country that pleased her and that she deemed as safe. Certainly she couldn't stay around Rutland, she couldn't be near her sister and mother in New York City, and she couldn't be near Salome in Florida. Wherever she would eventually settle, Ivy would always have Selma's phone number for Saturday morning calls from payphones in Manhattan. If Ivy ever said, "Make time!" Selma would know that she had to return to her box in Buffalo for an important letter from Rick Kimble.

Selma made it through the border at Rouses Point without any problems. It was just after midnight, and Selma knew that Salome would be finishing up at *The Careless Navigator*. Selma stopped at the first payphone she saw, removed one of the four rolls of quarters that she always kept in her glove compartment, and called Salome at work. Salome was devastated when told the story, and especially when Selma said, "I don't know if we'll ever be able to see each other again." Selma hung up the phone, got back into her car, sat and cried a few minutes, and then she drove west. She had a good *AAA* map, and although she didn't think that there would be an APB out on her now, nonetheless she decided to take smaller highways all the way to Buffalo. From Buffalo it would only be a few hours to Cleveland, and Cleveland was where Selma was going to alight for awhile.

Once in Cleveland, Selma would decide that she needed to do it again, she needed another identity after Amy Rosenberg. There would be too much financial activity with that name in the next several months. She would do her Amy Rosenberg banking in Buffalo, have an account there, withdraw all of the money in less than $3,000 increments, and then deposit that money in different increments, at a much later date, under her next name in her next bank account, in a galaxy far far away from Cleveland.

When she found her next name in *The Cleveland Plain Dealer* and tried to get a birth certificate, a letter was sent back that said:

> *To Whom It May Concern:*
>
> *We cannot issue a duplicate birth certificate for Elvira Johansen, because our records indicate that a death certificate was written just one week after her birth.*
>
> *Sincerely,*
>
> *Babs Kendal*
> *Cuyahoga County Bureau of Vital Statistics*

Selma learned that since 1980, with the advent of more sophisticated digitalized computer systems, a number of large cities were now cross-referencing their birth and death certificates.

On a pilgrimedge to Detroit a couple of months later, the library research of *The Detroit Free Press* produced the name of a child who had been born in Little Rock, Arkansas, and who had died in a car accident in Detroit three months later. Selma still hadn't figured out were she was going to permanently settle, but she knew that for the rest of her life she would always be known as Betty Lou Baker.

@@@@@@@@

For Thanksgiving of 1981, Salome, Anthony, Jack, Geneva, and the twins flew up to Burlington. The babies had been born in April, and neither Jack's parents nor Geneva's grandmother had seen anything but pictures so far. Jack had agreed to let Geneva name their children, and since they were fraternal twins, she had named them after the parents she barely remembered. And although little Sam Apple was asleep on his father's shoulder when he first met his grandfather at Burlington Airport, his sister, little

Lani—after Bubba had gotten close to her face and said, "WHYYY... look at this BEEEAUTIFUL little girl!"—punched Bubba smack in the nose. "WHYYY JEEESUS CHRIIIST!" Bubba said laughingly. "YOUUU want to hurt your old grandpa?" And then he lifted Lani into his arms, kissed her, and held her.

As they were leaving the terminal to go find Bluebird in the parking lot, they ran into Dr. Bill Wicks waiting on the arrival of his daughter and her family from California. "WHYYY JEEESUS CHRIIIST…I haven't seen YOUUU in months…Bill!" Bubba said.

"Hey Bubba. I'm waiting for Carolyn, Bob, and the kids."

"Bill, you KNOOOW Jack, Geneva, and Salome. I'd like YOUUU to MEEET my son-in-law Anthony."

"I met Anthony back in…1977 I guess…when he was first courting Salome. Nice seeing you again," Bill Wicks said.

"Nice seeing you again too," Anthony said and shook hands.

"And I'd like YOUUU to MEEET the BAAABIES…Sam over here is ASLEEEP on Jack's arm. And this little LAAADY here is Lani…and SHEEE just punched MEEEE in the nose!"

"Hello," Bill Wicks said quickly.

"WEEE got to GOOO…Pauline is preparing a big FEEEAST...but… WHYYY JEEESUS CHRIIIST…drop OOOVER some TIIIME!" Bubba said.

"Okay," Bill Wicks said.

On the way down Highway 7 to Rutland Bubba asked Jack, "SOOO… aren't the four of YOUUU real crowded in that MOOOTEL room?"

"We're going to buy a house in the next few years…Can't do that now…because you know I just opened *Apple Refrigeration* on Mad Beach this past August," Jack said.

"How's it GOOOING?" Bubba asked.

"Not bad," Jack said. "It's too early to tell yet, but we're getting by."

"We could more than just get by right now Mr. Apple, if your son wasn't such an honest man," Geneva said.

"What do YOUUU mean?" Bubba asked.

"What she means," Jack said, "Is that it would have been fairly easy to steal a number of accounts from *Tampa Bay Refrigeration…*"

"His customers love him," Geneva butted in with and then added, "And so do I."

"Thanks honey," Jack said. "I love you too. No Bubba…I just couldn't rip off Fred Watkins at *Tampa Bay Refrigeration*. He's been nothing but great to me."

"I'm proud of YOUUU!" Bubba said.

And this really amazed Jack. Was this the same man who had kicked the crap out of him when he was young…more times than he would like to remember? Was this the same man who had broken his sister's jaw six years ago…the human he had used his *Louisville Slugger* on…and on whom he had tried to go yard? 'Bubba has certainly softened up,' thought Jack. 'But I guess everything changes.' "Thanks Dad," Jack said.

"We're not in that small one-bedroom apartment at the motel anymore Mr. Apple," Geneva said.

Bubba, who was still a little dazed from having heard Jack call him 'Dad,' was slow to respond, "Where did YOUUU move?" Bubba asked.

"Anthony's brother, Felix, gave us his big three-bedroom two-bathroom place on the third floor of the motel in June, after Anthony and Salome moved into their house in Tampa. The apartment is actually a small house on the beach," Geneva said.

"Yeah…Felix is a great guy," Jack said. "Just before the babies were due, he said to Geneva and me, 'Hey look guys…Anthony and Salome are closing on that house in Tampa next month. After they move out, why don't you take my place? Walter Lee's old apartment is available, and all I really need is a one-bedroom place. Besides, I need to start writing again. I need the vibe of Jack Kerouac…which lives in that apartment!' And Jack continued, "So he moved his office phone and ringer, bumped our rent up just a little, and we moved into the bigger place on the third floor."

"How's your new PLAAACE Salome?" Bubba asked.

"It's nice," said a quiet Salome.

"It's in a real beautiful neighbor…it's zoned for great schools when we have kids…it's a four-bedroom three-bathroom Tudor…on a cobblestone street," Anthony said.

"How's the law practice GOOOING Anthony?" Bubba asked.

"Pretty good Mr. Apple…I just picked up two nice accounts this past week," Anthony said.

"YOUUU still working at your restaurant, Salome?" Bubba asked.

"Yep," Salome said.

"We both work at *The Careless Navigator* Tuesday through Saturday nights Mr. Apple. Salome is my boss," Geneva said.

"Does it take a long TIIIME now to drive to work from Tampa… Salome?" Bubba asked.

"Forty minutes," Salome said, continuing with her terse answers.

"I can't wait to EEEAT dinner," Bubba said, feeling hurt that there was apparently still nothing he could do or say to win Salome's forgiveness. He turned on the car radio to listen to the news in silence for the remainder of the trip home. When they pulled in front of the house he finally said, "Anthony…Geneva…call MEEE either 'Dad' or 'Bubba.' Anything but 'Mr. Apple.'"

The next night, after they had eaten Thanksgiving leftovers, and the entire family was either sitting around the big dining room table talking and drinking or sitting in the living room talking and drinking, Bubba said to Dick, "Let's GOOO get a cold one at the VFW hall…I'm TIIIRED of hearing all the gossip!"

"You know I don't drink anymore Bubba," said Dick.

"WHYYY JEEESUS CHRIIIST," said Bubba. Can YOUUU just keep MEEE company?"

"Sure," Dick said.

When they entered the VFW hall, Bubba and Dick noticed Bill Wicks down at the other end of the bar talking to cab driver Jebediah Witherspoon. They both had their backs to Bubba and Dick. Bubba ordered and received a beer, and then he and Dick walked towards Bill Wicks. As Bubba approached and was about to speak, he heard Bill Wicks say, "Bubba's kid just came back here with his nigger wife and zebra children."

"WHYYY JEEESUS CHRIIIST…did I hear YOUUU correctly? Would YOUUU care to REEEPEAT that to MYYY face? I never knew that YOUUU were a racist PIEEECE of shit Bill!" Bubba said angrily. A nervous Bill Wicks got off of his bar stool and turned toward Bubba. Bubba continued, "And you're a doctor TOOO!…YOUUU poor excuse for a HUUUMAN!" And then Bubba spat on the floor to show his disdain.

A somewhat drunken and angry Bill Wicks—an embarrassing newspaper story had appeared in *The Rutland Free Press* the day before Thanksgiving, in regards to his involvement in the currently sensational divorce case of Augusta vs. Maggie Smith—took his beer and tossed it into Bubba's face and said, "Go fuck yourself Bubba!"

Bubba reached out and grabbed Bill's arm, spun him around, put him into a full nelson, and from behind whispered into his ear, "Look Bill…I knooow you're embarrassed by the story in the paaaper…I knooow Augusta had deeetectives following youuu guys around in 1974…I knooow theeey had pictures of youuu two goooing into different moootels in Burlington and Plattsburgh…I know that Augusta forgaaave Maggie back then…she promised to stop seeeing you…but then Augusta caught youuu two again earlier this year…But don't taaake that out on myyy family Bill!" And then Bubba let Bill go.

"Fuck you Bubba!" Bill Wicks said, and then he hit Bubba on the cheek with not only Jebediah Witherspoon's beer, but with the schooner it came in. Bubba was cut and bleeding profusely from two different places on the left side of his face.

Dick Chumwell leaned in and cold-cocked Bill Wicks—dropped him like the Standard of Living. Dick looked down at Bill Wicks, spat on him, and then softly said, "Physician heal thyself!"

Once outside, Dick removed his coat, took off his flannel shirt, and he gave it to Bubba. He said, "Press this against your face with pressure…try and stop the bleeding!" Dick drove Bubba to the ER at Rutland General

Hospital. After they carefully cleaned out all of the tiny shards of glass, Bubba received four stitches just above his left eye and three stitches in his left cheek just below the eye. They got home a couple of hours later, and Dick explained to the remaining family what exactly had happened.

An hour after getting home, Sheriff Glenn came and arrested both Dick and Bubba for Assault. A very drunk Bill Wicks, forgetting what he had done at the bar, had filed a complaint. Pauline followed in Bluebird, and they were both out on bail within forty minutes. And although Bubba and Dick hadn't thought about filing any charges against Bill, since they were at the police station anyway, they decided to have him arrested. An hour later, Bill Wicks was picked up and booked for Assault also.

Two months later, after all three men had spent slightly more than twelve hundred dollars each on lawyers, through those lawyers, they had all worked an agreement with The State of Vermont. All three men pled guilty, and after Judge Harold Rheingold had lectured them on the repercussions of irresponsible drinking, all three men received probation. Bubba and Bill Wicks would serve their probations in Vermont, and Dick—after an agreement had been reached with his CO at Plattsburgh Air Force Base—would report to a civilian probation officer in downtown Plattsburgh, New York monthly.

@@@@@@@@

In March of 1982, Walter Lee and Annie Younger celebrated the first birthday of their daughter Lena. And although Walter Lee, Annie, and Lena had been traveling around Florida incessantly—maintaining quality control on the other three restaurants in Tampa, Orlando, and Miami—they loved the time they could spend at *The Careless Navigator* on Mad Beach, and they especially loved staying at their home in *The Breakers*. Recently they had been wavering on whether or not they wanted to pursue other restaurants in other cities. To be sure, they knew that they eventually wanted to sell the other places, just keep the original and remain on Mad Beach, once Lena was old enough to attend public school. And although Walter Lee had finished his graduate program, written and defended his dissertation, and received his Ph.D., he was still a little annoyed that he hadn't been able to go to Nigeria to gather data for the topic he had really wanted to research: *The Born African: Emigrating and Assimilation in White America*. Instead, since he had become such a big restaurant mogul and couldn't spend much time out of the United States, he had researched—he actually rented a kiosk in Tyrone Square Mall in St. Petersburg, and he would ask passing African-Americans to answer his questionnaire—and written: *Living in America: The Afro-American in the Modern South*. The dissertation had been purchased by *Logocentrician Publishing, Inc.*, in New York, Walter Lee had already worked with an editor and corrected all errata, and the book was due out within the next sixty days.

"Yeah, yeah, yeah…I know…" said Felix, after he had walked up to the beach table, and he heard Walter Lee tell the vacationing Bruiser and Eileen Apple that his book would be out by May, and Walter Lee, after having seen him approach had begun to smile. "People will be able to read it in English…right?"

Walter Lee laughed and said, "No 'Licks…I wasn't gonna kid you about that again."

"Yeah right…Scholar Lee," Felix said.

"My Aunt Clara…read your book…in French," Bruiser wheezed.

"Really…I wonder where she got it," Felix said. "Was she in Europe recently?"

"She got it…in Montreal at a…book store on Ste.…Catherine Street."

"Wow!" said Felix. "I'm being sold in North America…just thirty miles from *les Etats-Unis*!"

And Petomane came over, rubbed up against Felix's leg and thought, 'Both of you guys suck as writers.…*Catiline* by Jonson…Addison's *Cato*… *Cat on a Hot Tin Roof* by Williams…and the poetry of Catullus…now that's good writing! Meanwhile…you can feed me Round Boy!'

"Your kitty face will see grub soon enough, Peto!" Felix said.

Walter Lee went and picked up Lena, and then he walked back to Felix. "She's beautiful…Father Lee," Felix said.

"Yeah…she's my little tweetie," Walter Lee said while tickling Lena. "What I was going to ask you before…'Licks…How's the studio coming?"

"Almost finished," Felix said.

Walter Lee was referring to what Felix had done with the two storage rooms on the first floor. He had gotten rid of a bunch of unneeded stuff, and he had the wall knocked out between the rooms. Then he hired an acoustic engineer, to size up exactly what the room required. The big room had been totally soundproofed, and soon the place would be ready for band practice.

After Salome's advice to do volunteer work, Felix had found a twenty-five hour per week job with a local after school program. Felix had worked out a financial arrangement with Dora Larue, the motel's housekeeper for the past five years, and he had trained her to work in the office when needed. Between Dora, Geneva, and occasionally Annie or Walter Lee, Felix was always covered whenever he was away helping kids with their reading and writing.

On one hand, Salome had been correct, because Felix soon began feeling better about his life while he was helping others. On the other hand, Salome had been incorrect, because the volunteer work had put him no closer to a female 'heart of gold.' And since he was no longer chasing skirts, and the journal entries were slim pickings these days, and he didn't feel like beginning another story, a different idea had come to him immediately upon opening his eyes one morning. Music. Songs. Felix had a *Vox Continental* portable organ and a fifty-watt *Gibson* amplifier set up in his bedroom for years, and occasionally he would play in his neophyte way. And although he wasn't a great keyboardist, he had gotten pretty good at listening to the simpler Rock and Soul songs on the stereo and figuring out the chords for those songs. Felix had even managed to write some simple Rock songs. And even though the rudimentary music revealed Felix's lack of true audio panache, as a published novelist and a Man of Letters, his lyrics were really excellent.

One early evening, while walking on the beach, Felix saw a young man sitting on a blanket playing guitar and singing. Felix stood about twenty feet in back of the young man and listened. He was really good, but more than that, he featured a unique way of playing the acoustic guitar, by incorporating little lead jabs within the chords themselves. At the end of the song Felix told him how impressed he was. A musical conversation turned into a philosophical conversation turned into Felix suggesting that perhaps the young man might be able to work with some of Felix's songs. "The lyrics are great...but the music sucks," Felix had said.

And seventeen year-old K. J. Bauer had said, "That's just the opposite for me. I have no problem coming up with tight music, but I struggle with the lyrics."

And Felix, now almost six years beyond the age of when his generation had said to stop trusting people, had invited K. J. over to hear some of his tunes. K. J. immediately liked Felix's songs, and Felix immediately liked how K. J. rearranged them. That night they wrote their first song together. Taken from the play within the play of *Hamlet*, "The Mousetrap" featured the chorus: "*I saw you, watching me, watching you, watching the play unfold. I saw you, watching me, watching you, watching just what you had sold.*"

"We need to record this," K. J. had said.

"So let's get serious," Felix had said.

And indeed, Felix had gotten serious. Besides building the soundproofed studio, Felix had purchased a used *Hammond B-3* organ;
a *Leslie* speaker; a new *Roland D-50* synthesizer; a used *Altec/Lansing Voice of the Theatre* public address system, with *Shure* microphones and microphone stands; and a new *AIWA* eight-track recorder.

K. J. had a *Fender Stratocaster* electric guitar; an *Ovation* twelve-string acoustic/electric guitar; a *Fender Jazz Bass;* and a *Fender Super Reverb* amplifier. K. J. also had a *Boss* pedal rack for various guitar effects.

In May of 1982, after the studio was finished, and Felix and K. J. had written fifteen songs together, K. J. said, "We really need a bass player and a drummer. Let's get tight with twenty or thirty cover songs, and then we'll understand our groove when it comes to the four of us recording our own material." Felix agreed. And so Felix convinced two of his oldest friends in

St. Petersburg, Jay Biggs a bass player and Montgomery Butler a drummer, to come out to *The Breakers* and play. After playing three or four covers, as more of an experiment than anything, Felix and K. J. taught Jay and Montgomery "The Mousetrap." They practiced the song three times, and put it on tape in just one take. K. J.'s voice was particularly good on that track, so it was unanimously decided that he would be the lead singer, and that everybody else would provide backup vocals.

Petomane, who was in the studio listening to all of this, came by, meowed, and rubbed against Felix's leg. He thought, 'You guys suck…I like Cat Stevens…See?…Cat Stevens…Meanwhile…feed me…Round Boy!'

"Cool your kitty jets Peto," Felix said. "Or I'm gonna be force-feeding you *Purina Dog Chow* in just a few!"

In September of 1982, at Curtis Hixon Hall in Tampa, after opening up with their original material for *Kansas* and the headlining *Rush*, Felix's band, *Home Cooking*, was offered a record contract backstage by Billy Bob Bramlett, an A&R guy with Whizz-Cracker Records out of Valdosta, Georgia. They recorded their first album in Valdosta in December of 1982, but due to limited distribution, "Without Grease" came out in March of 1983 to accolades in the South, but virtual obscurity everywhere else. As Kurt Vonnegut wrote, "So it goes."

@@@@@@@@

In September of 1983, Lizzie Apple gave birth to a second girl. And although newly born Eve Apple had almost the exact face of her two year-old sister Nancy, her hair was almost white blonde in juxtaposition to Nancy's jet black locks. Lizzie was teaching Social Studies at Burlington Central High School and commuting two hours each way, and Jimson, who was working graveyard shift as a guard at the Northwest State Correctional Facility in Swanton, Vermont, forty miles north of Burlington, had a three hour commute each way. They had their small house in Rutland up for sale and were actively looking for a new place in Burlington.

Geneva Apple flew up to Vermont in September of 1983 and helped her grandmother relocate to an assisted living facility in Burlington. The farmhouse had become too much for Geneva's grandmother to manage alone, and the loneliness she felt since her husband had died was overwhelming. She was happy to move somewhere where she would be surrounded by older people. Geneva also helped to put together the sale of the Liberty farm to Bruiser and Eileen Apple. Jr. Liberty was living on a seven acre farm he had purchased near Middlebury, and he was very pleased to hear that Bruiser wanted his grandparents' old place. They were both doing well from the share of *The Careless Navigator* they had split, and they were both still involved in counter-cultural farming—albeit to a much lesser extent. They were growing just enough yearly to keep themselves in stash and to provide an annual limited special treat for their friends. Jr., who was a crackerjack mechanic, had opened a garage in downtown Middlebury.

Bruiser still took hunters to find bear during the season, but he was spending more time at the orchard these days. Bubba had told him that when he eventually got sick of running the business, Bruiser would be the heir apparent to their pomological empire. Bubba had also said, that eventually, he was sure that he and Pauline would move into a smaller house, so the farm house would be Bruiser's also. For now however, Bruiser and Eileen were excited by both their new digs and that Eileen was expecting their first child in January.

Dick and Cindy were expecting their third child in March, and recently they had purchased a nice four-bedroom three-bathroom house in Peru, New York, about twelve miles south of Plattsburgh. Dick, like Bubba, had just four months to go on his Assault probation. Dick also had three years to go in his current six-year Air Force hitch, having re-upped in 1980. Cindy was working fulltime on the 3-11 afternoon/evening shift as an RN at Champlain Valley Hospital in Plattsburgh, and Dick worked from 6 am. until 2 pm.

Jennifer and Colin had cleared the calendar, taken the whole summer off, and spent that time discovering Europe with Colin's children. Jennifer's miscarriage in 1982 had been extremely traumatic for her, but now she and Colin were trying again. Also, another big thing for Jennifer and Colin at the moment was that they had taken up sailing and had just purchased a twenty-five foot *Catalina* Swing Keel sailboat. (Petomane's favorite no doubt!) They had made a test run on Lake Bomoseen, and now they were excited about sailing this whole coming weekend on Lake Champlain.

Bubba and Pauline were getting along better than ever. They were happy to let Bruiser and Eileen run the business a few days per week, and they started to take little three or four day weekend junkets all around the North Country. One weekend they went to the 1,000 Island section of upstate New York, another weekend to Montreal and Quebec City, and still another weekend to Buffalo, Rochester, and Toronto. This coming weekend they were driving to Boston.

Walter Lee and Annie were spending less time on the road, and they seemed genuinely happy being on Mad Beach as much as possible. Occasionally, they would put ear muffs on Lena, and they'd all come in and listen to *Home Cooking* in the studio. Felix and K. J. had written a new album's worth of material; but after they were ready to go into the professional studio and record that new album, instead, the band had decided they wanted to shop around for another record company, and to hire an attorney to try and break their three-record deal with Whizz-Cracker Records. As far as Felix, K. J., Jay, and Montgomery were concerned, Whizz-Cracker hadn't lived up to their part of the agreement, because they hadn't bent over backwards to place "Without Grease," with any music store chains anywhere north of the Mason-Dixon Line.

"Well…sheeet Mr. 'Licks," Walter Lee said. "We be understandin' all de Shakespeare references in Dixie…dat why you be poplar down home… dem nordern Yankees ain't got de smarts to be knowing you. What dat tune from de last recurd…'Derrida's Dilemma?'…Why sheeet…Mr. 'Licks…dey not be knowing nutin bout no Deeeeconstucten in de nord!"

"You're a real panic…Tedious Lee," Felix said. "But since you mentioned Derrida…I got a letter from him yesterday."

"You're kidding," Walter Lee said.

"No I'm not. I sent him a copy of 'Without Grease' and I suggested that he listen to the 'Derrida's Dilemma' track."

"And he responded?" Walter Lee asked.

"I'll be right back," Felix said, and then he went to his apartment to retrieve the letter. He handed it to Walter Lee:

September 1983
Dear Mr. Kulpa,

Thank you for the record album. I enjoyed all of it, and particularly "Derrida's Dilemma." You seem to be having a hard time accepting my idea, that one writes before one speaks. Thus, you sing in the chorus of "Derrida's Dilemma":

"If I kick you in the balls,
will you write before you scream?
Or is this just a part of my Jungian dream?
If I kick you in the balls,
will you write before you scream?
Dear Mr. Derrida."

And that you tag the chorus with "Dear Mr. Derrida," which, of course, is an opening salutation…very interesting! And so I will now answer the question(s) that your thought provoking chorus asks. Ready? The answer is yes.

And now a comment from me on your prose: I enjoyed Tous Les Sieges Etaient Occupés. I was particularly impressed with, since I know you are not a native French speaker, your use of Contrepetrie. Since Contrepetrie is almost impossible to find in English, that you've understood and instructed your translator to use this device twice in your novel astounds me. In Chapter 2,

> *when your protagonist, Joyce Bloom, goes off to boarding school, and her Physical Education Instructor asks her what sport she would like to play. Joyce says that she doesn't know, and then she asks the instructor what she would suggest. And the instructor says, "Les filles aiment le penis en tension," or "Girls like a hard penis," instead of "Les filles aiment le tennis en pension," or "Girls in boarding school like tennis." Wonderful! And later in the novel, in Chapter 10, when Joyce is at a Jewish retreat in the mountains, and she's in deep thought, the French narrator says: "Joyce was in deep thought," and then the narrator adds, "S'asseoir sur la verge du rabin," or "Sitting on the rabbi's penis," instead of "S'asseoir sur la berge du ravin," or "Sitting on the edge of the ravine." Absolutely brilliant! Keep up the good work!*
>
> *Sincerely,*
>
> *Jacques Derrida*

"That's interesting," Walter Lee said. "Do you know French well enough to have thought of that stuff?"

"Absolutely not!" said Felix. "That must have been my wiseass translator, Jean-Luc Petitmalin. I think I need to call him!"

"Are you pissed off?" Walter Lee asked.

"I'm not sure yet. One thing is for sure…"

"What's that?" Walter Lee asked.

"Since I didn't really mean those lines the way they were put into the book in French…'letting the words speak for themselves' is absolute bullshit! Since I'm not the writer of those words…they don't speak for me. It may be time to write 'Derrida's Dilemma Part 2,'" Felix said.

"Good idea," said Walter Lee.

"Hey wait a minute…I just thought of a *Contrepetrie* in English… 'smart feller' and 'fart smeller'…I think I'll write Derrida back."

@@@@@@@@

By Thanksgiving of 1983, when Jack, Geneva, the twins, Salome, and Anthony all came home to Rutland, Salome was at a crossroads. She liked her job; she had been made manager of *The Careless Navigator*, she worked Tuesday through Friday from eleven until six and Saturday from eleven until four, and she had received a substantial pay raise. But all of the reading that Salome had been doing since leaving college—and lately because Anthony was hardly ever around—had been slowly changing her thinking. Salome was on a spiritual quest, and she was attempting to answer the one question that either has an answer, a multitude of answers, or no possible answer at all: "Why am I here?" And in an attempt to find her answer, in the past few years Salome had read a veritable mixed bag of literature, psychology, and religious texts. She would borrow these books from Felix's library, and then she would discuss them with him either when he'd come to Tampa once a month for dinner and a back shave, when he'd come into *The Careless Navigator* for an early dinner, or sometimes she would drive to Mad Beach early before work if Felix could give her an hour or two.

The books Felix had given her to read were just a small sampling of good stuff, and Felix had told her, "If you read my entire library, you'll be just about at the one-tenth of one percent mark...in terms of great books...And you'll be much smarter...because you'll realize just how stupid you really are!" Felix had given Salome: Dickens' *David Copperfield*, *Great Expectations*, and *A Tale of Two Cities*; *Jane Eyre* and *Wuthering Heights* by the Bronte sisters; *Pride and Prejudice* by Jane Austen; Mary Shelley's *Frankenstein*; Joyce's *Ulysses*; Shakespeare's *King Lear* and *Macbeth*; Twain's *The Adventures of Huckleberry Finn*; Melville's *Moby Dick*; Faulkner's *The Sound and the Fury*; Miller's *Death of a Salesman*, *The Crucible*, and *All My Sons*; Hansberry's *A Raisin in the Sun*; Kerouac's *The Dharma Bums*, for a sociological perspective of The Beats, and Kerouac's *Visions of Gerard*, for just great writing; Garcia-Marquez's *One Hundred Years of Solitude*; *Of Mice and Men*, by Steinbeck; poetry by Shakespeare, Shelley, Keats, Yeats, Marvell, Donne, Wordsworth, Milton, Lord Byron, Dickinson, Frost, Whitman, Ginsberg, and Olds; contemporary fiction by Kurt Vonnegut, John Irving, T. C. Boyle, John Barth, Umberto Eco, Philip Roth, Joseph Heller, Joyce Carol Oates, Tom Robbins, William Kotzwinkle, and Karen Loeb; and a final round of classics by Voltaire, Tolstoy, Kafka, Dostoevsky, and Hesse. When Felix had been a graduate student at NYU, one of his professors had told him, "You're here to be a student of literature, not a student of what you like." Felix only had Salome read what he liked.

Salome was a voracious reader, and after she had inhaled Felix's little sampling of literature that she either hadn't read or had just touched upon in college, she decided she wanted to explore Eastern religions in relation to human psychology. So Felix gave her: *Be Here Now*, by Baba Ram Dass; *Gestalt Therapy Verbatim*, by Fritz Perls; *Studies in Hysteria*, by Sigmund Freud; *The Third Eye*, by Lobsang Rampa; the *Bhagavad-Gita*, "The Song of the Blessed One," the most famous Hindu text; *The Brahma Sutras*, the most famous commentary on the *Upanishads*, another famous Hindu text; the *Mahabharata*, yet another sacred Hindu text; the *Srimad-Bhagavatam*, a Hare Krishna text; *The Analats Of Confucius*, commentary on Confucianism; the *TaoTe Ching*, a fifth century work on Buddhism, written by the Chinese hermit Lao Tzu; the *Akaranga Sutra*, the sacred text of Jainism; a couple of books about the Islamic *Qu'Rán*; a book about the Rosicrucian religion; commentary on the *Zohar*, the Jewish sacred book of Kabballa; and L. Ron Hubbard's *Dianetics: The Modern Science of Mental Health*, a book by the founder of Scientology.

During the past month Salome had begun reading The New Testament. Pauline was a Catholic who regularly attended Mass on Sunday mornings with her sister Clara, and she had regularly forced her children to go with her until they were about thirteen. Bubba, a Southern Baptist, never went to church. And other than for weddings and funerals, Salome hadn't been to church since 1973. But now, at this moment in her life, The New Testament was beginning to make sense to Salome.

"I'll cut the TURKEEEY," Bubba said. The food was placed on a long picnic table on one side of the dining room—dinner would be served buffet style—and second and third picnic tables had been placed perpendicularly along the ends of the large Maplewood dining room table forming a huge 'U.' This way Bubba Apple, Pauline Apple, Ethel Bouvier, Clara Small, Jennifer Morgan, Colin Morgan, James Morgan, Erika Morgan, Cindy Chumwell with either Samantha or Dick Jr., Dick Chumwell, Tonya Chumwell, Karla Chumwell, Bruiser Apple, Eileen Apple with either Karen or Conrad, Jack Apple, Geneva Apple, Lorelei Liberty, Sam Apple, Lani Apple, Jr. Liberty, Jimson Apple, Lizzie Apple, Nancy Apple, Eve Apple, Salome Kulpa, and Anthony Kulpa could all look at one another.

During dinner some of the adults drank wine and some drank beer. However, the large majority of the drinking adults, who were sitting at this Thanksgiving table in Bubba and Pauline's dining room, had been slamming vodka and tonics all afternoon. Fairly soon the verbiage began to get sloppy, and that which usually gets repressed was making its move from the brain to the mouth. (Upon returning to Mad Beach, when Jack would tell Felix what had gone on with his wacky drunken family during Thanksgiving, Felix, goofing on the theme song from the television show, *Cheers*, would sing: "*Sometimes you want to go, where everybody is drunk....And they're always glad you stunk...You want to go where people are sloshed, talking shit just the same...You want to go where everyone acts insane.*")

"It's so nice to see you again, Salome," a non-drinking Lorelei Liberty, grandmother of Geneva and Jr., said. "I guess it's been a few years."

"It's great...seeing you again...Ms. Liberty...I know Geneva... misses you," a getting-pretty-blended Salome said. Spiritual journey notwithstanding, Salome had been using a lot more alcohol since she had given up cocaine a few years ago.

"So when are you and Anthony going to give me a great-grandchild?" Salome's grandmother, Ethel Bouvier, walked up and asked.

"When...it...feels...right...don't...bother me with that!" Salome said.

"What? When it feels right? Don't bother me with that? What kind of an answer is that to your grandmother...to show her such disrespect? You and Anthony have been married for five years now. You just turned twenty-three this past August. Me asking you about great-grandchildren doesn't seem out of place!"

"Why are you being disrespectful to your grandma, Salome?" said Salome's aunt, Clara Small, having overheard the exchange between her mother and niece.

And Salome, who was feeling particularly touchy on this subject, having had this conversation over and over with Anthony, didn't feel like explaining it to her grandmother and aunt. Not only wasn't Anthony interested in children at the moment, lately he was no longer interested in sex with Salome either. They had had a major fight just an hour before heading to the airport to fly home for Thanksgiving. "You're out to ridiculous hours...where the hell do you go?" Salome had shouted at Anthony.

"You know the deal Salome, either I'm at *The Tampa Tavern* schmoozing with the big shot corporate types...trying to drum up business, or I'm having a meal with someone trying to do the same. I thought you were smart enough to understand that!"

"This coming home at four o'clock in the morning is absolute horseshit, Anthony. It has to stop! Is there another woman, Anthony?" Salome had asked.

"There's no other woman!" Anthony had answered—which wasn't exactly true. There was another woman—who the Brothers call "Girl." Cocaine. Anthony had promised Salome a year ago that he had quit, so in the past year when he had used, he had done so covertly. These days Anthony was either spending time every evening in Tampa with Simone Traxel, a fortyish-something Caucasian woman who dealt coke, or with Jesus Narizes, a thirtyish-something Cuban man who dealt coke. And these days it was worse than ever, because Anthony had discovered "freebasing" or smoking coke. When one freebased, one cooked the cocaine down to its pure rock form. Smoking that rock was many times more powerful than snorting lines, since powder coke always had other things added—so the dealers could add weight to the product to make more money—like the white powder baby laxative Mannitol. (Many years later, amongst those who didn't know any better, "Crack" would become popular. Crack is the pure cocaine rock mixed in with corn starch, but since it is a mixture, it is still less powerful than smoking just the rock itself or freebasing.) And addictive? People who freebase do stupid things to keep getting that rock, like deplete their bank accounts and lie to their friends and family. Expensive? Since only the pure rock is used and the rest is thrown away, it usually cost more than double to freebase than to snort—but since freebasing is so much more addictive, the user usually doesn't care how much is spent. Dangerous? Besides the obvious physical effects to the body, those who freebase using a mixture of baking soda and spring water with the powdered coke before cooking it down to a rock form, usually get greedy in terms of rock yield, and then they turn to other catalysts like ether, which produce more rock but are far more dangerous. It's fairly easy to blow oneself up or to ignite oneself on fire freebasing with either ether or other dangerous gases.

When Salome and Anthony had been snorting cocaine, they had been spending $800 per month. Now that Anthony was smoking cocaine, by himself he was spending monthly close to $2500. Anthony had only eaten a tiny Thanksgiving dinner, and Pauline had said, "Eat more Anthony! You're too skinny. Isn't my daughter feeding you?"

Salome looked around for Anthony but he was missing from the dining and living room. She assumed he was in the bathroom, but he was actually standing in the woods behind the Apple's house and smoking rock.

"Salome...just has to be...controversial," a fairly drunk—which was unusual for her—Cindy said. "If it's not...nude pictures...or an inability to forgive her father...it's being testy with our grandmother!"

"Maybe you've had too much drink," Dick said to Cindy.

"DON'T YOU...FUCKING TELL ME...THAT I'VE HAD...TOO MUCH TO DRINK, DICK!" Cindy shouted. And then Cindy, who had just received some medical test results back which said that she might have the beginnings of Multiple Sclerosis, and had told nobody, said, "YOU'RE A REAL ASSHOLE DICK!"

Dick, who had really reinvented himself since he had given up drinking, and was now considered by most of the family as more of an angel than an asshole, said nothing.

Bruiser leaned over to Dick and wheezed, "Miserable bitches...they never shut up!"

Jennifer, who was annoyed because Colin—who really hated family gatherings—had used his answering service again to feign an alleged medical emergency to bail him out of having to sit and talk after dinner, drunkenly said to Bruiser, "Who...are you... calling a bitch?...All guys...are selfish!...Besides their dicks...they think little of anybody else's...needs!"

"Who are you...calling selfish?" Bruiser angrily wheezed. "I ask to borrow...your fucking lawnmower...but you say no!...Is your...Lake Bomoseen home...lawnmower just too...good for me?"

"Hey Bruiser...everyone felt real...sorry for you...when you...lost your arm!" Jennifer said with anger. "But that...was years ago!...It's time...you realized...that not everyone in the family...is always going to...immediately respond positively...to your needs at any given moment!"

"LEAVE...BRUISER ALONE!" Cindy shouted. "HE'S DOING OKAY!"

Bubba got up to leave, he was going to just sit in his favorite chair in front of *The Apple House* for awhile. He said, "WHYYY JEEESUS CHRIIIST...I can't sit here and listen to YOUUU all bitch!"

"Well...maybe you...need to hear people bitch...every once in awhile now. Because...you never listened...to what anybody...else wanted in this family...for years!" A totally zonked Pauline said.

"WHYYY JEEESUS CHRIIIST Pauline...I've gotten much better at listening to what YOUUU and OURRR children want," a hurt Bubba said.

And Jennifer went into her Bubba imitation complete with the pointing finger, "WHYYY JEESUS CHRIIIST...it's OOOKAY to BREAAAKE MYYY daughter's jaw!"

"LEAVE DAD ALONE...YOU ASSHOLE!" Cindy shouted at Jennifer. "HE'S GONE...THROUGH ENOUGH HELL...FOR THAT!"

"WHO'S... AN ASSHOLE?" Jennifer barked. And then looking Cindy straight in the eye she said, "YOU...ALWAYS COVERED UP... YOUR ASSHOLE HUSBAND'S...ANTI-SOCIAL BEHAVIOR!...AND NOW... THAT HE'S NOT...DRINKING...HIS SHIT...IS AS PURE... AS THE WHITE SNOW!"

Bubba walked out of the house as Cindy was shouting at Jennifer, "YOU'VE ALWAYS THOUGHT...THAT YOU WERE...SO MUCH BETTER... THAN EVERYBODY ELSE IN THIS FAMILY!...YOU'RE A... PRETENTIOUS TWIT!"

"I'VE CERTAINLY...GOT MORE...GOING ON...THAN YOU! BIG DEAL...YOU MARRY...THE FIRST REAL...BOYFRIEND... YOU EVER HAD!...AND HE JOINS THE MILITARY!...PEOPLE WHO HAVE TO...JOIN THE MILITARY...IT'S BECAUSE...THEY DON'T HAVE THE SKILLS...TO MAKE IT...IN THE REAL WORLD!" Jennifer shouted at Cindy.

"WELL...AT LEAST...I DIDN'T HAVE...TO STEAL MY HUSBAND...FROM ANOTHER WIFE!" Cindy shouted back.

"I COULD HAVE HAD DICK...AT ANY TIME! ON MY WEDDING DAY...HE TOLD ME...THAT HE ALWAYS WANTED ME...THAT HE HAD SETTLED...FOR YOU!"

Cindy, who had looked around for Dick for some kind of confirmation or lack thereof in regards to Jennifer's last statement, and couldn't find him because he and Bruiser had slipped out to join Bubba in front of *The Apple House*, said, "THAT'S NOT TRUE!" And then she tossed what was left of her vodka and tonic into Jennifer's face and stormed out to find Dick.

Jennifer ran after Cindy, and outside just in front of the kitchen door, she grabbed Cindy's hair and shouted, "FUCK YOU!"

Cindy started pulling Jennifer's hair, and she screamed, "YOU ALWAYS...TOOK MY MONEY!"

And Jennifer shouted, "WHAT?" as they were dancing around pulling each other's hair.

"DAD...WOULD GIVE US MONEY...FOR MUSIC LESSONS

AFTER SCHOOL...YOU...WOULD ALWAYS...GO FIRST...WITH YOUR OBOE LESSON...THEN YOU...WOULD ALWAYS...CONVINCE ME...THAT I WASN'T...ANY GOOD...ON THE SAXOPHONE...AND THAT...WE SHOULD SPEND...THAT MONEY...FOR MY LESSON... ON ICE CREAM!"

A very inebriated Salome, who still couldn't find Anthony and couldn't stand anymore of this fighting, had taken the keys for Bluebird from the kitchen wall, and said nothing as she passed Cindy and Jennifer rolling on the ground now and still pulling each other's hair. She got into the car and took off. Bubba, Dick, and Bruiser all saw her as she blew past *The Apple House*.

"Well...YOU DID SUCK...as a musician," Jennifer said laughingly and stopped pulling Cindy's hair. "And the ice cream...was good!"

Cindy let go of Jennifer's hair, and laughingly said, "I did suck! And the ice cream was great!" And then she took a handful worth of snow and shoved it into Jennifer's face.

"WHY YOU..." Jennifer said laughingly, and she made a snowball and beaned Cindy in the head. And the two sisters started one bodacious snowball fight. Pretty soon, with the exception of Colin who was home reading, Bubba, Dick, and Bruiser who were talking quietly in front of *The Apple House*, Anthony who was in the woods smoking cocaine, and Salome who was drunkenly driving north on Highway 7, the rest of the family members were outside and throwing snowballs.

Salome was traveling too fast on Highway 7 for the slick road conditions, and just north of downtown Rutland as she went into an S curve, she lost control of the car and it spun 360 degrees three times before it smashed through a guard rail. The car ended up perched precariously over Rutland's largest ravine, the front wheels just dangling in space. Being too out of it still to even think about the repercussions of just getting out of the car, Salome opened the door and climbed out. And although the car swayed back and forth when she did that, it finally came to rest in the same position that Salome had left it. It took a few moments for what had just happened to sink into Salome's head. She decided to just wait there until help passed by. Sitting on the edge of the ravine, Salome said, "Thank you Jesus!" And in that moment she gave her life to Christ.

Bubba came along in a truck about thirty minutes later. When he saw her he said, "WHYYY JEEESUS CHRIIIST Salome...are YOUUU alright?"

A totally sober Salome came over to Bubba and threw her arms around him and said, "I'm going to be fine Dad. I gave my life to Jesus tonight."

"OOOKAY," Bubba said.

"And since Jesus gave his life for the sins of Mankind, and he has forgiven me for my sins," Salome said. "It seems as if the Christian thing to do is to not hold any grudges. I love you Dad, I'm sorry I was so wild when I was younger, and I forgive you for what you did eight years ago."

"Thank YOUUU SWEEETHEART. I love you. I'M SOOO sorry!"

"We'll never mention it again," Salome said. "But there is one favor I do need to ask you."

"Whatever YOUUU want dear," Bubba said.

"Please stop taking the Lord's name in vain. It's so irreverent…how you usually begin talking…with the 'WHYYY' and then the Lord's name," Salome said.

"OOOKAY," Bubba said.

CHAPTER TWELVE

And so it came to pass in the hot July of 1984 in the USA, that while the beautifully bourgeois danced in discos by night with their dangling gold spoons a rockin' to and fro to the beat of *The Bee Gees*, Donna Summers, and Rick James, and the financial fat cats spent their days figuring out how to spend all of the newfound wealth courteously created by the Reagan Administration's easing up of corporate taxes and restrictions, and the rest of the country—in a futile attempt to keep their collective legs from getting wet as a result of the Trickle Down Theory of Economics—were anesthetized by thirty-six different deodorant choices, ninety-seven different automobile choices, the latest fashion, the latest electronics, the latest light beer, the latest diet, the latest Broadway musical, summer reruns of *Saturday Night Live* and *Cheers*, Whizz-Cracker Records was forced by Z. Robert Schultz, recently hired Tampa music attorney and now business manager of the band, to void its deal with *Home Cooking*.

On a very rainy thirty-eighth birthday for Felix in August of 1984, he, K. J. Bauer, Jay Biggs with his wife and daughter, Montgomery Butler with his wife and son, and Z. Robert Schultz all arrived mid-afternoon at Heathrow Airport. *Home Cooking* was ready to record their second album as a band, and the first of a three album deal Z. Robert Schultz had negotiated with Decca/Deram Records of London. The deal centered on distribution, with various stages of record sales opening the next market. The album would be distributed throughout the UK first, then Europe, then the USA, and finally the rest of the world. *Home Cooking* would have one month's worth of studio time to complete their album, and Felix, with heartfelt thanks, had been allowed to put together a complex schedule of Jack, Geneva, Salome, Walter Lee, Annie, and Dora Larue to cover the daily maintenance and run the office of *The Breakers* while he was gone. Anthony, to Felix's disappointment, had said that he just couldn't handle it.

"Just think," Jay Biggs said when the plane had finally rolled to a stop, "It was twenty years ago that *The Beatles* flew in the opposite direction and found thousands of adoring fans waiting when they landed in New York!"

"I wouldn't hold my breath for that!" Felix said laughingly.

"I wish something would make you hold your breath…Damn!" Montgomery joked and then pinched his nose.

"You can hold this!" Felix said to Montgomery while grabbing his crotch.

"Yeah…that'll do if you only need to hold on to something for a real short time!" K. J. added.

"Hey…has anybody ever told you…that you're too much of a wiseass to be only nineteen?" Felix shot back.

"Everybody tells me that," K. J. said and then added, "It must be the company I keep!"

When everybody had disembarked and opened their umbrellas, K. J. looked around and saw one young lady with an umbrella and a **I LOVE HOME COOKING! I LOVE TOUS LES SIEGES ETAIENT OCCUPÉS!** sign standing behind a fence.

"Hey…looks like she's one of yours," K. J. said to Felix.

"How the hell did anyone know that we were arriving today?" Felix asked to no one in particular.

"That is kind of strange," Montgomery said.

"My curiosity has been piqued," Felix said, and then he added, "I'm gonna have to go and check her out."

"Hello there…thanks for standing out here in the rain with the sign," Felix said after he had walked to the fence. He noticed that the young lady was a very attractive brunette with beautiful hazel eyes, and that those beautiful hazel bedroom eyes were smiling at him.

"I'm a big fan!" said twenty-eight year old Sarah Fussell with an English accent.

"Thank you!" Felix said, and then he added, "I'm curious…how did you know that we'd be arriving now?"

"There was an item written in *The Buzz* last weekend," Sarah said.

"*The Buzz*?"

"That's the weekend entertainment supplement in *The London Sun*," Sarah said.

"I see," Felix said and then he added, "If you don't mind me asking, where and when did you read my novel?"

"I read it six years ago…when I was finishing college in Paris," Sarah said. "My roommate had read it…she recommended it. I loved it."

"What were you studying in Paris?"

"My degree is in French Literature."

"Wow…now my head is gonna get real swelled. A Woman of Letters in French has liked my novel!" Felix said schmoozing her and then added, "How about the album…where did you hear it?"

"When I stayed with me aunt, uncle, and cousins in Atlanta, Georgia for three weeks last summer," Sarah said. "A cousin had bought 'Without Grease,' and I liked it very much. I particularly liked 'Two Worlds Converge,' 'Derrida's Dilemma,' and 'I'll Be Around.' So I went to some huge record store…*Peaches*…in Atlanta and I purchased a copy before I returned home."

Felix smiled and thought, 'me aunt!' He loved hearing the English speak English. And he said, "Well…don't let any writer or artist ever lie to you and say that his or her Ego isn't incredibly stroked by fans," Felix said. "You've really made my day…jet lag and all!"

"Thank you."

"What's your name?"

"Sarah Fussell."

"Well…Sarah Fussell…I really do appreciate that you came here, but you should have stayed inside where it's dry! Did you take off from work today?" Felix asked.

"I just resigned from the last job," Sarah said. "I'm a waitress…and the owner of the establishment kept grabbing me bottom. I'm good at what I do…so I'm sure I can find another place."

"A degree in French Literature six years ago, and you prefer waitress work?"

"I find that menial work allows me to keep the mind clear…to pursue writing."

"Oh no!" Felix said, "A writer…another one of us!"

"I've been working on the first novel for five years."

"And I certainly know how much work is involved in writing a novel," Felix said. "Are you writing it in English or French?"

"Both," Sarah said. "I write a section of a chapter in English first, then I immediately translate it into French. I have two separate manuscripts."

"Wow!" Felix said and then added, "Can we give you a ride somewhere?"

"I was going to just take the train home," Sarah replied.

"Where do you live?"

"Me mum and dad own a flat in Covent Garden," Sarah said. "I live in the garret upstairs…private entrance…only see them a few times a week."

"I seem to remember that Covent Garden is downtown," Felix said. "We're heading downtown now…let us drop you off," he added.

Sarah said, "I'd love a lift from you!" Felix smiled, and then he walked over and asked an airport security guard to let her in. The security guard motioned for Sarah to walk about twenty feet to a locked gate, he opened it, Sarah walked onto the tarmac, and Felix came over and gave her a kiss on the cheek. "Thanks again for being such a dedicated fan," a truly flattered Felix said. And he thought, 'She didn't bring the book or album and ask me for an autograph…I'm impressed.'

Sarah rode to downtown London with everyone in the large limousine, and by the time they had reached Decca/Deram Records Felix asked, "Would you like to hang out with us today?" Sarah happily agreed.

As they were getting out of the limo and Sarah was busy talking with Jay, K. J. said *sotto voce* to Felix, "So…your first international groupie!"

"You're just jealous," Felix said laughingly and then added, "Because every time we play somewhere you're always the babe magnet!"

"I've done okay," K. J. said.

"Well sure you have," Felix said. "What a great deal for you…young and handsome…passionate guitar player…incredible lead singer…and you're showcased in front of three old farts twice your age!"

"I've seen you hook up before," K. J. said.

"Yeah…two groupies in two years…compared to your thirty or forty!" Felix said, and then he lightly jabbed K. J. with an elbow to the ribs. "But hey…I'm not jealous…it kind of feels like you're my son…so it's like I get this parental pride thing happening…when I see you stroll off after a show with some beautiful creature who makes my tongue hang out!"

"Thanks Pops!" K. J. said sarcastically. Felix acknowledged that moniker with an Italian salute.

After their forty minute meeting with Sir Reginald Mitchell, the man who would be producing their next album, and Clive Dorkus, the manager for Decca/Deram Records who was responsible for allocating funds for recording artists, Felix was the first one out of the boardroom. Sarah was sitting in the waiting room reading *Modern Rocker*, a magazine about today's Rock Music scene that was published by one of Decca/Deram's sister companies. "We're all gonna be staying and recording our album during the next month at this country estate the record company owns," Felix said to Sarah.

"Where is the estate?" Sarah asked.

"I was just told…that I'm really not supposed to tell anyone that."

"Oh!" a disappointed Sarah said.

"Yeah…but since Jay and Montgomery have their wives and kids staying there, I guess…if I had a woman…she'd be allowed to stay too!" Felix said, putting special emphasis on the last part of his statement.

Sarah's face lit up and she said, "Are you making me an offer?"

And Felix took both of Sarah's hands into his and said, "Sarah… look…you are young and beautiful. I'd have to be some kind of a blind schmuck to not desire you. But this is an unusual situation. If I had met you at a bar a few hours ago…who knows…we might have ended up going home together. But that's not how we met…and we haven't had a few hours to talk and drink. If you'd like to come with me…I'll make sure you have a separate bedroom…and we'll just see how the chemistry works for awhile. Okay?"

"Okay!" Sarah said, and then she added, "Can we swing by me flat on the way out of town so I can pack a suitcase?"

"No problem," Felix said. "I don't know what everybody else plans on doing for the next few hours, but we're all going out to dinner at *Trader Vic's* at 9:00, so I'll go with you in a cab to your place and we can hook back up with everybody at dinner."

"That sounds great!" Sarah said. "By the way…where is the country estate?"

"Someplace called Henley on Thames," Felix said.

"Henley on Thames is beautiful! That's about sixty kilometers from London."

"You've been there?"

"A few years ago," Sarah said. "The estates are extravagant and very expensive. Your record company must have spent a fortune buying or leasing a place there."

"Yeah…from what I just heard…Decca/Deram has three studios in this building…but they use them for more established artists. Those artists are supposed to have gotten their material to perfection…and are ready to record when they arrive at the studio. Most of those musicians already live around London…and have practice studios in their homes…or they rent space in town," Felix said. "Since the company doesn't want to waste expensive studio time when a group isn't from around here and needs studio space to practice before they record, they invested in the estate in Henley on Thames. I was told that has worked out well. There are practice studios on one side of the main house…and the recording studio is on the other. There are also several bedrooms and bathrooms in-between, plus a large kitchen and living area, so the musicians can just remain on the estate. I guess…the place is in the country far enough away from London to keep the newer recording artists from being too easily distracted."

"That sounds great!" Sarah said.

When they arrived in the taxi at Sarah's place in Covent Garden, at first she said, "Me mum's home…I'd like you to meet her." When they exited the cab however, and Sarah had taken another long look at Felix she said, "Let's use the private entrance to the garret…you'll meet Mum later." Once inside Sarah asked, "Would you like tea?"

Felix asked, "To drink or to smoke?"

"Both!" Sarah exclaimed.

"Both it is then!" Felix said. "I've got some special stuff with me… give me a minute...where's your bathroom?"

"The door to the loo is in the bedroom," Sarah said and then added playfully, "Would you like finger sandwiches? I love cucumber!"

Felix chuckled to himself and said as he was walking to the bathroom, "I'm not big on cucumber sandwiches myself…don't know too many guys who are…but I certainly want you to have all of the cucumber you'd like… me lady!" He could hear Sarah's laughter as he found the bathroom door.

In the bathroom Felix dropped trou and removed the taped plastic package from his right leg, thinking about a character in a short story, an old man named Lemon Brown in "The Treasure of Lemon Brown" by Walter Dean Meyers, who had done the same thing. 'But he had an old mouth harp and newspaper clippings from fifty years ago wrapped in his plastic,' Felix thought. Inside of Felix's plastic package, after the *Bounce* for the benefit of the dogs at Heathrow had been removed, was an ounce of some commercial marijuana and an ounce of Bruiser's incredible stuff. Felix had purchased three ounces from Bruiser last year—actually he had bartered days at the motel for the product—and he had kept this one ounce for special occasions.

Felix walked back into the living room and asked Sarah, "Do you have papers?"

"What kind of papers do you seek?" she asked.

And then imitating a Gestapo officer, Felix said, "Your papers please!" And then he said, "Something to roll the pot in."

"Oh," Sarah laughingly said. "You'll find the wraps and a tray in the drawer of the table next to the sofa."

After they had sipped and smoked tea and Felix had gotten Sarah totally snookered on Bruiser's stuff, Sarah gave Felix another long look and said, "God…do you turn me on!" And then she led Felix by the hand into the bedroom. Felix thought, 'Man…I'm glad I brought my razor over to Salome and Anthony's the other night!'

Later that night, after dinner, the entourage was taken by the same limo driver out to Henley on Thames. Felix and Sarah immediately claimed one of the beautiful bedrooms, Felix said "Goodnight," and then he and Sarah got back into doing that which they had done earlier. And it was good.

During the next month *Home Cooking* recorded their album "Brewin' Bitches," whose title was a spoof on Miles Younger' great jazz record of the late 1960's, "Bitches Brew." When it was finished, at Felix's suggestion, Decca/Deram Records got Jacques Derrida to write the album's liner notes. Here's what he wrote:

> *This sophomoric effort by Home Cooking is really quite interesting. If one examines the etymological meaning of "bitches," one finds that word to be the plural of "a female dog." Of*

course, if "bitch" is looked up in J. C. Hotten's The Slang Dictionary (20th Edition) the meaning also includes "a shrewish female human," and "a complaint." And although Mr. Miles Younger' album from circa 1968 seems to be ambiguous re: the title, since the album is an instrumental and the song titles refer neither to female dogs, female humans, nor complaints, for some reason unbeknownst to me, the songwriting team of Mr. Bauer and Mr. Kulpa have decided to slap Mr. Younger and his album title around a bit. (Which he may or may not deserve...Go figure!)

"Brewin' Bitches" begins with "Into the Cauldron," a slick rock piece featuring K. J. Bauer's passionate electric guitar lead floating high over the rhythm of the piece. This is a song destined to be a Rock Music anthem, much like Led Zeppelin's "Stairway to Heaven," and it juxtaposes the hot passion of romantic love with the void of that love in the cold soul. Then comes "Derrida's Dilemma Part 2," an acoustic number in which the question is posed: "Is a writer still responsible for his words, if the words get translated incorrectly?" And so, since this question is posed to me, my response is yes!

Other songs include "Double Double Toil and Trouble," obviously concerning itself with Macbeth's witches; "Let Her Stew," a song about the dating game; "Mystery Food," in which the sounds of people eating throughout is apparently diagetic to the text; "Vegetable World," "What Goes in Here Comes out There," "Beet Generation," in which the narrator seems to represent the decentralized transgressive Ego; "I Don't Like Broccoli (Michael's Song),""Super Sonic Broom," "Fried Eggs on Her Chest," and "Your Stomach is Bigger Than Your Eyes." The record ends with perhaps the best song on the album, "The Inner Bitch," in which the problem of the dichotomy between hot love and the cold soul, first mentioned in "Into the Cauldron" is resolved.

Finally, there is a hidden fourteenth track, "Root the Hedgehog," a preposterous tune about a Hedgehog named "Root," who emigrates to the USA, opens a SOHO club in New York City, catches a fatal sexually transmitted disease, and eventually gets buried in a dung heap back in his homeland. How the band persuaded Johnny Cash to fly to London to sing this little ditty remains a mystery to me. Bon Appetit!

One early morning in late August, at about the halfway point in recording the album, naked Felix and Sarah were surprised to find four men and a woman in suits standing in their bedroom. "What the hell is this all about?"

Felix yelled, while covering himself and Sarah up with a blanket.

"Decca/Deram has defaulted on their note for this estate," one of the men said. "My bank is repossessing this place and everything must be out in thirty days. We're just examining the property today."

'Aw shit!' Felix thought. 'Decca/Deram is in trouble. I wonder how this will effect the distribution of our album?' "I wish those A-holes had told us…at least…to expect company this morning!" Felix said to the man.

Jay, his wife and daughter, Montgomery's wife and son, and K. J. were all in the kitchen having breakfast while the suits were in the house. Unfortunately, Montgomery was sitting on the throne in a bathroom that connected the room he and his wife used with the room his son used. While sitting there, suddenly the door from his son's room opened and all five suits were in the bathroom and looking at him. Montgomery reached over and opened the door to his room and said, "This way folks," while gesturing with his hand. When an angry Montgomery saw Felix, Sarah, and everybody else sitting at the kitchen table, and he told what had happened, the room erupted in hysterical laughter. Felix mentioned his first written song, when he had been sixteen, "You Can't Crap on Company Time." Everybody was crying with laughter, even Montgomery's fourteen year-old son, who said, "I'm sorry Dad…that you couldn't take your dump in peace! I was wondering…when we get home…Can I invite my friends over to watch you crap?" And that made Montgomery laugh.

"Brewin' Bitches" came out to favorable reviews in late November of 1984, after everyone had already returned to Florida in late September. The plan was to put out two singles first and then the whole album itself, allowing just enough time and airplay to pique interest, but not too much time for people to have already moved on to the next thing. The singles would have about forty days of airplay in the UK before the entire album was released. People would have about two weeks of listening to the entire album, before the band would return in December to do a twenty night Christmas tour around the UK in support of the record. Decca/Deram released "Let Her Stew" as the first single on October 10th , and on November 5th they released the second single, "Beet Generation." Both singles received heavy rotation on the air from a number of stations around the UK, but whether that was the result of being great songs or payola is anybody's guess. The entire album was released on November 22nd about two weeks prior to the first scheduled live appearance of *Home Cooking* in London. Unfortunately, Decca/Deram folded, went financially kaput about a week after the release of the entire album, so the scheduled tour was cancelled. The band made a little bit of money from the record, but other than fifteen minutes of fame in the UK, "Brewin' Bitches" was destined for obscurity also. And since no other record company bought out the Decca/Deram label until about three years later, there was no place to record the second and third albums of *Home Cooking's* deal, and nobody to promote the band's current album after December of 1984.

Meanwhile, after Felix and Sarah had said a teary-eyed goodbye, both agreeing that the month had been fun but that they weren't meant to be long term, Officer Sarah Fussell of the London Metropolitan Police's narcotics squad filed the following report: "*Although Mr. Kulpa apparently brought in two ounces of marijuana to Heathrow for personal use, there is no indication that any band member in Home Cooking is involved in either cocaine smuggling or usage. However, a man who was known only as Dr. Feelgood, and who frequented the Henley on Thames estate regularly, would provide cocaine—he referred to it as 'Toot Uncommon'—for the production crew, and he appeared to be working for Decca/Deram, and specifically for Mr. Clive Dorkus. As we have suspected, Mr. Dorkus is responsible for the major importation of cocaine into the UK from the United States using Rock bands as couriers. However, Home Cooking is not one of those bands. Johnny Cash isn't smuggling cocaine either.*"

In February of 1985, K. J. was made an incredible offer. The lead singer/guitar player of the now famous three-piece band, *Triangulated Crossfire*, had been killed in a single car accident on a lonely highway in Melodeon, Texas. Since K. J. sounded like their now deceased lead singer and his guitar style was very similar, the two surviving band members asked him if he'd like to join. This band had been very successful with its five albums in the past ten years. "The Grassy Knoll," "The Magic Bullet Theory," "An Unusual Turn on Elm Street," "Who's Waiting in the Wings?" and "Back and to the Left," respectively, had all sold more than a million copies each. It was hard for K. J. to resist the offer, and Felix, Jay, and Montgomery all told him, without any hard feelings, that he'd be a schmuck to refuse. So K. J. decided to move to Austin, Texas and to join *Triangulated Crossfire*, and, of course, that was the end of *Home Cooking*. Jay and Montgomery would go back to their regular jobs, Jay as a manager for his father's plastic company in St. Petersburg, and Montgomery as an insurance agent with *CNA* in Tampa.

Felix would decide to go ahead and write his doctorial dissertation on Dickens' use of naming, especially in *David Copperfield*. "Do you realize, in *David Copperfield*, David has seven different names...depending on who is addressing him?" Felix told Walter Lee. "To understand the 'why' is to understand the plot's key!"

Walter Lee replied, "I remember when you told me about that in 1971." So Felix began again, that which he had started in 1971. The dissertation would take him ten months to complete, and he would commute to New York about once every six weeks to consult with his advising professor at NYU. After the dissertation was finished in December of 1985, and was successfully defended in February of 1986, Felix would finally receive his Ph.D. in May of 1986. And although there were no American publishing companies who expressed any interest, Felix was contacted by a company in Berlin who wanted to publish his dissertation as a book in German.

@@@@@@@@

In early February of 1984, after a sixty day notice, Salome left her position as manager of *The Careless Navigator*. Geneva Apple was offered the job and she readily accepted. Salome immediately began her new career in downtown Tampa as a telephone claims handler for *Grapefruit State Insurance*.

Salome had discovered close to a $15,000 shortage in her and Anthony's savings account in early December of 1983, and upon being confronted, Anthony had broken down and admitted that he was smoking cocaine and having a hard time quitting. Salome, with her newly discovered desire to be a good Christian, and specifically to be a good Christian wife, amazingly, had forgiven Anthony with only one "I'm very disappointed" thrown in. And Anthony, with his rediscovered desire to be a good husband, had voluntarily admitted himself into a highly successful drug rehabilitation program in Tampa. The program required a six week stay without visitors, and then six more weeks in which visitors were allowed. After the twelve weeks were over, the patient would be discharged and required to attend two weekly meetings for one year. Anthony was admitted into the "New Horizons" program on December 15th of 1983, and Salome, with the help of her husband's secretary, Rebecca Boulton, had cleared Anthony's calendar until the first of April in 1984. Those clients who couldn't wait that long for Anthony's legal services, were given the name of Manfred Chisum, another Tampa independent corporate attorney, who was Anthony's friend and a fellow Stetson alum from 1981. Salome had applied for and then taken the job with *Grapefruit State*, because she wanted to stay closer to her husband in Tampa all of the time and because it was just time for a change. By the time Felix and the band were ready to go to London in August of 1984, Felix felt reasonably certain that his brother had been cured of his addiction. And although Anthony allowed Felix to visit during the second six weeks of his rehabilitation program, and subsequently allowed him to come over to the house for dinner and a shave once a month, Anthony just went to work and came straight home. He never ventured out anywhere anymore, which included *The Breakers* on Mad Beach or just a simple dinner and movie out with his wife. And there were very few people who were allowed to visit him in Tampa. Other than Felix, only Walter Lee, Annie, Lena, and Jack, Geneva, Sam, and Lani were invited over. And when they would come over, they would notice not only how dark Anthony kept the house, but how nothing ever seemed to make him laugh anymore. Anthony's complete countenance had changed. The look in his eye was one of a defeated man.

In February of 1984, Salome had been befriended by Denise Walker at *Grapefruit State*. Denise had been working there for two years, and she had gone from the title of a general telephone claims handler (TCH) to a bodily injury telephone claims handler—the in-house joke with having that position was the acronym BITCH—to a claims adjustor. Denise was an African-American Born Again Christian, and she regularly attended a primarily African-American Pentecostal church about a half mile from where Salome lived. Salome explained that although she had started reading The New Testament in the King James Bible last year, that she had put that aside, gone back to Genesis, and had just finished The Old Testament. Salome said that now that she had understood The Old Covenant between God and the Jewish people, she was in a better position to understand The New Covenant and Christianity. Denise invited her to a Sunday service at her church, Salome went and felt totally at home. Salome particularly liked the twelve-piece Gospel band, as they were not only excellent musicians, but the sound of live music, along with the singing of hymns and other Gospel songs, seemed to add a deeper dimension to worshipping Jesus for Salome. She joined Denise's church, and although she regularly invited Anthony to come along on Sunday mornings, he would always decline. Not so much because Anthony wasn't searching for something meaningful in his life also, but rather because he felt alienated from people, and the notion of fellowshipping with other parishioners was more than he could handle.

When it came to sexual intimacy with his wife, by the summer of 1984 Anthony was confused and disillusioned. He still loved Salome and thought that she was the most beautiful woman in the world, but even though all of his equipment was functioning properly and he had no desire for any other woman, the problem was that he had lost desire period. There are those who have said that nothing else in the world feels like the incredible high that comes from smoking cocaine, and that once stopped, even sex pales in comparison. Still, Anthony was insecure about Salome. He hadn't realized yet that his wife, who was truly walking a Christian path, would never cheat on him with another man. Anthony knew that she needed, as most of us do, physical intimacy with her mate. Not wanting Salome to leave him for someone else, Anthony made sure to initiate sexual activity with her at least once a week, to act as if it meant the same thing to him now as it had in the past, and to perform the best he could—albeit in a perfunctory manner. Salome, who was perceptive enough to recognize all of this, said nothing discouraging to her husband. She did bring up having a child with Anthony every few months, but he kept saying that he wasn't psychological prepared for that yet.

Salome regularly prayed that she might once again see the fire in her husband's eyes.

And this was how Salome and Anthony lived through the rest of 1984 and 1985. They would always go out for dinner on August 6th with Jack and Geneva, to celebrate both couples' anniversary and Salome's birthday, but Anthony never wanted to go out for his own birthday on July 4th . "Too many people out and about," he would always say. Anthony had acquiesced to celebrating Salome's promotion to claims adjustor at *Grapefruit State* in September of 1985, but most of the time they stayed home. Besides going to work and church on Sunday, for the past two years Salome had been developing a good case of cabin fever. By the beginning of 1986, Salome was painfully aware that she hadn't been home to see her mom and dad in more than two years. Once, in late 1984, her parents wanted to fly down to Tampa and stay at Salome and Anthony's house during Christmas, but Anthony had thrown such a conniption that idea had been totally eighty-sixed. And other than an allowed day visit to their Tampa home by Bruiser, Eileen, Conrad, and three month old Karen Apple in early 1985, and Colin, Jennifer, and four month old Elaine Morgan a little later in 1985, besides her parents, Salome also hadn't seen Jimson, Lizzie and their two kids, Cindy, Dick, and their four kids (including the unmet third daughter Samantha and fourth daughter Rachael) in more than two years.

And every time that Salome would think about people she hadn't seen in awhile, she would cry hardest when she realized that it had been almost five years since she had heard from Selma. Salome thought about flying to JFK, just walking into the Museum of Natural History in Manhattan, finding Ivy Laplotski, and asking her if she could possibly share anything in regards to how Selma was doing. After that conversation Salome would take a bus to Rutland.

Salome didn't know that Ivy Laplotski had been busted by Fester Daily in 1982 for Aiding and Abetting a Federal Fugitive. She had cut a deal with the federal prosecutor and received one year in prison and four years on parole. She had lost her job at the museum and lost her apartment in Queens. She had also lost her mother while she was doing the downtime. Ivy was now living in Brooklyn and working at a *Payless* shoe store. Ivy hadn't been able to communicate with Selma while she was in jail, and Selma had moved yet again. Neither sister knew how to make contact. Selma did know that her mom had passed away however, because after hearing nothing for months, she had called the nursing home from a payphone in 1983 and asked for Mrs. Laplotski. A nurse had come on and asked, "Are you a relative?" And Selma had said, "I'm an old friend who has been living abroad." And the nurse had then expressed her sympathy and told Selma.

Salome was desperate to go home, but Anthony refused, and she was still afraid to leave him alone for too long. By early 1986 Salome decided to put her foot down a little. She said, "Anthony…I love you…you're my husband

and so far I've respected your wishes since your rehab program two years ago. But I'm telling you right now...this summer you and I are going to Rutland...with a few days in Manhattan first. We're going to stay in a luxurious hotel room, see a Broadway show, go out to eat at a few good restaurants, and then we're going to stay at my mom and dad's for a good ten days...Capice?" And Anthony said, "Okay," while he was thinking, 'That's months away...I'm sure I can figure a way to get out of it.'

@@@@@@@@

In late May of 1986 Dick Chumwell was contemplating leaving the military. He had been in the Air Force for sixteen years, the original four, and then two more "re-ups" of six years each. He had just finished his first year at Clinton County Community College in Plattsburgh, and although Dick wasn't sure yet, in what he wanted to pursue for a four-year degree, he was sure that he was sick of coming home with grease under his nails every day.

In late May of 1986 Bruiser and Eileen Apple were on vacation with their children in California for two weeks. They were taking a much deserved rest. Six months earlier they had opened a Michigan hot dog restaurant on the other side of Rutland from *Claire and Carl's.* They had figured that there were enough Michigan hot dog aficionados in the area to ensure that another place could succeed. And to make sure that they had an edge, unlike *Claire and Carl's*, their place, *Eileen's Michigans*, offered milk shakes. Bruiser had wheezed, "Why Jesus Christ...I had to open...a place to...keep from...going broke...at *Claire and Carl's*!" Bruiser and Eileen still had the split twenty-five percent share of *The Careless Navigator* on Mad Beach with Jr. Liberty, and recently Bruiser had turned Jr. down when he asked if they wanted to sell out to him. Bruiser had paid $25,000 for his half of the twenty-five percent interest eight years ago, and he had just turned down Jr.'s offer of $200,000. Bruiser was still a Vermont State Wilderness Guide, and he occasionally made money taking small groups to sightsee. He also made money using his dogs during bear season, charging high fees to serious and trying to be serious bear hunters. Since his coon dog Gertrude had died a year ago, Bruiser had pretty much given up flushing out raccoons as a business. Bruiser still worked primarily at the orchard during the week, and Eileen ran the hot dog restaurant. Bubba had agreed to take care of Bruiser's three dogs while he was away, and to make things easier and to keep the dogs from howling due to loneliness, he had had Bruiser bring the dogs to the orchard and to leave them in the old kennel by the barn.

In late May of 1986, Jennifer, Colin, and Elaine were spending a lot of time sailing on the weekends. And although there were rumors around Rutland General Hospital that Dr. Colin Morgan might be a philanderer, when questioned by Jennifer, he denied the assertion and Jennifer let it drop.

Meanwhile, Jennifer and Colin had recently added a huge new section onto their home, and they had also built a six-car carriage house with a mother-in-law apartment on top about one hundred yards from the house. One of Doc Colin's new passions was old automobiles, and he had purchased both a 1924 Model A and a 1968 Jaguar XKE. Both were in excellent shape and ran well.

In late May of 1986, Jimson, Lizzie, Nancy, and Eve Apple had just finished dessert in Pauline and Bubba's dining room and were getting ready to leave. "Sorry we have to run," Jimson said looking at his watch, "But I have to get in an hour early for a ten o'clock meeting tonight." Jimson was still working the graveyard shift at the correctional center, and, much to Lizzie's chagrin, he had decided that he preferred that shift. There was much less hassle during the night, a lot less confrontational situations with prisoners, and the pay differential was ten percent higher. Jimson and Lizzie had sold their small place in Rutland in January of 1984, and for more than two years they had been living in their beautiful five bedroom three and a half bathroom farm house on three acres just a few miles north of Burlington. It was just after seven o'clock, and with the two hour drive home, Jimson would have about fifteen minutes to kill at home before he had to leave for work. Jimson had only gotten about four hours sleep today, but Lizzie had just relaxed and read, since school had ended for the year. They had taken their daughters and picked up their new 1986 *Honda Accord* at the dealership earlier, and then they had made the impromptu drive to Rutland. "I don't know how you do it Mom," Lizzie said. "You bake apple pies in the morning, keep this house immaculate, and then whip up an incredible dinner for all of us on the spot!"

"I'm a tough little Indian!" Pauline said.

Later that night, after Pauline had kissed him and gone upstairs to sleep, just after Bubba had finished watching the eleven o'clock news in the downstairs den, he heard a gunshot. Then Bruiser's dogs began howling. "WHYYY...JEEES...Jumpin' JEEEHOSEPHAT!" Bubba said to nobody, practicing for a future Salome visit. "That sounded LIIIKE a shotgun from the Strattus PLAAACE!" But Bubba wasn't exactly certain what he had heard, since he had drunk a few more beers than usual today, and he thought, 'It might have just been a car's backfire.'

About fifteen minutes later, after one more beer, Bubba turned off the television, latched the screen door, closed and locked the front door, and was heading upstairs when he heard, "HEY APPLE...HERE'S YOUR...DEAD FUCKING DOG!" Bubba unlocked and opened the door, and saw through the screen door, one of Bruiser's dogs covered in blood lying dead about twenty feet away. The dog, "Bear," was Bruiser's oldest and best bear dog. Standing behind the dog with a twelve gauge shotgun resting on his shoulder, its barrels pointing back at Highway 7, was an inebriated Gus Strattus.

It had been another one of those nights in which he had desired his wife and his wife had refused.

"WHYYY JEEESUS CHRIIIST Strattus…did YOUUU kill one of MYYY son's dogs?" Bubba said loudly, feeling a little woozy from the beer.

"I'VE…BEEN TELLING YOU…FOR YEARS…APPLE…TO KEEP THOSE MANGY PIECE OF SHIT MUTTS…OFF OF MY PROPERTY. THIS DEAD SACK OF SHIT…JUST KILLED MY BEST ROOSTER."

"WHYYY somebody…should have put both YOUUU...and your noisy PIEEECE of shit cock into the bone yard…AAA long time AGOOO!" yelled sixty-six year-old Bubba.

"I WISH…YOU HAD BEEN THE ONE…WHO HAD TRIED!" screamed seventy-one year-old Gus Strattus.

"That dog cost MYYY son $2500...YOUUU ASSHOOOLE!" Bubba screamed back.

"WELL YOU… SHOULD HAVE MADE SURE…THAT DOG STAYED HOME!"

"WHYYY JEEESUS CHRIIIST…we'll DEEEDUCT $100...$50 for the rooster and $50 for the fence…in REEEPLACEMENT costs…and then YOUUU can give MYYY son…$2400 in REEEPLACEMENT costs…if HEEE can ever FIIIND…another fucking dog…who can TREEE bear like Bear did!" Bubba proposed.

"GO FUCK YOURSELF…APPLE!…I'VE… PUT UP WITH… ENOUGH OF YOUR SHIT FOR YEARS!...FROM YOUR REFUSAL…TO LET ME USE SOME OF YOUR WATER…WATER YOU WOULDN'T… HAVE EVEN MISSED…BACK IN 1950...AND I OFFERED TO PAY YOU!…BUT YOU WERE TOO… MUCH OF AN ASSHOLE…TO BE A GOOD NEIGHBOR!…AND THEN…YOU BUILT…THAT FUCKING BARN…IN 1952...TO BLOCK OUR VIEW!…YOU ASSHOLE…THE BACK…OF OUR ELEVATED HOME… IS TOTALLY GLASS… AND…UNTIL YOUR BARN WAS BUILT…WE HAD…AN UNOBSTRUCTED VIEW …ACROSS HIGHWAY 7...TO THE GREEN MOUNTAINS…AND YOU DID IT INTENTIONALLY! YOU…BUILT THAT FUCKING BARN…JUST THE EXACT SIZE…TO TOTALLY BLOCK OUR VIEW…FROM EVERYWHERE…IN THE HOUSE…YOU ASSHOLE!"

"WHYYY JEEESUS CHRIIIST…MYYY water is MYYY water…and it's not for sale!…And where I build MYYY barn is MYYY business!… Perhaps YOUUU NEEED to GOOO fuck yourself...and YOUUU need to do it TODAAAY!" Bubba screamed and then added, "And…don't think that WEEE don't KNOOOW who CIRCUUULATED that EUROPEEEAN men's magazine…with the NAAAKED pictures…of MYYY daughter in 1975… YOUUU rotten PIEEECE of shit!" Bubba yelled.

"I HOPE...YOU ENJOYED...LEARNING WHAT EVERYONE IN RUTLAND...FOUND OUT...WHAT A WHORE YOUR DAUGHTER REALLY IS!.. THINK ABOUT...HOW MANY MEN... THROUGHOUT EUROPE...JERKED OFF...TO HER NAKED PICTURES!"

"STRATTUS... I DON'T DOUBT...THAT YOU'UU'VE JERKED OFF TO HER PICTURES YOURSELF!...DON'T THINK III HAVEN'T NOOOTICED YOU STARING AT SALOME SINCE SHEEE WAS TEN FUCKING YEARS OLD...YOUUU FUCKING PERVERT!...BUT EVERYONE IN RUTLAND KNOOOWS ALSO...THAT YOUR WIFE HASN'T GIVEN YOUUU ANY IN MORE THAN TWENTY YEARS!"

"WHY YOU...!" Gus Strattus screamed as he approached the door.

Bubba quickly grabbed his loaded sixteen gauge shotgun from the rack on the wall next to the front door, pointed it at Gus Strattus through the screen door and screamed, "DON'T YOU TRYYY COMING INTO MYY HOUSE... STRATTUS!"

Gus Strattus went to reach for the handle of the screen door, and Bubba fired the shotgun. The force of the blast doubled-over Gus Strattus and then dropped him screaming to the ground. Bubba immediately put his shotgun back on the wall, and then he called Sheriff Roger Glenn at home. Gus Strattus was still screaming outside on the ground. Bubba knew that Gus wasn't that hurt, he wasn't going to die or anything, because Bubba had only kept rock salt in the shotgun. But rock salt can still do damage, depending on where it strikes the human body, and anyplace it strikes, it burns incredibly.

Sheriff Glenn arrived about fifteen minutes later with an ambulance from Rutland General Hospital following him. Both men were placed under arrest, but Gus was taken to the hospital and Bubba to the police station. Pauline, who had been awakened by all of the yelling and was on her way downstairs when Bubba had fired his shotgun, followed her husband to the police station in Bluebird. She then called Jeffery Green, the bailsman she had used before for Bubba and Dick, and after Sheriff Glenn called Wilson Smith, Rutland's District Attorney at home, and after a charge was officially made and the bail was set, Pauline paid and Bubba was allowed to leave. This process had taken slightly more than two and half hours, in which Bubba had stayed in a cell and Pauline in the waiting room, because the prosecutor refused to name the charge or charges and to call Judge Thompson at home for the appropriate bail, until Sheriff Glenn had had an opportunity to examine the crime scene and had also gotten Gus Strattus' prognosis from the hospital. Sheriff Glenn had gone back to Bubba's house with the crime scene kit and taken fingerprints from the handle of the screen door, and then went to the hospital and taken Gus Strattus' prints.

When the news had come in and Bubba was taken from his cell, Sheriff Glenn had told him that he was being charged with Attempted Homicide and the bond was $50,000. Pauline had written a check for $5,000 to Jeffrey Green, and signed the necessary papers putting a lien on their orchard, business, and house. "ATTEMPTED HOMICIDE?" Bubba had yelled. "WHYYY JEEESUS CHRIIIST Roger...that's fucking CRAAAZY! The bastard was TRYYYING to enter MYYY house! I was PROOOTECTING Pauline...which is MYYY right and DUUUTY!"

"Gus Strattus is going to live, but you blew his right testicle to smithereens Bubba! They had to remove that testicle!" Sheriff Glen had said.

"WHYYY JEEESUS CHRIIIST Roger...from what I've heard...HEEE hasn't been UUUSING much of his EEEQUIPMENT in the past twenty years ANYWAAAY," Bubba had said.

And then Sheriff Glen had added, "You better get a good attorney Bubba...There weren't any of Gus Stattus' fingerprints on the handle of your screen door. Self Defense isn't going to work unless you can prove he was coming into the house."

"WHYYY JEEESUS CHRIIIST Roger...HEEE was coming into MYYY house, and Pauline might have been shot...SHEEE was on the stairs BEEEHIND MEEE! Isn't HEEE being charged with anything? HEEE WAS ON MYYY PROPERTY WITH A FUCKING SHOTGUN!" Bubba had said.

"He was charged with Trespassing and Reckless Endangerment," Sheriff Glenn had said.

"WHYYY...JEEESUS CHRIIIST...," Bubba had said.

A few months later Bubba would go to trial. The New York City defense attorney he and Pauline would hire, Q. Harrison Albright, a junior member on the staff of F. Lee Bailey, would charge $15,000. Q. Harrison Albright was an excellent attorney. He would be able to get Judge Able Thompson to agree to a field trip. The jurors would get to see, that from where Bubba was standing behind the screen door inside of the house, it was impossible to tell when someone on the outside, leaning in toward the screen door, actually touched the door handle, or whose hand was still as far away as eight inches. And, of course, the ominous looking assistant, Big Joe Grazzle, who would be hired by Q. Harrison Albright, to play Gus Strattus in their dramatization, would just scare the dickens out of the jurors. Every time Big Joe would approach the screen door, with a twelve gauge shotgun on his shoulder, and yell what the defense would say over and over was what Gus Strattus had yelled on that night, "I'M GONNA KILL YOU APPLE!" the jurors, standing in the foyer of Bubba's house, would totally recoil in fright. And even though the District Attorney, Wilson Smith, would keep trying to make the point that Bubba should have waited until he saw the door actually open before discharging his weapon, Q. Harrison Albright, primarily due to Big Joe's acting skills and appearance, would be able to garner the needed empathy for Bubba.

The verdict: Not Guilty.

Chapter Thirteen

Many years later, in the late 1990's, Felix would be inseparable from his writing journal—even in his bed when he slept. The magnitude of the copious entries he would make, the total number of actual journal notebooks he would have to buy, Felix would be astounded by his inability to stop writing; and thankful, since he had not written this much since the 1969 to 1972 years, when he had laid the groundwork for *Tous Les Sieges Etaient Occupés.*

And although Felix knew and had spent time with Jennifer Apple Morgan on a few occasions by the late 1990's, it would be her stay at *The Breakers* in August of 1998, and the discussions on the beach under the big umbrella, that would be the necessary catalyst for Felix's then rediscovered prolificacy. Her story would open the flood gates for Felix, by providing the additional fodder for lengthy journal entries like, "*Such is the problematic nature of lies, and especially lies of omission,*" and "*whether what they don't hurts less or more.*" And after a particularly poignant conversation with Jennifer on the beach one evening, Felix would add to that journal entry in 2000, when he was developing the back-story for two characters in a new novel: *One of the less than enjoyable repercussions of a former lover or mate dating within a shared social or work circle, is that the other former lover or mate has to see the face of the new lover on a regular basis. And generally she or he thinks, "Gee...with all of the personal baring of my soul that I've shared with him or her about other failed relationships and other traumatic events in my life, topics that I'm real selective with whom I share, with all of the baring of his or her soul to me—which means that he or she also has the proclivity to talk openly about other relationships—no doubt I've now become the subject of pillow talk at times, and even though I might do the same thing to him or her with somebody else I'm currently seeing, I'm humane enough to keep it out of our shared social circle or workplace. But I have to look into the face regularly of somebody who now knows personal things about me.*" Felix would also add to his journal entry on assigning numerical values to childhood and present day relationships: *Charles Dickens wrote in David Copperfield, "There can be no disparity in marriage like unsuitability of mind and purpose." Yet are not those issues of "unsuitability" again issues of mathematical numerical assignments? And don't the numerical assignments change? When we are fifteen, and don't know yet what our own minds and purposes are let alone a prospective mate's, on a scale from +1 to +50, the physical attributes of the one we are romantically pursuing might be assigned a value of +50. When we are fifty that might change to +15, and at sixty-five have no value whatsoever.*

And what numerical value do we give to sex? (Assuming that we've chosen someone who, at least in this area, is of like mind and purpose.) It doesn't matter if Fab Magazine has named you and your mate each "One of the World's Ten Most Sexy," and everybody who buys Fab Magazine fantasizes about taking a tumble in the hay with you or (and) your mate. When a dating couple decides to have sexual intercourse, if it's good the first time, the Earth moves, the Moon winks, the angels sing, and the kitties cry. The second time, the Earth moves, the Moon winks, the angels sing, and the kitties cry—albeit for not quite so long. By the 100th time you've made love to the same person, the kitties have stopped crying altogether. By the 1000th time you've made love to the same person, you put on your miner's helmet, adjust the helmet light, check your box for messages, punch the time clock, and go to work. And I don't care how unromantic that may sound to some ghost who may be looking over my shoulder right now as I write these words in my private journal, but when sex becomes repetitive in both set and setting, the relationship is eventually either doomed or just relegated to the land of quiet desperation. So how do couples who are neither into Marin-county-hot-tub-mate-swapping nor infidelity keep it fresh and entertaining? (According to The Bible, in Genesis, Mankind was told "to be fruitful and multiply." But we were never told, "And have a real good time doing it," nor were we given instructions on how not to be bored. This may have been problematic for Adam and Eve, once they left the Garden, if we can assume that they didn't know "boredom" in the Garden—having spent most of their 900+ years together as outcasts—and at some point they must have felt as if they were punching the time clock also. From a Biblical perspective, if the only reason for sex is procreation—regardless of the double standard of polygamy back then that allowed men only to have multiple mates and might have been an answer, for at least one gender, to boredom—then it's not supposed to be for fun anyway. But since we were given these human psyches, and since we were given this human sexual equipment that requires mental as well as physical stimulation in order to have sex and to procreate, are we sinning if sex is indeed fun with our mates? Are we really coveting somebody else, or even being adulterous if our mate dresses up in different outfits and different wigs and pretends to be different people? Go figure!) Creativity. Either one or both people in a lengthy romantic relationship, a marriage, must be creative enough to keep the sexual intimacy fun and interesting. We make love with our minds not our bodies. Talk about extended foreplay: Sometimes I would call Tatiana at work and bug her all day long. I would elevate the sexual innuendo, and by the final conversation I would tell Tatiana everything that I was going to do to her when she got home. And then when she got home, sometimes she would be so turned on, she'd jump my bones in the foyer, barely crossing the threshold of the apartment, and I'd have to swing around and close the door while holding her.

And what numerical value do we assign to prospective mates in regards to similar hobbies, pastimes, philosophies, and that which we consider to be important in terms of "being yoked alike?" 'Well…Betty Lou likes to rock climb, so that's a big +50. But she doesn't like video games, so that's a big -50. She's a fun person to be with, so that's a big +50. But because she's so pretty, and I want her, and she knows that, she'll probably control me, so that's a big -50.' Billy Bob might think. 'Well…Billy Bob likes to dance, so that's a big +50. But he doesn't like cooking classes, so that's a big -50. He's a fun person to be with, and I can control him, so that's a big +50. But he lets me control him, and eventually he'll outgrow that, and he'll probably leave me, so that's a big -50,' Betty Lou might think. But as time passes, and all of the facades melt away from our true selves, when all of the mini mountains have been climbed, and all of the computers have been crashed, and all of the dances have been danced ad nauseam, and all of the secrets to all of the beloved epicurean delights have been revealed, what the fuck else will Billy Bob and Betty Lou creatively talk about? Will their repartee remain fresh and a turn on, or will it morph into the forced bad fiction of thirty minute television situational comedies?

And that's the most important thing in a long term relationship, that's the proper Biblical "sharing of the same yoke," that's what should get the +50 on the numerical scale of prospective mates: Intelligent Creative Conversation. Tatiana had it right, but I was too immature to understand it back then. As long as a prospective mate has the ability to turn you on, if you can entertain yourselves by staying in bed, drinking tea, and talking all day, with or without interludes of lovemaking, then you have what's needed to make a romantic relationship last. And the more differences between the two people, as long as there is a deep undercurrent of love and respect for each other, the more there is to talk about in bed. Differences in religious philosophy, art, music, literature, food choices, and clothes choices, mean so little when juxtaposed to respect, creativity, conversation, and knowing that your mate has the intellectual wherewithal to really understand you and your needs, and to cover your back in every situation. And even if one hates motorcycles, and needs to see this just metaphorically, it's feeling totally safe on the back of the motorcycle with the mate in control. It's also riding that motorcycle to places and events that one might not particularly like, and learning new skills that one might not particularly care about learning, but doing it, because of the joy it gives one's mate, is more than enough to make up for any personal inconvenience. The old question is relevant nonetheless: "Who is going to have the savoir faire, the smarts, and the creativity to keep you most entertained on a deserted island for years?" When we're younger, we usually lack the intellectual equipment to even visualize that question, when we're out shopping around for a mate. We tend to gravitate more toward "the red and the white," or the passion and innocence (lack of sophistication) the lower levels of love that Andrew Marvell characterizes in "The Garden." (Andrew Marvell also says in the poem, that it would be wiser for the young lovers to carve the name of the tree itself into the bark as opposed to the initials of the lovers, since the tree will last longer.) As we approach middle age, we tend to tally up similarities and differences with perspective mates, and the physical pleasures are still important, when evaluating the overall gestalt of the relationship. When we're older, although we are hopefully wiser, we become more aware of time running out, and then we seem to be more willing "to settle" for someone who we might have rejected when we were younger. I'm not totally sure. But I am sure that most of us would really rather not have our lives, end all alone, like Walt Whitman, in a room over a grocery store in Philadelphia.

@@@@@@@@

"Come on Betty Lou," Fred Larkin said, "I've been asking you out for weeks. Give a decent working man a chance!"

"It's not that I don't find you interesting or attractive Fred," Selma Greenwood said, "It's just been a long time since I've dated anybody."

And that was true. Since her husband had passed away in 1969, Selma had only been out with a few men in eighteen years. In 1975, when she was forty-three, she had gone out with *Rutland Taxi* driver Jebediah Witherspoon for a year. And although eventually they had become intimate, the relationship had gone nowhere. In 1977, a Stanford Professor of Psychology, Dr. Ira Cohen, had visited the library to do research while spending a week's vacation with a friend in Rutland. The attraction had been immediate with Selma, and a weeklong whirlwind tryst had ensued. Unfortunately, late in the week, Selma would catch the tail end of a phone conversation he was having with his wife, and that ended that. In 1981, when she was forty-nine, when she had to flee from the *Hotel Frontenac* after the conversation with Lizzie Apple, Selma was in a room directly across the hall from sixty year-old Dr. Miles Stone, a visiting widower and retired pediatrician she had met at a church social in Rutland a week earlier, and who had asked her to vacation with him in Quebec City. He had taken care of the separate room for Selma, and he had been disappointed when Selma had knocked on his door and explained that a family emergency had occurred and she had to leave. Now in 1987, at fifty-five, she was flattered that sixty-two year-old real estate agent Fred Larkin had shown interest in her. But the life of a fugitive is a life of being alone, at least not getting too close to other people, and although Selma had taken a chance with previous relationships, Fester Daily putting two and two together in 1981 had made her even more cautious.

There does come a point in a fugitive's life however, when the question must arise: Is my freedom worth the loneliness? And Selma had indeed been thinking just that recently. There were many times in the past several months, in which she had thought about surrendering to the police. At least then, Selma could be herself when talking to people in jail, she'd eventually get out of jail, and then she could spend the rest of her life without having to look over her shoulder and into every woodpile.

Selma hadn't spoken to her sister, or Salome, or her other Rutland friends in more than six years. She worked as a waitress at *The Piedmont Diner* in Atlanta, Georgia, deciding when she put together her last identity not to chance library work again. Her life was fairly simple, in that her apartment was off of Piedmont Road in Atlanta just three blocks from the restaurant. She knew that the chances of someone coming into the diner and recognizing her was a possibility, but she felt as if she had lessened that risk by working at a hash slinging mom and pop diner rather than a chain restaurant. Selma also knew that she could do better as a waitress working the night shift at a good place in Underground Atlanta, but Underground Atlanta had too many tourists and Selma was content staying off of the beaten path. The loneliness. Selma spent her leisure time at the main Atlanta Library downtown on Peachtree Street, going to museums in and around Atlanta, taking weekend car trips to obscure locations throughout the South, and seeing lots of movies. In late 1981, just before she had given up the name Amy Rosenberg and left the Buffalo and Cleveland areas forever, Selma noticed that the mail in Amy Rosenberg's post office box had been opened. Selma had immediately driven to a corner mailbox in Manhattan and sent a letter to Ivy in care of the Natural History Museum that said, "Box in Buffalo unsafe. Don't use!" Several months later, after having made the trip to Manhattan and mailed letters in care of the museum to Ivy two more times, Selma finally called the Museum of Natural History looking for her sister. Somebody came on the phone and said that Ivy was no longer in their employ. Fortunately, the letters to Ivy had contained no new alias, just a payphone number in Detroit and the hours on Saturday that Selma would hang out near the payphone waiting for the call. After months with no call, Selma had moved to Atlanta.

Recently, the extremely well-read Selma, had begun writing a novel in first person that, playing on Dostoevsky's title, she intended on calling *Notes from the Modern Underground.* Writing this thinly disguised *roman à clef* did occupy some of Selma's time, but mostly she still felt depressed. Dating Fred Larkin seemed like a good way to shake the blues.

"Okay Fred," Selma said, "I'll go out to dinner with you. If we don't click, we'll still talk whenever you come in here...right? We'll still remain friendly...right?"

"Of course Betty Lou!" Fred said with confidence. Actually Fred was confident that he could win Selma's heart. As to how he would react to her if she rejected him, Fred hadn't a clue.

"Well…how about this Saturday night?"

"That'll be fine Fred," Selma said. "What should I wear?"

"I was thinking about *Windows*," he said. "If I can still get a reservation. That place is fancy-shmantzy." Fred was talking about the restaurant that sat on top of the *Regency Hyatt Hotel* in downtown Atlanta on Peachtree Street. The walls of this restaurant were completely glass, and the whole place rotated around once an hour, giving the diner an incredible view of four states.

"Couldn't we go somewhere a bit more out of the way?" Selma asked, fearing the possibility of recognition at a tourist trap like *Windows*.

And Fred Larkin, assuming that Selma wanted a more intimate setting, was happy to change up and suggest this dark little French restaurant near Stone Mountain. "Let's go to *Le Rendez-Vous*, it's a nice French place," he said.

And Selma had agreed.

@@@@@@@@

In September of 1987, Felix received an interesting letter. It was from Eric Olsen, a Swede, who had been one of Felix's friends at NYU in 1968. Felix hadn't heard anything from or about him in nineteen years. The letter had been mailed from Stockholm:

> *Dear Felix,*
>
> *Hello! It's been more than 19 years! I hope you are doing well, and I guess that means I hope you're writing or have written another novel. Although it's 10 years-old now, I recently read Tous Les Sieges Etaient Occupés. It was an interesting read. I wasn't too happy with your character Ole Sorensen however, because he's basically a Swedish buffoon who can't even tie his shoelaces without falling on his face.*
>
> *I thought you and I had a nice friendship back then Felix. Obviously you felt the need to make me look stupid. (Your character's last name, Sorensen, was the name of my dorm at NYU. How many other Swedish friends did you have in 1968?) Please don't try to con me with, "This is just a work of fiction." As a tenured Professor of Swedish Literature at the University of Stockholm, I know better.*

Whatever dibbick you felt you needed to exorcise by ripping me a new one, I hope you feel better now. Friends?

Eric

And Felix immediately wrote back:

Dearest Eric,

I had no intention of "ripping you a new one," in my novel. Why would I want to do that? I remember you as a wonderful man, I always enjoyed your company, and you never did anything to piss me off. Honestly, and I hope this isn't worse than doing what you suggest I did, I didn't even think about you while I was writing the character of Ole Sorensen. I mean…I needed somebody Swedish, because the action takes place in that part of the world. I had already created the names of two Danish men, a German man, and a Dutch woman by the time Ole Sorensen is introduced. (I had a Finnish woman later in the story, remember?) So the only thinking about you that I probably did was to discount anybody with the first name of "Eric" or the last name of "Olsen." It becomes difficult in a novel, especially with all of the minor character names a writer uses, to make sure that those names don't come from the writer's real life. "Let's call this minor character 'Arthur.' Oh wait a minute, there's a man I know who lives in Apt. 5-F in my building named 'Arthur.' He'll think I'm writing about him!" In the case of Ole Sorensen, I got "Ole" from a short story I once read, "Swedish Midnight," whose protagonist was named Ole Johansen. I did take "Sorensen" from your old NYU dorm however, not because I had some agenda with you, but because I don't know a whole plethora of Swedish names. Please believe me…I always liked you. And please, I hope you'll consider taking a vacation to the west coast of Florida…my home…Madeira Beach. You'll have a nice room in my motel, and I'll show you around.

Friends Always!

Felix

In March of 1987, after resigning himself to the disappointing truth that Anthony was going to vacate his previous promise to run *The Breakers* for ten years, and that he could either sell and be done with Mad Beach or accept his apparent fate that he and the motel were to be yoked together forever, after the possibility of tenure was offered by the University of Tampa Bay, Dr. Felix Kulpa readily agreed to teach as a professor of Victorian Literature for the fall session in September of 1987. Felix was able to get Dora Larue to cover the office of *The Breakers* for the three mornings that he would be at school, and Jack covered during Felix's Wednesday evening class.

In September of 1987, after handing out the ambitious syllabus to his students on the first day of his first class, one young lady, upon glancing at the syllabus, said, "Dr. Kulpa. I can't believe we have to read *The Woman in White* by Wilke Collins. I read *Moonstone*, and I absolutely hated it!"

And Felix smiled and said, "Ms. Lipschitz, you're here to be a student of Victorian Literature, not a student of what you like!"

@@@@@@@@

By September of 1987 Salome had had enough of staying home every evening. And as if getting the same kind of rush that cocaine had given her up until seven years ago, Salome discovered that by being out and about she suddenly felt alive and vital again. She still loved her husband very much, but Anthony didn't seem to care if she stayed home anymore. When he wasn't working, he was content drinking beer and watching television in the dark alone. Walter Lee would regularly give Anthony grief over how dark he kept his house saying things like, "'Knee…when I lived my previous life…with my now deceased family in Chicago…If you knew how much we struggled to get the light into that apartment…If you knew how important the light was and what it meant to us, you'd know how miserable this darkness can make one feel!" And Anthony would just smile and go back to watching television. Anthony had figured out about six months ago that Salome's Christian values wouldn't allow her to cheat on him, and that lack of insecurity had manifested itself as no concern over where Salome went, no concern in keeping Salome happy by being hospitable to family and friends who were allowed over, and no concern over initiating bedroom activity.

When she wasn't working, Salome now had a complex schedule in her life. She went to a prayer meeting with Denise, at her church on Monday evenings; a Polish cooking class, on Tuesday evenings; a ballroom dancing class, at *Arthur Murray's*, on Wednesday evenings; a woman's discussion group, on Thursday evenings; and a visit with Jack, Geneva, Sam, Lani, Felix, Walter Lee, Anne, and Lena, at *The Breakers*, on Friday evenings. On Saturday afternoons, Salome took a class in French cooking, and she always went to church on Sunday mornings. Salome always stayed home on Saturday evenings, unless Denise, other friends from the office, or family on Mad Beach had tickets for an event and asked her to come along. Salome tried to make an exquisite meal for Anthony on Saturday evenings, some recipe that was usually expensive and difficult. But sullen Anthony was totally unappreciative when it came to the complex dinners that Salome fixed on those nights, and he would say, "So what country are we in tonight?"

And Salome would say, "I made you a wonderful *cordon bleu*," or "Wait until you taste this *canard á l'orange*," or "You're gonna love this borscht I made," or "This is the greatest miso soup, try it!"

And Anthony would say, "Look Salome...I like simple American, simple Italian...not northern Italian...a few simple seafood dishes, and a few Chinese dishes...that's it. Stop making me all of this other crap!"

And Salome would cry because she tried so hard to make Anthony's life at home enjoyable, and she felt that opening up his food horizons would restore some fire to his being. But she reluctantly did what her husband requested, except on the one Saturday night per month that Felix came over. Felix loved trying new and exotic foods.

Felix would joke and say things to Salome like, "So are we having the stir fried monkey hips or the candied goat anus tonight?"

And Salome would joke back with something like, "I hope you like the fish head *á l'orange* and the catfish intestine *ceviche!*"

Whatever it was that Salome cooked was usually excellent, and Felix would always make sure to give compliments on her great cooking. Felix would also always bring dessert and a bottle of wine, and before his monthly back shave, while they were drinking coffee and eating dessert, he and Salome would discuss some book. Lately, The Bible had been the book of choice. During these discussions Anthony would leave the table and watch television alone.

Felix, who was always concerned about his brother anyway, but who had sensed particular alarm back in 1985, when it had been more than a year after Anthony's "New Horizon" cocaine detoxification program and he was still extremely depressed, and having made a ton of money from his share of *The Careless Navigator*, had spent nearly $40,000 on a brand new *Aurora Cobra* two-seater convertible sports car—the Canadian replica of the original 289 *Ford* engine *A.C. Cobra*—for Anthony's 30th birthday. Anthony had been appreciative, he had hugged and kissed his brother on the cheek, but other than driving it back and forth to work, the car still hadn't brought Anthony the kind of joy that Felix had hoped it would. Salome had finally said in 1986, before heading up to Rutland alone during Bubba's trial, "When I get back, let's go find some two lane mountain blacktops in the Tennessee Smokies and see what this bad boy can do!"

And Anthony had responded, "Why don't you go? You can take the car...see if your friend Denise would like to go with you."

Now, in 1987, Felix was at a loss for how to help his brother get over his malaise. Felix had consulted a psychiatrist last year, paying him $150 for the hour, looking for a way to help Anthony. And the psychiatrist had told Felix,

"I can help him, but you have to get him in here." When delicately approached with this by Felix, Anthony had just rejected the idea, stating that he wouldn't discuss it, and that the psychiatrist couldn't tell him anything about himself that he didn't already know.

Many years later, in the late 1990's, Felix would write in his journal: *And that's the problem with those of us who have read a few psychology texts and think, because we intellectually understand various psychological models, that going to a therapist is a big waste of time. Once, when I was in a cynical mood, I said to Walter Lee's friend and psychotherapist from the 1960's, Chuck Coaker, "Isn't it interesting that the word 'therapist' is actually two words, 'the' and 'rapist.' I don't know what that means, but it's interesting nonetheless." But I was just being contrary on that day, because I do believe in psychotherapy. Psychotherapy usually works, because the patient vocalizes that which may have been understood intellectually in the mind, but only begins to actually complete the impasse and make the patient feel better when once vocalized. Say it aloud, feel better. And this notion might be paralleled in religion, and might answer the question: "Is it necessary for one to announce aloud that one has theologically accepted one path or another? Need an atheist announce that he or she is now a theist in order to be a theist? Need a theist announce that he or she is now a Christian in order to be a Christian?" If the answer is "Yes," then perhaps there is some correlation between religion and psychotherapy. Perhaps Freud needed to look a little further back in history, beyond classical Greece and two of its most famous tragedies, back to Adam and Eve, their tragedy, and both their pre-Fall and post-Fall Egos, to see, if after they had vocalized their guilt, if they actually felt better working "in the sweat of thy face" amongst the thorns and bristles. "As if they were New York City School Teachers."* Felix would add to this journal entry, in late 2004, after hearing a New York City Literacy Teacher complain.)

@@@@@@@@

By May of 1988, Bubba had had enough of Gus Strattus. After Gus Strattus had lost his right testicle, and The State of Vermont had lost its criminal case against Bubba in 1986, Gus, with the help of his nephew, an attorney in Burlington, had attempted in 1987, to bring a frivolous lawsuit against *Apple Apples, Inc.*, claiming that, as prosecutor Wilson Smith had said during the case, "Bubba should have waited until the door actually opened before firing and that Bubba had used excessive force," to force Bubba Apple to waste money on an attorney; but, to his credit, Rutland Judge Homer Morton, recognizing the lack of evidence and frivolity in the plaintiff's suit, summarily dismissed it, and gave Gus' nephew a verbal reprimand for wasting his time.

Since both the Strattus orchard and the Apple orchard were outside of the Rutland city limits, neither were subject to certain city ordinances. One of those ordinances was noise. In an attempt to annoy Bubba Apple, Gus

Strattus now had outside stereo speakers set up next to the property line fence by the barn, and he had made a tape with teary-eyed "my-gal-done-me-wrong-and-now-I-just-drink-beer" Country and Western Music intermixed with happy Greek Bouzouki Music, and that tape now blasted 24/7 on a loop. "WHYYY Jumpin' JEEEHOSOPHAT!" Bubba would say while pondering his kingdom in the bathroom of the barn. "Every time I TAAAKE a dump, I either have to hear Merle Haggard or VISUUUALIZE Anthony Quinn!"

Bubba would also complain about the smell in and around the barn, since subject to no city odor ordinances either, Gus Strattus had started a huge compost heap next to the stereo speakers, and placed a gigantic fan running off of a long extension cord behind it. (When told about this during one of his dinner, discussion, and back shave Saturday nights at Salome and Anthony's, Felix would say, "New York City might want to consider that big fan idea…to kinda blow the smell back at New Jersey." And Salome would say, "You're just kidding…right? New Jersey isn't that bad…it's actually pretty nice!" And Felix would counter with, "Yeah…well we all know which part of the Statue of Liberty faces New Jersey don't we!" And Salome would say, coming to the defense of New Jersyites everywhere, "Yeah…but her armpit faces Staten Island, New York!")

Since Ethel Bouvier had passed away in April of 1988 and had left her small Burlington house to Pauline and Clara, and since Clara was more than happy to let Pauline buyout her half share in the house at current market value, and since sixty-eight year-old Bubba and sixty year-old Pauline were tired of the apple business and particularly tired of Gus Strattus' shenanigans, in May of 1988 they decided to move to the small house in Burlington and to give the farmhouse, orchard, and business to Bruiser, Eileen, Karen and Conrad. This, of course, had to be worked out with the other children, since Bubba and Pauline's 1000 acres, farmhouse, and business were worth slightly more than \$3,000,000. With Bubba and Pauline's help, since the property, business, and farmhouse were completely paid off, Bruiser obtained a thirty year mortgage for \$3,000,000. Since Bubba and Pauline wanted \$1,000,000 for retirement, that meant the six Apple children would each receive approximately \$333,333 of the remaining \$2,000,000. Bruiser sent a check for \$333,333 to Jennifer, Cindy, Jack, Jimson, and Salome. Bruiser and Eileen were able to sell the old seven acre Liberty farm for \$125,000, so after adding \$75,000 of their own savings to that amount, plus adding their \$333,333.00 share from the loan, they were able to lower the principal on their 7.5% mortgage to slightly less than \$2,470,000. The monthly payments were still high, but between the profits from the orchard, *The Careless Navigator*, the Michigan hot dog restaurant, Bruiser's guide business, and Bruiser's hunting business, they were able to get by nicely.

Once they moved onto the property, Bruiser Apple, with Felix's help, figured out a way to fix Gus Strattus' wagon. Felix stopped by Rutland and stayed with Bruiser and Eileen for a couple of days in early June of 1988. Felix was taking a two week Canadian car vacation to Quebec and the Maritimes, so he decided to see his relatives in Burlington and Plattsburgh on the way. Having never been to Herman Melville's home, Arrowhead, in the Berkshires, Felix headed east off of I-87 in New York to Pittsfield, Massachusetts. After seeing the desk where Melville wrote *Moby Dick*, the window he looked out of at the mountaintop that looked like a white whale, and after seeing the hackneyed gift shop that Anthony and Salome had described in 1974, Felix continued up Highway 7 into Vermont. A couple of hours later in Rutland, Felix saw the **Apple Apples** sign on Highway 7. He pulled in for just a quick impromptu visit with Bruiser, Eileen, and the children, but after sharing a joint of Bruiser's Western Vermont Wacky Weed in the barn, Felix suddenly discovered that he was staying for a couple of days at Bruiser's. During those two days Felix met, partied, and was taken by Jr. Liberty out to look at this year's covert crop, had dinner and went sailing with Colin and Jennifer on Lake Bomoseen, and had a wonderful dinner prepared by Eileen with the invited guests Cindy, Dick, and children, Jimson, Lizzie, and children, and Bubba and Pauline. Somewhere during the dinner Bubba said to Felix, "WHYYY Jumpin' JEEEHOSOPHAT…your voice sounds familiar to MEEE! Have WEEE ever spoken BEEEFORE?"

And Felix assured Bubba that they had never met before. "You must think that I sound like my brother, Anthony," he said.

"That's not it," Bubba said. "I KNOOOW how Anthony sounds."

Later, in private, Pauline said to Felix, "OH MY GOD! You were Salome's lawyer on the phone in 1975!" And after Felix admitted that truth to Pauline she said, "Thank you! You saved my daughter back then," and then she gave Felix a big kiss on the cheek.

Felix and Bruiser found a high end electronics store in Burlington, and Bruiser spent a bundle on state of the art electronic equipment. Gus Strattus' equipment was totally antiquated in comparison to what Bruiser bought. Bruiser now had his six loud dogs in the old kennel next to the barn, and Felix noticed how the hounds barked loudly at the screaming guitar work in "The Inner Bitch," the thirteenth track on *Home Cooking*'s "Brewin' Bitches," and how they howled loudly at the fourteenth hidden track, "Root the Hedgehog," sung by Johnny Cash. Felix and Bruiser then prepared a 24/7 tape loop of those two songs, and after "mic-ing" the kennel and aiming the four huge speakers at Gus Strattus' house, what they got, besides the songs over and over again themselves, was an incredibly loud canine Greek chorus that alternated between barks and howls. And to deal with the Strattus smell issue, Felix dug a pit behind the barn and dumped in twenty dozen eggs and five pounds of sulfur. He and Bruiser then went and bought a larger industrial fan than Gus Strattus.' "Wait until a couple weeks of summer heat starts to cook those eggs!" Felix said.

In June of 1988 Jennifer caught Colin with another woman. Actually, unbeknownst to Colin and his paramour, on that Tuesday afternoon when he was supposed to be taking a seminar on some new gynecological technique at Burlington Mercy Hospital, but he and Rutland General Hospital Candystriper Becky Truman were frolicking in Room 112 of the Burlington *Days Inn*, was that Cindy Chumwell had seen them entering the room from her car on South Street on her way to Burlington Mercy Hospital for some advanced tests for Multiple Sclerosis that her physician in Plattsburgh wanted her to have, and that she had called Jennifer at *The Woman's Center* in Rutland from a payphone at the hospital immediately to report her findings. There were no patients in *The Woman's Center* at the time, and none were scheduled for appointments that afternoon, so Jennifer had closed down the center and literally flew up Highway 7 to the Burlington *Day's Inn* in her convertible *Mercedes 450 SL* with the top up. She made the trip, unimpeded by a speeding ticket, in less than ninety minutes. Jennifer pulled up next to her husband's car in the parking lot in front of Room 112. Colin and twenty year-old Becky were just exiting the room as Jennifer was about to knock. "You son of a bitch!" Jennifer had yelled at Colin, and then she had slapped him hard across the face.

Jennifer wouldn't allow Colin back into the house without Sheriff Glenn escorting him, and Colin had taken his clothes and some personal items and moved into a hotel room in Rutland. After two months of begging, an incredibly romantic dinner in Burlington, complete with a two carat emerald ring—Colin had bought the ring for Jennifer during a final weekend fling in New York City with Becky Truman—in August of 1988, Jennifer would finally acquiesce, forgive Colin, and let him move back in.

In June of 1988 Salome discovered that she was pregnant. The excitement she felt was mirrored by her family in Rutland, her family and friends on Mad Beach, Denise and her friends at work, in fact everyone but Anthony was excited. "Come on Anthony!" Salome had said, "Aren't you happy about having our own baby?"

And Anthony had just responded, "I guess," and then he had given his wife an obligatory kiss, grabbed a beer from the refrigerator, and sat back down in the dark to watch television.

Walter Lee Kulpa was born on March 9, 1989, and nobody flipped out more than Felix. Felix had wanted a child forever, and his brother's son, his first nephew, would be his son by proxy. Naming their son Walter Lee had been Salome's idea, but Anthony had agreed and Walter Lee Younger was too flattered and emotional to say much more than just, "Thank you," to Salome and Anthony. Later, when he could get the words out, Walter Lee said in private to Anthony, "You know 'Knee…if my son, Travis, had lived…he'd be two years older than you are now...your son might have been my first grandchild. I wish I could say the right words…to really let you see...just how deeply you and Salome have touched me... I am so honored." And Anthony, who really had to force himself anymore to be the touchy-feely person he had once been, got up and gave Walter Lee a big hug.

By the summer of 1989, Anthony had begun smoking cocaine again. He was never around, and despite the pleading by Salome, the admonitions from Walter Lee Younger, and the threats of "I'm gonna take you out and kick your ass if you don't start staying at home and taking care of your son and wife," by Felix, Anthony was gone most of the time. Salome, who would regularly call Felix and cry, was at least happy that Felix would come over several times a week and play with little Walter Lee. By early 1990, Anthony had moved into a room somewhere in downtown Tampa. A couple of months later, two hired goons showed up at Salome's door early one Monday morning demanding money. Anthony was more than $50,000 in debt to Jesus Narizes. The goons were contemplating doing a touch up job on Salome's face, and they gave her three days to come up with the money. Salome then called Anthony's office and left a message for him on his answering machine, but he never bothered getting back to her.

That was the end of the road as far as Salome was concerned. That Anthony could leave not only herself but their son in harm's way, Salome couldn't go through the rest of her life like that. She went to the bank to withdraw the $50,000 from their joint savings account to payoff Anthony's drug debt, but when she attempted to withdraw the funds she found that there was only about $1500 left in the account. After receiving their share of Salome's parents' business, along with their profits from *The Careless Navigator*, they had paid off the mortgage on their home in Tampa, and had renovated completely a small building in downtown Tampa they had bought to house Anthony's law office. They had equity, but they no longer had the $50,000. On the afternoon before her "goon deadline," Salome called Felix, told him what had happened, and he insisted on coming over and protecting her and little Walter Lee overnight. Felix slept on the couch, and the next morning, when the men showed up again, Felix answered the door and said, "My brother has apparently ripped off the money from his joint account with my sister-in-law. Is $50,000 the total amount of Anthony's drug debt? Because if it is, you can go with me to the bank in St. Petersburg right now, I'll give you the money, and that's that. I assume it was Jesus who hired you...I've known him for years, so please give him this message. Tell him that he's been paid, and not to issue Anthony any more credit...because there is nothing left. Tell Jesus, if he allows Anthony to run up another tab...that's on him...and he shouldn't come to Anthony's wife or me again looking for payment!" And then Felix took the threatening looking men to his bank to get them the money. From a payphone in the lobby of the bank, Felix called Jesus Narizes and spoke very carefully and cleverly to him on the phone—in case any law enforcement agencies were listening in—just to verify that these henchmen were his, that was indeed all of the money owed to him by Anthony, and to ask him if he knew of anymore drug debt of Anthony's with other dealers. "No more credit to Anthony." Jesus agreed, and Felix paid.

By early 1991, after a shady deal with a corporate client that was designed to make Anthony a whole bunch of money that he could smoke up had gone awry, the client complained to the Florida Bar Association's disciplinary committee. After a lengthy hearing, Anthony was disbarred. He could no longer practice in court, so he took his name off of the business cards and signs in front of his building, and he hired two other attorneys straight out of law school, used their names, and made them the courtroom junior partners. Although he usually stayed out of sight, Anthony was still the office manager for *Corporate Solutions, Inc.*, the legal firm he had started, and all of the cases were still discussed with him.

By late 1991 Salome filed divorce papers, and by 1992 the divorce was finalized. Salome was forced to sell the house in Tampa and give half of the money to Anthony, after Felix had been repaid. Salome then purchased a small condominium on Younger Island in Tampa for her and little Walter Lee. Anthony and Salome still had the twenty-five percent interest in *The Careless Navigator* on Mad Beach, and it became Salome's job to account for and forward quarterly Anthony's half of the profit from their share. In return, since Anthony didn't want to hang around with friends and family on Mad Beach anyway, he had given a signed proxy to Salome, and she voted the way she saw fit on corporate issues with *The Careless Navigator*. Anthony had won visitation rights with his son for every other weekend and every other holiday, but he very rarely took advantage of seeing little Walter Lee. He was very rarely straight enough to safely spend time with his son.

In late 1992, Salome took little three year-old Walter Lee and visited Anthony at work. And although Salome raised quite a ruckus with the assistant at the sliding glass window that separated the waiting room from the inner sanctum, Anthony had already given his junior partners, assistants, and security a heads up about the possibility of his "crazy ex" visiting work. The assistant, Bambi Waxler, with whom Anthony was currently smoking coke and *schtupping*, hung tough with Salome, and she threatened to call the cops if Salome didn't leave.

In early December of 1992, Felix went to Anthony's office one late afternoon and waited in the parking garage next to Anthony's *Cobra*. When Anthony finally came out of the office and saw Felix, before Felix could say anything, as Anthony was unlocking and starting up his car, he kept repeating, "It's the Felix Kulpa Show! It's the Felix Kulpa Show!" And then he drove away.

@@@@@@@@

In March of 1993, Felix had to take twenty-one year-old Petomaine to the vet's to be euthanized. And although the sad official diagnosis a year earlier had been Feline Leukemia, and the vet had wanted Felix to say goodbye at that time, Felix had opted instead for the medication and for taking Peto home, as long as it didn't seem as if the cat were suffering. At that time, Peto had looked up into Felix's face and thought, 'Before Dr. Mengele here...sitting in his "It-will-only-be-$395-to-kill-Peto" catbird seat...becomes the cataclysmic catalysis that catapults me into my fourth life...why not take me home and keep feeding me Round Boy...see?' And as if reading Peto's mind, that's exactly what Felix had done.

For the last year it had been hard on Felix, as Peto decided, no matter how many times Felix changed the litter weekly, that he would prefer using other places to relieve himself. Felix would regularly find that Peto had used the bathtub; Felix's shoes; the plants, sitting on top of the cupboard; the hibachi pot, sitting in the corner of the living room for decoration; and the floor in front of the litter box. And even though it had been diagnosed as Feline Leukemia, Peto acted as if he had Kitty Alzheimer's. He would decide that he was hungry, he was even more persistent, and it would be just ten minutes since he had been fed. Peto would rub up against Felix's leg and think, 'Feed me...Round Boy!' And Felix would say something like, "I just fed you Peto. But if you'd like some more *Purina Wildebeest Chow*, and you'll eat it before the roaches decide that I've opened up a buffet...it's yours." And Felix would feed Peto again, just so Peto could have his kitty thrill of being fed, then later Felix would dump the uneaten food. During this final year together, Peto became very affectionate to Felix. He had always been the type of cat who hated to be held or petted, but during his last year of life he wouldn't leave Felix alone. And Felix regularly gave Peto the attention he suddenly craved. Finally, it had gotten to the point that Peto was throwing up everything and he seemed to be suffering, so Felix decided that it was indeed time to bring him back to the vet.

After Petomaine had been given the goodbye kitty injection, he found his kitty mind free associating, as his third life was ending. He thought, in his Edward G. Robinson/Johnny Rocco voice, 'The horror! The horror! See? To leave now is a catastrophe! I always wanted to sail a catamaran to Catalonia or Catalina...Yes...and I've always wanted to catalogue the catalos and cattle of the Cathay people...Yes...and I always thought a trip to the Catskills would be cathartic...Yes...and I always wanted to make a cat's cradle and play marbles with a cat's-eye...Yes...and run crazy chasing a catcaller through the catkins...Yes...but I was always used as a cat's-paw...Yes...thoroughly catheterized in this catty biped society... Yes...and I love catsup on my catnip...Yes...and I always wanted to see inside of a Catholic cathedral and a CAT scan...Yes...and I always wanted to study catoptrics... Yes...and now it's hard to maintain this cathexis...Yes...somebody please find me a catholicon...See?...Yes!'

Chapter Fourteen

Four years later, in early September of 1998, as another hurricane approached the St. Petersburg area, Felix would write: *Hurricanes can be very disingenuous; sometimes they'll stand at the top of the elegant staircase, having already been announced as the guest of honor, with their invitations for the head table in hand, gaze upon all of the prepared accommodations below, hear the orchestra tuning, and then decide that some less in earnest seamy soirée fifty miles away in Podunkville would be more worth while attending. Meanwhile, down below, the caterer has already been paid too much for all of the eclectic delicacies that the guest of honor demands, and the grand hall has already been modified to please the guest of honor's eye; and although there will be a party anyway, so the money really isn't wasted, and the one stuck with the bill will eventually say, "Thank God she headed in a different direction!" after the gauche behavior of Ms. Hurricane, the bill payer can't help but deplore Ms. Hurricane's deceptive mutable nature.*

It was early Sunday morning, August 28, 1994, and as Hurricane Desdemona was preparing to greet the new work week by blowing open shutters, scattering debris, realigning coastal vertebrae, and douching the inland waterways between St. Petersburg and the beaches with a plié of bad news, Felix sat uneasily at his favorite table on the beach with his open stone-weighted-down writing journal, the umbrella having already been stashed.

For Mr. or Ms. Still-Working-Forty-Hours-Per-Week Northerner, in the winter, Florida was a one-week oasis sans cold on the Atlantic Ocean or Gulf of Mexico. And, of course, upon returning home, Mr. or Ms.

Northerner would discover that the snow had gathered, was playing canasta in the driveway and chuckling, knowing how much harder you now had to work to rid yourself of it, since you had actually displayed enough chutzpah to have taken a week off from your hell-frozen-over bailiwick and gone to Florida. For the snowbird retiree on a fixed income, Florida was sanctuary for a short season. It was time to head north, when the electric bills for air conditioning and the dry cleaning costs for the daily three sweaty outfit changes began to require one to refinance his or her mortgage. For the out-of-stater with ties to Florida, if bad weather were there, even if no personal property were at risk, there was always this sigh and thought about Florida, "My God...there's trouble in paradise!" For Felix Kulpa, who owned half of a heavily insured by *Grapefruit State* motel on Mad Beach that had recently been appraised at close to fifteen million dollars, although he didn't want to see people hurt or homeless, and he didn't really want any serious damage to his place that would require a major fixing and cleanup hassle, hurricanes at least represented change from the annual ten and a half months of sunshine and heat. Felix usually welcomed that change, but for some reason this morning he felt uneasy. He sensed that the approaching hurricane would only be the dropping of the first boot.

Yesterday, Felix had boarded up the motel when the last of the short-term guests had checked out at noon. The tenants in the two remaining annual apartments, Big John and Little John, the Gay couple in Apartment 6, and Dora Laurue, in Apartment 7, had already left for a few days. Jack, Geneva, and the twins, fortunately, had chosen the correct week to be on vacation at Bubba and Pauline's in Burlington. Walter Lee, Annie, and Lena were staying at their condo in Orlando. They had purchased the condo as an investment, but since *The Careless Navigator* in Orlando, just a few miles from *Disneyworld*, was the busiest of their three restaurants, a few times monthly they had to stay over and the condo had come in handy. In a few hours Felix would pick up Salome and little Walter Lee in Tampa, and they would all drive the ninety miles east to Walter Lee's place.

The category three hurricane was in the Gulf of Mexico about fifty miles due west of land, and it was paralleling the Florida coastline as it rushed north by northwest toward the Florida panhandle and Panama City Beach. At the moment, Desdemona was still about seven hours south of the St. Pete. area, but the winds were already blowing close to fifty miles per hour.

Felix was worried about his brother's evacuation plans. But since Anthony had moved in with Bambi Waxler in her apartment just north of Tampa in Temple Terrace, and he had never given Felix the address, and he was refusing to answer or return Felix's calls, there was nothing that Felix could do other than to hope that Anthony was okay.

Felix wrote in his journal: *I wish that I could help my brother out of his psychological quagmire. I know what it is that ails him, and it's a basic lack of trust...when it comes to other human beings. Anthony was abandoned way too young by our mother. And of course I was responsible at a number of levels for taking his dad away too. And then I went away to New York, and then he fell for Salome and she went away also. Anthony is probably afraid to love anyone too deeply anymore...including his son...including his ex-wife...because he fears that the person he loves might go away. And the only time that Anthony can forget that fear and be sociable, is when he is with others, for whom the coke pipe also shuts it all out. And in other news: It feels as if I'm getting ready to write again. Perhaps I can develop a protagonist who can help both me and Anthony. Perhaps I'm kidding myself. Because of my limited journal entries in the last twenty years, I thought that I had said everything I could possibly say in Tous Les Sieges Etaient Occupés. I thought that that 454 page pontification had been cathartic enough, and that I was on the path toward being able to live with myself finally, and maybe even learn how to forgive myself. The hurt I had always carried, like Anthony, over our mother's abandonment, the hurt over Tatiana's infidelities and our subsequent divorce in 1972, and the worse thing, the guilt I carried because my hatred of Terry had motivated me to cause her fall in 1961, and that fall had caused a medical condition that resulted in her death in 1971, and her death resulted in my father slowly withering away and then taking his own life in 1973—even though I was responsible for all of that—I had thought...in the past twenty years...that I had actually started to heal. Today...it feels as if that isn't the case.*

Yesterday, I had an interesting conversation with Montgomery Butler. He's always been a spiritual person, and he first turned me on to the Buddhist way of seeing life back in the summer of 1965, just before I headed off for my first year at NYU. At that time, he explained to me how the Ego tries to suppress the Self, and what he said then eventually led me to study Buddhism in my post-psychotropic drug days. I said to Montgomery, "I thought Mr. Guilt had vacated the premises permanently a long time ago. I mean...Remember? I sent Mr. Self around...he's still the town sheriff you know...and he tacked up a 454 page Eviction Notice on Mr. Guilt's door back in the 1970's...telling him that he hadn't been paying the rent...and that it was time to scram. But recently, I saw Mr. Guilt hanging out again with the Emotion Family. And when he sat down for the family dinner...his ass was occupying just way too many seats. So I yelled at him across the room...told him to get out. And then he got up...dropped trou...mooned me...and then flipped me the bird as he was heading out the door." And Montgomery said to me, "Apparently Mr. Self, as the sheriff, is falling down on the job! Tell him to get tougher with Mr. Guilt. As a matter of fact, tell him to switch to the other side of the law...and to waste Mr. Guilt organized crime execution style!" And that sounded like the thing to do and I told Montgomery, "Thanks." But I still can't help feeling that another long Eviction Notice may be coming first. The last thing that Montgomery had said to me before hanging up was, "Stay in touch...with your Self!" And the last thing that I had said to him was, "I would...but the long distance charges are killing me!"

@@@@@@@@

On this Sunday morning of August 28, 1994, Lizzie Apple was sitting on the leather recliner and watching *Sunday Morning* on CBS. Thirteen year-old daughter Nancy was still at her friend's sleepover in Burlington, and she would be returned around 5:00 this afternoon. Eleven year-old daughter Eve was still with her cousin Karen at Bruiser and Eileen's in Rutland, and she would be retrieved by Lizzie alone, to let Jimson sleep, at around 1:00 this afternoon. Then at 6:00 this evening, Jimson, Lizzie, Nancy, and Eve were all expected at Bubba and Pauline's for dinner with the visiting Jack, Geneva, Sam, and Lani. Jimson had just finished breakfast and was asleep. He still preferred the graveyard shift at the correction center, and the rotating schedule gave him two Saturday nights per month. When he had gotten home this Sunday morning, Lizzie had made him a large pancake and egg breakfast. Lizzie sat watching television alone, impervious to Charles Osgood on the screen, thinking about what had happened last night with Harold Williams.

Twenty years ago in 1974, when Lizzie, Jimson, and Harold had all been seniors in high school, Lizzie had momentarily succumbed to Harold Williams' money and charm. At the time she had been Jimson Apple's girlfriend for almost two years, and although their relationship had been—as most romantic relationships between the ages of fifteen and seventeen are—filled with moments of insecurity and overall teenage strife, for the most part they had seemed rock solid as a couple. But at the beginning of her senior year, Lizzie couldn't help but wonder if a long term relationship with Jimson Apple was really in the cards. She had always wanted to go away to college, and in particular, she had always fantasized about driving a British racing green with tan leather *MGB*, top down, radio blasting, returning cross country from a trip home to Vermont, heading over some bridge to her college dormitory in San Francisco. Lizzie instinctively knew that Jimson was destined to stay in Vermont and remain linked to his family's orchard forever, and so when twelfth grade had begun in September of 1973, Lizzie began backing off from Jimson. Two months later, the bold and very rich Harold Williams—his father was the Mr. Potter character from *It's a Wonderful Life*, owner of two banks, hand in all big business in Rutland and a chunk of it in Burlington—began writing Lizzie Mitner love poetry. At first Lizzie was appalled, and she had almost told Jimson. But upon deeper reflection, as she had walked home from school one afternoon and had detoured by the Williams mansion, she became flattered that Harold thought so highly of her, and respectful of his courage—since he obviously faced a major ass-pounding if she chose to tell Jimson—so she had decided that there was no harm in having another man love her silently. Harold's love hadn't been solicited anyway.

By December of 1973 Lizzie had not responded one way or the other to Harold's poetry, but then not sending the poems back and not saying anything to either Harold or Jimson was a response in itself. Harold was living quietly with his unrequited love, and Lizzie began feeling a sense of power—the power that is felt from another's silent love.

At Oscar Oswald's "my parents are in Europe for two weeks" New Years Eve party on Lake Bomoseen, after an argument in which Jimson had stormed off and had left her there alone, it was only natural for the waiting-in-the-wings Harold Williams to approach Lizzie, glass of champagne for her in hand, and ask her to step outside on the terrace. Lizzie had accepted, and several glasses later she and Harold had ended up in an upstairs bedroom with the door locked. And although Lizzie had maintained enough wherewithal to not do *everything* with Harold, they did roll around naked on the bed and do enough for Lizzie to decide to dump Jimson.

Jimson had taken it, at least on the surface, surprisingly well. He didn't date for awhile in early 1974, but by the time the prom had rolled around in late May, he had begun dating Penny Walters. Coincidentally, while he and Penny were hitting it for the first time in a motel room in Burlington after the prom, Lizzie and Harold were a floor up and on the other side of the same motel, attempting, for the first time, to do the same thing. In the case of Jimson and Penny, their good lovemaking would begin a bad relationship, that would last just a little more than three months until August of 1974. In the case of Lizzie and Harold, his equipment problems on that night would start to end their good relationship, but it wouldn't be officially over until just a little more than three months later in August of 1974.

Although Harold occasionally saw Lizzie out and about in Rutland and later in Burlington over the next twenty years, it was in June of 1994 when he had suddenly sat down with his coffee and scone at her table in the downtown Burlington *Starbuck's* and said, "I just have to tell you Lizzie...you're even more beautiful...twenty years later."

A flattered Lizzie had said, "It's good seeing you again Harold. You look great too. Should I tell Jimson about your nice compliment?"

"Maybe not," the recently divorced banker Harold Williams had smiled and said. Secretly, Harold was still embarrassed over his lack of sexual prowess on the night of their prom. In 1976, during his sophomore year at the University of Vermont, when he would meet the woman who would become his wife for seventeen years and the mother of his two children, Harold was neither sexually dysfunctional then, nor would he be during the duration of his marriage. What vexed Harold, when he reflected on the last twenty years, was that he knew that he had never really loved his wife as much as he had loved Lizzie. For some reason, on that prom night, Harold had felt too much love for Lizzie to just want to schtupp her. He had tried to drink her in, to experience her entire essence, but her sexual aggression became a turnoff to him—ergo, his equipment failure. Now, twenty years later, besides still being in love with Lizzie, it was hard for Harold to shut up his Ego when it told him, "Hey stud…you still have something to sexually prove to Lizzie Apple."

In Lizzie's mind, since she had recognized the limo that Jimson and Penny were using in the parking lot of the motel in Burlington on that prom night in 1974, and since she had assumed that Harold's poor performance was the result of the same, the notion that someone could be in love with her too deeply to just want to "do it" was a foreign concept. She had assumed back then that Harold was just too nervous about Jimson being in the same building. And since her love for Jimson had been reawakened on that night, as the jealousy alarm clock can sometimes do, she had said nothing to Harold but, "It's okay…don't worry about it." She had gone out a few more times with Harold, but other than a little kissing, she hadn't allowed anything more intimate again. Finally, she had told Harold that it was over, and a few weeks later she and Jimson had gotten back together again.

In June of 1994, after two hours of conversation in the *Starbuck's*, Lizzie could feel that Harold still loved her. And since things hadn't been that great with Jimson in the past few years—he was always too tired and irritable for romance, and when they did make love it was always hyper and lacking a true loving warmth, they never vacationed anywhere, and Lizzie was fed up with the arguments and being left alone most every night—the notion of having a fling with Harold Williams began to intrigue her. At thirty-seven, Lizzie understood that she needed more masculine attention in her life. During their conversation on that afternoon, Lizzie had shared her 1974 *MGB*/San Francisco fantasy with Harold, and Harold had replied, "I always had that same fantasy back then too! Yes!…San Francisco and a sports car…and then on down the Pacific Coast Highway to Los Angeles. But my choice would have been a convertible two-seater *Mercedes Roadster*."

During the next two months Lizzie met Harold, accidentally on purpose, at a number of public places. They would meet and talk on a bench in the large downtown park, talk while shopping at *Burlington Grocery*, and they even arranged appointments back to back with the dentist they both used, so they could have some time to talk in the waiting room.

Last night, August 27, 1994, Lizzie had instigated the journey from which there is no return. She had invited Harold over for a late dinner. Knowing what the invite would probably lead to, rather than drive his *Mercedes*, Harold had opted to ride his bicycle over and hide it in the woods next to Lizzie and Jimson's property. After their romantic dinner, after a few more glasses of wine and some smooching on the couch, Lizzie had led Harold upstairs to the master bedroom. And there on Lizzie and Jimson's bed, Lizzie and Harold had made love, a Sinatra C.D. playing—whenever Harold would reflect on that night "Witchcraft" would always come to mind—and Harold had not displayed any of the nervousness of prom night 1974. Lizzie had not had love made to her like that in a long time. And now, as *Sunday Morning* on CBS was ending with live pictures of Hurricane Desdemona in the Gulf of Mexico, and Lizzie had gotten off of the recliner and was getting ready for her five hour picking-up-the-child-with-an-hour-layover sojourn to Rutland and back, she realized that she had a major problem.

@@@@@@@@

Still, on this early Sunday morning of August 28, 1994, Ida Laplotski, aka Selma Underwood, aka Selma Greenwood, aka Amy Rosenberg, aka Betty Lou Baker, now known as Betty Lou Larkin, sat in the uncomfortable Stone Mountain Hospital chair next to her husband's bed. Fred, recovering from his second heart attack in four years, was still asleep.

Three years after they had begun dating, and two years after they had first knocked boots, Selma and Fred had married in October of 1990 while vacationing in the Smoky Mountains. They had found a little white chapel with a justice of the peace in Pigeon Forge, Tennessee, and for the first time in years Selma had experienced real joy. Fred had pushed the marriage issue for two whole years before it finally happened, and at the halfway point of his whining, he had produced a beautiful two carat brilliant cut diamond ring during an intimate dinner at the same French restaurant in Stone Mountain where they had had their first date. Selma hadn't wanted to accept it, but Fred had said, "Look Betty Lou…keep the ring for a year. Then, either give it back to me and I'll know that there's no chance, or put it on your finger and make me the happiest guy in the world. That is…"

"That is, what?" Selma had asked.

"That is…unless you've decided now…that it's over with us," Fred had said with a slightly raised eyebrow.

"No…I don't want it to be over," Selma had said. "But I'm just not ready to commit to marriage," she had added. But at Fred's insistence, Selma had kept the ring. Finally, on the first evening of their Smoky Mountain vacation, on the one-year anniversary of having been given the ring, Selma sat down for dinner in the gourmet restaurant of *The Smoky Mountain Inn* with the ring on. She had coyly kept her left hand out of sight during dinner, but when the cappuccino and hazelnut tort had been served, she had casually put her hand on the table. Totally aware that this was the last night in the year of Betty Lou's decision, it had taken Fred about twenty second to notice her hand. "This means…," he had said, taking her hand into his.

"This means what it means!" Selma had said.

Now, almost four years and two heart attacks later, Fred's cardiologist had just told Selma fifteen minutes ago in the hallway that Fred needed a quadruple bypass. A half hour later, sixty-nine year-old Fred woke up and said, “Betty Lou…my love. You see…I’m okay.”

“You’re not okay,” sixty-two year-old Selma said. “Dr. Finkelstein says that you need a quadruple bypass…and soon.”

“Come closer sweetheart,” Fred said. “Let me whisper in your ear.” Selma put her ear next to his mouth and Fred whispered, “Don’t worry…Ida. Before I let them cut me open, I’ll go to New York, find a private eye that I can trust, I’ll find your sister first, and then I’ll find your friend, Salome, in Florida. I’ll tell them both…the way you’ve come up with…how you can communicate with them. I’ll square-that-away for you…before any surgery.”

“You silly and wonderful man,” Selma said. “Do you really think that I want you to put lifesaving heart surgery off so that you can find my sister and friend first? You’re scheduled for surgery this Wednesday morning.”

“Let me put it off for a few weeks,” Fred whined.

“No way!” Selma insisted. Selma loved Fred, and she wanted to keep him around for awhile. Fred was a wonderful man, a good lover, and he covered her back. Selma didn’t think that Fred was the love of her life however, but then she hadn’t felt that way about Robert Greenwood, her first husband, either. Selma didn’t think that she had met *that* man yet. In her still unfinished manuscript, *Notes From the Modern Underground*, Selma’s protagonist, Rachael Trotsky, regularly reflected on her inability to find *the* love of her life. Selma kept that manuscript under lock and key, lest Fred read what was going on in his wife’s heart and get extremely hurt. Selma was content with Fred, and she hoped that they could be together until they were both quite old.

Unfortunately, much to Selma’s devastation, Fred Larkin died on the operating table the following Wednesday. And, of course, Selma had told Fred the truth about herself the night she had agreed to marry him. And Fred had wanted to take care of those errands in New York City and Florida for a long time. But between his aggressive real estate sales manner, because he really wanted to buy Selma a bigger and nicer house and take her on extended trips around the world, and his constant health problems, Fred had never gotten around to finding Salome or Ivy Laplotski for his wife.

@@@@@@@@

The winds were increasing in thirty minute increments as Hurricane Desdemona drew nearer, and if his glasses hadn’t been blown from his face and onto the sand as he leaned over to continue writing in his journal, Felix wouldn’t have seen the approaching Salome holding his nephew’s hand. Neither Salome nor little Walter Lee noticed Felix noticing them. Little Walter Lee was looking to his right, watching three or four seagulls fight for a piece of something on the beach. Salome was looking down. And in that moment in which Felix’s brain assimilated what his peripheral vision had just seen, and in that instant in which the question of ‘Why is she here now? I was supposed to pick them up in Tampa later,' reared its head, and in that nanosecond in which truth is just felt, a sudden chill ran up Felix's back and lodged in his neck. Felix rubbed his neck, saw the quick lightening flash over the Gulf of Mexico, and then he just *knew*.

"Hi Uncle Felix," Walter Lee said, throwing his arms in a hug around the sitting Felix. Felix leaned over, a tear already having been born and now escaping from his right eye onto his nephew's head, and kissed five year-old Walter Lee Kulpa on that tear on the top of his head. And then Walter Lee said, "Bye Uncle Felix," before he ran to go play with those same seagulls with whom he was still fascinated.

Salome stood behind Felix and said nothing. Felix, still rubbing the back of his neck, stared again out over the Gulf of Mexico, and he forced himself to say, "When and how did he die, Salome?"

Salome burst into tears, and then she leaned over to hold Felix from behind. She put her head on Felix's right shoulder and whaled, "I'm so sorry Felix…your brother…Walter Lee's father…still the husband of my heart…Oh Felix!"

"When…and how?" Felix squeaked out, the rain in his eyes warning of the approaching hurricane soon to be coming from his gut.

Salome, speaking slow and deliberately said, "His girlfriend…that b…oh I'm a Christian…so I won't say it…Bambi…His girlfriend Bambi…called police emergency…at about four o'clock this morning…when she noticed that Anthony had stopped breathing…and that he was turning blue…Christian or not…I will say that and I'm sure she waited until she had cleaned up all of the coke and coke pipes to make that call…time that might have saved him! The Temple Terrace Fire Department ambulance…came about fifteen minutes later…but it was too late. He killed himself smoking that devil drug! A massive heart attack! Only thirty-nine years-old and he gave himself to Satan!" Felix reached over his head with his right arm and stroked Salome's hair. "I need to be alone," he managed to get out. "You take Walter Lee and drive to Orlando."

"I need you…Felix!" Salome said. "Please…don't make me go through this…on my own. Please…don't make your nephew…go through this alone. And what about big Walter Lee?…Anthony…was a son to him…he needs you…I believe that eventually…Jesus…will help me…and my son…get through this on the inside…But we need…your physical presence…your family love…your shoulder…your strength…now. Please Felix…I beg you…this whole family needs you…please let's grieve together."

"You haven't told little Walter Lee yet, right?"

"I was hoping…I was praying…that you might have…the way…the strength to do that…for me."

"Did you call Walter Lee in Orlando?"

"You're…the first person…I've told," And Salome's crying became elevated again.

"I'll take you and little Walter Lee to Orlando, and I'll stay for awhile. But I don't know how long I'll stay there," Felix said, almost as if he were an automaton, since he wasn't even aware of the words he was saying. He was not aware either, at the moment, of some of what he had just heard. Later, upon reflection, he would be slightly annoyed with Salome for saying to him that Anthony "had given himself to Satan" because of Anthony's cocaine addiction.

Felix stood up, turned, and then he held Salome tightly as they cried together. Little Walter Lee, apparently disenchanted with the elusive seagulls, ran back to the table and asked, "Mommy…why are you and Uncle Felix crying?"

And Felix picked up Walter Lee, kissed him on the cheek, and then sat down with his nephew on his lap and said, "Hey buddy…you know that your daddy has been very sick for a long time."

"That's why he doesn't see me much Mommy said," Walter Lee said.

"Well buddy…I am so sorry to tell you this…" And somehow the words detoured around the huge lump, and Felix said, "The worst happened. Your daddy passed away."

And Walter Lee looked up into Felix's face and asked, "Daddy's with Jesus?"

"Daddy is with Jesus!" Salome said, drawing Walter Lee's attention to her, as she got down on one knee to hold her son while he was on Felix's lap.

Felix had only been an Atheist for a short time in the 1960's, before he had come to the realization that that position displayed as much hubris as the *Elmer Gantrys*, in their circus revival tents, asking for mega bucks. Unlike his brother, who had had no religious training, and had agreed to be baptized after Salome became a Born Again Christian, and before his son was born—not so much that Anthony suddenly became a Christian, but more because he was just theologically indifferent—Beverly Kulpa had sent Felix to Hebrew School from the time he was six years-old. Although she left when Felix was eleven, Frank Kulpa had insisted that he continue until he was thirteen and bar mitzvahed. Now, as an adult, Felix thought of himself as a Jew culturally and an Agnostic religiously. Felix also saw himself as a seeker; a seeker who would prefer to not be an Agnostic. For this reason, Felix showed absolutely no disrespect towards the religion that Salome practiced, and he would never do anything to undermine what she had taught her son.

"Daddy's with Jesus?" Walter Lee asked looking back up at his uncle.

"Your daddy is at peace now…in Heaven," Felix said.

And Walter Lee, the realization now of what he was hearing beginning to be understood, jumped off of Felix's lap and ran towards the beach. Felix stood up and looked at Salome, and she said, "I know that you'd be so much better at this…would you please go after him?" Felix nodded and headed off towards the beach. Salome said, "You will stick to our religious beliefs... what Walter Lee has been taught...please...Felix." And Felix nodded again.

Felix let Walter Lee keep running, he was about twenty yards ahead. Finally, Walter Lee just fell down on the beach. Felix walked up and heard his nephew bellowing into the sand. When Walter Lee saw his uncle, he suddenly stopped crying and wiped his eyes with his sandy arm. Felix said, "Hey buddy...let me get that." And Felix took off his black t-shirt and wiped the sand out of his nephew's eyes. "It's okay to cry Walter Lee," Felix said, cupping Walter Lee's face in his hand. "I'm crying too." Walter Lee threw his arms around Felix—as much of Felix as he could—and then Felix lifted Walter Lee onto his lap and held him close. As Felix held his nephew, 'God...if you do exist...after all of the fucking pain You've sent my way...by giving me a mother who didn't love me enough to stick around... after all of the misery I've had to endure because of my responsibility for Terry's accident...after all that Anthony had to endure...Okay...I understand if You needed to give me yet another Book of Job experience and take a sibling...But what about my nephew? Does that son have to pay...for the sins of his...uncle? Another Kulpa boy...and he too has to grow up without a parent?' ran through his mind.

The Wake was held the following Friday night, and an inconsolable Walter Lee Younger came out and sat next to Felix in the anteroom. "You're not going to say goodbye?" He asked Felix.

"I don't want to see him like this...human taxidermy...in a suit...in his coffin. I'd rather remember him as he was...the last time I saw him alive. I'll say my goodbye at the cemetery." And Walter Lee Younger leaned over and held Felix.

@@@@@@@@

On a late Saturday night/early Sunday morning in February of 1995, Jimson Apple came home sick from work at about four o'clock. Nancy and Eve were both at sleepovers, and Jimson assumed that Lizzie would be asleep. In an attempt to not wake her, rather than use the front door which always squeaked, Jimson unlocked and walked in stealthily through the kitchen door. What he saw in the kitchen was unbelievable to him, and it took Jimson a few seconds to comprehend the scene. There, bent over the center counter in the middle of the kitchen, was his naked wife getting schtupped by Harold Williams doggie style. Jimson withdrew his *Glock* 9 mm revolver, and he fired a round past their heads into the kitchen sink. The porcelain shards flew up from the surface of the sink, and one immediately became embedded in Harold Williams' naked behind.

"What the...?" Harold Williams yelled.

After he yelled, the immediate reaction to the gunshot had been for Harold and Lizzie to drop to the floor, and when they did that they looked up and saw Jimson pointing his weapon at them. “You fucking whore!” Jimson yelled. “I’m gonna put a round into each of your heads!” And then Jimson stuck the barrel of the gun to Harold’s temple, “You’re gonna go first... asshole! So the whore can experience that before she leaves this world!”

“Please…let me explain,” Lizzie cried out, as she tried slithering backwards on the linoleum tiled floor. “You haven’t loved me…for a long time!” She added.

“If that’s what you thought, you should have just left and filed for divorce…you fucking cunt!” And then Jimson turned his eyes back to Harold and said, “Ready to meet your maker…rich boy?”

“I’ll do…anything…if you’ll spare my life. Any amount of money you want…Jimson…I can give you the $20,000 I have at my house now…you can hold me hostage until the bank opens in the morning…And then I can give you more…Whatever you want…I’ll leave town…and never see your wife…again…Only please don’t take my life Jimson!”

At that moment an idea came to Jimson. He looked back at the small table that sat next to the kitchen door, and he saw the broken china dinner plate with the tube of *Krazy Glue* sitting next to it. This project, that was on his list of projects that Lizzie had wanted him to do later today, became an inspiration in the heat of the moment. Jimson, gun still aimed at Harold, walked over and got the tube of glue. The sewing kit was sitting on the same table waiting for one of Lizzie’s projects scheduled for later in the day, so Jimson popped open the top and took a straight pin from the pin cushion in the kit. He took the cap off of the glue, and he balanced the tube in this mouth, while he kept the gun on Harold with his right hand and used his left hand to prick the inner seal of the tube with the straight pin. “Stand up bitch!” He yelled at Lizzie. Lizzie got up, and as she did she grabbed her jeans to put on. “Leave the clothes on the floor bitch!” Jimson yelled. Lizzie complied, and then Jimson said, “Turn around against the counter.”

“So you can…shoot me in the back?” Lizzie cried out.

“If I kill you bitch,” Jimson said, “It will be facing you...so my pleased face is the last thing that you ever see! Now do what I said…you despicable piece of shit…or I’m gonna end you lover boy’s life right now!” And Lizzie did exactly what Jimson wanted. Jimson took the *Krazy Glue* and squirted it all over Lizzie’s rear end. He then took a sheet of paper towel, and rubbed it all around. “Stand up over here…asshole,” Jimson then said to Harold. Harold did what Jimson wanted. “Now press your belly real tight against my bitch’s ass.”

“But we’ll be stuck…if I,” Harold started to say.

“No shit Sherlock!” Jimson said, and then added, “I can see…besides being a rich piece of shit…you can think also!"

When Jimson was positive that they were stuck together, he picked up the kitchen phone and called Burlington Taxi. "I need a cab at 2436 Edgemont Drive in North Burlington. And make it quick, we need to get to Burlington Mercy Hospital's E. R. in a hurry!" The taxi dispatcher said he had a vacant cab in the neighborhood, so it would be less than five minutes. Jimson hung up the phone and took twenty dollars out of his wallet. He stuck the gun barrel back against Harold's head and held out the twenty dollars for him to take. "Here's the money for the cab ride asshole!" Jimson said. After Harold had taken the money, Jimson then forced the naked stuck together couple at gunpoint out of the front door of the house and onto the porch to await their cab.

At the hospital, the taxi driver removed his sweatshirt and tied it around Lizzie and Harold's midsection, to hide their private parts. Lizzie kept her arms up over her breasts as they walked into the emergency room, looking as if they had either been part of a West Village daisy chain, or they had just been watching an old *Lawrence Welk Show*, and they were practicing his top forty one hit wonder, "The Elephant Walk." After a lot of chuckling in the waiting area, and after the cab driver revealed everything he had heard during the ride over to said waiting area chucklers, one guy waiting for his college son, currently having a cast built on his arm, after he and a number of his UVM fraternity pals had been playing drunken midnight football, said, "If it had been me…I would have *Krazy Glued* the bastard's *nose* to my wife's ass!" The doctors were able to separate Lizzie and Harold using acetone to weaken the glue. (A procedure that hadn't been thought of yet in 1974, when Bubba had faced a similar glue experience!) When that ordeal was over, Harold Williams called the police to report what had happened.

Jimson Apple was picked up and booked for the felony of Assault and the misdemeanor of Discharging a Weapon. As part of the divorce agreement, since Harold and Lizzie were by then in a hurry to get married, the Assault felony charge was dropped. The Assistant District Attorney thought the Discharging a Weapon case was a little iffy also, and since Lizzie and Harold had decided not to testify, when he offered to accept a plea from Jimson on a lesser token misdemeanor, Jimson readily accepted. Jimson paid one hundred dollars and plead *Nolo* to Disturbing the Peace.

@@@@@@@@

In February of 1995, Dr. Colin Morgan was diagnosed with advanced Pancreatic Cancer, and in September of 1995 he passed away. Having gotten to know Colin and Jennifer during a previous stop in Rutland, Felix felt obliged to fly to Burlington with Salome, little Walter Lee, Jack, Geneva, Sam, and Lani for the funeral. Salome and Walter Lee were going to stay at

Bubba and Pauline's small place in Burlington, and Jack, Geneva, Sam, and Lani were staying at Jimson's place. Jimson had decided to keep the house, since he wanted a familiar place for his daughters whenever they stayed with him, and he was very happy—even though the tragedy of Colin's death did put a damper on things—to have his house filled with family.

Felix had elected instead, at Bruiser's insistence, to stay with him in Rutland. In fact, Bruiser was at the Burlington Airport to pick Felix up at the same time that Bubba was there to pick up everybody else.

"WHYYY Jumpin' JEHOSOPHATE Bruiser…WEEE could have found a PLAAACE for Anthony's brother in our house or at Jimson's. HEEE didn't have to go all the WAAAY down to Rutland. Jack, Geneva, and the kid are GOOOING to STAAAY at Jimson and Lizzie's ANYWAAAY," Bubba had said.

"Felix and I have…some major business with…*The Careless Navigator* to…discuss," Bruiser had wheezed. There really wasn't any major business to discuss, but Bruiser liked partying with Felix, and they didn't really get to see each other too often anymore.

Even though there was much sadness in the Apple family over the death of Colin, Felix had enjoyed his stay at Bruiser and Eileen's orchard in Rutland. When he returned to *The Breakers* a few days later, Felix found the letter that his father had written to him and Anthony in 1973, the letter that had taken more than twenty-two years to be delivered by the United States Post Office. Felix was overwhelmed by his father's letter, and for the next few weeks, after getting Dora Larue, Walter Lee, Annie, Geneva, and Jack to cover the motel's front office, all Felix did was stay in his apartment rereading the letter. Somewhere, during those two weeks, he heard himself saying in Hebrew the holiest of Jewish prayers, the *Schma*, and he also heard himself saying, "Thank you God…for my life."

@@@@@@@@

In late September 1995, Salome began dating Enrique Suave, another claims adjustor at *Grapefruit State*. After Salome had gotten closer to Enrique, Felix found that he was being asked to watch little Walter Lee more and more on the weekends. That was never a problem for Felix, as he loved spending time with his nephew. They would go fishing, see movies, go to Grapefruit League spring training baseball games, and walk around in *Tyrone Square Mall*. And if Felix needed an hour or two alone during those weekends, there were usually plenty of other family members at *The Breakers* to watch little Walter Lee for a while.

In late August of 1996, just after Walter Lee, Annie, Lena, Jack, Geneva, Sam, Lani, Salome, little Walter Lee, and Enrique Suave had all conspired and thrown a surprise fiftieth birthday party for Felix at *The*

Breakers—among the guests were K. J. Bauer and his band *Triangulated Crossfire*, who preformed on the private beach in back of the motel, while hundreds of uninvited guests stopped along the public beach behind Felix's property line—Salome confessed to Felix that she was becoming more and more annoyed with Enrique. "He saves all of his coins in a big jar, and then he sticks them in coin wrappers. When we go out, he carries those rolled coins and uses them to pay for dinner and everything else. It's just so tacky! It's almost as if his time with me is being represented by his spare change!"

In early February of 1997, Enrique broke up with Salome, telling her that she was "just too confining." Salome was hurt, and she spent a lot of time, both on the phone and in person, being consoled by Felix. Felix tried to help Salome, and he regularly referred to Enrique as "Mr. Transition Man." Felix had also just come out of a year-long relationship with Gail Lipschitz, his former student in 1987 at the University of Tampa Bay, when he had told her on New Years Eve, 1996, that he just wasn't interested in marrying her.

One Saturday afternoon, in May of 1997, after eight year-old Walter Lee had said goodbye to his mommy before going camping overnight with Jack, Geneva, Sam, Lani, and Lena in Ocala National Forest, Salome said, "It's almost four o'clock, Felix. Come here…I want to show you something." And sure enough, just like back in 1974 when Salome had first developed her theory in The Case of the Slippery Seagull Shit, the seagull squad came pretty close to laying their entire sortie on step thirty-two of the outside staircase. Salome had Felix walk with her up the stairs, and when they got to ground zero, she explained the theory that she had told Anthony twenty-three years ago. Felix was flabbergasted. Of all of his creative thoughts, of all of the scenarios that he had ever thought of from life that could be used in his fiction, what Salome told him on that day, had never even run through his mind. Felix immediately felt the truth in her theory. He knew that he wasn't absolved from having made the attempt to hurt Terry in 1961, but he now felt, deep in his soul, that he had not been responsible for her actual fall.

"I can't tell you how much what you've said as helped me today!" Felix said, while suddenly feeling that same Ca Thump Ca Thump for Salome that he had felt on Long Island in 1976.

"I can't tell you how much what you've said and done over the years has helped me! Starting with pretending to be my lawyer in 1975. I've always loved you for that," Salome said. "And what you did for Anthony on his thirtieth birthday…that expensive car…trying to get him excited by something in life again…And when you took care of Anthony's drug debt…and saved me from getting hurt by those thugs…And the loving way you've always taken care of your nephew…especially since his daddy died…Felix Kulpa…it would be very difficult for me to not love you." And then Salome reached up with both of her hands, and she held Felix's face while looking him deeply in the eyes. Felix removed her hands and began kissing them, and there on the landing between the thirty-second and thirty-third steps, their lips, tongues, and souls intertwined. In the background, somewhere off in the distance, *Rare Earth's* version of "Get Ready" was playing on somebody's radio. And while he was holding Salome tightly, Felix suddenly felt as if everything on his planet and in his life was perfectly in synch. Felix said aloud, "Thank you God."

The Sun

❖ ❖ ❖

Chapter Fifteen

After that incredible afternoon in early May of 1997 when Felix and Salome had melted into each other, fallen asleep, made dinner at midnight, and then stayed in bed talking until seven in the morning before falling asleep again, after fifty and thirty-six years respectively of individual life steps with a fading in and out of a nearly twenty-three-year *pas de deux* connection, after a *carpe diem* moment that felt to Felix as if it were the start of a nuclear chain reaction of *carpe diem* moments that would last a lifetime, and after eight year-old Walter Lee Kulpa had finished second grade, had said goodbye to his mother at Tampa International Airport, had gotten on the plane with Geneva Apple for the flight to Kennedy and connecting flight to Burlington to spend the summer with his grandparents, aunts, uncles, and cousins before being retrieved by Salome in mid-August, and after Salome had scheduled her annual four weeks of vacation in one big chunk—when she had become a claims manager with *Grapefruit State* two years ago, the extra week of vacation had been a nice perk—along with the begging for and receiving of two more months of unpaid leave after the vacation (in the last year Salome had saved *Grapefruit State* nearly two million dollars through her claims/investigative diligence) and after a complete schedule for covering the front desk of *The Breakers* for the entire summer had been assembled by Walter Lee Younger as a belated part two of a fiftieth birthday present, Felix and Salome began what was supposed to be a two-month whirlwind North American tour in early June of 1997 in part one of Walter Lee Younger's fiftieth birthday present to Felix, a brand new taken-from-the-showroom-the-first-week-it-was-introduced 1998 white with gray cloth interior *Volkswagen New Beetle*;

the car, a familiar face and sound even with its complete mechanical redesign, having been reintroduced after a twenty-year hiatus, represented warm memories for Felix, having thoroughly loved his previous 1963 and 1970 models, warm memories of which Walter Lee Younger was very much aware. After learning in July of 1996 that the car would be available the following May, on Felix's fiftieth birthday in August of 1996, Walter Lee had told him, "I got you something real nice... something you're gonna love...but you don't get it...homeboy...until next May."

And Felix had said, "What...you bought me that cotton plantation I always wanted?"

And Walter Lee had replied, "Well...sheeet no, Mr. 'Licks...I done got you a new crib...in de cracker nursing home! Dey got a space for your honky ass...available next May."

A couple of hours after Felix and Salome had left New Orleans, on the morning of the seventh day of June, heading west on I-10 on the next leg of their journey, a three-day visit with K. J. Bauer in Austin, Texas, Felix said, "Why don't we go to Montreal, Quebec City, Prince Edward Island, Nova Scotia, New Brunswick, and Maine late next month? Even with everyplace else we're going, we could work it so we could pick up Walter Lee in Burlington in mid-August, and then the three of us could stop in New York City for a few days on the way home. I'm sure seeing Manhattan for the first time, at eight, would blow Walter Lee's mind...give him something to dream about. Then we can visit *Kings Dominion*, Luray Caverns, and colonial Williamsburg in Virginia. That would be fun...and I'm sure Walter Lee would love those places too."

Felix and Salome planned on heading north to Dallas and then Oklahoma City, after leaving K.J.'s in Austin. From Oklahoma City they would drive northwest to Denver, and after Denver, visit Salome's old roommate from New York, Jaxie—with whom Salome had just recently been back in contact, and with whom Salome had finally told the truth re: her name and age—who was now married to a Mormon and living in Tooele, Utah, then head back south to the Grand Canyon, west to Las Vegas, and finally on to Los Angeles, where they were to spend the evening of June 20th with the vacationing Jr. Liberty, his wife, and their children. From Los Angeles, Felix and Salome would drive south to San Diego and Tijuana, and then back north slowly up the California coast into Oregon and Washington, where they were supposed to spend July 4th weekend in Seattle with Jay Biggs and his family.

In 1990, Jay Bigg's father had retired and left him sole ownership of *Plastic Fabricators* in St. Petersburg. Jay had built up sales, sold the company in 1995, and in 1996 satisfied his lifelong dream of living in Seattle, by purchasing a large direct mailing company, *Northwest Mailers*, and moving—with much protest from his wife and children—to Seattle in late August of 1996, just ten days after Felix's big fiftieth birthday bash. After the visit with Jay, Felix and Salome planned on seeing Vancouver. After Vancouver their itinerary was blank. Salome had said that she'd like to be back in Florida on the first of August, she wanted a week to relax, before heading to New York City to do some investigating as to the whereabouts of Selma Greenwood.

There had been no contact with Selma in sixteen years, and Salome had been told on the phone years ago by someone at the Natural History Museum in Manhattan that Ivy Laplotski was no longer an employee. Life had just gone on, with Anthony's drug addiction, the birth of her son, and then Anthony's death. Somehow sixteen years had gotten away from Salome. She could stand it no longer. She had to see Selma. Salome planned on just showing up at Ivy's apartment in Flushing—just to see if Ivy still resided there. Salome would then take the train to Burlington, stay a week, and then she and Walter Lee would fly out of Burlington Airport back to Tampa on August 24th.

Salome had lied and told Felix that there was an old friend, Selma Greenwood, with whom she had had a rift sixteen years ago, and that she wanted to find her in New York City, to finally set things right. Salome had also told Felix, that at one time the twenty-eight year older Selma had been her best friend. True to her word, Salome had never revealed that Selma's real name was Ida Laplotski to Felix, Anthony, or anybody else.

Felix continued, "We could head back east to New York City from Vancouver, so we'd have some time to look for your friend before driving up to the Maritimes."

Salome, riding in a very sexy pink sun dress, dark sunglasses, and big Savannah straw hat, was swaying to "Here Comes the Sun" on the currently playing *Beatles* C.D., and had her barefoot legs up on the huge dashboard of the *Beetle*. And along with the miles of smiles she had been receiving from passing male drivers in SUV's heading west on Interstate 10, she had also been aware—as had Felix—of the salutatory horn honks from the big riggers all morning. "I don't know, Felix," Salome said. "The trip sounds great, but I don't know if I'm prepared to let my family know that you and I are an item yet." 'I also don't want you knowing all of the details that would be involved in looking for Selma in New York City,' she also thought.

"Couldn't we just say that we took a Platonic vacation?" Felix asked.

"Bubba will never buy that. He's always had 'sexdar!'" Salome said.

"'Sexdar?'" Felix asked.

"Yeah…a kind of sex radar. If he thinks that two people are doing it, he's able to look into their eyes…even separately…at different places…and always tell for sure," Salome said.

"Your kidding!" Felix said.

"No…I'm not," Salome said. "Remember that incident in 1981 over Dr.

Bill Wicks' racist comments about Jack, Geneva, and the kids at the VFW hall in Rutland? That anger from Bill Wicks...that insanity...came on the heels of a published story about a divorcing couple, and Dr. Wicks' involvement with the wife. Well, in 1974, after everybody in town was satisfied with Bill Wick's explanation as to why his van had been in front of the Smith house all weekend when Mr. Smith had been gone but Ms. Smith had not, Bubba was the only one who kept saying, 'Bull...Poop!' Bubba said he looked into Bill Wicks' eyes, and he knew that he was doing Maggie Smith. He said he saw Maggie Smith at *Rutland Grocery* a week later, and that he looked into her eyes and he knew that she was riding...what did he call it...oh yeah...the 'Wicks Wascally Wabbit.' And even if he couldn't see it in our eyes...because we really *were* traveling Platonically...Bubba would start a rumor that we were lovers anyway...just for something to talk about. Like my old roommate Jaxie, he tells everything he knows, and half of what he doesn't."

"Is it really that big of a deal if your family knows the truth? They already know how much I love Walter Lee. And as long as you and I have known each other, wouldn't it just seem natural that you and I got together? I would think that they might be pleased."

"I'm sure...eventually...they will be pleased. I just think it's a little too soon to tell them," Salome said. And, 'The jury is still out on you and me anyway,' is what she thought.

"It isn't as if you and I began seeing each other immediately after Anthony's death or anything," Felix said. "It's been nearly three years since my brother died, and you and I have both had other relationships since then. I would also think that your family, especially your wise mother, would realize that both of us probably must have gone through some kind of a moral quandary...in terms of me choosing to be with my dead brother's ex-wife...and you choosing to be with your dead ex-husband's brother. I'm sure your family would figure out quickly...just how deep our love is...I mean... I'm fifty years old...I'm not interested in just having a casual thing with my...is it ex?...sister-in-law. I'm interested in being a family with you and Walter Lee, and maybe adding one of our own too."

"That's what I want too," Salome said. And, 'I'm just not sure yet,' is what she thought. But then Salome's mind went to a fantasy place and she asked, "Would you want a boy or a girl?"

"We already have Walter Lee...so a girl," Felix replied.

"Yeah...a daughter...I can see myself brushing her long hair," Salome said dreamy-eyed. "I've always loved the name...Thalia...Thalia Rose."

"Thalia Rose Kulpa it is then," Felix said. And then he added, "But if we had a boy...I'd want to name him...Frank...after my father. But that wouldn't have to be his first name. He could be called...Something Franklin Kulpa...that would be fine."

"Something Franklin Kulpa it is then," Salome said. And then she changed gears again and continued, "I just think we should be quiet with all of this…at least a little while longer. Look Felix…I'm a Born Again Christian. I believe that sex between a man and a woman should only happen after marriage. It was difficult for me with Enrique, because I knew that I needed a man, but we weren't married. Eventually he ditched me, because I refused to have complete sex with him…that's probably what he meant when he said that I was too 'confining.' I spoke many hours with my friend Denise, about how to handle being a widow and dating. She told me, and I later understood, that the more conservative members of the Pentecostal Church say, 'You get married once. You don't divorce. And if your mate dies, you stay chaste, without another mate…for life.' Those in my church who are in the middle-of-the-road, say, 'You don't divorce. But if your mate dies, it's okay to get married again.' And those who are more liberal in my church say, 'You shouldn't divorce, unless it's absolutely necessary.' But none of the three factions think that premarital sex is okay. Since I don't think fooling around sexually without penile/vaginal penetration is really sex, as I told you, what Enrique and I did, with protection, for the year, was really more mutual masturbation than sex. I'm still traumatized Felix, that you and I hit it the first day that we made out."

"It was more towards the evening," Felix said, while taking a sip from his bottle of water and then replacing it in the window cup holder.

"You know what I mean wise guy," Salome said. "The fact that you and I aren't married, and I not only let you hit it…but on our first date…I'm traumatized!…I've been asking Jesus for forgiveness!"

"Well…I spoke to Jesus about that too," Felix said, as he was lighting a cigarette. "And He said…"

"Hey…now you're being irreverent," Salome said.

"I'm sorry…forgive me…but I've got to tell you anyway…Jesus said to me, 'Felix…if My woman were as fine as Salome…I'd have a hard time doing what I'd think that I'd want Me to do…in regards to the flesh…too!'
And then Jesus smiled and gave me a big thumbs up!"

Salome smiled and said, "Like I said…irreverent," and then Salome took a swig of water from her bottle, just as they were driving through Beaumont, Texas.

"Look Salome," Felix said, as he put on his left blinker to pass the slowly decelerating big rig heading toward the approaching exit in the right lane, "In The Bible…when Adam was created…a rib was taken from him to create Eve. God must have thought this man and woman were joined together forever…and to my knowledge…He never had an official marriage ceremony. Later…after The Fall…outside of The Garden…marriage ceremonies began. And since men were allowed many wives…do you think the connection those ancient men had with *all* of their wives…was deeper and more loving…in God's Eye…than the connection I have with you? In other words,"

Felix continued, while staring up at a billboard along I-10 West with a panoramic view of downtown Houston that said, "**Nightlife in Houston: A Star in the Lone Star**," and at the same time taking another swig of water, "What we have…isn't just amorous caprice. You and I have been 'married'…or joined at the hip in some way or another…for much longer…nearly twenty-three years…and in considerably more earnestness… than any man from The Bible ever had…legally…with any wife…from at least wife number *two* through wife number *one thousand*…I think God wants 'marriage' to be a life long in earnest commitment between a man and a…'*a*' meaning 'one'…helpmate…and He really doesn't care if some mumble-jumble has been said in front of a priest, reverend, rabbi, justice of the peace, notary public, or the captain of an ocean liner first."

"Well…I'm more of a letter of the law…rather than a spirit of the law person," Salome said. "The letter of the law…calls for marriage before sex."

"Marriage as defined by the writings of man…in The Bible after The Fall?" Felix asked.

"Marriage as defined by God…after The Fall," Salome said.

"Well…to my mind…the only thing that God ever actually *wrote* in The Bible was The Ten Commandments. And my good friend Jacques Derrida would say that the only thing to be believed is the primary text…that which the author has *written*…not other writing in which the primary text gets interpreted."

"God spoke to people and told them what to write. Deconstruction doesn't apply to The Bible!" Salome said with some annoyance.

"Well…I'm not so sure about that," Felix said. "Anyway…in God's Ten Commandments…one of those commandments dealt with adultery… and another with coveting thy neighbor's wife," Felix said and then added after ditching the butt of the old one and lighting another cigarette, "So I guess it would have been just as wrong to covet Solomon's wife number two through wife number one thousand…as it would have been to covet his wife number one…a woman…I must add…who probably…at times…questioned the letter of the law!"

"I guess so," Salome said, not really wanting to have this discussion.

"So what about when 'the letter of the law' needed to be violated? When Moses lead the Children of Israel from out of their slavery in Egypt, he was breaking the Pharaoh's law."

"But he was listening to God's Law…and God's Law is always the top law…the law that 'the letter of the law' applies to the most," Salome said.

"Okay…so if the U.S. government comes around in the future… looking for little Walter Lee…to send his ass to some foreign land…to murder people…because some greedy imperialistic American corporations…have colluded and concocted some new *fakokta* war… somewhere far away from here…because it's economically pleasing…I guess you'll agree with the letter of God's Law then ...that Thou Shalt Not Murder...and we won't let them take Walter Lee to go murder," Felix said.

"I wouldn't want Walter Lee to go to jail," Salome said, while waving her hand to move Felix's smoke away from her face.

"Moses and the escaping Jews from Egypt all faced jail time...but they were listening to a higher law. I don't claim to have been God-inspired when I was involved in anti-Vietnam War demonstrations...I just knew...at that time...that murdering people in a foreign land to help feed the American economy...was wrong. Look Salome..." and Felix decided to ditch his cigarette butt on the highway and immediately light another, "In 1947, Ho Chi Minh, the leader of Vietnam, before the country was split into two parts, came to the United States and asked for help. He said...'Hey guys...you've got this thing called the Monroe Doctrine...and it says that there is to be no more colonization in North America. Well hey...we have the French up our asses in my part of the world...and we would really like them to get the hell out!...And since your baby...this wonderful Monroe Doctrine...kinda covers problems like ours...we thought you might be able to empathize... Hey...the French are your buddies...all joined at the hip and everything... you Allies just kicked Hitler's ass...and then your country scared the absolute shit out of everybody...two years ago...with those two atomic bombs on Japan...you're the big boys on the block!...I think the French would listen to your reasonable request...I mean...if you'll do this for my country...we'll be forever indebted to you...and we'll always be friends...However...if you can't help...I guess we can talk to the Soviet Union...or perhaps...China.' And we did nothing to help Ho Chi Minh, so he did indeed speak with China...and with their help...they kicked the shit out of the French in 1954. Then the United States saw an economic opportunity in Vietnam...since the French were gone...and so our country sent in two thousand 'advisors.' It was all about money, Salome, and I refused to murder people for that reason. I was packed and ready to be become a Canadian...if my lottery number hadn't been 316. And I'm no coward...If it had been World War II...and Hitler was putting my people in the ovens...I would have been the first one to join up. Of course...I would have had to join up in England...since the United States...totally aware of what Hitler was doing...decided not to get involved...at least officially... until the Japanese bombed Pearl Harbor much later...Our government even turned away Jewish boat people...who were just looking to get away from the Mengele Institute of Wacky Human Experimentation and *Schicklegruber's Bar-B-que*...But it wasn't in our government's interest to help those boat people at the time. Yeah...I would have gone to England in the 1930's to fight Hitler...but I wasn't going to Vietnam...to protect the almighty American corporate dollar...and I certainly wouldn't let my nephew bloody his hands...or lose his life...for that," Felix said, as he ditched his cigarette butt on the highway and lit another.

"If Walter Lee has to serve his country…then he'll serve his country," Salome said, unhappy with Felix's apparent disregard for the law, and also unhappy with his chain smoking.

"If there's a war going on…then I guess I'll have to knock you out… and hide my nephew…Anne Frank style…in an attic somewhere," Felix said, unhappy that Salome couldn't see what he saw as being morally correct.

The subject was changed, and then after a few more subjects Salome said, "I was just thinking about Crystal Thompson at work."

"You're on vacation…a much deserved vacation…why are you even thinking about work?" Felix asked.

"Well…I'm not thinking of work per se…just about this woman I work with…Crystal Thompson…Actually…she's in my unit…I'm her immediate supervisor…She just turned forty…and she's marrying a man who just turned thirty…I was thinking how skeeved I was about that," Salome said.

"Why?…because she's marrying a man ten years younger?"

"Yeah…I kinda like May-December relationships…when the man is older…But the other way…that's just too weird," Salome said.

"For somebody who has always been sensitive to the secondary status that women get…I'm surprised that an older woman marrying a younger man…would bother you," Felix said, just before ditching his cigarette butt and taking a much needed break from smoking.

"I'm against secondary status for women in society…but in The Bible…in marriages…the man was always older. I think God intended for a woman to be a man's helpmate. If the man and woman are approximately the same age…fine…If the man is older…fine," Salome said.

"I think the age…between two people who love each other…is irrelevant," Felix said, while rubbing his back in a bear-like way against the seat to relieve an itch. And then changing the subject he said, "Would you mind shaving my back when we finally stop for the night? I'm starting to itch!" After Anthony's death in 1994, Felix saw Salome and little Walter Lee two or three times a week in either Tampa or on Mad Beach. And once monthly, Salome was still happy to shave his back. But when Salome had begun dating Enrique, at his request, the back shaving had stopped, and Felix had suffered the torture of a couple of year's worth of professional back waxing. After Enrique was out of the picture however, Salome had asked and Felix had readily accepted her help again.

"Not that I mind shaving you," Salome said. "But I kind of like your hairy teddy bear-like self. You don't have to shave your back for me…so why not just be natural?" Felix thanked her for saying that, and he agreed that he'd rather stop worrying about it. He also added that he needed to stop at a pharmacy someplace, so he could take his shirt off in the parking lot and dump a whole can of medicated powder on his back. Salome smiled at the mental picture of that, and then her cell phone rang. They were still on I-10

West, with just an hour to go before reaching the Highway 71 cutoff to Austin. After that, it would be less than two hours northwest to K. J.'s mansion and recording studio.

"Hello," Salome said.

"Hi sweetheart," Pauline said.

"Mom!" Salome said. "What's up?"

"OH MY GOD!" Pauline said. "Nancy has run away. We now know she's heading down to Tampa to see you. I tried calling you at home…I thought you and your friend Denise might be back from New Orleans already."

"Uh…no…not yet," Salome said. And then holding the phone away from her mouth she added, "Oh no!"

"What's wrong?" Felix asked. But Salome just shook her head and held her finger up over her mouth in a "Shhh" sign.

"Why do you think she's heading to Tampa?" Salome asked her mom.

"OH MY GOD…she's been impossible ever since Lizzie divorced Jimson and married Harold Williams. She dresses like a whore, boys are calling her at all hours, and Jimson thinks she's doing drugs. She just failed every class in the eleventh grade…and she has to repeat the entire year! Lizzie discovered that most of Nancy's personal things…along with her suitcase…were missing from her bedroom last night…when she didn't come home. Lizzie called Jimson…Jimson took off from work…went and found Nancy's best friend…Brenda Carlton…at her parents' house late last night…put some pressure on her. Brenda admitted that she had seen Nancy…with a suitcase…in downtown Burlington at 5:30 yesterday afternoon…And that Nancy had said that she was leaving forever…but she didn't say where she was going…She promised to let Brenda know where she had settled…and she made Brenda promise…to be quiet about it. Jimson went to the train station…found out that the last train to New York had left at 3:00 yesterday afternoon…Then he went to the bus station…it was nearly one o'clock in the morning…took a recent picture of Nancy out of his wallet…showed it to the man at the ticket counter…The man said that he had only been on since eleven that evening…but he called the man who had worked before him at home, and that man gave Jimson his address. Jimson went over there…showed him Nancy's picture…and that man was able to identify Nancy…said that she had bought a one-way for the 6:14 to Tampa yesterday afternoon. She's going down to see you! Bubba wants to talk to you."

And before Salome could even respond Bubba was on the phone.

"WHYYY Jumpin' JEEEHOSOPHAT!" Bubba said, "Still running WIIILD around here! YOUUU have ALWAAAYS been a role model to Nancy…because YOUUU ran AWAAAY…and still managed to MAAAKE a DEEE-CENT life for yourself."

"But the times were different then Bubba…I was different then…I hadn't found Jesus yet," Salome said. And then Salome motioned to Felix to pull off of I-10 West at the approaching exit.

"I KNOOOW," Bubba said. "And I KNOOOW you'll do the RIIIGHT thing when Nancy ARRIIIVES…You'll convince her to GOOO back to school…and to GOOO back to Lizzie and Harold."

"I will do that…that's the best thing for her," Salome said, just before taking another swig of water from her water bottle.

"I love YOUUU Salome…Here's Mom," Bubba said, before handing the phone back to Pauline.

"PLEASE SALOME…you've got to convince her to come home!" Pauline said, worried that her sixteen year-old granddaughter didn't have the same savvy that Salome had at fourteen.

"I will…Mom," Salome said, and then added, "When will she arrive in Tampa?"

"She left at 6:14 yesterday afternoon…and with the layover in New York City…it takes thirty-three hours to Tampa. We figure she'll be in Tampa around three o'clock tomorrow morning."

"What will she do…if I'm still out of town?" Salome asked.

"She'll probably call Jack at *The Breakers*…and have him pick her up in Tampa," Pauline said, and then added, "Geneva is still up here…won't be back in Florida for another week."

Salome thought for a moment, and then realized what she had to do. Jack would be a good listener, and he would know the right way to handle his niece. But Salome knew that Nancy would probably have an easier time talking to her. As much as Salome wanted to continue this vacation with Felix, she knew that she had to be there for her niece. "Okay Mom…I'll be there at the bus station in Tampa when she arrives."

"I'm sorry if this cuts your New Orleans vacation a little short," Pauline said.

"That's okay Mom. Family comes first." And then Salome said goodbye and called the operator to get the phone number of Houston Airport.

Felix, who had exited as Salome had asked, and had parked the car on the side of a gas station waiting for Salome to finish her conversation with her parents said, "Houston Airport? What do you need with them?"

And in-between getting and dialing the number, Salome quickly explained what was happening.

"Shit!" was all that Felix said.

Salome's phone call produced information, but it wasn't information that Salome wanted to hear. The only airline with connecting flights that could get Salome back to Tampa in time to meet Nancy at the bus station was *Continental*, and their employees were currently on strike. "I don't know what I'm going to do," Salome said. "There's no way that I can find a flight back to Tampa before three o'clock tomorrow morning."

And then Felix did some figuring and said, "It's just about noon now. Even doing seventy the whole way…it's a seventeen hour trip…which would put us in Tampa…two hours after you need to be there. But I guess…we can do something about that." And then Felix reached into his glove compartment, pulled out his state of the art radar detector, matched up the *Velcro* with the other piece on the dash, plugged it into the cigarette lighter, and then said, "Shit!" once more.

"Will you please quit swearing? It's so irreverent," Salome said.

"Hey…wait a minute," Felix said. "I'm not taking God's name in vain…you never hear me say the G.D. expression…or the J.C. expression anymore…anything else…isn't irreverent."

"Any cursing…is blasphemous!" Salome said.

"Well…etymologically…what's blasphemous at one point in time and in one culture…changes. Do you think that God still holds us accountable for words like 'shucks' or 'doggone?'…those were considered curse words in eighteenth-century America…Does He expect someone growing up in Alabama to know that 'bloody' is a curse word in England?…And by the way, the word 'shit' came from a few centuries ago, when it was discovered that boats carrying manure couldn't allow that manure to come in contact with salt water. The result of that contact was a spontaneous explosion. So after that was figured out…the manure began being carried high in the ship's hull, and the containers were stamped 'SHIT,' which stood for 'Ship High In Transit.'"

An annoyed Salome said, "He expects you to be accountable for your language…in your particular place and time!"

"I see…and you know that," Felix said and then added, "So…when you've drunk too much…you get…"

"I get poopy-faced!" Salome said.

"Right!" Felix said, as he got the *Beetle* up to one hundred miles an hour on I-10 East. And then he added, "Well…we're gonna be in some deep poop…if I get busted driving at this speed." And then Felix thought, 'Deep poop?…I'm sorry…but that just doesn't sound as syntactically pleasing as deep shit!'

The important thing for Felix was spending uninterrupted time with Salome. But as he was speeding along he couldn't help but think, 'Heading back to Tampa…getting fucked out of this western vacation with Salome…is total horseshit!…*niece Nancy interruptus*…but I'll be real Christian about it.'

@@@@@@@@

In early 1995 Gus Strattus had passed away from a heart attack. His wife, Helen, after deciding in 1996 that a smaller place in Rutland would suit her better, had opted to sell the 300-acre orchard. Dick and Cindy Chumwell bought the Strattus place in the summer of 1996. Forty-three year-old Dick and forty-two year-old Cindy had decided that the Strattus orchard could yield enough profit to keep them financially secure the rest of their lives, and to the dismay of twelve year-old daughter Samantha Chumwell, who was looking forward to returning in September for the seventh grade at Peru Middle School, and eleven year-old daughter Rachael Chumwell, who was looking forward to starting same said school also in September, and Chief of Staff, Dr. James Horton, who hated to lose Cindy, his head RN at Champlain Valley Hospital for many years, Dick and Cindy had sold their house in Peru, New York, and moved to the orchard in Rutland in August of 1996. Eighteen year-old daughter Karla Chumwell, having graduated from Peru High School the previous May, had joined the Air Force. Basic training for her would begin in September of 1996. And twenty-one year-old daughter, Tonya Chumwell, who had her own apartment in Burlington—unbeknownst to her parents she was sharing it with pre-Law student Russell Andersen—was getting ready for her senior year in Nursing at UVM also in September of 1996. Meanwhile, Cindy's Multiple Sclerosis had gotten worse, and she was now totally blind in her left eye. Part of their decision to leave New York and to buy the orchard in Rutland, centered on Cindy's failing health. Every Friday she would inject herself with powerful medicine, and it was usually Tuesday before Cindy felt well enough to do much of anything. Cindy had decided that she could no longer work fulltime, but she didn't want to give up nursing completely. A nice solution had presented itself when Jennifer had said to Cindy, "If you guys buy the Strattus orchard…you can work at *The Woman's Center* part time. I could use another RN…and you could put together any schedule that works for you."

After Dr. Colin Morgan's death in September of 1995, there had been absolute business mayhem at *The Woman's Center*—in terms of finding another doctor who would buy Colin's practice, but allow Jennifer Morgan to retain fifty percent of the business. Jennifer also owned the building. Finally, Dr. Alan Portman had agreed to Jennifer's terms in May of 1996. That had been a big relief to Jennifer, who, since the reading of Colin's will in December of 1995, had to make major personnel changes at the office, and major personal changes in her lifestyle, and had to—outwardly at least—keep hidden her total shame, at just how mortified she was with what had been in Colin's will. Having her sister Cindy working with her, and more importantly having her now living near, had presented Jennifer with the chance to bond more closely with her sister, as Jennifer really needed an outlet for her anguish with someone she could trust, and she just wasn't ready yet to talk about things with a professional stranger for seventy-five dollars an hour.

The main reason that the Strattus orchard was an attractive deal for the Chumwells however, was that growing apples had been exactly what Dick had studied in college. After he had finished his last six-year commitment to

Uncle Sam, Dick Chumwell had taken a maintenance supervisory job with the Clinton County Parks Department in Plattsburgh. The job involved a lot of responsibility, and as a result, it had taken Dick nearly eight years, with his first two years of college credits from Clinton County College, until May of 1993, to get his BS degree in Horticulture from Plattsburgh State University. Dick then started a graduate program at UVM in Burlington in September of 1993, and in May of 1997, nearly a year after purchasing the orchard, he had just received his MS in Horticulture—with a concentration in Pomology. The science of growing apples had changed considerably since Bubba's time. Unfortunately, Bruiser still clung to his father's antiquated methods.

In June of 1997, while Felix and Salome were driving east on I-10 at Bonneville Salt Flats-like speeds, Dick was sitting at Bruiser and Eileen's dining room table drinking coffee. "Bruiser…you've got three mostly clear acres at the back of your property. One acre of that would be enough room for you to build your compost heap."

"Jesus fucking Christ I…finally got rid of…the smell of Gus…Strattus' shit pile two…years ago and now…you want to stink…up the place again," Bruiser wheezed. Although Bruiser still grew his annual small marijuana crop in a few different patches in the Bread Loaf Mountains organically, the notion of creating a compost heap that would accommodate nearly three hundred thousand apple trees yearly seemed absurd. "Do you realize the…work involved in growing…the apples we grow…and doing it organically?"

"Well that's how I'm doing it," Dick said. "And with organic *everything*…now being the new thing…I hate to hurt your business."

"It will hurt your…business when the people…tell you to go…fuck yourself with your…higher prices," Bruiser retorted with a wheeze.

Dick looked down at the floor and then looked up and said, "There is something else I wanted to ask you, Bruiser...and it's a big favor."

"What the fuck else…do you want? I…already said you could…build an aqueduct downstream…from the barn to…help you with your…weak water supply. And…the only reason I…agreed to that was…because you're married to…my sister."

"If I were to pay for the dismantling and rebuilding of your barn, would you mind moving it?"

"Why the fuck would…I want to move…the barn? Bubba built…it's where it is…and I'd like to…keep this place the…same!"

"Yeah Bruiser...but Bubba built it where it is to totally piss off Gus Strattus. The back of my house is all glass…and your sister and I would have an incredible view of the Green Mountains across Highway 7...if your barn was moved about 100 feet away from the property line."

"Well that's just too…fucking bad!" Bruiser wheezed. "Just because you decided...to become Johnny Appleseed...late in life, now...you expect me to...provide you with all...of these accommodations. I...already gave you free...water, and now you...want me to move...Bubba's barn. Fuck no!"

"You wouldn't have to do anything. I'd pay to have it totally done," Dick said.

"No!" Bruiser emphasized in-between coughs.

"I don't see why that would be a big deal," a very exhausted Eileen said, as she entered the dining room. Besides getting up very early every morning to bake—using Pauline's secret recipe—between thirty and fifty apple pies for the store and dining room, feeding and getting the children ready when they had school, and also feeding Bruiser and nearly thirty men breakfast when it was harvest season, she then had to open up the Michigan hot dog restaurant, get the steam table up and running by ten in the morning, and after whichever scheduled employee would arrive at eleven, speed home to take care of lunch for Bruiser and the workers at twelve thirty. Then, of course, she still had to prepare the family dinner. "Why not let your sister and family have a nice view? Certainly...Cindy is going through enough health-wise. Why not give her some extra happiness?" Eileen said.

And Bruiser, thinking how Dick had badmouthed him throughout the years—"Bruiser is just a crazy pothead"—and who didn't feel that inclined to grant him any more favors, just said, "No!" to his wife, as he grabbed the truck keys and slammed the screen door on his way out to run some errands. After he had started the truck and driven it back up by the kitchen door however, after thinking that he really would like to make Cindy's life more enjoyable, he jumped out of the truck and walked back in the house and said to Eileen in front of Dick, "Let the fucking bastard...do what he wants...Move the fucking barn...But not one penny is...coming out of my...pocket!" And then Bruiser hopped back into his still running truck and took off. As he was about to leave the property, he saw his son, thirteen year-old Conrad, playing by the front gate. "Come take a ride...with your old man," Bruiser said. And then Conrad climbed into the front seat while Bruiser was mumbling, "Son of a bitch!"

@@@@@@@@

"It's no problem, Fred," Jack Apple said, on this July afternoon in 1997, "What I can't scrape together, I can get from the bank. They already extended me a credit line that exceeds what I need, based on the collateral of my business." *Apple Refrigeration*, having begun on Mad Beach in August of 1981, had long since closed that store and opened a large four-story service and appliance center on Highway 19 in St. Petersburg. In the last sixteen years, Jack had also opened large refrigeration service center/appliance stores in Tampa, Clearwater, Orlando, Ocala, Daytona Beach, and Gainesville. And now, besides those seven stores, Fred Watkins wanted to sell his ten *Tampa Bay Refrigeration* stores to Jack. In St. Petersburg, Tampa, Clearwater, and Orlando, where Fred and Jack had been competitors, Jack would not only keep his own stores open, he would keep Fred's stores open under Fred's name, and reap the profits from whichever company the consumer used. In the six cities in which *Tampa Bay Refrigeration* currently operated but Jack did not, Tallahassee, Jacksonville, Bradenton, Sarasota, Naples, and Miami, Jack would takeover those stores and change the name to *Apple Refrigeration*.

Fred Watkins and Jack Apple had been friends for years, and although they were competitors, their friendship had always been very important. Fred was fond of saying, "I love Jack Apple...Hell if I needed refrigeration work, an appliance fixed, or a new appliance...if I didn't go to me...I'd go to him." Fred Watkins had always been impressed by how Jack had built his company from the ground up, having never stolen a major account from him. They had both agreed years ago, never to advertise in a nasty manner against each other, and to never go after each other's big accounts. And if a contracted business became unhappy with either refrigeration company—a situation that rarely occurred—there were no hard feelings if that customer switched. Now, sixteen years after having begun his business, a business that was already prosperous, it looked as if Jack and Geneva were going to become even wealthier.

Six years earlier, when they knew that they could finally afford it, Jack and Geneva had discussed moving from their apartment in *The Breakers* and buying a big house with a big yard on the water in mainland St. Petersburg. Geneva had said at the time, "As much as I love having the Gulf of Mexico in our backyard, it would probably be better for Sam and Lani to have a regular house with a big yard to play in."

Having heard this upon entering the room, ten year-old Lani Apple had said, "I don't want to leave here! I love living here!" And then Lani had gone off and explained the situation to her ten year-old twin brother, and Sam had come back into the living room and had expressed the same sentiment.

"I don't really want to leave here either!" Jack had said to Geneva, laughingly imitating Lani. And he too had added, "I love living here!"

And Geneva had concurred, staying and paying rent for their third floor three-bedroom two-bathroom 1400 square-foot apartment at *The Breakers*, was still more desirable than buying a house in St. Petersburg. And although Geneva really didn't have to work anymore, she still loved managing *The Careless Navigator*, and she certainly liked being able to just walk across Gulf Boulevard to go to work. Instead, Jack and Geneva had bought a three-bedroom two-bath Swiss chalet in the Smoky Mountains, and whenever they wanted something different, that was their getaway.

"It looks as if we can do this thing next week, Fred," Jack said.

"That's great Jack...I really want to close this deal, and then take a long vacation with Ethel around the world."

"Lucky man!" Jack said. "Okay Fred…I'll talk to you later in the week," Jack said before hanging up the phone.

Geneva walked into the living room and said, "Was that Fred?"

"Yeah sweetie…it's a done deal. Just think…*Apple Refrigeration*… seventeen stores!" And then goofing on a *Z Z Top* song, Jack added, "I'm bad…I'm seventeen stores wide!"

"Great!" Geneva said. And then she added, "By the way…it looks as if Sam and Lena Younger might be an item."

"They've been best friends since they were babies…what makes you think they're going to be 'an item?'" Jack asked.

"Sam told me yesterday. I saw him sitting in his room…just staring out of his window at the water…and I asked him what was the matter. He finally admitted…after a little motherly prying…that he loves Lena. He said he wanted to ask her to the junior prom two months ago…but he didn't have the nerve."

"I thought she had a date," Jack said.

"She did…but I think she waited for the last minute…for Sam to speak up."

"And Sam ended up just staying home."

"Anyway…I told Sam that his father would give him some advice…on how to approach a girl…if a boy likes her."

"Right!…if, at forty-one, I'm still 'with it' enough…to know what works these days," Jack said. And then he added, "I'm getting pretty ancient…you know."

And thirty-seven year-old Geneva said, "Not too ancient to be a father again…I hope…I'm pregnant!"

@@@@@@@@

In September of 1997, Walter Lee Younger celebrated his seventieth birthday. Walter Lee had been saying since Felix's fiftieth the year before, "Please don't give me a big surprise party like Felix's…I hate big parties." So, instead, Felix, Salome, little Walter Lee, niece Nancy, Jack, Geneva, Sam, and Lani, had taken Walter Lee, Annie, and Lena out for dinner at *The Garden Seat*, still one of the swankier restaurants in the St. Petersburg area. About a week before the September 11th dinner, Felix had said, "I got you something real nice for your seventieth birthday…but you don't get it…until the actual day of your birthday."

And Walter Lee had asked, "What'd you get me Mr. 'Licks?…A hair processing…a skin lightening job at de dermatology clinic…and a bed in de cracker nursing home next to yours?"

And Felix had replied, "No…Boy…I bought you your freedom…and a ticket north!"

What Felix had really bought Walter Lee was a brand new 1998 *Mercedes S 500*, a car that cost nearly thirteen hundred dollars for every year that Walter Lee had been on the planet. But the profits from *The Careless Navigator* and *The Breakers* were better than ever, and recently Felix had sold the film rights to *Tous Les Sieges Etaient Occupés* to a French filmmaking company for one hundred and fifty thousand dollars. Walter Lee was knocked out. "Wow...what a cruiser!" he said.

"Let's take it for a test ride up to *The Garden Seat* in Clearwater," Felix said.

"This will be great for riding to Tampa and back," Walter Lee said. Since selling the other restaurants in the state to a large chain who were planning to open up fifty more in the United States and Europe, Walter Lee and Annie had very little running around to do anymore. They kept the original restaurant only, so when they needed to, they would just walk across the street to *The Careless Navigator*. But Walter Lee Younger, having published three excellent books in his field, was now a full Professor of Anthropology in Tampa at the University of Tampa Bay, and he made that trip to Tampa three times a week. Having not published anything particularly important in English other than a few articles on Dickens, Felix was still an associate professor at the same university. On Wednesdays their schedules were the same, so Felix and Walter Lee always commuted together that one day.

After the dinner, Felix and Salome were standing alone in the huge garden of *The Garden Seat*, and Felix said, "I'm going nuts, Salome. Since Nancy moved in with you...it's been three months...and other than family outings...you and I haven't been alone. What's up? I'm hornier than a hoot owl!"

"I know," Salome said. "I mean...I've enjoyed the late night phone sex...but I'm in dire need for a visit from Winky!"

"Yeah...and Winky keeps calling out, 'Oh Cootie Cat...where are you?'" Felix said.

"Did you hear that message I left on your cell the other day?"

"You mean...about listening to Otis Redding...feeling frisky...and wanting to wrap your legs around my face?...Yeah...Winky and I both heard that! The question is...when?"

"I haven't wanted to leave Nancy alone with Walter Lee yet. Not that I don't trust her as a babysitter...I just want to be there...for her to keep talking," Salome said. "I still worry about her spending too much time... thinking...by herself. I was able to convince Lizzie and Jimson to let her stay with me this year...to repeat eleventh grade at Plant High School in Tampa. I enrolled her and she started there last week...the day after Labor Day...the same day I started back at *Grapefruit State*. I've been able to convince Nancy...to not smoke cigarettes...pot...not to look for any other drugs like coke or X...to only have an occasional glass of wine...with me...and to dress less provocatively. I also started bringing her to church on Sundays...and to our prayer meetings on Mondays along with Walter Lee. She's definitely changed...I just feel the need to be constantly around her...when she's not in school...and when I'm not working."

"I understand," Felix said. "But Winky...he's dumb...he doesn't appreciate no deep underlyin' motifs...he just knows...that something's missing!"

Salome laughed and said, "Well...I was thinking about this Sunday. Why don't you join Nancy, Walter Lee, and me for church in the morning? After church you can come with us to Denise's house for lunch. And after lunch, I promised Walter Lee that Nancy could take him and Denise's young son, Curtis, to that new *Disney* movie at the multiplex on West Shore Boulevard. While they are at the movies...we could reintroduce Winky to Ms. Cootie Cat...then you, Walter Lee, Nancy, and I could go out for nice dinner somewhere."

"Sounds like a wiener...er...winner!" Felix said.

On the following Sunday, after church and lunch at Denise's, Felix and Salome were in Salome's bedroom, attempting to get busy. After removing all of their clothes, Felix cupped Salome's face in his hands and began kissing her neck. "I love the nape of your neck...yum!" Felix said, and then added, as his kisses moved from Salome's neck to her face, "MMM...woman good! Woman...nutritious!" sounding like the *Frankenstein* creature.

"I'll bet I look like a big roast to you now...huh!" Salome said laughingly.

"My favorite kind of Sunday meal...MMM...woman roast!" Felix said, as he moved his mouth south from Salome's mouth, and headed down the happy trail...after a stop in the mountains...to the promised land.

"There's...no time for that," Salome said, as she repositioned herself, putting Winky into her own hands. Winky, having been awake since somewhere during the second hour of church, stood at attention and waited to be dressed. Once his coat was on, he was ready to reacquaint himself with his badly missed friend. Introductions were held up a few moment however, as the hosts were in slight disagreement as to the best venue for reintroducing the friends.

After Salome's speedy venue, complete with hair pulling, won out, and Felix got beyond his disappointment over not getting the slower, more loving method that he preferred—Felix could be what Salome wanted today as a character, but since he associated that type of hyper sex with more shallow flings than with true love making, he preferred a more 'total drinking in of the essence' approach most of the time—Salome completed the task quickly, and then said to Felix, "Would you hurry up already...and finish!"

Felix kept going a few more minutes and then pretended he had finished. Fortunately, Winky hadn't shut down from the aghast feeling Felix felt. Only one other woman had ever told Felix to hurry up before, and she was a twenty dollar hooker in Times Square; an attractive blonde with huge breasts she was, and Felix had literally run into her, when he came out of a midtown bar drunk his first week at NYU in 1965. It was twenty dollars for twenty minutes with her—she provided the condom—and twenty dollars also for the cheap motel. Under that kind of pressure, Felix hadn't finished with her either. There was no bathroom in the room of the cheap motel, and the image of the prostitute squatting and urinating in the corner, after Felix was allegedly done, was forever laser-burnt in his brain. Felix thought about giving Salome an earful—but he didn't.

@@@@@@@@

By November of 1997, Salome felt comfortable that her niece, Nancy, had adjusted to life in Tampa. Nancy was doing well in school, all A's at the moment except Math, in which she was struggling for a C, and she had become friendly with a nice group of kids in her class. Salome began asking Nancy to baby-sit on weekends, paid her well for doing that, and she had trusted Nancy—since their heart-to-hearts included all topics—with the information that she was seeing Felix.

"Where are you and Uncle Felix going this weekend?" Nancy asked on a Friday afternoon, just before Salome jetted in the *Cobra* to get Nancy and Walter Lee pizza before being picked up by Felix.

"We're going to Miami Beach. We're staying at the *Doral.* I left the phone number on the refrigerator…and you know my cell," Salome said.

"Do you have specific plans for down there…or are you just hanging out?" Nancy asked.

"We're going out for an early dinner at *Joe's Stone Crab* tomorrow night, and then we're going to see a new version of *Man of La Mancha* at the Coconut Grove Playhouse," Salome said.

"And church on Sunday morning? I'll walk to ours with Walter Lee."

"When we get there tonight…I'm gonna look in the phone book…or ask the concierge for a Pentecostal church nearby," Salome said.

On the following Sunday morning, Salome and Felix attended a service at the Miami Beach Pentecostal Church. The sermon on this morning was "Staying in Your Marriage No Matter What." After the preacher had spoken of Job, and how God never gave him more than he could handle, and equated Job's ordeal to marriage, he said, "God doesn't expect marriage to be easy Brothers and Sisters…He knows that marriage can be very challenging at times…But it's His will…that we struggle with ALL of those challenges…and stay in our marriages…no matter what. God knew what He was doing…when he took a rib from a man…and created a helpmate…and He doesn't recognize… divorce!"

After the service, complete with a twelve-piece band and chorus, the preacher, seeing Salome and knowing that he had never seen a parishioner in his church before who was quite as beautiful as her, approached and introduced himself. Felix, totally aware that this man had gravitated their way because of Salome's looks, stood quietly and let the man do his thing. "Sister," he said, "Is this your first time in this House of the Lord?"

And Salome said, "Why yes…we're just visiting from the other side of the state," and then Salome introduced herself and Felix.

"Are you a true believer?" He asked Salome as he looked into her eyes, and at the same time was shaking Felix's hand.

"Yes…yes I am!" Salome said.

And recognizing Felix's somewhat Semitic looks he turned and said, "And you?"

"My father was Catholic and my mother was Jewish," Felix said. "I believe in God…I've been reading what Jesus actually said in the Red Letter Edition of the King James Bible…but I'm not so sure if Jesus was the Messiah…and I'm not so sure if Jews even have to accept the New Covenant…or if God is happy with us sticking to the Old."

And the preacher reiterated John 3:16 to Felix and added, "I hope you see…the true light…in this lifetime."

And Felix said, "Perhaps…whatever that true light may be." And then Felix added, "but I have a question for you now."

"I'll be happy to answer any question…any question that God has given me the wisdom to answer."

"During your sermon," Felix began, "You said that men and women should stay together in a marriage no matter what. Do you think…if a woman is being continually physically abused by her husband…that she should stay in that marriage?"

"Yes…I do. But it's not what I think that matters…it's what God wants."

"So God wants a woman to stay in a marriage…a marriage in which she is getting continually beaten up?" Felix asked.

"Yes…He does," the preacher said.

"And if it were YOUR daughter?" Felix said with some annoyance. "You'd want her to stay in a house in which she was regularly getting the crap kicked out of her?"

"I would discuss with her…what's needed to be a good wife…yes," the preacher said.

"Are you freakin' nuts?" Felix asked. Salome, looking totally embarrassed by what Felix had said, instinctively moved several more inches away from him. Felix, recognizing Salome's body language as almost repulsion, said to her, "I'm going out front for a cigarette." And then thinking of something that Salome had said to him one Sunday afternoon in her bedroom, he added, "Hurry up and finish!" on his way out of the door. As he was walking out, Felix thought of an old line about, "He who argues with a fool…"

@@@@@@@@

For Valentines Day in 1998, Salome insisted that Felix attend a party at Denise's house. And although Pentecostal Christians don't celebrate Valentine's Day, it just happened that February 14th fell on a Saturday, so Denise had used that as an excuse for some good Christian fellowshipping complete with alcohol and games on a Saturday night.

One of the games involved two lines, boy/girl, boy/girl, but all couples were told to find someone other than the one with whom they had come to the party—to make things more interesting. The boys all had big vegetables or fruit stuck under their chins, and the object of the game was to pass the vegetable or fruit to the female in the line directly behind without using hands. Felix didn't really want to participate in this lame excuse for copping a feel with one's chin, but at Salome's insistence he played anyway. He had no particular interest in the woman standing on line behind him, but his interest was indeed piqued by the pagan Dutch dork in the other line, who was rubbing his chin on Salome's breasts. Felix thought, 'Those wacky Pentecostals…Gosh…they certainly know how to have a good time!'

After the produce portion of the party had passed, Salome sat down in the other room and kept talking with the Dutch dude. He was smoking a very expensive Cuban cigar, cigars that Denise's husband had handed out after the produce had been put back in the fridge. Curious Salome asked for a few puffs of his cigar, and watching this, Felix couldn't help but think of the Freudian implications. Felix had declined a cigar, and he also wasn't eating, just because he felt totally uncomfortable. He did strike up an interesting conversation with Denise's mother for fifteen or twenty minutes because she had approached him, but other than that, Felix had never liked just introducing himself to strangers and being forced to talk about either his life or theirs. Conversations with strangers that just happened, and might lead to friendships, were fine with Felix. But parties like this felt too forced. Salome had told him earlier, when he had said how much more he preferred smaller intimate gatherings of family and friends, "I have a list of ten things on my refrigerator called: 'What You Should Have Accomplished by the Time You're Thirty,' and one of those ten things is being able to handle yourself in any party atmosphere with strangers."

And Felix said, "Well I have a list of ten things on my refrigerator called: 'What You Should Have Accomplished by the Time You're Fifty,' and one of those ten things is knowing exactly where and with whom you want to spend time."

Felix sat by himself and did pretty much nothing for the next two hours while Salome worked the room, and finally he pulled her aside and said, "Let's split."

"It's only midnight!" She said, annoyed that Felix wanted to leave so early. But finally Salome acquiesced, they said their goodbyes to the host and hostess, and Felix started to drive Salome back to his place on Mad Beach. "I think I'd rather go home alone," Salome said. So Felix dropped Salome at her place on Younger Island, and she said a simple, "Goodnight!" as she exited the *Beetle* without looking back.

By May of 1998, Salome was tired of Felix and already interested in an adjustor at *Grapefruit State*, Pierce Rodman, a man ten years her junior, and she was looking for a way to end things with Felix. So after a dinner out one evening, which included Walter Lee and his friend, Curtis, after Walter Lee had sneezed in the backseat of the *Beetle*, held his hand over his mouth, which deflected his snot at a forty-five degree angle into Felix's neck, and after Felix had shot him a glance, and after a starved Felix had asked at least three times if anybody wanted an appetizer and the kids didn't want appetizers, and after only two appetizers arrived for Salome and himself and Salome had given away most of the food to the kids anyway, and after Felix had said, "Hey…I'll order 27 appetizers if that's what everybody wants…but I wanted one for myself…and can't we get our act together?" and after Salome had shot him a nasty glance, and after the ride back to Salome's on Younger Island, and after the kids had gone into Walter Lee's room to play, Salome said to Felix, "I love you Felix…but I'm not 'in love' with you."

"That will come in time. I'm 'in love' with you enough…there's enough there for the both of us."

"It's not enough for me," Salome said. And then she added what she had said to Anthony in 1974, "Yellow goes with blue, but it also goes with red, black, brown, and a number of other different colors."

"Says who?" asked Felix. "Who says any color goes with any color…some pinhead who thinks that he or she is some bastion of style? I like blue and green together…and perhaps yellow and orange with pink. Look Salome…I love you like I've loved no other woman in this life…and that's really saying something…because my first wife screwed me up for years. I don't care that we have a number of differences…and I don't care that sometimes we might disagree. Don't deny me the chance to express my annoyance…when it comes up. Certainly a little annoyance…has nothing to do with the big picture…how much I love you and Walter Lee."

"But that has to be a two-way street…and although I thought that I might get there...I haven't. I just don't love you like that," Salome said.

"I'm still sure that will come in time," a starting to feel desperate Felix said. "Look Salome...quite honestly...you can be a major pain in the ass. You're incredibly demanding...your stream of conscious way of how we spend our time together...starting off with one game plan...and then suddenly switching gears...most other men would be totally put off by that. But I see you as a wonderful breath of fresh air...I find it cute...most of the time...how your curiosity modifies our plans...And I know that you're exactly what's perfect for me in my life...because your changing keeps me feeling young. I know...that being with you forever...will add twenty years to my life. Hey I know that you're the *Energizer* bunny...and that no man could ever possibly keep up with you...but as I told you once before...if we were married...As long as I had some private writing time...I'd promise to run with you at least two nights per week...and you could go do your thing another three nights per week...I'd stay home and watch the kids...as long as you'd give me two nights a week to just stay home, cuddle up, and watch a good movie...And as long as the three nights a week that you run alone...there's no infidelity...I'd have no problem...But I know that there wouldn't be...because that would be in total opposition to your Christian values."

"None of that makes any difference," Salome said. "Felix...I just don't feel the same way inside that you do. I'm sorry...I know you're disappointed...but you'll just have to get over it. I know we'll always be close...and you are my son's uncle...but I need to move on."

Felix got up and walked toward the door. At the door, he turned back toward Salome and said, "What a loss...what a tragic loss," before walking outside and getting into his car.

@@@@@@@@

In August of 1998 Jennifer Apple Morgan arrived for a two-week stay at *The Breakers*. And although Salome had said that she could give Jennifer her evenings and weekends if she stayed with her on Younger Island—she had made a secret agreement with Pierce to appease him, that she would pretend to Jennifer to go into work at *Grapefruit State* on one of those days, and instead they would both take the day off and stay at his place—Jennifer had opted instead to stay on Mad Beach, so she could relax next to the Gulf of Mexico all day. Felix gave Jennifer the best room available and told her, "The two weeks are free...I want you to just enjoy yourself."

Jennifer was very appreciative of Felix's generosity, and because of his broken heart over Salome, and because of Jennifer's desire to talk, they both began sitting for hours together at the table in the backyard under the big umbrella, drinking Margaritas, smoking joints, and talking.

Felix told Jennifer, "I love your sister intensely…and I'm just beside myself with grief…over the ending of what we had."

"I know it hurts," Jennifer said. "Salome is beautiful…and very smart. But I can also see how her Christianity might interfere."

"Well…that's not the problem," Felix said. "I can live with whatever belief system she has…when it comes to God. And honestly…although she would have preferred it if I were a Christian…she knew that I might be open to that…with more study on my part…and that really wasn't the issue."

"So what was the issue?" Jennifer asked.

"She says she isn't in love with me…and there's absolutely nothing I can do to make her feel that way."

"Well…sometimes we don't know what 'being in love' really is. I remember how much she was 'in love' with Darius Malcovitch…and how she had blown off your brother…wasn't 'in love' with him either…it didn't feel the same as Darius. But eventually she must have decided that she was 'in love' with Anthony…because she married him, had a son with him, and tolerated most of his drug abuse."

"And I'm certainly not like my brother in that way," Felix said.

"No…you're not. Who knows what's going through her mind?…
You're an incredible man, Felix…I've heard about your adventures…and I knew I really liked you…when I heard how you had called up Bubba in 1975...and pretended to be Salome's lawyer," Jennifer said, as she took the last swallow of her Margarita.

"In 1976...after Darius' funeral on Long Island…I definitely got the vibe…that Salome had some romantic feelings for me. But that was before she re-hooked up with and eventually married my brother."

"Who knows…maybe she'll come to her senses…maybe not. At least you're not living a lie," Jennifer said with some anger.

"What do you mean?" Felix asked.

"Although I had caught Colin with his hand in the cookie jar…with another woman…and I had always known that he was a philanderer…I never knew…that for the better part of twenty years…that he was carrying on with Deannie Cox…our head RN at *The Woman's Center*. For the better part of twenty years!…That son of a bitch! At the reading of Colin's will I found out…after he had left her…nearly half of his estate!"

"I'm so sorry," Felix said. "That is absolutely terrible."

"For twenty years that bitch looked in my face…while she was sleeping with my husband…and pretended to be my friend. And she was a lot more than just an employee…We regularly went out together…either just the two of us…or with a small group of other women. I was the maid of honor at her wedding...although I suspect their marriage only lasted five years…because her husband caught wind of her long term affair with Colin. I don't know…after they divorced…he just left town."

"Isn't it just absolutely total horseshit...how some people can look into your face...and keep you shined on?" Felix asked.

"It's absolutely the worst thing to do to another human being," Jennifer said, the tears coming to her eyes.

Felix and Jennifer spoke at length about relationships and love several more times at the table under the umbrella during the next two weeks. As a result of those discussions, Felix found himself writing more in his journal than he had written in the past twenty years. Felix was still emotionally shaken, but he did feel somewhat better, once he put his feelings down on paper.

One night, with only three more days for Jennifer before she returned to Vermont, Jennifer just grabbed Felix and kissed him passionately. Felix enjoyed the kiss, and he didn't resist. Jennifer said, "You are an exceptional man...and I am so turned on by you. Would you please take me to bed?"

And Felix said, "You turn me on big time too...and Winky wants to give me a big thumbs up on what you just asked." But then Felix added, "But I'm still head over heels in love with Salome...and any possibility that we might ever have...in the future...would be totally gone...if she knew I took her older sister to bed."

"Would she have to know?" Jennifer asked, while reaching down to meet Winky.

Felix gently removed her hand, kissed it, and said, "No...but I'd know."

@@@@@@@@

In January of 1999 things were finished with Salome and Pierce Rodman. Salome had thought that she was in love with the man, and maybe in the beginning he had felt the same way too, but eventually the twenty-eight year-old junior buckaroo had come to the conclusion that Salome was just too restrictive, and that there was a lot more cootie cat out there for him to conquer. Salome was devastated, but she still maintained her cool veneer at work, even with Pierce, who worked in a cubicle not quite fifty feet away from her.

Other than a bullshit five minute call about her alleged concern in regards to an approaching hurricane the previous September, there had been no contact between Felix and Salome, and Felix missed both her and his nephew. Nancy Apple, finishing her senior year at Plant High School, still baby-sat for Salome, so Salome no longer needed Felix to do that. A few times however, Walter Lee had called saying, "I miss you Uncle Felix." And Felix had to tell Walter Lee that he was just real busy, even though he knew that it hurt his nephew, and that his nephew must think that he didn't love him anymore. It was a miserable situation for Felix, but seeing Salome just hurt too badly, and he was unable to camouflage that hurt, so he could just hang out with his nephew.

The craziness. Felix regularly read the astrology section in *The St. Petersburg Times*, looking for what was up with his and Salome's sign, Leo, and Felix also made several visits to psychics, looking for any glimmer of hope with Salome for the future. Finally, Felix had folded carefully the life-sized picture of Salome that he had taped to a wall in his bedroom—Felix, Salome, and Walter Lee all had their pictures taken at the Florida State Fair in Tampa, with the proviso that their three pictures, blown up to their actual heights, would be sent in the mail later—and carried it with him in his suitcase on a weeklong trip to Venice, Italy in February of 1999. Once there, Felix found an appliance store, and begged them to let him have an empty cardboard box that had once held a refrigerator. Felix set Salome's full-sized picture on top of the cardboard box, and using a box cutter, he carefully traced and cut the cardboard. Felix then glued Salome to the cardboard, and carrying it with him, he found a gondolier to take him and his cardboard Salome for a ride under the Bridge of Sighs. And there, under the bridge, Felix kissed his Salome facsimile and said, "Regardless of how you feel…I'll be in love with you forever."

By late June of 1999 Felix had given up. Salome was never going to change her mind, and Felix was sick and tired of his life. He knew he wanted to write a new novel, but he also knew that Mad Beach wasn't the place for it. He went to Walter Lee Younger and said, "Would you be interesting in buying *The Breakers*?"

Secretly, Walter Lee had always fantasized about owning the motel. But he loved Felix too much to see his adopted son do something so hasty. "You don't really want to sell this place. Why don't you just take off for awhile…I'm sure we can keep the place going for awhile without you."

And Felix said, "No Walter Lee…I need a big life change. I really want to sell. I also want to sell my twenty-five percent in *The Careless Navigator*."

"That's interesting too," Walter Lee said. "Salome called the other day…looking to do the same thing."

"Why?…Where are Salome and Walter Lee heading? Do they want to leave Tampa?"

"Salome said that last February, she applied to, and recently had been accepted in, graduate school at NYU. Apparently she's decided that she wants to be a literature professor…just like you…and she's starting classes there this coming September."

'Perhaps she'll learn something,' Felix thought. Then he said, "Well…half of this motel belongs to her anyway…so I was planning on giving her that money."

"Annie and I spoke about it…and there's enough money to give both you and Salome…the close to one million dollars each…that both of your twenty-five percents are worth. Annie and I would then own seventy-five percent of the restaurant, with Bruiser, Eileen, Jr., and his wife Daphne keeping the last twenty-five percent," Walter Lee said.

"Fine. And how about the motel?"

"I don't know…'Licks…how much do you want?"

"Well…it was appraised at fifteen million dollars in 1994...I'm sure it's worth more than that now…but I'm not out to gouge you…Hey…I love you Walter Lee."

"You know I love you too 'Licks…but business is business. I have money…and I have an almost unlimited credit line…but fifteen million plus would be hard to do."

"Well how about if you partnered-up with Jack and Geneva? I know Jack's business has almost doubled in the past few years…maybe he'd be interested," Felix said.

"That's a great idea," Walter Lee said, and then added, "Are you sure you really want to do this 'Licks?"

"I'm sure," Felix said. "I'll call Salome…to see if we can just unload this place…under market value. I don't really care. How about twelve million?"

"If you're sure…and Salome goes for that price…and Jack and Geneva agree…Bet!" Walter Lee said.

As hard as it was, Felix called Salome that evening and told her his plans. Salome said very little, but she was willing to accept half of twelve million dollars for the motel. Walter Lee Younger also discussed the motel with Jack and Geneva Apple, and they both agreed that they'd love to own half of the place.

In July of 1999, after Felix and Salome had each been paid—before their clever accountants had figured a way to keep Uncle Sam's cut as minimal as possible—one million dollars for their shares in *The Careless Navigator* and six million dollars for their portion of *The Breakers*, and after Walter Lee and Jack had helped Felix to move and store most of his worldly goods in the unused recording studio on the first floor, and after Walter Lee and Jack had said that he could leave his stuff in the first floor studio indefinitely, Felix left Mad Beach in his *Beetle* forever. He was going to complete that western journey that he and Salome had never finished, and then he was going to drive to Alaska, and buy a place somewhere remote. Felix wanted to hibernate and to write a new novel, and he wanted to be as far away from Salome as possible. As he headed over the Howard Franklin Bridge from St. Petersburg to Tampa, a biker on a *Harley* whizzed by him. As the traffic came to a near crawl at the middle of the bridge, Felix couldn't help but laugh when he was able to discern the white lettering on the back of the biker's black t-shirt. It read: **If you can read this, the bitch fell off!**

Chapter Sixteen

The unobstructed view across New York Harbor of the Twin Towers, downtown and part of midtown Manhattan, the Statue of Liberty, Ellis Island, Governors Island, the Brooklyn Bridge, the Manhattan Bridge, and the Williamsburg Bridge up the East River on the Eastside of Manhattan, and—on a particularly clear day—the George Washington Bridge nearly fifteen miles away up the Hudson on the Westside, downtown Brooklyn, Bayonne, Jersey City, the Staten Island Ferry Terminal, and the under construction Richmond County Stadium, where the Staten Island Yankees would eventually play, from the perpendicular northern and western all glass walls of her living room, had been the main selling point to Salome when she had purchased the fifth floor, with outside terrace, 1200 square foot, great room with loft, two-bedroom, one and half-bathroom, formal dining room, and eat-in kitchen corner condominium on the water in St. George, on the northern tip of Staten Island, next to the ferry terminal, for Nancy, Walter Lee, and herself in September of 1999. The building included a security gate for the one hundred and fifty yard walk along the water to the ferry, twenty-four hour human security, two assigned parking spaces for each apartment, one enclosed below the building, where Salome kept the two-seat *Cobra*, and one for guests or a second vehicle outside, where Salome kept her new 2000 *Jeep Grand Cherokee*, and individual huge storage closets on the first floor, also assigned by apartment. Located on the top floor, one floor above Salome, was the health club, complete with saunas, swimming pools, indoor racquetball courts, and an available physical trainer. Salome had paid $395,000 cash for the condo, and her monthly maintenance fee, mostly tax deductible, which included water, trash pick up, and insurance was eleven hundred and fifty dollars. Salome had the largest bedroom, Walter Lee the second bedroom, and the huge climb-up-ladder loft belonged to Nancy.

Nancy had begun her first semester in college at the Borough of Manhattan Community College on Chambers and West Streets in September, at the same time that Salome had begun graduate school in English at NYU. Nancy watched Walter Lee, called for takeout or made him dinner, on Monday and Wednesday evenings when Salome had classes. On those days, after her classes at BMCC, Nancy would head back to Staten Island, and walk over to the St. George Christian School, a few blocks from the apartment, and pick up Walter Lee from his fifth grade class' after school program by six o'clock. In the mornings, Salome would always stuff Walter Lee's lunchbox with fun and healthy foods, and, depending on the weather, either walk or drive him to school.

At NYU, with a total student body of nearly 50,000, and limited classroom space, all of the seats were occupied by the undergraduates during the day. Graduate school in English was held entirely in the shadows and eventual darkness, from six o'clock until nine forty-five, Monday through Thursday. Salome had a class from six to seven forty-five and another from eight to nine forty-five on Mondays, and a third class on Wednesdays from eight to nine forty-five. On Mondays and Wednesdays, after getting Walter Lee to school, Salome would catch the morning eight o'clock ferry to Manhattan, and be in the Village at NYU in the Bobst Library, already doing her research by nine. Salome had been able to cover the required research for her three graduate classes with the two full days in the library, and reading at home all day pretty much the rest of the week. Fortunately, Salome didn't have to work a job while going to graduate school, and she recognized just how lucky she was.

Nancy, on the other hand, had to work. Jimson and Lizzie each sent her money, and Salome paid her well and gave her free room and board for babysitting, and, if she had wanted to, Salome could have just given Nancy everything financially that she would ever need. But Salome felt that Nancy needed to learn how to balance classes, study, work, church, and a social life, to be a true 'Christian woman for all seasons,' so she insisted that Nancy have a job.

Nancy was taking a fulltime load at BMCC her first semester, and her classes were spread out from Monday through Thursday between nine in the morning and three in the afternoon. On Tuesdays and Thursdays she stayed in town and worked at *Village Burrito* on Bleeker Street from six o'clock until two in the morning. On Fridays, although she had no classes, Nancy also worked the same shift. Salome did worry about Nancy taking the late night ferry alone back to Staten Island, and, if she missed the two thirty boat, having to wait around an hour, with the homeless sleeping on benches in the terminal, for the three thirty boat. Nancy attempted to reassure Salome however, and she said, "It's no big deal!" in a response to Salome's concern.

Now, on this late Wednesday night/early Thursday morning of Thanksgiving in 1999, as Salome watched the first snowflakes of Winter over the harbor with a well lighted Manhattan in the background, again she was worried about Nancy. Since Salome had the day off from class on this holiday eve Wednesday, she had agreed to Nancy's request to attend a party in the East Village after classes at BMCC. But Salome had said to get home early, since they were leaving at six in the morning to drive to Rutland, to meet at Bruiser and Eileen's place at nine o'clock, so the women could go shopping for all of the extras that made the meal complete, and the men could get ready to watch the football games. Eileen and Bruiser had already purchased the turkeys, the potatoes—both sweet and regular—the turnips, and Eileen had made both the pumpkin and apple pies.

Pauline, Bubba, Jimson, Eve Apple, and a visiting Jack, Geneva, Lani, and twenty-month old, Lorelei, who, other than a grandma Pauline visit to *The Breakers* last year, and a grandpa Bubba pick up at the airport yesterday, no other Liberty or Apple of Vermont had yet met, were bringing all of the beer, wine, and other libations from Burlington, and they would be at Bruiser and Eileen's at nine. Jr. Liberty, his wife Daphne, his seven year-old son, Tyler, his four year-old daughter, Delie, and great-grandma Lorelei Liberty, would arrive later from Middlebury, and they were bringing yet more food. It was three o'clock in the morning, and Salome, Walter Lee, and Nancy were supposed to leave in three hours for Rutland, but Nancy still wasn't home. Salome had left three messages on Nancy's cell since midnight.

@@@@@@@@

"WWWRRROOOAAA...Asshole!" Major Doofus said, just because Felix had accidentally mentioned a certain female name, on this Thanksgiving Day in 1999.

"Knock it off...Major Doofus, or I'm gonna buy a kitty for you to play with!" Felix said to the parrot.

"WWWRRROOOAAA...Eat Me!"

When Felix had arrived in Alaska in August of 1999, looking for a cabin and some acreage, he had taken a room in an Anchorage motel for nearly a month, while Leslie O'Reily, his real estate agent at *Land Ho!*, the largest real estate agency in Anchorage, had sought out properties for him. Leslie had taken Felix to see many places, but nothing so far had knocked him out. Finally, on the Tuesday after Labor Day Weekend, Leslie had called Felix on his cell and said, "Good news...I have a place...but the circumstances are kinda strange."

And Felix had said, as he dried himself, since Leslie's call had gotten him out of the shower, "Strange?...what's strange?"

"Well...let me tell you about the place first," Leslie had said. "It's seven acres...a big log cabin...with two bedrooms, one bathroom, a big loft, a nice kitchen with a wood burning stove, and a huge stone fireplace...It's on a stream that runs out to the Salmon River. The place is twenty-five miles northwest of Palmer."

Felix thought, 'Twenty-five miles northwest of Palmer...and Palmer is about thirty-five miles due north of Anchorage...I can still drive to the big city in about an hour...weather permitting...in an emergency.' While in the shower, Felix had been thinking that he needed to buy a four wheel drive pick up truck. He had thought, 'Unlike my two old *VW Beetles*...that I could just push out of the snow...this *New Beetle* is twice the weight... besides...I need a vehicle that I can use to schlep a bunch of stuff...And I'll probably need to have a barn built...with heat...for the vehicles.'

"Oh yeah...Felix...the place has a half-finished basement, a wooden wraparound deck with a covered working hot tub, and a heated two-car barn," Leslie had added. "And...I believe...it comes with...whatever is inside the cabin and barn...and outside on the property...whatever's been left behind."

"What do you mean...'whatever's been left behind?'...And why are the circumstances...surrounding this property... strange?" Felix had asked.

"Well...the owner...the builder...Mr. Ferdinand Kingsley...he built the place...from a kit...with professional help...and they made all kinds of cool modifications...seven years ago...But Ferdinand Kingsley was a loner...and when he would come into Palmer...everybody said that he would act real strange...Although...the one time I spoke to him he was nice... Anyway... apparently he went bonkers last Friday...ran into the bank...told them that they could have...all of the possessions that he was leaving on his property...and then he signed off on everything...gave them power of attorney...told them to just ask enough for the place to cover what was left on the mortgage...and then Mr. Kingsley yelled something about...to 'Give him a ticket for an airplane...that he didn't have time for a fast train'...that..."

"I know," Felix had said, "'Lonely days were gone...he was going home...his baby...had wrote him a letter!'" Felix had laughingly added, impressed that the eleven year-younger Leslie knew the song by *The Boxtops.*

"That's right!" Leslie had said.

At forty-two, petite, short black-haired, blue-eyed Leslie O'Reily was kind of cute. She had been going through a divorce right at that time, and fifty-three year-old Felix had thought, 'Note to self...down the road...!'

Felix then had asked, "What did this Ferdinand Kingsley guy do for a living?...Why did he build the place...seven years ago?...What was he doing out there?"

And Leslie had replied, “Apparently…he was a failed novelist.”

“I’ll take it!…Cash!” Felix had said.

“Don’t you want to see the place and know the price?”

“I don’t care!” Felix had said. He was very pleased however, after he had fallen in love with the place, that he had only paid $135,000.

When Felix arrived with Leslie at what would become his property, as they had walked up to the door they heard, “WWWRRROOOAAA…Go Away!”

And Felix had looked at Leslie and said, “What the hell was that?”

When they entered the cabin, they had found the parrot, still with plenty of food, in his cage on a table in the living room. He had a nameplate under the cage that read: **Major Doofus**. Felix had said, “Major Doofus?”

And Major Doofus had said, “WWWRRROOOAAA…Eat Me!”

Later, Felix would learn that Major Doofus knew five things, and Felix would laugh, because this perverse parrot was a *Frankenstein*-like creation of the strange writer Ferdinand Kingsley, who had vacated these premises, and left this potty-mouthed parrot, for yet another strange writer to stumble upon. Whenever somebody approached the front door, Major Doofus would say, “Go Away!” Whenever he was hungry he would say, “Feed Me!” Whenever you said the parrot’s name he would say, “Eat Me!” And he would say, a misogynistic “Asshole!” whenever a female’s name was mentioned, and the politically incorrect “Homo!” whenever a man’s name was mentioned. And it mattered not what man or woman’s name was said, the bird had a better than 90% accuracy ratio on picking the correct gender.

And Major Doofus made no value judgments, it didn’t matter if you said, “Adolph Hitler!” or “Pope John Paul II!” the response was going to be, “WWWRRROOOAAA …Homo!” and “Tokyo Rose!” or “Mother Theresa!” would get a “WWWRRROOOAAA…Asshole!” You did have to say two or three names for Major Doofus to speak however, just “Sting!” or “Bono!” wouldn’t work. You’d have to say “Billy Bob!” or “Betty Lou!” or “John Rocker!” or “Warren Commission!” or “John Foster Dulles!” or “Hillary Rodham Clinton!”

There were some names that Major Doofus had a hard time discerning however, names that could be either male or female. Unfortunately, “Rene Descartes!” always got, “WWWRRROOOAAA… Asshole!” and “Billy Jean King!” always got, “WWWRRROOOAAA…Homo!” And Felix learned, that Major Doofus was just guessing with terms, either real or made up, that sounded like names. Just for fun, Felix liked to mix things up:

“Hey Major Doofus…”

“WWWRRROOOAAA…Eat Me!”

“Dumbshit Nasty Parrot!”

“WWWRRROOOAAA…Asshole!”

"Bathtub Sailor!"
"WWWRRROOOAAA...Homo!"
"Running Dog of Imperialism!"
"WWWRRROOOAAA...Asshole!"
"Choke the Chicken!"
"WWWRRROOOAAA...Homo!"
"Flog the Dolphin!"
"WWWRRROOOAAA...Asshole!"
"*The Silver Beatles*!"
"WWWRRROOOAAA...Homo!"
"Joseph Stalin!"
"WWWRRROOOAAA...Homo!"
"Lady Bird Johnson!"
"WWWRRROOOAAA...Asshole!"
"Lee Harvey Oswald!"
"WWWRRROOOAAA...Homo!"
"Clay Shaw!"
"WWWRRROOOAAA...Homo!"
"Limited Nuclear War!"
"WWWRRROOOAAA...Asshole!"
"Mark David Chapman"
"WWWRRROOOAAA...Homo!"
"Peace With Dignity!"
"WWWRRROOOAAA...Asshole!"
"Richard Nixon!"
"WWWRRROOOAAA...Homo!"
"Trickle Down Economy!"
"WWWRRROOOAAA...Asshole!"
"Walt the Wanker!"
"WWWRRROOOAAA...Homo!"
"The Ugly American!"
"WWWRRROOOAAA...Asshole!"

Along with Major Doofus, Ferdinand Kingsley had also left an extensive library; and functional, albeit cheaply made, hardwood furniture; including a bed, night table, chest of drawers, cushioned sofa and chair, dining room set with hutch, and a large writing desk and chair. Felix had to buy very little in the way of furniture, except he did allow himself the luxury of a nice comfortable swivel writing chair to go with the desk, and a blue leather covered *Lazy Boy* recliner, both of which he brought home in his recently purchased used 1996 *Ford* four wheel drive pick up truck. Felix had also bought a new *Honda* generator at the same time, for emergencies. Since the cabin had no phone, and Felix's cell phone had precarious reception there, Felix paid to have phone lines brought out to his property on the electric line poles, which also allowed him a dial up internet connection for his *Apple* computer. Finally, Felix had a satellite dish installed, for when he felt like watching television.

A typical day for Felix usually began with lots of coffee and some fresh baked *Pillsbury* biscuits, and plenty of writing from four in the morning until around eleven. Then he took a two hour nap, woke up and did some editing on what he had written earlier in the day, and then he would do some outdoor activity of either chopping wood or fishing. He was currently stuffed to the gills with fish in his freezer—he had to fry up a batch of it last weekend to make room for all of the *Pillsbury* biscuit dough canisters he had purchased at *Palmer Groceries*—so Felix had been concentrating on filling his huge covered wood shed with enough logs for the year. Felix figured about 4,000 logs would suffice, between constant use of the fireplace and the wood burning stove in the kitchen. Felix had electric heat in the cabin and car barn also, but he kept those thermostats down to just sixty degrees. After wood chopping, Felix would eat dinner, and then spend a couple of hours either reading The New Testament or reading commentary about The New Testament, from the left behind library of Ferdinand Kingsley or from the Internet. After reading, Felix usually ended his day with an hour or two of television, with the *BBC News* as the last thing, before crashing in the bed he had moved from the larger bedroom to up in his loft. This move, allowed Felix to watch and listen to the wood crackling in the huge stone fireplace at night. He had decided that was a relaxing way to fall asleep. Felix was usually in bed no later than ten thirty every night.

Felix had finally come up with how he was going to construct his new novel. He liked the idea of juxtaposing his protagonist to the rest of society, and for that reason, he found that using a plural first person present tense narrator in *Mad Beach* was an interesting voice. The novel began:

> *Rotund Roy Cassier sits quietly on Mad Beach watching us all. We sashay by, our bronzed biceps bulging, our sun-drenched expressions reflected in the tide's ebb. We promenade like prima donnas, the soft white sand sticking to our feet. And when our momentary flirtation with Nature has finally exorcised our weekend dibbick, and we've drunk the last of our Sunday soma from our Saturday golden chalice, we pile into our prodigious driving machines, and head back to the mainland, paying the toll takers for the trips as we go. We get ready for our Monday lives. We downshift the Sun.*
>
> *Not so Roy Cassier, writer, beach bum, and eclectic extraordinaire. Here on Mad Beach he has no Monday life.*

Felix had known for years, that regardless of the emotionally scarred baggage he carried, he was still fortunate. He could have been broke all of his life, and he knew, that had his life been a life of poverty, along with all of the hurt he already had, that he too might have made the same choice his father had made in 1973. Felix also realized, that those he knew and cared about, Walter Lee Younger and his family, K. J. Bauer, Jay Biggs, Montgomery Butler, and the whole Apple Family, were also very fortunate. Nobody in Felix's emotional sphere was financially suffering. As a matter of fact, everybody Felix knew well, was fairly well off. Salome had to work in New York City when she had first moved away from Rutland, but eventually, both by marrying Anthony and investing in *The Careless Navigator*, and her share of the proceeds from her parents' orchard, she had put herself into a reasonable financial situation. The only person who Felix knew well, who had ever suffered from a lack of money, until he was in his forties was Walter Lee Younger. And Walter Lee's road to money had been a big highway of sorrow. So Felix decided that the characters in his novel, unlike his own life, would all be suffering from financial hardship. He wrote in his journal: *Sure…my protagonist, Roy Cassier, sits on Mad Beach all day…looking at us with a so-called existential eye…but hey…he sits there because he's broke. At the start of our story…yeah…Roy is well-read and very bright, but he hasn't a pot to piss in! We may not understand the dichotomy of Nature as he does, with his knowledge of the seventeenth-century Metaphysical Poets, but we get to go home and sleep in a bed! By the end of the novel…Roy will be okay. He starts off 'on the beach,' waxing philosophic in his writing journal, about what's phony and what's real…but he needs to learn some more societal assimilation lessons first, before he can leave the 'mad beach.' He needs to learn that we all have to do things that we'd rather not do, and to quote one of those Metaphysical Poets he loves, "No man is an island." Conversely, the woman he loves and who recently dumped him, Judziah Cromwell, who is also seen through the first person plural present tense eye, and by the end of the novel, she'll be okay also…But she goes from total societal and religious assimilation in her mind, and being psychologically beaten down in a marriage, to worrying about the superficial and the Ego strokes she can get, to finally being able to sit by herself on the beach…and tell the difference between what's real and what's phony…what's her Ego and what's her true Self.*

Today was a holiday, so things were a little different. Today Felix got to watch his favorite football team, the Tampa Bay Buccaneers. The two football games, a Thanksgiving tradition, featured the Tampa Bay Buccaneers visiting the Detroit Lions for the first game. (Many centuries earlier, it would have been the Rome Christians visiting the Detroit Lions.) This game had already started at eight thirty in the morning Alaska time, and now, as the game was ending just after eleven—Tampa Bay having been thoroughly devoured by Detroit—and just before the Green Bay Packers began game two at Dallas against the Cowboys, Felix said, "Well…Major

Doofus…I'm getting hungry!"

And Major Doofus said, "WWWRRROOOAAA…Eat Me!"

And Felix said, "YUMMM…Baked Stuffed Parrot!…"

And Major Doofus said, "WWWRRROOOAAA…Homo!"

And Felix said, "Ah…a New Thanksgiving Tradition!"

And Major Doofus said, "WWWRRROOOAAA…Asshole!"

And then Felix stopped by his desk and reread the letter he had typed on the computer to Salome. He printed it out, and would later mail it via Walter Lee, since he didn't have Salome's new address.

Dear Salome,

You know…after so much religious discussion with you…about The New Testament…my curiosity was piqued. As you know…I had already read exactly what Jesus had said—that which was written in red in the Red Letter Edition of The King James Bible—but that, of course, was out of context. I've since gone back and read The New Testament from cover to cover. I've also spent a lot of time reading modern Christian commentary—some of which was left behind in the library of this cabin I bought, the rest from the Internet—trying to under- stand the different philosophies in the different types of Christianity. I studied Methodists, Lutherans, and Presbyterians. I looked at Christian Science and Jehovah Witnesses. I examined the Catholics. (What's the deal with the Catholics? They've come up with all of this stuff that Jesus never asked for. Worshipping saints? Kissing some Monsignor's ring? Confession in a booth? Saying a bunch of "Hail Marys" as an act of contrition for sin?)

But of all the different denominations of Christianity I've studied so far, next to that wild Southern Baptist group who actually handle poisonous snakes as part of their Sunday service, far and away, the Pentecostals seem to be the most on the fringe. Pentecostalism seems almost heretical. I'm sorry Salome…but the Apostle Paul says, "Come, let us reason together." He doesn't hand you a brown paper bag with chicken bones and snake rattles inside, and say, "Shake this up, work yourself into a frenzy, mumble some gibberish, and you'll be one with Jesus!" Not only did Jesus never request that, there's no place in The Bible where there's a directive to do that.

From what I understand, the ancient Jews celebrated the Pentecost…the "Feast of Weeks" on the fiftieth day after Passover. Their festival included the offering of the first fruit of the harvest season to God. The Christians began celebrating the holiday as being fifty days after Easter, and called It

"Whitsunday," because of the white garments worn during the mass baptisms. For Christians, on Pentecost Sunday, a passage that might be heard would be from John (20:19-23) which tells of a visit of the Risen Christ to the Disciples huddled in fear. "Peace be with you," Jesus says. "As the Father sent Me, so I am sending you." Then Jesus breathed on them and said, "Receive the Holy Spirit." So, if one is a Christian, one could say from that passage, "We are God-breathed." It seems to me, for the Christian, the Pentecost celebrates that reality; and, this unifying spirit, that crossed the boundaries of language, race, and culture, would be manifested through the episode of "the fiery tongues."

But Salome...do you really think it took a Bible assignment by Charles Parham to his students at the Bethel Bible College, to investigate the "baptism of the Spirit" or the Pentecostal Blessing, for the world to suddenly discover, in Topeka, Kansas, in 1900, that a true Christian is so touched during this blessing, that suddenly he or she begins speaking nonsensically, but others in the church understand? Charles Parham was a Methodist reverend who broke away, and along with William J. Seymour's Azusa Revival in Los Angeles in 1906...suddenly...they come up with a whole new way for Christians to worship Jesus...1900 years later?

A portion of the long passage in The Bible that speaks of "the fiery tongues" is in Acts 2:5-8: "And there were dwelling at Jerusalem Jews, devout men, out of every nation under heaven. Now when this was noised abroad, the multitude came together, and were confounded, because that every man heard them speak in his own language. And they were all amazed and marveled, saying one to another, Behold, are not all these which speak Galilaeans? And how hear we every man in our tongue, wherein we were born?"

It seems apparent to me, Salome, and most Christians would say, that the Holy Spirit filled the Disciples, and God allowed all listeners to hear His Word in his own language. His own language...Salome...and I could find no evidence in The New Testament...of anything else. There is no mention of everybody understanding just one special prayer language...a language that nobody had ever heard before...some secret code. More likely, it was like something that a friend of mine in New York told me on the phone last year, something he had experienced a couple of years ago at a Calvary Evangelical Church in New Jersey. My friend heard a man get up during the service and begin preaching in Croatian. The problem was, and it was well-documented by many people who knew this man his whole life, he knew absolutely nothing about Croatia and its language. Another man in the church, the only speaker of Croatian there that day, got up and exclaimed, "My God…He's talking to me!" That…to my mind…is more in line with what the Pentecost section in The Bible is describing.

Okay…The New Testament was originally written in Aramaic and Greek, and then translated into Latin. In Latin, "lingua" means "tongue," and its derivative "language." Although we don't use the expression so much anymore, it used to be fairly common to say, "Do you speak the English tongue?" "Do you speak the French tongue?" etc. So "the fiery tongues" probably means "the fiery language." And whether or not flames actually appeared over the heads of the Apostles literally, or "fiery tongues" is just a metaphor for "preaching God's word with extreme passion," and "over the heads of the Apostles," is just a metaphor for "beyond the knowledge of the Apostles at that moment," I don't know. But the fact that what the people heard from the Apostles wasn't some special language that had never been heard before, but each individual's own language, is supported right there in the text.

You know…even among Pentecostals, there is no absolute consensus on doctrine, except for the glossolalia, the Spirit baptism, and the practice of "charismata" (gifts of the Holy Spirit). Anyway…to my mind…the notion of frenzied gibberish, seems almost like an anathema to Christianity. That's the way it looks…from my seat on the bus.

Please tell my nephew, that I love and miss him very much. Is there a possibility that he could either spend all or part of next summer up here in Alaska with me? You know I'd take good care of Walter Lee. Please let me know.

Hope you're well.
From far away,
Felix

@@@@@@@@

The pigeons all scattered as the drunk old bag lady stepped dangerously close, just as she had entered through the Fifth Avenue Arch of Washington Square Park in New York City on this Thanksgiving Day in 1999. "Out of my way!" The woman belligerently yelled at the birds, "Or it's pigeon stew tonight!"

A very tattered-looking old man, who had been walking towards Fifth Avenue from the inside of the park said, "Hey Bev...can you help me out?"

The lady who called herself "Bev," and said it was short for "Beverage," said, "Who are you?...Do you work for the government?"

"It's me...Ralphie-boy...Bev...Don't you remember?...I'm your friend."

"Ralphie-boy?...And you're not with the government?"

"I'm not with the government...Don't you remember?...I used to be a teacher?...Ralphie-boy Feldman?"

"Ralphie-boy Feldman...you used to teach high school English in Brooklyn...I remember...Ralphie-boy...how are you?"

"I'm okay Bev...can you help me out?"

"No *problemo* Ralphie-boy...here." And then she removed a three-quarters full pint of cheap vodka from her coat and handed it to him. "I'm fine for now, you can have this." Ralphie-boy thanked her, took the bottle, and headed back into the park. Seventy-seven year-old Bev headed into the park also, but she instinctively turned east towards a particular group of benches. She knew she was supposed to wait there for somebody, but she could remember neither for whom nor for what reason.

@@@@@@@@

"I'm gonna call Uncle Bruiser and Aunt Eileen's, honey, and say hello from us to the whole family, before this turkey is ready to come out of the oven. So could you lower the football game a bit?" Lena Younger Apple asked her husband Sam, from the kitchen of their small one-bedroom rental apartment in Atlanta, on this Thanksgiving Day in 1999.

"Okay sweetie," Sam Apple said from the sectional sofa. "And after that, let's call your parents at *The Breakers* and say hello also."

"They were going to Jamaica for the Thanksgiving weekend... remember?"

"Oh yeah...I forgot."

Actually, Walter Lee and Annie Younger were in their *Mercedes* on I-75 in Atlanta. They were going to stay on the sectional sofa that folded out into a queen-sized bed in Sam and Lena's apartment for the Thanksgiving weekend, and they would be arriving at any moment. Sam knew, but it was meant as a big surprise for Lena.

Not as big of a surprise as when Sam and Lena had called home and told both sides of the family that they had eloped the previous weekend. They had both graduated high school at seventeen in June of 1998, and they had both applied to and had been accepted as undergraduates at Mercer College in Atlanta. Lena wanted to go to Mercer as an undergraduate, because she figured that it would be easier to get into their fine medical school, if she had already been an Honor Roll undergraduate there. Sam wanted to be a lawyer, and Mercer had a fine law school also, but primarily Sam wanted to be with Lena, so Mercer had been the obvious choice for him.

They began school in Atlanta in September of 1998, each staying in the required freshman dormitory. In late May of 1999, after their freshman final exams, they had rented this small apartment in a complex in the northern part of the city. Both sides of the family had been told of their decision to live together after they had moved into the apartment; and, since it was assumed that Sam and Lena were going to eventually get married, that had come as no shock. But everybody was totally surprised the previous week, surprised and disappointed, when told that Sam and Lena had eloped. Annie had said, "My only child…and I don't get to see her get married?"

Walter Lee had told Sam that he had also wanted to see his daughter get married, so Sam had suggested that they drive up to Atlanta for the Thanksgiving weekend. Lena didn't know that her parents were coming for the weekend, and nobody but Sam knew, that he had put together another wedding, rented the recreation hall of the apartment complex, hired a minister, hired a caterer, hired a band, and had invited classmates from Mercer and selected residents from the apartment complex for the following evening. Sam had covertly tried to persuade his parents to come to Atlanta for the weekend also, but they had already made plans and paid for tickets to Burlington. Sam had hired a professional photographer, who, besides the still shots, was quite excellent at video taping. At least Sam's parents and sisters would get a nice video tape of the event.

@@@@@@@@

The Sun was just setting, as Salome watched through her western glass living room wall Bayonne, New Jersey in the background, and the ferry terminal and stadium in the foreground. And sitting there unnoticed through the northern glass living room wall, on this early warm evening in late May of 2000, was the already darkening Manhattan skyline. Salome's second semester in graduate school at NYU had just ended, and this semester had been a snooze compared to her first. And, of course, switching from the College of Arts and Science graduate program in English and American Literature, to the School of Education graduate program in Secondary English Education, had made all of the difference.

The first semester had been a nightmare for Salome, with her class in Chaucer and her class in the Seventeenth-Century Metaphysical Poets. Her twenty-page paper on "The Fawn: A Symbol for Sexual Innocence in Marvell's Poem," won her a B from her Seventeenth-Century Metaphysical Poets Professor. However, "Political Symbolism in 'The Miller's Tale,'" was only worth a B- from her Chaucer Professor. In graduate school in English and American Literature, a B- was tantamount to an F. Only nine classes were required for the Masters Degree, and one was allowed a B- in only two of them. And even her third class, Early Colonial American Literature, which had been her concentration as an undergraduate at the University of Tampa Bay, was incredibly difficult. The three classes together, required at least twenty-five hundred pages of reading a week, and more, if one wanted to be 'the apple of the professor's eye.' Salome had managed, with incredibly difficulty, to crank out a twenty page B+ paper on "Religious Heresy: The Dialogues Between Carwin and Others in Charles B. Brown's Novel of 1792," in her Early Colonial American Literature Class. Salome's professors, when hearing of her personal tragedy, were all sympathetic, however. By early January of 2000, Salome had come to the realization that she really wasn't a writer. She knew that her three papers were really all below a B, by NYU English graduate school standards, and that she had won sympathy grade-wise from at least two of her professors. So in late January, with the help of the Head of Graduate Studies for the College of Arts and Science, Salome switched to the School of Education. Salome knew, that writing scholarly articles for publication, for the rest of her life, in order to maintain tenure at a college or university, was not her forte. But she also knew that she could become a great secondary school English teacher.

Salome walked away from the living room glass, and she went over to the large gold framed Victorian mirror on the wall that separated her living room from her dining room, and she looked at herself. She had cut her hair extremely short, and had substituted big black framed glasses for her contact lenses to cover up her attractive face. She was also dressing very matronly these days, doing everything possible to downplay her sexual appeal to men. She went to church three or four times per week, and she regularly asked Jesus for forgiveness. Salome had decided that it had been her running away at fourteen, her pagan drug usage, and her Sodom and Gomorrah-like sexual encounters with men out of wedlock, that had been responsible for Nancy's abduction, rape, and subsequent murder on Thanksgiving eve of 1999. Somebody needed to pay for what Salome had done, and God had chosen Nancy. And on this May evening of 2000, the newspaper stories from late December of 1999, were omnipresent in Salome's mind. The stories that told how Stanley Robards and Nancy Apple, two freshmen from BMCC at a Thanksgiving party in the East Village, had been smooching in Stanley's parked car on 10th Street and Avenue D, and were surprised by Robert Smith, and ordered at gunpoint to drive him to New Jersey, where outside of Morristown they were robbed, Nancy was raped—while Stanley had been knocked out by the gun butt—and then they were both shot dead and dumped into the Passaic River. Robert Smith had then driven the car into Pennsylvania, where he was stopped by a state trooper for speeding. Robert Smith pulled a gun on the trooper, and the trooper had shot him dead. And after the bodies had been found in the river and identified and tied in with the license on the stopped car, and after the bodies had been closely examined by the coroner, it had been fairly easy to put the events together. Jimson Apple had been seeing a psychologist since this had happened, and Lizzie Williams, who was carrying her first child with Harold and had miscarried due to the stress, had then suffered a nervous breakdown. For Salome, it was all about guilt, and her notion of God exacting some kind of a payment because of her.

@@@@@@@@

"Hello," Felix said on this early June afternoon of 2000, when he answered his telephone. He had been sitting in his blue leather *Lazy Boy* thinking about his nephew, how Salome had never responded to his inquiry about the summer, but how she probably needed to stay close to her son this summer, after Walter Lee had told him on the phone about Nancy. He was also thinking about the letter he had written to Salome, expressing more than just sympathy, but imploring her to not feel guilty for that which she could not control.

"Hello Felix, it's David Summers." David Summers owned *Summers Detective Agency*, the largest and most prestigious detective agency in the United States. Felix had a notion, before leaving Mad Beach, to hire a private detective. And since he knew that he would be passing through Denver on his way to Alaska in July of 1999, he had made and kept an appointment with David Summers at that time.

"David Summers!" Felix said.

"WWWRRROOOAAA...Homo!" Major Doofus said.

"Yo...Major Doofus...be quiet...or next Thanksgiving..."

"WWWRRROOOAAA...Eat me!" Major Doofus said.

"What's up David? Any leads?" Felix asked, turning away from Major Doofus, so the parrot didn't think he was being addressed.

"Did I interrupt something?" David Summers asked laughingly.

"No...it's just my Dumbshit Nasty Parrot!" Felix said, turning back and looking at Major Doofus.

"WWWRRROOOAAA...Asshole!" Major Doofus said.

"And yes, I do have a lead on your mother," David Summers said. "My sources tell me that she was collecting social security, under the name of Beverly Kulpa, at a post office box in Manhattan in 1987 and 1988, and then that file is closed and marked 'deceased.'"

"So she died in New York City sometime in 1988 or 1989?"

"Maybe," David Summers said. "But didn't you tell me that your mother's maiden name was Jenkowitz?"

"Yeah."

"Coincidentally...at the same lower eastside post office box address…since 1990...somebody by the name of B. Jenko has been collecting both social security checks and pension checks."

"Pension checks? So you're saying that my mother worked someplace for many years under an assumed name?"

"Yeah…but there's something even stranger, Felix," David Summers said. "The checks she gets are from the Mongoose Electronics Corporation. My deep sources tell me that the Mongoose Electronics Corporation…is actually a front for the CIA."

"So you're telling me…that my seventy-seven year-old mother, changed her name, is still alive, lives in New York City, and is retired from the CIA?"

"Apparently so," David Summers said.

Chapter Seventeen

"Wow...what did you think of that?" asked C. Wel Rellim, Dean of the Eighth Grade, after taking a puff on his cigarette. He was seated on "The Veranda," the large stone slab that jettisoned out from the front wall of the school, a few feet from the entrance of Essex Street Middle School #234, on the lower Eastside of Manhattan, talking with Christopher Jeremy, an eighth grade English Teacher, on this first day of school for teachers, the Tuesday after Labor Day in September of 2000.

"Absolutely gorgeous!" Christopher said, and then he took a puff on his own cigarette. Both men, smart, jokesters, and single—fifty-four year-old C. Wel had been married and divorced years ago and twenty-eight year-old Christopher had never bothered—were referring to the late twentyish-something attractive Chinese woman, apparently a new addition to the staff, who had just walked into the school, and would end up at the teacher's continental breakfast in the auditorium. The breakfast was the school principal's idea, a way to ease the faculty into four days of boring staff development, before the children returned on the following Monday.

"I'd like *that* for breakfast!" C. Wel said with a big smile.

"Yeah...but then you'd be hungry again...in just a couple of hours!" Christopher fired back. As they were laughing, the familiar faces of returning teachers approached. C. Wel and Christopher said hello to Vivia Crane, Toni Talton, Mary Kohn, and Alex Silver. "Welcome back to hell!" Christopher said to twenty-eight year-old Ali Hillson, another English Teacher.

"What...with just one year here...and you're already jaded?" Ali laughingly asked.

"So it should take me the extra years here…that you have in…to become that way?" Christopher joked back.

"At least I'm not cynical about the kids…I have a chance…we have a chance to fix them…before my husband and his colleagues have to." She was referring to her husband's vocation of being a police officer in New York City. "It's just that the yearly changes they give us…always some new *fakokta* program…some new way to teach…that's going to make all of the difference in the world. I wish the Board of Education would just trust the veteran teachers to do their jobs…without all of the new ridiculous stuff annually," Ali said.

"I understand that we're no longer English Teachers this year…now we're called Language Arts Teachers," Christopher said. "And also now… before each daily ten minute "mini" lesson…you know, before the kids allegedly get all of their meaningful learning done in groups…now each child is supposed to stand at his desk, and rub his or her belly twenty-five times with the left hand, while rubbing his or her head with the right hand…the same number of times."

"That will improve motor coordination...which will enhance academic performance!" Ali laughed. Then she added, "We'll have a four point rubric chart on our classroom walls, to grade the kids on how they rub."

"Yeah," Christopher said. "Two points will be 'Approaching Rubbing Standards.'"

Ali laughed and then turned to C. Wel and said, "My…don't you look svelte! You must have played a lot of racquetball this summer. And that George Hamilton-like tan! You look pretty good for a fifty-four year-old dirty old man."

And before C. Wel could respond Christopher said, "Actually…C. Wel took his dingy out on Long Island Sound…the weekend after school ended last June…and he was just adrift all summer long in the Atlantic. The Coast Guard finally found his lost, bathtub sailor, burnt, eating-raw-sea-shit-and-drinking-rainwater emaciated ass last week!"

"Hey fuck you porky…and I've got your dingy right here…but it's really the QEII!" C. Well said to Christopher. And then he pinched some of Christopher's belly fat and added, "Floating adrift without a few meals this summer wouldn't have hurt you." And then he turned to Ali and joked, "Why don't you do something productive, Blondie…like stay home and make some babies with your husband?"

Ali Hillson laughed and then walked into the school. "Great…I love having my balls broken on the first day!" C. Wel said, and then he lit another cigarette.

Other familiar faces, Heath Brown, Theresa Saperstein, Regina Roberts, Nancy Dupree, Steve Sutherland, and Deana Thomas walked by and said hello to C. Wel and Christopher. Then they both saw Salome as she walked past and entered the school.

"SCHWINGGG!" Christopher said. "Who was *that*?"

"Don't know," C. Wel said, "But she's a total knockout…even with the short hair, granny dress, and big glasses."

After Salome had switched to the School of Education at NYU, she had become a part of an accelerated fellows program. This program allowed her to complete her MA in English Education and to become provisionally certified in just two semesters. She had finished half of her Education credits between late January and mid-May of 2000, and the second half between June and August, while doing her required student teaching, with supervision, during summer school from June 29th until August 11th.

Salome had been assigned to a summer school program at a middle school in the Bronx. She had been very fortunate, in that she had learned much about how to teach middle school English to children while in the Bronx. In the Bronx she had been teamed with a seasoned professional. On the last day of summer school, Salome had received her appointment to Essex Street for September. This Monday would be her first solo flight as a teacher, and Salome was hoping that the four days of staff development would ease some of her jitters. After Salome ate half of a bagel, she sat down in a fold-down hard wooden seat in the auditorium, and she rubbed her belly nervously.

Actually, that jittery feeling had been inside of Salome since this past December, after hearing the tragic news about Nancy. To be sure there were several trips to church weekly, but Salome had begun overeating at that time, as a way to cope with the tragedy. And then the way in which she coped with the feeling of being bloated from the overeating, was to rub her belly. Now, although she had gone back to her normal amount of food consumption, whenever she ate anything, she would rub her belly.

During her very first trip to Europe this past August after summer school, to celebrate her fortieth birthday and her new profession, in which she had taken Walter Lee, as she and her eleven year-old son sat outside at a small café in Paris drinking cappuccinos and eating napoleons, Salome began rubbing her belly. Although she was only ten pounds over her normal weight, it was all in one location. Walter Lee had said, "Mom… rubbing your large pot belly…is not going to make it go away!"

And Salome had laughed, gotten up and tickled her son, and then rubbed his mouth and said, "Maybe…I can make this large mouth go away!"

At 8:45, forty-five year-old African-American Principal Jonathan Greely, a veteran of teaching English in New York City for a total of ten years in two different schools, an assistant principal for a total of five years at three different schools, and principal at Essex Street for five years, asked the auditorium of noisy teachers to stop talking and to move down front, so he could begin the program. After a few brief announcements, who got married, who got engaged, who had a child, who died, who published a novel, etc., Principal Greely said, "I know…as teachers…we all get stuck in our own particular groove…as to the best way to teach our students. We are often reticent…to try something new. This year, our school has been mandated to use the program, *Students Can Achieve More* (SCAM). Your department heads, when we break into our departmental meetings, will explain in detail, how the SCAM program will be utilized in your particular field." After some mumbling from disgruntled teachers, Principal Greely continued, "Although she won't be here until tomorrow, due to a family tragedy, Ms. Othella Fender will again be our Sixth Grade Assistant Principal this year. Our hearts and prayers go out to Ms. Fender, at this time of her bereavement. Mr. James Winkler…" And then Principal Greely pointed to his right at an older balding man holding a stack of papers to be distributed to the teachers, "will continue as our Seventh Grade Assistant Principal. But now I would like to introduce a newcomer to our Essex Street family. Our new Eighth Grade Assistant Principal, and the new Head of Language Arts, Dr. Lipzelda Merkin."

Dr. Merkin stood up in the front row and faced the faculty. She was a stout Irish woman in her early forties, with shoulder-length frizzy auburn hair, and her facial expression was almost robotic. "Principal Greely, Assistant Principal Winkler, and staff...I would like to take this opportunity…to say what a privilege it is to be a supervisor at Essex Street Middle School… and I am sure that we will all work together to have a great year…to help our wee ones learn…and to finally get off of the state's list," and then Dr. Merkin sat down. The "list" that she was referring to was the Corrective Action list, which meant that a school in New York was not producing high enough math and reading scores from its student body. And, of course, being labeled a Corrective Action school, meant that all of this federal and state money was thrown at the school, along with new programs like SCAM, to try and correct the academic deficiencies. After three years of Corrective Action status, if there wasn't enough improvement, a school became a SURR school. A SURR school was a School Under Regents Review, which meant that the state took the school over, dumped even more state and federal money there, added even more new-fangled programs, removed the principal and assistant principals, and reassigned about sixty-five percent of the faculty. After a few years under SURR status, if a school still wasn't improving enough, that school was just closed down. Essex Street never had this problem, until three years ago, when another middle school in the same district had been shut down by the state, and about seventy percent of that student body had been transferred to Essex Street.

Most of the teachers at Essex Street were excellent, and they knew exactly how to teach, no matter how hard a student tried not to learn. The frustration for most teachers was two-fold: First, there was the time wasted with new programs. For what had been English but was now Language Arts, classes were taught in two-period blocks of eighty-six minutes. Last year, part of the requirement for teachers in *that* program, *Students Tackling and Understanding Possibilities Independently and with Detail* (STUPID) had been close to the same as the new SCAM program in which they were about to be educated; but it was different enough, with SCAM's own version of "education-speak," so that yet another private corporation could turn a profit on a school's educational woes.

The federal mandate of, "No Child Left Behind," was really just the federal government saying, "Hey…we don't know what to do about our educational problems…in fact…we've figured out that the 'dummying down' of our American society can actually be financially advantageous to our economic agenda…But hey…come up with some clever doctorial dissertation while you're in graduate school in your Schools of Education…and we don't even care if it's just old rehashed Edna Rosenblatt from the 1930's…with her concept of group cooperative education…And especially if you're a person of color…we'll be happy to throw you a bunch of money…and to watch you fail also."

The eighty-six minute double period would begin with thirty minutes of independent reading, with students choosing either Young Adult Fiction short novels, short story collections, plays, poetry, or nonfiction biographies, autobiographies, and "How to" books. This idea most English teachers endorsed, because most English teachers recognized the importance in just reading—no matter what was being read. (Christopher Jeremy had said last year, "Hell…It was *Penthouse Magazine* and the "Forum" section that got me reading…then I graduated to Henry Miller's, *The Tropic of Cancer*!") And the notion, when forced to read, because a rubric grade of one to four was being given daily during the independent reading segment that the child would choose something that wasn't too difficult—a typical classroom library had two to three hundred books, most at the grade's own reading level, but enough either lower or higher books to accommodate all students—as opposed to a teacher handing out the same story to be read, with some students having great difficulty understanding it, and other students bored that it was beneath them, was a good idea. The important thing was to get the child reading. (Independent Reading Rubric: 1=Below Standards When Independently Reading, which meant that the child was just fooling around during reading time, and when asked questions about what he or she was reading, for teacher anecdotals, he or she would just look back at the teacher with a blank expression; 2=Approaching Standards When Independently Reading, which meant that the child was kind of reading and kind of fooling around during reading time, and when asked questions about what he or she was reading, the child could say something like, "I'm reading *Black Beauty*, and it's about a horse;" 3=Meeting Standards When Independently Reading, which meant that the child only occasionally fooled around during reading time, and he or she could answer a number of questions about what he or she was reading; 4=Beyond Meeting Standards When Independently Reading, which meant that the child rarely fooled around, and he or she could answer just about any question the teacher put forth about the text, and with great detail.)

After the independent reading however, most English teachers wanted to be free to teach new material in a chronologically intelligent order. Some of those lessons could be taught in ten to fifteen minutes, with some of those lessons indeed receiving positive reinforcement from intelligent group activity designed intelligently by the teacher. But there were other lessons—although group activity later to prepare for a quiz might be a good idea—that just needed to be taught straight up to students individually in thirty to forty minutes. And then the unthinkable might have to occur, in that the student might actually have to go home, study, and memorize how to spell and what the definitions were, for this week's twenty-word vocabulary quiz. There was really no other way to learn certain things other than to just go home and study.

Christopher Jeremy had said last year, "When I took Biology in high school, I was forced to learn the names of all of the bones in the human body…so I went home and studied and studied. I can still recite the names to this day. And you know…it didn't kill me…having to learn them. And no amount of group activity in the world would have replaced the needed memorization." Christopher Jeremy had also said last year, "With all of the time being accounted for during a typical STUPID two-period block, there really isn't time to just read to my students. Although individual reading daily is important, I also feel that reading a story, in which each student's eyes are focused on the English that has been written on the page, and each student's ears are hearing the teacher pronounce the words correctly, and with the teacher stopping and explaining main idea, details, inferences, and foreshadowing devices while being engaged with the text as a class, is a great way to help our students in their understanding of both the literature and the language structure. And since our brain, even if we hate the story we're being forced to look at and listen to, steals syntax from the professional writing in front of us, when I read to my students, it helps their writing also. But there's little time to do that…with this STUPID program."

And this, of course, led to the second complaint of most teachers: some parents, usually of the worst students, weren't supervising and asking to see the homework that a child had brought home. Ali Hillson had said last year to Christopher Jeremy and Social Studies Teacher Heath Brown, "I called the father of one of my students last week and told him that his son wasn't studying, and that he was failing my class. The father said to me, 'What the hell do you want me to do about it?' And I said, 'Gee…I don't know…I guess if you want your son to succeed, you'll spend some time with him each evening…and ask him what he learned in school today…ask to see his homework…and then look at that homework when it's been completed.'" And he then told me that he and his wife both worked two jobs, and there just wasn't time to check his son's homework nightly. I told him I understood, I told him I empathized, but I also told him that my job was to teach his son…not to raise him. He told me to 'F off,' and then he hung up on me."

"Some of these parents should be rounded up and arrested for Educational Neglect," Heath had said.

"I have an idea," Christopher had said. "A bunch of teachers should rent a flat bed truck and a few bull horns. Then, on a Saturday morning, we should pull up in front of the homes of our worst students, and announce through the bull horns, so the whole neighborhood can hear, what a shitty job those parents are doing!"

"I was in a bookstore last week," Principal Greely continued in the auditorium, "and I saw this children's picture book...and it intrigued me. I thought, in light of how difficult it is for some of us to change how we teach, that this book would be a propos for the first day of staff development." And then Principal Greely read and showed the pictures of the children's book, *Somebody Moved My Cheese.* This was a cute story, and the message was clearly, "Don't get uptight when things get changed around!"

After the story, Christopher Jeremy raised his hand. And, after being recognized by Principal Greely, Christopher just had to ask, "What if one is lactose intolerant?"

That received a good laugh in the auditorium. Even Salome laughed, which since last November, had only occurred a few other times. Principal Greely said to Christopher, "You would be the one to think of that!"

After the paperwork had been handed out to the teachers, and Principal Greely had gone over "The Law Refresher," that which a teacher could not do with a student, such as send the student to the teacher's cafeteria to get the teacher's lunch, and that which a teacher had to do as a "mandated reporter," such as report any knowledge of child abuse at home, he told the various subject areas which rooms were being used for the meetings. All Language Arts Teachers had to report to the library.

Once everyone was seated in the library, Dr. Lipzelda Merkin addressed the fourteen teachers. Christopher Jeremy noticed, that once again this year, he was the only male in the department. "It is very important that your lessons are chunked together in ten minute mini lessons. The best learning comes from small ten minute lessons," she said.

Christopher raised his hand and was recognized. "What if one just has to teach a maxi lesson?" he asked. That got a laugh, and he continued, "I teach my kids three tenses of a verb, simple present, past, and future all at in one lesson. If I teach the verb 'to walk,' as an example, I can get them to understand first, second, and third person, in present, past, and future tenses, using boxes on the board with pronouns, explaining how all names, either people or objects are third person, and modeling plenty of sentence examples in thirty to forty minutes. Doing my lesson after their thirty minutes of independent reading, will still leave sixteen to twenty-six minutes for group work, in which various sentences are written on the board, with the verb form left blank, and after the sentence, in parenthesis, which tense of the verb form is to be used. And they have to figure out person, which isn't that difficult, they see on the board from the boxes that if it's "I" or "We" at the beginning of a sentence it has to be first person, if the sentence starts with "You" it has to be second person, and everything else is either singular or plural third person. These sentences are solved in the group, and that reinforces the lesson I've taught. That is a very effective lesson. With all due respect, Ms. Merkin, with all there is to teach these kids before their state tests in January, I'd rather not blow off three days teaching this in three ten minute segments, when the kids I taught last year, even the ones who were 'a few fries short of a happy meal,' understood everything in just one big thirty minute teacher-directed lesson."

"What is your name…sir?" Dr. Merkin asked.

"Mr. Jeremy."

"Mr. Jeremy…first of all…my name is *Dr.* Merkin. Secondly…some of our children are just a wee bit 'challenged.' We *never* describe them as you did."

"Sorry for the colorful non-politically correct description…but what about my point? That not always…but sometimes our kids can learn what needs to be learned in a thirty minute lesson."

"I'm sorry Mr. Jeremy, but the district mandates that we 'chunk'… that we teach in ten minute mini lessons…and you will comply."

And Christopher said he would, and then he whispered to Ali Hillson, "Only when I know that she might be coming around."

"You're such a rebel," Ali whispered back.

"Hey…my room is gonna look like 'Rubric City.' Everything will seem to be in perfect alignment with the SCAM method. But then I'll teach the way I know will work. Fuck their 'this year's flavor' style of education."

@@@@@@@@

The Rutland Tattler
by
Jebediah Witherspoon

Howdy friends, and welcome to a special Christmas 2000 edition of The Rutland Tattler. Much has been happening in our fine community, so without further ado, let's get to it.

How about that Apple family? Has there ever been an edition of The Tattler column in any Rutland Free Press, at least since 1982, when I began writing it, that hasn't included at least two or three items about the Apple family?

Congratulations are in order to Jennifer Apple Morgan, 48, at The Woman's Center, and her husband-to-be, Dr. Alan Portman, 58, the OBGYN who bought her deceased husband's practice, and then, apparently, began practicing other things with Jennifer. The two just announced a June Wedding. Since Dr. Portman is Jewish, we say "Mazel Tov!"

And on the subject of Apple marriages, up in Burlington, prison guard Jimson Apple, 43, was married for the second time during this past Thanksgiving weekend, to Officer Diana O'Malley, 38, a ten-year veteran of the Burlington Police Department. If you will recall, Jimson Apple was involved in that "sticky" business with his ex-wife, Lizzie Mitner Apple Williams, 43, and Rutland native son and now resident of Burlington, multi-millionaire and current husband of Lizzie Mitner Apple Williams, Harold Williams, 43, in which, forever after, Harold and Lizzie Williams would always be known as "The Stuck Up Couple From Burlington." And, on a much more somber note, it was Jimson and Lizzie Mitner Apple Williams' daughter, Nancy, 18, who, just one short year ago, was found brutally murdered and raped in New Jersey. Our hearts still go out to them. We also understand that Lizzie Mitner Apple Williams, having miscarried a child last year (a boy five months along) is now out of Greenwood Sanitarium in Rutland, back home, and we're proud to announce, pregnant (a girl three months along).

And while we're still in Burlington, we understand native son Bubba Apple, 80, the

man who many years ago blew the right testicle off of the now deceased Gus Strattus, is in Burlington Mercy Hospital, and quite ill. Our prayers go out to this colorful character who, for years, was a legend in these here parts.

And on the subject of legends, another Apple, Cindy Apple Chumwell, 47, married

to Dick Chumwell, 48, besides having the only organic apple growing business in Rutland, having had the foresight to know that would be the next big thing, just announced a July wedding for their eldest daughter, Tonya, 25, to Burlington criminal defense attorney, Russell Andersen, 27.

Finally, while still on the subject of Rutland legends, Blanchard Apple Jr., aka Bruiser Apple, 45, has just purchased property within the city limits of Rutland. When asked why he wanted the four-apartment unit, Bruiser Apple wheezed..."So my family can...get away from it...all out at the...orchard and just relax...in beautiful downtown Rutland...Besides, it's an investment...the rent I make...from the three units...makes me money and...gives my family a...free apartment." Free rent and profit notwithstanding, this reporter thinks that Bruiser Apple has his eye on a city council seat, and maybe even the mayor's chair, in an attempt to change zoning

to include Rutland County, not just the city of Rutland. This zoning change ploy might be a way to hurt his brother-in-law's business, by evoking the city of Rutland's Smell Ordinance, which would stop Dick Chumwell from using manure and compost on his adjacent property.

Buying the four-unit apartment building, in downtown Rutland, might just be a way for Bruiser Apple to establish residency within the city limits. We'll have to wait and see, but this reporter believes that "Mayor" Apple might not sound too unusual in the future.

In other Rutland gossip, Dr. Bill Wicks, 79, the "other man" in the sensational Smith divorce of years ago, said recently, that there is absolutely no truth to the rumor, that soon, circulating on the Internet, there will be real, non-composite photographs of him, from years ago, having sex with barnyard animals.

Dr. Wicks also went on to say...

@@@@@@@@

"So it turned out...that B. Jenko was African-American?" Walter Lee Younger asked Felix on the phone. It was New Years Day 2001, and Felix had called from Alaska to say hello.

"What did Felix say?" Annie Younger asked her husband.

"Hang on...'Licks...let me tell Annie." And then Walter Lee took a sip of his now-getting-cold chamomile tea and said, "That detective agency 'Licks hired out of Denver, sent an operative to watch the post office box in Manhattan...you know...the box where Beverly Kulpa had been getting her social security checks until the late 1980's...until social security labeled her 'deceased'...and then somebody using the name of B. Jenko...which is pretty close to 'Lick's mother's maiden name...Beverly Jenkowitz...started getting both her social security and apparently CIA pension checks at that same box...from 1990 on..."

"So did they find Felix's mom?"

"Well no," Walter Lee said. "The female operative watched the box on the first and second of last month...when social security and pension checks are usually sent...and on the early evening of December 2nd, an African-American woman came into the post office, opened the B. Jenko box, and removed the checks. The operative carefully followed the woman from the post office to where she lived, just about seven blocks away on Allen Street in the lower eastside of Manhattan. The apartment's mailbox also had B. Jenko's name. The next day, after B. Jenko had left, the operative broke into her apartment and looked through all of her stuff. She reported back to her boss in Denver, and he just reported to 'Licks, that B. Jenko lives alone, there's no sign of another woman living with her, in fact, there are neither pictures out nor albums of pictures anywhere in the drawers of her apartment. B. Jenko seems to be a total loner."

"Well...that's kind of strange," Annie said. "You would think, an old woman, living alone, would at least have a picture or two of *somebody* out... something that would remind her of either her youth...or loved ones missed... and at the very least...even if not out...she would have a few picture albums in her drawers."

"I think you're right!" Walter Lee said, and then he stood up while he still cradled the phone between his ear and shoulder, and pulled Annie onto his lap, kissed her on the back of the neck, and said, "I knew it was more than just your peppered fish...the reason why I married you."

And Annie whispered into Walter Lee's ear, "I thought it was because I was so good in bed!"

And Walter Lee said, "That too," before he said to Felix, "Annie thinks it is pretty unusual...for an older woman living alone...to not have some kind of pictures either out or in albums in drawers...that either remind her of when she was young...or loved ones who have died along the way."

And then Felix, in his mind, first got angry with David Summers, thinking that this fancy detective agency he had paid a lot of money to, should have thought of that, then Felix got angry with himself, thinking that as a writer of fiction, he should have thought of that, but then he remembered that he also hadn't thought of Salome's theory, in "The Case of the Slippery Seagull Shit" either, from after Terry's fall in 1961 until Salome had explained it all to him in 1997. So Felix said nothing but, "I'm going to discuss Annie's theory with the detective agency, that something isn't quite right inside that apartment."

Then Walter Lee said, "By the way...Lena and Sam called earlier from Atlanta...Lena is preggers...and they're expecting around the end of July."

"Congratulations...Grandfather Lee!" Felix said.

"Thanks," Walter Lee said. "Jack and Geneva don't know yet…They took Lorelei, Lani, and the new boyfriend Lani met at the University of Tampa Bay…camping for the weekend in Ocala National Forest. I tried to get them on their cells…they must be out of range." Then he added, "I got called by the State Department last week!" After Felix asked why, Walter Lee continued, "Yeah…this bozo called me up and said, 'Dr. Younger…the Mauritanian Ambassador is very unhappy with the article you just had published in *The New York Times*. To write an article, talking about how blacks still enslave blacks currently…in Mauritania…doesn't help the United States government at all.' And I said, 'Okay…but it's true.' And he said, 'And then to say…that the Mauritanian Ambassador…has slave help from his country working for him in New York…' 'But that's true too,' I said. And then he said, 'With all due respect Dr. Younger…we need to keep Mauritania happy. Not only do they have oil and uranium that we need…but they serve as a civilized bookend…on the west coast of Africa…along with Egypt on the east coast…to help keep those more radical countries in the middle between them…The Sudan, Libya, Algeria, and Tunisia…in check. We don't want to piss off the Mauritanians!' And I said, 'Sorry about that…but the United States' agenda doesn't concern me…I'm just concerned with the truth.'"

"And what did the State Department dude say then?" Felix asked.

"He told me…'Life is pretty good for you these days Dr. Younger…but that could all change.'"

"Wow…that sounds pretty ominous!" Felix said.

"I'll be seventy-four next September. This is 2001. I don't frighten that easily anymore, 'Licks. I can move into any housing subdivision in this country that I want to…and I can write whatever I want to also."

"I don't know…Dangerous Lee…There are probably some subdivisions in Idaho…that you might want to avoid," Felix said.

"I can move anywhere…and write anything," Walter Lee said.

"God…I certainly hope so," Felix said.

@@@@@@@@

"Finally…I was worried about you, Bev," The seventy-two year-old African-American woman said to the seventy-eight year-old white woman, as the seventy-eight year-old white woman made her way toward the appropriate part of Battery Park, next to the Staten Island Ferry Terminal, on this Thursday evening in early April of 2001.

"Are you with the government?" Beverly Jenkowitz Kulpa asked as she approached the African-American woman.

"No Bev…it's your best friend…Joanne…remember me? I'm the one who gets your checks and cashes them…and then brings you your money every Thursday night."

"Are you with the government?" Beverly asked again.

"I used to be...years ago...just like you. Don't you remember? I'm helping you to avoid the government, Bev...That's why you live out on the streets...and have me bring you your money."

"Joanne?"

"Joanne Watson...remember now?"

"Yes...you're my best friend Joanne."

"Okay Bev...remember how we do this?"

"Right pocket money," Bev said, "Left pocket instructions!"

"That's right...Bev. And when do you look at the instructions...to remind you where we are meeting?" Joanne asked.

"Every Thursday, when the sun is going down."

"Good girl...Bev. Now you know...next Thursday at ten o'clock...it's just inside of Central Park...at West 72nd Street...near the Strawberry Fields plaque...right? And you'll look in the left inside pocket of your coat...to remember where we're meeting..."

"Next Thursday...as the sun is going down."

"Very good...Bev. Now here's this week's money. Put it away in..."

"In the right inside pocket of my coat," Beverly Jenkowitz Kulpa said.

@@@@@@@@

"Please excuse this interruption...but there till ee a mormal lanceee in dey tolin ley this 'ternoon," The public address system crackled in Christopher Jeremy's room.

Christopher asked his eighth grade Language Arts students, during their quiet independent reading time, "Could anybody make out that announcement?"

"I couldn't understand it at all, Mr. J.," Juan Hernandez said.

"Me neither," Julie Crawford said.

Christopher Jeremy looked across the hall, and saw that Salome Apple's door was open. She taught seventh grade Language Arts, but at the moment she had a preparatory period, and she was working at her desk. It was already late April 2001, and Christopher had been wanting to ask Salome out all year. But at the beginning of the year, she had been so aloof. And although there had been moments of small talk in the hall between classes, at lunch in the teacher's cafeteria, and at the weekly Language Arts meeting, it had only been in the last month that Christopher had felt as if he might be making some headway toward having a chance. Christopher noticed that Salome now laughed more at his jokes, and that she had begun growing her hair out, she was obviously wearing contact lenses these days, and her clothing had become considerably less conservative. "Keep reading quietly guys...I'm leaving the door open...I need to ask Ms. Apple if she could understand that announcement." And then Christopher stuck his head in Salome's room and said, "Hey Salome...did you understand that announcement?"

"Absolutely not, Chris," Salome said.

"It sounded to me like, 'There will be a formal dance in the bowling alley this afternoon!'" Chris said.

That blew Salome away, and she laughed harder than she had laughed in three years, since when her son was eight, and they had been out with Felix, and Salome had told Walter Lee, "Since your grandmother was Jewish, you'll always be welcome in Israel," and Walter Lee had asked, "But weren't Jewish people being killed in Germany just because they were Jewish?" And Felix had said, "Yes, during World War II," and then he and Salome had explained about Hitler's attempt at genocide, and Walter Lee had said, "But I have such *little* Jewish blood, Mommy!"

"I just love your laugh," Christopher said.

"Well...you're a real funny guy," Salome said.

"Would you like to go out sometime?" Christopher asked.

"I'd love to," Salome said. Actually, since Bubba had had a quadruple bypass in January, was recovering nicely at home, and she didn't have to worry about her mom as much, and since time itself had begun to ease some of the pain and guilt she had felt over Nancy's murder on her watch, Salome had been thinking in the past two months, that she'd like to go out with Christopher, and that he kind of reminded her of a young Felix. Even though Christopher was twelve years younger than she was, that was a prejudice that she had long since outgrown. Her only concern had been his religion, or lack thereof. Christopher had told everyone that he was an Atheist. Although Salome didn't think that she could ever be with someone long term who didn't believe in God, Christopher made her laugh, and that was exactly what she needed at this time in her life. Besides, there was the issue of Salome's curiosity. Perhaps it was what Joni Mitchell sang in "A Case of You," that, "I'm frightened by the Devil, and I'm drawn to those ones who aren't afraid."

"Well...this Friday night my band is playing on Staten Island, and this Saturday night, the off-off-off Broadway musical I wrote is opening in Manhattan, on Ludlow Street, just a little south of Houston. I realize that if you went with me to either of those events, it wouldn't be the traditional dinner and movie first date!"

"I live on Staten Island...where is your band playing?"

"In the Great Kills section on Nelson Avenue, at a place called *The Swiss Chalet*," Christopher said.

"I think I know where that is," Salome said. "I didn't even know you were a musician...what do you play?"

"I play guitar and I sing," Christopher Jeremy said. "I'm in a band with my fifty year-old father, Ron, he plays keyboards and also sings. The drummer, John, is his age. The bass player, Arturo, is my age. We call ourselves, *Disabled Dad*, and we play rock from both the Sixties…my dad's thing…which he sings…and the Nineties…my thing...which I sing."

"Wow…how long have you guys been playing together?" Curious Salome asked.

"For three years now," Christopher said. "I got my Masters in Education from Columbia University five years ago, and then I joined the Peace Corps. I spent one year in Burkina Faso teaching, practicing guitar, and I wrote a couple of plays. When I got back to New York three years ago, my dad and his friend John the drummer, wanted to put together a band. They thought I sounded pretty good, and I had known Arturo the bass player for years. Voila! There's my story!"

"Wow," Salome said again. "Tell me about your play," she added.

"Uh…I think maybe I should wait until after the first date…to tell you about my play. Do you want to go hear us play Friday night?"

"That sounds great…I'm sure I can get my son's regular sitter from my building."

"That would be wonderful," Christopher said.

"What time do you start?"

"Nine o'clock until one…we play four sets of forty-five minutes each."

"Okay…but we get out of school at two-forty on Friday afternoon…and you have to eat dinner…Do you want to come to my place on Staten Island for dinner…before the show?"

"I'd love to," Christopher said, "But I have to get the equipment out of the basement of my place in East Elmhurst…and the other three guys get off from work between five and six. Anyway…they usually don't get to my place until around six thirty, and then it takes about thirty minutes to pack up, and then we still have to drive in rush hour traffic to Staten Island, set up, and be ready to start at nine. There's just no way I ever have time when we play on a Friday night, to do more than just drive through a hamburger joint on the way. Could I get a rain check on your generous offer?"

"I'll do better than that," Salome said. "You do what you have to do, and I'll bring dinner for you, your dad, and the other two guys, at *The Swiss Chalet* at eight-thirty."

"Wow," said Christopher, already sounding like Salome. And then he heard something that sounded like Ca Thump Ca Thump.

Chapter Eighteen

"I'll go down to the basement...and get the money from my asshole boss," Monte Vandenburg, the bartender and manager of *The Swiss Chalet*, said. It was already two-twenty in the morning, *Disabled Dad* had stopped playing at one-ten, had packed the van and car entirely by one-fifty, and now were sitting around having a few beers, waiting to be paid the promised $300 for the four sets of music, on this late Friday night/early Saturday morning in late April of 2001. Christopher sat away from the other band members, at a table in the dark, canoodling with Salome, not caring that they hadn't been paid yet, just hoping that this evening would never end. He finally asked Salome, "When does your babysitter expect you home?"

"I told her two, but she usually just sleeps over in the upstairs loft. She lives in my building with her parents. She'll call me...if she needs me."

The "to die for" linguini, shrimp, scallops, with pesto sauce, along with the incredible antipasto salad, doused in extra virgin olive oil and balsamic vinegar, complete with rolled prosciutto, artichoke hearts, and fresh mozzarella balls, the fresh bread, and the tiramisu dessert, that Salome had brought to *The Swiss Chalet* for Christopher and his band mates, and was plentiful enough to also feed the bartender/manager, his two assistants, and Salome herself, was perhaps the nicest thing that a woman had ever done for Christopher. And, upon reflecting on just that, Christopher had thought, 'Well...perhaps the *second* nicest thing!' Christopher's dad, the rest of the band, and the *Swiss Chalet* staff had all been knocked out by the food.

Disabled Dad had opened the first set with a twin-pack, Christopher singing Billy Joel's, "Out Here in No Man's Land," which, by its very chord structure, segued nicely into Christopher's father singing *The Spencer Younger Group's*, "Give Me Some Lovin.'" Salome was immediately impressed with how good the band sounded. Christopher then announced to the crowd, just before the last song of the first set, "We'd like to end this set with a song from the early 1980's. We rarely do songs from that time period, but this is a group that both my father and I have always liked. Unfortunately, they only recorded two hard-to-find records." And then *Disabled Dad* covered *Home Cooking's*, "The Inner Bitch."

After the song and set were finished, Salome had said to Christopher, "Hey...I know those guys in *Home Cooking*...in fact the keyboard player and one of the writers of the songs, Felix Kulpa, is the brother of my deceased husband...and my son's uncle." And although Christopher had been interested in hearing about Felix and stories about *Home Cooking* from Salome, when they stepped outside for the band's fifteen-minute break, he had leaned up against the side of his van and taken Salome into his arms and kissed her passionately. Salome was very excited by that kiss, it had been awhile since she had been kissed like that.

The last set of the evening had ended with yet another deviation from *Disabled Dad's* eclectic 1960's and 1990's only music, a song from the late 1970's, that featured Christopher's singing and incredible guitar work, *Pink Floyd's*, "Comfortably Numb." That song went over so well—the crowd was really into it—that the band, by popular demand, had agreed to an encore. "What would you like to hear?" Christopher asked the crowd.

Monte yelled from behind the bar, "Do you know *Pink Floyd's*, "Wish You Were Here?"

Christopher said from the stage, after discussing it with the others, "We know the music...but nobody remembers all of the lyrics."

Then Monte yelled back, "I know the lyrics." So Monte was invited up, the band played "Wish You Were Here," and Monte did a great job of singing it. Christopher and his father provided the backup vocals.

But now it was approaching two-thirty, and Christopher's dad was getting a little testy. Finally, Monte came up the stairs from the basement, $300 in hand, and said, "Sorry it took so long for my boss to get his shit together!" Everybody thanked Monte and left.

Outside, Christopher walked Salome to her car. Leaning up against the front fender of Salome's *Cobra*, they made out some more.

"Get a room," said two girls walking across the parking lot.

"It would be nice if there were a place to go," Christopher said.

"Follow me back to my place. You'll have to leave your van on the street...I don't have an extra spot."

"Well actually...with all of the equipment inside...I'd rather not leave it on the street. I could have my dad drive it home however, and I guess I can figure out how to get home later."

"I'm sure we'll figure something out…later," And then Salome kissed Christopher again, and Christopher went to find his dad and give him the van keys. When he returned, he and Salome both climbed into the *Cobra*. "You'll have to be real quiet at my place…don't want anybody waking up."

Christopher assured her that he would be as quiet as the proverbial church mouse. And then he smiled and thought, 'I wonder how quiet you're gonna be?'

Inside of her apartment, Salome led Christopher by the hand to her bedroom. And there, reverting to her old pre-Felix way of thinking, Salome and Christopher did almost everything, as quietly as possible.

At six o'clock in the morning, Salome woke Christopher up and said, "We need to get you out of here…before everybody wakes up."

"No problem," Christopher said. "I'll take the ferry next door, and then grab a train back to Queens."

"I'm getting dressed…I'm gonna drive you home," Salome said.

"Don't be ridiculous. You just relax in bed…I'm sure you're tired. It was a hard week at school…I'll see you later tonight."

"I don't want my man having to take public transportation all the way back to Queens at six o'clock in the morning!" Salome said.

"Oh…so I'm 'your man' now?" Christopher smiled and asked, as he was putting his jeans on.

"I think so," Salome said. "Am I your woman?"

Christopher looked at her lovingly, nodded, kissed her, and then said, "Don't worry about me and public transportation…Salome…believe me… I'm gonna be floating on air…all of the way home."

"Okay…if you're sure," Salome said. Then she asked, "So we're gonna meet at *Katz's Deli* at six o'clock this evening?"

"Yeah…if that's what you want for dinner," Christopher said. "We can go anywhere you want to eat…but the play starts at eight…and I have to be at the theatre near *Katz's* at seven…But if you want…we could go out somewhere after the play is over…at around ten."

"I'm kinda jonesing for a pastrami sandwich…so let's meet at *Katz's* at six, have a sandwich, and then after the play, we can go down to Little Italy for dessert."

"Sounds good," Christopher said.

The play started precisely at eight o'clock, with the small theatre's other thirty-one seats, all occupied by patrons who had paid five dollars each. Earlier, at four o'clock in the morning, while snuggling up on the bed in the afterglow of passion, when Christopher had explained his play to her, Salome had been a bit skeeved at first. She had said, "Work…for the GOOOD… Christopher…toward the LIIIGHT...away from the DAAARK. Your play sounds EEEVIL!" And Christopher had said, "It isn't EEEVIL...it's just funny!" But now, as she sat next to Christopher the author, upon hearing the opening number and seeing the entire audience laughing hysterically at the writing of her twelve year-younger boyfriend, Salome basked in the Ego-stroke and managed to laugh, even though she still thought what she was seeing was pretty perverse. Christopher Jeremy's play was called *Back to Uranus*. The edition of *Playblurb*, that was distributed at the small *La Puanteur Theatre* on Ludlow Street, had the following synopsis:

This science fiction play is a variation on the standard Romeo and Juliet star-crossed lovers theme, and most of the action takes place in the 1990's. In this version, Romeo Managoo, an Uranusian, is in love with Juliet Port o' let, an Earthling. And, of course, neither of their families approve.

The Uranusians had accidentally crash landed their space ship in the early 1970's at the Staten Island Dump. They've kept their ship hidden, using a cloak, under a trash pile for years, waiting for that time, when world technology would finally catch up, the microchip would be developed, and they could head back to Uranus.

Although the Uranusians look just like Earthlings on the outside, the male Uransians have two penises and the females two vaginas. Fortunately, since the ship was en route to Earth on a long-term anthropological and scientific survey anyway, in which the one-world Ministry of Science had sent their people to just blend in and observe Earth life, with an eye towards "normalcy," an equal number of males and females had been assigned to the mission. Unfortunately—at least from the Uranusian government's point of view—a number of the thirty-four women and thirty-four men were Gay, and others who were Hetero, were just plain appalled by some of their shipmates. This, of course, created some sexual imbalance in regards to "normalcy," so, unbeknownst to either the leaders at home or on Earth, a number of Uransusians had been doing the "interplanetary bop" with Earthlings on the Q-T. It was strictly verboten for the Uranusians to become involved physically with other species, but so far none of the Earthlings had complained, so none of the Uranusians had been busted. Tragically, this won't be the case with Romeo Managoo and Juliet Port o' let. They meet in an Astronomy class at the College of Staten Island, and they both are immediately smitten. They desire each other for several weeks, and finally Romeo tells Juliet that he's an alien. Juliet doesn't believe him, and she says, "You're just saying that...so you can end things with me...before they've even had a chance to begin."

Romeo finally convinces Juliet that he isn't kidding, that he is indeed from another planet, and, when they go to bed, things are going to be slightly different. He prepares Juliet for what to expect, and, after she makes love to Romeo for the first time, she immediately decides to leave it all behind, and to travel back to Uranus with him.

Juliet's family and friends are surprised and devastated, when, in the midst of a big argument with her parents, Juliet fesses up that her love interest and his family are from another planet, and that she will be returning there with them. They report Romeo and his family to the United States Air Force, and some general from Project Bluebook shows up and asks a bunch of questions (in song!).

Meanwhile, Romeo's parents, leaders of the Uranusians on Earth, are working hard on the spaceship under a mound of trash at the Staten Island Dump. They are the last to finally catch wind of the tip off to the United States government, from their son's "I'm so sorry this happened!" teary-eyed confession, so they decide it is time to move the ship, until it is fixed, and they are ready to depart. They find another trash dump—their sensors malfunction so they don't realize it's toxic—in Bayonne, New Jersey, and, in the middle of the night, using just one-quarter impulse power and their cloaking device, they move their vessel.

Romeo's parents and colleagues are also surprised and devastated, when they finally learn, that Romeo has broken Uranusian law, by being intimate with and falling in love with an Earthling. They angrily tell him, "NO!" when he says that he wants to take Juliet with him, back to Uranus.

But nobody is more devastated than Lt. Spacey Brownstar, the Uranusian female who is in love with Romeo. A woman scorned, she leaves New York, and ends up living for awhile in Los Angeles, with brothers who are Siamese twins.

The play ends "tragically," when Lt. Brownstar returns to confront Romeo and Juliet, and they all end up dead in the toxic waste in Bayonne, New Jersey.

Christopher Jeremy had recorded all of the music for the play in his basement. He used his father's *Roland* keyboard for all of the orchestra instruments, his drum machine for the percussion, and he then added guitar and bass, and mixed everything on his eight-track recorder. A DAT was made, and the actors sang along with the instrumental tape on stage.
The musical began with the title song, with the entire cast singing:

We're going back to Uranus someday.
Back where the people are so gay.
Where the Sun don't shine, most of the time,
Back to Uranus this May.

We're going back to Uranus real soon.
Back where the 'roids hide the Moon.
Where the south wind blows, into your nose,
Back to Uranus this June.

The men only sing:

Many years ago, when we needed some,

We'd pray twice, at the Orifice of Hairpie.
But since we had to go,
Where they have just one,
We've learned to love their Moon,
And their K-Y.

The women only sing:

Many years ago, when we needed some,
We'd pray twice, at the Monument of Steel.
But since we had to go,
Where they have just one,
We've learned to love a snack,
Not a full meal.

The entire cast sings:

We're going back to Uranus in July.
Back where you fly the red-eye.
Where you neither smoke crack, nor read Balzac,
Back to Uranus in July.

We're going back to Uranus someday.
Back where the people are so gay.
Where the Sun don't shine, most of the time,
Back to Uranus this May.

@@@@@@@@

It was a Thursday night in late May 2001, and Beverly Jenkowitz Kulpa had read the instructions in her left inside coat pocket a couple of hours earlier, while she had been sitting on a bench in Tompkins Square Park near Tenth Street and Avenue B drinking vodka. She walked into Madison Square Park at Madison Avenue and Broadway, caddy-cornered from the Flatiron Building, at a few minutes before ten o'clock, carrying something wrapped in a handkerchief. She knew that she was supposed to walk on the cement path's forty-five degree angle to the benches next to the statue, and to deliver what was currently wrapped in her hand to somebody there. But she had no idea why.

"Bev…Hi Bev…it's me," Joanne said.

"Do you work for the government?" Bev asked.

"I haven't worked for the government in a long time…Remember Bev…we used to work for the government together…I'm your best friend...Joanne Watson...remember?"

"Joanne...I remember now," Bev said.

"Is that the dead bird and knife wrapped in a handkerchief in your right hand?" Joanne asked.

"Yes," Bev said.

"Did anybody see you kill that bird?"

"No," Bev said and then added, "I did exactly what you said...and what the instructions...the ones wrapped in the handkerchief...with the package of birdseed...and the package of peanuts...and the knife...that were in the left inside pocket of my coat...told me to do."

"And when are you supposed to read those instructions?" Joanne asked.

"On Thursday...as the sun is going down," Bev said. And then Bev reached into her left inside coat pocket and pulled out the sheet of notebook paper and read, "You must kill a bird without anybody seeing...use the birdseed, peanuts, and knife to help you...wrap the dead bird and knife..."

"You needn't read anymore...I wrote those instructions," Joanne said.

"Why did you want...a dead bird?" Bev asked.

"I told you...I can't just bring you your money every Thursday night anymore...I have to ask you for things...from now on...and you have to bring them...for your money." And then Bev handed Joanne the handkerchief with the dead bird and knife inside, and the old instructions, and Joanne handed Bev the weekly envelope of money and asked, "Where does this money go?"

And Bev said, "In the inside right pocket of my coat."

And Joanne, who was carrying a big *Lord and Taylor* shopping bag with clean underwear, socks, jeans, undershirt, sweatshirt, and toiletries inside for Bev, said, "Follow me to the restroom in this park. I'm going to help you to clean up a bit."

As she and Bev walked towards the restroom, without Bev seeing, Joanne opened the handkerchief to make sure that Bev had carried out her mission successfully. Joanne then tossed the dead bird into a garbage can near the restroom, and used the handkerchief to wipe off the knife. Once in the restroom, Joanne covertly flushed the handkerchief and instructions down the toilet, reached into the *Lord and Taylor* bag, removed a black t-shirt from the bag, wrapped it around the knife and this week's instructions, and then handed it all to Bev and said, "Where does this black t-shirt, this knife, and these instructions go?"

"Inside my coat...in my left pocket," Bev said.

"And when do you read them?"

"On Thursday...as the sun is going down." And then Joanne helped to clean up and change Bev, before leaving her in the restroom of Madison Square Park, throwing away her old clothes in a trash can, and walking off into the night.

@@@@@@@@

"I am very disappointed with these reading scores," Dr. Lipzelda Merkin said, at the weekly scheduled fifth period Language Arts meeting in early June 2001. The eighth graders had taken the state ELA reading, writing, and listening test in mid-January, and the seventh graders had taken their city CTB reading test in early April, and it was always early June before the results were known for both.

"I don't think it's practical," Ali Hillson said, "with how much these kids don't know...by the time they arrive in September for their eighth grade year...for the Board of Education to expect them to learn it all...by the time they take their ELA test in January."

"You are being paid well...to make sure you teach them...what they need to know...by mid-January," Dr. Merkin said.

"That isn't very realistic," said Vivia Crane, an eighth grade Language Arts teacher of many years. "When I was in school, I could already spell, and I had a considerably larger vocabulary then most of the eighth graders I teach now. And I understood subject/predicate agreement, and the difference between a sentence and a fragment. These children come to us with limited abilities, and then we are expected to fix them in just four months."

"Ms. Crane," Dr. Merkin said, "I've noticed all year...that your room is very sparse. You need more student generated work on your walls...on your bulletin boards. I hope you'll keep that in mind...for next year."

"More eye candy," Ali Hillson whispered to Christopher Jeremy.

"More 'smoke and mirrors,'" Christopher whispered backed.

"With all due respect Ms. Merkin," Vivia Crane said.

"That's *Dr.* Merkin," Dr. Merkin interrupted.

"*Dr.* Merkin," Vivia said. "I don't see how more poorly written student generated work on my walls...is going to solve the problem. The problem is...our children come to us with an unfortunate lack of skills. I know...by the end of the year...I have helped them. I know...by mid-January when they take the ELA test...I have helped them. I just can't possibly help them enough...in only four months."

"Ms. Crane," Dr. Merkin said. "Many educators...men and women smarter than you and me..."

'That should be "you and *I*,"' Vivia Crane thought.

"...have come up with what really works in the classroom... irregardless of what you may think."

'No such word as *irregardless*,' Vivia Crane thought.

"And if the SCAM program is followed...complete with lots of student generated work all around the classroom," Dr. Merkin continued. "We should be able to see higher reading scores."

"You put an infinite number of chimpanzees...in an infinite number of rooms...with an infinite number of typewriters...and they'll come up with an infinite number of new programs for us to use in the classroom!" Christopher whispered to Vivia, while Dr. Merkin was still pontificating.

"Ms. Merkin," Vivia continued, "I can worry about covering my walls with student work...or I can worry about getting them ready for the test in mid-January..."

"That's *Dr.* Merkin," Dr. Merkin said.

Just then the public address system crackled, "Pleads accuse dis in..errect...shen...Dwill Dakow Merkin...sleaze crawl...x...tension...101. Aden...Dwill Dakow Merkin...sleaze crawl...x...tension...101. Tak...two."

Dr. Merkin walked over to the school phone in the gray box on the wall and made her call. While she was talking, Toni Talton, another eighth grade Language Arts teacher, said to Ali, Christopher, Vivia, Salome, and Theresa Saperstein, "This pacing calendar that the city gave us...is pretty whacked out! According to this, we're not supposed to teach the compare/contrast essay until February...and we're not supposed to teach poetry until April. That makes no sense...since one of the three essays they must write for the ELA test in mid-January is a compare/contrast essay..."

"And sometimes...on the ELA test...one of the things that gets compared/contrasted with an article...is a poem," Theresa Saperstein said.

"Or sometimes...there's a poem...with five or six questions about it in the multiple choice part of the test, " Ali said.

"And sometimes...the questions are impossible to answer," Christopher said. "Did anybody notice...on last January's test...the ambiguous essay question? After the kids had to read two articles...one on President Woodrow Wilson's wife...the other about President FDR's wife...and how they both had worked for women's rights...and then write an essay...using information from both articles...on this question: **What progress have women made in American society in this century?**"

"What's wrong with that question?" Theresa Saperstein asked.

"Well...since 2000 officially ended the last century...and when they took the test it was mid-January 2001...if I were grading a kid's essay...and that child responded...'Gee, I'd love to answer your essay question, but since this century is just two weeks old, it's pretty impossible for me to tell yet, what progress women have made so far'...I'd have to give that kid the highest mark possible...for thinking!"

"I never noticed that!" Theresa said, with everyone else having that in-regards-to-how-the-educational-system-in-this-country-is-run-it-just-figures- look on their faces.

Salome sat and listened. As a seventh grade Language Arts teacher, all she just had to deal with was the city's CTB test. That test was all multiple choice, so Salome's responsibility was to make sure that her children, after reading the articles, could answer the standard different types of multiple choice questions. Salome taught the children as she had been taught, by Iris Heilweil, the seasoned Language Arts Teacher at the Bronx middle school where Salome had student-taught last summer: you should always read the questions first, then read the article, and put check marks in the article when something seems familiar from the questions you've already read, then answer the questions, by going back to what you've checked off in the article.

"I know there's always a poem with multiple choice questions on the CTB," Salome said. "I knew I had to teach my guys poetry before this past April…so hopefully, they'll remember some of what they've been taught…by the time you get them for eighth grade."

"Unfortunately…they remember squat!" Christopher said.

"That's not totally true," Toni Talton said. "They don't remember the terms by name. When I ask if anybody knows what an 'alliteration' is… hardly anybody ever knows. But when I give an example of it…everybody remembers what it is then."

"That's a good point," Theresa Saperstein said.

"That's why teaching these kids vocabulary…is so important," Christopher said. "We should make these kids learn twenty new words a week…complete with proper sentence writing using the new words… along with synonyms and antonyms. If we teach them twenty new words a week…that will be close to 250 new words by the ELA test. Hell…because of their poor vocabularies…some of our kids can neither understand certain key elements in the articles they read nor answer some of the questions after the articles…and that's with already having taught them…how to figure out a word in context…by all of the surrounding words."

"And the poetry words…like 'alliteration'…should definitely be part of those 250," Salome said.

"I have to see Mr. Rellim," Dr. Merkin said, once she had hung up the school phone in its gray box. "Mr. Greely isn't in the building…and an administrative decision has to made…in regards to a student. Please carry on with your discussion. At next week's meeting…I'm expecting each of you to tell me…how you…personally…can help to improve your children's test scores next year."

After Dr. Merkin had left the room Christopher said, "One thing that would help…if we had somebody other than Lippy Merkin running Language Arts…you know…somebody competent!"

"'Lippy' Merkin?" A still annoyed by Dr. Merkin's, 'You're paid well to teach' comment, Ali Hillson, laughingly asked.

"I think that's a great moniker!" Toni Talton added while laughing.

"That sounds like a horse's name!" Theresa Saperstein said. "When I go out to *Belmont* this Friday afternoon…I'm gonna to see if there's a 'Lippy

Merkin' running in any of the races."

"I've never been to a horserace," Salome said. Then she asked Theresa, "Is it fun?"

"Yeah…and I usually win a few dollars," Theresa said and then added, "I'm going with a few other teachers from here…right after school on Friday…Would you like to join us, Salome?"

And curious Salome said that she would, and she added, "I'll go for the experience of just watching it…I'm a Born Again Christian…I don't gamble."

After the meeting, when Christopher and Salome were sitting together in the teacher's cafeteria, before any other teacher got there for sixth period lunch, Christopher said, "I thought you were coming home with me on Friday afternoon…and then going to our gig in Hoboken later."

"I'll go to *Belmont* with Theresa after school, and then I'll drive to Hoboken later…and meet you at *Phil's Back Door*…before you start playing at nine o'clock."

"Yeah…okay," Christopher said. "It's just that my mom looks forward to your company too."

"She's going…right? So just tell her that I'll see her at the club…to save me a seat next to her."

"Okay," Christopher said and then added, "Actually…I'd kinda like to go with you to *Belmont* on Friday."

"You and I can do that some other time," Salome said. "Besides…if you went…you'd be hanging all over me. I don't want anybody here to know that you and I are an item."

"Well that kinda annoys me," Christopher said. "Are you embarrassed by me?"

"Absolutely not…you're my man," Salome said, while trying to get the elusive piece of green *Jell-o*, which was kindly provided for dessert on the teacher's lunch *du jour*, to stay on the plastic "spork."

"So…if I'm 'your man,' why can't people know?" Christopher asked, just a wee bit too loud for Salome's taste.

"Shhh!…Enquiring minds want to know!" Salome said, repeating the slogan of one of the gossip tabloids.

"But there's nobody within earshot," Christopher said. "Besides…I'm so happy that you're my girlfriend…I'd like to go on the school's public address system and announce it to everybody!"

"I'm sure our students would love that," Salome said, just before she finally ate the piece of elusive *Jell-o*.

"The announcement would be: 'Tease defuse dis in…serr ection! Dis is

Mr. Jeremy…an die wood…dike to say…dat die…dasbsulutleeqz…crqslovesqt Ms. Apple!'"

"I'm sure that would get us noticed," Salome said.

"Well…what about the end term party in three weeks? Am I buying tickets for us this week to go together?"

"Yeah…I wouldn't want to miss that," Salome said.

"I assume we're going together…I assume we're going to be sitting together…eating together…dancing together. Won't the faculty have it all figured out in just three weeks?"

"Well…I wanted to talk to you about that. Why don't we take Marsha Bootress with us…she lives on Staten Island…not too far from me…and then it will look as if the three of us just went Platonically."

"You don't think it would look strange to her…if I came all the way from Queens…to pick you two up on Staten Island? She would know she was being used as a…as a…damn…there's a word for it," Christopher said.

"I don't know the word," Salome said.

The word Christopher was looking for was "beard."

"That's why…I'm going to pick Marsha up…then the two of us will pick you up in Queens…since you're kinda on the way to the party at *Douglaston Manor* on Long Island anyway."

"And…after the party…we don't get to go home together?" Christopher asked.

"Not that night…but we do have the whole summer," Salome said. "My son will be with his uncle in Alaska for the last three weeks in July, and then he'll be in Vermont for the first three weeks in August. Other than when I'm in Vermont the first week in August, we'll have plenty of time alone."

"Okay…sure," Christopher said, as he dropped both of their semi-empty styrofoam trays into the trash. But, upon imagining the end term party, his woman dressed to the nines and dancing in her sexy manner, he still wasn't happy that he would have to go home alone that night.

And then, in the dark hallway that connected the teacher's cafeteria to the stairs back up to the first floor, after looking around to make sure they were alone, Salome said, "Give me some sugar," and Christopher quickly obliged.

After lunch, Salome had a seventh period class and Christopher had a preparatory period. Christopher went out to the veranda to grab a quick smoke, before returning to his room to grade homework. When he got outside he saw an angry C. Wel.

"Hey buddy…what's up?" he asked C. Wel.

"That bitch…*Herr* doctor!…is a total piece of work! Okay…you know that Greely is out of the building today, right?"

"Yeah," Christopher said.

"So Madame Merkin is in charge...she's number one on the pecking order...as the Grade Eight AP," C. Wel said.

"That's *Dr.* Merkin," Christopher said.

"Well...Dr. Dumbshit doesn't want to call the police...and she doesn't want to suspend this slime bucket eighth grader...who just molested a seventh grade girl...in the girl's bathroom on the third floor. I've got him cooling his jets in my office...and the girl is in with the school nurse. This sleazeball, James Diaz, should already be doing time on Riker's. I bring the crying girl to see Dr. Dumbshit, and she says, 'We'll start an investigation...
but I really don't want to write an administrative letter of suspense now...and have to take a trip to the district office...and I really don't want to get the police involved...not without talking to Mr. Greely first. We only have three weeks of school left this year.' And I ask her what we're supposed to do with James Diaz...shouldn't we at least put him in in-house suspension for the rest of the year...and she tells me, 'return him to his class.' Meanwhile, the other kids have already gotten wind of this...and I guess, when asshole goes back to class, the other guys will know... 'hey...it's okay to walk into the girl's bathroom...and to grab a seventh grader's tits.'"

"This douche bag just walked into a girl's bathroom...and felt up a seventh grader?" Christopher asked.

"Apparently...it was an Anatomy assignment," C. Wel said sarcastically, while lighting a cigarette.

"It's too bad that Lippy Merkin doesn't have the balls to make the right call," Christopher said, while lighting another cigarette himself.

"'Lippy' Merkin?" C. Wel said, just before his belly laugh temporarily diffused his annoyance.

@@@@@@@@

"Uncle Felix!" Twelve year-old Walter Lee Kulpa had said, when he had gotten off the plane at O'Hare Airport in Chicago, on that Saturday during the second week of July 2001, just before he hugged his uncle. He had added, "You've lost weight! I can actually put my arms totally around you now!"

And Felix had said, "It's not that...it's that you've gotten so big!" It had been three years since Felix had seen more than just photographs of his nephew. Salome was letting Walter Lee spend three weeks with him in Alaska, but since it required two plane changes after leaving JFK, one in Chicago and one in Seattle, she had insisted that Felix meet her son in Chicago and escort him the rest of the way. Felix had agreed. Felix had also agreed to fly with his nephew all the way back to Burlington in time for the Apple family reunion the weekend of August fifth, since, by Walter Lee avoiding a return trip to JFK and going directly to Burlington instead, that gave Felix a few more days with him. Salome had reluctantly agreed to that, but she really didn't want Felix hanging around in Rutland or Burlington with her family, while she was there. Felix was aware that Salome would probably be uncomfortable with him being around her, but he had thought, 'I don't care what she's comfortable with. I like her family…so too bad. I'll bring her something for her forty-first birthday…and then I'll go see my aunt in Plattsburgh.'

On this morning in Alaska, Felix was drinking coffee, eating biscuits, and quietly working on his novel at the computer when his nephew surprised him. "Walter Lee!" Felix said, while looking at the clock on his desk. "It's not even five o'clock yet…how come you're up so early?"

"I couldn't sleep, Uncle Felix."

"Well here…have some biscuits…I'll go get you a glass of milk."

"Couldn't I have coffee instead?"

"I don't think so…Walter Lee. You're only twelve…your mom probably doesn't want you drinking coffee."

"She let me drink cappuccino with her…when we were in Europe last summer."

"Well…that was probably just a special occasion," Felix said.

"Being with my uncle…after three years…in Alaska…is pretty special too!"

And Felix was just knocked out by his nephew, by his thinking, to see a twelve year-old mind working with its, "I was allowed to do this…so I should be allowed to…" reasoning made Felix laugh. "Tell you what…why don't we go into Anchorage for an afternoon movie and a nice meal tonight…and I'll let you have a cappuccino with dessert."

"That sounds great, Uncle Felix."

Felix had modified his lifestyle to accommodate his nephew's visit, but he was happy to do so. First of all, there would be no fooling around with Leslie O'Reily for three weeks, the woman he had been seeing off and on for more than six months. He had finally asked her out for last New Years Eve, and they had "painted the town red" (Anchorage). Felix and Leslie ended up spending the night back at her place in Palmer, since her eleven year-old daughter was spending the holiday with her father in Anchorage. Second, since Felix really didn't want his nephew reporting back to Salome about his perverse parrot, he had convinced Leslie to keep Major Doofus for three weeks. Finally, every day was designed for Walter Lee's entertainment. Other than the times they had camped out, Felix would get up, make coffee and biscuits, and work on his novel at four o'clock every morning, since Walter Lee usually slept in until nine. But once Walter Lee was up, until he was exhausted and ready for sleep around ten every evening—which was fine with Felix, he was tired too, having no late morning nap—the whole day was dedicated to Walter Lee. So far, besides the overnight camping trips—one just a few miles from Felix's cabin in the woods, and one hours away at Mt. McKinley National Park for three days, in which they had gotten to snow ski in July—they had been out on Felix's small boat fishing twice, and they had taken a day hike once.

On the way to Anchorage in Felix's *Beetle* Walter Lee said, "I wish you, Mom, and I could be a family."

Felix was taken aback by that, and he felt himself getting misty-eyed. He hadn't been aware, that apparently Walter Lee was aware, that he and Salome had been an item between 1997 and 1998. He said, "Well…it just wasn't meant to be. But hey…Walter Lee…I'm still your uncle…and I don't have any children of my own…so it kinda feels as if you're my son anyway."

And Walter Lee leaned over in the *Beetle* and hugged his uncle. Then he said, "Maybe things would have been better…for you and Mom…if you believed in Jesus."

"I never said that I didn't believe in Jesus," Felix said.

"Well…Mom says that you believe in Him differently than we do."

"I see," Felix said. He didn't really want to subvert anything that Salome had taught Walter Lee—Felix assumed that his nephew had never seen his scathing letter to her about Pentecostalism in late 1999—but he also didn't want his nephew to misunderstand him. "You know…Walter Lee," Felix said. "It's particularly hard…for someone who sees himself culturally as a Jew…to totally accept Christianity. And it's not necessarily that Christianity is wrong. It's probably…because Jewish people have had it rammed down their throats…and then are killed in some instances…if they don't accept it. From the days of the Spanish Inquisition…to Adolph Hitler's ovens…it's always been, 'Hey JEW!…you better learn to believe in Jesus!' The truth is…after reading The New Testament twice…and after reading a ton of scholarly commentary on Christianity…I think I do accept it. But The New Testament itself…talks about having to come to that conclusion on your own…that nobody can make you see something…that you can't see yourself."

"So you now believe that Jesus is the Son of God?"

"Well you know…I had always believed that Jesus was a great prophet, like Moses…but I had never believed that he was the Messiah…because I was taught in Hebrew school…when I was young…that the Messiah hadn't come yet…and the whole essence of Judaism…was waiting for the true Messiah to come. But now…I have decided…and I didn't come to this decision easily…but I did come to it freely myself… under no duress…that yes…Jesus was the Messiah…and he was indeed the Son of God."

"Wow," Walter Lee said, sounding like his mother. "I think Mom will be happy to hear that."

"Well…even though I now accept Jesus as the Messiah…I still don't accept your mother's way of worshipping Him."

"I understand," Felix's wise twelve year-old nephew said. "You don't believe in the Pentecostal church."

"You've got it," Felix said.

"I understand...Actually, I've heard Mom say before, that the really important thing...is that a person believe in Jesus...and that the church you go to...isn't nearly as important."

"Well that's good to know," Felix said. "My way of thinking is more in the Evangelical way of looking at Christianity."

"Is that like the *Jews for Jesus* church?"

Felix was totally blown away with just how smart his twelve year-old nephew was. "Yeah...I think so. If I were an actual member of a church... I'd probably join those guys. They thoroughly accept Jewish roots, celebrate all of the Jewish holidays...in fact...they're Jewish. They just say, 'Stop waiting for the Messiah...He's already come.'"

"Have you been baptized?" Walter Lee asked his uncle.

"No...I haven't," Felix said.

"You need to do that, no matter what church you join," Walter Lee said.

"Yeah?" Felix asked. And, of course, Felix already knew that. He was just waiting for the right time and place to take that final step.

"Why don't you do that this afternoon...in Anchorage? I'd rather see that...than see a movie," Walter Lee said.

"Really?" Felix asked.

"Really!" Walter Lee said.

"Okay," Felix said. "There's a *Jews for Jesus* church in Anchorage... we can stop there."

When they arrived at the church and walked inside, Felix and Walter Lee were greeted by a man of about Felix's age. "Howdy Felix," said Harry Goldberg, Doctor of Divinity, pastor of the church, former Tampa Bay area resident, avid Tampa Bay Buccaneers fan, and nearly three-month friend of Felix Kulpa. "Is this your nephew...Walter Lee?"

Felix nodded, and Walter Lee said, "Uncle Felix...how does he know you?"

And Dr. Goldberg said, "Your uncle has been coming here on Sundays for...I don't know...I guess...close to three months. And after services, your uncle and I have spent some time talking about Jesus."

"Well...we've also spent some time watching football too...Doc Harry!" Felix said.

"Yeah...we've also watched some football too," Dr. Goldberg repeated.

"So you've already been baptized?" Walter Lee asked his uncle.

"No...Walter Lee. Your uncle said he was waiting until you came to Alaska...so you could witness it."

And Walter Lee gave his uncle another big hug.

@@@@@@@@

"I'm over here...Bev," Joanne said to Bev, from the bench next to the entrance of the carousel in Central Park, on this Friday night in early August of 2001.

"Are you with the government?" Bev asked.

"No Bev...I'm Joanne Watson...your best friend...remember? I'm so proud of you! You read the instructions..."

"On Thursday night...just after the sun goes down."

"And those instructions said..."

"To be here on Friday night for my money. I don't understand...it's always been Thursday night before. I'm confused," Bev said.

"I know you're confused Bev," Joanne said. "That's why I'm so proud of you! I knew...reading those instructions on Thursday...that told you that you'd have to wait until Friday at ten o'clock...might confuse you. I was hoping you'd be able to figure it out. As a matter of fact...I was here on Thursday night...just in case you weren't able to figure it out."

"I'm confused...this was different," Bev said.

"But you did wonderfully," Joanne said. "In the future...you're going to be getting more instructions...that will have you meet me at different times, places, and days...for your money. It's important...that you try to follow those instructions."

"I always keep the instructions in my left inside coat pocket until..."

"Until when...Bev?"

"Until Thursday...just after the sun goes down."

"Let me have the instruction sheet," Joanne said. And Bev handed them to her. "Now here's your envelope of money. Where does this go?"

"In my coat...in the inside right pocket."

"Good girl! Now here are your new instructions...to be read..."

"Next Thursday...just after the sun goes down."

"Excellent!" Joanne said, and then she added, "Do you have any friends in Van Cortland Park?"

"I have my old friend...Ralphie-boy...he usually hangs out...way up there...at least five days a week."

"Well...your instructions...the ones that you read..."

"On Thursday...just after the sun goes down."

"Good girl! Your instructions next week are going to have you meet me in Van Cortland Park. We'll be meeting way uptown for awhile...as a matter of fact...I don't want you to come south of 96th Street...until after the first of November. From now on...for the next three months...you're to stay north of 96th Street. Your instructions will tell you more...when you read them..."

"On Thursday...just after the sun goes down."

@@@@@@@@

It was Bubba who met Felix and Walter Lee at Burlington Airport on the Saturday afternoon in early August 2001, and he said, "WHYYY Jumpin' JEEEHOSOPHAT…it's been forever…since I've seen YOUUU!"

"Nice to see you again, Mr. Apple," Felix said.

"PLEEESE…call me Bubba! And how is MYYY grandson?" And then Bubba gave Walter Lee a big hug.

"Hi Grandpa…is Mom with Grandma?"

"No Walter Lee…SHEEE'S down at Bruiser and Eileen's in Rutland. SHEEE said she would be back…LAAATER tonight."

"But today's her birthday…and Uncle Felix brought her something."

"I KNOOOW…Walter Lee. We're all TAAAKING your mom out for dinner tomorrow NIIIGHT…in Montreal. Your mom said…she would PREEEFER doing that." Walter Lee saw something in the gift store that intrigued him, and when he went to look at the item, Bubba looked at Felix.

"Right!" Felix said. "When I'm at my aunt's in Plattsburgh…and I can't possibly come along. I get it."

"I'm SOOO sorry, Felix," Bubba said. "I TAAAKE it…that you and Salome…have some history…and I TAAAKE it…that it's more than just BEEEING brother-in-law and sister-in-law."

Felix, remembering what Salome had told him once about Bubba Apple's "sexdar," said, "Truthfully…Mr. Apple…Bubba…you'll have to discuss that with Salome. Meanwhile…I got this painting for her birthday…if you'll just give it to her…I'd appreciate it." And then Felix handed Bubba the wrapped twenty-four inch by eighteen inch gift. The black and white painting, called "Your Majesty," had been done by a gifted Inuit artist, and it featured an Inuit princess, whose face looked amazingly like Salome's, sitting on her throne, with numerous men on their knees surrounding her, all holding the gifts they were offering, high above their heads. "I think I'll rent a car…hang out in Burlington for a bit…and then drive over to Plattsburgh tonight," Felix said.

"When do YOUUU head back to Alaska?" Bubba asked.

"I leave here early Tuesday morning," Felix said

"I'm sorry…about ALLL of this," Bubba said.

"Me too," Felix said.

Walter Lee came back, apparently disenchanted with whatever he had been checking out in the gift store and said, "You're leaving now, Uncle Felix?"

"Yeah…I'm gonna rent a car here…and just head across the lake to Plattsburgh. I'll miss you Walter Lee," Felix said, and then he lifted Walter Lee up, kissed him on both cheeks, and gave him a big bear hug.

"I'll really miss you too, Uncle Felix," Walter Lee said, while hugging

Felix. "Thanks for a great time in Alaska this summer, and thanks for letting me share a part of something so important to you. I hope, in the future, we can spend more time together."

"I hope so too Walter Lee." And Felix walked away, thinking just how much he loved his nephew.

@@@@@@@@

September 11, 2001. Walter Lee Younger's 74th birthday. Other than Felix—since he had been writing and was impervious to the news—everybody else, including Lena, Sam, and their baby, Adam, forgot to call Walter Lee until the next day. Salome closed all of the windows in the apartment and all of the drapes on her northern glass wall, and that's the way they would remain for several months.

Chapter Nineteen

It was nearly seven o'clock on a Tuesday evening in late February of 2002, and as the intensity of the snowfall began to make 86th Street in the Bayridge section of Brooklyn almost impossible to navigate, Selma Greenwood was fortunate, in that she had been able to quickly grab the handrail and maintain her balance, as she had begun to slip while ascending the stairs of the R Train Station. Once on the street, still shaken by her nearly injurious close call—the horizontal snow was so blinding—seventy year-old Selma was concerned about whether she still had the physical wherewithal to make the three-block walk home. She had just returned from Manhattan, where she had met clandestinely in a booth at the *Homer Café*, on Tenth Street just off of Sixth Avenue, with her editor, Eleanor Devine, and she had heard the reasons why *In Your Face Publishing* was scared to distribute her *Notes From the Modern Underground* at this time.

In January of 2001, Selma had solicited *In Your Face Publishing* from a phone booth in Atlanta upon finishing her manuscript, and reading in *The Writer's Market*, that they were a publishing house who specialized in manuscripts like hers; and, having seen Eleanor Devine's name as a senior editor on their website, and after conning a secretary into believing that she was Eleanor's sister, Selma was able to get her on the phone. She then apologized for her lie, quickly piqued her interest, and upon Eleanor Devine swearing herself to secrecy, Selma told her that she was really Ida Laplotski, and why she had been on the run from the FBI since 1966. *In Your Face* was very interested in reading her story. Selma set up a time for exactly one month later when she would call Eleanor, and then she had driven to Detroit, and mailed her manuscript from a corner mailbox. She rented a room, and when she finally spoke again to Eleanor in February of 2001, Selma had been pleased to hear that *In Your Face* wanted to publish her novel. She paid a second month's rent, and a couple of weeks later, the publishing house mailed a contract and advance check to Betty Lou Baker in care of the old Detroit post office box. She then signed the contract in front of a notary and mailed it back—she had used her newly renewed Betty Lou Baker Michigan driver license—and although Selma still had close to $1500 in a bank account there in the name of Betty Lou Baker, she elected instead to just cash the $5,000 advance check at a check cashing joint downtown, before heading back to Atlanta. Later, even though Selma and Eleanor were able to do some editing work, from a payphone in Atlanta's Piedmont Park to Eleanor's desk phone on the thirty-third floor of the Chrysler Building in Manhattan for a couple of months, it was eventually decided that Selma needed to be in New York.

Selma had rented her one-bedroom apartment at 88th Street and Gelstan Avenue in Bayridge in May of 2001, and she and Eleanor Devine met between then and late July in different parks and cafés. The novel was finally printed and bound in late August, and it was supposed to be distributed in late September. September 11th changed all of that.

Selma had a feeling, after September 11th, that *In Your Face* might be reticent to distribute a novel about a leftist who accidentally blows up the wrong building, a building that the federal government had earmarked for demolition anyway, is on the run, but successfully eludes capture for more than thirty-five years. So, as September morphed into October, and October finally said, "See ya!" Selma had demonstrated incredible patience, for a first time published novelist waiting for the world to see her or his first book. Then, in late November, when she could stand it no longer, Selma had called Eleanor at work. She couldn't get through to her, and every time Selma called during the next month, an underling would come on and give some lame excuse as to why Eleanor was not available. Finally, in late December of 2001, just before the Christmas holiday, Selma disguised herself with a blonde wig, hat, and big dark glasses, and went to the Chrysler Building. On the thirty-third floor, she just blew past *In Your Face Publishing's* main receptionist. She then found Eleanor's office, burst in, and yelled, "So what's the deal, Eleanor? I'm Betty Lou Baker...remember me?"

And Eleanor had said, "Betty Lou Baker...I finally get to meet you!...What a surprise!" And then Eleanor had gotten up from behind her desk and whispered into Selma's ear, "Ida...you need to get out of here. You should know...in fact I thought you did know...that the CIA reads everything before it's published with a major publishing house in this country...and before it's catalogued with the Library of Congress...That old movie...*Three Days of the Condor*...with Robert Redford...was pretty much right on the money...Your book has generated a lot of heat...in light of

September 11th… I've already had the FBI…and I think the NSA…up here interviewing me…I told them that all the editing work had been done with you over the phone…and that I had never met you…that I thought your name was Betty Lou Baker…and that you lived in Detroit…in fact we had mailed your contract and advance check to your post office box there…and I assumed you were always calling me from there…that you said you were deeply in debt…couldn't afford to turn your phone back on…even with the $5,000 advance…and that you would always call me at a set time from a payphone… And then they had asked me…'Weren't you in the least bit…you know…suspicious…that the author…Betty Lou Baker…who we now know is really Ida Laplotski…was living a lifestyle very similar to her protagonist Rachel Trotsky?'…And I told them, 'It hadn't occurred to me.' And then they tapped my phone…and I heard they sent agents to your box in Detroit…had you on videotape…cashing your advance check in downtown Detroit…That's why I haven't spoken with you…They've always watched what we publish here fairly close anyway…*In Your Face* has always had a reputation for taking chances…for publishing material that was edgy…That started in the early 1960's…when we published Ben Hecht's book… *Perfidy*…in which Mr. Hecht…a Jew…had lambasted the State of Israel for all of their terrorism...all of the bloody things they had to do… including secret deals with the Nazis…in becoming an independent state…He discussed the loss of innocent life…with the bombings…etc…and the difference between when one is called a "terrorist"…or called a "patriot." We managed to slip that one by the CIA… someone must have been sleeping…but six weeks after it came out…it was mysteriously withdrawn from all of the book store and library shelves everywhere in North America…Look Ida…I'll meet you at the *Homer Café* on Tenth Street just west of Sixth Avenue, in the West Village…," And then Eleanor walked back over to her desk and looked at her calendar, and then she came back and continued whispering in Selma's ear, "two months exactly from today…at four o'clock. Be there. I should have a better handle on what's going to happen with your book at that time…Now get the hell out of here!"

Earlier this afternoon, while sitting in the restaurant's booth, Eleanor had told Selma, "They're afraid to distribute it. That $5,000 advance might be all you ever see."

"So…if I give the $5,000 back…will *In Your Face* tear up my contract…so perhaps I can find another publishing house with more balls?" Selma had asked.

"You're not gonna find...bigger balls...than *In Your Face*," Eleanor had said. "I think, in a couple of years, this novel will go over well. I'd suggest that…in the meantime…you just write another novel. You're an excellent writer Ida…try writing a good story…that isn't so much of a *roman à clef* on the bombing of a building. Then later, we can get *Notes From the*

Modern Underground distributed," Eleanor had added.

And Selma had said, "Well…I don't really need the money…my dear Fred left me plenty…so maybe I will try to write something different." And then Selma had added, "But, if down the road, I decide to give the $5,000 back, will *In Your Face* destroy the contract then?"

"Probably," Eleanor had said and added, "But we've already printed and bound the first 10,000 copies. I'm sure my bosses would want to get paid something for that…perhaps a percentage…if it finally gets distributed."

Selma was reflecting on that conversation with Eleanor, when she ducked into a bodega that she had never used before on 85th Street and Fourth Avenue to pick up a few items. She usually shopped at the larger grocery store on the corner of 92nd Street and Gelstan, but today, with the ridiculous amount of snow, she just wanted the quickest store possible. When she went to pay for her items, the Korean man behind the counter said, "I'm glad you came back. You left your plastic bag…with your bottle of wine…on the counter a few minutes ago."

And Selma said, "I wasn't in here a few minutes ago…I left nothing on your counter."

"But Miss Ivy…I've known you for many years," James Kim said.

Selma immediately recognized what was happening, and she felt her heart palpitate with excitement. She said, "I'm sorry…I almost fell on the subway steps a few minutes ago…I'm just not thinking clearly today." And then Selma paid for the items she wanted, and she took the already paid for bottle of *Merlot* in the plastic bag, and she said, "I'm sorry…I'm feeling really confused…can you tell me where I live?"

"Sure…Ms. Ivy…I've certainly delivered enough to your place throughout the years…You live in the apartment building on 83rd Street and Third Avenue…called *The Ambassador*…and you are in apartment 4-F," James Kim said.

"Thank you so very much…Mr….Mr…,"

"Mr. Kim…Are you sure that you didn't bang your head? Are you going to be okay?"

"I'll be fine…Mr. Kim," Selma said.

"Just the same…my car is parked right out in front at a meter…let me get my son to watch the register for a few minutes…I'll drive you home," James Kim said.

"That's okay…Mr. Kim…it's terrible driving out there…and I wouldn't want you to lose your spot."

"If you're sure…Ms. Ivy."

Selma said she was sure, left the store, and walked down Fourth Avenue to Eighty-Third Street and hung a right. As she turned, she almost ran into an exhausted Ivy Laplotski. Ivy, having worked ten hours at the downtown Brooklyn *Payless Shoe Source*, in her capacity today as for the past seven years, as a district manager responsible for eight stores, in this, her twentieth and last year before retirement, a pension, and social security, who was totally pissed off at having forgotten the wine, and begrudgingly heading back to the bodega in the heavy snow to retrieve that which she had forgotten, said, "Hey...watch where the hell you're going!"

Selma said, "I'm still thirty minutes older than you...show a little respect!"

And then Ivy looked closely into Selma's face and said, "Ida...my dear sister Ida...it's been more than twenty years!"

Selma held up the bottle of *Merlot* and said, "I brought something for us to celebrate with...but I thought you had better taste!"

Ivy laughed and said, "Well...I only bought that swill...because they were out of *Ripple* and *MD 20-20*!" And there, on that corner in Brooklyn, in the freezing horizontal snow, the twins, Ida and Ivy Laplotski, with their special homing pigeon-like umbilicus radar, had found each other, after twenty years, in a city of eight million; and, like those of us who have ever body-surfed it, and are truly moved by the awesome wave of human emotion, they laughed, cried, and embraced.

@@@@@@@@

In early May of 2002, about thirteen months after they had started dating, and about seven months after they had started having intercourse, as they sat drinking coffee, having just finished a late lunch in the small Spanish restaurant a couple of blocks away from Essex Street Middle School, and while Salome was rubbing her belly after the meal in her customary way, she told Christopher that it was over between them.

"Why?" a devastated Christopher asked.

"Yellow goes with blue, goes with black, goes with red, etc. Just because we have a number of things in common, doesn't mean that we're meant to be together long term," Salome said.

"Then why were we talking about marriage and naming fictional children...if you weren't in earnest?" Christopher asked.

"I was in earnest...I wanted to see if we could work out long term...I decided that we could not. Do you think you were used?" Salome asked.

"I'm not sure yet," Christopher said. "But I do know...that you knew...I was an Atheist right from jump...so you must have known we'd never be long term back then also...so why did you pump sunshine up my skirt...with talk of marriage and children?" And Christopher, who had paid the bill and was ready to go, started to walk out of the restaurant.

"Wait a minute," Salome said, "If I were head over heels in love with somebody...I could love him, even if he were an Atheist...I could also live with him in a cardboard box under the Brooklyn Bridge."

That notion didn't particularly ring true to Christopher and he said, "Yeah…sure." And he added, "Well I guess I can't make you be in love with me…but that doesn't change the fact that I am with you."

They left the restaurant and walked in silence back to school. After signing back in at the main office, they walked silently back to their individual classrooms to teach the final period of the day.

After pm homeroom, when the kids had left, Salome walked into Christopher's classroom and said, "Look Christopher…you've been nothing but wonderful to me…a perfect gentleman…and…at a time in my life when I really needed someone…you came through and rocked my world in many ways…I'll always love you for that…I hope you can be my closest friend…I just know it isn't meant to be…I know you're disappointed…I know this is going to be painful…for me too…so why don't we wait until this summer to deal with that pain…there are only two months left in the school year…why don't we keep going out…just like we are now…until the last day of school…then… we can say goodbye for the summer…and when we see each other…when school starts the following September…we will be great close friends and colleagues."

That notion seemed a little creepy to Christopher, as if he were on death row awaiting the needle, but given the choice between no Salome as his woman for the rest of his life, or no Salome as his woman for the rest of his life after eight more weeks, he decided that the latter was more desirable than the former. "Okay," he said.

"And we won't date other people at the school…as a measure of respect for each other…okay?" Salome asked. But then Salome immediately felt her *faux pas*. She already knew, the next in line was on staff too.

"Okay," Christopher said and then added, as he was preparing to leave the room, to drive home, grade a few essays, eat dinner, and then have band practice, "Goodnight…can I still call you at our regular time later?"

"Of course," Salome said. "We'll keep everything exactly like it is until the last day of school."

After Christopher left, Salome remained in his room looking at the student work on the walls. Through the windows of his classroom, she saw Christopher drive by in his van. She then turned off Christopher's lights, and locked his door, with the universal key that most teachers have. As she was walking across the hall to her classroom, Salome saw Peter Proffilacto, the Italian thirty year-old rookie science teacher, who, from what had been recently discussed in the ladies room, saw himself as God's gift to women. One story concerned a recent party at another Essex Street science teacher's house, Betty Levin, a party to celebrate her new Masters Degree, in which apparently the young Don Juan had asked every single woman in the place if she wanted to sleep with him. Later, all of the women got together in the kitchen and compared notes. Salome hadn't attended that party, but she had heard the story. It didn't surprise her however, because even though she had only mentioned it and then downplayed it a few times in the past year, just to get a rise out of Christopher, in reality Peter Proffilacto had been hitting heavily on her all year. And much in the same way that some misguided women think that '*I* can be the one' who can turn that Gay guy straight, and, much in the same way that other misguided women are attracted by and think that '*I* can be the one' who can turn that troubled James Dean/Marlon Brando/Fonzie-type bad boy around, Salome had to admit to herself, she was kind of fascinated with the notion, and she had thought recently, 'I wonder if *I* could be the one to stop his cooty cat chasing ways.' Peter followed Salome into her room to schmooze a bit. He had seen Christopher Jeremy leave for the day also.

In early 2000, before becoming a Christian, thinking about his previous relationship with Salome, Felix had written an entry in his journal, an entry that would find its way into *Mad Beach* as part of the story between his characters Roy Cassier and Judziah Cromwell:

Perhaps, in a relationship, we should learn to just keep our big mouths shut until we're sure. And if one speaks of marriage too early, the response from the other should be, "Let's not have this conversation for one year. One year from today, if we're still together, I'll speak to you of marriage and family." Because when couples play fantasy games, like looking at engagement rings, and talking about where they're going to get married, how the wedding will be done, what they're going to name their children, what kind of a house they're going to buy, how they're going to furnish that house, how they can be together despite differences in taste, religion, and philosophy, the inference is clearly that they are beyond having serious objections that might block the union. If they are not beyond those objections, if they are still in the "wait and see" mode, then they should just shut the fuck up! As a matter of fact, most people, most of the time, should just shut the fuck up!

And Felix had turned to Major Doofus and said, "Shut the Fuck Up!"

And Major Doofus had said, "WWWRRROOOAAA...Asshole!"

In another journal entry he wrote in Alaska in early 2000, an entry that was added on the backs of pages he had written in the late 1990's on Mad Beach, in regards to former lovers dating within the same social or work circle, Felix wrote: *I need to come up with a good back story, as to what has pushed Roy Cassier into such a deep psychological funk. And, no doubt, a woman or women are involved. There needs to be an infidelity issue, but I'd rather it not be exactly like my marriage to Tatiana, as I already covered that in "Tous Les Siege Etaient Occupés." So rather than have an unfaithful wife with three different lovers in five years, I think I'll change around the story that Jennifer Apple told me on Mad Beach in 1998, and make it about a wife cheating with the same man...for twenty years. But twenty years is a wee bit too long, so I'll make it fifteen. And it will be a deathbed confession.*

Okay...at the moment, Roy Cassier is completely broke. He was fired from his teaching position at the University of Tampa Bay, because he mooned his dipshit boss,

Professor Joseph Bayard. He's been evicted from his apartment, and he had to sell his car. He's been sitting on Mad Beach writing, sleeping under a small bridge that connects Mad Beach to St. Petersburg, washing up in the public restroom on Mad Beach's public beach, keeping a change of clothes hidden in a plastic garbage bag inside of a wall, behind some broken sheet rock, at the twenty-four hour laundromat, for something to wear when he washes his clothes weekly, and he sweeps the parking lot of a small Mad Beach strip shopping center for two hours daily, which gives him just enough money for food and cigarettes.

So let's do this...Roy is a widower, and a few years ago, just before she died from breast cancer, during a deathbed confession, he finds out that his wife, Jill, had been sleeping with one of his so-called friends on and off for nearly fifteen years. He asks her, "Why didn't you just divorce me? If you didn't want to be with me exclusively, if I bored you, if you hated my lovemaking, why didn't you just divorce me?" And she replies, "I love you.

You are the love of my life. I love being with you. I love our lovemaking... It's just...over the years...I've needed the excitement of a regular rendezvous with another man...and I don't know why." And Roy thinks, but doesn't say, since she's dieing, and it would be cruel to say, 'You were just being greedy. Hey...I've always put up with your bullshit...but you gave another man the gravy?' And although the mental image of his naked wife in bed with this guy is tormenting, the worse feelings come later, when he realizes that he had been managed by his wife and her lover for a long time. The notion of a hidden agenda between the woman he loved and her lover, that personal information about his life was being shared with another man, and that the once or twice monthly he would see the guy himself, and on those occasions he apparently was getting just a big shine on job, is even worse to Roy than imagining what they look like together in bed doing it.

Okay...so a year after she's gone, Roy begins dating again. After one three-month fling with a waitress, he starts going out with a colleague in his department, Judziah Cromwell, another literature professor at the University of Tampa Bay. After awhile, he finds that he's totally in love with her, and he shares the horror story of his wife's deathbed confession. A year later, however, after numerous discussions of marriage, children, and lots of house hunting, and also after Judziah has been hit on regularly for most of the year by another professor in the same department who she thinks is cute, Judziah decides that she doesn't feel the same way about Roy, and she wants to end it. Roy is blown away by this, but he realizes that he can't make anyone be in love with him. Roy and Judziah do make an agreement, since there are billions of people on the planet to date, out of respect for each other, not to date anybody else in the building. Judziah immediately violates this agreement, with the professor in their department who had been hitting on her all year. And, at times, during pillow talk, no doubt, she brings up all kinds of personal stuff about Roy with her new lover. She also involves him in managing Roy for a year, in a futile attempt at deception. And even though there is a big difference between a wife seeing another man for a fifteen-year period, and a former lover breaking an agreement, to Roy, who sits on Mad Beach with his writing journal, it's all infidelity nonetheless. Roy writes in his journal: "The mathematics of one situation having been longer, with a wife, with less of a frequency of me having to see the other man, in juxtaposition to the other situation being much shorter, with a girlfriend, but with a far greater frequency of me having to see the dickhead where I work, since I loved both women deeply, the difference in scenarios matters not, it all feels about the same—just another disingenuous duplicitous diva with a greedy Ego agenda. And just another opportunistic douche bag peckerwood Jolly Roger, who doesn't have enough savoir faire in his limited worldly experience to understand—regardless of any encouragement the woman gives—the two basic good guy principles: 1) You don't mess around with another man's wife…that's a given always. 2) You don't piss on another man's leg, by hitting heavily on his girlfriend, until after that relationship is officially over. And you especially don't do that, in the same building where the other guy works, unless your message is either balls-to-the-wall arrogance, or complete stupidity."

Before he was fired from the university, Roy had thought, 'Hey…if a year or two go by, and this other guy has put a ring on Judziah's finger, well I guess I'll just have to use the machine in the departmental restroom to dry off my leg, before wishing her well. Either way, I won't discuss much with her beyond the weather ever again.'

In June of 2002, on their last weekend together before the end of the school year, Salome wouldn't have sex because of her monthly visitor, so Christopher asked, "Can I have a raincheck…even if it's…after my execution…on the last day of school?"

And Salome smiled and said, "Sure…I'll give you a cooty cat raincheck…for one last time." At that moment, still bedazzled and shattered, Christopher didn't reflect on just how weird and perverse the raincheck for later sex thing really was. He did decide that he'd do it right, however. It would be a night to remember. Since Salome had this fantasy about being pulled over by a threatening Southern cop with a voice like Harry Conick Jr.'s, and having sex with him as a way of getting out of the ticket, Christopher decided that he would rent a Southern cop's uniform from a costume shop, have a nice room waiting in a midtown Manhattan hotel, and he'd have a dressed to the nines Salome wait for him in the hotel bar. After awhile, he would walk down to the bar in his uniform, approach Salome, and say, "Excuse me missy…do you own that *Cobra* parked outside? Well…I'm afraid we got us a sit-u-a-tion." He would walk Salome outside, she'd ask if there was something she could do in lieu of a ticket, and he would tell her that he had some "hard" work upstairs…and if she were willing to "do that hard work" he might consider not giving her the ticket. Then, with most of his uniform still on, after some tuning up, he would hammer her hard, and then keep hammering her, and then hammer her some more—until people two floors away heard her squeal.

When school ended at the end of June, Salome went home to Rutland for a week. When she returned, she and Christopher were two of the four Language Arts teachers who were working summer school at Essex Street for the extra money. A week after summer school began, the second week of July, Christopher brought up the raincheck thing that Thursday afternoon in Salome's room after classes had ended.

"Look at you…all doe-eyed and everything…but I can't do that Christopher. I've already started to heal." And, of course, she had also started seeing Peter Proffilacto.

Christopher didn't feel like dating that summer, so, when summer school ended after the first week in August, he just went camping by himself in the Adirondacks. On Labor Day, the day before he had to be back at school, Salome gave him a quick five minute call, in regards to stories on the news about a major fire, that caused a number of houses to burn down on the Saturday before Labor Day in the East Elmhurst section of Queens. Salome said she was concerned.

The next day, during and after the continental breakfast in the auditorium, Salome ignored Christopher. Thirteen year-old Walter Lee was there, since his St. George Christian School would not open until the next day, and Salome couldn't get the sitter. He came over and sat next to Christopher and talked to him, while Salome walked by three times and didn't say a word. 'I guess her little five minute phone call of concern yesterday, was just a way to dispose of me today,' Christopher thought.

After Walter Lee had gone off to play with another boy whose teacher mom was also stuck without a sitter for the day, Peter Proffilacto came by and said hello to Christopher. Of course he couldn't look Christopher in the eye, as he was too busy looking over Christopher's shoulder at Salome, to make sure that she saw that he had done exactly what he had been coached to do.

A couple of days later, Christopher was just getting into his van at the end of the school day, when Salome walked by heading toward the subway. Christopher waved, but she ignored him. Since he was stuck in traffic and just creeping along, there were three more times when he pulled up next to the walking Salome, honked his horn, waved, and said, "Hey Salome." Salome totally ignored him.

The next morning, as he was walking to his classroom on the first floor, he happened to walk by Peter Proffilacto, who was standing in front of the science lab. Peter gave Christopher a cold steely-eyed "you're-stalking-my-girlfriend" stare, and Christopher said, as he passed, "I only charge a dollar for a photo." By this time, Christopher was starting to figure out that Salome and Peter were an item, and that her "Let's not date anybody else on the faculty" agreement was total horseshit.

About a week later in early October of 2002, as Christopher was getting into his van after school on a Friday night, Salome walked by, then turned and said, "Christopher Jeremy…you're really the pits…you can't say hello to an old close friend?"

"Right back at you," Christopher said. "You're the one who has been acting as if I don't even exist."

"No I haven't," Salome said. And, of course, she had indeed been acting that exact way.

Felix had written in his journal recently: *It's always so obvious, when guilt about one's actions toward another person, makes one treat that other person even more rotten.*

"Let's have lunch together at school one day this week," she added, and Christopher agreed.

The following Wednesday, after the Language Arts meeting, in which much arguing had occurred, because each teacher felt as if there were no real objective way for Dr. Merkin to evaluate each teacher's progress with this year's program, *Children Reading And Participating* (CRAP) Christopher mentioned that he had been invited to a traditional Japanese Wedding in Brooklyn. Salome said, "I've always wanted to see a traditional Japanese Wedding."

And while they were sharing their first meal together in a long time in Salome's room, Christopher said, "Well…the invitation to the wedding is for this Saturday night…and it's for me and a date. Would you like to go as my Platonic date?" And Salome said she'd love to.

And then Salome mentioned that she had just paid sixty-five dollars to join *eharmony.com*, she had completed her personality profile, and that she was hoping to find someone online who was more similar to her. Then she asked Christopher if he'd read her profile and make some suggestions.

"Right…I really want to help you to be even more attractive to some other guy," Christopher said. He thought, 'Why bother with the ruse? I already know that you're with Prophylactic Boy.'

"Help a damsel in distress," Salome said. "I am so frisky! I'm gonna have to rent a porn film soon! Hmmm…I wonder…could I have sex again with you…Christopher Jeremy? Probably not."

Christopher thought about reminding her of his raincheck, but then he thought, 'This is all bullshit anyway. She's already hooked up. She's not horny, she's just mouthing these words to try and deflect the truth.'

That Saturday night they met in Brooklyn at the Japanese wedding, and they made plans to go to a club, drink a couple of beers, and listen to music after the wedding. But somewhere during the evening, while visiting the ladies room, Salome had called on her cell and hooked up with Peter for later, so she feigned exhaustion, said goodbye to Christopher immediately after the wedding, and they each went their separate ways.

A week later, since the sixth grade dean was out sick, C. Wel Rellim had the assignment of bringing the sixth graders around the school to check out the eighth grade classrooms. Salome, standing by her door when the kids came out of Peter Proffilacto's science room, squealed loudly, "He's the best science teacher in the school!" Hearing this, Christopher wanted to vomit. He just closed his classroom door instead.

A couple of weeks later, in mid-November, the day of the parent-teacher conferences, during the four hours break between afternoon and evening conferences, as Christopher walked towards his room and passed Salome, she said, "Hello." Christopher just ignored her, as he was unlocking his classroom door. "You can't say hello anymore?" Salome asked. "You must really hate my guts!"

"You just had to bring it…all up in here…in my face…with Prophylactic Boy…didn't you…I mean…I was nothing but great to you…did everything for you…but obviously…how I felt…our agreements…mattered squat to you!" Christopher said. "Oh…I know…you two are just so in love…Hey…maybe you'll marry…makes no difference…what are you…42?…he'll be long gone…by the time you're 50...and other than being forced into seeing each other every other week…if there's joint custody with a child…he'll just be a fading blip on your radar by then…And then you'll be a two-time loser…because you've already lost my friendship…But hey…to answer your previous statement…No…I don't hate your guts…The opposite of love isn't hate…it's total imperviousness." And as he was walking into his room he said, just loud enough for her to hear, "I see dead people!…This is all just personification!… I'm having a conversation with the furniture…the office sofa…the building… the office garage."

And, of course, as Bruce Springsteen sang, in "Prove it All Night," "You want it…you take it…you pay the price."

@@@@@@@@

It was December 2, 2002 at four o'clock in the morning, and, after too much Condoleeza Rice the previous day, as Felix sat downloading in Camp Cheney, he realized that it had been nearly three months since he had sent his completed manuscript, *Mad Beach*, to Dee Dee Symington, his literary agent in New York City. It had also been nearly three months since he had written anything. But on this morning, as he sat in camp drinking coffee, using the sink counter as his coffee cup holder, various philosophic quandaries were bouncing around in Felix's head.

First, there was the Major Doofus profanity issue. Although Felix still maintained, as he had argued with Salome, that so-called swear words (in the future, "Bush Backer" might be considered profane) other than the G.D. or J.C. expressions, were not blasphemous, he was beginning to understand

Salome's reticence in using off-color language. She just hadn't made the best argument. In Felix's mind, it was becoming a high road versus low road issue. That, given the choice, it's better to take the high road, with both people and language. And since off-color language infers low road, perhaps it would be best to leave it behind. Besides, if one really just can't restrain oneself from using the tongue or pen as a knife, there are always better words or tropes to use, in any language's vocabulary, than the words heard on the street. (Consider this: Although yelling "Asshole!" at the home plate ump, at Yankee Stadium, will probably get a bigger laugh, yelling, "He's Oedipus Rex, early and late in the play!" will probably introduce you to some fine eclectic people, who will later become life-long friends.) Felix felt, as a Christian, he needed to take the high road. And it wasn't so much that he hadn't figured that out when he considered himself a Jew only, it was just that the "leap of faith" for him into Christianity, had begun to focus his attention away from the narrow, sometimes perverse world of his fictive characters, with their emotional dilemmas, and into the wider real or surreal world of everyday political and moral dilemmas. And somehow, spewing out phrases for Major Doofus to either reply, "WWWRRROOOAAA... Asshole!" or "WWWRRROOOAAA...Homo!" or "WWWRRROOOAAA ...Eat Me!" just didn't feel like a very high road kind of thing to do anymore. Felix had stopped speaking to Major Doofus. Even though he knew exactly whenit was time for Major Doofus to eat, Felix had begun holding back the food, just so the parrot could at least say, "WWWRRROOOAAA...Feed Me!" Felix did worry, since Major Doofus was used to much more daily dialogue, if it were psychologically hurting the parrot to speak so much less. Felix had decided that Major Doofus needed a new home.

Second, there was the issue of Felix's writing. Although he now accepted Jesus as the Messiah, it still didn't change his continual need to write away his own psychological angst, and what he saw as the angst of most people. Felix would never be the type of Christian who felt that since he was saved when this life was over, he didn't have to actively get involved in trying to physically save those who were suffering here. He now understood the trope from The New Testament, that "good deeds alone are not enough," but he also understood that just believing in Jesus was not enough either. And, of course, charity was always a good deed. Felix had gone out in the past three Augusts, just as it was starting to get cold at night, and purchased at least twenty new heavy coats each year, which he took around and gave to homeless people in Anchorage, along with a fifty dollar bill each. Felix also had given a few thousand dollars each year, to both the Anchorage Free Clinic and a downtown soup kitchen that fed the homeless. But Felix felt he needed to do more. He had no intention of trying to "save" others, in a religious sense, through his writing. Felix was a writer of fiction, not a preacher of The Word. And in trying to write the best story possible, it was necessary for

Felix to keep open both a cynical and romantic eye. And yes, people who do bad things in novels usually get punished later in those novels, and yes, great nobility in a character is always welcomed in a novel, so Felix had tried, by the end of *Mad Beach*, and he would continue to try, in whatever else God let him live long enough to write, to lead the reader to higher ground, a place that at least pointed upward toward God. But it was Felix's job first and foremost to tell a good story. Once he left his fictive world however, Felix had begun feeling that he needed to be heard in other ways too. Remembering back to the Anti-Vietnam War Movement of the late 1960's, Felix was thinking that it was time for him to again get involved, this time as a Christian, in the current Anti-Iraq War Movement. There wasn't much happening in Anchorage along that front, so, as Felix sat in Camp Cheney drinking coffee, thinking about how much money the Vice President's former company, *Halliburton*, was making from the war in Iraq, thinking about how no so-called "Weapons of Mass Destruction" had been found in Iraq, thinking about how most of the plane hijackers on 9/11 were Saudi, Osama bin Laden was Saudi (although his family was originally from Yemen) and that the airplanes carrying bin Laden's family were the only jets allowed in the air in the United States immediately after the attack on 9/11, and thinking that the next time he ate at *Khyber Pass* he would try the Jerry Rice, Felix decided that it was time he left Alaska and headed to New York City.

Third, although Felix didn't want to see women thrown in jail for having an abortion, as a Christian, he could no longer endorse abortion either. Felix thought, 'Just as I don't want my tax dollars supporting the war in Iraq, I also do not want that money going to fund abortion. Yes, I do understand, that without federal financial intervention, only women with money might be able to afford an abortion from a licensed doctor, and that the poor women might again turn to coat hangers and seeking out shady people in alleyways. But the public has had decades to be educated on what the repercussions and responsibilities are when it comes to having sex, so I refuse, as a Christian, to fund what I see as being immoral, and that which is the byproduct of somebody's stupidity.' Felix wasn't against stem cell research, but he did fear that that new industry might encourage women to have abortions for profit.

Finally, there was the issue of sex itself. Felix had decided, he was no longer interested in sleeping with anyone to whom he wasn't married. And, since Leslie was still in love with her ex-husband, and he was still in love with Salome, he had to tell Leslie that they could no longer just be bed buddies. Felix, still sitting in Camp Cheney, was thinking about how gracious Leslie had been when he had told her that, and that they would always remain close, when the telephone rang. Naked Felix got off of the throne, and walked carefully toward the kitchen to answer the call. Not carefully enough however, as he stubbed his right big toe on the coffee table in front of the sofa. "Son of a bitch!" Felix yelled out, hobbling on his left foot, while trying to keep his cheeks together.

"WWWRRROOOAAA...Homo!" Major Doofus said.

"Hello?" Felix said, thinking, even though it had only been twelve weeks since he had mailed his manuscript off, that it might be Hollywood calling, offering him a deal, telling him that they had cast Paul Giamatti to play Roy Cassier and Angelina Jolie to play Judziah Cromwell in the movie version of *Mad Beach*. But nobody was on the other end of the phone, and no message had been left. "That's just bullshit!" Felix said, his toe still throbbing, thinking that it would have probably been a made-for-T.V. movie offer anyway, starring Drew Carey and Paris Hilton.

"WWWRRROOOAAA...Asshole!" Major Doofus said.

Felix, still hobbling on his left foot, and feeling the need for more quality downloading, had made his way back to Camp Cheney, when the phone rang again. He quickly used some toilet paper as a plug, and then he hobbled, more carefully this time, yet with great aggressiveness, to the portable phone in the kitchen. "Hello?" He said, with the portable phone to his ear, as he made his way back again to camp with lightning-like speed.

"Hello...Felix? Is that YOUUU?" said eighty-two year-old Bubba Apple, under heavy medication, from his bed in Burlington Mercy Hospital, the advanced liver cancer having almost entirely consumed him.

"Mr. Apple?" Felix said, now sitting comfortably.

"Please call MEEE Bubba already."

"Alright...Bubba...Are you here in Alaska?"

"No...I'm DIIIEING here in a hospital bed in Burlington. They left MEEE here to DIIIE!"

"What's wrong...Mr...Bubba?"

"Advanced liver cancer. They SAAAY I only have short a TIIIME left. I wanted to SPEEEAK to YOUUU Felix...before I leave this world. By the WAAAY...would YOUUU know what time it is?...Don't have my watch."

"Well...it's just a little after 4 am my time, so in Burlington, it's a little past eight o'clock in the morning," Felix said, having wrapped things up in camp, and now fixing himself another cup of coffee in the kitchen.

"I'm sorry to call SOOO early," Bubba said.

"Nonsense...I'm up at this time every morning writing. And I'm sorry to hear that you are so sick...Bubba," Felix said.

"Then I'm SOOO sorry to bother YOUUU while you ARRRE writing. How's that book of yours coming ANYWAAAY?"

"I finished that novel...it's called *Mad Beach*...and I mailed it to my literary agent in New York City three months ago. I'm just writing observations in my journal now...I haven't a clue as to what kind of a story I'm going to write next. I'm kind of interested in seeing what happens with *Mad Beach*...as that will probably influence my writing direction," Felix said.

"I'm sure YOUUU will make a lot of MONEEEY writing, Felix. YOUUU ARRRE one of the smartest PEEEOPLE I've ever KNOOOWN."

"Thank you...Bubba. I don't know how true that is...but I'm very flattered anyway."

"Oh...YOUUU ARRRE very smart, Felix. YOUUU certainly fooled MEEE...back in 1975...when YOUUU pretended to BEEE Salome's lawyer!"

"So you know about that!" Felix said. "Listen Mr...eh...Bubba...I..."

"Don't APOLOOOGIZE! It was a GREAAAT performance, Felix. And you did the right thing. I was a TOOOTAL asshole back then. I wasn't a very good father. YOUUU did the RIIIGHT thing...by helping MYYY daughter. And SHEEE has gone on to BEEE alright. I'm very proud that SHEEE'S a New York City school teacher," Bubba said.

"That is pretty remarkable," Felix said, thinking back to Salome, from the first time he met her in 1974, when she was a fourteen year-old runaway. "But you were a fine father Bubba...when it came to the essentials. True, back then, you may have lacked somewhat in sensitivity, but hey...all of your children had food in their bellies, clothes on their backs, and a nice roof over their heads...And that was because you got up early...and busted your ass every single day!"

"That is SOOO kind of YOUUU to SAAAY," Bubba said. "BACKKK to Salome a minute. I KNOOOW...that YOUUU have ALWAAAYS loved her deeply," Bubba said, and then he continued, "Look Felix...I'm SOOO sorry...if I'm stepping on sensitive ground here...but I KNOOW...I'm not going to BEEE around much longer...so PLEEEASE let MEEE just talk."

"Please Bubba...say anything you feel like saying," Felix said, with that old lump in his throat over Salome beginning again.

"I KNOOW that YOUUU wanted to BEEE with her and my grandson...as her husband...and she turned YOUUU down...And I can't think of anybody who would have been better for her...than YOUUU."

"Well...that's ancient history. She already deemed me unworthy...and we've both moved on to other people," Felix said, not really wanting to have this conversation.

"Well...that MAAAY be how things are now...and that MAAAY be how they stay...But I'd like to LEEEAVE this world...and I guess I have NOOO choice in the matter...KNOOOWING that my daughter has YOUUU in her corner...Look Felix...YOUUU were wonderful to my son, Jack, when HEEE first moved into your MOOOTEL...and YOUUU helped him to BEEEGIN a life that led to a successful career. YOUUU have always been wonderful to Geneva and their children...MYYY grandchildren...also...In 1978...when Bruiser was at his LOOOWEST point...your MOOTEL...and his involvement with that restaurant...SAAAVED Bruiser's life...When Jennifer was at her LOOOWEST...after she found out that her BASTTTARD husband had another woman for nearly twenty years...YOUUU were wonderful to her...at your

MOOOTEL...she came back from Florida...in 1998...with a SMIIILE on her face...And what YOUUU did...for your brother, Anthony...Salome's husband...BUYYYING him that car...to pick up his spirits...and then STOPPPING Salome and Walter Lee from getting HURRRT...by PAAAYING off Anthony's drug debt...YOUUU ARRRE one incredible man, Felix...and YOUUU have always been there for my family...and I KNOOOW...that somewhere DEEEP in her heart...Salome has always IDOLIIIZED you...from WAAAY back in 1975...when YOUUU PLAAAYED her lawyer," Bubba said, and then jokingly added..."In fact...I was ALWAAAYS afraid...that YOUUU might STEEEAL Pauline away from MEEE...she loves YOUUU so much."

And Felix, having thought in the past, that maybe at one time he had been the object of a crush by the young Salome, the type of crush that starts in a young girl's mind and is fantasized about for years, and that perhaps his romantic relationship with her in 1997, had just been a way for her to satisfy her youthful curiosity. And that, after awhile, especially when the sex had segued from slow, loving, and romantic, into a hyper thing, maybe she had indeed just satisfied her curiosity, which once satisfied, had turned the sex, as a byproduct of their romantic relationship, into more of an obligatory than a loving thing in her mind, thus the relationship had come to an end. "You know I care about you and your family very much," Felix said. "And yes...I am still in love with Salome...but she's made it clear...she isn't interested."

"I KNOOW," Bubba said. "But EEEVEN if YOUUU both never have the REEELATIONSHIP that YOUUU once had in the late 1990's...Would YOUUU PLEEEASE promise MEEE...that after I LEEEAVE this world...that YOUUU will keep a close eye out for her ANYWAAAY?... Jack and Geneva will be fine...SOOO will Jennifer...SOOO will Bruiser...SOOO will Cindy, Jimson, and the grandchildren...And Pauline will be surrounded by family... But I worry about Salome...She doesn't even KNOOOW...that she has ALWAAAYS been my favorite...And I worry about her FIIINDING the wrong man...that her life will get MESSSED up...PLEEEASE Felix...promise that YOUUU will ALWAAAYS watch out for Salome and Walter Lee...and that YOUUU will ALWAAAYS be a rock they can LEEEAN on," Bubba said.

"I promise," Felix said, wondering how he'd work out the logistics to that promise.

"God Bless YOUUU...Felix Kulpa," Bubba said.

"God Bless you too...Mr. Apple," Felix said.

Five days later, on December 9, 2002, Bubba Apple passed away in his sleep. Walter Lee Younger called Felix to tell him, and after the phone call, Felix cried. The funeral was four days later, and all of the children were solemn. Pauline was inconsolable. Bruiser delivered the eulogy. He began

with, "My dad…my best friend." Since there was only another week until the ten-day December school recess anyway, Salome took the week off before the Winter break, and she stayed in Burlington at her mom's house.
When she returned to Staten island on New Years Day, Salome found, from Felix, a sympathy card with the following letter inside:

Dear Salome,

I was saddened deeply, to hear about the passing of your father. Regardless of the problems you two had in the past (most of which, I understand, were cleared up after you became a Christian in the early 1980's) I know how much you loved him. (And I think about, how much I loved and miss my father too.) I just want you to know, that your father called me from the hospital, five days before he died, and we had a wonderful conversation. He told me, and it might surprise you to know, that you were always his favorite, that he had always admired your brains and your b—— (guts)! He said, that even when he had acted like a total jerk, that he had always loved you, and that he had never really forgiven himself for breaking your jaw. He also asked me, to always "be in your corner." In fact, he made me promise that I would. With that promise in mind, besides being the biological uncle to your son, I would also like to always be a sounding board and a shoulder for you too. I know that there are some uncomfortable things between us, that we'll probably need to discuss in the future—if you're willing. I'm moving to New York City, when Winter ends, and the Al-Can is passable. Probably in the next few months (hopefully because I've sold my novel!) and besides asking to see Walter Lee, I would like us to communicate regularly again. (There's nobody's conversation, who've I've ever enjoyed and missed more.) Meanwhile, if you'd like to talk, I've included my phone number, just in case you've misplaced it, and you can call me 24/7, for any reason.

Take care of yourself,
Felix

@@@@@@@@

Clothed in a nice dress, cleaned up with a haircut, with phony press credentials displayed around her neck, eighty-two year-old Beverly Jenkowitz Kulpa, snaked her way through the Bryant Park crowd, and positioned herself right up at the front of the runway, on this warm afternoon in May of

2003. Today's event featured female celebrities modeling for famous designers, and Beverly had approached her mission zone at precisely the right time, just as Joanne Watson had trained her repeatedly to do. She was going to verbally ambush somebody on the runway, much in the same way that one of Howard Stern's crew, "Stuttering John," would do to celebrities. The only difference, Beverly's question would be for monitoring purposes, since Joanne Watson's boss wanted to see just how many people turned in the direction of the verbal confrontation, and for just how long. They wanted a time reading, as to just how effective of a diversion Beverly Jenkowitz Kulpa could create.

Martha Stewart strutted slowly down the runway in her bodacious *Jonathan Dingus* chartreuse sari with made-from-old-tire-and-inner-tube sandles, and when she got to the end, just after she finally smiled, but just before she could push out her hips and make an exaggerated turn, Beverly Jenkowitz Kulpa yelled out: "YOU'RE INVOLVED IN INSIDE TRADING, AND ALL OF YOUR EMPLOYEES SAY YOU ARE A RACIST BITCH! YOU'RE INVOLVED IN INSIDE TRADING, AND ALL OF YOUR EMPLOYEES SAY YOU ARE A RACIST BITCH!" And then Beverly gave Martha Stewart an Italian salute, and escaped through the pandemonium of the shocked crowd.

@@@@@@@@

In early May of 2003, after Felix had heard from Dee Dee that *Dreck Publishing* wanted to publish *Mad Beach*, he had made all of the necessary arrangements, before leaving Alaska. He sold his pick up truck and most of the furniture. Unfortunately, Felix felt, with the war in Iraq escalating, that down the road, conscription might rear its ugly little head in America once again. And, worrying about all of the Apple boys, but especially his fourteen year-old nephew, Walter Lee, Felix had decided that his hard-to-find cabin in Alaska might be useful, in the future, as a hideout. Fortunately, Felix had been befriended by Thutmose Romitu, his closest neighbor two miles away, an Egyptian, who had both joined the Anchorage *Jews for Jesus* church at about the same time as Felix, and who was in charge of computer operations at *The First Palmer Bank*. Since the bank had just merged with *The Alaskan National Bank*, and the new parent bank had cleaned house with the exception of Thutmose, he had been placed in a unique situation to help Felix. And since Thutmose Romitu was simpatico with Felix in regards to being staunchly against the war in Iraq, he not only was willing to help Felix, but he was the actual architect of the plan.

Thutmose's cabin, heated car barn, and ten acres, were worth about the same as Felix's place on seven acres. The cabins were about the same size, and what Thutmose's place lacked in amenities, it made up for in extra acreage.

To make sure that Thutmose was comfortable with the deal, Felix insisted that he accept an additional $20,000 as a differential. Thutmose simply changed Felix's free and clear mortgage, on the bank's computer, into his own name, and he showed it as a sale from Felix Kulpa to Thutmose Romitu. Thutmose had been left a sizeable fortune by his father, so there would be nothing unusual about him making the purchase. Felix would deposit the money into his account, and then in smaller amounts, Felix would withdraw the amount of the check plus $20,000 from his accounts in Florida and New York, and by the end of the following year, he would fly to Seattle to meet Thutmose, and give him the cash in one lump sum. Meanwhile, Thutmose, with his wife and son, would move into Felix's cabin after he left. Thutmose had forwarded all of that information to the title company, the Hall of Records, and the utility companies. He still kept his own place in his name, and, with just a handshake agreement, assured Felix, that any nephew who arrived in Alaska, after a phone call from Felix, would receive Thutmose's cabin and property, and the title would be transferred to him. To be sure that a nephew of Felix's couldn't be traced to Thutmose's old cabin, it was decided that he would arrive with a complete phony background and identification. Felix said, that somewhere along the way to New York City in his *Beetle*, he would stop for a while in a larger city, and do research, find a male child who had died as a baby, rent a room under that dead infant's name, and put together a false identity for a young male, using the address of the room where he was staying. Before he left Alaska, with Thutmose's permission, Felix had told Leslie O'Reily the truth about the property switch, and Leslie had agreed, if needed, to watch over his nephew in Alaska.

When Felix left Alaska, on an early morning in late May of 2003, he had the backseat of his *Beetle* packed so high, he could barely see out of the rearview mirror. On the passenger seat in his cage sat Major Doofus. Felix had decided, of all the people he knew, Bruiser Apple would probably enjoy Major Doofus the most. Felix planned on taking I-90 across the United States, and then dropping Major Doofus off with Bruiser in Rutland.

When Felix stopped at Canadian Customs at the Tok, Alaska crossing, everything went smoothly. But, four days later, leaving Alberta, Canada, for Sweet Grass, Montana, at United States Customs, Major Doofus decided to act up.

The United States Border Patrol Officer was wearing two hearing aids, and as he result, he was very loud when he spoke, "Have you ANYTHING TO DECLARE?"

And Major Doofus said, "WWWRRROOOAAA...HOMO!"

Since the Border Patrol Officer was also Gay, he was more than a bit annoyed hearing the parrot. "That's a REAL NASTY PARROT!" he said.

And Major Doofus said, "WWWRRROOOAAA...ASSHOLE!"

"I don't know if we like nasty parrots entering the United States," he said. And Felix thought, 'What about Tony Blair?' He then stuck his head inside of the *Beetle*, and he saw the nameplate on the bottom of the cage. "MAJOR DOOFUS…EH?" He said.

And Major Doofus said, "WWWRRROOOAAA…Eat Me!"

After Felix explained that the parrot had come with the cabin he had purchased in Alaska, and that somebody else had taught him how to be nasty, and, as a Christian, he had decided to get rid of the parrot, and that he was now heading to Vermont to leave Major Doofus with one of his heathen friends, the Border Patrol Officer let Felix pass.

Felix arrived in Minneapolis two days later, and he rented a room for a month. He did his library research, and he found a white male baby, who had been born in Rapid City, South Dakota fifteen years ago, and, at two years of age, had accidentally fallen into his aunt's pool in St. Paul and drown. Felix put together a birth certificate, a social security card, and a passport for Arnold Hirshensen during the next month in Minneapolis, and then he headed to Bruiser and Eileen's in Rutland.

He arrived in Rutland very late on the Wednesday after the July 4th holiday, and Bruiser was delighted with the present. Eileen was not so thrilled. But after Bruiser had wheezed, "Aw come on Eileen…I'll take Major Doofus…with me to city…council meetings," she, still very much proud that her husband had won a city council seat in Rutland last year, acquiesced. Then Bruiser told Felix, "Salome is up here…and in the hospital…she had major surgery…yesterday."

"What's wrong with her?" Felix asked with true concern.

"Mom made us all…swear to secrecy what…is wrong with Salome…because Salome doesn't want…anyone outside of the…family to know the…truth. In fact I…shouldn't have even told…you that, but for…some reason I thought…that Bubba would have…wanted me to."

"But I can't go see her?" Felix asked.

"No. She would be…totally embarrassed and she…would never talk to…me again."

Later that night at two-thirty, when everyone was sleeping soundly, Felix snuck out of the house and drove to the hospital. He figured that she was in ICU, so after seeing in the lobby that ICU was on the fifth floor, he walked up the five flights of stairs. When he sneaked a peak out from the staircase doors, he could see two women wearing white uniforms, down at the far end of the hall. Fortunately, the angle in which they were sitting, would conceal him from them, if he were quiet.

Felix tip-toed down the hall, looking in through the doors of the rooms at people asleep in bed, with each one wired up electronically to the monitoring screen where the two women in white sat. Suddenly, an Italian-looking man of approximately thirty years of age, wearing a heavily grimaced face, stepped out from one of the rooms, and quietly walked past Felix. For an instant their eyes locked, but then he disappeared through the door that led to the same staircase that Felix had used.

Felix approached the door from which the other man had fled, looked in, and the first thing he noticed was Salome's beautiful red hair. Stealthily, Felix walked up to the bed. The next thing he noticed was the smooth skin on Salome's neck, and then her bank lamp green eyes. Then he noticed her angelic face, and he smiled. The fifth thing he noticed, since the bed sheet was pulled off of her, was that one of her beautiful breasts was trying to poke it's way out of the hospital gown, and then he noticed her cute belly button. The seventh thing he noticed, was that she had a colostomy bag attached to her left side.

Felix now understood in an instant, and his first reaction was to hop into bed, hold her, and kiss her all over. But he knew that she would be embarrassed, if she opened her eyes, and his was the face that she gazed upon. So very gingerly, Felix covered her up with the sheet, and then he left her room and the fifth floor using the same stairs.

Salome would eventually tell Felix, thirteen months later in August of 2004, what had happened. She would tell him that she had been constipated for two weeks, and during the July 4th weekend of 2003 in Rutland, she had woken up at Jennifer's in agony. At the hospital they gave her a CAT scan, and a large tumor in the lower colon had been discovered. That tumor was causing the blockage. Then they had performed an emergency colostomy, so there would be a place for the waste to go. A month later, after she had healed from the initial surgery, they had removed the tumor from her lower colon during a second operation. The tumor was cancerous, and also the pathology showed that some of the cancer cells had traveled and broken into healthy tissue. The solution was several protocols of chemo and radiation therapy, and once cancer free, they would reverse the colostomy. That reversal would come during the Winter recess from school in December of 2003, but by June of 2004, not only would the cancer be back, but they would discover a new tumor twice as big as the original. Immediately after school had ended in June of 2004, eight weeks after the second tumor had been excised, Salome was given a permanent colostomy—her entire colon removed.

In July of 2003, before her first surgery, Salome had called Peter Proffilacto to tell him, that she had decided to go ahead the next day, while in Rutland, and have the needed surgery to correct a "woman's problem." He had whined that she had to go to Rutland for a week in the first place, seeing it as just a week taken away from their planned road trip out west, while Walter Lee stayed with relatives in Vermont. He hadn't wanted to go with her to Vermont, so he just remained in New York City pouting. He would start to feel guilty about things on Wednesday however, so he would drive to Rutland to surprise her in the middle of the night. He would get her room number over the phone from New York, and he would be told that she didn't have a phone in her room in ICU. When he would see the colostomy bag, he would be totally skeeved. But since nobody, but some older guy on the fifth floor of the hospital in ICU, would see him, he would decide to at least be a little classy, and to not tell anyone about Salome's plight, or to tell Salome herself that he knew.

The day after he would come to Rutland and then immediately return to New York, Salome would call him in New York during the afternoon. She would know that the colostomy bag was going to be a problem in her relationship with Peter, and she would know that she wanted to tell him and show him in person. She would naively think however, that their love would overcome that as an obstacle. The minute she would get him on the phone however, he would say, "Listen Salome…I've been thinking…And I think our relationship is a bit too confining…I think that we should date other people." Peter Proffilacto's words would cut her deeper than any surgeon's scalpel.

Felix sat until dawn on a bench next to a small duck pond on the hospital grounds. His whimpering was more like a silent scream that just couldn't be extracted, and he would then suddenly break into meaningless gibberish. He needed to cry, but he was just too overwhelmed with grief to do that. He did manage to pull it together just a little when he saw the first light of dawn, because he realized that he needed to get back to Bruiser's, before anyone woke up and thought that he might have gone to the hospital to see Salome. Felix truly loved Salome, and he would never mention to anyone what he knew. The last thing he said, one of the only things that had made any sense in the past few hours, before he left the bench by the little duck pond was, "Dear God…why couldn't it have been me instead?" And, of course, it just doesn't work that way.

CHAPTER TWENTY

'Just like the announcements being made *ad nauseam* both in the terminal and on the Staten Island Ferry,' Felix thought, walking in Manhattan's West Village with his old friend and current landlord, Michael Keigh, on this beautiful August 16th evening in 2003. They were celebrating Felix's fifty-seventh birthday, having just devoured wonderful Mexican food at *Tortilla Flats* on Washington Street, and now they were heading towards *The Bottom Line* on 4th Street to see the ten o'clock show of *The K. J. Bauer Band*. Felix's old writing partner from the *Home Cooking* days, had recently left *Triangulated Crossfire*, moved from Austin, Texas to Manhattan, and put together his own four-piece group. Tonight at ten o'clock was their maiden voyage, and it was a hot ticket. When Felix had called K. J. on his cell earlier in the day for two tickets to the sold out show, K. J. had told him that it was a slam dunk, to pick them up at the box office.

"I'm thinking about digitally changing those bullshit subway escalator announcements…I think I can hack my way into the MTA system… and then one day…rather than sitting…waiting for a train…and having to hear over and over the MTA's ideas on proper escalator usage…instead… people will hear: 'Please do not fart or masturbate while on the escalator…as the liquid and vapors will bollocks up the sensitive equipment…Please do not perform cartwheels, D and C's, wisdom tooth extraction, or sheep shearing while on the escalator…as those activities require expensive city and state licenses… and we have no way of monitoring you…when you're mobile!'" Michael Keigh said, with a churlish attitude and a grin. And if anybody could hack into the MTA's announcement system, it was surely Michael. Besides being a real estate and financial wizard—one of his properties, where Felix currently lived, was the six-story apartment building in which he had been a renter, and Felix and Tatiana had sublet in 1966, on 10th Street between Avenues C and D—Michael was also a great bass player, a computer-hacking genius, and an overall smart man.

"Yeah…I was just thinking about all of the Staten Island Ferry announcements," Felix said. "I was waiting for my nephew last week in the Manhattan terminal, and every thirty seconds I was bombarded with messages about, 'The K-9 dogs are for your security…all backpacks, bags, and luggage are subject to search…thank you for your cooperation.' The next day…when Walter Lee had to go back…just for fun…since I hadn't ridden it in over thirty years…I took the ferry with him to Staten Island and then immediately took it back…and on the trip there…we could hardly hear ourselves talk…on the trip back I didn't care…Anyway…I think that the MTA, the Staten Island Ferry, and the City of New York are all in cahoots with the companies who make MP3 and portable CD players…that they're getting a big kickback…You know…annoy people enough with announcements…so the only recourse is to buy a portable device that cranks the music directly into your ears."

"Agreed," Michael said with a smile. Then he asked, "Hey…do you remember that song…the one we made up on the ferry…I think it was in 1966? You know…we got real baked at my place…and we decided a ride on the Staten Island Ferry would be fun."

"I don't remember the lyrics," Felix said, while having to adjust his position on the street, yet again, for somebody who was walking directly at him. "I do remember the annoying shoeshine guy…he carried a shoeshine box and big pillow…and he would get down on his knees and shine your shoes for a dollar...and that you could hear him bellow, 'SHINE!' throughout the boat." Felix, now used to four years of serenity in the Alaskan wilderness, was having a hard time readjusting to the noise pollution in Manhattan.

"That's it!" Michael said. "I remember the chorus now…We came up with: *'Out of this shit, and into something else. Obscurity sucks, I don't need no fucking shine!'* "

"Right," Felix said. "In early 1966...before I had met Tatiana…when we were both fledgling artists…you as a musician…and me as a writer…and we both dreamed of making it big."

"You've done alright, Felix…You've got your second novel coming out in November…And your two *Home Cooking* albums are cult classics. "

"Well…the journey so far…hasn't been the journey that I envisioned in 1966...but I guess I'm not complaining," Felix said. And then Felix thought of all the missing people in his life, and he started to tear up. Recently, he had been particularly feeling the absence of his brother. He was able to stop from crying before Michael detected, and he continued, "You're the one who has made the serious money, Michael...You own what...seven buildings in lower Manhattan...you've got big *machers*...from all over the world...paying you large fees for your financial consultation...and...from what I heard at your place earlier...you still play a mean bass."

"Yeah...well...I would have preferred to have made my money playing Rock Music," Michael said with a smile. But then, as somebody on the sidewalk was walking right at him, Michael's smile gave way to a grimace, as he just stopped and made the other person walk around him. "I'm really getting fed up with assholes...who always expect other people to move out of their way on the sidewalk."

"I think people should be required to know basketball...to take a test...to know the difference between a block and a charge...before being allowed to walk on the streets of Manhattan," Felix said. "I try to be real decent about it...real Christian...but I too am getting tired of people always expecting me to be the one to move...It's almost as if I have a big sign on my shoulders that reads: 'I'm a big guy...and I'll be happy to get out of your way if you get in my face.'"

"I know," Michael said. "You mentioned the Staten Island Ferry...last year I had to take it...So I'm waiting up near the front for the big glass doors to open...they start to open...I'm clearly one of the first people through...and this young black dude...in his late teens...pushes me out of the way to get through the door...I say, 'Excuse me!' and he gives me one of these looks...You know...the 'Who do you think you are you cracker asshole?' type of looks. And I say, 'Oh I see...because I'm white...I have to back away from my position at the door...and you get to go through first, huh!'...And then he mumbles something to his friend about 'whitey'...So I say, 'Yo...look sonny...this ain't no Rosa Parks deal...it ain't a racial issue...it's a human issue...I was in position at the door first...and you didn't need to be so fucking aggressive...pushing me out of the way...and you're lucky that I didn't knock your ass out...which I could have easily done...and still can if you like...and when I'm done with you...I'll take care of your homey too...if he wants to dance...But hey...just so you know...I was out in the streets fighting for your rights...in the 1960's...before you were even a sperm cell in your daddy's nut sack! Now go home and tell your mama...she raised a stupid kid!'"

"So what did he say then?" Felix asked.

"Nothing...he just gave me another look...and then I had to see his boxer shorts...as he walked away with his pants so low...it looked as if he were carrying a major load."

"Well I certainly understand African-American angst...my best friend...Dr. Walter Lee Younger...has written several books on the subject...But if Walter Lee had witnessed your scene, not only would he have agreed with you, he would have gotten all up in the face of the kid himself,"

Felix said.

"Wait a minute...Dr. Walter Lee Younger...the radical anthropologist? I read, *Tokenism: The Corporate African-American Executive*, a few years ago...and I've read several of his articles... The guy is brilliant!...But didn't I meet him back in the summer of 1969? He came up here from your motel in Florida, and he spent a couple of days in The City with you and Tatiana before you guys went to Woodstock."

"That's right," Felix said.

"Yeah...you and Tatiana were having dinner with him...outside...at the *Life Café* on 10th Street and Avenue B...and I walked by, you made the introduction, and I sat down. I drank a beer and shot the shit at your table for fifteen or twenty minutes," Michael said. "I can't believe that's the same guy from way back then...I remember that he was real funny...I remember him saying...that one of his favorite things...was showing up at a stuffy Caucasian party and asking, 'Where the white women at?' I had no idea that he wrote brilliant books."

"Well...he hadn't written them then. In fact...he didn't even start college...if going to college is some kind of litmus test that earmarks the potential for a life of brilliance...until 1974...But Walter Lee was already very well-read by the time he began college...As for you having a beer with us in 1969...I seem to remember that...but I keep having these 'senior moments'... I don't remember so well anymore," Felix said.

"Well...that happens...when you're a crusty fifty-seven year old!" Michael laughed.

"Oh I see...you're still a year away from said crust deposits!" "'Miles and miles to go...before I sleep'...in a nursing home!" Michael laughingly said.

"Yeah...I've been thinking lately about just moving into the fade out farm now...why bother with the next twenty or thirty years?" Felix said, just before a huge woman, assuming that nobody could possibly be walking on the sidewalk as she exited, walked out of a chic dress store for big women on Greenwich Avenue carrying six bags, and immediately plowed into him.

"I'm so sorry!" She said in earnest.

"Hey...we're all human...forget about it," Felix said.

After they had walked about a half block, Michael said, "You really let Kate Smith off of the hook back there. If it had been me, I would have said something like, 'It's called "There Are Other People on the Planet Besides Yourself," look into it!'"

"I know...I probably would have said something like that to her...a few years ago. And if I were writing a story...no doubt, one of my characters would say something like that to her. But I know what it is to be fat...and to have to buy clothes at a specialty store. I mean...it's been years since I've had to do that...but I do remember that I felt embarrassment. I would imagine...for a woman...it would be even worse," Felix said.

"My God man...do you really think...that you can live your whole life...without getting angry with all of these assholes out here? Look at them... they're sheep!" Michael said.

"Most of them I call 'Bling-Blingites,'" Felix said. "Take a good look on the street...It's Darwinian Evolution...our species now has a cell phone appendage."

"What a circus on the subway...now that it's 'hot.' Between the *Palm Pilots* and *Blackberrys*...added to the CD and MP3's...," Michael said.

"I know," Felix said, while quickly noticing and avoiding something funky on the sidewalk. "It's a digital ballet of meaninglessness...and a way to avoid real contact with other human beings. We seem to prefer our human contact online these days. But if we don't know the person to whom we are e-mailing or IMing, then we can't see the facial expressions, the body language...that which...at times...tells so much more than the written word."

"Sheep!" Michael said, and then added, "It isn't whether the glass is half full or half empty...the fucking glass is totally empty...and they're just using smoke and mirrors...to try and convince us that it might be half full! Look at them...never an original thought...their half-lives are hackneyed hellholes of hysteria and ho-hum...and they actually think that electing John Kerry next year will make a difference...Lib-er-als!...*The Peter Principle* personified!" Michael said.

"*The Peter Principle*?...Oh yeah...I remember...that 'eventually everybody reaches their own level of incompetence.' From some of the 'Yes sir...yes sir...three bags full!' attitude I see from our so-called elected leaders...people who should rise up in disgust...over the political shenanigans in Washington...I would say that *The Peter Principle* nails it!"

"Sheep!" Michael bellowed, sounding like a character late in *David Copperfield*.

"Hey...that was always the difference between the Soviet Union and the United States. There was no charade in Soviet government. If you joined the Communist Party and always endorsed their position, life was easier for you, because the Communist Party's position was how the country was going to be run...Deal with it...But in the United States...there's this deceptive dance between what's supposed to be the left and the right...And while this show goes on for the public's entertainment...the real stuff goes on behind the scenes...anyway."

"And those poor souls who now immigrate...know not...that they will take over...in their rightful positions...at the bottom of the pyramid scheme," Michael said. Michael continued, "Lately I've been thinking...that we need to modify the Statue of Liberty...Instead of the torch...she should hold up a yellow cab...And her other arm...should be down in her crotch...And the gold plaque with Emma Lazarus' 'The New Colossus' should be removed... and replaced with these words: 'I'VE GOT YOUR NEW FOUND FREEDOM...RIGHT HERE!'"

"That's funny!" Felix said, and then he stopped to tie his shoelace.

"Sheep!" Michael bellowed again. "Give me your ignorant masses... yearning to be schtupped...without the *Vaseline*!"

"I agree," Felix said. "As citizens of this country and this planet...we must learn...that there are forces at work...forces interested only in profit... and scenarios created...designed only to hurt us...and to kill our young in superfluous warfare...so that we are not only bled dry financially...but the lifeblood of a family...its living members...are bled dry also...all so the armaments industry can make theirs...And I pity the person who can't see that...But at a personal level...how I interact with people individually...and I'm not going to change the quote...because some of the wording might not be deemed 'politically correct' in 2003...as John Lennon once said, 'When you have a retarded child in the family, you don't smash his teeth in, and then make him stand outside of the door. You extend a helping hand.' I see the wisdom in that...that seems like a Christian way to be...not in my writings...in which I'll bash the Fabianistic oligarchic and plutocratic profiteers...to whom life has little value...every time all of the time...but in most of my one on one dealings with other human beings...in the last couple of years especially...I've tried to be more compassionate...However...I'm still a human being with a temper...And on certain days, when sufficiently provoked of course, I might choose to either 'ed-u-ma-cate' the dorkus who pisses me off...with a verbal vivisection...or perhaps show her or him something up close... something that Neil Armstrong once saw. I'd rather save my angst for my writing, however...And now...my angst is political...
everything has been put into place...since September 11th...since the congressional passing of the Patriot Act...to not only turn this country into a 1950's House of Un-American Activities circus...but to bring conscription back also," Felix said.

"We should drag our so-called congressional representatives...out onto the White House lawn...and just kick the crap out of them...then arrest them...and throw the book at them!"

"A Harold Robbins novel for misdemeanors...a Tom Robbins novel for felonies!"

"Right!" Michael said, and then added, "Or send them off to LSD Reeducation Centers...like in the 1960's cult classic...*Wild in the Streets*!"

"Yeah," Felix said, and then added, "By the way... did you ever watch *The X-Files*...that Sunday evening television series?"

"Just a few shows...why?"

"Did you ever see those three bozos...'The Lone Gunmen'...who were occasionally part of the show?"

"Yeah...I remember them," Michael said.

"Well there was a spin off show called *The Lone Gunmen*...and the pilot episode...in March of 2001...remember...I'm saying March of 2001...was all about a U.S. governmental plan...to fly a commercial airline into the World Trade Center...to make it appear as if terrorists hijacked the plane...all to garner the support of both the politicians and the people...so we could sell more weaponry...more 'smart bombs,' etc...and crank up the armaments industry...an industry on the wane since Vietnam...The only difference between the show and real life...in the show it was to be done at night...with the possibility of a loss of hundreds...not thousands...In the show...the plane was actually being flown by remote control from the ground...and the pilots could do nothing to override...And in the show...one of The Lone Gunmen is able to hack into the computer controlling the plane...so what was to be a tragedy...turns out to be just a near miss."

"Get out of town!" Michael said. "And this was on television six months before September 11th?"

"That's right," Felix said. "They only made thirteen episodes of *The Lone Gunmen*, and other than the pilot episode, the rest are kind of silly. But there's this beautiful woman...Indian or Pakistani...Zuleikha Robinson is the actor's name...and she's worth watching...even if the shows are stupid!"

"Thanks for the heads up on that." Michael said. "Meanwhile...when we get to *The Bottom Line*...the first round is on me...TO THE PATRIOT ACT!" Michael said, raising his hand, pretending as if he were holding a goblet of libation.

"TO THE PATRIOT ACT THEN!" Felix said, imitating the toast.

A couple of years later, in 2005, when Congress was deciding on renewing the Patriot Act, Michael would post the following on Walter Lee Younger's *The Mad Beach Center for Free Expression* website: *"And the Younger Bush said, 'Let the price of freedom be Freedom.' And the People seemed dubious at first. So the Younger Bush wagged his tail, causing the attached flag to flutter in the fetid winds. Inspired, the People cheered and renewed the Patriot Act. In their delirious enthusiasm, the Supremes abolished property rights. Thus commenced the blessed era of freedomless freedom for all. And the Great White Father reigned for some time, benevolently distributing what remained of the Black Blood from the Sands to the deserving freedomless free. Amen."*

When Felix and Michael arrived at *The Bottom Line*, Felix scooped their tickets from the box office, and they were immediately seated in front.

Being huge fans of *Home Cooking*, Christopher Jeremy and his father were sitting in the back bleachers, and they noticed Felix. Christopher had been in Europe, when the tickets had become available in person only at *The Bottom Line's* box office. His father had blown off work and waited, with a sleeping bag, in front of the place all night, to get their tickets.

The opening act that night, from Florida, *The Dangling Chads*, were very good, yet they still needed just a wee bit of polish.

The K. J. Bauer Band was extremely tight, and the crowd seemed to like all of the new material. When it came time for an encore, K. J. went over and whispered something into his keyboard player's ear. The keyboard player nodded, and then he left the stage. K. J. said, "Thanks everybody for coming...you've been great. We'd like to end with something old...from the mid 1980's...when I played with my first band...*Home Cooking*...And since I see that my old writing partner and band mate...Felix Kulpa...is sitting down front...Felix...you'd better come up here...Plaudits.

"I think I've forgotten most of our stuff!" Felix yelled back.

"Come on up...I'll remind you...you old fart! Hey everybody...it's Felix's fifty-seventh birthday today!" The thirty-eight year-old K. J. Bauer said. More plaudits. When Felix made it up to the keyboard, K. J. whispered, "You thought I forgot...Dad?"

And Felix said, "You've done real well for yourself...Send money... Son!" K. J. laughed, and then he reminded Felix of his keyboard and harmony parts in "The Inner Bitch," before they played it perfectly.

For Christopher Jeremy and his dad, it was a perfect show.

@@@@@@@@

"Hey man...I've been waiting to talk to you...how was Europe?" Fifty-seven year-old C. Wel Rellim asked thirty-one year-old Christopher Jeremy, as Christopher approached the stone slab veranda in front of Essex Street Middle School, on this first day back to school in early September of 2003.

Christopher sat down, lit a cigarette, and said, "I had a great time... Sorry I didn't get around to e-mailing you when I got back...but the day after I came back I went to a show with my dad...and the next day my grandmother in Florida passed away...so we ended up in the Hollywood area for about a week."

"I thought she had passed away a couple of years ago, and left you her house and money," C. Wel said.

"That was my other grandmother," Christopher said. "When I got back from Florida, I went camping in the Adirondacks until a few days ago...What did you do all summer?"

"I was in Florida too...I drove down to Tallahassee and saw my son and his wife...My son manages a chic restaurant there," C. Wel said, after lighting a cigarette. "So talk about Europe already!"

"When I got to Heathrow...it was close to midnight...and the train to downtown London wasn't running...Fortunately...the guy I sat next to on the plane...had a car at the airport...He was heading into downtown...so he saved me the hefty cab fare...I had reservations for three nights at this old hotel...in the Southwark area...and after seeing London...I was going to travel by train to Scotland...then see the western part of

England...Liverpool and Manchester...take the ferry to Ireland...and then return to London for a day or two...before arriving in Amsterdam...where I had a two-day reservation waiting at a hostel."

"So...that's what you did?"

"Well...it didn't turn out that way...I met this woman..."

"Ah ha!...Things never turn out the way you've planned...when there's a woman involved," C. Wel said.

"True...Anyway...the day after I arrived in London...I hiked everywhere...and late in the afternoon...I ended up at the Dickens House on Doughty Street...I met Loretta there."

"Loretta?" C. Wel asked.

"Loretta Steinberg...her father is a German Jew...her mother English Anglican...'Steinberg' is her maiden name...she's divorced...has been for two years...She's thirty-five...with an eleven year-old daughter...She lives in Kiel, Germany...She's in charge of the marketing division of a huge corporation in Hamburg...forty-five miles from Kiel...and she commutes from her house by train...or she drives in...She makes a ton of money..."

"Never mind that shit," C. Wel said. "What does she look like?"

"Right...let's get down to what matters!" Christopher said. "She's very pretty...about 115 pounds...five feet six inches...longish auburn hair...blue eyes...nice facial features."

"So what happened?"

"She was raised in London...went to school there...and when she was a teenager...her father's company transferred him to Berlin...They were in Berlin for two years...and then they transferred him to Hamburg...She went to college in London...her father got her a job in marketing with his company in Hamburg...she got married...had a child...got divorced...and bought a house in Kiel."

"I didn't ask for a biography of this broad," C. Wel said. "I asked... what happened?"

"Right...enquiring minds want to know...Okay...so Loretta has always loved Victorian Literature...and especially Dickens...She'd been to the Dickens House once before...and we were the only two in the place... other than the curator...and we started talking Victorian Literature...then we started talking about everything else in the world...and the place was closing...so we left together...started walking towards the tube...and then we both decided we were hungry...I said that I wanted great fish n' chips...we ended up taking a taxi instead...to this place she knew...then we walked around London for a few more hours...and I walked her to her hotel."

"That was it?"

"Well...for that night...She was traveling with her aunt...sharing a hotel room...and they were heading back to her aunt's place in Antwerp by train the next morning...Loretta had driven from Kiel to Antwerp...and left her car at her aunt's house…Loretta was then going to drive to Amsterdam… spend one day there…and then return to Kiel…for her mother's sixtieth birthday…a day later."

"So?" C. Wel said impatiently, just before lighting another cigarette.

"What started as a simple goodnight kiss…in front of the hotel…evolved into several periods…plus overtime…of tonsil hockey."

"Ah ha!"

"And then she asked me…if I wanted to travel to Germany with her…that she had almost another two weeks of vacation left…that her daughter was with her ex-husband…I said to myself, 'Self…do you really want to see Edinburgh, Liverpool, Manchester, and Dublin…or would you prefer exploring this beautiful woman's anatomy?'"

"Tough choice…huh!" C. Wel said with a smirk.

"Naturally…I decided…Fuck the haggis…*The Beatles*…and Joyce."

"Naturally," C. Wel said, thinking that that sounded like a song written and sung by Dion, late in 1968, after the Robert Kennedy assassination.

"So…she traveled with her aunt to Antwerp…I took a later train to Amsterdam…we met in Amsterdam…I stayed with her at her ritzy hotel… and the next day we drove to Germany…it took about six hours…then she left me at her place…while she picked up her daughter and brought her daughter over to see grandma…on grandma's sixtieth…and then…after returning her daughter to her ex-husband…she picked me up…and we went out to dinner with her mom…which was kind of weird…sitting with the mom of the woman I'd just met…but to whom I'd already given my bratwurst!"

"Right…she got your *Vienna Sausage*," C. Wel laughingly said. "So go on with your adventure!"

"We hung out at her place a few days…went to Hamburg…went to the Reeperbahn District and the *Ratskeller*…the club where *The Beatles* played in the early 1960's…before their fame…Then we drove around the Upper Rhine Valley area…she showed me all of these beautiful places…we stayed at an incredible B & B…and then a couple of days later…we took the all night ferry from Kiel…across the Baltic Sea…to Copenhagen…and spent a couple of days in Denmark…then we came back to Germany…and it was time for her to get her daughter…so I took a train to Geneva…spent ten days at a friend's place there…spent a day in Paris…then headed home."

"Wow…are you going to keep seeing her?" C. Wel asked.

"I guess…she's a wonderful person…and very sexy…but she lives more than 5,000 miles away…and I have no intention of moving to Germany," Christopher said. "We have e-mailed and spoken twice…since I've been back, and I called her a few times from Geneva."

"And you wouldn't want to be with her enough…to move to Germany?"

"If she were here…I would definitely pursue things…However…I'm trying to keep my emotions on a more even keel..."

"Nice pun," C. Wel said, and then he added, "A more even keel...than with your ex?...Oh yeah...I saw Salome walk by...a few moments ago...She said hello...but I could tell that she was unhappy...maybe it ended...with her and Proffilacto," C. Wel said.

"You've seen a ghost?"

"Okay...right...I've got it," C. Wel said.

"Well anyway...at least Loretta was a nice diversion from some of the online stuff from last year," Christopher said.

"Yeah...I thought the ladies were easy...playing in a rock band."

"Well...last November and December...I was still thinking about 'The Ghost,'...and I really wasn't in the mood to date. By New Years Eve I had my shit together...but New Years Eve was the last gig for *Disabled Dad*... our bass player joined the Navy...and my dad is making some kind of weird movies these days...in his spare time...so the days of groupies were gone."

"So...online dating...sucks?" C. Wel asked, while lighting another cigarette.

"Let me have one of yours...I'm out," Christopher said. "Yeah," Christopher lit his cigarette, "I told you about most of the twelve online dates I had...last year."

"I remember...that one of them you nailed on the first date...and then you didn't call her back," C. Wel said.

"Yeah...and the intelligent...funny one...with no picture posted...who said she was 'statuesque'..."

"But was really 'fatuesque'...I remember...she was like 300 pounds?"

"That's the fact Jack!...But I remember now...you were away at some dean seminar...the last week of school last year...I never told you about my adventures with the psycho dentist from Stony Brook."

"Never heard that one...do tell," said C. Wel.

"*Psycho dentist...qu'est-ce c'est?*" Christopher sang, just like *The Talking Heads* song..."Okay...so I'm e-mailing back and forth with this pretty dentist...her name is Signe...she has some nice pictures posted...she's a good looking blonde with big hooters...and she's ten years older than I."

"What's up...with you and these older women?" C. Wel asked.

"Hell...I don't know...but let me finish this story...this happened on the Friday...the last Friday before the final three days of school the following week...The night before...she and I were IMing...and suddenly she writes, 'I want you! Drive to my house in Stony Brook...now!' And I write back, 'Wow Signe...that would be so cool...but my van is in the shop until late Saturday afternoon...and from where I live in East Elmhurst...to get to the Long Island Railroad right now...would be difficult...and I have to teach in the morning.' She sends me her phone number...asks me to call her...I do...and we agree to get together the next day...Friday...after school...I'll go to Penn Station…take the Long Island Railroad…ride a train to Stony Brook…and she'll pick me up…The problem is…what do I bring?…Since I have this Saturday morning English class I teach…at a Chinese learning center in downtown Brooklyn…and I have to be there by nine…and it was going to be a complicated subway journey anyway…not having my van…so…I think, 'If I get lucky in Stony Brook tonight…I probably won't have time to stop by my place in Queens…before heading to work in Brooklyn on Saturday morning…so I need a change of clothes…and toiletries with me…but I don't want to arrive in Stony Brook…carrying a suitcase…as that looks kind of presumptuous' …So I decided, 'fuck grading any essays this weekend…I'll leave my grade book and the essays in my desk at school…and I'll use my book bag for clothes'…which is what I do…She meets me at the station…or rather she waits in her car and honks at me… when I go outside to have a cigarette…I get in her car…she doesn't say a word…the car smells like a winery…and she just takes my hand in hers."

"Bingo!" C. Wel said.

"Yeah…well it gets better…First of all…I am totally starved…since I had to take the subway to get to school that morning…and I'm running late…I blow off breakfast…And since I teach six classes on Friday…and during my lunch period I had a parent show up…I haven't eaten all day…I had figured she'd meet me at the station…we'd go for a few drinks and a nice dinner somewhere in Stony Brook…and then…if I got lucky…she'd invite me back to her house…I say, 'Hey Signe…I'm starved…let's go get a nice meal someplace'…And she says, 'I have plenty of food back at my place…I'll feed you'…And I say, 'Cool'…and she proceeds to drive out of the station's parking lot…the wrong way…I see two different drivers give her the finger…And then on the street…she immediately runs a stop sign…So I say, 'You better let me drive'…she agrees…and somehow she gives me coherent directions to her place…We pull up into the driveway of this beautiful Victorian house…on a large shady lot in a posh neighborhood …and I notice that she has her dental practice…in the lower part of the house…We enter the house…it's beautiful…I put my book bag down in the foyer…I start to exam the living room…and she says, 'Come upstairs!'

"Bingo!" C. Wel said again.

"I walk upstairs with her…but I'm thinking, 'Yeah…this is cool…but I'm starving!…Please feed me…before you fuck me'…We get to her bedroom…and she immediately removes all of her clothes…climbs onto the bed…and says, 'Please just hold me Christopher.'"

"So what did you do next?…Come on…give it up!"

"Naturally…I removed all of my clothes…climbed onto the bed…and held her…Hey…I figured that I was dealing with wounded gash…And I didn't mind listening to all of her problems…as foreplay…But damn…I'm starved…So I listen for an hour…and she excuses herself to go downstairs to the kitchen...and I say, 'Would you have something downstairs... something I could make a sandwich out of?' And she says, 'I'll take care of it'...When she returns...she has an opened bottle of wine and two glasses...but no sandwich...So I drink some wine with her...one glass for me...three glasses for her...and pretty soon she starts to feel frisky...And I'm thinking, 'I need fuel to fuck'...but it makes no difference...she's already plucking my large grape vine in the dark," Christopher said.

"More like a raisin in the sun!" wise-cracked C. Wel.

"Hey...you're as funny...as Lippy Merkin is competent!...No really C. Wel...that was funny...Back to my adventure...I decide, 'What the hell...I guess I'm gonna fuck before I feed'...and I hop off of the bed...to get a condom from my pants pocket...She sees the condom and yells, 'No way! I hate those things'...And I'm thinking, 'What the fuck...she's a dentist and everything...she has to understand something about public health issues'...but we get into an argument about it...the sex is put on hold...and we end up just talking in bed...and eventually we fall asleep...I'm sleeping soundly... and I awake to discover...that she's taking a Sonoma Valley tour of my grape vine again...I see the clock on the nightstand...it says eleven o'clock...and I see that she's brought another bottle of wine upstairs...but still no sandwich...She stops her vine tasting tour...pours me some wine...I drink my one glass...she drinks her three...and by now...she's so loaded and horny...I can wear a rubber wet suit to bed...and she'll still do me...So I get the prophylactic...and I boink her a couple of times...We both fall asleep...and when I wake up again...I notice that I just have time to quickly clean up and dress...and to make the last possible train back to the city...the 5:30...that will get me to Penn Station...so I can get a subway...and make it to work on time in Brooklyn...I need her to drive me to the station...and she's zonked out...I finally get her up...I get to the station with two minutes to go before the train...I kiss her hung over ass goodbye... I'm so hungry I'm feeling faint...And I find a candy machine with peanut butter crackers in the station...It takes my dollar and returns nothing...I try four quarters instead... It takes my four quarters and returns nothing...So I have to wait until I get to Penn Station...to get a couple of breakfast sandwiches at *Roy Rogers* to go...before heading to work in Brooklyn on the R Train."

"That's quite an adventure," C. Wel said.

"Yeah...well the story isn't over...I get home from work...and she's sent me eight e-mails...and left four messages on my phone...She's saying things like, 'Please move in with me...I'll take care of you...You can use my *Mercedes* to drive to work...I want to take care of you'...And I'm thinking, 'Right...after one wacky night'...So I ignore her messages...and she starts to cyber-stalk me...I get continual IM's and e-mails...she won't stop calling...so finally I write her a real nice e-mail...and explain that I'm still getting over a previous relationship...and yadda, yadda, yadda...how I'm going to

Europe...and I wish her well...and then the e-mails and phone messages start getting nasty...I'm glad she didn't know...specifically where I lived or worked...When I returned from Europe...I noticed that the e-mails and phone messages had stopped...about two weeks after I had left."

"Not the woman...you want to hook up with...you'd probably wake up to find...that your junior grape vine had been cut off...and she was walking on it...That would make you whine!" C. Wel wise-cracked.

"Man...you're in rare form today...you must have taken a healthy one...before school this morning!" Christopher said. "And yeah...I guess most men get emasculated by a woman...somewhere along the line...But it's so much better...when it remains a metaphor!"

"But this babe in Germany...isn't like that...right?"

"Nah...she's cool...so far," Christopher said, as he put out his cigarette. Heath Brown had just made it to school, so C. Wel and Christopher both said hello, and the three men made their way into the continental breakfast in the auditorium.

At 8:45 Principal Greely called the auditorium to order, made the usual first day announcements, and then told the faculty to head into the gymnasium. In the gym, speaking through a microphone that was hooked up to a small amplifier, Principal Greely announced, "One of the things that makes our school great...is being able to work together with our colleagues...If we can work with each other...we can work best with our children...With that thought in mind...I would like us to all break into eight-person groups...you'll find which group you're in...listed over here on this wall...and I would like us to do a little exercise...an exercise designed by psychologists...working with corporate human resource departments... designed to break down...some of the walls...we may have with our colleagues. " After the groups were put together, Principal Greely handed a rubber chicken to one person in each group and said, "The idea here...is that you flip the rubber chicken around the group quickly... establishing a rhythm and a trust with each other." Christopher noticed, after the activity began, that Salome was sitting by herself in the bleachers. Principal Greely walked over to her, apparently looking for an explanation as to why she wasn't participating, and whatever she said he accepted and walked away. Christopher also noticed that Peter Proffilacto was in his group standing at nine o'clock, so the second time Christopher was tossed the chicken, he looked at Alex Silver standing at twelve o'clock, but he flung the bird at nine, and beaned a caught-off-guard Peter in the face. "My bad," is all he said.

At the end of the exercise, Christopher was the one who ended up with the chicken in his group, and he had the awesome responsibility of returning it to the big plastic garbage bag up near the amplifier. As he walked across the gymnasium floor, in an exaggerated manner, he choked his chicken for the entire faculty to see.

Ten minutes later, Christopher was in the library with the other Language Arts Teachers. He chose a place to sit, as far away from Salome as possible. They were learning that they were no longer Language Arts Teachers, Dr. Merkin had just said, "From this day forth...thee shall be known as Literacy Teachers!" And it was good. A rose by any other name...Dr. Merkin continued her chest-thumping "By-Golly-We're-Gonna-Do-Big-Things-This-Year-In Literacy," rap, but since most of the bemused teachers were ignoring her, her poignant pontification passed into a mere pusillanimous parlance. Then she said, "We have a new program in Literacy this year...and I'm counting on you...to be able to implement the necessary changes...into your lesson plans."

"Shit!" A number of teachers said individually *sotto voce*, but collectively it was loud.

"Here we go again!" Ali Hillson whispered to Christopher. Christopher just held his nose.

"This year...we are very pleased...here at Essex Street Middle School #234...to have been chosen...to participate in the *Students Understanding Conceptual Keystones Earmarking Recognition* Program (SUCKER)...and today...we will discuss some of the SUCKER strategy. One strategy...is called 'The Circle Jump' ...and we will demonstrate that right now... Please move your chairs into two circles...a smaller circle...with eight chairs...and a larger circle around the smaller circle...with another eight chairs...Now teachers..."

The teachers were vocalizing discontent about having to move, and again, the *sotto voce* individual "Bullshits!" all came together as one loud protest.

"Okay," Dr. Merkin continued, "In 'The Circle Jump'...the teacher asks questions to the inner circle...the inner circle turn to the student sitting immediately behind...in the outer circle...called the "researcher"...and the researcher...has five minutes...to use any classroom tools necessary...to provide his inner group partner...with the correct answer...The next question...is given when the "researchers"...all move up one seat...to facilitate...somebody new...in the inner circle."

"Excuse me Ms. Merkin," Vivia Crane said, her eyes flashing with anger and annoyance.

"That's *Dr.* Merkin," Dr. Merkin said.

"Oh no," Christopher whispered to Ali Hillson, "It looks as if Vivia is getting ready to do one of her famous Viviasections on Lippy!"

"Dr. Merkin...this game is all well and good...but it presumes that our children...not only know 'something'...but that they also know...how to go about finding...that which they do not know...True...by the time they get finished with my class…they will know how to do research…And if you want me to play this game…with them then…I will gladly oblige…But if you really expect me…to waste valuable class time…with something as futile as this…"

"Ms. Crane," Dr. Merkin said, "If I was in charge…"

'It's the subjunctive…"If I *were* in charge"' Viva Crane thought.

"I would certainly allow…a seasoned teacher like yourself…to make her case…as to why this won't work…but we are mandated by the District to participate in this program...So I must insist…that you participate," Dr. Merkin said.

"Excuse me…Ms. Merkin," Christopher said.

"That's *Dr.* Merkin," Dr. Merkin said.

"So when doing 'The Circle Jerk'…the person on the outside…is the pivot man?" That cracked up Ali Hillson, and she had a hard time containing her laughter.

"It's called 'The Circle Jump'…Mr. Jeremy…And I guess you could say…that the outside people…are pivot people…yes."

Just then the intercom announced: "A ten son…dwill Dakow Merkin…go hell…p…a pear rat…in da orifice?…Deill Dakow Merkin…go hell…p…a pear rat…in da orifice?…Prince…al Gree… e…is…not… beer… A din…Prince…al…Gree…e…is…not…beer…Tank du!"

"Please teachers…please keep trying 'The Circle Jump' while I'm gone…I have to go help a parent…in the office…When I come back…show me…demonstrate for me…how you can make this work in your class," Dr. Merkin said.

"Sure we will…we'll get right on it!" Christopher said.

Salome sat by herself and said nothing, but after Dr. Merkin had left the library, Toni Talton went over and sat at Salome's table.

@@@@@@@@

On New Years Day 2004, on the flight back from Berlin—Loretta's Christmas present to him—Christopher Jeremy decided to learn German, and to move to Germany after the school year ended in June. Loretta's company, one of Germany's largest conglomerates, *Getmutlichorchloch GMbH*, makers of high fiber content dietary supplements, thermometers, digital cameras, MP3 players, beer, pretzels, canned salmon, mercurochrome, paregoric, shoe-trees, closet organizers, French dressing, ball bearings, and ben-wa balls had several large conversational English classes for their executives, and Loretta said that she could land Christopher a good job, if he learned just the most rudimentary German.

On New Years Day 2004, Dick Chumwell sat at Bruiser Apple's dining room table eating a traditional Apple New Years Day Irish boiled dinner, of corned beef, cabbage, carrots, and potatoes. Sitting at the table also were his wife Cindy Apple Chumwell, two of their four daughters, Samantha and Rachael, Bruiser and Eileen Apple, one of their two children, Karen, Jimson Apple, his second wife, Diana O'Malley Apple, Jimson's daughter and Diana's step-daughter, Eve, Salome Apple, Walter Lee Kulpa, and Pauline. "Look Bruiser," Dick said. "I know that you're going to run for mayor of Rutland... you'll declare your candidacy in the next sixty days...for November's election...And I know that your primary agenda...is to extend the Smell Ordinance out here...all just to stop me...from using...MANURE ON MY TREES!" Dick said, with just a wee bit too much volume and emphasis.

"WWWRRROOOAAA...Homo!" Major Doofus said from the living room.

"Well I always knew...that you were a...real bright fellow, Dick," Bruiser wheezed.

"I love coming over here...and having to listen to commentary from your perverse parrot...Major Doofus!"

Major Doofus, now thinking that he was being fully engaged in conversation, said from the living room, "WWWRRROOOAAA...Eat Me!"

"That's a REAL NASTY PARROT!" Pauline said, just a little too loud.

"WWWRRROOOAAA...Asshole!" Major Doofus replied.

"I'll show you asshole!" Pauline said, "When I stuff you...like a ROCK CORNISH HEN!"

"WWWRRROOOAAA...Homo!" Major Doofus said.

"I'm going to move Major Doofus' cage...up to our bedroom," Eileen said, getting up from the table.

"WWWRRROOOAAA...Eat Me!" Major Doofus said.

When the parrot was gone, Dick continued what he had started, "I think I can make us both happy, Bruiser...I've just ordered a new system... featuring the latest *ORGANOPAC* machine...it's a closed system...that takes fresh garbage...and fresh manure...it doesn't have to ferment...like in a compost heap...and mixed it with ordinary sand...and time release pellets...it makes a smell-free organic fertilizer for the trees...And what's really remarkable...is that the machine extends whatever it's fed...about twenty fold," Dick said.

"Why should I give...a fuck about all...of that. I'm still...growing my apples the...way they've been grown...here for years," Bruiser wheezed, before taking a swig of beer.

"Yeah...I know Bruiser...Look...I really think you'd be a good mayor for Rutland...even with your perverse parrot...you have a lot of great ideas for this city...But if I were to fertilize your entire orchard...my way this year...using your everyday household garbage...and using the manure I supplement it with...manure that the diary farms are happy to let me have...If I save you the expense and hassle of having to fertilize at all this year...and prove to you how easy my way is…and that the same system on one clear cut acre of your land next year…and I'll even buy the system for you…is the way to go…and that annually…this will only cost you about five percent more than doing it the old fashioned way…would you please consider…changing your mind…and not making the Smell Ordinance…something that you aggressively pursue…if you're elected?…The truth is, this year, you'll only smell manure for about a month," Dick said. "The way it works…there's only about one month per year…in which you have to put up with any smell."

"Well Dick, I'm not…an unreasonable man…if you want to…do all of that…all of that work…and it costs me…nothing, I'll entertain the…notion to go your…way, and to forget…about making the Smell Ordinance…my main focus if…elected," Bruiser wheezed.

"Do you mean that honestly…or are you just shining us on?" Cindy Chumwell asked.

"No sis, I mean…it," Bruiser replied.

"Sorry to change the subject," Pauline said. "But Eve, are you really thinking about going to graduate school at NYU's Stern Business School in Manhattan?"

"Yeah Grandma…I think an MBA from there…will offer me a better opportunity…to become an executive in business…Besides…Manhattan is the American center of business," Eve Apple said.

"I worry about you…being in Manhattan," Pauline said, and then she looked at her son, Jimson, whose eyes said the same thing. "You just can't go to graduate school for business…at UVM?" Pauline asked her granddaughter.

"I could Grandma…but like I said…I think an MBA from NYU would be more prestigious…for my future…But I do understand your concern… Grandma…and Dad," Eve said, looking at her father. So far, Jimson hadn't said a derogatory word to his daughter about moving to Manhattan, and Eve was especially moved that he had forced himself to keep quiet about it.

Jimson looked lovingly at his daughter, and just smiled. She didn't see the mist in his eyes.

After dinner, Pauline whispered to Salome, "You hardly ate two bites of food…dear daughter…You look very thin."

"We ate too early in the day for me…I don't want my system working…the bag being used…on the ride back to Staten Island…with my son in the car…So far…I've figured out…that if I eat at six o'clock every evening…my bag fills up by ten…I quietly drain it in my own bathroom at home…with the door closed and the window open…and I spray *Ozium* …and Walter Lee is unaware of what I'm doing…In the morning…when I get up at six o'clock…there's some more overnight drainage…which I clean out and then soak the bag in the bathroom sink for awhile…And this procedure…has kept anybody at school from knowing."

"Well…your son knows."

"I know…but we don't talk about it…and I don't want to do anything…that grosses him out."

On New Years Day 2004, sitting in *The Careless Navigator* on Mad Beach and having dinner, were Walter Lee and Annie Younger, Jack and Geneva Apple, and Jack and Geneva's almost six year-old daughter, Lorelei.

"Now that Lani is finishing her MBA at the University of Tampa Bay…and she plans on marrying David in June…and she loves working here…I've been thinking about retiring," said forty-four year old Geneva Liberty Apple. "How would you feel…Annie…Walter Lee…if my daughter took over?"

"We love Lani," Annie said. "But eventually…we're gonna sell the restaurant…Walter Lee is going to be seventy-seven in September…I'm going to be sixty-nine this year…we'd like to travel more…and not worry about *The Careless Navigator*."

"I'm thinking about selling my business too," said forty-eight year-old Jack Apple. "And Geneva and I…also…are thinking about traveling more."

"Yeah…and eventually…we're going to have to hire a few more people to run *The Breakers*," Annie said. "There's more work there daily… than Dora Larue can handle now…and that's with our help."

"I've been thinking lately," Walter Lee began, "and I'd like everybody's opinion on this…that we should just close up *The Breakers*…for daily room rentals…Keep our apartments to live in…but no longer rent rooms to the general public…I mean we can let Dora stay in her place as long as she wants…and we can keep on paying her…to handle maintenance and cleaning work…John and John can stay in their apartment as long as they like too."

"What would you want to use all of the vacant rooms for?" Jack asked.

"Well…we surely don't need the money from room rentals…I was thinking about turning the place…into an anthropological research center…a publishing center…and a home for counter-cultural expression," Walter Lee said. "And music can be a part of that too…since our good friend, Felix, saw fit to build a recording studio on the first floor."

@@@@@@@@

"Hello…this is Michael Bloomberg…and I'm the King of New York City…um…I mean mayor…Please pay attention to this MTA announcement…While our public address system…at times…operates at volumes that can blast young children and little old ladies onto the third rail…most of the time it is garbled…and in keeping with that tradition…my introduction will be the only intelligible thing you'll hear…Now the message: You the Sheeple…must not chew gum and think…while riding on the escalator…Please no copulating on the escalator…as that may result in offspring…afflicted with a face like mine…And after a final settlement of the ten-year contract dispute with their union…asking MTA employees for directions…could result in arrest and fines and or imprisonment…Any attempt to sue the MTA…New York City…or *moi*…Monarch Bloomberg… or any of my faithful vassals…for any injuries…theft of property…or other mishaps…while riding on the escalator…or for that matter…while riding on a city subway or bus…may result in accidental shooting…for resisting arrest…whilst attempting escape…But that's okay…the meaning of life can still be understood…if you watch Charlie Rose on Bloomberg Television… And bad things always come in threes…so term limits have been extended to three consecutive terms in office…While we strive to keep the fare reasonable at two dollars per ride… the necessary gas masks to filter out PCB's endemic throughout the subway system…can be rented at fifty dollars per ride…We hope you enjoy your adventure…and we thank you for choosing the Manhattan Transit System…and now a word from Washington… and Emperor George Dubya Bush"…"My fellow 'merkins… Please help to remove me from my position of power…and to restore me to my rightful position…as being caricaturally inadequate to my own ambitions…by attending the large Anti-Iraq War Rally… tomorrow…July 17th 2004...in Washington Square Park at one o'clock…Music will be provided by *The K. J. Bower Band*…And speeches will be delivered by novelist Felix Kulpa, and noted radical anthropologist and author, Dr. Walter Lee Younger…Be there…or be square!" The message kept repeating on a digital loop, with synthesized Bloomberg and Bush voices, from rush hour on Thursday July 15th until the MTA—along with Mayor Bloomberg's Emergency Task Force working with the FBI—managed to hack beyond all of the lockouts of administrative passwords, and get beyond all of the encrypted firewalls that Michael Keigh had installed. They were finally able to stop the message at just after three o'clock on Saturday afternoon, the rally already two hours old, and *The K. J. Bauer Band* having just finished their set.

Felix was standing on the makeshift stage. He began, speaking into the microphone, "The war in Iraq, is yet another attempt at selling the people of this country…on the notion…that killing is justified…all in the name of 'democracy.' And although I could stand up here…and give you a history lesson of involvement in Vietnam…And I could stand up here and tell you…as a Christian…how appalled I am seeing senseless murder committed worldwide…all instigated by greedy imperialistic American corporations… instead…I would rather you hear the words of somebody from a long time ago…from the 1930's…somebody I heard quoted in this very park…in 1966...by somebody who changed my life."

Selma Greenwood, standing about thirty yards back from the stage, wearing the same blonde wig with dark sunglasses disguise she had once worn to visit Eleanor Devine at the Chrysler Building, heard Felix allude to her and her speech of thirty-eight years ago, and she looked up at him. There was something about his presence, something in the way he carried himself. Seventy-two year old Selma thought, 'And that voice!' just before she felt Ca Thump Ca Thump truly for the first time in her life. She thought about finding her sister in the park—Ivy was there, but she was keeping away from her wanted-by-the-FBI sister—and telling her, that there was something that really turned her on about this guy speaking, Felix Kulpa. She looked away from the stage, and suddenly her eyes spotted something else. There, standing down front at approximately the same distance away from the stage, but on the other end, was a woman with the reddest hair she had ever seen, save one. Selma finally saw the woman's face, and the excitement overwhelmed her. She carefully snaked her way through the fifty or so people right up front, and tapped the woman with red hair on the shoulder.

Salome turned around and said, "Yes?"

And Selma leaned forward and whispered in her ear, "My dearest Salome…the daughter I never had…it's been too long."

Salome, immediately recognizing Selma's voice, turned quickly around and exclaimed, "Selma…my dearest and sweetest friend Selma…Oh how I've missed you!" And Salome embraced Selma, but not too hard, she didn't want her old friend to feel the bag.

"We can't really catch up here," Selma said, while looking around. "But this rally is supposed to wrap up around four o'clock…Meet me at the *Homer Café*…on Sixth Avenue and Tenth Street…at four-thirty…we'll eat and talk."

And Felix continued, "This speech is called, 'War is a Racket,' and it was delivered in the 1930's, by Major General Smedley Darlington Butler, a man who was decorated two times with the Congressional Medal of Honor, a man who was a Republican candidate for Senate, and a man who spent most of his life in the Marine Corps." And Felix began the entire thirteen-page speech, just as Ida Laplotski had in 1966.

After the first ten minutes, Selma, still standing behind Salome, whispered in her ear, "Do you know anything about this guy…Felix Kulpa? I haven't read his new novel yet…and I never read his first book either…but I did hear a record from his old band, *Home Cooking*, once. They sounded pretty good."

"Felix is my son's uncle…my deceased husband was Felix's brother."

"My God…Salome! I didn't even know that you had married…given birth…and that your husband had died…I'm so sorry," Selma whispered.

"My husband died ten years-ago…He was an incurable druggie…he liked to smoke cocaine…and then three years later…I started seeing Felix…that didn't work out…Although I've communicated with him…I really haven't seen him for more than six years…until today."

Selma gave Salome a deep look in the eyes…trying to see if Salome were in love with Felix…she didn't see that in her eyes…and she said, "Well I think he's beautiful!" Felix continued with Major General Butler's speech:

> *"To hell with war! I am not a fool, as to believe that war is a thing of the past. I know the people do not want war, but there is no use in saying we cannot be pushed into another war. Looking back, Woodrow Wilson was re-elected in 1916 on a platform that he had 'kept us out of war' and on the implied promise that he would 'keep us out of war.' Yet, five months later, he asked Congress to declare war on Germany. In that five-month interval, the people had not been asked whether they had changed their minds. The 4,000,000 young men who put on uniforms and marched or sailed away were not asked whether they wanted to go forth to suffer and die. Then what caused our government to change its mind so suddenly? Money.*
> *An allied commission, it may be recalled, came over shortly before the war declaration and called on the President. The President summoned a group of advisers. The head of the commission spoke. Stripped of its diplomatic language, this is what he told the President and his advisors: 'There is no use kidding ourselves any longer. The cause of the allies is lost. We now owe you (American bankers, American munitions makers, American speculators, American exporters) five or six billion dollars. If we lose (and without the help of the United States we must lose) we, England, France, and Italy, cannot pay back this money. And Germany won't. So…' "*

"This is Ida Laplotski…arrest her," Eighty-six year-old, long retired from the FBI, Fester Daily said to the young New York City cop he had commandeered, after he had spotted Ida Laplotski, down by the stage, blonde wig and all, talking to another woman. Ida had been the only fugitive in his long illustrious career who had ever successfully eluded him. And now, as his days were growing shorter, but his intuition had remained sharp, accurately predicting that Ida Laplotski would probably be at this rally, he could go to meet his Maker having batted 1000.

"You must have me confused with someone else," Selma said. "My name is Betty Lou Baker."

"Right!" Fester Daily said. "Betty Lou Baker...noted author of the published...yet still undistributed novel...*Notes From the Modern Underground*...Not a bad piece of writing I must say...Your big mistake... Ida...was coming back to New York."

Felix was just finishing his speech, when he noticed an older looking woman, obviously wearing a blonde wig, being escorted out of the park in handcuffs. He also thought he had seen Salome in the crowd, but there was no time to keep looking, as he had to introduce Dr. Walter Lee Younger. And never mind his speech, or Major General Butler's speech, Felix, having read the text already of Walter Lee's speech, knew that when the crowd heard Walter Lee, they would not only be totally pissed off, but they would probably get mobilized to actually do something. Walter Lee had facts, as to why military action in the Middle East was totally unjustified and being staged, and that what was being sold by President Bush...was a total sham.

As Selma was being escorted out of the park, her sister, Ivy Laplotski, buying some goo-goo gee-gaws at a table set up for Anti-Iraq War t-shirts, buttons, and posters, saw what was happening. Selma said as she passed, "Ivy...get me a great lawyer...spare no expense...and then find out where they're taking me...and bail me out!"

Dr. Walter Lee Younger, having been introduced by Felix, began his speech. As he was talking, suddenly this scruffy old bag lady, up close to the stage, in approximately the same place as where Selma had once stood, yelled out: "YOU WERE RESPONSIBLE FOR YOUR WHOLE FAMILY BEING KILLED IN CHICAGO...YOU SHOULD HAVE TAKEN THE DEAL... AND NOT MOVED INTO CLYBOURNE PARK!"

Felix suddenly recognized the voice, he wasn't sure who it was, but he recognized it. And for some reason he didn't look toward it. Instinctively, he felt it was a diversion, so he looked in the opposite direction instead, at the Shimka Building of NYU. He looked up, and then he saw the rifle barrel, pointing out of a window on the seventh floor.

"YOU WERE RESPONSIBLE FOR YOUR WHOLE FAMILY BEING KILLED IN CHICAGO...YOU SHOULD HAVE TAKEN THE DEAL...AND NOT MOVED INTO CLYBOURNE PARK!" Beverly Jenkowitz Kulpa screamed again, before giving Walter Lee an Italian salute and then scampering through the crowd.

Walter Lee was to the left of Felix, and instantaneously, when he saw the rifle barrel protruding out from the window, Felix just tackled Walter Lee and pushed him over to his left, while partially covering him. The rifle shot rang out, and Felix lost consciousness, as he felt the excruciating pain of the *Remington* 308 bullet entering his body.

Chapter Twenty-one

"Live Lee...it's good to see your cotton-picking face!" Felix said dreamily, on this Sunday evening, July 18th, 2004, from on his stomach, in a semi-private room, on the seventh floor of St. Vincent Hospital, at 7th Avenue and 12th Street in Manhattan.

"Well sheeet Mr. 'Licks...I done picked de south forty today...slopped de hogs...den carried an 'portant message from Boss Man Jim to Mistuah Charlie...and I still had de time to come here...so I could see your cracker ass smilin' at me...de minute I done come into de room!" Walter Lee Younger said.

Felix could feel the cold air-conditioned air on his derrière, and with his right hand, he reached back and felt the tape and gauze on his right cheek. He was also aware of an I.V. hook up in his left arm, and he said, "Is the other side of my ass exposed too?"

"It was when I walked in here...twenty minutes ago...I thought, 'Sheeet...Mr. 'Licks is done givin' me cheek again!'...and then I covered you up."

Felix tried to move onto his left side, so he could more easily see Walter Lee on his right, but there were straps and some kind of space age-material blocks...that were keeping him wedged in one position. "Yeah...I remember now...man...whatever they're pumping into my veins is pretty good...I am wasted!...And earlier...my surgeon...Dr. Abramoff...said I had to stay in this position for forty-eight hours...before I could turn onto my side."

"I saw him in the hall in front of your room...He didn't want to say much...but then I explained that you've been my son for more than thirty years...so he told me...that bullet did some serious muscle damage to the right cheek of your ass...and that it would be awhile...before you could lie on your back."

"Yeah...he told me that the bullet chipped the top part of a bone in my right leg too...and that I'll probably...be walking with a limp...from now on. Great...a gimp with a limp...and my ass will always let me know...whether it's sun...outside...or snow!" And then Felix reached under his right leg, and felt more gauze and tape there too.

"Apparently...you got lucky with the exit wound...after the bone knick...Mr. Bullet done left gracefully!" Walter Lee said, and then he lightly rubbed Felix's head. "Seriously 'Licks...you saved my life...you took a bullet...meant for me...I love you man." And then Walter Lee squeezed Felix's right hand. "How did you know...when everybody else was looking at that crazy woman...to look in the other direction?"

"It's strange...I heard that woman shouting at you...I recognized her voice...and for some reason...something in my mind said, 'Look the other way!'...So that's what I did...and my eyes started at the bottom of the Shimka Building...and quickly went up...and then I saw the rifle barrel... pointing out from the window...aimed in our direction."

"You say that you recognized that woman's voice...in the park?"

"Yeah...it was my mother's voice...Beverly Kulpa...While it was all happening...there was just too much going on...for me to piece it all together then...But with what David Summers told me...that my mother was alive...in New York...and retired from the CIA...when I woke up in the recovery room...the first thought that came to my mind was...that was my mother's voice in the park."

"So maybe she isn't retired...quite yet...from the CIA...How old is she?" Walter Lee asked.

"By my figuring...she would be eighty-three now."

"Eighty-three...and still working for the CIA?"

"That doesn't make much sense," Felix said, and then he added, "Perhaps she doesn't know she's working for them."

"Perhaps," Walter Lee said.

"Either that or..."

"Or what?" asked Walter Lee.

"Or...she was not only a cold, impervious mother...in regards to having absolutely nothing to do with her children since 1957...but that she could also allow her own son...to be put in life-threatening danger...in the line of fire...is almost inconceivable!" Felix angrily said.

"It's hard to believe...than any mother...could be that cruel," Walter Lee said.

"Well...it did happen to Tony on *The Sopranos*...In the first season... his mom...put a contract out on him...but that was fiction!"

"Seriously," Walter Lee said. "My gut tells me…and my gut has been remarkably accurate…since around 1963...that your mom doesn't know what she's doing…doesn't know what she's saying…I sensed that in her voice… not the hurtful words that she said…but a sense of her being programmed…to say those words."

"You're probably right…Perceptive Lee," Felix said. "What's happening… police-wise…to find the shooter?" He added.

"It's still under investigation. I saw *NBC Nightly News* out in the waiting room a little while ago…and they reported that the FBI had found no prints on the rifle…and allegedly…they had found neither the shooter…nor the old lady in the park."

"Right!" Felix said.

"I was questioned by four different FBI agents…and then some other suit…who just said that he worked for the government…I think he was with Homeland Security."

"What was the deal with the woman…the one with the blonde wig… up close to the stage…who was arrested during my speech?" Felix asked.

"That was Ida Laplotski."

"You're kidding!…Really?…Ida Laplotski?…Man…you know…she's always been a hero of mine…I can't believe that she came to hear us speak…and was finally apprehended…after thirty-eight years."

"Yeah," Walter Lee said. "Apparently some old retired FBI agent spotted her."

"I'm real sorry to hear that…it's ironic…after I met Tatiana in the same park in 1966…with Ida giving the speech…the FBI…who had everyone at that rally on film…kept calling…before we even knew about the Birmingham bombing…asking if Tatiana or I knew her whereabouts…I'm very flattered… that she came to hear us speak…But I wish she would have stayed away."

"Well…she's being held in federal custody."

"What about the phony MTA announcement in the subway?"

"That was mentioned on the news too," Walter Lee said. "Although they didn't repeat the text of the message…It's interesting how none of the fourth estate…is mentioning or printing the text of that subway message. Although…'The Old Gray Lady' printed two excerpts. They mentioned that the voice of Bloomberg had said, 'Please don't copulate on the escalators,' and that the voice of Bush had advertised the rally, and then had ended with 'Be there or be square!'"

Felix laughed and whispered, "That Michael…he did a fine job!"

Walter Lee laughed, and then he leaned over and whispered in Felix's ear, "Michael called me on my cell earlier today…I told him that there was probably a governmental trace on all of my incoming and outgoing calls…and he said…'Don't worry…I've rerouted everything…this call will get traced back to Dick Cheney's personal cell phone...And wait until they finally piece together where the message in the subway originated...I've taken them on a cyber journey!...They'll start with the computer of a Bloomberg aide in Gracie Mansion...that will lead them to Martha Stewart's personal laptop... from there the trace goes to Pat Robertson's computer in Virginia...then to the computer H. Rap Brown is currently using in his prison's library in Atlanta...then to Tony Blair's personal computer at 10 Downing Street...then to Hillary Rodham Clinton's laptop...then to Alec Baldwin's computer in Hollywood...then to Trey Parker's computer in Colorado...and finally...after six or seven more locations...it ends up smack dab at Dubya's computer in the Oval Office.'...And I laughed so hard...I just had to sit my ass down."

Felix was laughing so hard his sutures hurt. "That Michael...pure genius...It's too bad we weren't cyber...during the 1960's!" And then Felix became more serious, "It's too bad that nobody in the park got to hear your speech... after the shooting...Your speech would have inflicted considerably more damage...on Washington...than this bullet did to me."

"Well...along with the complete text of what Michael put on the public address system in the subway...I'm also putting my speech online...it will be easy to access from the home page of *The Mad Beach Center for Free Expression* website. We already get close to 2,000 hits per day...and now that the whole world knows about what happened...at Saturday's rally in Washington Square Park...I imagine my speech will be seen by more people than we could have ever imagined."

"Once again...Dangerous Lee...be careful!...The 'powers that be' don't like you very much...and they usually don't let one live...who has become bigger than the game. "

"Yeah...but I've got a lot of light on me right now...and especially with the high visibility of what we're doing at *The Breakers*...I told the FBI... and the press...that I had been threatened by a Mr. Tom Mullock from the State Department...because of my article on Mauritania...They checked him out...and found out that a Mr. Tom Mullock didn't work for the State Department."

"Naturally!" Felix said.

"I also told the press and the FBI...that I was sure that bullet...had been meant for me...and not you...Seriously 'Licks...I don't think they'd have the nerve...to come after my nearly seventy-seven year-old black ass again!"

"I hope you're right...Confident Lee...I hope you're right." But as he said those words, Felix was suddenly hit by a wave of complete exhaustion, and he shut his eyes. "Hey Walter Lee," he kind of mumbled. "How am I supposed to take a leak?"

"You have a bag attached to the bed...apparently you've been..." Walter Lee said.

But before he could finish, Felix had already reached under himself with his right arm and mumbled, "Yeah…I see…Winky has a straw…" And then just before he drifted off and Walter Lee left for the evening, Felix heard his unknown Room-727-Bed-A-heavily-medicated roommate, mumble while dreaming, "We're all gonna get…a deadly flu… from the birds…and Donald Rumsfeld….he used to be…on the Board of Directors…of *Tamiflu*."

Felix dreamt he was ten years-old again, and it was a Thursday night. On Thursday nights Beverly Kulpa played *Mah Jong*, and Frank Kulpa would watch Felix and his brother, one year-old Anthony. Felix's dad would always allow him to stay up and watch television way past his normal mom-mandated eight-thirty bedtime, and Frank would also produce hidden candy, *Fritos* and soda pop—those food items which Beverly totally ignored, when doing the weekly shopping at the Mad Beach *Publix*. On those Thursday nights out, when Beverly would return just after midnight, Felix would have barely a thirty minute jump, on being in bed, prior to her arrival. And, of course, if one year-old Anthony were wailing his lungs out, that was always a good excuse for being awake—when Beverly looked in on him.

On this late summer evening in July of 2004, as Felix dreamt he was back in 1956, when his bedroom was still his bedroom alone, and Anthony's crib was still in his parents' bedroom, and Anthony was screaming loud in that room, he kept seeing his mother doing the same thing over and over. It was a Thursday night. She had just returned. She was still all dressed up. She would open Felix's door and look in. She would see Felix awake, lying in the dark. "Go to sleep now," is all she would say. Felix would try to ask her a question, but he could never quite get the words to that question out of his mouth, before she closed the door.

On this particular night, in this particular dream however, Felix is finally able, in his fifty-seven year-old voice, to ask his mother, before she closes the door: "If you're playing *Mah Jong* with four other women regularly on Thursday nights, and you're rotating between the homes of the players, how come, every fifth Thursday night, you're not playing here?" And his mom just smiles and closes the door.

And, of course, what Beverly Jenkowitz Kulpa had really been doing for the government on those Thursdays nights until 1957, and, before having met and wed Frank, how, as a child, because of *her* father's involvement with the same agency, how she had been—unbeknownst to her—used as a guinea pig for a newly invented experimental drug, and subsequently recruited just out of high school, by the Intelligence Section of the Department of Navy in the early 1940's—before it was called the CIA in 1947—and what she had been doing during the two years in which Frank Kulpa was away overseas finishing his Navy hitch towards the end of World War II, and everything else she had been doing for the government since, mostly without her own complete understanding, is a whole 'nother story—and just way too long and complicated to be discussed here.

"Felix...Are you okay?" Salome asked, sitting in a chair to the right of him, and holding his right hand. "You've been saying over and over, 'How come Mom?' and 'What's the answer Mom?'...you're having a bad dream."

Felix opened his eyes and said, "Salome...you came to see me!"

"Well of course I wanted to see you...shot in the park and all."

"I thought I saw you at the rally...down front...stage right."

"I was there," Salome said. "Oh...and thanks for mooning me...on the way into your room...it reminded me of myself...thirty years ago...It will be thirty years...in a few weeks...on August 6th...That was the day...I was hitchhiking south on Highway 7...the day I met your brother."

Felix, not wanting to think about his brother at the moment, said, "Sorry about the moon...Salome...but you should feel honored...Mayor Bloomberg got one also...when he came to see me...earlier today."

"Well...since one side is totally covered up with gauze and tape...I guess I just got half-mooned!" Salome said. "I pulled the sheet over you."

"Thank you...and I half-apologize," Felix said, and then he added, "I'm glad you came to the rally yesterday....I'm glad that your politics are anti-war...sorry about the scary conclusion."

"Of course I'm against war, Felix...although I'm not so sure...if we shouldn't just support this current administration...just a little longer...and give President Bush a chance."

Since the last thing Felix felt like doing at the moment was arguing politics with Salome, he just said, "Okay."

"No actually...I went to the rally yesterday...because two of my favorite people in the world...were speaking...Walter Lee...and you."

"Am I still one of your favorite people?" Felix asked. "I mean... although there's been some negativity between us...The letter I wrote...after Bubba's passing...wanting to be friends again...but so far...no reply."

"There have been changes in my life...of which you know nothing...so don't take...the standoffishness...too personally," Salome said.

Felix, realizing at that moment, that the answer to the question, the question since a year ago, when he had snuck into Salome's hospital room in Rutland, that he had never asked anyone, 'Is Salome's medical condition temporary or permanent?' was no doubt permanent, understood what Salome was alluding to now, and he decided not to talk about her standoffishness. "Okay...since it will be your forty-fourth birthday on August 6th...and I should be up and around by then...how about you let me take you...and my nephew...out for a nice birthday dinner...somewhere in Manhattan...your choice."

"Nah...thanks Felix...but I'm not really into going out to dinner much these days...I just eat...simple foods...at home."

Felix wanted to curse himself, for not having deduced that, and he said,

"Well...could I come over to your place...stay just a little while...and eat some simple foods with you and Walter Lee...on your birthday?"

Salome gave Felix a grin and said, "I don't know Felix...you certainly hammered me hard in *Mad Beach*."

"Oh...so you've read it?"

"Of course I've read it...You do a pretty thorough hatchet job on your Judziah Cromwell character."

"But she's okay...by the end of the story."

"Yeah...but there was a lot of stuff in there...in the relationship between Roy Cassier and Judziah...that had absolutely nothing to do with our relationship...Felix!" Salome said with some annoyance.

"Of course not...Judziah was a composite of you, Tatiana, and Sylvia Morton...and maybe a couple of other women thrown in too...I mean...some things were amplified in the writing...that were downplayed in real life...and other things that were more important in real life...were downplayed in the novel...it's more about what works in the story...As an example...the stuff about Judziah... dating someone else in the same workplace...breaking an agreement...after her relationship was over with Roy...that was inspired and inverted...from stories your sister...Jennifer...told me on Mad Beach in August of 1998...things concerning her deceased husband...You never, ever did anything like that to me," Felix said.

"No I didn't," Salome said, as she felt the chill in her neck—that sudden acute realization—that that was exactly what she had done to Christopher.

"So don't take it personally...Besides...that relationship...is just a small part of a multi-faceted whole story...Also...most of my characters... are broke...and that certainly isn't us...or any of our friends."

"True," Salome said.

"So...how did you like the whole book...just as a read?" Felix asked.

"It was a good read...the first person plural present tense voice is interesting...I liked that...even though Roy and Judziah get juxtaposed to the rest of the human race...by the end...they're just like the rest of us anyway."

"That's a perfect critique!" Felix said. "That's exactly what I was hoping the reader would see."

"I saw an article...in *The New York Post* the other day...that your first novel, *All the Seats Were Occupied*, will be available in paperback, in English, this October."

"Yeah...after twenty-seven years...finally available in the language in which it was written," Felix said, and then he asked, "Didn't I see you talking to Ida Laplotski...in the park...during my speech?"

"You know her?"

"Well yeah...she's always been special to me...I alluded to her in my speech yesterday...she was the one who read the entire Major General Butler

'War is a Racket' Speech in 1966...the same speech I read yesterday…in the same park…and she was the magical connection…the conduit I guess… that hooked me up with Tatiana."

"Well Felix…I hope you don't get mad at me…but I had a thirty-year promise with her…with Selma Greenwood…to not tell anybody…that she was really Ida Laplotski…so I had to lie to you in 1997...And I never told Anthony or my family either…I never told another human…I hadn't seen her since the late 1970's…until yesterday…I hadn't spoken to her since 1981...seeing her in the park yesterday was a total surprise!"

"Wait a minute…Selma Greenwood…your older friend from Rutland…the one you were going to look for in New York in August of 1997...until your niece ran away…and came to live with you in Tampa?"

"Right," Salome said, not wanting to think about her slain niece. "I've known her…from since I was a little girl…as Selma Greenwood…the Head Librarian at the downtown Rutland Library."

"When did you find out that she was really Ida?" Felix asked.

"In 1974...after I had runaway…when I called her from New York City…and she was afraid that Bubba…would get the FBI involved in looking for me…and because of how close she and I were…the FBI might question her heavily…and possibly fingerprint her…She hooked me up with her twin sister in Queens… remember?…And the heat was taken off of both of us…at least until those nude pictures of me…showed up in Rutland in 1975."

"And then I helped to get the heat off of you," Felix said, offering a gentle reminder of his lawyer performance, for perhaps yet more kudos from Salome.

"Yeah…you did," was all she said about that. "When the FBI came to Rutland…in 1981...looking for Selma…I was in Florida at *The Breakers…* and when my mom told me about it on the phone…that Selma Greenwood was actually somebody else…and wanted by the FBI…I acted real surprised…even though…the night before…Selma had already called me from the road…and told me...that she didn't know…when we would see each other again."

"Have you spoken to Ida Laplotski…since her arrest?" A somewhat disappointed Felix asked.

"No…but I went with her sister, Ivy, to find Ida a lawyer. We got her Q. Harrison Albright...the same guy who represented Bubba...and got him off…during that shooting incident in 1986."

"I remember," Felix said. "When Bubba shot off his neighbor's…"

"That right," Salome said. "I called the office of Q. Harrison Albright in Manhattan late yesterday afternoon...on my cell from the park…Ivy was with me…after Ida had been taken away…and I got their answering service…The operator told me to hold on...they contacted Q. Harrison Albright…He came on the phone…and coincidentally…it turned out he had an unusual…early catered Saturday dinner meeting happening in his office with a client at six…so he told me to bring Ivy…and to come right over…We went and saw him…his office is on the eightieth floor of the Empire State Building...and he promised…when he was finished with his other client…that he would go down to The Tombs…the city jail where the FBI is holding Ida…to see her… and to see about her bail…Anyway…he called Ivy…and she called me…late last night…There is no bail for Selma…she has to stay in jail…until Monday morning…when a federal judge…will hear from both the defense and prosecution…and then set bail."

"It will probably be sky high…viewed as an act of heinous terrorism…in light of September 11th," Felix said, and then he added, "I don't know Ida's financial situation…but if you get a chance to speak with her or her lawyer…if she needs money for anything…I'll help her…and so will Walter Lee."

"I'm sure Selma…Ida…will appreciate that…but I already offered her money…she said she has plenty…so far," Salome said.

"Okay," Felix said, and then he shut his eyes. With his eyes shut he asked, "Did you see Walter Lee here?"

"Yeah…I ran into him out in the hallway…We've spoken on the phone a number of times…over the years…since I've left Florida…but it's been since 1999...since I've actually seen him…He looks great!… Anyway…when I saw him…he had just left your room…said you were sleeping…so I went and drank some coffee…and then came back up here…I'd been sitting here about thirty minutes…when you started to have your nightmare."

"It's been longer…since you've actually seen me," Felix said.

"I know…since 1998," Salome said. "You look like you've lost a bunch of weight…and that you're more muscular…better toned."

"That's cause I chopped a load of wood…for nearly four years…in Alaska."

"Well…it's hard to get the complete picture…Felix…you know…from the angle you're giving the camera…at the moment, " Salome laughed.

Sounding just like Elvis, Felix said, "Thank you very much!" Then he said, "And how's my nephew?"

"He's fine…he has this crush…on another fifteen year-old…in his class at St. George Christian School…And this summer…they're hanging around together…at the St. George Christian Day Camp…a few blocks away from the school…She's a cute girl…named 'Jenny,'" Salome said.

"'Jenny'…that's wonderful," Felix said, as he was starting to nod. And then he opened his eyes and said, "May I…please…come over to your place…for just an hour or so…on your birthday…Saturday, August 6th?…I promise…I'll leave when you tell me to."

"I guess so," Salome said, and then she added, "If you're up to it…and you're able to walk around...Meanwhile…I see now…that you're starting to fall asleep… I'll come back late tomorrow afternoon…with Walter Lee."

"Promise?" a very sleepy Felix asked.

"Promise."

"That would be so nice…Salome…," Felix said, just before he fell asleep for the rest of the night.

@@@@@@@@

On August 6th, 2004, Felix, walking with a slight limp, using the beautifully handmade mahogany walking stick that Walter Lee Younger had bought him in the West Village—the top had the perfectly carved head of William F. Buckley, wearing a Yankees cap, with the brim to the side like a South Bronx homey—rang the buzzer to Salome's condo on Staten Island. And although the walk from the ferry terminal to Salome's building was less than 350 yards, because his leg still bothered him when walking, Felix elected to pay the five dollars for a car service to her front door instead.

After having been buzzed in, and then taking the elevator up to the fifth floor, Felix said, "Happy Birthday," at the threshold of Salome's door, and then he handed her a wrapped present. The present was obviously a record album.

"Thanks Felix," Salome said, after motioning him in, closing the door, and taking the present. "Would you like some wine?"

"Sure," Felix said. "I'll drink a toast to you…on your forty-fourth."

"Is *Merlot* okay?"

"Yeah…I like *Merlot*." After Salome had opened the bottle and poured a glass for Felix he toasted her and said, "Here's looking at you kid!"

"Thanks," Salome said. "I'm really worth looking at…these days," she added sarcastically. And before Felix could protest she asked, "Can I open this gift now?" Felix nodded, and so Salome delicately removed the "Happy Birthday!" red and blue balloon wrapping paper. Salome said, "Wow! Where on Earth did you find this?"

"In a second hand record store on Bleeker Street."

"*The Rutles*…I've missed this album badly…since Anthony…,"

"Yeah…I remember…he was out of his mind at the motel…and he decided to use the album to play *Frisbee* with the Gulf of Mexico."

"Yeah…I've been looking to replace this album…"

"I know," Felix said. "For about twenty-five years."

"Thanks again, Felix," Salome said. "This is such a funny album!" And then she kissed Felix on the cheek. (An historical note: *The Rutles* goof on songs by *The Beatles*, by mixing different parts of different songs, and making the lyrics funny. "Help" becomes "Ouch," etc.)

"Well…having seen you a few times in the past month…when you've visited me in the hospital…I just thought…you needed a gift that would make you laugh."

"That's pretty perceptive of you," Salome said, and then she added, "But then you've always been…one of the more perceptive people…in this world."

"Thank you…perceptive enough to know…that something is troubling you deeply," Felix said, and then he changed the subject, "Where's my handsome nephew, anyway?"

"He said he just had to go over to Jenny's place…his girlfriend's place…her parents have a condo in the building next door."

"Well that's too bad…I'm greedy…I always love seeing Walter Lee. He knew I was coming over today…on your birthday…didn't he?"

"To tell you the truth Felix…he left intentionally…I think he wanted us to have some time…to talk…alone…In fact…he said that he wouldn't come home…until I called him. "

Felix thought, 'I am so proud of Walter Lee…He's such a smart kid.' "That sounds like a good idea...that we have some time to talk alone."

"Oh…come over here a minute Felix," Salome said, and then Felix set down his wine glass on the coffee table, and he followed her into the hallway. "I have another one of your birthday presents…displayed here." And Felix looked up and saw "Your Majesty," the black and white Inuit painting he had given Salome three years earlier, the painting that featured men all kneeling and holding gifts above their heads, for a princess on a throne, a princess who looked remarkably like Salome. "I guess you think…this represents me!"

Felix, not really wanting to discuss anything negative about her with her, stuff that he may have once thought or written, said, "I just thought that the princess…or queen…looked like you...that's all."

"Right!" Salome said with a smile. She looked closely into Felix's eyes, and he could see the twinkle in hers. "That was me…to a T…don't try to be nice…Felix…You may have changed around some of the details in the story…in regards to your main characters and their relationship in *Mad Beach*…but there's still plenty of your slice and dice left…for me personally! That picture, 'Your Majesty,' is exactly how you see me…me on a throne… men worshipping at my feet…at my beckon…for any whim…Don't deny it…that's how you see me."

"Well it may have been how I *saw* you…three years ago…before I wrote the negative stuff out of me…But it's not how I see you now."

"Oh yeah?" Salome asked suspiciously. "What's different about me now?"

"You seem to carry…the burden of tragedy…in your countenance… these days," Felix said, trying very hard not to reveal too much. "Perhaps it was the tragedy of your niece…,"

"Yeah, yeah, yeah…Nancy's abduction, rape, and murder changed my life…Bubba's death…and your letter shortly afterwards…did too."

"I wanted you to know…just how much he really loved you."

And Salome started to cry before spitting out, "I really loved him too…He was a good man…confused at times…but that was because of his World War Two head injury…and then the car accident in Manhattan a couple of years later…But I guess…being one of six children…being the youngest… with all of the others taking my father's time…'Please take me to my music lesson,'…'Please take me to basketball practice,'…'Please come watch me compete in the wrestling tournament,'…I was always just the baby who was dragged along…I guess…until I read your letter…I had just never felt…as if I were 'special' to Bubba…since all of my brothers and sisters had their own 'things'…by the time I came along…there seemed to be no more time left…for me to figure out my 'thing.' All I had going for me…was my looks."

"I won't deny…as I stand here and look at you…at forty-four…you are still the most hauntingly beautiful woman…I've ever seen…But Salome…it's your mind… our conversations…that I've been missing the most since 1998," Felix said. "And I'm real picky…about with whom I spend my time…especially…since I'm almost fifty-eight…and I see the end of my life approaching…unlike thirty years ago…when I thought I'd live forever…So I certainly don't want to waste a minute…with some boring individual who can't think…or some humdrum individual…who doesn't have the ability to see the world…with a creative or humorous eye…even if that eye sees things in a completely different way than I…So no…don't ever think…that you are only about your good looks…there is just so much more…to Salome Apple...so much more that transcends her good looks."

Salome, somewhat taken aback by all of Felix's accolades, said, "I guess I've demanded that all men treat me like a princess…and I guess I've taken out my disappointment…on all men…my disappointment…that my father never treated me that way…And I guess…even though I really tried with Anthony…I've always been too demanding with men…so Felix…you not only pegged me in your novel…but that painting you bought me…says it all. I've been incredibly selfish. "

"I see…so this is '*The Salome Really Sucks Hour*,' brought to us by *Kleenex* no doubt. I can see Tammy Faye Baker doing the thirty-second ad, 'Friends…after a heavy day of crying…with all of this heavy makeup I wear…nothing cleans up the mess better…than *Kleenex*.'"

"Right!…so I'm just feeling sorry for myself…huh!" Salome said angrily. "I thought I had already paid for my sins…that when Nancy died…that was payment enough…I said, 'Jesus…I know that I was wild when I was young…and I did some bad things…I sinned…I'm so sorry that Nancy had to suffer the consequence of that'…And I thought I had started fresh again…But then I fell for a man…an Atheist…had sex out of wedlock with him…and then fell for another man and did the same thing…so I hadn't learned my lesson…and Jesus needed me to finally learn…so He…"

"It doesn't work like that," Felix said. "If you're a Christian…then you know…that once you've accepted Jesus…your sins go to 'Crudville'… and you go on without them…And if you transgress…then you just ask…in earnest…and that's the key…asking in earnest…for forgiveness again…and then you go on from there…God doesn't say, 'Listen…I know We had a deal…but I'm in the mood for a little Godly payback…so "Katie…bar the door!"'"

"There are all sorts of examples of God's revenge in The Bible…Can you say, 'Noah and the Flood' and 'Sodom and Gomorrah?'"

"But those were whole communities…or whole races…that He needed to set straight…Very rarely does God get involved in Earthly payback on an individual basis…I'm sure He figures…that there will be time enough for that…if you remain a sinner…after this life is over."

Salome immediately jumped up from the living room sofa and said, "Take a good look at me Felix…What do you see?"

Felix stood up and faced her and said, "I see the woman I love."

"I'll be right back," Salome said, and then she added, "You need to get over me," but the last three words dropped off as she left the room, so Felix didn't hear that part.

Salome came back a few minutes later, and she was wearing a large silk black bathrobe with a huge blue and gold peacock. She went to the front door and latched the chain. Then she turned to Felix and said, "Take a good look at me Felix." And then she dropped the robe to reveal her naked self and said, "What do you see now?"

Felix, who had remained standing, using his walking stick for balance, the entire time in which Salome had been out of the room, faced her and said, "I see the woman I love."

"Look closer!" Salome said. "Describe specific things about me… things you see!"

"The first thing I see is your beautiful red, red hair…I've always loved running my fingers through your hair…then I see the smooth skin on the nape of your neck…my favorite place to kiss…Next I see your unbelievably bright green eyes…the eyes I love watching me…when I sleep…then I see your mesmerizing angelic face…the face I love watching…when you sleep…The fifth thing I see is your beautiful left breast…I'm particularly partial to that breast…since it's closer to your heart…then I see your cute little belly button…and the seventh thing I see is that you have a colostomy bag."

"Oh Felix…you're just too slick with the words…you say such beautiful…poetic…things at times," Salome said, as she covered up with her robe. "And if this were 'The Ugly Duckling'…all of the impressionable children would 'ooh and ah'…and leave the theatre thinking, 'I can be homely…and still find true love'...But this isn't fiction... Felix...this is real life...and there is absolutely nothing attractive about me...having a bag of feces attached to my side...So get over it Felix...get over your romantic notions about how love should be...that stuff like this doesn't matter...because it does matter...Do you still want to take me to bed Felix?...How about right now?...Are you up for a *ménage à trois*...you know...you, me, and the bag?...How about it Felix?" And then Salome collapsed to the floor in tears and grief.

Felix got down on the floor and held Salome, and he said, "I've loved you...from the depths of my heart...for so long...nothing about you turns me off...Please just marry me!"

And Salome sat up and looked Felix in the eyes and said, "I'm not in love with you Felix."

"I know," Felix said. "But marry me anyway...you can be yourself around me...you don't need to hide anything...and you need somebody to give you love...everyday...Let me be the one...let me help."

"Felix...I really do love you...I can't express...just how grateful I am that you would throwaway your life...to take care of me...it shows...just how Christian you really are."

"It isn't about being Christian," Felix said. "It's because I love you... I'm crazy about you...I want to spend my life with you...I want to share everything with you...even that which is unpleasant...No...a good Christian...would do this for a stranger...A better Christian...for his enemy."

"Even though you love me," Salome said. "What you're offering...is still very Christian...In fact...I'll tell you...it's tempting...I'm starting two weeks of chemo therapy next week...I'll be in the hospital for fourteen days... and then I'll begin radiation...two nights a week...in late September...for eight weeks...I just hope...I have the wherewithal...to take care of Walter Lee...and to keep teaching school during all of this."

"So let me share your life...I'll cook...take care of the apartment...do the laundry...take care of Walter Lee...drive you to radiation and then wait...I'll drive you to school in Manhattan everyday...and then pick you up...so all you have to worry about is teaching...and getting better...I'll even grade and correct...your seventh graders' essays for you...Let me help... Salome...Marry me!"

"I just can't do that Felix...I can't marry someone with whom I'm not in love."

"I understand...but let me take care of you...anyway."

"Well...I don't know what I'm going to do with Walter Lee next week...I had thought that my mother was going to be home in Burlington... while I was in the hospital for two weeks having the chemo...so I was going to ask her to watch Walter Lee...send him up there on a train...But it turns out…that my mother is taking a car trip in Canada…with my Aunt Clara…starting next week…So then I thought about you…asking you…if Walter Lee could stay at your place in Manhattan…But I'm sure he'd prefer staying here…and continuing at camp for the rest of the summer…with his girlfriend… So…how would you feel about staying here…in my condo for two weeks?…You can stay up in the loft…you'd have privacy up there."

"I'd love to stay here…in your condo…for two lifetimes… Salome… I'll stay here as long as you'll let me."

"Thank you Felix."

"Oh Salome…"

"What?"

"You know when you asked me…a little while ago…if I were still interested in making love to you?…" And Salome looked up into Felix's face, and she saw him grinning from ear to ear. "I was wondering…since it's your birthday…"

Salome was touched, and she said, "Not today...It ain't happening! But it's something…that we both might want to explore…in the near future."

And Felix smiled, because all he really wanted to do with the rest of his life—other than to keep writing—was to spend time exploring with Salome.

@@@@@@@@

"I got an e-mail from Christopher last week," C. Wel Rellim said to Ali Hillson, while sitting outside on the veranda, on this first day back to school in early September, 2004. "He said that he's real happy with his job… he likes living in Kiel…and that things are going well with his woman."

"What was her name?...I forgot," Ali said.

"Loretta."

"Are they living together?"

"No," C. Wel said. "He's renting a room in this guy's house in Kiel… And he and Loretta see each other on the sly…She's taking her time… introducing him to her daughter…easing into things…He said a year from now…they'll probably get married."

"I'm glad he's happy…but I miss him already…Literacy meetings won't be quite the same…without his humor."

"Yeah…I miss him too," C. Wel said. "But at least I still have you Blondie…to bust my balls on a regular basis!" And Ali laughed.

Christopher Jeremy and Loretta Steinberg would marry in 2005, and have a son, Justin in 2007. Christopher's parents would rent out and manage his property in East Elmhurst until late 2009, when, after Christopher and Loretta had a daughter, Rebecca, they would move back from Germany—with Donna, Loretta's daughter from her previous marriage—to the East Elmhurst house. Loretta would transfer to the New York office of

Getmutlichorchloch GMbH, and Donna would begin her first year of NYU. Christopher would get back into teaching for the New York City Board of Education in September of 2010. Since Essex Street Middle School kept losing Literacy Teachers annually—Vivia Crane would retire in 2005, Salome would leave in 2005, Toni Talton would say "See ya!" in 2009, as would Theresa Saperstein—Principal Greely would be happy having Christopher back for the 2010-2011 school year.

Christopher Jeremy's first year back, would be C. Wel's last year after forty years of service with the New York City Board of Education. He would retire from Essex Street in June of 2011, at sixty-five. The year before he would retire, he would meet, date, and marry a fifty-three year-old woman who had been a student of his the first year he had taught Science, long before he had become a dean. He would just run into her in *Roosevelt Field Mall* on Long Island, and because she had had a crush on him since being his student, a simple conversation would segue into *amore*. She was a wealthy widow with two grown children and a grandchild, and after his retirement, she and C. Wel would spend the rest of their days traveling the globe a good eight months of every year. The other four months, they would live in her mansion on Sands Point.

It was probably missing Christopher's humor, later that day, during the first Literacy meeting of the year, that became the sine qua non for Ali Hillson's acceptance of the metaphorical torch of jocularity, in becoming the new vocal *Humor Laureate* of the Literacy Department.

"Welcome back," Dr. Merkin said. "This year…at Essex Street Middle School…we are pleased to have been chosen…to participate in a wonderful new Literacy program…*Forging Academic Reading Techniques* (FART). I know that we…as seasoned professionals…will be able to implement this new wonderful program…into our individual teaching styles…and pass muster…when the District Supervisor comes to observe."

And then Dr. Merkin explained the new program, which mostly had to do with a new desk-alignment. Instead of typical groups of four, or "buddy" groups of two, now the class would be set up in three-person triangles.

"I guess…Ms. Merkin…this is going to make all of the difference in the world," Ali Hillson said. "I think it just stinks!"

"That's *Dr.* Merkin," Dr. Merkin said, and then she added, "You know…Ms. Hillson…every now and then…you just have to think…outside of the box!"

And without missing a beat Ali Hillson said, "I have this twenty-year old cat…'Whiskers'…and lately…when I get home in the afternoon…I've noticed that he's been 'thinking outside of the box'…and I find it most annoying!" That received a thunderous laugh, and even Salome had tears in her eyes.

Ali Hillson would stay at Essex Street Middle School for another ten years, until she was forty-two, but she would get to retire in 2014, after she and her husband won millions on a lucky *Lotto* ticket. During her remaining time at Essex Street, she would give birth thrice: her first child, a daughter Morgan, in September of 2005, and twins, a son Austin and a daughter Jordan, in June of 2008.

During the next several years in Literacy, many new programs would be implemented and disregarded at Essex Street Middle School #234: In 2005, *Deciding on Responsible Keystones* (DORK); in 2006, *Noting Insightfully in Mandatory Reading the Official Details* (NIMROD); and in 2007, the ever popular *Students Can Understand More Basic Units of Controlled Keystone Educational Technique* (SCUM BUCKET). Finally, in 2008, a recently published book by Dr. Lipzelda Merkin, would catch the attention of the newly elected President of the United States, Hillary Rodham Clinton. President Clinton would tap Dr. Lipzelda Merkin to become the nation's new Secretary of Education, and her book, *Children Assimilating Crucial Academics* (CACA) would become the way Literacy would be taught by educational villagers for many years in the future. In fact, the federally mandated No Child Left Behind Act would be officially changed to the CACA Act in 2010. It takes a village...idiot.

@@@@@@@@

By early October of 2004, Salome was feeling pretty miserable. The chemo in August had been bad enough, but the radiation protocol was just totally zapping her energy. Miraculously, Salome had lost hardly any hair.

During this time, Felix had been staying in the loft of her condo on Staten Island. After the initial chemo therapy in August, although Salome had originally thought that Felix would only be around for two weeks, she had to admit to herself, that his help was invaluable. She finally asked him to stay. Felix did everything that he had said he would do for her, and since commuting was physically difficult, Felix would drive her to school in Manhattan each morning. Salome would teach, and then Felix would drive back to Manhattan and pick her up. The rest of the day Salome could just lie down and watch television in her bedroom at home—unless she had to go for a radiation treatment.

One day, as Peter Proffilacto was walking into school, he saw Felix dropping off Salome, and he recognized Felix, from having passed him on the fifth floor of Rutland General Hospital, in the summer of 2003. Salome only spoke to Peter when she absolutely had to, and although eventually she would have to tell Principal Greely about her health problem—there would be several days in which she was just too sick to get out of bed—other than Toni Talton, to whom Salome told everything, nobody else at the school knew anything about either her health or her relationship with Felix. Peter

Proffilacto would never really know who Felix was, and he would never understand the nature of the relationship between Salome and Felix.

One night Salome whispered to Felix, since Walter Lee was in the other room, "I think I'm ready for some of that exploring…you know…Mr. Winky and Ms. Cootie Cat exploring…that you mentioned on my birthday."

"You know…I am too," Felix said. "But I'd prefer it…if we were married."

Salome kind of looked askew at Felix and said, "You really want to marry me…don't you."

"It's really all I need…to make me a happy man."

"Okay," Salome said.

"Okay…what?…that you know that marrying you will make me a happy man…or okay…you'll marry me?"

"Okay…I'll marry you."

And Felix and Salome kissed passionately, before he asked, "When?"

"I've been thinking lately…Felix…that I would be more comfortable… going back…as a Christian…to the Christianity that I was first taught… Catholicism…I think I want to become a Catholic again…and I know I want to be married in Rutland at St. John's."

"How's that gonna work?" Felix asked. "And yes…my father was Catholic, but I was raised in my mom's faith, Judaism…And although I'm now a Christian, I'm an Evangelical Christian…no priest will let me marry in the Catholic church."

"I know," Salome said, giving Felix this soft eye-to-eye look.

"You want me to become a Catholic."

"Would you do that for me?" Salome asked, already knowing the answer.

"Of course…it's believing in Jesus that's important…the venue really isn't."

After a phone call to Father Andrews, a meeting was set up for the following Saturday in Rutland at St. John's. Father Andrews said, "Although about eight hours of refresher instruction from me…say two Saturday mornings here…four hours each…will be fine for you Salome…In your case…Felix…I would really need to instruct you for about six months…in order to feel comfortable…marrying you and Salome in this church."

"What if…after Salome's final four hours…you ask me any question on Catholicism…including various Christian scholarly textual debate…since the beginning of the religion…and I can intelligently answer …any question you put forth…on any ritual…belief…or theory…and quote you anybody… or any line from The Bible…would you consider marrying us sooner…rather than later?" Felix asked.

And Father Andrews smiled and said, "You really think…you're that smart?"

And Felix said, "I know that 'Pride' is one of The Seven Deadly Sins…so

I'll let you answer that question...after I've been tested."

"Okay," Father Andrews said, with a twinkle in his eye. And he thought, 'I'm going to come up with some questions that are real barnburners!'

And so it came to pass, that Felix did exactly as he said he would, and a totally impressed Father Andrews agreed to marry Salome and Felix at St. John's in Rutland on Saturday, December 2, 2004.

@@@@@@@@

One afternoon in late October of 2004, while in Las Vegas on vacation with her live in boyfriend of several years, David Horowitz—another MBA candidate at the University of Tampa Bay—after feeling sick, visiting a doctor, and discovering that she was two months gone, Lani Apple convinced David that they should get married at *Elvis' Love Me Tender Chapel o' Love*. Jack and Geneva Apple, when told the news on the phone later in the day, were thoroughly pissed off to learn, that yet again, they would miss the wedding of their child. But Lani said, "Don't worry Mom...we want to get married again...a real big wedding...on the beach behind *The Breakers*...You can help us plan that...for three or four months from now." And although still a bit annoyed, that did take some of the sting away for Jack and Geneva.

About this same time in late October, Jack and Geneva Apple had just purchased half of *The Careless Navigator* from Walter Lee and Annie Younger. This arrangement had been in the works for awhile, as Walter Lee and Annie wanted to spend more time on the gulf side of Gulf Boulevard, engaged in *The Mad Beach Center for Free Expression* work, and to also travel more and spend less time in the restaurant. And since Lani Apple and David Horowitz had done such an incredible job of running the place the previous summer, and since the partnership in *The Breakers* had always been such smooth sailing, selling half of the restaurant to Jack and Geneva seemed like the intelligent thing to do. David and Lani would run *The Careless Navigator* successfully for many years. And when they would eventually retire, their children would keep running the place.

Jack and Geneva Apple would eventually sell all seventeen of their *Apple Refrigeration and Appliance Center* stores in 2008, and they would spend more time working at the *Free Expression Center* in *The Breakers*, and more time traveling also. Son Sam Apple would pass his Georgia State Bar Examination in 2007, and he would open up a small family law practice in downtown Atlanta on Peachtree Street. Lena Younger Apple would finish medical school at Mercer College in 2008, and then begin her internship and residency at *Grady Memorial Hospital* in Atlanta. In 2011 she would become a fully certified surgeon. In 2012, when son Adam would be fourteen and in ninth grade, and daughter Susan would be ten and in fifth grade, and husband Sam would be doing very well, despite all of his *pro bono* work, Lena would convince the family that they should move for awhile to Nigeria. One of Lena's colleagues while in medical school would be Nigerian, and she would regularly speak of the need for good surgeons to practice in her homeland. And although Lena Apple wouldn't want to spend the rest of her life away from the United States, the notion of spending some time in Nigeria would feel right. Since she had been a small girl, she had always heard about the aunt she had never known, Beneatha, and that aunt's dream of becoming a doctor and moving to Nigeria. The explosion in Clybourne Park that had deferred Aunt Beneatha's dream, had become Lena's secret inner drive, the fire in her belly, that which would help her in her most trying times to maintain perfect grades all through college and medical school, and to become an incredible surgeon. Lena Younger Apple would want to give something back, something to her influential yet unknown aunt. Sam would go along with his wife's idea, because he loved her so much. He would say, "But what am I supposed to do? They probably have very little need for a Georgia lawyer!" And Lena would convince him that she was sure he could put his time to good use somehow. So Sam would decide to take a quick six-month introductory course in Nursing before they would leave later in the year, since he would figure that was something he could do that would help, and it would also allow him to work with his wife. And, of course, the kids would complain about the move. They would arrive in Nigeria in January of 2013, and return to the United States in the summer of 2015. In 2016, Lena would open up a family medical practice in *The Breakers*, and Sam, after passing his Florida Bar Examination, would open up a family law practice there too. Sam would also represent *The Free Expression Center* in all of its legal doings. Both Sam and Lena would continue working *pro bono* for many clients and patients for the rest of their lives. Walter Lee Younger, who knew that his sister Beneatha had always been an inspiration to his daughter, would remark to Annie, upon learning in 2012 that their daughter and her family were moving to Nigeria, "She touches me…in the deepest part of my soul. What a magnificent daughter we've raised!"

One summer day in 2016, while incredibly beautiful eighteen year-old recently-graduated-from-high-school Lorelei Apple would be sunbathing in a bikini out behind *The Breakers*, she would be spotted by a model agent. One thing would lead to another, and eventually, for about seven years, Lorelei Apple would become the number one supermodel in the world. Pictures of Lorelei would grace every major magazine. When she would eventually give up modeling at twenty-seven for marriage and family, she would retire a multi-millionaire.

In early November of 2004, Jimson Apple and his wife Diane visited Eve Apple in her dormitory at NYU in Manhattan. Eve had just begun working on her MBA in September. Jimson pulled Eve aside and whispered, "Eve… my darling daughter…We wanted to tell you in person…and we hope you're okay with it...Diane is pregnant." Since Eve's mother, Lizzie, had had two miscarriages with her step-father Harold, Eve was truly elated at finally having a sibling again.

Eve asked, "So what are you going to name my brother or sister?" Blanchard "Bubba" Apple III would be born in September of 2005. In September of 2010, when Bubba Apple would just be beginning kindergarten in Burlington, Eve Apple would just be beginning her third year working in Manhattan for the marketing division of *Getmutlichorchloch GMbH*. Coincidentally, her new boss would be Loretta Jeremy.

In early November of 2004, Dick and Cindy Chumwell were elated to learn that their eldest daughter, twenty-nine year-old Tonya Andersen, was pregnant with twins, and that they would arrive in June of 2005. Meanwhile, Cindy's Multiple Sclerosis was under control with medication, but her vision would keep getting worse. For the next twenty years, there would always be a Chumwell involved with the 300-acre organic orchard on Highway 7 in Rutland. Unfortunately, in 2025, thanks to privatized eminent domain laws, the State of Vermont would force the Chumwells to sell their orchard, so the *Rutland Village Shopping Mall*—complete with an amusement park, water park, and boardwalk—could be built there right next to Highway 7. Bruiser Apple's 1000-acre orchard would become a big parking lot and service road.

In early November of 2004, Jennifer Apple Morgan Portman broke her leg badly while skiing in the Italian Alps. Along on that vacation was her husband of more than three years Alan, her daughter Elaine Morgan Retenski, Elaine's husband Greg, Elaine and Greg's child, Jimmy, Jennifer's stepchildren from Colin, James and Erika, their mates, their children, and Alan's two children, their mates and children also. Jennifer called Pauline from her hospital room in Cortina, Italy, with the news of her compound fracture, and Pauline said, "OH MY GOD!" Jennifer, in the next couple of years, would require a few more surgeries. Her leg would eventually feel great again in 2008, after the third surgery, and she and Alan would keep skiing and be very happy for the rest of their lives.

In early November of 2004, along with George W. Bush's reelection as President of the United States, Bruiser Apple would win his first mayoral race in Rutland. This would be the start of five wins in a row, and the very popular Bruiser Apple, with his gruff style and his nasty parrot, would remain Mayor of Rutland until his retirement in 2024. One of the colorful stories that would circulate around on the news wire services in 2008, would be about Mayor Apple's parrot, Major Doofus. That initial story would pique the interest of one of the writers for *60 Minutes* on *CBS*, and since *CBS* would purchase *Showtime* in late 2007—so they could own an uncensored major cable network—they would send the ancient ninety year-old Mike Wallace to interview both Bruiser and his parrot, for the kickoff of a new *Showtime* show, *60 Uncensored Minutes*. Bruiser really wouldn't want to do the interview, so his stipulation would be that the interview would take place in his office, with Major Doofus present.

"So why did you want to become...MAYOR OF RUTLAND?" A decrepitated Mike Wallace, with a hearing aid, would ask.

"WWWRRROOOAAA...Homo!" Major Doofus would say.

"Great," A frustrated Mike Wallace would say. And then addressing Major Doofus he would add, "I'm sure our Gay listeners will appreciate that response... MAJOR DOOFUS."

"WWWRRROOOAAA...Eat Me!" Major Doofus would say.

"Is there anything you'd like to say?" Turning away from the bird, a getting-very-annoyed Mike Wallace would ask Bruiser.

And pointing to the parrot, Bruiser would wheeze, "He does all of...my talking for me!"

And an angry Mike Wallace, having made an apparently wasted four-hour car trip from Manhattan to Rutland, would say, "I see...I guess this interview just isn't going to work out...In fact...this may be one of the most futile interviews I've ever conducted...Thanks for being so cooperative... Mr. Mayor...and thanks a lot...MAJOR DOOFUS!"

"WWWRRROOOAAA...Eat Me!" Major Doofus would say.

"I've been a reporter for many years...Don't you like the way...I've DONE MY JOB?" Mike Wallace would ask the bird before leaving.

"WWWRRROOOAAA...Asshole!" Major Doofus would reply.

On Saturday, December 2, 2004, Felix and Salome were married in Rutland at St. John's. The entire family was there, and on the Friday night before the wedding, arriving from Florida were Walter Lee and Annie Younger, Jack, Geneva, and Lorelei Apple, and the recently married Lani Apple Horowitz with her husband David. They rented a minivan at Burlington Airport, spent the night at the *Burlington Sheraton*, and the next day drove to Rutland. Sam, Lena, and Adam Apple arrived from Atlanta early Saturday morning, rented at car at the airport, checked in at the *Burlington Sheraton*, changed, and barely got to the wedding in Rutland on time. Jr. Liberty, his wife, his two children, and his ninety year-old grandmother, Lorelei Liberty, would arrive at the church at the same time as Sam, Lena, and Adam, just minutes before the wedding began. Due to Salome's health, since everything was being downscaled at her request, there had been neither a rehearsal the day before nor a rehearsal dinner. Father Andrews told those involved in the ceremony to just show up an hour early.

Felix's nephew, fifteen year-old Walter Lee Kulpa was his best man, and Geneva Apple was Salome's maid of honor. Felix said to Walter Lee, "I hope...me marrying your mom...is okay with you."

And Walter Lee Kulpa said, "I love you Uncle Felix...I'm very happy…but I have a question."

"What?" Felix asked, putting his arm around his nephew.

"Would you mind if I called you 'Dad?'"

And Felix was speechless.

Meanwhile, Walter Lee Younger was talking with Salome. He said, "It was more than thirty years ago when I first met you…I liked you then…but I love you now…On this…your wedding day… to another son…I want you to know…that I've considered you my daughter…for a long time…And I'm still moved beyond words…that your only child…was named after me."

Salome began to cry, and then she hugged Walter Lee and said, "Thank you…Walter Lee…I've considered you my second father…for a long time also."

The wedding was simple, as was the dinner afterwards. Although several family members had suggested that Salome and Felix have their reception at *The Burlington Manor*, complete with a gourmet meal and dancing, everybody understood Salome's request for just a plain nice dinner at the *Burlington Sheraton*, with just a couple hours of conversation in lieu of dancing. When Salome was finally exhausted after dinner, she and Felix hugged and kissed everybody, and then retired to their honeymoon suite in the motel. There was to be no honeymoon, as Salome had to begin her next protocol of a week's worth of chemo therapy in three days. So in the morning, before leaving Burlington to drive back to Staten Island, they picked up their son at his grandma Pauline's house, and they visited with her for a couple of hours before leaving.

@@@@@@@@

In July of 2005 Salome said to Felix, "I think I'm going to have to tell Principal Greely…that I resign…I'm just too weak to handle it anymore."

"You're really under no obligation to say anything…until the first day of school…why don't you just wait and see how you feel in late August?"

And Salome lovingly took Felix's hand into hers and said, "My darling husband…it's not going to get any better."

Although Salome was currently in remission, another cancerous tumor had been discovered in her lower colon cavity in February of 2005. After the surgery, there had been two one-week stays in the hospital for chemo, and two eight-week radiation protocols of twice a week. Now, in July, two months after her last radiation treatment, Salome was still incredibly weak.

Salome waited another thirty days before calling Principal Greely. He wasn't at the school, he was on vacation like all public school teachers and administrators who don't work summer school, but the summer school secretary said that he would be home, back from Europe, in three days. Salome waited four more days, got him at home on the phone, and she resigned her teaching position.

"Why don't you just take a leave of absence this year…and if you feel better…you can come back the following year?" Principal Greely asked. And although Salome felt inside that she would never return, she agreed to call it 'a leave of absence,' rather than a 'resignation.'

@@@@@@@@

During the eighteen months between July 2005 and January 2007, Salome had three more surgeries to remove tumors that turned out to be cancerous in both her lower and upper colon cavity. And along with each surgery, after six weeks of recovery time, came one week in the hospital for chemo, and two eight-week radiation protocols of twice a week, each protocol separated by six weeks. But when the pathology revealed in March of 2007 that her "Type A" cancer had not only traveled, but was breaking through the cell walls of otherwise healthy organs, like her liver and pancreas, Salome said to Felix, while in the hospital on Staten Island, "I'm in deep trouble," and she started to cry uncontrollably. Felix immediately climbed onto the right side of her bed and held her. She sobbed, "I don't want to die!"

And Felix, who knew that he had to be her rock, but was having a difficult time at this moment maintaining his composure said, "I know there's absolutely nothing I can say that won't sound trite…I can just hold you and keep giving you love…but it seems to me…that none of us ever really want to die…whether we're forty-six or ninety-six…and that the throat lump would be just as intense…at ninety-six…but we would simply see it as being more inevitable…than at forty-six."

And Salome looked up at Felix through her tears and nodded. Felix continued, "You're a good Christian…Salome…You've prayed to God and to Jesus…Now's the time…to really believe…that this life is just a momentary stop…on the way to something better…And also…please…please know… that if I could make that journey for you…I would."

"I love you Felix," Salome said while snuggling up in Felix's arms even closer. "And when I do pray and apologize for my past transgressions…and when I ask for help and forgiveness…and to be accepted into Heaven…I always ask Jesus to watch over our son, and the rest of the Apple and Younger families…but then at the end of my prayers…I always save mentioning you until then Felix…because there's always just so much I want to say…I always ask Jesus to watch over you…to help you make it through… when I'm no longer around…"

Upon hearing those words, Felix completely broke down sobbing, "I don't want you to die Salome!"

And Salome turned in the bed and started to rub Felix's hair, and to kiss him all over his face. She continued, "I know…even though my death will deeply hurt our son…and especially my mom…something tells me…that you're gonna have…the hardest time of anybody accepting it…that regardless of your faith in the next world…my death is going to sit like a large rock inside of you for a long time…And I don't want that for you Felix…so I regularly ask Jesus to watch over you…and to help you move on…Please tell me that you'll be able to move on."

Felix's sorrow was in another gear, much as it had been that night by the hospital's duck pond in Rutland, he could barely speak. From somewhere inside of himself he was able to mumble, "I don't want to live…if you're no longer alive on this planet…I want to die…just a second or two after you."

"Don't ever say that again Felix!" Salome said loudly in Felix's face.

Felix was then able to pull some of his composure back and he said, "I always loved the way…that Milton handled the incident of 'The Forbidden Fruit'…in *Paradise Lost*…In his version…Adam tells Eve, 'It makes no difference if I eat the forbidden fruit. You already did. And since I could never stay here without you, I was condemned too when you ate.'"

"You're just such a romantic Felix…but that's one of the reasons I love you," Salome said while closing her eyes. Felix closed his eyes too, and they both fell asleep in the hospital bed.

@@@@@@@@

In June of 2007, after another stay in Staten Island Metropolitan Hospital, Salome's oncologist told her and Felix about this new experimental program in the treatment of colon cancer, being used—of all places—at Rutland General Hospital in Vermont. The program involved placing a radioactive seed directly into the cancerous region of the colon. Felix looked into the program, saw that it had beyond a normal ratio of success, so after discussing it with Salome and her surgeon, it was decided that she should be admitted into that program.

In early July, Felix and Walter Lee drove Salome up to Rutland and checked her in at Rutland General Hospital. Since Walter Lee didn't have school, he and Felix stayed at Bruiser and Eileen's place all during July and August. In late August they came back to Staten Island however, since Felix had to buy Walter Lee new clothes for his senior year at St. George Christian High School, which began two days after Labor Day. The plan was for Walter Lee to attend school, and then on Friday afternoons, he and Felix would drive up to Rutland every weekend. They would mostly stay in Salome's hospital room until Sunday night, and then drive back to Staten Island for the school week ahead. Meanwhile, other family members always kept vigil in Salome's room. Rarely was Salome ever left alone.

On September 11th , Felix called Walter Lee Younger to wish him a happy eightieth birthday. Felix said, "I'm sorry Walter Lee...I wanted to get you something really nice...but..."

"Don't you say another word 'Licks," Walter Lee said. "I know what you're going through...at least I think I know...You just focus all of your energy...all of your love...on that wife of yours in the hospital."

"Thanks for letting me off of the hook...Dad," Felix said. Although Felix and Walter Lee had had a father-son relationship for the longest time, that was the first time that Felix had ever called him 'Dad.'

"I love you...Son," was all Walter Lee said, before hanging up the phone, and wiping the tears from his eyes.

Walter Lee Younger was in great shape at eighty, as was Annie Harrison Younger at seventy-two. Neither of them had smoked for nearly thirty years, and other than one or two fish dinners per week at their restaurant, they were both vegetarians. They also worked out for at least an hour every morning, and they regularly walked two miles on the beach every evening. They both would live very long and healthy lives, and Walter Lee would publish five more books in his lifetime.

Seventy-nine year-old Pauline Apple was in great shape also. She would live many more years, and get to know many more great-grandchildren. And those great-grandchildren would be very fortunate.

On a beautiful Fall afternoon in Rutland, on a Saturday in early October of 2007, Felix said to Salome, "It looks as if Bush has garnered enough congressional support...to bring the draft back in January of next year...Now that we have troops in Iraq, Iran, Afghanistan, Indonesia, Syria, and Lebanon, our all-volunteer military just isn't cutting it anymore...I'm not gonna let our son...go off to be killed someplace for a stupid reason!"

"If Walter Lee has to serve his country...he will," Salome said, reiterating the same belief she had espoused during their failed trip out West in 1997 in Felix's *Beetle*. "In fact...just so there's no misunderstanding... I want you to promise me Felix...when I'm no longer around...that you won't do anything to interfere...if Walter Lee gets drafted."

Felix, recognizing that this was a losing battle, and hating that he had to lie to the woman he loved, said, "I promise." And Felix thought, 'I love you with all of my heart Salome...I'll love you forever...and I'll do every other single thing...that you've made me promise to do...including moving on with my life after you're gone...and not allowing your death...to totally shut me down forever...But I'm sorry dear wife...this one time I have to lie to you...Because I'm gonna protect our son...the last Kulpa in the family...And I refuse to let him die or bloody his hands...all so somebody somewhere turns a profit.'

In early November of 2007, Salome began having problems with fistulas. She was leaking everywhere, and she had to suffer the indignity of being diapered, as well as wearing the colostomy bag. She had all kinds of tubes running into her, including an I.V. for her only source of food intake. Also, she was heavily medicated on morphine, and the doses had to be steadily increased—to keep her pain-free. With a medicated haze in her eyes, one Saturday afternoon she told Felix, "I think Selma…Ida…has a crush on you."

"What?" Felix asked, truly amazed at what Salome had just said.

"That day…in the park…she asked me…about you…I told her…she said she thought you were…magnificent…I agreed…She couldn't stop talking about you."

"That's ridiculous," Felix said. "I love you…so I don't care about other women…Besides…I'm sixty-one…"

"She's seventy-five!" A dreamy Salome said.

"You're the woman I love," Felix said. But he couldn't help thinking about Ida Laplotski just a little too. After all, she was a hero of his.

Ida had gone to trial in November of 2004, and fortunately, because Q. Harrison Albright was an excellent attorney, Ida had only been sentenced to forty-eight months. Considering what the climate was in America in 2004, in regards to a defendant being perceived as a terrorist, Q. Harrison Albright had said, "They wanted to give you twenty years…with no chance of parole." With good behavior, Ida Laplotski could be out of jail the first week of this coming December, which was less than a month away.

Very late on Saturday, December 7th , Salome woke up and asked Felix,

"Is it Monday yet?"

"No Baby Doll," Felix said. "It's still Saturday…at least for another fifteen minutes."

On Monday, December 9, 2007, at 8:50 in the evening, while Felix was cooking dinner on Staten Island for Walter Lee and himself, the phone rang. It was Jennifer. "I'm so sorry Felix…but she's gone," is what Jennifer said. It was exactly five years to the day of Bubba's death.

"We'll be right there," is all Felix could say, before he hung up the phone. All he had to do was to walk into Walter Lee's room for Walter Lee to know, his expression having said it all. After holding each other and crying, Felix put the food away, they both got ready, and then they drove to Rutland.

@@@@@@@@

The wake was on Wednesday night, December 11th, and the funeral the following day. Felix had no desire to view her body, so during the wake, as he had done at his brother's, Felix sat alone in the anteroom. And just like before, Walter Lee Younger came over and sat beside him. This time however, Felix asked to be left alone.

Felix neither heard a word during the funeral at St. John's Church, nor knew when the service was over. And since he was on the aisle in the first pew, people were waiting for him to begin the processional. His legs were rubbery—even with his walking stick—when he finally began to walk, so he needed Walter Lee on his left and Walter Lee on his right to help him.

At the cemetery, after the burial ceremony—compassionately, the actual lowering of the casket into the ground was to be done when everybody had gone—after people had left for Jennifer's place on Lake Bomoseen, Felix thought he was standing alone, with his walking stick, as he looked at the casket perched above the hole in the ground.

"Hi Felix," a voice said. Felix turned and saw Ivy and Ida Laplotski. And although they were twins, he was able to discern that the woman on his left was Ida.

"Hi Ida," Felix said to the woman on his left. "And you must be Ivy," he said to the woman on his right.

That kind of reinforced Ida's Ca Thump Ca Thump for Felix from Washington Square Park in 2004, and she said, "I can't believe it...you're the first person...other than our mother...who has ever been able to tell us apart...Even our father couldn't do that!"

"You've always been a hero of mine...Ida...I would sense you anywhere," Felix said.

"Even though we've never met each other until today, I feel as if I've known you all of my life...While I was doing the downtime...in the Harvorfield Federal Detention Center...in Egg Harbor, New Jersey...I read... *Mad Beach*...and *All the Seats Were Occupied*...and I loved them both... Also... I heard 'Brewin' Bitches' years ago...thought it was great music!"

"What...you don't know 'Without Grease?'"

"Nope...Never heard that one."

"I'll get you a copy of 'Without Grease' and 'Brewin' Bitches' too," Felix said. "And by the way," he added. "I bought...on the first day it came out a few weeks ago...and read in Salome's hospital room...in just one day...since I couldn't stop reading it...*Notes From the Modern Underground* ...I absolutely loved it!"

"Thank you very much!" Ida said. Then she added, "Are you working on anything new?"

And Felix said, "Not at the moment...but I'm thinking about a story...based on the entire Apple family...I would just move it somewhere else...perhaps way upstate in New York...since I know that area pretty well...and change the family's name of course...perhaps to something that begins with a 'B'...I'm not really ready to write anything...at the moment."

Ida, having a hard time with her own composure, when it came to thinking about her forty-seven year-old deceased friend Salome, said, "I'm so very, very sorry that you have to go through this...if you need somebody to talk to...I'm here for you."

And Felix felt his eyes growing moist, because he knew he needed just that. He'd been unable to talk about Salome since her death. It felt as if he had *Krazy Glue* lodged in his throat. He said, "It's too bad that we don't have a camera... I'd love to have my picture...taken with you!"

"I have a small *Polaroid* camera in my purse," Ivy Laplotski said. "You guys stand together...right here...I'll take your picture."

Felix stood, walking stick in his right hand, his left arm around Ida.

"Smile for the camera," Ivy said.

WHIRRR...CLICK...WHIRRR

And the slowly developing picture was placed into Felix's hand.

fin